ONLY VILLAINS DO THAT

BOOK 1

D. D. WEBB

Podium

Cover design by Dalia and Sam

ISBN: 978-1-0394-5780-5

Published in 2024 by Podium Publishing
www.podiumaudio.com

ONLY VILLAINS DO THAT

1

In Which the Dark Lord Technically Doesn't Push a Girl in Front of a Train

Ugh, I wish the train would come. One of these smelly otaku is going to grope me; I just know it. You wouldn't believe what I'm seeing, Keiko! One of them is carrying a body pillow! *Yes*, with an anime character on it. I *know*! This is why I hate coming to Akihabara."

If she wasn't so annoying, the spectacle she was making of herself—talking on her phone at the top of her lungs—might have made me nostalgic for California, where that kind of behavior is tolerated. You *don't* make a scene on a train platform in Japan.

"Oh my god, one of them is staring at my ass," the annoying girl notified Keiko in a stage whisper that projected beautifully across the platform. "I swear, if he comes any closer I'll scream."

Nobody here was carrying a body pillow. I'd worked in Akihabara for two years and never once saw somebody do that, and I have *seen* some shit. This girl was a walking gyaru caricature, from the school uniform tucked and pinned into a stripper outfit to the platinum-bleached hair and over-the-top makeup.

"Wait, don't go, Keiko!" the gyaru whined. "I'm all alone here and—oh, fine, I understand. Bye. Bitch," she added in a tone just slightly lower after ending the call. The motion of tucking her phone into her tiny purse caused her to turn slightly to her left, which brought the nearest cluster of fellow travelers—including me—into her view. Most of the normal people who had the misfortune to get stuck in this crowd were politely pretending the rude idiot didn't exist, as normal people do. I was the only one staring right at her.

"What are *you* looking at?" she snapped, glaring back at me.

"I'd need a team of anthropologists to answer that question."

She looked shocked, and someone nearby muffled a laugh, though of course most were continuing to politely ignore the spectacle. You're also not supposed to snap back at rude people in Japan. Man, I couldn't wait to make the move to San Diego. One more year of saving . . .

"Fucking otaku," the girl sneered, roughly shoving the phone the rest of the way into her purse and turning away with her nose stuck in the air in the same violent motion.

That, despite my determination not to give the bitch the satisfaction, brought a scowl to my own face. I can put up with a lot, but lumping me in with those losers was going too far. At that moment the voice over the PA system announced the imminent arrival of the train, though, and I bit my tongue. No point in getting into it now. She wasn't worth the trouble anyway.

Immediately to my right, a guy stepped forward and bent over. He was clearly one of the special-edition hunters, carrying a shopping bag with a square bulge the exact size of the stupid game I'd been handing out all day, his t-shirt featuring one of the characters from it. Chubby fellow, not quite to the point of being obese, unkempt hair in need of a trim. And, to judge by its greasy sheen, a wash.

"Excuse me," the chubby boy said to her, straightening up. "You—"

"*Ugh*," she growled, stepping in the other direction without looking at him. "Don't talk to me, creep."

He actually reached toward her. "I'm sorry, but—"

"Get *away*," she squawked. "Don't touch me, pervert! I'll scream!"

She had sidestepped as far as she could without plowing into a mixed crowd of salarymen and scruffy nerds, avoiding eye contact with Fat Boy. Thus, she'd managed not to see the object he was trying to hold out—her phone. She must have dropped it when trying to put it away and snarl at me at the same time.

The otaku froze in panic, all his stunted social impulses put into conflict. He stood there, holding out her phone, failing to catch her eye, and now he was afraid to speak to her again. I couldn't help feeling for the guy, though personally I wouldn't have bothered. Why go to the trouble for the sake of such a worthless excuse for a human? I'd have just given it to the next station employee, if not tossed it in the trash. Well, there were only seconds before the train arrived, so unless he screwed up his courage and she suddenly developed some common sense, they were both out of luck.

I couldn't say what moved me, except that after a long day at a job I hated I was even more tired of everybody's shit than usual. Before I even thought about it, I found myself stepping forward and plucking the phone from his hand. The tubby guy was too surprised to resist, instead turning to gape at me as I held up the phone.

"Look at that," I said loudly, "she didn't even lock it. Hey, how much you wanna bet she's got nudes on here?"

He stammered helplessly, but the gyaru turned to look. The expression on her face was the most satisfying thing I'd seen all day.

"My phone," she shrieked, her voice rapidly climbing as she pointed dramatically at me. "*He stole my phone!*"

"No, you stupid bitch," I retorted, raising my voice. I'm not much for yelling, especially in public, but with everyone turning to stare at this spectacle, I wanted to make it clear what had really happened. "You *dropped* your phone. This guy was trying to return it to you while you were cursing at him for it. If you don't have the basic sense to look after your things, at *least* try not to be an asshole to people who are just trying to be nice to you. I don't even know why anyone would bother."

By public standards of behavior, mine was at least as bad as hers now, but . . . screw it. Sometimes you've gotta rub someone's nose in their own stupidity.

I tossed the phone to her before she could begin shouting again, already turning away. That meant I only caught the amusing spectacle of her fumbling to catch it out of the corner of my eye, but so be it. I was done with this idiot.

The next second, though, gasps and a couple of shouts from the onlookers made me turn back, just in time to see her stumble toward the edge of the platform. The phone bounced from her hands, arcing out over the tracks, and the fool lunged after it, realizing her mistake too late. She was already screaming and pinwheeling her arms as she lurched into space.

And that, of course, was the moment the train arrived. Slowing as it prepared to stop, but we were close to the end of the platform in the direction it was coming from. It wasn't going to be slow enough.

It was strange how time seemed to slow down when you were staring at an onrush of tragedy. Even as my own pulse spiked in my throat, it seemed as if the girl was soaring out over the tracks in slow motion. It couldn't possibly have taken more than a split second to hit her, but I had plenty of time for my whole chest to tighten and to think about how the effect was just like a movie, how I'd read that the human brain did this when it was in extreme danger, and how as much as I had despised the stupid brat I hadn't wanted to *kill* her. In that frozen moment all I could feel was crushing guilt.

Then the moment passed, and she didn't die, and I was left very confused. More relieved than I wanted to admit, but mostly confused.

I stared at the girl for a few more seconds before I was really willing to believe what I was seeing. She hung there, mid-fall, suspended in the air off the edge of the platform, right in front of the train. As if she were frozen in time.

In fact, so was the train. So was *everything*. The station had gone dead silent, I realized, which was chilling. Nothing in the vicinity of Tokyo is *ever* silent. People thronged the platform like statues, the closest in various poses of shock as they'd been caught in the process of seeing the girl fall, while others farther back could have been a painting of any crowd of Akihabara travelers waiting for a train.

Suddenly, I was alone in a frozen world.

"Huh."

Almost alone. I whirled at the voice and found the fat guy from before still moving. Actually, he was in the process of testing our new situation by poking a salaryman in the shoulder. It apparently wasn't hard to move the frozen people, to judge by how far he was able to tip the guy.

"Force equals mass times acceleration," I said, and he jumped violently. Apparently he hadn't noticed I was still alive either. "We're moving incredibly fast relative to anybody else here. That's probably gonna leave a hell of a bruise."

"Oh," he said nervously, and very gently tried to move the salaryman back into position, doubtless making it worse. "Sorry."

I sighed, turning in a full circle to take in the uncanny sight. "What the *hell* is going on here?"

"Everyone's frozen in time," my chubby fellow survivor said.

"Bullshit. That doesn't make *any* sense."

"Well, look around you!"

"Light has to move for us to see, dumbass. If time was frozen, light wouldn't travel and we'd be blind. Also, just moving through the air would be like getting sandblasted from the friction."

"Oh," he said again, peering closely at me. "Are . . . you a physicist?"

"No, I'm a musician," I said, annoyed and well aware that my store clerk uniform told a different story. But whatever; that was just a job I had, not who I was. "But I paid attention in school instead of daydreaming about anime tits. I don't know *what* this is; all I know is it doesn't make sense. Are we the only ones?"

"Good question," he agreed, then raised his voice. "Hello! Can anyone else hear me?"

Silence.

"Anyone?" he repeated.

"I guess that answers that," I said, grunting. "I wonder why the effect skipped the two of us."

"Maybe there's something special about us!"

I could see the dawning hope shining in his eyes, as if this was one of his video games and we were the chosen ones. A scenario like that had to be the lifelong dream of an otaku. Best to crush that before he started acting *really* weird.

"There is nothing special about anyone," I snapped. "The universe is random unfeeling chaos, and humans are just a particularly aggressive species of upright monkey. Don't go looking for purpose in this. The question *now* is, what are we doing to do?"

We looked at each other, and then away at the immobilized world all around us. I turned in a complete circle, just to make sure I hadn't missed anything. Nope. Creepy frozen train station.

Fat Boy cleared his throat. "Well, uh. I'm Shinonome Yoshi."

I don't care. I didn't say that, though; if he was the only other person awake in . . . How far did this extend? The station? Akihabara? Tokyo? The *world?* I obviously needed to know what to call my new companion, even if he was just a hopeless otaku.

"Omura Seiji," I introduced myself curtly.

"It's nice to—"

"We'd better go look around, see how far this extends," I said, turning back toward the station's entrance.

"Wait!"

I turned and gave him an impatient look. He was pointing back at the edge of the platform, where the girl was still suspended in the air in front of the train.

"Omura-san, aren't you forgetting something? We need to save her before we do anything else!"

Oh. Actually, I *had* forgotten, to my extreme embarrassment. I hate being embarrassed. My instinct is always to cover it up with cockiness.

"Why?" I asked, looking past him at the hanging gyaru with a smirk.

His expression was satisfyingly shocked. "Wh— She could *die*! What if time starts up and she's still hanging there? This is a chance to save her!"

"Oh, please, were you listening? Why is the world better off with her in it?"

The poor guy stared at me in outraged horror. After a moment, he started stammering incredulously.

"Relax, Yoshi, I'm kidding," I finally said. I patted him on the shoulder as I stepped past. "I guess you're right; it's no good leaving her there when it costs nothing to rescue her. I'd feel bad if time started up again and she got splattered. Hm . . . This might be tricky."

She was just past the edge of the platform, frozen in the act of leaping forward; the only part of her still within easy reach was one foot, which was down nearly at platform level. Even that we would have to really stretch to grasp. I knelt at the edge and started to reach toward her leg, but had a thought and withdrew my hand.

"When you touched that guy, did anything happen?" I asked, looking up at Yoshi, who had come to stand next to me. "I mean, did it feel different from normal?"

"Actually, yeah." He frowned, thinking. "It was weird. It felt almost like he was . . . stuck in jelly."

"Jelly."

"Or glue, or . . . Like there was some force holding him in place. It wasn't too powerful. I could push him through it, but he definitely had more inertia than normal."

"Makes sense," I agreed, standing up. "It'd take something like that to keep her from falling . . . Well, that's no good. If she's gonna be hard to move, we just don't have much leverage with the only part of her we can reach. We'd need to touch her near the top."

He sighed, studying the girl. The way her body was angled, she was well out of reach from the knees up, with her arms stretched forward trying to catch her phone. I couldn't help but wonder whether this was worth the hassle. This was not someone who was any use to society after all. I snuck a glance at Yoshi's determined expression and said nothing, though. Tubby nerd though he was, there was no telling how long I'd be stuck with nobody else for company.

Besides, I suppose you can't just let someone *die*, no matter how worth-less they are.

"I think I can reach her hair," he said, "if I stand at the very edge of the platform and lean out. If you'll stand back and hold my other hand for balance, I should be able to pull her in."

"You wanna yank a girl by her hair? Ouch."

"Well, do you have a better idea?"

"I guess 'let her fall' isn't what you want to hear." He gave me another look, and I grinned back. "Didn't think so. Well, if you think I'm gonna carry *your* weight . . ."

I trailed off, reconsidering. The prospect of being the anchor for both *his* fat ass and the girl was not appealing. I had started to suggest I should be the one to reach for her, since he was obviously better suited to be a living counterweight, but I suddenly realized we still had no idea what had caused time to stop, or how long it might last. If it suddenly started up again, I did not want to be the one stretching out in front of the oncoming train.

"No, I guess I don't have a better idea," I said instead. "Well, let's get this over with."

He stepped up to the edge of the platform, a look of such ostentatious determination on his face that I had to roll my eyes. Bracing himself right on the brink, he held one hand back toward me. "Ready?"

I grimaced, but set my own stance and reached out to take his hand, then grimaced again, harder. His palms were damp. I had to get a two-handed grip on his wrist to be reasonably certain he wasn't going to slip right out of my grasp.

Then he began to lean forward over the tracks, reaching out toward the stupid girl we were for some reason going to all this trouble for, and immediately almost dragged us both over the edge. Gritting my teeth, I leaned backward as far as I could manage while still holding on to his arm, and even so, the weight pulled me forward. My shoes slipped on the platform's surface, yielding one centimeter at a time as he strained to reach. Yoshi's fingers brushed an outstretched lock of her frozen, bleach-blonde hair, and my own foot came to rest against his.

That was it, nowhere else to slide. If this didn't work in the next few seconds, we were both going over the edge.

"Lucky for me you're so trim and petite," I grated against the strain. "Otherwise this would be *really hard*."

"Got her!" he gasped, finally getting a fistful of hair. Yoshi heaved his entire weight backward with the most immediate result that I went sprawling onto the concrete, losing my grip on his hand. I was forced to execute a desperate crab scuttle backward before having the chance to get my feet under me, as he immediately began to topple, the girl's weight adding to his momentum and overcoming his balance. Yoshi staggered, and for a second I felt the very real fear that I was about to be crushed under a pile of dumbasses.

He caught his balance, though, to my relief. I scrambled back upright while Yoshi carefully steadied the frozen girl. That proved difficult as she was stuck in a leaping pose which wasn't well suited to standing up. As I brushed off my clothes, he finally settled for lowering her to lie awkwardly on the platform. The position looked uncomfortable, but it would beat the alternative of falling on her face when time started up again.

If it did.

Yoshi apparently agreed, as he continued to fuss over her for a minute, his hands hovering as if he wanted to try moving her limbs into a better pose but was afraid to.

"Well, cop a feel if you're going to," I said. "Otherwise, we should probably get moving."

"I would *never* do something like that!" he exclaimed, glaring up at me in a picture of reproach.

"Of course you wouldn't," I replied. Yeah, I know my otaku; he'd never do something like that—while anybody was watching. "Now come *on*. Unless we figure out what's going on—"

Suddenly, the light in the station changed. Nobody else started moving again. In fact, the other people around us began to seem as if they were fading from view as gloomy shadows rose in the corners, and a bright light shone down upon the two of us as if from some massive spotlight hidden behind the ceiling.

"Oh, what the hell *now*?" I demanded.

Yoshi and I turned in a circle, back-to-back, to seek the source of whatever fresh nonsense was unfolding. For a few moments, there was nothing, and we made a complete revolution before coming to a stop, shifting positions to look questioningly at each other. By the look on his face, he had no better ideas than I did. No surprise there.

Both of us jumped when the powerful tone of a bell resonated through the silent station, lingering on the air for long seconds afterward. It rang a second time, and this time we managed not to make fools of ourselves. Though this time it was accompanied by the appearance of two more spotlights, shining onto points on the concrete floor a few meters in front of us.

The bell rang a third time, and something burst down from above through the spotlights with the force of an explosion—not a physical one, but bringing an intensity of light that forced Yoshi and I to cover our eyes and look away. It lasted only for an instant, though. Hesitantly, afraid of what I was going to see, I lowered my hand from my face and looked up again.

Two goddesses had arrived in Akihabara Station.

I could think of no other way to describe them. One was a very pale blonde with white highlights; the other had hair of purple streaked with blue. The first wore an ornate gown of white and crimson with golden trim, while the second wore a much skimpier garment that matched her hair while showing off a lot of pale skin. They both had distinctly European features, but even so, my first thought was that they looked like anime cosplayers. That wasn't an uncommon sight around Akihabara.

Except these two were floating more than a meter off the ground. And glowing. In fact, both the mysterious, sourceless spotlights and the station's own lighting seemed to have shut off, leaving them as the only source of illumination.

"G-goddesses?" Yoshi stammered. See, it wasn't just me.

The blonde one floated forward, and while I couldn't actually hear a choir of angels singing, it really seemed there ought to be. Leaning forward in midair, she extended one hand down toward Yoshi. On her face was the purest expression of kindness and gentleness I had ever seen. It immediately made me think she had to be up to no good. Nobody who's actually that benevolent makes a spectacle of it.

"Shinonome Yoshi," the golden goddess said in a breathy soprano, "you are pure of heart, brave in the face of struggle, and most importantly, willing to help others, even when it avails you nothing. Long have I searched for one such as you."

"Are you *kidding* me?" I heard myself ask out loud.

"What I ask of you is no small thing," she continued with solemn tenderness, ignoring me. "You will face untold hardship, and the fates of many will hang upon your courage. If you—"

"Yes!" he blurted, gazing up at her in outright worship, his rapturous expression making me cringe. How many hours must this kid have wasted daydreaming about this *exact* situation, while knowing that in a rational world no such thing could ever possibly happen?

"Be warned, and do not take this lightly," the goddess told him ever so gently. "Another world cries out for your help, a realm of unending struggle which will test you to your limits."

"I'll do it!"

"But if you endure, through that very hardship, you will learn to unlock the potential you have long sensed within yourself. What say you, Shinonome Yoshi? Will you take up the mantle of a hero?"

"*Yes*," he cried desperately. "Please give me this chance! I won't disappoint you!"

"Seriously?" I asked, looking back and forth between them. Neither acknowledged me.

"Then take my hand, young hero," she said in her soft, gentle tone, extending her hand farther. Slowly and reverently, Yoshi reached out to grab her delicate fingers in his big, sweaty mitt.

She lifted him right off the ground as if his flabby bulk weighed nothing, and the pair of them levitated slowly upward in their own column of light, toward the ceiling of the station.

"She is *obviously* conning you!" I exclaimed. "Please tell me you can't possibly be this naive!"

But then, with a final blinding flash, they were gone.

"Idiot," I said, staring up at the spot from which they'd disappeared. "Welp, he's dead."

That was when the other goddess shifted around right in front of me, and I winced, mentally cursing myself for forgetting she was there. While the blonde goddess had floated elegantly, this one swam through the air like a fish, deliberately showing off the long lines of her body and letting the train of her dress drift along behind her as if it too were suspended in water.

She was smiling down at me and, unlike the other goddess, her smile was in no way gentle or kind.

"Omura Seiji," she said with an avid grin, "you really are a contemptible piece of shit."

2

In Which the Dark Lord Bends Over Backward

"Well, fuck you, too, lady."

Yes, that was the first thing I said to the goddess. I won't defend it as an intelligent move, but what can I say? I've always been kind of a mouth.

Fortunately, she didn't seem to mind too much.

"And that," she said with a self-satisfied smirk, "is why I chose you. I've had strategic masterminds, cruel tyrants, thuggish bullies . . . Every manner of villain I could think of to try. But it all gets so *rote*, you know? Once in a while, I like to shake things up. And so here we are, Seiji—me, the Goddess of Evil, and you, a rude, pushy, self-centered dick. This is going to be such *fun!*"

"I'm gonna stop you right there," I said, holding up one hand. "I see why you might be confused, what with that hopeless dork your friend just picked up, and all these otaku in the station right now, but *I am not one of them.* Okay? I'm *not* an . . . an isekai protagonist. I have a career, goals, and plans, and I know what a vagina feels like. I've got a *personality.* And if you'll excuse me, I'm just gonna go get back to those. So, good luck with your . . . whatever it is. I'm sure *any* one of these socially maladjusted simps would be delighted to sign up. Just look for the ones who look like they've never seen sunlight. You've got a *wealth* of choices here."

"Aww, *Seiji,*" she cooed, squirming closer with an eel-like motion of her whole body that might have been sexy, had this whole situation not been setting off danger signals. The goddess reached for my face, and I instinctively leaned away; she just kept reaching until she gently placed her fingertips under my chin. "But I don't *want* any of these other socially maladjusted simps. I want *you.* And you seem to have misunderstood something."

In a flash, her hand surged forward, seizing me by the throat. For such a dainty-looking thing, she had an *amazingly* strong grip, and in the next moment I found myself dangling from her grasp, struggling to draw breath and clutching her wrist ineffectually.

"I," the goddess said sweetly, holding me right up to her face so I had a front-row seat for the most viciously psychotic grin I had ever seen, "was not *asking* you."

She held me that way just long enough to make her point. Just to drive home who was top dog here.

Then she dropped me. I hit the floor hard, acquiring a painful bruise on my tailbone, coughing and clutching my sore neck.

The goddess floated over me, looking down her nose with a maliciously triumphant expression, just drinking in the sight of me humiliated at her feet.

"You know," I said, my voice raspy, "you'd actually be pretty cute if you'd stop throwing out yandere vibes."

There went my mouth again . . . but still. Bullies just want to feel they have power over somebody. There was probably no way to win against an insane cosmic entity like this, but I could at least not give her the satisfaction.

But the purple-haired goddess only smiled wider, as if my backtalk was exactly what she wanted to hear.

"For someone who professes to hate otaku so much," she said sweetly, "you sure are up to date on their terminology, Seiji."

Oh, you bitch.

"And for someone who calls herself the *Goddess* of Evil, you sure do like to pick on people weaker than you. What, too risky to slap people around if they can slap back?"

That brought a full-throated laugh of apparent delight. "Oooh, we're going to have such *fun* together! I *knew* I was right to pick you. I had a good feeling about you right off the bat. Allow me to introduce myself!"

She floated backward and upward, positioning herself even higher above me, and rather than bow or do anything remotely polite or normal, she spread her arms wide as if inviting me to behold the spectacle that was her.

"I am Virya, the Lady of Malice, the Mistress of the Night, the Paragon of Mischief, and She Who Rules the Dark!"

Virya leaned forward, extending one hand—palm down with fingers curled, as if she expected me to kiss her fingers.

"And I am your new goddess."

Needless to say, I didn't reach for her hand.

"I'm an atheist."

"Of course you are, Seiji," she said with withering condescension. "It *takes* someone who only worships at the altar of his own ego to meet a goddess in the flesh and act the way *you* do. But that's all right; I don't require prayers from you. In fact, where you're going, praying won't help you."

"I'm not going *anywhere* with you, lady."

"Oh, you are just too *precious*! Behold!"

Again, she flung her arms wide, this time swiveling in midair to face away from me, and only then did I realize that Akihabara Station was gone. When had that happened? Being choked out and thrown around is surprisingly distracting. I was now sitting on a patch of . . . It wasn't the floor of the station. In fact, it looked as if the round circle of light the goddesses had projected was somehow solid enough to hold me up even with the actual floor gone. All around was an infinite sky glittering with stars. I had never *seen* so many stars, even in the countryside; it was as if there was no empty space left between them. They were colorful jewels far more brilliant than the plain white dots you could see from Earth.

At her gesture, though, something appeared in the distance; it grew rapidly as if we were rushing toward it, until I could tell it was a sphere. In fact, a planet. We'd have to be moving at nearly the speed of light to be approaching it so fast, but after the frozen train station I already knew goddesses weren't constrained by physics.

Unless, as I still desperately hoped, this was all some kind of illusion or trick. It had to be, surely. Right?

"Welcome," Virya said proudly, "to Ephemera. Our world."

We had drawn close enough for me to see details, settling into what I guess would be a low orbit. Except . . .

There were no oceans, only vast empty spaces where they should be. Of the landmasses, there were none large enough to be called continents, but only sprawling archipelagos, most of the islands connected by a series of thin land bridges. I could see some of the colossal stone spires holding up the islands, rising up from the world's core. Below the mostly missing surface between the islands was endlessly swirling mist that seemed not to come up even to sea level. Deep down where the core should have been, there was a steady glow illuminating the subterranean clouds, making shifting patterns of crimson and golden light that filtered through the fog. As far as I could tell, despite the shattered state of the planet itself, the surfaces of the surviving islands were not unlike the surface of Earth, complete with green forests and plains, plus areas that looked purple and blue. Different colored vegetation, maybe? There were snowcapped mountains, lakes and rivers, the latter of which tumbled off the stark edges of the world into the infinite abyss below. It was just . . . a broken shell of a world, wrapped around a hollow space filled with mist.

"Wow," I said, unimpressed. "What'd you do? Drop it down the stairs?"

"Oh, you know how it is," Virya replied with an offhanded shrug. "There was . . . an incident. I'll admit, things got a little out of hand in some of our early games."

"This is your idea of a little out of hand? What the hell kind of *game* does something like this to an entire planet?"

"Do you have any idea what it is like to be a goddess, Omura Seiji?" she mused, gazing down at Ephemera.

"So far, it seems bitchier than I would've thought."

"Well, it's *boring*!" Virya spun around and lunged at me faster than I could react, seizing me by the shoulders. She clutched me hard enough to leave fingertip-sized bruises, glaring wide-eyed and with bared teeth into my face. "Imagine it, if you can! Absolute power, the ability to do *anything* you can think of . . . but only on *one world*. You can't leave, can't explore the cosmos, can't even *die*. How long do you think it would take to run out of every possible thing there is to do?"

"I guess that depends on how much imagination you've got."

Okay, so maybe that wasn't the smartest observation to make under those circumstances, but it was the only thing that came to mind. Fortunately for me, she seemed to agree.

"*Exactly!*" Grinning, Virya gave me one last squeeze (ow) before releasing me and swirling away. She began to drift horizontally around my little island of light, like a goldfish circling its bowl. "You saw my sister, Sanora—she's all I have, really. Everybody else lives fifty, a hundred years at the *most*. After a while, there's just no point in getting attached to them. For all these eons it's been just Sanora and me, cooped up with only each other and our increasingly stale little world and an ever-changing parade of little people no more significant than mayflies. We've had to do *something* to keep from going insane out of sheer tedium."

"I don't think it's working."

"So we invented our game." She didn't answer me, which was probably for the best. "Good versus Evil! And you know what, Seiji? It's actually a lot of fun!"

"I'm happy for you."

"The game is *always* in session, you see, in one form or another. All those tiny little people down there, they're born into it; it's all they know. They are on the side of Evil or Good, they live, fight each other, make more little people, and die off. It makes an ever-changing selection of game pieces—a wonderful device to keep it interesting!"

"Has anybody ever sat you down and had a conversation about just how fucked up that is?"

"Oh, don't pretend you care about anybody but yourself," she chided, grinning at me as she idly swam through the air around me. "You, of all people. Ah, but where was I? Even though the game of Good and Evil is eternally ongoing, there are actual *sessions*, you see. They begin when my dear sister and I choose our key pieces. The Champions of Sanora and Virya, the Hero and the Dark Lord! Our most potent weapons. Do you play chess, Seiji?"

"I prefer shogi."

Actually, I preferred video games—specifically offline ones that didn't require me to interact with anyone—but I was not in the habit of admitting to any interests that were even otaku-adjacent. Once you get that stink on you, it *never* comes off.

"Well, Seiji, *you* can think of yourself as my queen." She drifted in front of me, planted her elbows on nothing in midair, and propped her chin in her hands, smiling sweetly. "My strongest piece, the one which can move with virtually no limits, strike harder than any other, wreak the *greatest* havoc in my name!"

"Well, gee, you sure know how to make a guy feel special."

"So!" She swirled away again, spinning in an exuberant ring above my head. "You'll be wanting to know the *rules* of this game!"

"I literally cannot imagine caring less about anything. What I *want* is to go home."

"At first, you see, we designed it to be sort of a free-form battle royale kind of thing. We added magic to the world, made it freely available to all people, and just let them go at each other. And . . . you see what happened." Virya glided past, gesturing at the shattered world below. "But it all worked out in the end! Ephemera makes a *much* better game board as it is now, with nice built-in limits on things like how people can move from one island to another, and how many people can be supported on any one place. It's all so much more *orderly*. We learned that lesson on the importance of limitations in a proper game; there's a *system* in place now. It has simple rules, keeps anybody from getting too powerful, and ensures the game is fair and *fun* for everybody!"

"Uh-huh." I took out my phone. It worked, but there was no signal. So either this *was* another world, or her illusion extended to little details like that.

"You may want to pay attention, Seiji. The object of the game is simple—the Dark Lord tries to conquer all of Ephemera, and the Hero tries to stop him . . . to the death. You—and your little friend from a moment ago—will live and die by the rules of this contest. Literally."

"You want me to murder *Yoshi*?" I demanded. "That poor, tubby nerd-boy your sister's manipulated into thinking that all this bullshit is his fantasy come to life? Fuck you! That kid can't be more than fifteen. I'm not doing it."

"You seem awfully confident you'll have a choice in the matter," she cooed, swirling around me uncomfortably close. "That poor, tubby nerd-boy is getting the same head start you are. *And* there's the fact of why she picked him—that man-child has spent his whole life hiding from reality and craving the fantasy of being a Hero. Now he is one. Do you *really* think he's going to ask questions when the beautiful Goddess who made all his dreams come true tells him to go kill a Dark Lord?"

Virya had practically coiled herself around me—she was amazingly flexible—and now came up with her grinning face right alongside my head.

"Especially since he's *met* you, Seiji. Oh, for only a few minutes, yes, but what kind of impression do you think you left? Be honest—if *you* were in *his* position, would you question for a moment that Omura Seiji was an evil bastard who needed a sword in the chest?"

For the first time, she'd left me without a ready response. Maybe because it was the first time she was *right*. If there was one thing I understood, it was that human beings are stupid, selfish, aggressive animals. *Especially* otaku like Shinonome Yoshi who'd gone their whole lives with barely one toe dipped in actual reality. He wasn't going to question orders from a pretty goddess who brought his favorite isekai fantasy to life; I vividly remembered the desperate joy on his face when she'd offered him the hero gig. That dumb fat-ass was gonna come at me with everything he had.

Of course, helpful goddess or no, he was still . . . Yoshi. I couldn't imagine any possible suite of isekai cheat powers that would render that boy anything but hopeless. Even if I did end up having to fight him, maybe I didn't have to go for the kill.

I'd murder Virya in an instant if I could, but I just didn't have it in me to start planning the death of a dumb teenager whose only crime was being a dumb teenager. Yoshi was as much a victim of this as I was, even if he didn't realize it.

"Yes, I thought that might finally get through to you," she murmured, smugness incarnate. "Now that we're all on the same page, let me clarify the rules. You—"

"There's one thing you haven't taken into account, you know," I interrupted.

She swam back in front of me, looking no less smug than before. "Oh, *do* tell. I expect this will be absolutely *priceless*."

"Well, it's like I already said," I informed her, calmly and with a smile. People who think they're making a point by getting red in the face and shouting only reveal their ignorance; there is nothing like proper Japanese social graces to emphasize a searing verbal takedown. "I'm not doing it. You set all this up because you're bored, right? Then you should consider my responses thus far and ask yourself whether a man who'll criticize you right to your face is going to dance for your amusement. I don't care about your silly game, I have no interest in your broken wreck of a planet, and I have absolutely no quarrel with Shinonome Yoshi. I'm not about to waste my time conquering people I don't know in the name of someone I don't like. My *sole* emotional stake in this, Virya, is that I think you're a cunt, and if the options are death or being your champion . . . well, darling, *you* aren't the more attractive prospect between the two." I smiled more widely, keeping my tone pleasant. "So fuck you, fuck your sister, and fuck the eternal battle of Good and Evil. I'm out. If you want someone to play a living RPG character, you could've picked almost *anyone* else from that train station. And hey, you still can! Really, this isn't going to work out well for you, so you might as well just send me back to Akihabara and get yourself a better Dark Lord."

The goddess just gazed down at me in silence, her expression thoughtful.

"Actually," I said after a pause, "now that I think of it, you *did* make me miss my train. So if you could just set me down in Yokohama—"

Virya didn't move, but something seized my whole body in an iron grasp and wrenched me out of place. I broke off with a strangled gasp as I was physically bent over backward, nearly double. I could feel muscles and ligaments stretching beyond their capacity, my spine flexing until the vertebrae ground against each other so hard I could practically *hear* them.

And then the force holding me began to twist me to the side, and I'm not ashamed to admit that this wrenched a scream out of me. A strangled one; with my neck bent backward farther than it was meant to go, my windpipe was compressed enough that I could barely breathe.

"Now, Seiji," the goddess said in a tone of kindly reproof, like a teacher correcting a child, "that's not how this works. I chose *you*. It wasn't an accident, and your opinion was not asked. What do you think the point is of grabbing people from Earth to fill these roles? There are thousands right here on Ephemera who'd love nothing more than to be named a champion of a goddess. Bringing in fresh blood who don't know how things work here is the *point*. And like I said . . . I picked you for a *reason*."

My arms were yanked out to the sides by an unseen grip, and then slowly twisted in opposite directions until I could feel the strain in every joint; I was sure my shoulders were about to dislocate. Despite having just learned to conserve air by keeping quiet, I couldn't completely repress a whimper of pain.

"I promise you, little boy," Virya crooned, sounding like she was coming closer, "you are *going* to entertain me. You can either do it by putting up a good fight against the Hero, and have all the fun of gaining fortune, power, and glory in the process . . . *or*, I can just keep you here, let a more amenable Dark Lord do your job, and spend the entire time finding new ways to make you scream. I should warn you, these games tend to go on for several years, at least. Often decades. So if that's the way you want it, say the word! Just be aware that by the time I allow you the reprieve of death, you will *thank* me for the mercy."

My spine cracked audibly, prompting a muffled shriek. With both feet firmly pressed to the floor, I had been bent so far backward that the crown of my head finally came to rest on the ground. Having your limbs bent just a little too far doesn't *sound* so terrible, in theory, but I had never experienced pain like that in my life. It takes a *lot* to shut me up, but she did it.

"Oh, sweetie, I know," Virya went on, her smirking visage appearing in my vision as she apparently flowed up over the agonized arch of my body. Upside down, she descended until her purple hair pooled on the floor, holding my panicked eyes while she spoke. "You're just so used to thinking you're *better* than everyone else. You, Seiji, with the oh-so-unique backstory that makes all your bullshit justified. The amateur musician saving up to go seek his fortune in California, the child of two cultures, caught between them and feeling himself superior to both, the son of a broken family that just . . . how very sad . . . *doesn't understand him*. And so you walk around sneering at everybody, telling yourself you are surrounded by inferior idiots who don't deserve your respect. Contriving to despise both your homelands by judging each only from the standards of the other, and carefully not thinking about the *stunning* hypocrisy of that."

She grinned and laid a gentle hand against the side of my face, that tender gesture in contrast to the agony her twisting was wreaking through my entire body. The strangled noise that emerged from my throat was hard to describe; I was stretched too far to manage a proper sob. My lungs just didn't have the necessary room to expand.

"You're an asshole, Omura Seiji," Virya informed me. "Oh, I know—you think you're unique, that you're *different.* The only real person in a world of NPCs, justified and entitled to treat everyone the way you do. Because that is exactly what *every* bog-standard asshole thinks." She leaned in closer, batting her eyelashes. "*You. Are. Not. Special.*"

Virya stared at me that way for a few eternally long seconds, the vindictively cruel pleasure she was taking in my suffering peeking through her cheerful facade.

Then, abruptly, the pressure let up and I collapsed onto my back, gasping. The sudden absence of intense, all-over pain was such a relief it took me a few seconds to even notice I'd landed in a really uncomfortable position, with my legs and one arm tucked under myself awkwardly. In carefully straightening myself out, I discovered that having all my joints yanked hard the wrong way and held there was the kind of experience I wouldn't get over quickly. Everything still hurt; I was going to be feeling this for days at least. At least she'd been careful enough not to break any bones.

"Until now, that is." Virya gazed down at me with insufferable self-satisfaction. "I have *made* you special. In Japan, you were a nobody with delusions of grandeur, and you can protest all you like, but you know it was never going to be any different in America. On Ephemera, you are *important.* You *will* do what I tell you, Seiji. And in the end? You'll thank me for this. Maybe not soon, but you will."

I got carefully to my feet, wincing and flexing my fingers to make sure they were undamaged. Looking up at the smug goddess, I made the decision that if I was going to be some kind of Dark Lord, it wouldn't be the forces of Good I set out to destroy. I had *one* enemy on this world, and it wasn't Shinonome Yoshi.

"Well, smart mouth?" she asked sweetly. "Nothing to say this time?"

I had to clear my throat twice; the recent strain on my neck had made my voice a bit raspy.

"What the hell do you mean, *amateur?* Bitch, conjure up my guitar and yourself some dry panties; I'm about to rock your universe."

Virya laughed with almost childlike glee. "It's not even that I think you're going to *win,* Seiji, but oh, what fun this will be! I've never had a Dark Lord *quite* like you. Win or lose, this is going to be a hell of a show! And now, before we put you to work, you should meet your familiar."

"My what?"

"It was part of those *rules* you were too cool to listen to. Have it your way, little Dark Lord; now you get to learn as you go. Fortunately, this will help with that."

She snapped her fingers, producing a shower of sparks and a puff of smoke. When it cleared a second later, there was a little monster hovering before me.

Barely bigger than a rat, it resembled nothing so much as a large black gecko, with the addition of buzzing wasp wings that kept it floating in the air at the level of my shoulder. Its eyes were crimson, which would maybe have looked sinister except that the overall impression the creature gave was . . . Well, it was cute. For some reason, I found that even more exasperating.

"Your familiar will serve as your guide," Virya intoned. "As you grow in power, he will gain skills, increasing your ability to gather intelligence about your enemies and providing you a great strategic advantage. The bond between you is struck when you give him a name. Now, Seiji, what is your familiar called?"

I gave the little wasp-lizard a sidelong look of disgust. It gazed back, its little tongue darting out to taste the air.

"Ah, ah," Virya interjected when I opened my mouth, grinning down at me. "I suggest you take this seriously, Seiji. You will be heavily dependent on this little fellow, and there will be no second chance to name him. You'd best pick something you won't mind hearing every day for the rest of your life."

That only deepened my antipathy, of course. Fuck, I didn't care—I didn't care about *any* of this. What was a good name for a little fantasy spirit lizard? I don't even *like* fantasy.

"I dunno," I said impatiently. "Bilbo?"

"The bond is struck!" Virya exclaimed gleefully, spinning off on another circuit of the empty space around me.

"And so it is," the familiar agreed in a squeaky little voice that I already knew was going to get on my nerves the longer I had to hear it. "Pleased to meetcha, boss! By your will, I am called Biribo."

I glared at him; he tasted the air again and grinned back. So that was how it was going to be? I'm stuck with a little helper-demon that intends to give me a hard time?

"Listen here, you little shit—"

"There's just one final thing you need," Virya cut me off. "You and Yoshi are both starting with certain advantages, but it's just no *fun* if you have the exact same set of powers!"

"Wait, what powers?"

Biribo tasted the air again. "Wait, did you seriously not listen to the rules?"

"He felt it was more important to tell me how ungrateful he was for my generosity," Virya smirked. "Now, you'll need one additional power . . . an extra advantage that will differentiate you from the Hero in style and approach. But what's your area of expertise, hm? Might, magic, or wisdom?"

Wisdom, obviously. My greatest strength was my understanding of how people worked and how to leverage that. Watching the dark goddess's pensive expression, I had the disconcerting feeling she could tell what I was thinking, and didn't agree.

"I think we'll make you a sorcerer," she mused, her lips curling up further. "Yes, I will augment your magical skill. Your Gift of the Goddess shall be . . . spell combination!"

"Ooh!" Biribo did a little loop-de-loop in excitement. "We haven't seen that one in forever! Gonna be interesting, boss!"

"And so, you are ready for your adventure to begin," Virya proclaimed. "Go forth, Lord Seiji, and conquer in my name! Destroy your enemies, sub-due your rivals, and above all . . ." She winked, grinning insufferably. "Be sure to put on a good show for me."

"I guess it may be a long time before I see you again, Virya," I said solemnly, "so let me just get this out while I still have the chance. I sincerely hope someone you love survives a protracted battle with bone cancer, only to perish in a gasoline fire. While you watch."

Biribo made a strangled squeak. "Uh, boss, you know she can . . ."

"Oh, Seiji," she giggled, "you should know better. People like you and I don't love anybody but ourselves. *That's* why I like you. Now go knock 'em dead, tiger."

Unsurprisingly, it was I who was immediately knocked—not dead, at least, but down. A sudden burst of force shoved me straight through whatever invisible surface had been holding me up, and I found myself plummeting toward the broken surface of Ephemera at horrifying speed.

I'll freely admit I screamed and flailed my arms in panic. I'm a musician, not a paratrooper.

"Wheeeeee!" Biribo crowed, which caused me to notice for the first time that he was clinging to my left shoulder with all four clawed limbs, his wasplike wings and tail trailing straight up with the force of our descent. "This is the best part!"

I didn't actually know how long it should take to descend from orbit to the surface, but we were clearly going much faster than that; the ground loomed up at a speed that meant we'd hit in seconds. We should *definitely* have been burning from atmospheric friction, but that didn't happen. With my familiar in tow, I plunged straight at one of the larger archipelagos, toward a narrower stretch of islands between two larger clusters. One island in particular raced to meet us, affording me a view of purplish forests, a mountain, a lake with what looked like ice floating in the middle, and a town or city amid green plains, and then we were zooming straight into the forest. I just barely had time to get a glimpse of a large stone structure before Biribo and I slammed right into its roof.

Except we didn't hit the roof, but landed somehow in an interior room. I staggered slightly as my feet touched the floor; it was an awkward landing, but at least it wasn't the lethal impact I'd expected from that descent.

As traumatic as the fall had been, I immediately had other things on my mind. We were in a dimly lit stone room, with cobweb-strewn shelves along one wall and a single rough table in the center. There were three men already there, and one of them was dead.

He sat in the only intact chair pulled up next to the table, lolling against its back with his arms hanging limply at his sides and his head leaning backward in a way that made a grotesque spectacle of the still-bleeding slash across his throat. I could see straight down his trachea, and had to immediately suppress the heaving of my stomach.

It wasn't hard to tell how he'd died either. The two other men in the room were staring at me in confusion. Both were carrying swords. One was smeared with blood along one edge.

"Yeah," I said aloud, "this seems about right."

3

In Which the Dark Lord
Has the Run of the Place

Who the *fuck* is this guy?" the one with the bloody sword shouted, straightening up and pointing it at me. "How'd he get in— Hey, you!"

"He musta been with the peddler," said the other one, who looked more nervous. "How come you didn't see him come in?"

"*You* were supposed to be watching— You know what, never mind, doesn't really matter."

"What's that . . . hey, what kinda animal is that?"

Biribo darted around behind my head, which I ignored. My attention was on the murderer, who started around the table toward me with a determined expression I did not like at all. I looked at him, at his companion's slightly more uncertain face, at the freshly slain corpse, and found my mind was a complete white blank. Never in my life had I ever imagined being in a situation like this.

So I can't explain what happened next, and I certainly won't take the blame for it.

"Halt!" I thundered, my voice echoing in the cramped stone chamber. Straightening up to my full height, I threw out one hand in a dramatic gesture, ignoring the jabbering voice in the back of my head demanding what the hell I was doing. "Insolent swine! You *dare* raise a weapon to the Champion of Virya? *Kneel* before the Dark Lord, and *perhaps* you shall find me . . . merciful."

They both stopped, staring. I must say I've always had a good stage presence, even when I don't know what the hell is going on.

"Aw, Kasser, he's just a crazy guy," the nervous thug said, reaching over to pull his companion's sleeve. "Do we really have to . . ."

"A *rich* crazy guy," Kasser retorted, eyeing me up and down. Rich? I didn't know where he was getting *that*; I was still in my store uniform. "It doesn't matter. Rocco said no intruders."

"But—"

"You *know* this is why we're always stuck on guard duty?" Kasser burst out, rounding on him. "You know that, right? You and your bleeding heart!"

The second guy frowned reproachfully. "You always said you liked that about me."

"I *like* it, but you *know* what the gang's like about weakness! What if Rocco decides to make some kind of example out of you and I'm not there, huh?"

"You guys seem like you're in the middle of something," I heard myself say. "Sorry, was this a bad time? My mistake, I'll just come back later."

They both turned on me again.

"Uh, boss, what're you *doing*?" Biribo hissed in my ear.

Good fucking question.

"We'll talk about this *later*, Harold," Kasser said, drawing in a deep breath and stepping toward me again, bloody sword at the ready.

I did the only thing I could come up with and kicked a chair toward him—not the one with a body in it. Unfortunately, that worked out poorly for both of us. The room contained the table—currently strewn with scrolls of paper and a spreading bloodstain—and two chairs, all of which I'd taken for wood at first glance. It was *not* wood. I had expected it to bounce toward Kasser and hopefully tangle his legs; instead the thing rocked forward abruptly. It was much heavier than I'd expected. Its back tipped to catch him in the stomach, which doubled him over with a *whoof* as the breath was driven from his lungs. I didn't come out much better, limping backward with a foot suddenly throbbing with pain.

Was that thing made of *stone*? No, it wasn't *that* heavy, not quite. I didn't have any time to mull the question over; I was fully occupied with retreating on a foot that I was mostly sure wasn't broken.

The room had two doors, which I noticed upon frantically looking around for them. Maybe a more experienced Dark Lord would have cased his exits immediately on arrival, but I was new at this and pretty distracted. One door was past the two thugs, the table, and the corpse—the other, behind me up a short flight of stairs which followed the arc of the curved wall. My injured foot throbbed harder at the prospect of climbing that at speed, but I didn't hesitate; getting past them wasn't really an option.

Fortunately, Harold stopped to make sure his friend was all right before chasing me, so I made it to the top before they came after me. His distraction was the only reason I managed it; my entire body still ached too much from Virya's recent handling to climb stairs in a hurry, and that wasn't even counting my freshly hurt foot. All my joints screamed in protest and my entire back twinged painfully with every step. I made undignified sounds as I climbed, but I climbed anyway. It was that, or get murdered.

The steps curved up the side of the rounded wall with no railing and terminated at a door, which I'd first taken for wood and learned, to my regret, was the same heavier-than-wood-but-lighter-than-stone material as the furniture when I rammed into it with my shoulder. It opened, allowing me to stumble through, but I gained a fresh bruise for my trouble.

I slammed the door behind me, turned to take stock of my new surroundings, and had to pause and stare.

It was a fortress. A medieval stone structure that could've been plucked from anywhere in Europe. It was also falling apart, portions of it looking half-collapsed, the crenelations on the wall right next to me worn down to rounded nubs. I'd just come from a squat corner tower and was now standing on an outer wall of the fortress, with exterior stairs down to a courtyard below on my left and a door into what looked like the central keep just a few meters straight ahead. The courtyard was strewn with junk—piles of hay in the corners, parts of two broken wagons, and various detritus—that I didn't take in too clearly because most of my attention was in the other direction. To my right, outside the fortress, was a forest.

Sort of.

There was nothing green. There were no leaves, no *trees*. Staring out across a panorama of multicolored nonsense, I felt a wave of vertigo that had nothing to do with being on top of a wall; for a second my brain couldn't make *sense* of the shapes I was seeing, but then perspective snapped into place, and I realized that this "forest" resembled nothing so much as a coral reef. I could see segmented dome-like structures covered in pulsating growths, colossal upright plates and fins of some hard material whose edges trailed feathery fronds that swayed too languorously to be propelled by the wind, and branching structures of spikes and blunt curves, which also had growths of living tissue emerging from strategic apertures. The colors tended toward blue and violet, with accents of yellow, green, and pink, and a heavy mixture of enormous spiky vines of vivid red that climbed over a lot of the other structures.

The fortress . . . I could sort of place. Virya had talked about a game; this ruin in fact looked exactly like something out of Skyrim. That forest, though. I might be on another world, but it clearly wasn't going to be a run-of-the-mill quasi-European medieval fantasy. This world was *alien*.

"Uh, boss?" Biribo prompted, buzzing in front of my face and blocking the view. "It's scenic and all, but maybe you should keep running?"

"Shit," I agreed, then turned to bolt way too fast and almost fell over because my foot was still in agony, and so was everything else. Way to start your Champion off right, Virya.

At the other end of this short stretch of wall was a door into the main keep, so that was where I went, limping as expeditiously as I could manage. It was a lot closer and less exposed than trying to descend the worn steps to the courtyard, and I was already hearing angry shouts from behind me. I made it to the door and hauled it open, hurling myself through and tugging it shut—like the other door, it was made of long planks of something that was heavier than wood but lighter than stone.

This place might as well be a labyrinth for all I knew of the layout. I wasted a precious second frozen in indecision—should I run to the opposite end of the hall I was now in, or try to hide behind one of the doors lining it?

Splitting the difference, I set off down the corridor as fast as my screaming legs could propel me; may as well not lose precious seconds while coming to a decision. It was eerie how clear and alert my mind felt, but then again my life had never been in physical danger before. Adrenaline is a hell of a drug.

"In here, boss!" Biribo shouted, zipping past me and diving to pull at the handle of one of the doors, the one nearest the end. He apparently wasn't strong enough to turn it, but I caught up in moments and got myself through, shutting the door scarcely a second before I heard the one down at the end of the hall open. Kasser's outraged cursing was only slightly muffled by the door behind me.

This was another corridor; I set off stumbling down it as quietly as I could. There were more doors down near the end, leading to who knew what.

"I'm open to suggestions," I hissed. "Aren't you supposed to be *helpful?* Get me out of this!"

"We gotta get you set up with some skills, boss," Biribo whispered, hovering right next to my ear. "Fortunately, the goddess dropped you right where you can start with some magic! Obvious choice, what with you bein' specialized for it and all."

"I don't *know* any fucking magic!"

"Right, not yet. You learn spells from magic scrolls, and we landed *right* on top of a starter set! That's what was all over that table back there, with the dead guy."

Despite the urgency of the situation, I had to pause and turn an incredulous stare on him, my hand on the latch of the next door, which I'd chosen at random.

"And . . . it didn't occur to you to mention this *before* we left that room?"

"Hey, it was a tense situation! I'm pretty sure you made the right call getting the hell away from the guys trying to murder you. Not that one, you'll get cornered in there. Door on the left."

I released the latch and grabbed the one he'd indicated, slipping inside and shutting the door after me as quietly as possible. I could still hear the footsteps and grunting of my pursuers, and couldn't tell how close they were due to the echoes and intervening walls.

We were now on a small landing overlooking a dining hall. There were dishes with the remains of food on several of the tables, and paths through the detritus on the floor to indicate this room was actively used, though nobody was here at the moment. Whoever lived here did so in squalor, though. What looked like squashed tumbleweeds were strewn across the floor, there was broken furniture piled in one corner, moss and vines climbed the walls, and from the rafters hung weird trailing things like tattered lace in shades of black and purple. If that was what the local cobwebs looked like, I was not looking forward to meeting this planet's spiders.

This position felt painfully exposed, so I limped forward, trying to balance speed and stealth around the pain. I had to brace myself with one hand along the wall, where the lichen that lived in this room had been rubbed away by people doing exactly that.

"Okay, then I guess we need to double back," I muttered as I descended. "Shit. Can you guide me another way to that tower?"

"Risky, boss," Biribo objected, buzzing in a complete circle around my head. "Gotta either go across the courtyard or back through the upper halls where they're actively lookin' for us."

"I fucking *know* it's risky, but it's either that or escape outta here into Hell Forest and get eaten by a xenomorph!"

"What's a—never mind, I got another idea. I can carry magic scrolls one at a time. They're not heavy. If you cut across the mess hall through that door, you'll come to the stables. Should be easy to hide in there, and they probably won't expect you made it this far down. Most intruders won't have a familiar guiding 'em!"

"One spell at a time, huh," I grunted. "All right, fine, get me the most powerful spell in the batch, then."

"Comin' right up!" he chirped, then swooped off—toward an upper window, I noted, not the door through which we'd come.

I limped across the mess hall, suddenly alone, and fortunately, with the presence of mind to try to walk through the established paths rather than leave a trail by disarranging the plant matter strewn all around.

I had to leave the cleared path to reach the door Biribo had indicated, but hopefully I wouldn't leave too obvious a trail. The handle was stiff, the hinges rusted, and the door partially blocked by something beyond. I cringed as I dug my heels in and forced it open, both because of the noise and what this did to my recently tortured body.

Beyond was darkness and a truly incredible stench, which I ignored while turning to push the door shut again. Only once the room was secured did I pause to get my bearings, which I immediately regretted.

This being a stable would account for the smell—a blend of rot, manure, and rotted manure. It was also pitch-black, with only dim light at the front door onto the courtyard. Either Ephemera's sun was farther away than Earth's or it was evening, because the dimness outside did nothing to illuminate the stable more than a meter or two inside. Worse, once I was shut into the darkness, there were *sounds*.

Sourceless, inscrutable *skittering* sounds. Rustling, eerie little squeaks that didn't resemble any rodent I'd ever heard . . . Abortive rushes of frantic tapping that made me envision a centipede the size of a cat, wearing horse-shoes. You'd expect rats and spiders in a disused stable, but remembering my glimpse of the alien forest outside, I was excruciatingly aware that I had no idea what kind of creepy-crawlies would live here. After a few seconds of this, I became aware that the only thing I could hear besides the pitter-patter of tiny horrors was my own labored breathing.

It was the first moment I'd had to catch my breath since landing on this ridiculous hell planet; it figured all I had to breathe was ancient stable funk. Adrenaline thrummed in my body, muting the pain and urging me to *move*, to *do* something, despite the fact that what I needed to do right now was stay put and hide. I began creeping toward the open front doors, stepping as carefully as I could in the darkness, mostly just to keep in motion, and winc-ing at every crunch and rustle underfoot. Adrenaline was a great thing while it was up, but once it faded, the crash could reduce a person to a helpless, blubbering wreck. I'd only read about that and was not looking forward to the firsthand experience.

The courtyard outside was mostly as I remembered it from my previous brief glimpse, I observed as I crept closer. Dim, strewn with trash . . . I hesitated, pressing myself against the wall next to the door, listening. I could hear Kasser and Harold stomping and shouting . . . somewhere? I had no sense of the layout, and the echoes were confusing. Another thought intruded—my hand was pressed against the wall and it felt *weird*. It wasn't wood, or stone. Now that I thought about it, I'd not been paying much attention to the architecture for obvious reasons, but I had vague impressions of the walls and rafters of the areas I'd passed through being oddly colored. The doors and furniture were made of something that resembled wood at a glance but was heavier. What the hell were these people building with?

"Boss!"

To my abject embarrassment, I shrieked like a girl when Biribo zipped around the corner and almost smacked me in the face. He dropped the scroll he'd been holding, and by sheer reflex I grabbed it, fumbling and nearly dropping it into the muck at my feet before getting a grip.

"Yo, maybe keep the volume down?" he suggested, flittering back around the door frame to check outside. "We're sorta tryin' to be discreet here."

"Thanks for the tip, asshole," I growled, holding up the scroll. It was a simple roll of what looked like parchment, bound with a thin red ribbon. In the darkness of the stable, though, I noticed a faint lightness about it, a glow which hadn't been visible in the tower. Or maybe I'd just been too distracted then to take note; it was pretty subtle. "Okay, how's this thing work? How do I get the magic out?"

"You've got the Blessing of Magic, so all you gotta do is read it to learn the spell."

I reached for the ribbon, but before I could touch it, the red strip suddenly came undone, allowing the scroll to partially unfurl. Automatic opening? Neat. I yanked the scroll fully open, almost hard enough to tear it, and beheld lines of text in shimmering ink set against a faintly luminous surface.

I didn't have a chance to start reading; the words immediately lifted straight up off the parchment, glowing brighter, and the scroll itself disintegrated under my fingers into motes of light. The text seemed to loom large in my vision, as if my consciousness were narrowed down to a pinpoint focused upon it, and I felt a strange *pressure* inside my head. All around me existence lit up, and the filthy stable vanished. For one brief moment, I was alone in a world of light, cocooned within a sphere of radiance upon which were meticulously arranged symbols I couldn't read. Even if I wasn't able to consciously parse the text, I could *sense* its purpose, the crucial part of it burned directly into my mind so that when the entire thing vanished a second later, I had a brand-new magic spell lodged in my consciousness.

Heal.

I turned incredulously to Biribo, blinking. "Are you fucking serious? A *healing* spell?"

His tongue flicked out. "You asked for the most powerful spell in the batch, boss. That was it. By, like, several orders of magnitude."

"What the *fuck* am I supposed to do with a healing spell?"

"Is . . . Is that a trick question?"

Here we are, getting chased by armed bandits, and instead of fireballs or lightning bolts, this idiot brings me a scroll of Heal. Of all the . . . Well, on second thought, it wasn't like I didn't have a use for it.

"Ugh, *fine*. How am I supposed to cast it?"

"Oh, it's super easy once you've learned the spell!" he said, now darting back and forth with enthusiasm. "Just takes focus! Focus on your target and focus on the spell in your mind, and the rest is magic! Most Blessed will say the name of the spell out loud to cast it; vocalization helps with concentration. You can learn to cast silently, but verbalizing's a good practice to start with 'til you've got the hang of it."

This felt idiotic, but it wasn't like I had many options. And I *could* focus on it better than I would've expected; the spell had a *weight* in my mind that felt distinct from my own thoughts. Concentrating on my own aching body and the foreign presence of the spell inside my brain, I could feel it *pushing* at me. Something wanted to break through, to bridge the connection. I gave it a final shove.

"Heal!"

Vivid pink light burst around me, regrettably illuminating the squalor of my decomposing surroundings and causing a horde of alarmingly multi-limbed shapes to scamper back to the shadows, but this time I wasn't paying any attention to that.

I was actually sort of amazed that it worked.

There was a rush of cool, tingling sensations, concentrating on my back, my joints, my heavily bruised foot, and other areas that had recently been abused, and then . . . nothing. No pain. In fact, I felt really good, though at least part of that was probably the adrenaline still buzzing in my system. Apparently Heal didn't get rid of that.

"All *right*," I said aloud, invigorated despite myself. I rolled my shoulders and flexed both my hands. "Now we're talking."

"See? Tolja that was a great spell," Biribo enthused, doing a complete loop around my head.

I snatched him out of the air and clamped my other hand over his face, listening to noises from behind us. They were muffled by the intervening not-stone wall, but as they drew closer, the shouts became more distinct.

". . . like it came from over there!"

"The old stables?"

"Shit," I muttered, tossing Biribo outside and dashing after him, on legs that suddenly worked *perfectly*. Fixing the damage Virya had done to my body improved the odds, but I was still stuck in this moldering castle with bandits trying to kill me. I was still unarmed, completely ignorant of everything on this planet, and possessing only one Ephemera-related skill, with zero offensive utility. The only real advantage I had was that casting magic was stupidly easy, now that I had the trick. If I could heal anything, instantly . . . As long as they didn't manage to lop my head off in one blow, then if nothing else I could stay alive and outlast them.

"Well," I said aloud as I jogged toward a tower, which I hoped was the one with the spell scrolls in it, "I guess I know what I'll be doing for the *entire* rest of the day."

4

In Which the Dark Lord
Lets His Little Light Shine

I made it almost the whole way across the courtyard before my pursuers latched onto my trail again.

"There he is!" Kasser's furious voice bellowed from behind me. I didn't waste time looking back, but it sounded like he'd made it to the big stable entrance. Crossing the last few meters in two bounds, I seized the door handle and flung myself inside, even as his footsteps pounded across the courtyard after me.

It was darker than I remembered inside, with only a faint illumination from an arrow loop high above, but I could see the dim shape of a chair where I'd left it after kicking it at Kasser. Prepared for the weight this time, I grabbed and hauled the chair to the door, tipping it up and jamming the back under the latch, seconds before the door rattled with an impact. I could hear him grunting and swearing on the other side, the door shaking as he apparently rammed his shoulder into it repeatedly, but he didn't have the leverage to overcome the chair braced against it.

Eat physics, asshole.

I turned and went for the table, only to discover that it was broken and its pieces dumped in a corner with the feeble light from the arrow loop beaming onto it. Also, there was no corpse, none of the sconces even had torches in them, and the stairs were on the wrong side of the room. All this led me to one inescapable conclusion.

"Uh, boss?" Biribo said oh so helpfully. "This isn't the same tower."

"*Thank you*," I snarled. "Okay, then we just have to get back to it. The towers will be connected by the battlements, right?"

"Well, yeah, but the section between here and that one is collapsed; there's no walking surface."

"*Fuck.*"

"It's okay!" He did another zoom around my head, as if he thought that was encouraging or something. "I can bring you more scrolls!"

"One at a time, while I run for my fucking life through this broken-down dump of a maze?"

"Hey, I didn't say it was a *perfect* solution. You don't usually get those in life."

"*Ugh*. Fine, what's my best route out of here?"

"Up the stairs, back along the only stretch of wall you can walk on. It'll take you back into the main keep. Then you can try to lose 'em in the corridors, there's lots of little rooms up there. Don't worry, as your familiar I can find you anywhere. Okay, be right back!"

"*Wait!*" I managed to grab him by the tail as he started to zoom away again. "Weren't there any combat spells in that pile?"

"Well, sort of. I mean, not a lot in the way of direct damage, but . . ."

"Seriously? No fire, no lightning?"

"Well, there *was* a fire spell . . ."

"Good! Bring me that!"

His forked tongue flicked out. "Uh, okay boss, but that's more for, like, starting campfires than throwing fireballs at people."

"I'll *take* it!" Maybe if I at least set something on fire I could trap them in it, perhaps make burning barricades.

"You're the boss," Biribo said doubtfully, and shot upward to vanish through the arrow loop the second I released him.

I wasted no more time making my way up the stairs; Kasser had already stopped hammering on the door, which meant the two of them were back-tracking to cut off my only other exit from this tower. Actually, thinking on that, I slowed as I topped the last steps. There was another door up there on the landing, made of that non-wood material and with a big crack down the middle. I pressed my face to the crack and peered out.

No sign of anyone. Opening the door, I poked my head out and looked down below. Yep, they were already gone from the floor entrance of the tower, and I couldn't hear anyone moving. Which meant they were halfway through the fortress, heading for the battlements to cut off my escape.

I slammed the door shut and raced back down to retrace my steps, darting back across the empty courtyard into the stable.

It was as dark, smelly, and full of skittering horrors as I remembered, but luckily my pursuers had been less conscientious than I about closing doors behind themselves, and even in the darkness I could see the open aperture back to the mess hall. I made it through in seconds and paused there, considering.

There was a heavy front door leading to I didn't know what, a second balcony with a second door into more upstairs corridors, or the way I'd initially come through. I went for the latter, both because it was—very slightly—more familiar and because it stood to reason that if Kasser and Harold were going for the other tower, they wouldn't be in that particular stretch of halls. So, zipping up the stairs much faster than I'd come down them minutes ago, I found myself bitterly reflecting on the fact that, in addition to an immediate threat to my life, this whole situation had turned into some kind of slapstick sketch. Just to add insult to injury.

It didn't help that I immediately got lost. Turns out one guided passage through a mess of doors and corridors isn't enough to figure out where everything is.

Fortunately, Biribo found me before I'd had a chance to get myself too turned around, zooming around the corridor with another scroll dangling from his little claws. "Hey, good thinking, boss! Looks like you got the drop on 'em for the moment!"

"Any idea where they are?" I snatched the scroll from him. Its ribbon—this one orange—broke apart the second it was in my hands, reinforcing my curiosity about exactly how that worked. At the moment I had much more pressing matters, though, so I yanked the scroll open and stared down at the words; they began lifting off the page and dissolving into light.

The sensation was the same—the pressure in my head and momentary feeling of being somewhere *else*, while all around me inscrutable likes of text shimmered and then faded, though this time the whole thing was faster and looked less complicated than the previous one. I guess Biribo was right; Heal must've been a more powerful spell. Regardless, I now found I'd absorbed the knowledge and power of Spark, which my newfound innate sense of it told me would ignite a small flame in any combustible material.

Okay, not the fireballs I was hoping for, but something I could use.

Biribo had waited for me to no longer be distracted by learning the spell and answered my question. "Still goin' across the battlements toward the other tower as of a minute ago, boss. They're probably realizing you're not in it by now. Both of 'em are sticking together instead of splitting up to flank you, so we're not dealin' with tactical minds here."

"All right, perfect. Is there an intersection or something where I can block off access from their side of the fortress?"

"Not that they can't go around, but there's a spot up here where you can slow 'em down! Follow me!"

He led me on a short dash down a corridor and around a corner to a landing, then onto the battlements and a flight of stairs descending into gloom below. I skidded to a stop, looking around quickly, and backtracked to the nearest side door behind me. Luck was still with me; I found a small table, big enough to block a doorway but not too unwieldy for me to drag. Okay, a little more unwieldy than I'd been expecting, as I immediately discovered—it was as heavy as everything else here, but I managed, hauling it back onto the landing and propping it up against the doorway with a groan of effort.

Healed or not, the last few years spent playing music, browsing the internet, and working my sedentary store job had not exactly left me in peak physical condition.

Dusting off my hands, I stepped back, focused on the table, and pointed. "**Spark!**"

Absolutely nothing happened. Not even the sense of indefinable something I'd felt in my head when casting Heal. Frowning, I tried again, more insistently. "**Spark!**"

"Hey, what was that? Was that him?" a voice sounded from the near distance beyond my improvised barricade, immediately followed by approaching footsteps. Shit.

"Spark, dammit!"

"Uh, boss?"

I rounded on him. "You brought me a broken spell!"

Biribo's little gecko face wasn't super expressive, but I had the distinct sense he was looking at me like I was a slow-witted child. "Boss, uh . . . Akorshil is . . . not flammable."

"What the *fuck* is akorshil? Can you people not just make furniture out of wood like any *normal* country?"

He managed to look absolutely aghast. "*Furniture*? Out of *wood*? Are you completely off your rocker?"

"What the fuck is this!" Kasser's familiar voice exclaimed from right outside the upright table. Half of his face appeared in the gap left by the angle at which I'd left it. "*There* you are!"

I pointed at him. "**Spark!**"

Well, the magic worked anyway. I felt it in my mind this time, and a tiny flame like a birthday candle appeared on his shirt, prompting him to jerk back out of view to the accompaniment of slapping sounds as he put himself out. "*Ow*! You asshole, I'm gonna—"

I could get the gist without hearing the details, so I pelted down the stairs rather than waiting for him to finish his threat. Behind me came the sound of my table crashing back down. I was already proceeding at an unsafe pace for stairs in the dark, so it wasn't any real surprise when I lost my footing and went tumbling down the last few meters, acquiring a nice set of bruises, bonking my head, and hearing a distinct cracking sound from the general direction of my rib cage.

The good news was that this no longer presented the game over it should have. Not vocalizing it this time, I sought the sense of Heal that I could still feel lingering in my brain, and pink light burst around me, illuminating the two men proceeding after me at a much more careful pace; obviously they were more familiar with the treacherousness of this staircase. More importantly, I was instantly back in perfect condition. Well, perfect for an admittedly out-of-shape guitarist.

I rolled through the nearest door, only getting to my feet once I was through, and slammed it shut; this one had been propped open with a bucket, fortunately empty. Also, blessedly, it had a bar to block it closed. Only seconds after I'd slapped that into place, the door banged with the impact of a shoulder, followed by Kasser's furious voice.

"You can keep this up all night, corebait; I'm still gonna gut you at the end of it!"

"You seem like you're having an episode, buddy," I called back. "How about I talk to your friend instead? You still with us, Harry?"

The door thudded again, and eyeing the rattling latch, I decided a little fortification was in order. There was another heavy table nearby, which I upended, sending a lot of dishes clattering to the floor, and shoved it across the flagstones to brace against the base of the bar.

Only then did I take stock of my new surroundings. I was in a medieval kitchen, with a large fireplace still smoldering with embers; rather than a stack of wood, there was a bin haphazardly stuffed with feathery branches and a barrel on the other side of that, mostly filled with some kind of oil. Other than that, could've been right out of a historical illustration. Also, there were unwashed dishes strewn everywhere among a mess of other implements, all with half-eaten food on them. There were a few torches burning in the room, giving me my first clear look at the horrifying, multilimbed arthropods, varying in size from that of roaches to rats, which went scurrying away into the corners, or in some cases, brazenly continued scavenging the leftovers. The smell was . . . well, it was better than the stable.

"Mother of god. These people are *eating* stuff they cook in here? No wonder they're so grumpy. Hey, what's that? Can I get out that way?"

Aside from the door I'd just blocked off, there were two others, and also a gaping hole in the wall where stones had been knocked down and haphazardly piled alongside it. This arrangement emphasized the odd shape and coloration of the stones used. Actually, I wasn't certain it was stone at all, now that I looked more closely; but I was more interested in the dark, dirt-walled tunnel beyond.

"For a given value of 'out,'" said Biribo. "That leads to the goblin tunnels, boss. Whole different set o' problems down there."

"Motherfucking isekai," I hissed, and picked one of the other doors at random.

It led me right back into the mess hall from before.

"Okay, let's try this again," I said, dashing between tables to the big front door. "This leads in the general direction of the courtyard, right?"

"Straight shot, dead ahead! And it's a short run from there to the tower with the rest of the scrolls!"

"*Finally*, some progress." Past the mess hall doors was a broad antechamber piled with barrels and other junk; there was a flight of stairs leading up to the next floor and a few smaller doors off to the sides. I bolted right past them, heading for the big double doors directly opposite the dining hall.

Then I had to slide to an awkward halt again, as one of them was pulled open from the outside, and I found myself uncomfortably close to sword range of Harold, who was apparently more shrewd than his companion.

"H-hold it!" he stammered, brandishing his weapon and looking very uncomfortable with this whole situation.

Was he *nervous*? Under other circumstances I might've sympathized with the guy. I have a low opinion of humanity in general, but the fact is most people will not try to kill another human being unless they're trained to or are in a desperate situation where they feel they have no choice. Without knowing Harold's story, I could tell from one look at his expression he wasn't enjoying this either, but whatever had brought him here, he *was* aiming a sword at me, so without thinking I hit back with literally the only thing I had at hand.

Snatching Biribo out of the air by his tail, I hurled him straight into Harold's face. Based on the screaming which ensued, it was hard to say which of them was more horrified. I'm thinking probably Harold, since I know the trauma of having a cockroach suddenly fly right into your eyes, and I figure that's gotta be magnified exponentially if the cockroach in question is a quasi lizard bigger than a squirrel which curses at you.

"Harold!"

And that was Kasser, having found a route around my roadblock in the kitchen, now pounding across the mess hall toward me and looking somehow even madder than during our last conversation.

With both open exits blocked by enemies, I went for the closest escape route, which was the stairs. I bounded up three at a time, leaving those two to sort themselves out.

Biribo returned to his customary place, buzzing along at my shoulder, and also clearly unhappy.

"A familiar is *not* a bludgeoning instrument, boss!" he snapped. "We gotta get you some proper weapons—"

"And whose job is *that?*" I shot back, pointing at a passing arrow loop as we ascended through the second floor. "Spells! *Now!*"

He buzzed off without another word. It occurred to me that maybe I should've been more specific, but time was a factor, and it wasn't like I knew what the options were. For the moment I concentrated on escaping.

At the third landing, I changed tactics. From here the path diverged. I could go up more stairs through a heavy door, or down a side corridor. Instead, I skittered around behind the stairwell itself and crouched down, folding my body into the darkness and forcing myself to breathe slowly and deeply. Which was physically painful, given how badly my lungs wanted to pant and gasp, but I did it anyway. This was a risk, of course; if they looked back here, I was effectively cornered, but so far I'd not tried hiding, and I was gambling that they wouldn't expect it.

Right on cue, stomping feet ascended the stairs and paused; I didn't peek out to see, holding myself as still as possible.

"Fuck," Kasser exclaimed, his favorite word. "Where'd that bastard . . ."

"The ramparts door hasn't been opened. He either went up the watchtower or backtracked down the hall toward the barracks."

"He wouldn't've gone up; he'd just get cornered up there. Fucker's probably doubling back again."

"Okay, you follow that way to cut him off, and I can flank him like before."

"Be *careful.* He may be unarmed, but this guy is clearly insane, and I'm pretty sure he's Blessed."

"You be careful, too."

Two sets of footsteps departed; from my hidden position I could see Kasser running down the hallway I had elected not to take, while Harold descended the stairs back toward the mess hall. So this corridor must lead back into the main complex? Good to know.

Almost the second they were gone, a rapid buzzing heralded the arrival of Biribo, who dropped another scroll into my hands, this one with a black ribbon.

"Finally," I muttered, unrolling it as soon as the ribbon broke. Text blazed, and for a moment my world vanished into darkness and luminous lines of writing accompanied by pressure in my head, and I was left with a new spell, plus intuitive knowledge of its name and use.

Enamor: a spell which made the caster's sexual advances irresistible to the victim, the effect broken upon . . . consummation.

"Are you. Fucking. *Kidding* me?" I very calmly inquired of my familiar.

He tasted the air. "We're runnin' low on options, boss, and I think I mentioned the available scrolls don't offer much in the way of offensive firepower. I figured, at least—"

"Hey!"

Oh, great; Kasser was returning down the hall. Apparently, activating a spell scroll made enough noise to be detectable, at least to someone who was looking for it.

"You motherf— Are you using up those scrolls?"

He raised his sword, charging at me, and I found myself in agreement with Biribo about desperate times and measures.

"Sorry about this, man," I muttered, pointing at him and cringing. Sure, he was trying to kill me, but there's some shit you just don't *do* to a person. Unless it's that or death. "**Enamor!**"

Kasser stumbled to a stop, raising his sword defensively and frowning in concern. "What was that? What did you just do?"

Absolutely nothing, which I could tell even without his failure to be suddenly panting after my body. Magic caused a distinctive sensation in the mind when activated, and I had not felt it. This was just like trying to use Spark on that non-combustible table made of whatever it was; something about the target prevented the spell from activating.

"Why, it's quite simple, my good man," I said, putting on my most evil grin. "I have just cast an insidious spell to cause you— Oh my god! What is *that?*"

I pointed past his shoulder, and he turned to look, because as much of a cliché as that is, most people *will* look unless they're expecting the trick. I was off, running up the stairs, painfully aware that I was now cornering myself just as they'd said a minute ago, but I could hear Harold coming up from below, no doubt drawn by our voices. No other option.

"Explain," I snarled at Biribo while climbing.

"Huh," he mused. "I guess you're not gay after all."

"Fucking *what?*"

"Enamor's an influence spell, boss; it derives its effect from the caster's mental state. That one in particular will only work on somebody you're sexually attracted to."

You know, I could almost learn to live with my life being insanely dangerous and surrounded by medieval squalor, but did it really need to be a dark comedy on top of it all? That just seemed excessive.

"Yeah? Well maybe I *am* gay and that guy just isn't my type. You ever think of that?"

"Boss, if you were gay, you'd have noticed that dude is *everyone's* type. Did you *see* those smoky eyes? Mmm."

"I hate you so much."

"Hey, gimme a break! If it had worked, it at least woulda taken him out of the fight. It was a fifty-fifty chance."

"Statistically, more like one in ten."

"That's not how statistics work, boss. For a single instance with a binary outcome—"

"Just go get me more *spells!*"

He did a quick loop around my head as I reached the next landing. "Remember the goddess gave you a special ability! Try using spell combination!"

"How?"

"Focus on more than one spell at a time, see if you can mash any of 'em together. Should be pretty intuitive once you get the trick. Be right back!"

He zoomed away, prompting cursing from my pursuers as he buzzed them on the way down the stairs. Fortunately, I was in a furnished landing. There was a table and two chairs set nearby, which I immediately put to good use by grabbing one of the handy seats and hurling it down the staircase.

The heavy stuff—what had Biribo called it? Akorshil?—bounced pretty well for being weightier than wood. Harold and Kasser yelled and tried to avoid it, and I got the pleasure of seeing only one of them succeed; Harold pressed himself against the wall. My improvised missile nailed Kasser right in the midsection and they both went tumbling down. Even better, Harold turned back to rescue his friend rather than push the pursuit.

That was the extent of the good news, as I had now, indeed, cornered myself. There was only one door up here, which I immediately went through, and that was the end of the chase. I now stood on a round platform looming above the fortress. This spot had a glorious view of the surrounding alien forest and absolutely nothing I could use.

I kicked the door shut, hoping to buy a precious half second.

Spell combination. Okay, what did I have to work with? Heal, Spark, and Enamor.

"I'm fine, just *go*! Get the son of a bitch!" Feet pounded up the stairs; I tried to brace myself against the door.

Enamor was apparently as useless against these guys as it was horrifying, for which I was almost grateful. That was a disgusting spell, and I felt slimy for even knowing it. But Heal and Spark? What could I even *do* with that?

The door shook and I was almost dislodged as Harold impacted it from the other side; I rallied and pushed back against it.

Heal. Responding to the pressure in my mind, pink light exploded and little else happened; I'd taken no injury since the last time, but the soreness in my calves from running upstairs disappeared. Spark did nothing at all, as there was nothing flammable up here except my clothes, which I wasn't about to burn.

Tiring of our little push-of-war, Harold backed up, got a running start, and slammed his body into the door again, nearly flinging me back. I barely rallied, and he was already gaining ground. The guy was a medieval bandit; obviously he was physically stronger than a sedentary musician from comfortable modern Japan.

In a way, the uselessness of Spark helped; by focusing on the heavy sense of Spark in my mind without actually triggering it, I could experience the sensation more closely. As I focused on it, I felt my awareness expand. It was like the moment in which I learned a spell from a scroll. Flickering around me, I could see lines of unreadable text imprinted on reality. Like some kind of computer code instructing the universe on how to make the spell work.

And now . . . **Heal**. The two existing simultaneously was almost too much pressure; I winced and was pushed back another centimeter. But then the text—the *code*—started to move. The process wasn't automatic or perfect.

Reaching out with my mind, I tried to force them together and they resisted. But approached more gently, lines slipped, adjusting and interlacing . . .

Harold's sword crashed through the gap he'd made in the door and I leaped backward instinctively to avoid being stabbed. The door banged fully open and the man himself lunged out, glaring furiously at me with an expression completely unlike his previously hesitant attitude. It seemed he was *not* pleased about me dropping a chair on his buddy.

I retreated, my back quickly coming up against the ramparts, still desperately trying to jam the two spells together in my mind, not that I was even sure what good that would do if I succeeded. I just had no other ideas.

Harold raised his sword, baring his teeth, and at that moment it *clicked*. I felt them combine, and a *new* spell was suddenly a fresh weight in my consciousness.

I pointed at him and shouted the brand-new incantation the instant it was clear enough in my head.

"Immolate!"

Harold went up like a bonfire.

5

In Which the Dark Lord's Home is His Castle

I've heard that burning to death is the most painful way to go. The way Harold screamed made me believe it.

I felt frozen, suddenly sick at what I'd done as the man dissolved into flame. An inferno had erupted inside his body, and every centimeter of him was either crisped completely black or venting concentrated fire. Skin charred, cracked, and it poured smoke and little flickers; every hole in his head blazed orange, and I swear I could see the moment his eyeballs boiled away. It was the most horrific spectacle I had ever beheld, and the fact that *I* had done this to another living person left me utterly paralyzed with shock.

The sound of his sword clattering to the floor was lost in the noise of Harold's screams as he buckled to his knees; I tried to back away, but was already pressed against the ramparts, and any further movement threatened to tip me over.

And then . . . it receded. The flames faded, and to my amazement, everything charred on him regenerated right before my eyes. As the fire died, his skin smoothed out, eyes re-forming out of seemingly nothing. Even his hair grew back.

In the next moment we were left in silence, staring at each other in shock. It took me a further second to grasp what had happened. It was still a healing spell, a powerful one. I had just added an extra component. And so, it had healed him. Fully.

With *fire*.

Harold, too, came to an obvious realization—he was now alone on a rooftop with someone who could do *that*. Clumsily, he snatched up his fallen sword and tried to launch a wild swing at me. Maybe being chased around the fortress had primed survival instincts that had been atrophied from a lifetime spent in a first world country, but despite my horror at this terrible thing I'd done, I didn't hesitate for an instant.

"**Immolate!**"

"*What did you do to him!?*"

There was Kasser, yet again, standing in the doorway and looking a bit worse for wear after his tumble down the staircase, and also utterly sick at the sight of Harold thrashing about and being burned from the inside out, again.

A strange calm had descended upon me. It was almost like the last moment before the combined spell had formed in my mind; I had the indefinable sense that things were slotting into place, as they should be.

"Oh, him?" I had to raise my voice a bit to be clear above Harold's anguished wailing, crouching to collect his sword from where he'd dropped it again to step past him toward Kasser. "Well, it's a bit complicated to explain. Why don't I show you?"

The noise Kasser made was just as wordless and primal, though his was a roar of pure rage as he charged me, sword first.

This time I just focused my mind, not bothering to vocalize it.

Immolate.

He burst into flames just as neatly as his companion, collapsing to his knees midlunge. It was amazing how quickly I'd gotten over my shock and revulsion at inflicting this spell; it still wasn't fun to watch, but knowing the suffering was temporary changed the equation for me. Actually, a distant part of me wondered, did that make it even worse? This was no combat spell; it was effectively just an implement of torture. What was the difference between me doing this and what Virya did to me?

Of course, that question had an immediate answer. Virya was torturing someone who posed no threat to her, purely for her own sick satisfaction. *These* guys had been trying to murder me a minute ago, and had been very close to succeeding. I had exactly one way of stopping them, so . . . here we were.

Collecting Kasser's sword, too, I chucked it over the parapet. Funny, now that I looked closely, the swords were scimitars and clearly not made of metal. I might almost have taken the material for black glass, except for the oddly organic pattern on the blades. Well, I decided to examine that later, just holding Harold's blade at my side for now.

Harold was in the fetal position by the time his friend stopped burning. Kasser scuttled away from me, all his rage of the last several minutes gone in an expression of pure terror as he retreated to press his back against the battlements. They were fine, I knew—physically. But the *looks* on their faces . . . The way it was them fleeing from me . . . The sudden reversal in our relationship up until now . . .

Never mind shock or guilt over causing such pain. In that moment, with my enemies cowering at my feet, I was overcome by such an all-encompassing sense of *vindication* that everything else faded away.

This was . . . *This was right.* Those who opposed me *should* be on the ground before me, gibbering in terror and submission. I raised my head, staring down at fallen foes, and behind them I could see a thousand shades of every idiot I'd ever met in Japan or California who deserved to be set on fire but was protected by the laws of a comfortable modern world. Every asshole who *dared* look down on me as if *I* were less than them, from my stuffed-shirt father to that sweaty jackass just this morning who'd wanted his precious special edition but hadn't bothered to pre-order—

And then suddenly I became consciously aware of the direction my thoughts were taking, and it all vanished like a popped soap bubble, leaving me sick with guilt. Maybe Virya hadn't been wrong to choose me after all . . .

I backed up, eyes on them, sword ready to swing . . . but more realistically, since I knew nothing about hand-to-hand combat, prepared to cast another Immolate. I'm pretty sure it was the latter prospect which kept them both glued to the battlements, as far from me as they could physically get while I retreated to the door. I stepped back through and pulled it shut behind me.

This one also had a bar. I lowered it into place, trapping Kasser and Harold on the roof, and slumped backward against the wall.

"Oh, wow. Looks like you got this sorted out, huh? Figured out the spell combination, then?" Biribo saved me from having to process any of that by returning with another scroll.

Mechanically, I held out a hand without answering him and he dropped the scroll into it. As soon as I moved my other hand toward it with the intent to unroll, the ribbon broke. So they responded to intention? Cool. I felt strangely abstract as I opened the scroll, activating the magic and absorbing the words, feeling the spell take shape in my mind.

Summon Slime.

I breathed in and then back out, slowly. A few minutes ago, this would have made me *very* angry. Right now, I was just too tired.

"Biribo?"

"Boss?"

"Is there *any* chance that on Ephemera, slimes are huge, fearsome monsters befitting the demonic armies of the Dark Lord?"

He flicked out his tongue, and I had the distinct impression his little lizard face was grinning at me. "Well, now that we've got the luxury of time to experiment, seems like there's a good way to find out!"

"Indeed. **Summon Slime**."

It popped into being on the floor by my feet, a gelatinous orb roughly the size of a honeydew melon. Mostly transparent with a pale blue hue and no visible features. Just . . . a blob.

As we both stared in silence, the slime extended a gooey pseudopod to probe at the wall next to it, then began oozing slowly across the floor.

"Yeah," I said, hearing the weariness in my own voice, "that seems about right. Welp, looks like I've just conquered my first castle. Let's go see what we're working with."

"So for most people, Blessings are mutually exclusive. You get one, and that's all you get?"

"Bingo—that's for everybody except the Hero and the Dark Lord. You two have all three Blessings, plus an extra gift from your patron goddess."

"Right, spell combination . . ." Which I'd already been practicing while listening to Biribo talk. Combining Spark with Summon Slime resulted in a slime that was perpetually on fire; combining Heal with it summoned a bright pink slime which glowed like my Heal spell, and presumably had healing properties though I had refrained from injuring myself to test that.

"And where do these Blessings come from?"

"Oh, several possible sources. Most commonly, a Spirit gives 'em as a reward for performing its task. Some of the more veteran Blessed can get artifacts or spells that enable them to bestow Blessings on others, but that's really rare. Occasionally, the goddesses will give one out directly to a chosen individual. It's also a pretty common reward for vanquishing the final boss of a dungeon, in the unlikely event someone who's not already Blessed manages to do that."

Every explanation only raised more questions. Spirits? Dungeons? Final bosses? That last bit in particular made my eyelid start to twitch, and I focused my attention back on directing the burning slime to crawl back and forth across the floor. I could *almost* deal with being stuck with an impossible task on this weird-ass planet, but adding honest-to-god video game mechanics to the mix just seemed insulting.

"And . . . there's three kinds of Blessings," I said slowly, also trying to compel the fire slime to climb up a table leg. The stuff it was made from, akorshil, showed no ill effect from the heat and flame.

"Far as most folks are concerned, two," Biribo said, flicking his tongue out at me. "The Blessing of Wisdom is so rare a lot of people don't even know it exists. Of the few who *have* it, most keep it a secret. That kind of advantage is maximized by nobody knowing you've got it."

"And that's the one that gives you a familiar."

"Your personal spy and advisor; that's the biggest benefit! Also gives you the ability to understand and speak any language. And later on, as you develop it, potentially some more exotic benefits."

That explained that; I'd only noticed belatedly that Harold and Kasser had definitely not been yelling at me—or me at them—in Japanese. The local language was so intuitive, I'd just used it without even realizing the difference.

"Hm. So it's the other two Blessings that let you actively use magic."

"Yup. The Blessing of Might allows you to use artifacts, pieces of equipment which have magical effects, and the Blessing of Magic . . . well, that's the one you've been using already."

"Right. Scrolls and spells. So, these artifacts . . . what kinds of things are they?"

"Oh, all kinds! Most commonly weapons, armor, clothing, or jewelry. Each one'll have a specific effect but there's way too many to describe. Like a sword that'll cut through most anything, or armor that'll protect from magic; those are pretty basic ones. Rarer artifacts can have *really* fancy powers!"

"Okay. And how do I get artifacts and more spells?" After the slime one, there had been only two more scrolls in the pile that the unfortunate peddler had unknowingly bequeathed to me—Tame Beast and Spirit Bond. The first enabled me to control the slimes I could now summon. The second was useless so far, as its purpose was to share magical attributes between the caster and the target, and slimes didn't have any of those. It could come in handy later, though, when I found more exotic monsters. So far, it seemed the peddler had been carrying a basic monster-tamer package of spells, plus Spark, Enamor, and Heal. Spark was a common enough survival spell, mostly used for campfires and lanterns and the like; Enamor was uncommon and of a more . . . specific sort of utility. Heal, my familiar insisted, was an incredibly rare and powerful spell, which had no business being in the same collection as the others.

"Same places you get the Blessings in the first place, mostly," Biribo answered. "That's the main reason Blessed tend to keep going off adventuring. That's the kinda stuff you gotta do to get new spells and artifacts."

"Gotcha." I made the fire slime crawl back down. They didn't move quickly, and when I wasn't using Tame Beast to exert my will directly, they just sort of burbled around, like the glowing pink slime nearby was doing.

"Hm. Any idea what extra power Yoshi got?"

"No tellin', boss. If he's smart, you won't find out until it's too late."

As ominous as that phrasing was, Yoshi did not strike me as the cunning type. "I guess it'd be asking too much for Virya to give her champion a helping hand against the Hero, since she's kidnapped me to this medieval shithole and all . . ."

I turned my attention back to experimenting with spell combination. I had the trick down of summoning a spell in my mind without firing it off, and then adding others, but apparently I couldn't just jam any old spell together any way I wanted. When I worked at it, the glowing symbols I could see in my mind's eye would shift and rearrange themselves in response to my will, but there was apparently an underlying logic to it that I didn't understand. Spells didn't all *fit* together, or only in certain ways, and since I couldn't actually read any of the magical notation, I was working completely blind. Basically I was trying to code software in a programming language I didn't know, while also being a displaced musician who knew fuck all about coding to begin with.

"Not to nitpick, boss, but Virya's already leaned on the scales a *lot* for you."

"Oh, please. Leaned how, exactly?"

"Simple—that Heal spell. That is a *major* piece of magic that had no business being in that peddler's basic collection."

"Pff. If the Goddess of Evil wanted to give the Dark Lord an extra piece of magic, why the hell would she pick Heal?"

"Seriously? To keep your ass alive while you're getting your feet under you. *Plus*, and you may wanna pay attention to this part because it's important, there are consequences if she's *caught* cheating, so it's much smarter for her not to give you something destructive and attention-getting. The goddesses are supposed to be hands-off with the Hero and the Dark Lord. Rules of the game. If Yoshi or Sanora *catch* Virya giving you any special treatment, then Sanora gets a free move. Heal is a lot less likely to draw their notice than Asteroid Strike."

That broke my concentration. The half-combined spells I was trying to mash together flickered out, and the tamed fire slime started wandering off without my attention.

"A . . . free move? Like what, exactly?"

"She's not allowed to *kill* you, but there's a lot you can live through, boss."

"Ominous. Is Heal really that big a deal?"

"Lemme put it this way, boss. If someone Blessed with Magic decided to specialize in healing, they might start with, say, Close Laceration or Numb Pain. As they exercised their Blessing, got more spells, and gained the power to use 'em, they could add stuff like Antivenom, Suppress Fever, Set Bone, Reconstitute—"

"Okay, I *get* it. There are a lot of different healing spells."

"Most of 'em very specific. A healing-specialized sorcerer is basically just a doctor with low overhead; they'll have a bunch of different options to treat various medical issues, just like practicing medicine the hard way. What *you've* got is the absolute pinnacle of all healing magic. The ability to heal any injury or disease instantly, with no effort. Boss, kingdoms would go to war to control a sorcerer who could do that. There is *no* way that scroll just happened to be in the possession of some rando who was trying to peddle basic beginner spells to bandits out in the middle of nowhere."

"I see," I murmured, activating the magic again. It made sense when he put it like that, but I still couldn't find it in me to be grateful to Virya. Her boredom and selfishness was the reason I'd been plucked out of my life and dumped here. As far as I was concerned, we wouldn't be square until I'd used Immolate on *her* a few times. "Wait, does this mean Sanora will try to cheat, too?"

"As long as it's not where you or Virya can see? Absolutely. They both cheat; it's why they've got that rule."

"So much for being the Goddess of Good."

"It's all a game to them, boss. Good and evil are just words to anybody who's got any amount of control over the world. I don't think those are gonna fit together. What're you trying to do?"

"Not trying to *do* anything, just getting a feel for it." I had been attempting to connect Enamor and Spirit Bond at that point, which I was pretty sure wouldn't even do anything useful if it worked. I was only still poking at it because I had the frustrating feeling that they were *close* to connecting and I was missing something. As I mentally pushed them together, the luminous sigils of magic kept shifting around as if they were *trying* to connect and couldn't quite find a way. If I could just understand how, it could help me create actually helpful spells once I found some more scrolls . . . "So you can see my half-formed spells, huh?"

"Well, I *am* your familiar. Don't worry, it's just you and me. Anybody else watching won't be able to see it."

"Can you read this gobbledygook? It would help a *lot* if I knew what these symbols meant. I thought I should be able to speak every language?"

"Uh, sorry, boss, but the foundational code that makes reality work isn't on that list. I kinda figure the goddesses don't want you messing around with that."

"Typical."

"Hum. Think about it in terms of what they do, and the limitations on 'em. Enamor only works on people you're sexually attracted to and has a very specific and limited result. Spirit Bond only works on monsters but results in a more general sharing of magic."

"I see, I see . . . you're right, they're both connecting sort of spells, just with very different rules. Similar, but not compatible."

"Exactly!"

"Here's a thought . . ."

It was hard, adding a third spell to the mix; my concentration was stretched to the limit to focus on all three at once. I suspected three was going to be the hard limit on how many spells I could mix into a single combo. Already the strain of keeping all three active in my consciousness forced me to lose focus on *what* I was doing. I'd been pushing and pulling at Enamor and Spirit Bond, noting the different ways the magical sigils shifted around me when I flexed my mind at them. Now, it was all I could do to hold all three concepts in my awareness.

To my surprise, they suddenly snapped together of their own volition, as if the third component was exactly what the others had been waiting for. Blinking in shock at the sudden removal of the mental pressure, I found myself in possession of a brand-new spell—**Enjoin**.

"Huh," Biribo said aloud. "That's, uh . . . no offense, boss, but . . ."

"No, you're not wrong," I admitted, studying the shape of it in my mind. Once it was a complete spell I could intuitively understand what it did and how, unlike when I was trying to make different spells fit together. "That's interesting, though. It's basically a spell with the input conditions of Enamor and the output of Spirit Bond. So . . . I can share magical powers . . . with a monster . . . as long as I wanna fuck it."

"Right. You made a completely useless spell. Unless you got some *serious* issues, I mean, and hey, here on Team Evil we don't judge—"

"Just shut up. What if there's a hot girl with magic I might want to absorb? Could be useful for that."

"Boss, the only magic people can learn is Blessings, and you've already got more than anybody else except the Hero."

"Hm. What about a sexy sorceress who knows better spells than I do?"

"I'm kinda spitballin', boss, but I don't think it works like that. Spirit Bond shares natural magical gifts, which only certain non-human creatures have. Spells learned by a Blessing are a different category of thing."

"Right." I sighed, then grinned. "Okay, fine, I made a completely useless spell. Still wasn't wasted time. I'm getting a handle on how the system works. Do you notice how Tame Beast doesn't actually *do* anything in that mix? It's like . . . its code was able to make the code of the other two work together across their incompatibility. So it has no conditions *or* output, it's just . . . spare parts."

"Well . . . It connected a spell that only works on people with a spell that only works on monsters, so I guess from a certain point of view, a 'beast' is halfway between—" Biribo suddenly buzzed upward another meter, turning to face the front doors of the mess hall where I'd been experimenting. "Heads up, boss. Looks like mom and dad are comin' home."

"Right." I carefully straightened my clothes, wishing I had something more impressive to wear than the polo shirt and slacks of my store uniform. "Here's hoping this goes better than with the *last* bandits we met."

"Long as they don't actually succeed in killing you, boss, I don't see how it could go worse."

"Thanks, Biribo. Thank you for that."

"Anytime, boss. I got your back."

I took the time to mentally direct the slimes to hide from view. Biribo had said smarter animals would be trickier to control, but slimes were such simpler creatures, so connecting my mind to theirs would completely overwhelm whatever motive they had. I could move them as easily as my own hands.

The mess hall was divided, with most of the tables in its main open area and a raised dais with a single long table where the fort's commander and officers would eat. It was up on that raised platform that I was currently carrying out my magical experiments. Most of the dais had been given over to disorganized storage, and to judge by the dust on the floor, didn't see much use. In fact, most of the tables in the main area were equally dusty, leaving only one with a cleared area around it and dishes still strewn across. Apparently this was a small gang, no more than a handful of people.

I could hear them now, voices and indeterminate sounds that might have been a scuffle, coming from the front of the hall and growing louder. The moment they opened the front door, it all became much louder—and more confusing, as the shouts and laughs echoed in the cavernous space. I lurked half-behind a stack of barrels, breathing slowly in one of the old anti-stage fright exercises my piano tutor had taught me. Not that I'd had stage fright in years, but fear was fear, and this was rather urgent. These were *bandits*. Murdering, plundering barbarians; Kasser and Harold had killed a man just for breaking in here and tried to do the same to me, and there were just two of them.

But I wasn't the same hapless refugee who'd been dumped in their laps. I had Heal if things went wrong, and more immediately . . . Immolate was almost as horrifying to watch as it probably was to be subjected to. I could definitely intimidate a few medieval thugs into submission now. I'd have to do something appalling, but I'd had time to psych myself up to it this time. Make my grand entrance that I'd practiced in my head, identify and combust the leader, start giving orders . . . it would work. It would have to.

Then they came swaggering in through the mess hall doors, and in a turn of events I should really have learned to expect by now, all my careful plans got run over by a truck and sent to another world.

There were five of the bandits. I didn't inspect them too closely beyond identifying the apparent leader by the way the others hung back and looked to him. He was a big man, at least a head taller than me, with a coarse beard and his long hair in braids. Three of the others were carrying bundles and objects I didn't really register, and set about laying them out on one of the tables. The leader, meanwhile, was laughing in a booming voice and casually tossed his own burden across another table.

The burden in question was a girl.

"Finally, home sweet home," he chortled, grabbing his victim by the neck and pressing her face-down into the tabletop. She was a fighter, snarling nonstop and struggling despite having her arms bound behind her; she aimed what looked like a powerful kick at his groin, but the bandit leader twisted aside, taking the blow to his hip. In annoyance, he lifted his captive's head up and smashed it back down, momentarily stunning her. All without seeming to even register he was in a fight. "Where the fuck are those two ass berries? See if I leave them in charge of anything again."

"Boss, do you gotta do that where we *eat*?" one of his followers objected. It was a woman, I noticed with some surprise, deep-voiced and nearly as burly as the leader, but definitely female. The smallest of the bandits was half-hiding behind her, while the other two men hung back.

He leered at her. "You can stay an' watch if you want, Goose. Don't say I never took ya anywhere romantic."

Then he started tugging at his captive's clothes, and I found myself stepping out into the open.

This was not how I'd planned to do this, but . . . fuck, I couldn't just let *this* go on. Maybe I was still feeling guilty for trying something similar on Kasser, even if that had been an act of desperation. Now, if only I had a *plan* for this and wasn't thrown back into improvising . . .

"Ara, ara, ara," I drawled, projecting as if I were on stage. Everyone in the room stopped what they were doing and turned to stare at me—even the captive woman, twisting her neck to blink in my direction past the blood trickling down her forehead. Meanwhile, I found myself wishing to trip and break my neck. *Really*, first confrontation with the bandit gang, and here I am channeling the spirit of my cranky grandmother. I was *so* off my game.

Still, the Omuras didn't raise a quitter, despite what they probably think, and I've pushed past too many embarrassing foibles on stage to let a thing like that slow me down.

"Just who raised you, boy?" I demanded of the bandit leader, affecting a condescending tone. "Release that young lady immediately. I will not have a guest in my castle so shamefully mistreated by my own staff."

They all continued to gape at me. Well, I can certainly carry a conversation by myself.

"I am Omura Seiji," I proclaimed, raising my chin and smirking. "The Champion of Virya, the Dark Lord sent to subdue this land. And *you* lucky mongrels have the honor of being my first minions. You may bow."

6

In Which the Dark Lord Meets the Gang

They continued to stare. I stared back, as imperiously as I could manage, focusing on my breathing, projecting outward confidence. I couldn't help noting that all of these people had swords, except the captive.

"*Well?*" I prompted, raising an eyebrow. I could've just opened by Immolating the leader—Rocco, I think Kasser had said his name was—and he would've deserved it just for what I'd *seen* him do, let alone the rest of his life of banditry. But this was a *performance*. There were certain rhythms to it; I had to build tension, strike the right notes at the right moments. That was the difference between music and noise.

"What in the f—" Rocco blinked twice, then took one hand off the woman he was pinning down to draw his sword. "This freak better've killed those two idiots, or I'm gonna do it slower. Sakin, hold her."

"Sakin," I interjected, as Rocco released her and one of his lackeys sidled forward to obey, "untie her, and then keep your greasy fingers to yourself."

"Okay, you little shit, that does it." Rocco let go of her entirely, ignoring the ensuing scuffle as she got a head start delivering mule kicks to Sakin without waiting to learn what he decided to do, and made it two long strides toward me.

Even knowing the horror I was about to unleash, *this* time I felt pure satisfaction in forming the spell in my mind and then pushing it silently into reality.

Immolate.

Rocco combusted like a firework. The next moment was all howling chaos as he dropped his sword, falling to his knees as his flesh dissolved into flame and charcoal, managing to scream intermittently as hellfire and healing magic fought for the condition of his lungs. The rest of the bandits all yelled in alarm, backing away from their boss, and their prisoner took the opportunity to roll herself across the table, away from Sakin, tumbling awkwardly to the floor. She didn't immediately get up, and I couldn't see her behind the tables from the dais; I really hoped she hadn't accidentally broken her skull or something in the fall. That would be a bitterly ironic end to her adventure.

"Boss," Biribo murmured directly in my ear, which would've made me jump violently had I not been in stage presence mode and ignoring all outside stimuli, "artifacts. On the table, there."

I noted them without him needing to point; deposited among the rest of the spoils on one of the tables were a shirt of chain mail and a big two-handed sword, both notably fancier in design than anything the bandits were wearing, and subtly glowing.

"They don't actually glow," Biribo explained quietly while I made myself gaze impassively down at Rocco burning. "That's your Blessing of Might. It'll let you pick 'em out from other objects that way. That armor is impervious to penetration and resistant to blunt force, and will draw incoming attacks toward itself and away from unarmored body parts. The sword gives the wielder an instinctive mastery of greatsword fighting."

I cut my eyes to the side and nodded subtly, and he retreated, flicking his tongue out once. So the little shit *could* take a hint, when he felt like it.

The fires consuming Rocco were diminishing, so I judged it was time to approach. One languid step at a time, I descended the stairs from the dais and made my unhurried way down the central aisle between rows of tables. The remaining bandits were already backed away from their boss; as I drew closer, three of them pressed themselves further back until they were against the walls. Sakin just stood there glancing back and forth between me and Rocco with an idly curious expression that gave no indication at all he was watching a man burning alive.

I came to a stop about three meters distant from Rocco as the fire at last faded, leaving him whole, gasping for breath, and down on his hands and knees. He raised his head, revealing a haunted expression, and the first thing he saw was me looming over him.

Looking smug. And I only slightly had to fake it. This was an ugly situation and I did not *enjoy* the spectacle of a human being in the extremity of pain; I especially didn't like being the cause of it. But at the same time, there was a certain satisfaction in seeing brutal karma befall a piece of shit like this. And, I had to admit further satisfaction at the sight of a man who'd moments ago offered me violence was now on his knees before me.

"So," I said lightly into the labored silence which followed. "Who's in charge here?"

"You . . . son of a . . ." Rocco pushed himself unsteadily upright, having to grip a nearby table for leverage. His sword had fallen out of easy reach, but he found the spirit to glare at me. "*I'm* the boss of this gang."

"Oh? **Immolate**."

Down he went, leaving behind a trail of sparks and an ear-splitting howl of anguish.

Off to my left, the bound woman's head appeared above the height of the tables; she had rolled herself out of range of Sakin and the others—and me—and was now watching this situation with a wary expression. Despite the blood still running down her face, she looked alert. Good, probably no head trauma then.

While waiting for Rocco's current doom to subside, I studied the bandits. All of them, including their captive, as well as Kasser and Harold, had medium brown skin and wavy black hair. They were clearly all of one ethnicity, though it was one I couldn't quite place in Earth terms. The coloration might have been North African, but they tended to have prominent cheekbones and aquiline noses like some European populations. Plus some exotic features that had probably emerged from mutations after their ancestors were brought here—all of them possessed oddly shaped eyebrows, not the smooth arch I was accustomed to, but sharply bending down in acute angles above the outer corner of the eye. Also their eyes were light in color, pale but vivid shades of green and blue, which was striking; lighter eye pigmentation is tied to lighter pigmentation in general, which is why you don't usually see that in people with skin and hair like theirs. The captive woman's eyes were a pale gold unlike anything I'd seen on a human. So not just lighter pigmentation, but a different kind?

I suspended my musings because Rocco was once more passing out of the worst of it. I fixed my stare on him, diligently keeping my expression neutral despite the horrible spectacle.

Eventually he was again gasping and slumped to the floor, but unharmed. His clothes were singed and smoking in several places, but not on fire. Maybe they used less combustible material than the cloth I was familiar with?

"Let's try this again," I said, projecting calm. "Who is in charge here?"

Rocco looked up at me, opened his mouth, then shut it. I could practically see his primitive brain struggling to figure out the correct answer.

Sakin loudly cleared his throat. I fixed my stare on him, and he made an odd gesture, placing his open right hand atop his left, palms down at chest level, and then lowering them to the level of his waist. "Why, you are, Lord Seiji."

It occurred to me belatedly that I had yet to ascertain whether the given name or family name went first in this country. Oh well, Lord Seiji suited me fine either way. Better that than my parents' name.

"Finally, we are making progress," I said, and he gave me a pleased smile. Yeah, something was definitely wrong with this guy; he'd shown no emotional response at all to anything he'd just seen. "Ah, ah! Stay down, Rocco. It suits you."

The (former) leader of the bandits had been laboriously getting to his feet, but froze at my command. I could see the conflict written all over his face as rage warred with fear. For a moment, I was afraid I'd have to Immolate him again, but fear won out. Baring his teeth and visibly seething, Rocco sank back down to his knees and lowered his head. I suspected just so I couldn't see his expression, but for now, that would do.

Silence fell. I let it hang for a moment, a grand pause to build tension under their apprehensive stares.

"Biribo," I said finally, strolling at the same unhurried pace toward the table on which the spoils were piled, "Virya told me this Good versus Evil business is a *game* the goddesses play. Tell me . . . how gamelike is it? Mechanically speaking, that is. Are there levels? Skill points?"

"I, uh, don't really know what you mean by levels and skill points, boss," my familiar replied uncertainly. "They're *goddesses*. Life an' death is only a game to the likes of them. For everybody else down here, it's just . . . life."

Good. That would've been *too* stupid.

"I see," I said aloud, picking up the sword. It wasn't as heavy as I would have expected, despite being nearly as long as I was tall. And also not made of metal. The blade was a deep blue in color, single-edged and straight for most of its length, with the last third or so tapering as it curved to one side. An intricate tracery of what looked like silver was inlaid into the lowest part of the blade, stemming from the cross hilt, which was also apparently silver and wrought in an elaborate shape that made it look like it was woven together from strands of metal. It looked way too delicate for an implement of violence, but there wasn't so much as a nick or dent on it anywhere.

Furthermore, upon picking it up, I felt something *resonate*. It was an almost indefinable sensation, but a familiar one after I'd spent time practicing my Blessing of Magic. This was the Blessing of Might, then—the artifact's inherent power connecting with mine. Completely unintentionally, I found myself adjusting my posture and stance as I suddenly became a master swordsman.

"In a video game," I mused aloud, turning and pacing slowly back the other way, "bandits would be procedurally generated to give the player something to kill. In an anime, the drawing and voice acting would show them being over-the-top evil, all sinister grins and wicked chuckling at their lascivious designs on the heroine. Speaking of which, Sakin, I believe I gave you an order."

"Ah, yes." Sakin did that odd gesture again. "My humble apologies, Lord Seiji. I was distracted by all the drama."

He approached the bound woman again, and she naturally backed up, snarling at him.

"It's all right," I said to her directly, pitching my voice lower. The look she leveled at me wasn't one bit more trusting than that which she directed at Sakin, so I elaborated. "He's just going to untie you. And if he does anything *else* to you, he dies. Everyone clear on this?"

"Clear as the sky, my lord," Sakin assured me, still calm and cheerful at having his life threatened by a man who could set people on fire with his mind. Either a *really* good actor or a psychopath, by my guess. Probably the latter, since he'd ended up in a bandit gang.

The woman didn't look any less suspicious, but this time she held still while the creepy bandit stepped around behind her and worked at her bindings. To his credit, he appeared to be obeying me, touching the ropes and nothing else.

"In real life, however," I continued, "banditry is the hallmark of a failing state. Not *just* because it shows that the local authorities don't have the military strength to put down bandit gangs, but because of simple human nature. Humans are social animals, and the vast majority of people will follow most of the rules, most of the time, if they can. We all *want* to have connections to others, to feel that we belong, that we are part of something greater than ourselves. It is one of the most fundamental human drives. So when whole groups of people are turning their backs on civilization, living wild and preying upon others . . . Well, it only happens when those people have been denied the opportunity to participate *fairly* in society."

I stopped in the central aisle, studying them all again. The captive was untied and had immediately put another table between herself and Sakin, but after that was just standing, watching.

"Most of you are here, in the damn howling wilderness, because this is the best you can do. Isn't that right? I'm pretty sure I know what *that* guy's deal is," I said in a dry tone, looking pointedly at Sakin, who grinned as if I was paying him a compliment. "And . . . what're you, a leper?" One of the other bandits had bandages wrapped heavily around his head and hands, leaving openings only for him to see and breathe through. What little skin I could see looked gray and weirdly cracked. He ducked his head and mumbled something in response, shrinking back away from the others. "I'm sure you each have your own fascinating stories," I said, glancing at the big woman, Goose. The smallest of the bandits was still half-hiding behind her, peeking warily at me; on closer inspection I realized that was also a woman. Or a girl; she looked hardly out of her teens. "The details don't matter much, to be frank. Just know that in a well-run country, with adequate social services *and* law enforcement, you would be back in your homes and towns, going about productive work, being part of the whole."

I paused again, for effect.

"That is . . . *most* of you. *You*, though."

It was astonishingly easy to manipulate the unwieldy-looking greatsword, thanks to its innate magic and my Blessing. I neatly slipped the tip under Rocco's chin and with the smallest nudge, forced him to raise his head and look at me.

"Oh, you're loving this life, aren't you?" I drawled. "Little bandit king in his broken-down wreck of a castle. There are always a few. The people who are the reason the rest of us *need* police and armies. Malcontents who just don't give a shit about anyone but themselves, who *jump* on the opportunity to steal and kill and rape and generally push other people around. I bet you think you're pretty hot stuff, huh?"

He glared pure hatred at me, tendons standing out on his neck as he clenched his jaw, but he said nothing.

"Y'know the truth, though?" I added, leaning toward him and affecting a conspiratorial tone. "The *truth*, Rocco, is that being an asshole who can't function in civilized company doesn't make you a big bad lone wolf. The truth is that you're just missing the vital pieces of your brain that would enable you to get along the way a human is meant to. The truth is that *you are not special*. You're just *weak*."

That was more than his manly pride could bear. He broke with a roar, shoving the blade aside as he surged back upright and lunged at me with bare fists.

I'd been expecting something of the kind, of course, but even so, it was way easier to evade him than it should have been, thanks to the sword's magic. I neatly sidestepped, my body flowing by instinct through martial forms I had never actually practiced and letting the ungainly brute stumble past me. I could easily have killed him in several ways by now, and nearly did on pure reflex thanks to the sword's borrowed expertise, but aside from bringing the weapon up to a ready position, I refrained from striking back.

With that anyway.

"Immolate."

Rocco faceplanted as he burst into flame, curling up into a piteous fetal position and howling in agony. I stepped back, sweeping another considering look across the thoroughly cowed bandits, my eyes coming to rest on the last member of our little party.

She tensed as I stepped toward her, but I kept the sword lowered at my side. The woman was rubbing her wrists, where red marks showed the bandits had been none too gentle when binding her. She also had bloodied knuckles, scrapes all over her hands, a black eye, and blood still steadily trickling down her face from where Rocco had bashed her head into the table. And that was just what I could see outside her clothes.

"Heal."

Pink light burst around her, causing her to jump in startlement and then . . . It probably said something about the woman's character that her reaction to confusion was to step toward me with a fist raised rather than flee, but she immediately stopped, taking stock of her new situation.

"What did you do?"

"Really?" I raised an eyebrow. "If you can't tell from the state of yourself, I'd think the name of the spell says it all."

She looked down at her hands, flexing her now undamaged fingers, then back up at me. Her expression had been downgraded from open distrust to wariness. "Thank you."

"You are welcome," I said in my most magnanimous tone. "As I said before, I am Omura Seiji."

Slowly, she nodded.

"And . . ." I prompted. "That would make you . . . ?"

Finally the suspicious look faltered, letting a hint of self-consciousness peek through. "Oh. I am Delavada Aster."

"Hajimemashite."

"Uh . . . what?"

"Never mind. And what shall I call you, Delavada Aster? I ask because different cultures arrange names differently, and I've only just arrived here. I'm afraid I don't know the rules yet."

"Oh. Delavada is my family name. You can call me Aster." She hesitated. "My . . . lord?"

"Aster it is then." I looked over at Rocco, who had managed to pull himself together again with the flames once more fading. His breathing was even more labored than before, but he was already shoving himself back upright.

That was the way of it, in all the cheesy stories, right? The hero saves the fair maiden from the cliché ravishing of a cliché bandit, and in gratitude she joins his party for adventure, romance, and . . .

But I wasn't the hero of this story, and frankly this woman didn't strike me as the damsel in distress type; so far she'd done a lot of kicking and snarling and hadn't screamed or cried once. And in a flash of inspiration, I suddenly had a better idea.

There was still blood on her face, but with the actual wounds gone, I noticed that Aster was, in fact, quite pretty. Now, I enjoy a pretty lady as much as the next guy, but I generally wouldn't focus on such details at a time like this, except that it enabled me to test out the fruits of my previous labor. Focusing on her golden eyes, I brought forth the recently created spell to the forefront of my mind, and gave it that last mental *push* to bring it out into the world.

Enjoin.

Had I not been looking right at her eyes, I might have missed it; I nearly did anyway. The golden corona of light that briefly swirled in each of her irises was almost the same as their base color. Then she blinked and took a step back, scowling.

"What was that? What did you just do?"

Instead of answering, I smiled and stepped closer, shifting my grip on the greatsword to offer it to her, hilt-first.

Aster's gaze dropped to the weapon. She frowned, and then looked back up at me. "It's . . . glowing."

"Not exactly. You can just see the magic in it now."

Her eyes widened in comprehension, and she inhaled sharply. That was all, for a moment, until I extended the handle of the sword toward her again. After another pause, Aster finally reached out and wrapped her fingers around it.

I almost stumbled when it left my grasp; there was a moment in which I felt hopelessly clumsy and off-balance, with the loss of the sword's artificially granted athleticism. It passed quickly, though, and then Aster straightened her own spine, blinking, and subconsciously shifted her feet exactly the way I had done upon picking it up.

Having just handed this stranger a deadly weapon, I turned my back on her, because I was fairly confident she wasn't motivated to use it on *me*, and because an expression of trust can be a power move. People are more kindly disposed toward someone who shows them generosity, a principle of human nature which has been leveraged by salesmen, cult recruiters, and pickup artists since time immemorial. No reason it shouldn't work for a Dark Lord.

"Now, as a newcomer here," I lectured, ambling back toward the central aisle and taking cold satisfaction in the way Rocco almost fell over himself backing away from me now, "I'm aware that some of the . . . *nuances* are going over my head. The broad strokes I can see, but on reflection, perhaps I'm not the best person to pass judgment on you lot. I believe that right belongs to the victims of your crimes. Those who are still alive anyway. So!" I turned around and leaned against the edge of a table, gesturing grandly. "Aster, you know what they did. I'll leave their fates in your hands."

Freshly healed, empowered with the Blessing and with a lethal artifact in her hands, the woman, who moments ago had been a beaten captive turned a wide-eyed stare on the bandits, most of whom immediately pressed themselves against the walls, having already backed up as far as they physically could in the room. I noted that Goose was deliberately shielding the young girl with her body. The guy in the bandages had his shoulders hunched, wringing his hands nervously. Sakin continued to look intrigued by it all.

Then Aster's gaze fell on Rocco, and her expression changed. So did his; I could actually see him realizing just how fucked he was.

She took a step toward him; he tried to retreat, ran into a table, and half-stumbled, almost losing his feet.

"Uh, boss," Biribo hissed in my ear, distracting me from the show. "You just gave *all the powers of the Dark Lord* to some chick you literally just picked up off the floor. Are you *sure* you know what you're doing?"

Of course I didn't fucking know what I was doing. Was that a real question?

"You seem able to pick up on invisible magic crap," I murmured back. "What can you tell me? How well did it work on her?"

"It . . . looks like she's got the *use* of your Blessings. It's weird, doesn't look like a normally Blessed person. The Blessing of Wisdom won't function for her since she hasn't been issued a familiar, and she doesn't have your gift of spell combination. Or any of the spells you know, I don't think."

"Mm. So she can also use spells and artifacts now, but will have to get her own."

He didn't answer, falling silent as Aster pressed Rocco against the wall, the tip of the sword resting against his chest.

"Well?" she growled. "Anything to say for yourself, asshole?"

He glared at her, chest rising and falling rapidly with labored breathing. For a moment, I thought he was actually going to try to argue on his own behalf, but then his face contorted into a feral sneer.

"Fuck you, little bitch!"

"That was not the correct answer," I murmured.

Rocco knocked the blade aside with one meaty forearm and tried to lunge at Aster, but he was no match for the artifact's power. In a single fluid motion, so fast it was almost invisible to the naked eye, she sidestepped, tripped him, and brought down the huge blade in a flashing arc.

The bandit leader hit the floor with two separate thumps, and then a couple smaller ones as his head bounced away. Blood spread across the floor with astonishing speed, as his still-pumping heart sprayed it from the stump of his neck.

I spent the next few moments in concentration and self-control. I could *not* afford to let my performance slip; these thugs needed to see me as calm and in charge or they'd turn on me like the wild dogs they practically were. Keeping my face composed, I fought down the nausea, suppressed the sudden shock of it. I mean, I had set this up myself with at least a strong suspicion this was how it was going to end, but it's another thing to *see* violence like that right in front of you. God, the smell. I'd never realized blood had a smell. I guess you only notice when there's a *lot* of it present, fresh and piping hot.

Aster was looking at me, I realized, and it was hard to interpret her expression. I just nodded at her once, rearranging my features to hopefully convey approval. I was getting myself back under control, but didn't quite trust my voice yet.

She turned, bloody sword at the ready, to study the rest of the bandits again. Her stare settled on Sakin.

"You." Aster pointed the blade at him; Rocco's blood dripped from its edge across a table. "*You* would've climbed onto me as soon as he was done."

"I surely would have," Sakin agreed without hesitation. "Because Rocco *expected* it. Believe me, you never wanted to fall short of his expectations. The other two lads who got left behind on guard duty, they were never willing to have a go at captives, and Rocco kicked them both around like pump balls because of it. Thankfully, we never have to worry about that again. Speaking of which, Lord Seiji, *did* you kill Kasser and Harold? Not to second-guess you or anything, my lord, but they always seemed like decent sorts to me."

"Those decent sorts murdered a peddler just before I got here," I remarked, pleased to find my voice perfectly even.

Sakin shrugged fatalistically. "Well, again. That's life out here in the wilderness. If they hadn't, Rocco would've made one of them bloody the other, and make 'em pick which did which. That's what he did last time. Oh, but Miss Aster, don't worry about Donon over there. He was off the hook when it came to women, thanks to his, y'know, condition."

Bandage Guy hunched his shoulders and pressed himself harder against the wall.

Aster lowered the sword, turning to glare at Goose. "And *you*. You're a woman, but you would've stood aside and *let* him do that? How many times *have* you stood back and watched?"

"Survival isn't easy, or guaranteed," Goose said in a tight voice, extending one brawny arm to press the girl behind her back into the wall. "Those of us who have something to protect have to . . . to do what we have to."

Aster stared at her in silence, then shifted her gaze to the younger girl. Then, with a sigh, she bent and grabbed one of the fluffy dried plants strewing the floor and began wiping blood off the sword with it.

"Really?" I prompted. "That explanation is good enough for you?"

"It's like you said, Lord Seiji," she replied, raising her eyes to meet mine with not a sign of fear. "And like she said. Life is hard all over. We all have had to do things we'd rather not. *Most* of us didn't choose to be in this situation, but . . . we make do."

"Well spoken." I straightened up, stepping out into the aisle. "Very well, then. Are there any further complaints concerning the new chain of command around here?"

All of them shook their heads, except Sakin, who made that hand gesture again.

"Good. Aster, I'm sorry about the awful day you must be having. You're of course welcome to enjoy my hospitality until you feel recovered enough to return home."

"I don't . . ." Aster's eyes fell upon the beheaded body of Rocco. "They killed my party. I don't have anywhere to go."

"I am sorry for your loss. That being the case, please make yourself at home. The rest of my new *employees* will treat you with the utmost respect;

you have my blessing to stab them if they do not. Now then! One of you kindly head up to the tower and let Harold and Kasser in; they're locked out on the roof. Do appraise them of the change in leadership. The rest of you, clean this up." I gestured casually at Rocco's cooling corpse. "Meanwhile, Aster, let's have a discussion about this *situation* we're both in."

7

In Which the Dark Lord Takes a Walk in the Woods

So that was how my first day as the Dark Lord ended. I'd left Akihabara in the afternoon and apparently arrived on Ephemera in what was the early evening local time, but given how much of that had been spent running around in various states of stress, I was more than ready to collapse by the time I felt safe to do so. I took over Rocco's room, since it was the biggest and he had the best stuff, barricaded the door in case one of the barbarians I'd conquered got any funny ideas, and to my own surprise managed to sleep for a few hours despite my ongoing worry about . . . well, everything.

Worry, and anger. To hell with conquering Ephemera, and screw going to war with Yoshi. I was gunning for Virya. Obviously I had no idea where to even start with that, and would have to play along until I came up with something, but it was fantasies of vengeance against the goddess that turned into troubled dreams as I drifted off.

First thing the next morning I was on the road with a small escort. My brief discussion with Aster the night before had given me a general outline of my immediate predicament. Sitting in a broken-down fortress in the middle of the terrifying alien wilderness wasn't going to get me anywhere, so I set out to investigate what was apparently the only city on this island.

"Gwyllthean," I said very carefully, for the eighth time.

"Very good!" Aster replied with an approving nod. "Well . . . close enough. Anyone would know what you meant."

"Thanks," I said, even more sourly than usual. "So, Gwyllthean, on the island of Dount."

"*Dount*," she corrected.

"That's what I said."

"You keep saying Dounto," Donon added, in what I'm sure he thought was a helpful tone. "It's just *Dount*—one syllable."

Donon's previous condition was why I'd brought him; my Heal had fixed it instantly, but apparently the disease was considered incurable, and the night before he had been weeping with gratitude. It was extremely awkward. He and Aster represented the closest thing I had to loyalty from any of these medieval brutes, so here they were.

Biribo buzzed in a complete circle around my head, making Donon shy back. "Heh, the boss has a bit of a—"

"*Silence, minion. So, Dount,*" I continued after a loaded pause in which I was not sassed any further, "which is the northernmost island in the kingdom of . . ."

I turned to Aster in defeat.

"Fflyr Dlemathlys," she reminded me.

"What the *hell* is that obscene pile of noises?" I complained. "It's like if Polish cheated on Swahili with Welsh and their bastard came out harelipped! *Anyway,* we're on the outskirts of the tiny, disorganized kingdom of . . . whatever . . . which itself is on the northern border of the Empire of . . . Lancor?"

"Lancor, yes," Aster said with a smile.

"You remembered one!" Donon added encouragingly, and I very generously did not set him on fire.

"Right. And Lancor is considered the bastion of civilization in this part of the world."

"Yup," he said, nodding. "I lived there for a couple years. Great place, very clean and orderly. I, uh, wasn't a bandit then."

"So, basically, this island is the ass end of nowhere."

"Well . . . basically," Aster agreed, sighing.

"Thanks, Virya," I muttered.

"Yeah, you *should* thank her," said Biribo. "Whaddaya think would happen to a brand spankin' new Dark Lord who got his start in a big, well-organized country teeming with temple knights and Blessed clerics of Sanora, huh? You landed in a fortified base, far from any power that'd oppose you, with pretty much the biggest and most potent concentration of forces one guy can take over with a handful of basic spells."

"Ngf," I grunted, unwilling to give Virya—or Biribo—credit for anything.

"Also you got proximity to monster races that're culturally Viryan," Biribo continued. "Fflyr Dlemathlys is an explicitly Sanorite country run by elves and with a mostly human population. North Watch is out on the border of Viryan territory."

"It's true, Lord Seiji," Donon added. "You can see the lizardfolk swamp from the battlements when the weather's clear; they're Viryan."

"The local lizardfolk tribe are basically a vassal state of the naga colony in the lake past the swamp," Biribo continued, "and the naga serve the same role for the dark elf nation beyond. Each protecting the borders of the next."

"Matryoshka dolls of monster people," I muttered, pausing in the road and turning to look back. We had only just set out from the gates, and I could see the overgrown remains of the road extending past the fortress in the other direction, toward a mountain which rose out of the coral-like foliage beyond. "So, wait, if these people worship Virya, and I'm the Dark Lord, maybe I should go visit them first."

Biribo darted directly in front of my face, waving his little arms frantically. "Bad idea, boss! Trust me, Viryans respect *strength*. You wanna be more established before you approach them. They'll follow a powerful Dark Lord, yeah, but some jackass showing up *claiming* to be the Dark Lord with nothing to back him up but a couple spells and a handful of bandits is likely to end up dead. No offense."

"I'm *not* a bandit," Aster protested.

He flicked out his tongue at her. "Sorry, doll, but you humans all look alike to them."

I turned and resumed course, studying the path as we went. The actual road beneath us looked like it had been extremely well-constructed, once, being made of large, closely fitted stones and remarkably smooth. There wasn't even anything growing out of the cracks between them; that was how expert the masonry had been when it was laid. At this point it had been left untended for so long I couldn't even tell how wide the road was, thanks to underbrush creeping across it from both sides. And "creeping" was definitely the word; it consisted of webs of crimson tendrils, or swollen protuberances from the giant coral-like structures nearby. No visible plant life as I understood it.

"Here in the khora forest is beastfolk territory," Biribo continued to lecture as we walked. "They're kind of a buffer zone, both cos they're comfortable among the khora, and because the tribes aren't Sanorite or Viryan. So even though the Fflyr tend to scuffle with them, there's never been a serious push to clear them out. It's too useful to not have a border with Viryans, who'd be openly hostile."

"North Watch is in the catfolk tribe's territory," Donon added. "Rocco used to buy 'em off with a share of our loot so they'd leave us alone."

"Hm." That sounded like it could be useful. From what I knew of Earth's history, societies like that tended to exist because bigger, more well-organized cultures denied them access to the necessary resources to advance—and then, adding insult to injury, usually acted as if there was some inherent defect in the "lesser" race that made them more "savage." Such treatment stoked resentment, and resentment could be leveraged . . . "Wait, so given all that, I get why North Watch was abandoned by the kingdom, but why was it built in the first place? Just as a border fort to keep an eye on the lizardfolk?"

"Fflyr Dlemathlys doesn't really secure the Viryan border these days, that's what the beastfolk in the khora forest are for," Aster chimed in. "No, they only bother fortifying the land bridges to other islands. And there used to *be* one up here, less than a limn from the fortress. But over a hundred years ago, the bridge collapsed, so . . . there'd be no point in keeping the fortress manned even if the kingdom had troops to spare for it, which it doesn't."

"Limn?" That word didn't automatically translate in my head.

Aster gave me a sidelong look. "You . . . don't know what limns are?"

"It's a unit of measurement," Biribo explained. "The Dark Lord is from a *long* way away, folks. We're gonna have to explain a lot of stuff you take for granted."

"How far?" Donon asked. "I've never seen a human who looked like you, Lord Seiji. Uh, you *are* human, right?"

Great, so the locals had no frame of reference for Asians. That could be potentially useful, or extremely hazardous, depending on how the racism happened to manifest here. I was taking it as a given that there would *be* racism, because I know what people are like. With luck, I could parlay my "exotic" appearance for notoriety; without luck, I might have to Immolate somebody.

"How big is a limn, exactly?" I asked aloud.

"A limn is five hundred and twenty-four dhils," Aster recited. "A dhil is ninety-six strides. A stride is defined as the average distance of an adult male elf's step. Strides are further broken down into thirteen ridds to measure smaller things."

Again, I came to a stop. The others turned to look at me curiously as I raised my face to stare at the sky between fronds and branches of . . . khora, they were called? I wouldn't have thought it possible, but these fucking people had *actually* come up with a stupider way to measure things than the American system. I didn't even want to know what the weights were.

"Thank you, Aster," I said, very calmly.

"You're welcome, Lord Seiji."

"In the future, if we happen to find ourselves in the thick of battle, I may ask you to repeat that explanation."

"Um . . . all right? But why in battle?"

"Because it fills me with rage and the urgent desire to murder someone."

I couldn't really blame them for staring at me in confused silence. There just wasn't anything more to be said on this subject, so I blew out a heavy sigh and resumed walking.

"I'm sorry," Donon suddenly blurted out, after we'd walked for a few minutes without speaking.

I looked over my shoulder. "Why? What'd you do?"

"Uh, sorry, my lord, I was talking to Miss Aster," he said, ducking his head. "About . . . y'know. The . . ."

"Well, *you* didn't try to have a go at me," she said, eyes forward and face blank.

He was dry-washing his hands now, his eyes downcast.

"Yeah, and I wouldn't've. Actually it was the one thing I, uh, appreciated about being . . . you know. Rocco didn't want me *tainting* any girls he caught, so at least I never had to . . . go along with his . . ." He trailed off, swallowing so hard I could hear it even with my back turned. "I, uh, I meant about your friends."

The ensuing silence was excruciating. Fortunately, or perhaps not, Donon didn't know when to quit.

"I know it probably doesn't help or anything and *sorry* is never enough, but . . . I am."

Aster let him twist in the wind for another few seconds before letting out a soft sigh.

"Jarind's father was a friend of my father's. He was . . . sort of like a cousin."

"Oh," Donon said in a quietly miserable voice.

"Right. So as 'almost family' he *only* grabbed my ass now and again," Aster went on, her voice growing progressively more bitter with every word, "and didn't crawl on top of me at night like he did Dannit. *Yet*, anyway. She and I both put up with it because being a registered adventurer is about the only life available to women that's not housewife, priestess, or sex worker; and if I stuck with it long enough, I had a chance of getting a Blessing. Dannit did. *But*, our party was registered under Jarind's name, so he controlled the purse strings. We slept in whatever inn or campsite Jarind took us to, and got only whatever coin he felt like handing out. I don't know Dannit's story, but the King's taxmen took everything my family had, to cover some debt they said my father owed when he died, and I was probably lucky they didn't take *me*. So there was nowhere else I could go if he kicked me out." She hesitated, and I glanced sidelong at her, observing her face twisting in an acidic scowl. "No one's going to mourn Jarind. Dannit . . . deserved better. You know, when Rocco first grabbed me, I was actually grateful she'd died in the trap and wouldn't have to . . . I didn't know Lord Seiji was waiting at the other end of that ordeal. Now . . ."

This time, the silence lingered, and I let it. I mean, what can you *say* to that?

Today, I was wearing the chain mail artifact over my polo shirt. It didn't have an immediately detectable effect like the sword; apparently it would only kick in if I was attacked. As an incidental effect, though, it changed shape to fit me precisely when I put it on, and was now snug over my clothes and amazingly comfortable. I actually didn't hate the look; the mail itself was glossy and finely woven, and it had supple, silvery embellishments at the collar, hems, and seams that prevented it from looking too plain.

Aster still had the sword, for the simple reason that I hadn't asked for it back. And *that* was also to avoid the risk of looking weak, because if she wasn't inclined to hand it over, I didn't have any way of making her, being that . . . well, she was the one with the sword. My only means of coercing people to obey me were Immolate and Enamor; the first I wasn't willing to use on anybody who wasn't actively engaged in some kind of violence that I urgently needed to stop, and the second was just an utterly disgusting spell that should never be used on anyone. I felt guilty enough for having tried it on Kasser.

This raised questions, though, to which I gave voice. "So, wait. You said this Dannit was Blessed. With Might?"

Aster shook her head. "Magic."

"Ah. So the artifacts were Jarind's. These are some pretty potent artifacts, aren't they, Biribo?"

"They're better than average beginner gear, boss. This Jarind guy must've been a pretty solid adventurer to have the two of 'em."

"Sorry if bringing this up is a painful subject, but I am completely perplexed how those greasy idiots managed to kill two Blessed without taking so much as a scratch. No offense, Donon."

"None taken, Lord Seiji; you're not wrong."

"It was a trap," Aster said, grimacing. "A pit trap—vines covering a hole with spikes at the bottom. The fact that I was the only one *not* Blessed probably saved my life. Jarind always made me walk behind, carrying the baggage."

Oof. That had probably not been a quick death, then. If I remembered right, traps like that were banned by the Geneva Convention, and for good reason.

"Anyway," she went on, quieter now, "I'm not . . . That is, I understand. We do what we have to. Here I am, following the *actual* Dark Lord around because he's already a better leader than my last one."

"I'd be flattered if you hadn't just explained what a low bar that is."

"My point is, I'm in no position to judge. I won't say I'm . . . Well, I don't really know what to feel about all this, honestly. I'm having a weird couple of days."

"Man, I know *that* feeling," I muttered.

"Can't have been easy for you either," Aster added, glancing over her shoulder at Donon, who continued to trail along awkwardly behind us. "I only caught a glimpse between those bandages before Lord Seiji healed you, but was that what it looked like?"

Donon hunched his shoulders even further. I was starting to feel legitimately sorry for the guy. ". . . yeah."

"What was up with that, by the way?" I asked. "It can't have been *too* contagious if Rocco and the gang let you stick around."

"Oh, it's not contagious in the usual ways," Biribo said brightly. "Gobrot is a venereal disease, boss. It's actually not transmissible between humans, but people who start showing the skin condition are pretty seriously ostracized in most human societies, cos of where you get it."

"Oh?"

"Goblins," Biribo said with malicious relish.

"Ah. So, he . . ."

"He's a monsterfucker," Aster explained.

"They're *not monsters!*" Both of us stopped and turned around in surprise; Donon's timid demeanor had abruptly vanished, and he looked like he was about to start preaching fire and brimstone. "Goblins are as much people as you or me!"

"That's the opposite of an endorsement," I said, openly skeptical. "By and large, people are shit. I haven't actually *seen* a goblin. Are they small green critters on this world, like in the fiction where I'm from?"

"That's a basically solid description," Aster agreed.

"Hah. Well, Donny boy, I guess it's better you'd go after goblins than *actual* children, since I assume that's the—"

"Oh, don't even *start* with that!" Donon shouted, clearly forgetting who he was talking to in his sudden and inexplicable passion. "That is a slanderous rumor made up by bigots and fools! Goblins don't look even *slightly* like human children—especially the women! They're not just shrunk down people, you know; the proportions are *just* different enough to be *perfect*, don't you see? Smaller features look bigger on a smaller body; even the most modest set of curves makes a voluptuous goddess of a little green woman! And those adorable ears, the cute little button noses . . . The fact that their pretty little faces are conveniently *right* at waist height, why . . . If there was a goblin brothel in *every* city on Ephemera, there would be peace and happiness all across the land!"

Total silence descended; even the nearby animal noises had ceased in response to his yelling. All three of us just stared at him, completely dumbfounded.

Then Biribo burst out laughing so hard he actually fell out of the air and began rolling around on the ground.

"*Wow,*" said Aster.

"All right, then." I turned back around and resumed walking. "That was . . . interesting. Donon, we need to get along without creating a ruckus when we reach . . ." I hesitated, concentrating on my pronunciation. "*Gwyllthean.* So, no yelling, and you are not to discuss goblins under any circumstances."

"Yes, Lord Seiji," he mumbled, trailing along behind again.

"Waist height," Aster muttered, shaking her head. "Have you seen the *teeth* on them? If I had a dick, I would *not* stick it in—"

"Okay, we can talk about something else now," I interjected. "How much trouble is my appearance going to cause in town? Is this one of those places where foreigners aren't welcome in the shops?"

"That won't be a problem," Aster assured me. "Dount still has a land bridge aside from the one that leads to the kingdom's mainland, and the road passes right through Gwyllthean. It's a stop on several big trade routes, the last one before the capital where prices are higher. So, lots of merchant activity and adventurers passing through. I've never seen anyone who looks quite like you, Lord Seiji, but people are used to seeing foreigners. They'll probably like you, in fact, because you're rich."

I frowned; Kasser had said the same, now that I thought about it. "*Why* is it you think I'm rich?"

She gave me a perplexed look, as if this should be obvious. "Your clothes."

My what? I looked down at myself; though it was now partially hidden by the mail artifact, I was wearing my game store uniform, hardly upper-class attire.

But then I looked at what Aster and Donon were wearing, and it clicked. Not only were their clothes scruffy from overuse, I suddenly noted they were made of coarse fabrics in drab colors, pieces of leather that didn't look properly cured, and held together with thick, equally rough-looking thread.

My outfit, by contrast, featured smooth synthetic fabrics, vivid artificial dyes, and precise machine stitching. The fact that it marked me as a low-wage shop clerk was a social perception, and one that didn't exist here. Even the katakana of the store logo embroidered on my polo shirt was just a meaningless decoration to anyone who didn't recognize Japanese. In fact, a decoration of such quality that a working-class person in Fflyr Dlemathlys would never dream of having it on their clothes. Where I was from, these were cheap garments, but in a medieval country I *did* look rich.

And that gave me another idea.

"Hold up," I ordered, coming to a stop and pulling at the mail tunic. Like the ribbons on the spell scrolls, it responded to intent, obligingly loosening as soon as I was attempting to take it off. I tugged it over my head, straightened my shirt, and handed the artifact to Aster. "Here, put this on."

She blinked, looking from my eyes to the armor before hesitantly reaching to take it. "Are . . . you sure, my lord?"

"Congratulations, you're my bodyguard now," I informed her. "If anyone asks, I'm a foreign nobleman, you don't know from where. You are in my employ on account of being Blessed with Might and possessing these valuable artifacts."

"Well . . . that has the advantage of being true," she agreed.

"Which means, Aster, you're going to have to *be* my bodyguard; this is not just a ruse. I don't have the chain mail, so if anybody comes at me with violent intent, I'll need you to deal with it."

"I can do that," she said, propping the sword against a nearby sprawl of hard khora that protruded over half the road. She shrugged out of the harness for the greatsword and then her coat and pulled the mail over her head. "If you're that worried about it, though, you *could* just wear the artifact."

"And in the future I may, if I'm expecting to be attacked. But for the time being, this is not that kind of game. I won't be able to avoid drawing a certain amount of attention just in the course of figuring out how things stand in

Gwyllthean, but I don't want to advertise who and what I am yet. That means *both* of you need to be discreet, understand?"

"Of course."

"Ah . . . yes, Lord Seiji, not a word," Donon said, distracted. I followed the direction of his gaze which led me to Aster's chest.

Once it was on a person, the artifact molded itself to fit them snugly. And it was *really* snug.

"So it's not just goblins for you then, I take it?" I asked sweetly.

Aster turned a scowl on him, and quickly shrugged back into her jacket while he stammered and averted his eyes.

"So, uh . . . What's my role then, Lord Seiji?" Donon asked nervously. By this point I couldn't tell if he was actually nervous, or if that was just his personality. The guy seemed to have two settings—afraid of everything, and worked up about how much he loved goblin women.

This was the caliber of talent I was working with. Some Dark Lord.

"In the rear with the gear," I said, grinning at him. "A nobleman needs a servant after all."

"Ah! Thank you, my lord." Donon visibly brightened up, which I admit puzzled me. I'd been ribbing him, but apparently this was an esteemed position here? Little moments like this made me painfully aware I had no common sense in this country, or this *world*. If I could make it through a one-day trip to the city to get a sense of what was going on and how I could turn it to my advantage *without* embarrassing myself in public, I was going to call that a win.

Speaking of which . . .

"How far from here *is* Gwyllthean?" I asked as we resumed walking.

"Hard to judge as there's no *straight* path, but it's a good limn or so," said Aster.

My left eyelid began to twitch.

8

In Which the Dark Lord Goes to Town

The sky on Ephemera was weird. During the day it was a deep purple, with stars faintly visible even when the sun was high, fading to a rosy pink all around the horizon. I had my first clear sight of this when we emerged from the khora forest, along with some more pleasant details.

"Plants!" I exclaimed, unable to contain my relief. "There are *plants*!"

"Yes, Lord Seiji," Aster replied in the carefully neutral tone of someone whose dangerous boss is being laughably stupid.

"Hey, I'm not crazy. Virya dropped me right in North Watch and I haven't seen anything but the khora forest. I thought that was just what everything was like here."

"Oh. Well, no, khora forests aren't uncommon, but they are sort of unique. Most places where people live have more green plants."

Not that the plants in question were impressive specimens. They were scraggly weeds and scrub bushes that started to appear along the sides of the road as it emerged from the alien overgrowth of the khora biome, and rather unassuming fields of grass to either side. I was just relieved to see more familiar green foliage, even as the rest of the scenery was actually more interesting.

There were still khora out here, but instead of growing in the wild profusion of the forest, they were in neat rows marching into the distance to either side of the road, with even spacing between them. To my right were orderly domes of what looked like house-sized brain coral, complete with lazily waving fronds emerging from between the lumped folds of their hard shells; to the left rose an orchard of antler-like structures that towered over three stories in height, deep gold in color and topped with flat fins from which sprouted moving tendrils.

"So . . . you farm these khora things, then? What are they for?"

I made it several more steps before I realized they'd both stopped. Turning around, I beheld Aster and Donon staring at me as if I'd sprouted a second head.

Biribo cackled, zooming in circles above me. "Guys, I really wasn't kidding! The boss is gonna need some *really* basic stuff explained to him."

Aster cleared her throat. "Right, well . . . Um, khora are used for *everything*, Lord Seiji. There are a few species that're edible or have medicinal properties—the flesh inside, that is—but mostly, we use the shells."

"Right, so there's three kinds," Donon cut in, nodding eagerly. "Akorthist is the heaviest and hardest, and comes in the biggest chunks. It's also brittle, though, so it's tricky to carve without breaking it. Akorshil is softer and *slightly* flexible. I think the official standard for akorshil is it's soft enough to hammer nails into, but you can also carve it into more complicated shapes without breaking it. And akornin is the hardest yet, but it's more likely to bend than fracture if you push it too hard."

"Also, akornin doesn't come from khora," Aster added. "It's from the shells of animals. So it only comes in smaller pieces, and it's rarer and more expensive. The hardest to work with as well. Basically any blades you see will be made of akornin." She pulled the greatsword from its harness, holding it up so the deep blue color gleamed in the sun. "The ones not made from metal, that is, but those are pretty uncommon."

I looked back and forth at the two fields flanking the road. "So . . . which is . . ."

"Those're both akorthist khora, boss," said Biribo. "These are categories, not species. There are hundreds of kinds of khora; people divide them up based on what they're used for."

"So . . . North Watch is made from . . ."

"The walls are akorthist blocks," he said. "Akorshil is used for the beams, the floors, some of the inner supports and wall panels. And doors, stuff like that."

In other words, these people relied on crustacean-based analogues for stone, wood, and metal. Wait, why would they *need* a biological alternative to wood? I couldn't help noticing I hadn't seen a single tree in this alleged "forest." For that matter . . .

"Why not just build with stone? Surely it's more durable." North Watch's state of erosion made it look like it had been abandoned considerably longer than a hundred years.

"Stone?" Somehow, the two of them looked even more aghast; Donon held up his hands in a crossed gesture in front of his throat while speaking. "You mean, like what the *ground* is made of?"

"Ah, boss . . ." Biribo buzzed lower to speak right in my ear. "You may've noticed on the way down that Ephemera is made of archipelagos, suspended above an empty space of a planet with a fiery core far below. In basically every culture on this world, digging up the ground is a major taboo."

"How do you lay foundations for buildings, then?"

Aster shrugged. "Foundation-laying involves lots of prayers from priests and will often have people Blessed with Magic supervising in case something goes wrong. The early stages of construction always involve a big ceremony."

"I'm guessing you people don't have cellars, then."

"What's a cellar?"

I stared at her for a moment, processing, then turned and resumed walking. Seconds later, footsteps hastened along behind me as they caught up.

"So, there are no oceans," I murmured. "Where do you get your water from?"

"Rain, and natural springs. Those feed streams and rivers. An ocean is a source of water, then?"

"Hmm. Do you do much fishing?"

"Fishing?"

I looked back at her, pantomiming casting a rod. "You know, to get fish. Animals that live in the water. For food."

Aster frowned in puzzlement; it was Donon who answered in a hesitant voice. "There are animals that *go* in the water? Some of them are edible. I know geese like to swim. Also there are predatory shellbacks that hide in streams and jump out to grab you. Maybe there are more water animals in the big lake? Nobody goes there, though. Nothing like that in the rivers around here."

I scrubbed at my eyes with both fists. "And I don't suppose you eat any, say, grain crops that grow in the water."

"Grain? From water?" Aster frowned even harder. "What country *do* you come from, Lord Seiji?"

"So, no fish, and no rice. This is hell. I am in hell. Wait, these springs you mentioned. Are there any onsen?" Oh, that was a bad sign; the Japanese word came out of my mouth automatically, which probably meant this language didn't have a word for the concept. I tried combining two more basic ones. "Hot springs?"

Again, my two followers exchanged an incredulous look.

"Why would a spring ever be *hot?*" Donon asked.

I just trudged on down the road, adding another tally to the list of crimes for which I meant to punish Virya someday. Obviously, the water cycle wouldn't function normally on a broken shell of a planet like this, so the goddesses were using their magic to cheat and keep everybody alive. You'd think they could have done more than the bare minimum.

As the road brought us closer to civilization, Biribo ended up tucked inside Aster's coat; it was the only garment between the three of us big enough to conceal him. Even so, he made for a suspicious bulge at her waist when he squirmed around, but at least the garment was baggy enough below the ribs to hide him, so long as she kept it buttoned.

"I could do with less complaining," she commented after we had to endure his muffled grumbling for a few minutes. "Plenty would kill to be in your position, little man."

Biribo's triangular black head popped out of the neckline of the jacket. "Lady, I'm a magical flying lizard. What do *I* care about a pair of tits? I can tell you from here that they're a *lot* less soft when covered in *freaking chain mail!*"

"You can feel free to belly flop on him if the whining gets too bad," I told her.

"I will take that under advisement, Lord Seiji," Aster said gravely.

By the time we turned off the last backcountry lane onto a broad, paved road—paved in blocks of dull yellow akorthist; Aster and Donon failed to understand why I laughed—there was no avoiding people. It wasn't crowded, exactly, Dount being the backwater it was, but there were pedestrians, farmers in carts, and merchant trains. The most popular choice of animal for pulling vehicles were burly things that looked like stocky, bowlegged goats almost the size of cows. Occasionally, a person would ride past on a horse, and once I saw a woman in armor dash past, astride a huge feathered thing shaped like a velociraptor.

Aster stepped close to me and began speaking in a quiet tone, unprompted. "Fflyr Dlemathlys belongs to the elves, Lord Seiji."

I glanced up and down the road. "Elves? I don't see any." Goblins and elves. Someone had clearly tried to recreate a standard sword-and-sorcery world here without removing the native flora and fauna first. Dear god, were there any *people* on this planet before Virya and Sanora arrived? I didn't doubt for a second they'd drop a genocide from orbit on whoever was in the way of their fun . . .

"Believe me, if an elf were on the road, you'd know, though you still might not see them. They'd be in a carriage or palanquin, with a whole procession of servants and armed guards. It's possible to never encounter an elf at all, if you're poor enough; there aren't that many of them, and they move exclusively in the upper echelons of society. That's my point, all Fflyr elves are nobility, automatically. I'm telling you this, my lord, because you need to watch for people's coloration. See that man, the one on the horse?"

She didn't rudely point, just jerked her head, and I followed the gesture to a fellow astride a sleek black mare, wearing clothing much fancier than mine. He was blonde, and quite pale, with a broad-brimmed hat protecting his complexion from the sun. I caught a glimpse of his features as he glanced to one side while riding on ahead; though his coloring was practically Scandinavian, I wouldn't quite peg him as European. The eyes were the wrong shape, cheekbones too high and prominent, with an oddly pointed yet understated nose and chin and sharply defined jawline. Plus those weird, quirked eyebrows like all the Dount people seemed to have.

"Pale skin, straight yellow hair, and dark eyes are signs of elvish blood," Aster continued quietly. "A person's social rank is determined by how much elf they have in them. Someone colored like that is a nobleman by default. Be careful around people with lighter but not pale skin and brown hair rather than black; it can be hard to tell their rank at a glance, and they can get you in trouble if they don't feel you've been respectful enough. But if you show them *too* much deference, that can offend a higher-ranking noble if they happen to see it."

"A racial caste system," I muttered. "Okay, Ephemera, you can stop. I already hate you; I don't need a new reason every ten minutes."

I took a quick look around at the people passing along the road with fresh eyes.

Most were like Aster and the bandits—brown, sharp-featured, with wavy or curly black hair. So, commoners. I saw a few more indeterminate individuals such as she'd mentioned, with a lighter complexion and hair that was straighter and browner without approaching blonde. Notably, they were all better-dressed than the commoners, which afforded me the opportunity to observe that the Fflyr standard of "well-dressed" was straight up tacky—vivid jewel colors and excessive, gaudy embellishments. There were no other nobles about, now that the guy on the horse had disappeared over the rise ahead.

People were also giving the three of us a decently wide berth and not staring, despite the fact that I was the only person in sight with Asian features.

I'd put that down to my well-made clothing and Aster's big sword, plus a peasant's fear of antagonizing a rich man with his own personal thug, but now I had to wonder.

"So where do *I* fit on this sliding scale, exactly?"

"Foreigners aren't considered part of the system," she explained. "There's a whole lot of Fflyr history I can go into if you want—"

"Hard pass, don't care."

"—but the short version is the elves consider it their religious duty to keep the local people in line, and what other groups of humans do isn't their business. So, as long as you don't overtly insult or offend a noble, nobody's going to expect you to know your place. Donon and I can probably get away with a bit more, too, since we're obviously your servants, but even so I *wouldn't push it.*"

Those last few words were delivered over her shoulder to Donon, who raised his hands in surrender.

"Hey, I'm not an idiot! Nobody wants trouble with the pales. I thought we were tryin' to avoid attention anyway."

"Too right," I agreed, then fell silent as we topped the hill and I beheld my first sight of the city of Gwyllthean.

City? Town? I had no frame of reference for how big or important this was relative to a medieval society. It was certainly smaller than a midsized Japanese town, but *far* more dense; I wasn't sure how to guess how many people lived there. Also the class system I'd just been learning about was obvious at a glance in its construction.

Gwyllthean was built on a broad, domed hill, with an outer wall around what looked like its base. Outside the wall was an untidy sprawl of buildings that seemed to consist of most of the city's total size; inside there was another, smaller wall halfway up the hill marking off an interior district from the middle ring. The buildings inside each tier of walls grew progressively fancier, and rising up from the center was a towering palace. That much looked normal enough, as medieval towns went. But because this was Ephemera, the city not only got richer but *weirder* as it climbed toward its apex.

The lowest, poorest section looked normal enough, though more colorful than I'd have expected of a medieval town due to being made of khora rather than wood and stone. The real strangeness began with the walls—both tiers were pale blue, buttressed by dull reddish columns and topped by a violet strip of battlements. Also, they arced *outward* a considerable distance, leaving the areas below them in the shadow of a convex overhang. The effect was visually very cool; it didn't look particularly stable, but I figured the shape would make them basically impossible to climb, so it did serve a defensive purpose. Inside the first ring of walls were domes and spires with odd, organic-looking trim. Rooftops were all that was visible, so I couldn't tell anything of the buildings below from this angle. The next tier up made the effect more pronounced, as the buildings there rose higher over the walls, and were even more fanciful in their shape and color, consisting entirely of curved forms like seashells and river-carved rocks. And above it all loomed the palace.

One of my childhood treasures was a set of English-language Dr. Seuss books given to me by my grandmother in California; the structure at the center of Gwyllthean looked to me like something he would have designed. It was all gold and ivory and blue and purple, all irregular and organic shapes; overall a sweeping spiral structure like a seashell standing on its broad end but embellished with more spiraling towers, colonnades, protruding and overhanging wings, and a *lot* of it sticking out from the base in sweeping curves, rather like the walls to loom menacingly over the uppermost tier of the town.

Clearly they didn't have earthquakes here.

"Hey, Aster. What am I looking at?"

"That's Gwyllthean, Lord Seiji."

I bit back a retort, which was somewhat against my nature, but we *were* trying to be discreet, and there was no point in hiding Biribo if I was just gonna start a fracas right in the middle of traffic.

"Yes, I got that, thank you," I replied with admirable patience. "Leaving aside how there's no way in hell this was built without *deep* foundations . . . why does it go from being built like a normal city to . . . whatever the hell is going on with that big building in the middle?"

She glanced at me, then around. Nobody was walking close or looking at us, but she still lowered her voice.

"The section of the city outside the walls is the poorest district, my lord. Traditional Fflyr architecture emphasizes using the least individual pieces of akorthist and akorshil possible, but the big pieces are very valuable. So basically, people down in the Gutters just build out of whatever bricks and planks they can get. As you go higher up toward the palace, the people get richer, and so they can afford to buy and transport larger pieces of natural akorthist, and pay architects to design *around* whatever big chunks they obtain. So those buildings end up shaped more like the natural khora. Basically, the richer a building's owners are, the more organic it'll look."

"Huh." Made sense; the palace really did look like something that had grown naturally, or been shaped by wind and rain. And now that I squinted, even from this distance it *looked* like the walls were single huge chunks of pale blue akorthist, connected by the red columns. That would help explain their odd shape. And in fact, they weren't quite as *regular* as city walls in historical illustrations, varying slightly in height along the battlements.

Aster cleared her throat and shifted to walk closer to me again before speaking in the same soft tone. "So, Lord Seiji, I hope I'm not being presumptuous, and please don't think I'm challenging you. I didn't want to give that impression, but we're almost there, and I can't help—"

"Just spit it out, woman. I'm not going to punish anybody for asking reasonable questions; that would be insane."

She gave me a loaded look. "Your definition of insanity is common practice for nobles in this country, my lord. But thank you, if you don't mind . . . What exactly do you intend to *do* in Gwyllthean? I could probably be more helpful if I knew what your plan was."

Well . . . that actually was putting me on the spot. There was the concern that I barely knew either of the people following me and wasn't willing to reveal my full plans to them just yet, but that dilemma was made much easier by the fact that I had no plans to speak of, just a selection of half-baked ideas.

"I don't know if you've picked this up from context, but I am not from around here."

"I've had that impression, my lord," she said solemnly.

I also glanced around, discreetly, making sure there was no one nearby. A merchant wagon train was lumbering past on the opposite side of the road; the noise of the wheels and animals made a nice cover. "By *here* I mean Ephemera."

Aster gave me a surprised look, but not as surprised as I might have expected. "Oh. It's true, then?"

"That depends on what 'it' is."

"That Heroes and Dark Lords are called from another world? It's been a century and a half since the last pair, so at this point there's just myth and rumor . . ."

"Well, it's certainly true this time. So to answer your question . . . I want to get a look around."

"That's . . ." She frowned quizzically. "That's it?"

"That's it. I need to understand . . . what I'm working with. *Everything.* Politics, economics. Military. What commoners' lives are like. More things than I can even think of to name. Before I can make concrete plans, I need to *understand* what's happening here, how this country works, and how I can operate within and against it. And I don't have time to dawdle. It'll be my ass if Virya gets bored waiting for me to do something. Not to mention the Hero is out there, and I wouldn't put it past that dumbass to let himself get manipulated into murdering me even if all I do is walk around petting puppies and feeding orphans."

"I see," she murmured. "Well . . . there are some things I can show you, of course, and explain. There's a lot I *don't* know, but some things I imagine could be useful. You should see the King's Guild, to begin with. I also need to stop there at some point soon. With your permission, my lord."

I gave her a sidelong look, considering.

"Why *are* you so willing to help, Aster? Just gratitude that I saved you from the bandits?"

"You didn't save me from the bandits," she said softly. "You gave me the power to save *myself* from them. That makes all the difference in the world. Aside from the fact that I only keep my Blessing if I work for you? I won't deny I have *reservations*, Lord Seiji. Everything I've been taught since I was old enough to hear it makes Virya and her Dark Lords out to be the very essence of evil. Destruction, suffering, all of that."

She trailed off, frowning ahead into the distance in deep thought.

"But?" I prompted after a moment.

"But," Aster agreed, "having met you, and having thought about how Fflyr Dlemathlys already works . . . Maybe I'm rushing to conclusions, but I can't help wondering if you wouldn't actually be *better* than the way things are now. I'm already pretty sure you wouldn't be worse."

"Hm. It's that bad, huh?"

Her expression darkened further. "If you're not a noble, or at least rich—and a man, to boot—it isn't great."

"It's a pretty shit country, Lord Seiji," Donon agreed from behind us, not troubling to moderate his voice. "Why, the nobles—"

We both turned to glare at him and he broke off, eyes going wide. Then he glanced furtively about. Fortunately, we were somewhat distant from any pedestrians, but one of the armored guards riding along the tail end of the passing merchant caravan gave Donon an amused look and shook his head.

"Also," I amended my stated agenda, "let's try to avoid getting ourselves arrested, murdered, or otherwise inconvenienced by the powers that be, yeah?"

A muffled but clearly derisive noise emerged from inside Aster's jacket.

9

In Which the Dark Lord Makes a Friend

We arrived at Gwyllthean in the afternoon, having walked for most of the day. That gave me an idea how far it was from my evil lair, even accounting for the roundabout route we'd taken, and it was a favorable distance—I had access to civilization but a comfortable amount of space from it. I could get to town at need, but should have advance warning if they tried to march an army at me. This also spared me having to develop a mental frame of reference for how far a limn was because I *refused* on principle to have that bullshit in my brain.

Though the Gutters were outside the walls, there were watchtowers at intervals beyond them, including one standing right alongside the main road; once past that periphery, I guessed we were in Gwyllthean proper. From there, the road itself began to rise in a long ramp toward the gate in the first wall—which I noted was housed in a towering fortification and loomed over twice the height of the wall itself. From this close, I could see that the aptly named Gutters seemed to have partially flooded foundations, with their clearly unplanned layout connected by a hodgepodge of rough streets, canals, and bridges of varying quality. Lesser ramps down from the main road connected them at intervals, looking almost tacked on as afterthoughts to the well-built central avenue.

I was quickly preoccupied by discovering what happens when a medieval city is built over a bunch of canals—it smells like a family of fish drowned in pig feces, and then a family of enemy fish pelted their funeral with rotten eggs. I mentally scratched visiting Venice off my list of things to do if I ever got back to Earth.

Donon cleared his throat loudly behind me. "Ah, begging your pardon, Lord Seiji . . . not to overstep or nothing, but . . ."

"I'm actively in need of insights here, Donon. If you have any thoughts you can share *without getting us in trouble*, please do."

"Of course, my lord. Just wanted to point out in case it was useful . . ." He jogged forward to walk on the other side of me from Aster, pointing ahead and toward one side of the long ramp we were currently ascending toward the gates. "In the Gutters, the rule is the better, nicer areas are closer to the walls, but up there is an exception. Right around the northwest gate, in the shadow of the outer walls, the streets reached directly by the steepest ramps . . . That's where you go if you got shady business. *Expensive* shady business."

"*Hmm.* This is useful information. Thank you, Donon. Well done."

He puffed up so visibly it made me uncomfortable. How hard up was this guy for validation?

Aster cleared her throat. "While, uh, I can see how bandits and criminals might be useful to you, Lord Seiji, it might be smarter to start . . . lower? There are plenty of sketchy areas in the Gutters. The people in the High Lows are *dangerous.*"

I just nodded, thinking ahead. Donon and Aster were hinting at organized crime, which sounded like exactly what the Dark Lord needed. That'd be a tough crowd to get in with, but worst case I could Immolate people until they learned to behave.

Among the people coming in and out through the gates, my eye caught two men who turned onto one of the ramps leading down to the streets Donon had just indicated. They made a more conventional parallel to me and Aster, in fact. A well-dressed man accompanied by a heavily armed thug. Except that the man wore local rich-people fashion, in tight pants and a loose shirt with a heavily embroidered thigh-length coat, which was dyed a vivid blue beneath all of its decorations to match his cobalt-colored and gold-trimmed leather boots. He was also blonde beneath his broad-brimmed hat, wearing a rapier at his waist, and had that expression that rich people get where I couldn't tell if he was sneering or his face was just shaped that way. His bodyguard was more conventional, too—a tall, broad-shouldered man with both a club and short sword hanging from his belt, nothing on him apparently elaborate enough to be an artifact.

"Perfect," I said aloud, changing my course and lengthening my stride to pursue them down the ramp.

"Lord Seiji?" Aster hissed. "What are you *doing?*"

"Isn't it obvious?" I grinned at her and made a languid gesture at the nobleman ahead, currently striding down into criminal territory with all the confidence of someone who owns the place. "I'm gonna go make friends with that guy. He seems nice."

If I hadn't been saving the battery on my phone for emergencies, I would've taken a picture of her face. That expression was worth preserving.

"My lord," she continued to mutter, leaning close to me as we descended, "if I failed to make it clear enough, nobles are dangerous, and criminals are dangerous, and *this* looks like *both*."

"You know who else is dangerous? The fuckin' Dark Lord. Best behavior now, people, it's time to be sociable."

She subsided, looking magnificently displeased at everything. Behind me I swear I could hear Donon gulp.

I turned onto the ramp, bringing the pair ahead back into sight; they were already more than halfway down. Being the closest to the city gates and thus highest up, the ramp was taller and longer than any of the others we'd passed, and at its top, where it joined the much larger ramp of the road leading to the gates, it was above the level of most of the rooftops below. The nobleman and his bodyguard had just passed into the shadow of a looming structure ahead. I lengthened my stride, Aster keeping pace and Donon trotting along behind.

The bodyguard was good; he kept watch all around, even occasionally glancing behind. Thus, he noticed us just seconds after we began our pursuit as part of a random sweep. His head-turning became immediately less random, glancing back over his shoulder twice more over the next ten seconds and clearly taking note of the distance between us shortening. After the third glance, he lowered his head slightly toward his employer. I was, of course, too distant to hear anything, but in the next moment the nobleman also glanced back at us. Thereafter he did not look again, though the bodyguard began keeping a regular watch on us. I noted that while the lord rested a hand on the hilt of his rapier, they didn't increase their pace. Confident fellows, then.

Aster tried once more, pitching her voice low. "Men like that are not going to appreciate being approached in public by strangers, Lord Seiji."

"Let me worry about that. Defend me if either goes on the offensive, but otherwise mind your manners."

She pressed her lips together and exhaled an angry sigh through her nose.

The street below this ramp was quiet, to a point that was downright strange for an urban area at this time of afternoon. By the look of the buildings lining it, there might not necessarily be many people about; they had large doors and few windows, which suggested warehouses. Still, there should be *someone*, unless . . . Actually I didn't know unless what, though it was a safe bet it had to do with the kind of business I'd been warned was conducted in these parts. It was noticeably darker, especially once we passed down below the level of the surrounding rooftops. The outward-arching city walls hung directly overhead here, which felt unsettling and oppressive. I knew they had to be structurally sound, somehow, but it *felt* like they were about to collapse on us any second.

The dimness and isolation set a perfect mood for the moment, just after the three of us reached the base of the ramp with our quarry only a few meters ahead, when both men suddenly stopped and turned. Smoothly drawing his rapier in the process of pivoting, the nobleman held it forward and pointed down, at the ready but not overtly threatening me. Yet.

"Strange to see a fellow traveler passing through *this* of all places," he said, staring icily at me. At his side, the bodyguard was less subtle, taking up both his cudgel and short sword and bracing his feet in a stance I recognized as menacing, despite my lack of martial arts skill.

Out of the corner of my eye, I saw Aster start to reach for the greatsword handle protruding over her shoulder in response, which was an aggressive posture I did *not* want to take here. I held up one hand; she lowered hers and both she and Donon hesitated, letting me continue two steps ahead.

I stopped out of rapier range, of course, and not so far ahead of Aster that she couldn't intervene. Almost unbidden, the mental weight that was Immolate formed in my mind and hovered there, ready to be deployed. The nobleman's black eyes fixed on me, suspicious and cold.

"It's funny you would say so," I replied in a cheerful tone. Almost reflexively my body fell into a cocky semi-slouch as I slipped into the stage persona I used for performing at classic rock venues. "If it's not obvious at a glance, I am newly arrived in your lovely country! And just as I was coming to the city, my local guides here happened to mention that these streets were best avoided by a man of means and taste."

"Excellent advice." His tone did not warm in the slightest, but at least the rapier didn't move.

"So imagine my surprise when the very next thing I saw was a man obviously possessing both," I gestured grandly at his clothes, and he narrowed his eyes in response, "accompanied by a walking pile of muscle, heading down into this very street!"

"If your response to *that* was to walk up and strike up a conversation, you're as foolish as Conzart."

Who? Or what? Never mind, the cultural references here weren't important. "Only if I meant to pry into your business." I let my own smile diminish to a more reserved level. "I assure you, sir, I'm not even slightly curious what brings you here. I just pegged you as the kind of person who would know where an enterprising fresh face in the city could go looking for profitable opportunity!" I paused for effect, then lowered my voice conspiratorially. "And maybe it would reflect well on you in the eyes of those looking for talent if you directed it to them."

He stared at me in chilling silence; the bodyguard's fingers flexed on his weapons, but at least he made no further moves. I did notice the bigger man's eyes had cut past me to fix on Aster, and while I couldn't see what *she* was doing, I hoped it wasn't going to escalate this while I was trying to be diplomatic.

After the moment had drawn out for several tense seconds, the nobleman finally lowered his rapier slightly—keeping it out and at the ready, but aimed toward the side rather than at my feet. He glanced at his goon as if for confirmation before returning his stare to me.

"Are you completely insane?"

I might've been offended if it wasn't such a valid question.

"Well, damn, I hope not," I said, grinning broadly and spreading my hands in a disarming gesture. "I'd say, rather, that I am . . . liberated."

"From sanity?"

"From *everything*. I wasn't exaggerating; I have *just* arrived in . . ." I hesitated, then decided not to try pronouncing Fflyr Dlemathlys in front of someone who probably had an emotional attachment to the name. ". . . in this land. I've not even ventured inside the walls yet. Yes, I am free—of the, shall we say, *issues* which caused me to leave my homeland, and of such mundane concerns as lodging, food, and the like. What you see is what there is—myself, my skills, the contents of my pockets, and these two moderately useful strays I've picked up. Now, I could dither around, look for an inn or something, feel sorry for myself, and drown my frustrations . . . but I'm more the type to look for opportunity than remain content with disappointment."

"Opportunity," he repeated, skepticism heavy in his voice. "And you somehow picked *me* as a source of it."

"Perhaps I have misjudged you, my friend, in which case I apologize. But, circumstantially, it does seem you might be connected to the sort of business that offers high risk and equally high reward. The only way to live, isn't it? Especially for a man with no roots in this country."

Another pause fell, in which he continued to stare at me, but this time I thought his expression was more pensive. Suggesting that I was on the run from political trouble in my own country hopefully helped; that was a narrative I felt an aristocrat would be more likely to relate to.

"What about it, then?" I prompted. "Not that I'm hitting you up for a job, you understand. But perhaps you can point a guy in the direction of where to peddle my . . . humble tricks?"

I gestured at the ground between us, releasing the block of congealed thought that was Immolate and activating another spell—**Summon Fire Slime**.

It burst into being out of nowhere, immediately prompting both of them to skip backward, the nobleman with an agility and reflexive lift of his sword which told me that yes, he did indeed know how to use it. His bodyguard moved as well, not only back from the slime but in front of his master, both weapons at the ready.

"It's all right!" I assured them cheerfully, raising both hands. "Just a harmless little demonstration! It's completely under my control."

Tame Beast, I added to the slime in order to back that up, then pointed back and forth slowly, making it slide across the ground between us. Slimes, as I had already discovered, don't move quickly, but I was able to make it ripple in interesting ways, extending little pseudopods of burning goo and creating tiny puffs of the fire that coated it naturally.

"Now *that* is a thing worth seeing," the noble said at last, still keeping his distance but brushing his bodyguard aside with the flat of his sword. The speed with which the big man moved in response to such light pressure suggested he was used to being pushed around this way. "A fire elemental, is it? That's a rare spell, stranger."

"Huh," the other fellow grunted. "Looks kinda like a slime."

"A slime." The noble tore his eyes from it to direct an utterly withering look at his companion. "Which is on *fire*. I do not pay you for your conversational skills or scintillating insights, you chunk of gristle, nor do I need you to continually demonstrate what a poor bargain that would be. Speak with your fists or not at all, and only when directed."

"My lord," the man replied stoically. The lack of reaction suggested he was equally used to being spoken to thusly. I already didn't like this aristocrat, but I didn't need to; he was a means to an end.

"So," the noble said, again studying me. "A foreigner, and a silent caster, with access to . . . exotic spells rarely seen on Dount. *And* an enterprising spirit with an eye for opportunity. On the other hand, friend, you show rather more ambition than sense."

"I'll cop to that," I said in my most agreeable tone, "but really, isn't that an equally useful trait? Under the right circumstances anyway."

"Perhaps." Finally, he sheathed the rapier, his expression relaxing somewhat. "If you're that new to the country, you've done well to already have acquired Dountol servants. Particularly Blessed specimens." His eyes cut to Aster, flicking to the handle of her sword and the collar of her mail shirt. At least, I assumed that was what he was looking at; her loose jacket obscured both the shape of her chest and the bundle of Biribo still hidden in it.

"Oh, these two? They were just what was lying around," I demurred airily. "Aster has already proved a surprisingly valuable find, and the boy . . . well, he only has to carry things and follow. I will honestly be impressed if he finds a way to screw *that* up."

The nobleman's lip curled up in an effete sneer. "Never underestimate the ability of lowborn to bungle simple tasks, my friend."

Oh yeah, fuck *this* guy. But I could still use him, and if he had me pegged as a fellow noble it meant my act was working as intended. "True, true. It's the same wherever one goes, is it not?"

"Indeed. I am not, I regret to inform you, in a position to *recruit* new . . . talent."

I kept my own smile in place. "*But . . . ?*"

"But," he agreed, nodding almost imperceptibly, "I do believe I know someone who might be interested in interviewing you."

"I would be absolutely thrilled to meet them!" Success! At the very least I could learn how the dark side of Gwyllthean operated, and perhaps if the terms were agreeable, it would suit my interests to let myself be recruited.

"Obviously," my new acquaintance continued in a drier tone, "my associates are mindful of both their pride and security. I should forewarn you that we have short manners with those of hostile or duplicitous intent."

"Oh, but of course. Severed fingers, shattered kneecaps, plucked eyeballs, all the classics. I fancy I'm familiar with the broad strokes."

The bodyguard grimaced deeply; his employer just raised his eyebrows. "Hell's revels, what an . . . *imaginative* people yours must be. We Fflyr simply kill our enemies and dump them over the rim."

"Straightforward and efficient! I think I'm going to like it here."

He made a peculiar gesture—right hand in front of the heart, palm down, then rotated it palm up and moved it in a horizontal line across his chest before letting it fall. "I am Lord Arider of Clan Olumnach."

"Hajimemashite. I am . . . Lord Seiji of Clan Omura."

Lord Arider's expression tightened subtly. "We don't bow in Fflyr Dlemathlys, Lord Seiji. As you become acquainted with our history, you will understand why, but to begin, consider it a point of etiquette."

Oh. I hadn't even registered that I'd done it; bowing was just second nature.

"Ah, forgive me. I appreciate the instruction, Lord Arider."

"So. It is *Lord* Seiji, then?" His eyes flicked briefly over my outfit—with curiosity, but not skepticism. Evidently, cheap Japanese fabric matched up well against the best Fflyr Dlemathlys had to offer, and he was willing to accept the style as being foreign, like my face and accent.

"That is a translation, of course. I suspect if I went around introducing myself as Seiji-sama, no one would know what I meant." Hm. That was actually the first time I'd heard the title in my native language. Maybe I *should* have people call me Seiji-sama. It had a nice ring to it.

"Quite so. Perhaps later we can discuss how the different systems of rank align. For now, I'm afraid you have caught me in the middle of an errand."

"Ah yes, and here I am, making you late! Profound apologies, Lord Arider. If you'll kindly direct me to the next person to whom I should speak, I'll cease taking up your time."

"No one there would see you without an introduction," he said with a knowing little smile. "This . . . will not take long, and is not excessively sensitive in nature. I must admit, I have been relegated to the role of delivery boy—but only because there are matters my clan *cannot* entrust to lesser talents." He gave his bodyguard a pointed stare; the man just stood there in long-suffering patience. "If you are not busy at present . . . ?"

"My time is yours!"

Arider nodded once and gave my fire slime a significant look. Oh, right . . . I didn't actually know how to get rid of these things, they couldn't be banished the same way they were summoned. My previous fire slime back at North Watch had been left in a cauldron in the kitchen; the other two were just . . . around, somewhere. Fortunately we were still in the Gutters and there was a narrow gap between two nearby buildings at the base of which was a drain. I directed the slime into this; it oozed through the bars, there came a splash and a sizzle, and the awareness of it in my head from Tame Beast fizzled out.

Alas, poor slime, we hardly knew you.

10

In Which the Dark Lord Immediately Unmakes a Friend

My new asshole friend, Lord Arider of Clan Olumnach, whom I had no immediate plans to betray but had a feeling that was where this relationship would end up, took a step to the side and paced around the end of the ramp. Beckoning me with a courteous gesture, he proceeded into the space alongside it, which I now saw formed an alleyway between the side of the ramp and the arch of the city wall. Up ahead, the alley turned into a tunnel as it passed beneath the much larger ramp of the main road, directly below the gates.

I fell into step alongside him, keeping up my insouciant swagger and noting that he moved with a similar gait. Apparently, there was some overlap between the mannerisms of aristocrats and rock stars. Arider's bodyguard came up behind us—uncomfortably close, actually, to the point I almost imagined I could feel his breath. Right; I'd stepped into what had been his position at his master's side. I started to say something, but caught Arider glancing at me sidelong with a faint yet distinctly smug little smirk pulling at the corner of his mouth, and immediately decided not to give him the satisfaction. Or any satisfaction, ever. Aster and Donon trailed along behind, so I held my peace, reasoning that if Muscle Man tried anything, she'd see and take him out.

"What country *did* you say you were from, Lord Seiji?"

The sudden interruption of my inner monologue caused me to momentarily fumble. "Ah—Japan."

"Oh? Did you forget for a moment?" The smirk widened.

I naturally wanted to punch it off his face, but that was clearly the reaction he was digging for, so instead I gave him a cocky grin.

"We call it Nihon, but Japan is the . . . international name. I thought it might be more familiar to you."

"Ah? I can't say I've heard of either name, and I *have* had the benefit of a proper education. How far is this country?"

Fortunately, I'd had time to come up with an answer to this during the day-long walk to Gwyllthean.

"To be quite honest, I have no idea of either distance or direction. My arrival here . . . Well, it came at a convenient time for me to get out of the country; though this was not at all the method I would have chosen." Not even a lie, I'd been saving up for my move to the States for seven years. "I encountered a, shall we say, magical mishap of a nature I could not have predicted."

The plan here was to then play coy and try to leverage my vague hint to build mystery and interest, but Arider immediately nodded as if he knew exactly what I was talking about.

"Ah yes, several of my clan have had that happen when giving unwise answers to the Spirit on our estate—mostly of the older generations, but one of my cousins got himself disappeared messing about with the wretched thing, as if he didn't know better. My great-uncle is the only one to have made it back, years after the fact, and let us know the damned Spirit was sending people who annoyed it to the far end of the archipelago. You're fortunate, Seiji; you might have ended up disintegrated instead of translocated. Spirits are not to be taken lightly."

"Indeed, the goddess was watching over me," I said solemnly, filing away this information. Biribo had mentioned Spirits, too. I didn't know what that was, but stories about mischievous yokai or fae or whatever exist in most cultures; apparently, on Ephemera they were a bit more literal.

"Well, we shall soon see," he replied, again putting on that knowing little smirk. Still in active performance mode, I didn't tense up or make a face in reply, though my sense of danger heightened. Arider was obviously testing me . . . which wasn't unreasonable in his position. "In fact, if you'll indulge me, why not a little test of your vaunted abilities right now?"

At that moment, we passed into the darkness of the tunnel.

"What did you have in mind, Arider?" I kept my tone as light as my gait, but couldn't shake the feeling he saw through my performance. People of his class *lived* by projecting carefully crafted impressions; he wasn't going to be as easy to take in as the girls who hung around the rock venues I'd played.

"As your retainers informed you, this area of the Gutters caters to those on *discreet* business."

"I did note the odd lack of warm bodies on the street."

"Mm, yes. A mix of factors; most business done here is held well after dark, and those I am out to visit encourage the locals to give us . . . privacy. For our advantage, and their own. But no one rules absolutely, least of all the elite among the scum. There are always dissident factions, and hidden motives."

"I'm not sure what you're asking of me, Lord Arider. I think I mentioned I'm new here; I'm the last person who would know about the local factions."

He stopped; I stopped. The bodyguard finally gave us a bit of space. Arider turned to look at me directly, the light from the tunnel's entrance casting half his face in dramatic shadow. I didn't dare take my eyes off him beyond shifting enough to keep his escort within my peripheral vision; only the shuffling of their footsteps reassured me that Aster and Donon were still at hand.

"What do you think of the architecture?"

It was dim, not dark. This tunnel was narrow enough to feel cramped with all of us in it, but it wasn't long. The light in the Gutters beyond was low, thanks to the overhanging walls, but it was enough to reveal the path, if only just. Still, there were shadows, deep and nearly black ones, cast by the pillars and buttresses of carved akorthist holding up the weight of the main road over our heads.

"What little I can see of it?" I took my eyes off him to glance pointedly around the tunnel. "Seems to provide, shall we say, plenty of opportunity. I probably wouldn't step foot in here without the escort of someone who knows the area, *and* my armed backup."

"You have sharp eyes, and wits! But we already established that." His smirk was an unsettling carnival mask in the half-lit dimness. "Let us say I am . . . curious. You are a man of unusual talents; do they include the ability to spot a foe in the darkness?"

I studied his eyes for a moment. They glinted amid the shadows, knowing and predatory. Then I took one deliberate step back from him, which almost put me against the wall of the tunnel—except that it didn't. What I had taken for a wall was an alcove, black as outer space, between two support pillars. I finally tore my eyes off Arider's and panned them around the tunnel, what I could see of it from this angle. Those pillars were closer together than it seemed like they should be, plus longer than they were wide, creating oddly deep gaps between them. At head height, just below where the tunnel's ceiling began to arch, they were carved into moldings that formed a lip just barely wide enough for someone to brace a foot on, though the space above wasn't big enough for a person to crouch there.

"Looks to me like anything could be hidden in here," I said at last, glancing past Arider's bodyguard to my own. Aster had one hand over her shoulder, clutching the handle of her greatsword, though she hadn't drawn it yet. That huge thing would put her at a serious disadvantage in these tight quarters. So would Arider's rapier, though the bodyguard's cudgel and short sword were well-served by the space. "Frankly . . . you would have to tell me. It all comes down to *who* you expect *might* be lurking in here."

"True enough, if elementary. Ah well—don't feel bad, Lord Seiji. It doesn't reflect poorly upon you. One would need to be a goblin to spot anything hidden in this darkness." But his words said one thing while his tone and expression mocked my inability. "And as you said! It all becomes so much more clear when one knows *what to expect!*"

Arider whipped around so fast I didn't even realize what he was doing until there came a shrill cry from the darkness ahead, followed by a rustling thump, and the aristocrat was standing there holding out one arm and sneering victoriously.

I half-stepped forward, leaning around the pillar to look where he was pointing. A shape was curled up piteously on the ground, and I experienced the sickening realization of what I'd missed. An *adult* couldn't hide in the shadows above the alcoves, but a child? There was room for that. And now, a child lay on the ground, curled around his midsection, having fallen and facing us so that I could see what happened.

The handle of a knife stuck out of his belly. Arider had thrown a knife. He'd spotted the watcher, drawn and hurled the weapon with pinpoint accuracy in the dimness at an almost fully concealed target. There was enough light streaming in from the far exit of the tunnel to glint on the pool of blood spreading across the ground.

He'd knifed a child. The kid couldn't have been more than ten years old. He hadn't even blinked; it had been faster than my eyes could follow.

My decision to fuck around with this guy *might* have been in error.

"Nightlady, take me," Donon whispered, the hoarse oath echoing in the tunnel.

"Now there's a bit of local trivia it'll behoove you to learn, Lord Seiji," Arider drawled casually, as if he were chatting about fashion or his favorite food. "Here in the Gutters, the Gutter Rats are *always* watching. Local orphans and castoffs, gathered up and put to work doing this and that. The man they answer to ostensibly works for . . . well, you'll come to know him in time. But he is not above peddling information to other interested parties. They know every hiding place and bolt-hole; it's all but impossible to evade their sneaking little eyes. And so, one must *manage* them."

I realized that I'd let shock crack my facade, and Arider's sneer was as much for my lack of composure as the great victory he'd just achieved by *knifing a child*. The boy's raspy breathing filled my ears, far louder than it actually was, punctuated by whimpers of pain and terror.

Lord Arider drew his rapier and flicked its tip in lazy figure eights a centimeter above the ground while he continued to lecture me.

"It does not do to be *too* heavy-handed with them, you see. Rats are easy enough to kill, but the Nest remembers. Business becomes unnecessarily complicated if they are all stirred up against you. On the other hand, one cannot allow them to get the idea that they have impunity. The method *I* have hit upon is to . . . roll the dice, let us say." The shadows made his grin a gargoyle's sneer as he flicked the sword contemptuously at the wounded child. "Maim a Rat and let him stagger home, if he can. Sometimes they die, but what of it? Nothing of value is lost, and the rest of them expect no better from life. Sometimes they *live*, and if you've given them a prominent enough scar, why, such badges of piteousness are quite the asset in the beggar's trade. It's an elegant solution, if I do say so myself! Reinforcing their *proper* position while providing them a means to profit by it, if they have the strength to survive."

"What an . . . imaginative people you are after all," I heard myself say in a wooden voice. Funny; I actually don't remember deciding to answer him out loud.

Arider's grin widened, glinting in the faint light. "Well, I suppose you have a point. But alas! In this case, I seem to have erred. A clean stab through the gut might kill, or might not; it's tricky to predict these things. If he lives, though, that is *hardly* a useful scar. He'd have to go about half-naked to capitalize upon it—surely an excessive indignity, even for a beggar brat. No, we must leave him a more *fitting* badge of honor. Geurild, break the Rat's arm. Make it complicated enough that it won't heal properly. The *left* arm, mind—let us not be needlessly cruel."

The beefy man's shoulders moved in a sigh and he clenched his jaw. Clearly not as sadistic as his master, he was not enjoying this prospect. But he obeyed, pulling out his cudgel and trudging around behind Arider toward the fallen boy.

"Okay, that's enough of that," I said, stepping fully out of the alcove. I was well within the rapier's reach, but Arider just held it to the side, watching me smugly. "You've made your point, Lord Arider. Call off your dog."

"Why, Lord Seiji," he purred, "of all things, I would not have taken you for a *soft-hearted* man."

"Soft?" I whispered. "You think I'm soft?"

"It's just a Gutter Rat," he sneered. "They'll only take advantage if you throw them a crumb. Don't worry; we'll harden you up quickly. That, or you won't survive."

It was the strangest sensation, the terrifying icy calm which suddenly hung over me like a weighted blanket. Beyond it I could distantly feel confusion, panic, revulsion, but they didn't affect me. My body moved, my mouth worked on its own, and the weight of a spell coalesced in my consciousness, pushing to the forefront, begging to be unleashed.

"In my mother's country, they have a proverb," I said. "A piece of advice from one of their greatest leaders. 'Speak softly, and carry a big stick.'"

Lord Arider's face went blank, and I found I could read him far more clearly, all of a sudden. The tension of his grip on the sword, his intent expression free of mockery . . . He had seen the change in my demeanor and suddenly intuited that despite my alleged soft-heartedness and lack of a visible weapon, he was in danger.

Time seemed to freeze around us, one second drawing out almost as it had in Akihabara Station. This was no magic, though, but a trick played by the human brain in response to immediate peril. Aster had gone rigid, sword half-drawn, her eyes darting between Arider and myself. Geurild, almost at the fallen Gutter Rat, paused and turned back toward us, sensing a threat.

The boy let out a muffled sob, squelching in his own blood as he curled up.

Arider's arm twitched; a trained swordsman, he was fast enough to kill in a split second, but the sword never reached me. With my eyes intent on him and my mind alight with that strange dissociative clarity, he was not faster than thought.

Immolate, you son of a bitch.

Cheery firelight blossomed in the tunnel, driving away the shadows to the accompaniment of Lord Arider's scream of agony. The sword clanged to the ground and he staggered back, holding up his hands before his face as if he could still see them turn to charred meat on blackened sticks of bone with his eyeballs already boiled away. Back he stumbled, falling to his knees in the alcove opposite me, and it was strange how, despite *everything*, I couldn't find any satisfaction in finally burning that smirk off his face.

A sense of ineffable rightness, sure as if I'd restored some upset balance, but no personal pleasure. In that moment, the thought suddenly in the fore front of my mind was that Virya was wasting an awful lot of time and energy bringing me here from across the galaxy to play Dark Lord when Ephemera already had people as evil as this just walking around.

Fortunately, Aster was more attentive to our surroundings than I, and my next sight was her dashing across the light source Arider made to intercept Geurild, who'd come at me with both weapons. She had managed to get the greatsword out and immediately drove him back.

By all logic she shouldn't have been able to wield that thing at all in such tight confines; it was about as long as she was tall. The power of its enchantment made all the difference, though. Aster spun continuously, keeping the huge length of the blade folded practically against her body and using her own constant pivoting to compensate for the inability to properly swing it. Geurild was much better able to deploy his short sword and club, not to mention standing head and shoulders taller than her, but he found himself trying to fight a very angry woman-sized drill bit and giving ground as she spun at him, deflecting his blows and forcing him back.

A bellow of pain echoed in the tunnel as she inflicted a cut on his arm. That sword should have taken the arm *off* and gone halfway through his torso if she'd been able to give it a full swing, but even the acute angle at which she moved it made blood splatter the wall and caused him to lose his grip on the cudgel.

The light was beginning to fade as Arider started to peter out. Based on past examples, he'd only burn for a few more seconds, but I took the risk of turning my back to him because there was something more important to deal with. Aster had pushed Geurild back past the fallen Gutter Rat, meaning I could get close without risking a sword in the face. I stepped to his side, ignoring the bloody squelching around my shoes, and knelt down.

The boy grimaced and tried to back away. I grabbed his shoulder.

"It's okay. You're gonna be all right. I need you to hold still, okay? This is gonna hurt like a bitch for a second, but I'll fix it."

You never, *ever* pull out the foreign object impaling someone. I wasn't actually trained in first aid, but even I knew that—the knife was the only thing preventing him from bleeding out. Leave it for the medical professionals to handle. But that was advice for people who don't have bullshit overpowered healing magic, which I couldn't exactly use with the weapon still *in* him.

Grabbing the handle, I yanked it free, flinging the knife away behind me with the same motion. I grimaced, he screamed, and I seized the magic before the blood loss could take him any further.

Heal!

Pink light burst in the tunnel, overwhelming the last flickers of Arider's Immolation. The boy gasped, and with amazing speed, skittered to his feet, clutching his suddenly unwounded stomach. His expression a twisted blend of panic and awe, he looked down at it, then back at me.

"There we go," I said, realizing I was breathing heavily as if I'd just done something actually difficult. "You should be—"

He turned and scampered, dashing past Aster out the opposite end of the tunnel.

"... ingrate," I accused. Well, on the other hand, I guess I couldn't begrudge the kid that reaction. Getting the hell out of there was just good sense.

Only now did I realize quiet had descended. Slowly, I straightened back up, taking stock.

Geurild was dead, slumped half into one of the alcoves in his own spreading pool of blood. I couldn't even see what the fatal wound was, but he didn't appear to be breathing, and that was a *lot* of blood. Aster stood over him, sword at the ready, her whole body heaving as she regained her own breath. There was a noticeable rent in her jacket, baring the unmarred chain mail beneath it; the artifact had done its job well.

From behind me, silence. I turned slowly, already dreading what I would find.

Arider was no longer burning. He was, in fact, no longer doing much of anything except lying on the floor with Donon standing over him, blood dripping from his hands. The long, thin knife Arider had thrown at the orphan boy was now buried up to its hilt in his left eye.

Donon was also struggling to breathe, though his problem appeared to be nerves. He was shaking violently, wide-eyed and aghast, his hands trembling hard enough to cause droplets of noble blood to flicker across the ground.

"I . . . I had to," Donon wheezed. "He was . . . he . . ."

"Good work, Donon," I said hoarsely.

Biribo landed on my shoulder, causing me to jump. I hadn't even noticed when he'd left Aster's jacket. Given what she'd just been up to, that was clearly a wise decision, though.

"Welcome to Gwyllthean, boss," my familiar said. "Hope you enjoy your fuckin' stay."

I inhaled slowly, just to be sure I could do it smoothly. Yep, minimal trembling and no sign of any damage. To me, anyway. God, this whole place stank of blood now.

"I . . . I . . . he . . . we were fightin' them," Donon stammered. "It's . . . m'lord, I didn't . . . he was gonna kill a *kid*. For fun! Even *Rocco* didn't do shit like that, and, and, you don't wanna *know* what Rocco—"

"Donon." I made my voice even, projecting from the diaphragm. It echoed powerfully in the tunnel, cutting him off. "Thanks for having my back. You did good. Biribo, are we . . . I mean, were there any other witnesses?"

"Y'mean, other than the one you let get away?" Biribo's wings buzzed, and he departed my shoulder to hover around as usual. "Nope, we got privacy. I wouldn't expect to have it *long*, so might I suggest *not* standing around over the two freshly murdered corpses any longer than necessary?"

"Uh-huh, so, you've got pretty keen senses, then? You're sure?"

He flicked out his tongue at me in annoyance. "I'm a familiar, boss. Information gathering is what I do. It's what I *am*."

"And are there ways to interfere with your . . . ability?"

"Well . . . I mean, there *are* artifacts and spells that can mess with familiars' senses, and Void magic is . . . That is, I'd be *really* surprised to find anybody with skills like that skulking around the slums of a midsized border town, boss. We're as clear as we can reasonably expect to be. *For now*."

I nodded, taking another steadying breath. Through my mouth, trying to ignore the stink of blood. "Right. Well. Yep, *this* turned into a grand champion fuckup."

"Lord Seiji, you walked up to a rich criminal and asked to be recruited," Aster said in exasperation. "The surprising part is not that the whole thing went tits up in the weeds, it's that for a couple minutes there it was *working*."

I just nodded again, not trusting my voice. The revelation that she was *right* had shaken me more than I wanted to reveal. This, I could not deny, had been an unnecessary disaster caused by me recklessly trying to seize what I thought *might* be an opportunity, with no plan and zero knowledge of the situation. I went off half-cocked, and now two people were dead.

Next time, it might be *my* people.

Or *me*.

"Hell's revels," Donon exclaimed. I turned to find him holding a hefty sack, which I assumed had been previously hidden inside the loose cut of

Lord Arider's coat, based on the fact that said coat was now spread open and half-pulled off him.

"Christ on a bike, man, are you *looting the bodies?*"

"He may as well," Biribo opined. "If you leave 'em lyin' in a place like this, they'll be stripped bare in minutes anyway. Might as well be by us, since we actually did the killing."

"*We?*" Aster muttered.

"Lord Seiji, you really should see this." Donon held up the sack, opening its top. "This, uh . . . This is a *lot* of money."

I stepped over, craning my neck to look. Then frowned, reached forward, and grabbed a few coins.

The sack was *full* of coins. It was bulging, and bigger than a grapefruit. For the moment, though, I didn't think about their value, or how the hell Arider had been concealing this so well that I hadn't noticed the bulge in his coat . . . I held up the coins to the light, studying them.

They were gleaming and glossy as if freshly minted. Their weight suggested metal, but the color . . . All of them, in different denominations, were made of at least two metals fused together. Some pale material like platinum seemed to predominate, but there were outer rims and inlaid patterns of crimson, gold, white, and even blue. They had neatly ridged edges, intricate cutouts, highly detailed engravings, and all of them were utterly flawless, not even dingy from use.

"Are these . . . normal coins, here?" I asked.

"Those are all higher-value denominations," Aster replied, her own eyes practically bulging. "Hell's revels, I've never actually seen a white halo in person. Lord Seiji, this is . . . this is a *lot* of money."

"But they're *normal coins?*"

"Normal? I mean, they're coins. I'm not sure what you're asking."

No, she wouldn't be. But I was standing here, in a medieval society, which appeared not to have indoor plumbing and which built its buildings out of shells and didn't even use metal for weapons, looking at an example of metallurgy so sophisticated I was pretty sure the national treasuries of twenty-first century Earth could not have produced anything this elaborate and flawless.

Every new thing I learned about Ephemera was either grotesquely fucked up or just plain *weird*. Why couldn't I have landed in one of those bog-standard, quasi-European fantasy isekai Yoshi probably liked? I'd have had a better idea what to do with that, at least. Why did it all have to be so *fucking weird?*

I cleared my throat. "As someone who's new here and has no mental frame of reference for the value of coinage . . . how *much* money are we looking at here? Put it in context for me."

Aster and Donon shared a loaded look, apparently lost for words. It was Biribo who answered.

"For this? On the Fflyr mainland you could buy a comfortable manor in the countryside with enough grounds to be self-sustaining, *furnish* it, and pay a staff to work the fields until the harvests came in and it could support itself."

My two henchpeople nodded gravely, still apparently tongue-tied by the wealth on display before them.

"And this," I said slowly, "was being carried by a nobleman . . . on a mysterious errand . . . to the criminal district of town."

They nodded again.

I took another long look at the bodies we'd left lying in the Gutters.

". . . I think we should get the fuck outta here."

Biribo buzzed his wings furiously. "Oh, do ya *think* so?"

11

In Which the Dark Lord Dresses for the Part

The next morning I found myself having a nice breakfast at a charming little inn which catered to Gwyllthean's wealthy class of travelers and reflecting on how damn surreal everything was. Life on Ephemera so far seemed to consist of cycles of tedium and terrifying violence. I'd spent the previous day on the road, pondering and chatting with my companions, occasionally casting a self-Heal because my legs were *not* accustomed to that kind of hiking, and then suddenly it was all bloodshed and fire in a dark tunnel under the city gates.

The inn was very nice, though. Primitive, but far more comfortable than North Watch. There were even indoor toilets . . . sort of. I preferred to psych myself up for my next unavoidable visit to one by not thinking about it.

We had gotten inside the walls the evening before with no issue, after dipping our shoes in a canal to scrub the blood off and hustling back up to the city gates. I'd finally opted to take Biribo's and Donon's advice out of pragmatism, and had taken everything of value from our victims, which amounted to some pocket change from the bodyguard and his short sword, now hanging at Donon's belt. Arider had had a collapsible telescope, a fancy ring with an engraved signet, and his rapier, which Donon carried thoroughly wrapped up in Geurild's coat in case someone recognized it.

And the money, of course. Obviously the disappearance of that amount of cash was going to piss someone off, at least as much as Lord Arider's untimely demise, but dammit, I needed funds. Anyway, I planned to be safely inside the walls for the rest of this trip, until I got out of Gwyllthean entirely.

In the nicer section of the city, finding an inn had been easy; this one was close to the gates, catering to merchants and lower nobility. After seeing my money, the management fell over themselves to find me a comfortable room, with smaller rooms adjacent for my two "servants."

So here I was, the next morning, having breakfast in the common room. Not knowing my social rank due to my foreign features, the staff had placed me on the upper tier of the multi-leveled space, which was reserved for higher nobles; there was a foursome of highborn youth off to my left meeting for breakfast, all of them pale and blonde.

Breakfast was a bowl of spiced meat porridge—gross to look at or describe, but quite tasty—a piece of tough flatbread smeared with a surprisingly sour purple jam, and a tall cup of hot tea, which was crimson in color and had a strong spicy-sweet flavor a little like citrus and cinnamon. I spent most of my meal sneaking glances at the noble kids at the next table over, who were carrying on as loudly as overprivileged teenagers in any culture on any planet.

Two boys, two girls; about Yoshi's age or a little older, at a guess. The boys were dressed as Arider had been. Noblemen's fashion was apparently tight pants and loose shirts—with ruffles, ugh—a heavy, loose-cut overcoat which fell to midthigh, and knee-high leather boots. It seemed the coat and boots had to match. Women's fashion here was more interesting to me, as it had less analog to anything I'd seen on Earth. Both girls had on some kind of tight leotard or pants-and-shirt combo which covered them from ankle to wrist and halfway up the neck. Over that they wore very loose kimono-like short robes, falling to the knee and elbow and open at the neck to an extent that would show a *lot* of cleavage if there wasn't more tight fabric under it. The loose design was offset by having the entire waist from hips to bust tightly wrapped by what looked like a single strip of incredibly long ribbon encircling them dozens of times.

Boys and girls alike wore jewelry, all of which was *wood*. Intricately cut and highly polished, but all wood, with no precious stones or metals in sight.

"Stimion gone courting?" one of the boys suddenly said, looking directly at me. In fact, all four were looking at me, and I belatedly realized I'd forgotten to sneak glances and had been staring at them.

"Beg pardon?" I replied.

He smirked, his buddy guffawed, and both girls giggled shrilly. God, I hate teenagers.

"I see you're *new* in Fflyr Dlemathlys, stranger," he said, speaking slowly as if addressing a half-wit, to the visible mirth of his gang. "Around here, we try to gawk at young ladies with a little more *discretion*."

Little shits, I could boil you alive in your fancy pants . . . That was no way to defuse a situation, though.

I stood up abruptly, causing all four to stiffen in alarm, but I repeated the gesture Lord Arider had used yesterday—right hand over heart, rotate it palm up, horizontal across the chest. I'd practiced it in my room last night, and probably still wasn't doing it quite right, but if they could tell I was a foreigner, the effort would count for something.

"Sumimasen deshita. Humble apologies, kids, I'm terribly sorry to disturb your breakfast. Truth be told, I *am* new on Dount and trying to study how to fit in."

"Aww," the darker-haired of the girls cooed, smiling flirtatiously up at me, to the clear annoyance of the boy next to her.

"Conzart at the theater," he muttered.

The other girl smacked his shoulder with the back of her hand, scowling in reproach and retorting, "Conzart takes the doorman's oath! Honestly, Finneder, how often do we meet a foreigner with actual manners? Don't be Lhaetha in the fields."

"Welcome to Gwyllthean," the first boy said to me, looking a little more relaxed. "Make sure you spend some time in the bookshops—the ones in the upper circle, if you've the means."

I raised my eyebrows, pleasantly surprised. "You have bookshops here?"

All four burst out laughing.

"You *are* Tagamin among the wood, stranger," said the more flirtatious of the girls. She leaned toward me, smirking and letting her eyes go half-lidded. "Why, maybe I should take you around on a tour myself. Hmm?" Finneder controlled his expression fairly well, but his complexion was getting noticeably redder.

"I may take you up on that in about . . . four years, dear," I replied, prompting a little moue of disappointment from her and a peal of laughter from the other girl. Even if the kid wasn't *way* too young for me, I can tell when a girl is just trying to rile up her boyfriend. "To be truthful, I was admiring your attire. Fashions are very different where I am from, as you can see. I don't suppose you kids could point me to a good place to get myself more locally styled?"

Both girls and one of the boys perked up like children who'd been offered candy. "*Ooooh!*"

A little over an hour later, I was feeling much more charitable toward the noble teens.

I stepped back outside the tailor's shop in the middle ring attired as a Fflyr nobleman, in a black pants-and-shirt combo with a deep crimson overcoat and boots trimmed with gold. It seemed the fashion for the rich and powerful in Fflyr Dlemathlys was what was called "dictator chic" back on Earth—lots of gold, wildly excessive decorative flourishes, and generally tacky and tasteless. The other aristocrats I'd seen looked like they were cosplaying RPG characters.

Speaking of which . . .

"Hey, Aster," I said as we paused on the street outside the shop.

"Lord Seiji?"

"Those female-shaped mannequins in there." I glanced at the ornate door through which we'd just passed, bringing my trio to a stop outside where we weren't obstructing it. "The ones wearing leather armor with nothing across the chest. What was up with *that*?"

"Ah." She nodded and touched the intricate collar of the chain mail tunic beneath her own new coat. "You noticed how this shifted to perfectly fit whoever put it on? Most artifact armor does that. But a *lot* of artifacts, when a woman wears them, will also physically change to only cover the boobs. So there's crafted armor for female adventurers to supplement artifacts and protect our, y'know, organs. And modesty."

I closed my eyes, drew in a deep breath, and let it out slowly before opening them again. We were already getting fewer stares from passersby now that I was dressed like a local, but I had a feeling that shouting in the street about how the goddesses themselves were *fucking otaku morons* would still lead to unnecessary trouble.

I'd bought Aster a new coat to replace her torn one—more modest than mine, since a lowborn putting on airs could apparently get in serious trouble here—and Donon was carrying some bundles of additional clothing to take back to North Watch with us. So that was one task sorted.

"Speaking of which, Lord Seiji," Aster continued, still watching me warily, "you remember I told you about the King's Guild, right?"

"Ah yes, the adventurer thing. You want to go there next?"

"If you don't have anything more immediate to do, my lord. I *do* have something I need to do there, and I think getting a look at how the adventurers operate will be useful for your, ah . . . goals."

"Sounds like as good a starting point as any. Lead the way. You going to be okay with all that, Donon?" I asked over my shoulder as we set out up the street. "We've got a *long* walk back."

"Kind of you to ask, Lord Seiji, but no need to worry about me!" he said with a grin. "None of this is heavy. Not even awkward, the way it hangs on my back."

"Right on. Let me know if you have any trouble." I suspected people around here might find it odd a nobleman would express concern for one of his servants, if my impression of how this place ran so far was correct, but nobody was paying us much attention. Also, fuck 'em. Donon was a good dude. "So, Aster, you can start with the name. Why isn't it called the Adventurer's Guild?"

"Bit of a story, that," she began to narrate as we walked. "Fflyr Dlemathlys didn't used to have any real organization for adventurers. Some of the bigger parties had political pull, and the clans would sponsor Blessed individuals, but on the whole it was kind of a free-for-all. The King's Guild is one of the reforms launched by Lord Vanderhoen. It was . . . ten years ago? Nine or ten. Supposedly, he modeled it on the Lancor system. Now there's government funding, it's all organized, there are rules . . . Adventurers get protection from political crap the clans pull, and citizens get protection from rogue adventurers. *That* used to be a big problem; some of the more infamous parties were practically bandit gangs."

I had tuned out most of the latter part of her speech, my attention having hung on one earlier detail. "Lord who, now?"

"Oh, Lord Vanderhoen," she said in a disinterested tone. "He's some foreigner who turned up about twelve . . . fifteen years ago? Something like that. Somehow he got popular and got a position as the King's advisor. He's done a lot of reforms, most of them pretty well-liked with the people, though the clans don't care for him as much. Like the King's Guild, a lot of his programs have transferred power from them back toward the Crown." She lowered her voice. "Some people say he basically runs Fflyr Dlemathlys, but I'd be careful where you repeat that."

"Hm. What else can you tell me about him?"

Aster shrugged, giving me a bemused sidelong look. "That, basically. This guy hangs out with the *King*, I have no idea how he lives his life. I thought we were talking about the guild?"

"Right, of course."

It was . . . probably a coincidence. Names were just collections of sounds, and similar ones could pop up independently, in different places and languages. I'd already met one guy here called Harold. So a guy shows up from nowhere, weasels his way into the King's ear, starts reorganizing the whole kingdom to its betterment—that was a thing real people had done in historical times. If it wasn't for the fact that he had a distinctively Dutch surname, it probably wouldn't even occur to me to question it.

Obviously, there was some means of transit between Ephemera and Earth. Virya had made it sound like this Hero versus Dark Lord thing was the only show in town, but might she and Sanora be running more than one game at a time? A planet is an awfully big playing field, even a shattered remnant of one like this. For that matter . . . What if Virya and Sanora weren't the only two players?

I definitely needed to learn more about this Vanderhoen character.

I realized Aster was still talking.

". . . shouldn't be a problem, given the terms of the party's charter. Jarind didn't have any family, so it'd be customary for the artifacts to fall to the surviving party member anyway. The only question is me being able to use them; the Guild keeps records of who is and isn't Blessed. What, ah, would you like to tell them, Lord Seiji?"

"What . . . do you think we should tell them?" I ventured.

"As little as possible. It's plausible if you don't want to reveal how you got me a Blessing. The clans all have their secrets; just say you're a nobleman and they'll probably let it go. I'd . . . like to not lie any more than we absolutely have to. Not that I'm going soft on you!" she hastily added.

"Nope, I'm totally with you on that one. Lies require maintenance. They lead to more lies and ultimately a big pain in the ass to keep running. I'd much rather keep things simple."

Aster nodded, then pitched her voice lower. "It's just up ahead, Lord Seiji. We should probably think about being overheard from here."

The building she nodded to had a couple of people out front chatting quietly—people wearing incongruously mismatched outfits of gorgeously elaborate pieces of armor over far plainer ensembles of leather and cloth, and displaying weapons. I would've been able to guess those *Final Fantasy*-looking scraps were artifacts even without the subtle glow they put off to my Blessed eyes. Aster took the lead as we stepped inside, passing the loitering adventurers with an exchange of mute nods. Just inside the building, she paused, turning to me and speaking in a low voice.

"I'll be as quick as I can, Lord Seiji, but dealing with clerks and bureaucrats is . . . well . . ."

"Say no more."

"The front area here is open to visitors, so feel free to look around. You might learn something useful. Just don't try to go up or down the stairs at the back and no one will question you. And Donon . . . don't touch anything. I'll be done as quick as I can."

"What does *that* mean?" Donon asked in a hushed but irked tone as Aster hustled off toward a row of occupied desks. "Does she think I'm some kind of idiot? Do I *seem* like an idiot?"

"I think she's just nervous. Don't take it personally."

"If you say so, Lord Seiji."

I wandered aimlessly off to the side, just to be out of the doorway, peering about. The room was quite spacious and pretty well lit, morning sunlight beaming in through irregularly placed round windows near the ceiling. There was a clear path from the door to the stairs at the back dividing the open ground floor, with support pillars lining it. On one side of the room were tables and benches, and a counter in the back—clearly a tavern or restaurant, most likely catering to the adventurers who had business here. Even at this hour of the morning there were a handful sitting at the tables. On the other side of the room, the half in which I stood, was actual adventuring business. Mirroring the bar counter on the tavern side was the row of desks toward which Aster now strode.

I had to chuckle at the sight. There were three clerks on duty—a sour-faced old man; a middle-aged fellow, who was the first overweight person I'd seen on Ephemera; and a scrawny, nervous-looking youth, who was my age at the absolute most. I had only seen a few fantasy anime featuring adventurer guilds, but the trope always seemed to include cute girls working behind the desks. I guess the people who make anime don't stop to consider what kind of person historically ended up working in a government-run bureaucracy in medieval times.

And speaking of anime . . .

"Whoa, check out Goblin Slayer over there," I murmured.

"Lord Seiji?" Donon asked uncertainly. I just shook my head, still studying the man standing in front of the desks, clad from head to toe in gleaming plate armor that looked as if it could have been wrought from pure silver. Black chain mail showed through the gaps at the joints, and he had a visor covering his face, with only slits to see through. Not a centimeter of skin showed. It was *fancy* armor, with silver wings on the helmet, extravagant engravings on every piece, golden embellishments, and a dashing tabard of crimson and white trimmed with more gold over it. I didn't need the subtle glow around him to know that armor was made entirely of artifacts. Or maybe was a single artifact made of multiple pieces?

Red, white, and gold . . . the colors Sanora had been wearing. I decided to give this guy a wide berth.

The armored man was speaking with the chubby clerk; the young clerk leaned on his elbow, visibly bored, while Aster talked with the old one. I couldn't tell if he was unhappy with what he was hearing or just unhappy in general, as older people stuck in desk jobs tended to get.

I spotted a notice board and wandered over to peruse the requests listed. There was a standing bounty for information that led to the apprehension of Void cultists, and another for intelligence on dark elves. Unusual goblin activity had been noted recently, including rumor that a Goblin King had risen; adventurers were advised to be cautious in anti-goblin operations until more was known. In the southwest region of Dount near the khora forest there continued to be sightings of undead, indicating a potential pattern. The King's Guild suspected a necromancer and was interested in funding an expedition to investigate, but would only pay for confirmation and success, so I suspected that notice was going to sit there untouched until there was a much bigger mess to clean up than a few stray zombies. Also, something called Soulfire had appeared on the estates of Clan Ardyllen, which was making it accessible to anyone interested. That was it, no further detail; apparently everyone was just expected to understand what that meant.

Then I turned around, saw something on the other side of the room, which had been out of view from the door, and forgot everything else.

I crossed the chamber as swiftly as I could manage without breaking into a run, coming to a stop before the object positioned against one outer wall of the tavern area, tucked away in a little alcove made by the rippling shape of the great khora shell from which the building was made.

They had a piano.

Sort of.

The keys were made of khora, of course—the "white" ones were a dull yellow like old ivory, the "black" was a purple so dark it was *almost* black, with lighter striations of blue. The keyboard itself had an odd shape, too, arranged in a slightly concave arc, as if in an effort to be ergonomic. Also, the sounds presumably came from the hammers hidden behind its body, striking the blades rising up from the back like the pipes of an organ, fanning outward in a configuration that reminded me of a peacock's spread tail. Differences aside, it had obviously been designed along the pattern of an Earth piano.

Almost hesitantly, I stepped up to the instrument, reached out, and pressed middle C.

One of the blades vibrated and its tone filled the air. It was definitely not *quite* a piano. The sound was something between a xylophone and a steel drum. I tapped it more gently and then harder—good, it had weighted keys to enable volume control. No pedals, I discovered upon leaning over to check.

"Ugh. Why does every clod who wanders in here feel the need to poke at that thing? If you don't know how to *play* it, kindly don't fill the room with discordant noise. It's too early."

Slowly, I turned around to confront whatever fresh pest *this* was.

She was a woman in her twenties, wearing narrow spectacles and a garment in a similar style to the young noblewomen from the inn—a heavy, kimono-like affair with an enormous length of narrow ribbon wrapped countless times around the waist to form a sort of external corset. Her robe had longer skirts and sleeves than theirs, though, and a higher neckline. It was white with gold trim, the ribbon scarlet and also with golden edges. Again, Sanora's colors.

I took note of her complexion. A few shades lighter than Aster's—her hair brown with a slight curl, eyes likewise a medium brown. So . . . on the cusp of lower nobility from upper peasantry? I did not know the nuances of this stupid caste system and was personally offended by the reality that sooner or later I was going to have to learn them.

"Do *you* play?" I asked.

"Do I *look* like a musician?" she countered, arching one eyebrow.

"You don't look like much of anything," I replied. "You *sound* like one of those people with more opinions than knowledge. Or do you normally start your day criticizing people for things *you* can't do?"

I turned my back on her incensed stammering, sat down on the stool placed before the quasi piano, and placed my hands on the keys.

The keyboard's arced shape made it different, but not too bad. I flexed my hand, and filled the room with music.

At first I kept my eyes opened and focused on where I was putting my fingers. Between the curved keyboard and the fact that the keys were a bit stiffer and heavier than I was used to, it demanded some concentration. It did not impede me, though. I've been playing since I've been speaking; I have fingers like steel springs and know a keyboard more intimately than my own body.

And after the last two days, I wasn't about to screw around with a warmup. I went straight to one of my favorites—Rachmaninoff's Rhapsody on a

Theme of Paganini, one of those pieces so beloved as to be almost cliché. Of course, only hipsters care about nonsense like that. It is well-known for a reason; it's one of those compositions that *never* loses its power, no matter how often it's heard. The pure expression of gentle passion in musical form, swelling and undulating in a perfect flow.

I started off admittedly a tad wooden, due to the unfamiliar instrument and because I was two days out of practice. And the experience was *somewhat* diminished by the strange, almost metallic tone, but . . . well, it worked. It was different, definitely, but not worse. Quickly enough, I fell back into it, and just blissfully lost myself. My eyes drifted shut, my fingers knowing their work and settling into the new arrangement after only a few infinitesimal missteps. Everything fell away—Ephemera, Virya, all of this horrible nonsense. There was just the purity of music. The bliss.

It was almost disorienting when the piece ended. I felt . . . lighter, and yet somewhat drained. It's strange how different a familiar experience like playing the piano can become after a series of events that leaves you desperately longing for *some* kind of familiarity.

I had really needed that.

Applause met the end of my performance, from several corners of the room. There were only a handful of people present so early in the day, but at least a few of them appreciated Rachmaninoff. They had damn well *better*.

"You're good," the woman in glasses said. To my surprise she had not stormed off in a huff and was still standing right there, now studying me with an appraising look.

"I know," I replied.

Her mouth tugged to one side in an almost-grimace. "Did it have to be so . . . schmaltzy, though? Don't you know any *proper* music?"

"Has anyone ever told you that your lips are the perfect shape for slapping?"

She curled the aforementioned lips up into a sneer. "Nobody *says* things like that."

"They will, if this is how you normally talk to people. Very well, then!" I shook my fingers and hovered them over the keys, looking up at her expectantly. "What, in your opinion, constitutes *proper* music?"

"Nothing so . . . overwrought." Folding her arms, she sniffed imperiously at me. "Haven't you ever been to a temple service? Keyboard music is meant to be transcendent. Elevating the mind and spirit above base passions, not . . . indulging and *inflaming* them like that."

"Ahh, I catch your drift. Well, how about this?"

If it's church music you want, you can't go wrong with J.S. Bach, so I gave her his "Prelude in C Major." Classical, mathematical, *simple*, a piece upon which centuries of young pianists have trained as they learned their way around a keyboard. A plain series of ascending arpeggios, five notes each, with never more than three keys pressed down at a time. Simple, but still lovely.

I'd chosen it in part to mock her, though I expected the joke to soar over her head; only someone moderately versed in classical music would recognize how mechanistic and easy this prelude is compared to Rachmaninoff. I had to admit, though, this piece actually sounded better in this instrument's slightly metallic voice than the more intricate Russian number. Which made sense; Bach was from before the pianoforte and actually wrote for the harpsichord.

I got more applause at the end of it, though less than previously, which I didn't mind. I liked Rachmaninoff better, too.

"Now, *that* was lovely," my prickly new acquaintance said, finally giving me a smile. "You should play more like that one."

"Lady, I don't tell you how to stand around being snippy at people—and believe me, I could. Kindly don't tell me how to play the keyboard. You can, however, *ask* me. I do take requests, when I'm in the mood."

"Ah, Lord Seiji?" Donon poked his head around the corner. "That was really pretty, but I think you may wanna come look at this."

Following his gesture, I swiveled around on the stool to behold Aster still standing at the desk, staring over at me with a wide-eyed, helpless expression. The elderly clerk was scowling at her, the younger one had come over and was scribbling furiously on documents at the same desk, and the guy in the shiny armor had now joined them, looming ominously over Aster.

Well, crap.

"Ugh." I stood up, giving the keys one last regretful caress as I stepped away from them. "I have to do *everything* myself."

12

In Which the Dark Lord
Takes a Level in Bard

L ord Seiji," Aster said in clear relief as I approached.

The three men around her all turned to study me, the young clerk blinking owlishly, the old one controlling his expression better, and the one behind a visor . . . behind a visor.

"Aster, is there some sort of problem here?"

"Ah," the disapproving-looking old man said in a voice as creaky as an old boat, "you would be this . . . foreign lord young Miss Delavada reports saved her from bandits?"

I did not care for his tone, and after a split second of hesitation, I realized that not caring for his tone *exactly* matched the cover story we were using. What aristocrat would let some doddering file clerk cop that kind of attitude with him?

Straightening my spine, I raised my chin and stared down my nose at him—challenging, as he was taller than I, but I managed. "Yes, I suppose I am *this* foreign lord. And who might *you* be?"

His expression and tone did not change in the slightest, but he made that hand gesture Sakin had the night before—right hand over left at chest level, then folding the arms down to the waist. "No disrespect was meant, Lord . . . Seiji, was it?" He glanced to the side, nodding at the young clerk, who scribbled something down on a sheet of paper. "We must simply be precise about such a serious matter as the demise of nearly an entire registered adventuring party. It is also of interest to the King's Guild if a new arrival in Fflyr Dlemathlys is a Blessed of sufficient power to single-handedly defeat an entire bandit gang."

Which told me I wasn't going to get anywhere with hauteur and bullying.

There is nothing in nature more unresponsive to pressure than a bureaucrat confident in the full weight of a government agency behind him.

I thought as rapidly as I ever had, not even sparing the attention to kick myself for not working up a plan for this situation beforehand. How much could I afford to reveal? How to keep the lies minimal enough to avoid being caught in one while also covering my ass and Aster's?

"Really, defeat the bandits? Is that what you told them?" I gave Aster my most sardonic look before turning back to the clerk, projecting my best insouciant facade. "I think she may be overly enamored of my assistance. Understandable, I suppose—it did result in saving her life. But no, I simply spooked them into running. I happen to possess a few . . . minor spells of a medical nature. Nothing too fancy, but they *do* make pretty flashing lights when cast, and that was enough to encourage a handful of bandit dregs to try their luck elsewhere rather than tangling with a Blessed. Criminals are a superstitious and cowardly lot," I added with a smirk. "Ironically, the oafs bolted before they had a chance to find out they could almost certainly have taken me out more easily than the adventurers."

"I see," he said, his voice and expression revealing nothing. I couldn't tell if he disapproved of our story in particular or our existence in general. "And with these . . . medical spells, you were unable to render aid to Miss Delavada's fallen comrades?"

"It was too late," Aster said quietly. Her face was strained; I wondered how many times he'd made her go through this while I was noodling about on the not-piano. "It was a trap—a pit in the ground, full of spears. We didn't even have the chance to fight."

"I see," the old clerk repeated, just as stiffly and without looking at her. "And what is the exact location of this trap, Lord Seiji?"

"I have absolutely no idea," I replied, not hiding my exasperation. "I barely know where I am *now*. Aster led me here, and I'd likely have wandered into the khora forest by now without her. It's only my third day on Dount."

"I did describe it in detail, with directions, Mr. Tisch," Aster said, glancing at the younger clerk who was still taking notes. "Do you need me to repeat—"

"That will not be necessary, Miss Delavada," Tisch interrupted, turning his gimlet stare on her. "We must be as certain as possible in the case of such a serious . . . incident. Any corroborating account is of benefit. Another party will have to be dispatched, to retrieve the remains, locate the bandits' headquarters, and clear them out."

Uh-oh. This time, I carefully kept my expression blank. Before I could think of something to interject, though, the fellow in the heavy armor suit placed one gauntleted hand on Aster's shoulder, making her jump.

"We all mourn your loss, Adventurer Aster," he said, his voice echoing slightly through the slits in his visor. "The loss of companions . . . it is a fact with which we all live, but it never grows easier. I am grateful to you, Lord Seiji, for saving at least one of our own."

"I'm . . . just glad I was able to," I said warily. Was there a reason this guy kept his face covered while having a polite conversation indoors? "I'm sorry I wasn't there soon enough to help the others. It was just luck I managed to aid Aster."

"You'd just have fallen into the trap, too, Lord Seiji," she said with a wan smile.

I shrugged, repressing annoyance at myself. I may be the worst example of a Japanese person on two whole planets, but the compulsion to apologize still rears up sometimes. "Yeah, I know. Still."

"Still," agreed Armor Man, nodding his helmet at me once. "One always abhors the deaths of others. Even when we could have done nothing to prevent it, the guilt remains. Remember, Aster," he added, squeezing her shoulder briefly, "that guilt is only emotion. If you could have saved them, I am certain you would have done so. You are not to blame."

Poor Aster looked tongue-tied, opening and closing her mouth slightly while staring up at him. He let go of her shoulder, turning back to me.

"Have you considered joining the King's Guild, Lord Seiji?"

"*Me?*"

He nodded again. "Blessed are always welcome among our ranks—and in particular, those Blessed with Magic and in possession of healing spells are most sought after. We suffer a perennial lack of healers. Here in Fflyr Dlemathlys, adventuring under the Guild's aegis is considered an honorable pursuit for noblemen as well. With your rank and abilities, I could personally guarantee you a position among an advanced party and the Guild's most generous tier of compensation."

He could? With fresh eyes, I took note of Aster's starstruck expression, the fact that the disapproving Guild clerk hadn't dared interrupt him to bring this conversation back on track, and his allover suit of very fancy armor, which was clearly a powerful artifact. Belatedly, it occurred to me that I was dealing with someone actually important here.

"That's an interesting idea," I said, very carefully. "I think grubbing around in dungeons killing monsters is not the life I envisioned for myself, however."

"It is not a life for everyone," he agreed, his echoing voice solemn. "The offer remains valid, should you reconsider. The Guild would be glad of your talents."

Tisch cleared his throat, sparing me from further awkwardness. "All that being settled, there is the matter of inheritance. I see you are in possession of the artifacts registered to Adventurer Jarind Delostinon, Miss Delavada. Per your party's contract, that is proper. Since Lord Seiji has deigned to join us, may the Guild have an explanation for your acquisition of the Blessing of Might necessary to *use* them?"

I was ready for that one, at least. "Is the Guild accustomed to prying into the family business of lords?"

"Certainly not," the metal-plated celebrity said, emphatic and with his helmet pointed right at Tisch.

"It is not the Guild's intent to *pry*," he replied in what may have been the driest tone I'd ever heard. "Especially into the business of the clans. The interest of thoroughness compels me to ask, but a detailed answer is not necessary. That being the case," Tisch droned on, reaching over and unerringly retrieving a paper from the middle of the pile the younger clerk was working on, "the only remaining matter is bereavement insurance. Adventurer Delostinon opted to include it in his party contract and faithfully paid dues. The death of party members in the course of a sanctioned King's Guild quest means a payment of twelve gold halos per deceased, to be divided evenly among all surviving registered party members." His eyes darted back and forth across the document, then he set it down on the desk's surface and pushed it toward Aster, along with a pen and a pot of ink. "The King's Guild thus authorizes a one-time payment of twenty-four gold halos to Delavada Aster, with his Majesty's condolences and thanks for your brave service. Sign in the designated space, please."

"Oh, I . . . I don't . . ." To my surprise, Aster seemed mostly upset by this, looking at me and then at Tisch in consternation and not moving to take the pen. "I don't need . . . That is, I've agreed to work for Lord Seiji, so I . . ." She swallowed heavily and it occurred to me we hadn't actually discussed compensation for her bodyguard services. "Is that . . . I don't think it feels *right* to . . ."

"Aster." The armored man touched her shoulder again—lightly and just for a second this time to get her attention. His voice was much gentler, which was an odd effect with the way it echoed out of his helmet. "Your party leader not only approved these arrangements, but made regular payments to keep them up. This was his affirmative will, not a mistake. You are not taking advantage, but honoring his wishes. Those funds are yours, to ensure your well-being now that they are gone."

She stared blankly up at him. "Jarind was probably hoping to get a payout if he got me or Dannit killed."

Mr. Tisch sniffed in loud disapproval, but the armored adventurer was not put off.

"Even so, these are the arrangements he made. You are no less entitled to these funds. There is nothing about which you need feel guilty, Adventurer Aster."

"Is there a statute of limitations on the insurance payout?" I asked, seeing Aster still in the grip of some kind of emotional crisis. "Some kind of time constraint?"

Tisch sniffed again. "Certainly not. Miss Delavada can collect it at any time."

"Then you don't have to deal with this right now, if you don't want to," I said, directly to Aster. "Take time to process all this, and come back to get your money if and when you feel ready. It's not like I'll let you go hungry in the meantime."

"A wise suggestion," the armored man agreed, nodding at me again. "Would that be agreeable to you, Aster?"

"I . . . yeah, that sounds . . . good. Thank you, Lord Seiji."

"Indeed," he said. "I am glad to see that after such a terrible event, Aster has at least gained the patronage of such a decent person. Truly, Lord Seiji, the goddess must have set you upon her path."

I just smiled as blandly as I could manage. Not touching that one.

Mr. Tisch emitted a long-suffering sigh, loudly shuffling his forms back into a stack. "Very well, then. If you have no *further* information to report, Miss Delavada, then that will be all. *Next!*"

We all turned to look behind us.

There was no one in line.

"That was *Rhydion!*" Aster practically shouted once we were safely a block from the King's Guild. "Rhydion talked to me! What's he even doing on Dount? I thought he worked around the capital!"

"That would be the guy in the armor, then?" I asked. "He's a big deal, then."

"The *guy* in the—" Aster caught herself midoutburst and made a visible effort to moderate her delivery. "Yes, Lord Seiji, he's *easily* the foremost adventurer in Fflyr Dlemathlys. He's our only sanctified paladin of Sanora, ordained not only by Fflyrdylle's Radiant Convocation but the Radiant Temple Knights of Lancor! The man has single-handedly slain *three* khorodects and completed the only recorded solo clear of Cairnarrien! I heard he even fought at the warclan front in eastern Darkmarch!"

"You cannot possibly imagine that collection of words means anything to me. More immediately . . ." I flicked my eyes across the street, trying not to *look* like I was looking around, and lowered my voice when I beheld no one in our immediate vicinity. "I guess we need to get back to the fortress pronto, now that you've set another adventuring party to hunt us down."

"What? I what? When?" She frowned at me.

Donon cleared his throat behind us. "Ah, beggin' your pardon, Lord Seiji? That won't be an issue. Rocco always had our traps set a *long* way from North Watch. Nobody who finds it will find a trail back there."

"Oh. Good." I glanced around again, less surreptitiously, just to verify there was nobody within earshot.

"Even *I* knew that," said Aster, now scowling at me in reproach. "Do you think I'm an idiot?"

"Ah . . ." I cast about for a change of topic. "So, those kids at the inn. Did you notice all their jewelry was made of *wood*?"

Her expression said she had made a note of the unsubtle deflection, but she didn't press me on it. "Well, sure. They were rich."

I drew in a steadying breath. Yep, all right, I felt emotionally prepared now. Time to learn more stupid, horrible facts about this stupid, horrible world.

"Okay. *Why* is wood rare?"

Donon and Aster exchanged a loaded look.

"Would you two quit *doing* that?" I exclaimed. "We have *established* I'm an outsider here and I need things explained. Just answer questions without making a sideshow production of 'I can't believe he doesn't know this!'"

"Sorry, Lord Seiji," Aster said in a more subdued tone. "Well, basically, trees are really hard to grow. Bugs and crawns love to eat living wood. Once it's all cut and properly varnished it's fine, but while the tree's alive, they go crazy for it."

"*What* is a crawn? And don't do that thing again! I'm watching you."

"Crawns are vermin, Lord Seiji," Donon explained. "Basically, most pests are either rodents, birds, or crawns; there's a bunch of different types. Crawns are the ones with shells. If you were in the kitchen at North Watch you probably saw some."

"Ah."

"Right, so," Aster continued, "to grow trees, you basically need a space large enough to have several, but fully enclosed by walls, and be able to afford enchantments and alchemy, have a bunch of dogs and cats on the site to chase pests, a staff to check them basically constantly . . . I've heard to do it successfully you need at least one person Blessed with Magic who knows healing spells and is willing to, uh, be a gardener."

"Is wood more common where you're from, Lord Seiji?" Donon asked.

I sighed. "We build houses with it. And burn it for campfires."

We walked on in silence, neither of them finding anything to say in response to that. I suspected they didn't believe me.

"Wait," I said suddenly, overtaken by a sinking feeling. "If you don't have wood widely available . . . I guess that means you don't have guitars."

I hated this planet. I hated it *so very much*.

"What?" Aster tilted her head. "Of course we have guitar—ah!"

She yelped, and I think started to reflexively go for her sword, when I suddenly whirled and grabbed her by the shoulders.

"*Show me!*"

Another hour later, we were strolling down the road outside Gwyllthean's gates, descending the long ramp through the Gutters to the main trade road, and I was happier than I'd been since landing on this godforsaken shithole of a world.

Fflyr guitars were thinner than the wooden acoustic guitars back home, but about the thickness of an electric guitar so it wasn't unfamiliar to hold. Akorshil didn't have the same resonant qualities as wood, so the hollow body contained a set of akornin blades which vibrated along with the strings and were tuned by positioning padded clamps along their length. So it was a bit of a pain to tune, as you had to adjust both the strings and the blades, but I *loved* the sound. It was deeper and more complex than any guitar I'd played before.

My own new Fflyr guitar was made of sky blue akorshil and hung around my neck on an embroidered strap, which was where it had been since I had purchased it from the luthier.

"So you're just going to walk around playing that, then?" Aster asked as we reached the end of the ramp, about halfway through the Gutters. Streets opened onto the main road here, but we were caught in the flow of traffic heading out, ignoring the shouts of vendors and the trickle of people turning on and off side streets.

I turned to grin at her and strummed a louder chord.

"I only ask," Aster continued with a long-suffering look, "because I thought you were trying to project a certain *image*, Lord Seiji. Walking down the road playing the guitar is more 'wandering minstrel' than 'nobleman.'"

"Aw, let 'em look," Donon piped up. He was carrying the case my new instrument had come with. "Nobles do much weirder stuff than this and nobody tells 'em a thing about it. That's the whole benefit of *being* a noble, isn't it? Besides, he's really good. I dunno how much you heard back at the Guild, but the man's a sorcerer on the keyboard."

"You know what, Donon? You *get* me." I slipped into the intro riff from Bon Jovi's "Dead or Alive," and winked at a highborn woman passing by on a horse, receiving a flirtatious smile in response. "Let me have my fun, Aster. I have so very little."

Strolling along, strumming my guitar and mulling my plans, we made it all the way to the outskirts of the city without further incident. Then, just beyond the watchtower, somebody threw a rock at me.

"*Hey!*" I exclaimed, whirling to confront the direction from which the pebble had sailed, nearly grazing my face. After being chased all over North Watch I wasn't too upset at the prospect of being beaned with a rock, but if this asshole so much as chipped my guitar . . .

The culprit was immediately identifiable, and in fact it appeared the rock was meant specifically to get my attention. It was impossible to miss the ragged-looking child currently grinning at me and bouncing another rock on his palm.

Seeing he had my eyes, he dropped the rock, waved, then turned and dashed away around the corner of the closest broken-down old warehouse. Actually, a lot of the structures here on the outskirts looked abandoned and neglected, so there were plenty of places to hide. A second later his head poked out and he beckoned with one hand.

"Hey," said Donon, "that's that kid! The one from . . . you know."

"Are you sure?" Aster demanded.

"Pretty sure. I thought at the time, he looks a lot like my cousin did when we were little sprouts."

I didn't need his confirmation; I had seen the boy much closer than either of them the night before, and got a good look just now.

"It's him. And . . . apparently he would like a word."

"Could be a trap," Aster said tersely, drawing her sword.

"Could be. It *also* could be an opportunity. Let's go check it out. Be on the alert, though."

"Then I'm going first," she stated, starting forward at a slow walk and constantly swiveling her head to watch the nearby fences and drainage ditch, the only places that could possibly hide a person. "Be ready to use your healing magic on me if I get jumped."

"Well," I drawled, "*yes*, your Highness, but only because you asked so courteously."

"If you want me to be your bodyguard, then I'm your bodyguard," Aster retorted, still looking at the surroundings and not me as we proceeded at a careful pace. "Jarind had us do work like this for nobles a few times. Rule number one is that when the client is in danger, the bodyguard is in charge. *Behind me*, Lord Seiji."

"I *am* behind you!"

"Good."

The flap of her outer coat pocket popped open and a tiny triangular head emerged. "It's no trap, guys, there's nobody within earshot but the kid."

"Thanks, Biribo," Aster muttered, not relaxing at all.

"Just doin' my job," he replied, ducking back down. A second later, one little black claw reached up to pull the pocket flap closed.

Aster was the first past the corner, shifting the huge sword to an over-handed grip with its tip pointed, as I saw when I made it around, at the boy. He was standing there in the shade of the warehouse, hidden from the road, with his hands raised but not looking otherwise too worried.

His ratty shirt had a large hole at the belly. It looked like a good effort had been made to get the bloodstain out, but the entire lower half of it was suspiciously brown and stiff.

"Well, well, look who it is," I said, handing my guitar to Donon, who knelt to tuck it carefully into its case. "You look a lot more chipper than the *last* time I saw you. Why do I get the feeling you didn't chase us all the way out here to say a belated 'thank you?'"

"Cos you ain't stupid, obviously," he said with a grin. "Believe me, I know. I ain't stupid either; I figured out your whole plan. *That's* why I came to find you—cos I'm either on your side, or I'm a loose end. And I don't wanna get tied up, but more important, I know whose crew I wanna be with when it all goes down."

Aster and Donon both shifted to look at me inquisitively.

"My *whole* plan?" I mused. "You have a pretty high opinion of yourself, squirt. Okay, you have my attention—now impress me. What is my *whole* plan?"

I was really interested in hearing this. The kid had only seen me when I was bumbling around in a panic after an extremely ill-advised impulse had gone horribly awry.

"Both ends against the middle!" he said brightly. "Clan Olumnach and Lady Gray are the only two players powerful enough to matter in shady business in Gwyllthean, maybe on all of Dount. So there's nobody who dares stand up to 'em, 'cept each other. And cos of that, everybody knows *nobody* would be daft enough to hit 'em both at once! So I'm glad to let you know it worked like a charm. After your move last night, the Olumnachs are roaring mad about their boy getting knifed, Lady Gray's roaring mad about all her money going missing, and cos nobody knows anyone else was even *there*, they blame each other. It's been heating up all night, and neither side's backing off or hearing any smooth talk. It's gonna be blades out by sundown, I'll bet. For stakes like this, things won't calm down for a *good* long while. And as long as they're tearing each other up, the whole city'll be ripe for the taking!"

Oh.

Oops.

13

In Which the Dark Lord Experiences the Horror of Self-Awareness

Ephemera was giving me plenty of practice at maintaining a stage presence. I seized that familiar poise and wrapped it around myself like a fluffy blanket, continuing to look aloof and amused at the kid and giving no outward sign of the loop for which he'd just knocked me.

"Ara, ara, ara, sounds like they're off to a good start. Reacting a bit faster than I'd expected, but oh well! You can only predict the behavior of people like that up to a point after all."

Dear god, Seiji, *shut up*. I really needed to work on this habit of babbling to cover my unease. Apparently Grandmother's "aras" compulsively came out when I was flustered, which meant I needed to clamp down on that before anyone else noticed the tell.

"See? Tolja I had it worked out. I'm smarter than I look." He puffed up his chest, smirking insufferably at me, and I had the fleeting thought that this fresh desire to smack him must be what talking to *me* felt like. "And something *else* I figured out is, since I'm the only one who saw what went down . . . well, it's like I said."

"You're with me or against me," I agreed, keeping myself as inscrutable as possible while I inwardly scrambled for a way to seize control of this conversation.

He nodded, his expression going serious. "Yeah, I . . . Well, it took me a bit to put it together, so, sorry for running out on you. And *thanks*. Y'know, for the magic." He unconsciously touched his midsection where the knife had been driven most of the way through his thin stomach. "I didn't get what you were doin' until I had time to think on it, but I get it now."

"Hmm. Tell me what you *get*, and I'll tell you how close you are." I really hoped I looked as wise and in control as I was trying to.

"Well, at first I thought maybe it was cos you were soft, like the Olumnach lord said." He flashed me a cheeky grin. "But that didn't hold, cos you lured him into that tunnel for an ambush with your pet muscle, took out him and his goon, *and* lifted a shitload of Lady Gray's gold. That's some *cold* maneuvering right there."

"*Pet muscle?*" Aster repeated from behind me.

I held up a hand for silence, then nodded to the boy. "Go on."

"So I got thinking," he said eagerly, "and this is something I've seen before. Me and most of the Rats—hell, most lowlifes in the Gutters—it's all take what you can and fuck whoever gets in your way, right? But the *real* crews, like the Olumnachs and Lady Gray's outfit, they stick *together*. Even the bully boys back at the Nest always got their little crew of bootlickers; they don't go alone. Nobody makes it big without backup. You're building a *crew*, and I almost missed my invite. But I figured it out!" He nodded furiously. "I ain't told nobody what I saw. I want *in*. You need Rat business done, right? Eyes and quick fingers all over the Gutters, that's what we do."

He straightened up, lifting his chin proudly, and thumped a fist into his thin chest.

"Gilder's your guy, Lord Seiji! You need eyes on the Gutters, and I got 'em. Just say the word!"

Well, what the fuck was I supposed to do about *this*? Mindful that my own hasty action had created this situation and it could have been *so much worse*, I tried frantically to think ahead and in the meanwhile stalled for time with a little theater.

"See, Aster?" I said, turning to give her a little half smirk. "I told you he had potential."

She returned a silent but deeply expressive stare. Aster was good at those.

"Here, now," said Donon, "how'd you know he's called Lord Seiji?"

"I been following you and listening," Gilder retorted, grinning again. "That's what I *do*! Only thing I couldn't figure out, though, Lord Seiji, is how'd you know I'd come back? You musta had *something* on me, otherwise you'd'a been proper fucked if I told somebody you was the one who did it. A cold operator doesn't take that kinda risk without havin' a leash to pull. What was it?"

I experienced the unique sensation of hearing my inner monologue emit a continuous high-pitched scream.

"Ah, ah," I chided aloud, putting on a smirk and wagging a finger at him. "Walk before you run, child. We're just starting out here. In time, you'll learn more about how I do things. Surely you don't expect me to start handing out my own secrets like candy?"

Wait. Was candy expensive here? Did they even *have* sugar?

"All right, all right, I got you." Gilder just nodded back, not even seeming disappointed. "We'll get there."

"Working for me is still going to have its risks," I continued, still stalling for time while struggling against the white noise in my head to think up a scheme out of this that wouldn't make the situation worse or require me to do something unacceptable. Silencing the kid like Arider had tried to was just not on the table. I'd crossed some moral boundaries already and doubtless would cross more, but there had to be some hard lines *somewhere*, and child murder was way on the wrong side of any of them. But what could I *do* with him? Leaving him loose in Gwyllthean unsupervised was a security risk . . . but was taking him back to North Watch any better? Then he'd know where I was based, and I'd have nowhere to retreat to if he turned on me anyway. The question of what was *right* wasn't much easier. Obviously letting an orphan continue to live on the streets when I could help him out was appalling, but honestly, would he be any better off in a crumbling ruin among bandits surrounded by an alien forest full of cat people and god knew what else?

It was only after speaking that I realized my stalling tactic had offered him a cogent reason to turn on me. Fortunately Gilder replied before I could mull too deeply upon how much I deserved to be kicked in the head for how badly I was bungling this.

"Hey, you gotta take risks to get rewards," he said, thumping his chest again. "I know the score. Me, I ain't gonna be a Gutter Rat my whole life, get me? I got *dreams*. I'm gonna be an *adventurer*, and not some graydisc Gutter-grubber neither. I'm gonna get a Blessing and get rich, and live in a shell mansion in the inner quarter, and eat pepper mutton every day! I'm gonna marry a yellow-haired highborn lady with huge knockers and keep twenty mistresses around town to bang! But none of that's happening if nothing changes around the Gutters, see? The Gutters are practically a workshop for people like me to get worked *on*. You either get broke and thrown out with the rest of the scrap, or hammered into a tool for the likes of Lady Gray to use. Until *she* breaks you and throws you out. Fuck that. You're the only real option that's come along in forever, Lord Seiji. I'm with *you*."

I could only stare at him for a moment. I'm not great with children, but I was *certain* he couldn't be any more than ten years old.

"Well," I said finally, "those are some grand and . . . extremely specific dreams."

"Boy knows what's good in life," Donon said sagely.

"Except that you want the knockers on the mistresses," Aster added, equally solemn. "You want to marry a petite blonde; that's more fashionable among the pales."

"I meant the pepper mutton, but go off, I guess."

"Aster, how much change do we have after shopping?" She was handling the money, on account of her coat having the biggest and sturdiest pockets. My new Fflyr-style nobleman's coat was loose-cut and would be handy for concealing things the way Arider had, but you needed actual pockets or fasteners on the inside to do that, and either those didn't come standard or I'd been cheated. Given how much I'd annoyed the tailor, could be either.

"Lord Seiji, I don't want to seem inconsiderate, but you should be *careful* about giving a lot of money to somebody like . . . Gilder, was it? If the other Gutter Rats *see* him with a bunch of cash they'll just roll him for it."

"She's not wrong, Lord Seiji," Gilder agreed with a displeased grimace. "Not that I wouldn't love a pocketful, but I show up at the Nest with anything too nice, and it'll just get took from me, along with a chunk of my ass. And there ain't any safe stash spots in the Gutters. We Rats have a game where we sniff out each other's stashes."

"I appreciate the concern, you two, but you'll be glad to know I am not, in fact, a complete idiot." Man, *I* would be glad to know that at this point. "That is why I asked for *change*. I'm not gonna hand the kid a blue halo." That was one of the denominations whose name I'd heard; at some point I needed to have Aster walk me through what each was worth. "I *do* want to make sure all my people are taken care of. Let's get Gilder set up with something to put a meal in him. Anything else you need right now, kid?"

"Hell's revels, Lord Seiji, a meal is *always* what I need," he chirped, again with that big infectious grin. "If you're feeling generous, I won't turn down a few discs for something hot from the vendors! Anything nicer'll have to wait 'til I got safer digs and protection."

"And that day will come," I promised, "but it has to be one step at a time."

"I get it," he nodded. "You're just getting started and I gotta earn cred. What's next, boss man?"

Fortunately, I finally had an answer. The preceding byplay had bought me enough time to come to a conclusion—I had to put the boy to work, here in Gwyllthean. Whether or not it was ethical, it was my only *strategic* option right now. Since I was not willing to silence him, I needed him firmly on my side, which meant I needed him to keep thinking I was an ice-cold mastermind who'd spared him in order to put him to use in my schemes— which meant he needed to be put to actual use in an actual scheme. As soon as he realized that my maneuvers up until now had been random bumbling, and he was objectively better off with one of the established powers, I'd have *all* of the established powers climbing up my ass with sharp implements. I couldn't even afford to reveal ignorance by asking who the hell Lady Gray was or what the deal was with Clan Olumnach.

"First off," I said, "I need to go monitor business elsewhere and may not be back in Gwyllthean for a few days. How can I find you?"

"Hah!" Gilder's irrepressible grin only got wider. "You don't find the Gutter Rats, Lord Seiji; we find you. Just dally a little next time you're passing down the road on the way to the walls. You'll be noted, face like yours, and I can make sure word gets to me. Then I can find you anywhere outside the walls."

"That sounds like you'll be relying on others. That's a good strategy to get through life, but at this stage, I need to be *careful* who knows I'm a person of interest."

"I gotcha, don't worry," he said, nodding. "The Rats trade favors, and I got friends. I just gotta spin a story about how I got a rich mark interested in you, and nobody'll ask questions so long as I cut 'em in. Pales are always having each other followed around, and the smart ones know to use the Rats. Means I'll need a few coins to hand out, though."

"That won't be a problem. Good, I'm glad to hear you've thought that through, because that was my first assignment for you—I'm going to need more eyes and ears on the street than just yours."

"I know people!" He beamed.

I held up a warning finger. "*Carefully*, Gilder. Only Rats you person- ally know and trust. Preferably those who'll stay loyal as long as I look after them—because that is the deal, let me make that clear. Stick by me and I will stick by you. I have coin and healing magic, and between them I can solve a lot of problems for you."

"Gotta be careful with that, Lord Seiji," he said, going serious again. "If Uncle Gently spots you poaching Rats from him, he'll run to Lady Gray and she'll round on you."

"Mm." So that was the guy running the Gutter Rats organization? Worth knowing. "To be clear, he answers to Lady Gray?"

"*Everybody* in the Gutters answers to Lady Gray, one way or another. Uncle Gently keeps us separate from her organization, but he also gives her info at cost or free and pays his protection money. She likes having the Rats answering to somebody who'll lick her toes for her."

"Then that's good advice for us both. Slow and careful. No overt recruitment yet—for the time being, sound people out, see if you can sus out who's interested and trustworthy."

"You got it, boss man!" The grin returned in a flash. "I got a few names I can start with, and I'll see about roping up more."

"Good man."

Aster handed him a few coins, which he bounced on his palm, beaming. "Anything else, Lord Seiji?"

"I'll be interested in general rumors and information, especially on how business between the Olumnachs and Lady Gray's people progresses. For now, though, focus on building me a network. You're getting in on the ground floor, Gilder. Don't screw this up, and you're heading for a high place in my organization."

He grinned so hard I thought I might have to heal his face.

"Won't let you down, Lord Seiji. You'll see for yourself—Gilder's a man of his word. Just gimme a couple days, I'll have results for you!"

Gilder turned and scrambled off back toward the warren of outbuildings that led to the Gutters before I could say anything else. Manners aside, it was just as well. That conversation was wearing down my equanimity.

Much as I wanted to stand there and stew for a few minutes, I turned without another word and proceeded back toward the main road, Aster and Donon falling into step with me. I hadn't been in that much of a hurry before, but after talking with Gilder, the urge to get the hell out of Gwyllthean was a constant itch between my shoulder blades. And now that I no longer had to actively put on a face, the weight of my screwup was truly settling in.

My god in heaven. I had walked into the equivalent of yakuza turf, gotten a major player killed, waltzed off with a small—or not so small?—fortune in ill-gotten cash, *let a witness escape*, and then gone on about my evening as if nothing had happened. By Virya's *taint*, I'd spent a leisurely night and morning sleeping, dining, shopping around town . . . It was just luck, pure clueless *luck* that the boy I'd let get away had been smart and ambitious but not *too* smart and ambitious, in just the right amount to decide to throw in with me. He was probably the only one; any other Rat would almost certainly have squealed on me, and I'd have been dead before dawn, along with Aster and Donon.

It was all I could do to keep putting one foot in front of the other, fast enough to stay a bit ahead of Aster so she couldn't see me laboring not to cry.

I couldn't do this. I could *not do this*. Dark Lord? It was pushing my capabilities to their limits to pull off Morally Ambiguous Asshole. It had been two days, and I'd already gotten multiple people killed, a majority of them by accident, and started a fucking gang war. I didn't know what I was doing and I was going to *die* and . . .

And there was nothing to be done about it. This was the situation I was in. There was no one I could trust or turn to. Either I figured this shit out and made it work, or . . .

Left foot, right foot. Just one in front of the other, for now. I just had to keep pressing on.

The nice thing about having a hike that took most of a day to complete was that it provided ample time for me to get my frantically racing brain back under control. By the time we reached North Watch, dark was falling and I was relatively calm. Second-guessing myself, of course—in hindsight I wasn't at all sure leaving Gilder loose in Gwyllthean had been the right call, either for me or him. But it was done now. I'd done my best to plan ahead while walking rather than dwelling on my mistakes up until now.

I'd also taken the guitar back from Donon, both because strumming it while strolling did wonders to calm me and because it was the heaviest single thing we'd purchased, and despite what he'd said, I didn't feel right making him carry everything by himself.

Biribo had of course vacated Aster's coat as soon as we were out of sight of Gwyllthean, and now reported to me as we drew close to the old fortress. "One person on watch, boss. Looks like the girl, Twigs. She's seen us—not aiming a weapon."

I nodded in silence; familiars were useful for more than general exposition.

Thus, I was not surprised when Twigs popped out of the shadows of the gatehouse when we returned and made that descending gesture of folded hands which I had started to interpret as what the Fflyr did instead of bowing.

"Welcome back, Lord Seiji. I hope your journey was successful."

I stopped, studying her closely. In truth, I had paid Twigs almost no attention before; she was just the skinny girl Goose was protective of. Now, I noted her poised delivery and looked more carefully. She was almost painfully thin—hence the nickname, no doubt—and dirty. As in, her cheeks had dirt on them, smeared in a pattern that looked deliberate. It completely failed to conceal the fact that her skin was quite pale compared to the rest of the bandits. She also wore a big, baggy, beret-like hat over her head, but the wisps of hair which poked out were straight and a very light brown.

Interesting.

"Thank you, Twigs," I said aloud. "Any news? Who's still here?"

She hesitated. "We've all been doing as you ordered, Lord Seiji. No one has left. I doubt anyone will. All of us . . . It's like you said, that night when you arrived. We have nowhere else to go."

"I see. Very good, then, carry on."

Twigs folded her hands down again and slipped back into the tower.

The doors to the keep were standing open, a pile of broken furniture and containers heaped on one side of the entry, and a smaller pile of dust and obvious trash on the other. I gave them barely a glance, mostly focusing on the sounds of a rant in progress as I crossed through the foyer into the big mess hall which was the apparent heart of the fortress.

"I'm getting *sick* of this! Just because I never set out to be a bandit doesn't mean I wanted to be a fucking *maid* either. I mean, come on, what is even the *point* of this? Look at this fucking dump! How the hell is any of this even going to help, huh? Tell me that!"

Actually, I observed upon entering the mess hall—quietly—it looked a lot better already. The foyer had been cleared of junk, swept, and had the streamer-like alien cobwebs cleared out, and now most of that had been done in the big hall as well. There were still piles of things up on the dais around the head table, but they looked better organized, at least. The walls were clean of moss, the torches had been replaced, and the room was far better illuminated than before. I had observed at the inn in Gwyllthean that polished akorshil was actually rather beautiful under torchlight, but this was the first time I had seen the effect in my own castle. The tables were nicely clean and showing off the almost luminous golden grain in their grayish-ivory surface.

Altogether, the place was shaping up nicely. You'd never know it from the way Kasser was carrying on, though.

He was facing the other end of the hall, toward the dais, and I got the pleasure of seeing him actually throw down his broom in frustration. "This is just fucking *stupid*. Why should we be doing this just cos that demented asshole said so, huh? What kind of fucking idiot goes around claiming to be the Dark Lord? He's gonna get a bunch of adventurers coming to kill his ass, and then *we'll* all go down with him!"

"Uh, Kasser," Goose started to warn him.

Kasser had a full head of steam, though, and rolled right over her. "If a crazy guy with killer fire magic wanted to go raiding, I mean, sure, *that* at least makes sense! But *this*? He wants us to *clean* the *fortress*? What the fuck is a little cleaning going to do for this shithole, anyway?"

"Kasser!" Harold said urgently, staring at me with wide eyes.

"I've had it!" Kasser kicked his fallen broom. "I'm not doing this bullshit anymore! What's Lord Freakjob gonna do about it, anyway? I don't see *his* ass here lending a hand. At least if he did, maybe he'd see how fucking dumb this whole fucking idea is!"

He finally worked himself to a stop, shoulders heaving with exertion, and only then looked around at the other three bandits for approval.

Harold was clutching his hands at his throat, looking terrified. Goose just heaved a resigned sigh and went back to sweeping by the door. Sakin was grinning as if his birthday had come early.

I could actually see, even from behind, the moment Kasser figured it out. His labored breathing abruptly stilled, and then he hunched in on himself, shoulders clenching up. Very slowly, he turned around to find me standing barely a meter behind him, wearing a polite little smile.

"Feel better?" I asked pleasantly.

Kasser whimpered.

"Cleaning the fortress serves multiple purposes," I explained, keeping my tone amiable. "The most immediate benefit, of course, is that when the fortress is *clean*, we don't have to live in filth. I realize you're accustomed to thinking of yourselves as the dregs of humanity, and while you may have a point, you are still all human beings. *That* is a mixed blessing at the absolute best, but all people deserve some basic dignity. Not living in squalor is better for your health, your pride, and your overall well-being."

"In addition, the *act* of cleaning gives its own blessings. By laboring together to maintain the space in which we live and work, the group improves its own cohesion and gains respect—for one another, and for our shared environment. These bonds are what differentiate a group united in common purpose from a miscellaneous rabble. Besides, there's just not a lot to *do* around here while we're in between raiding jobs, is there? Performing useful tasks is a much more mentally and physically healthy way to fill the time than sitting around waiting for our hair to turn gray."

"Where I am from, these are the first things children learn. The first years of education are devoted to social and practical skills, and all students are expected to take part in continuing to develop their work ethic and social bonds by cleaning and maintaining their shared spaces. I realize you lot are a little old to begin learning, but I have faith in you."

I fell silent, still giving him a benign smile. Kasser swallowed heavily, clearly waiting for more. I waited until he finally opened his mouth to speak to deliver the last bit.

"If you ever have questions about my orders, Kasser, please feel free to ask me. I certainly won't punish someone for expressing reasonable concerns. It's my belief that people are best able to carry out my instructions when they *understand* them. Don't you think so?"

"Yes, Lord Seiji," he said in a very small voice.

I nodded graciously. "Carry on, then."

He folded his hands downward in a hasty gesture, then bent to retrieve his broom and started to scuffle away toward Harold.

I crossed the space between us in a few rapid, silent strides, only speaking again when I was right behind him.

"And Kasser."

He flinched violently, nearly dropping the broom.

I rested one hand on his shoulder, continuing to give him the same pleasant smile when he slowly turned a dread-filled face to look at me.

"Complaining about one's boss is a time-honored tradition, as venerable as the institution of bosses themselves. Far be it from me to begrudge my employees one of life's simple pleasures. But when speaking of the Dark Lord, let's try to keep the obscenities to a minimum, shall we?"

He gibbered in a series of squeaks, not producing anything I could parse as words, and eventually managed a jerky nod.

I clapped him on the shoulder. "Good man."

"You got a real way with people, boss," Biribo said as I turned and strolled away.

Sakin loudly cleared his throat, then folded his hands down when I turned to look at him. "Please understand I'm not complaining, Lord Seiji, but just out of curiosity . . . How long do you want us to keep cleaning the fortress?"

"Until it is clean, obviously."

"Ah." His expression, as usual, didn't waver. "You're the boss, of course. But, just for reference . . . This is a fortress meant to garrison several hundred soldiers, left to rot for more than a century, and there are six of us. Seven, counting Miss Aster."

"Seven so far," I corrected. "Don't worry, Sakin, I won't have you over-working yourselves. Take breaks, don't skip meals, be sure to stay hydrated, and make progress as you can. We'll get there."

"As you say, Lord Seiji," he said, visibly bemused, and went back to sorting through the contents of a crate.

"Welcome back, Lord Seiji," said Goose, leaning her broom against the wall.

"Thank you, Goose. I trust all's well here? You've all done fine work so far; I'm impressed."

"Thanks, my lord, we've tried. Ah, sorry, I know you must've had a long walk to get here, but . . . you've got a visitor waiting for you."

I came to a stop, blinking at her.

"Excuse me, I have a what?"

14

In Which the Dark Lord Plans Ahead

There were goblins in my kitchen. Well, at least the kitchen was *clean* now.

"There he is!" I was greeted effusively by a little green man roughly a meter tall, who hopped down from the chair upon which he'd been perched to spread his arms and grin up at me in welcome. "The famous Lord Seiji himself! Soon as I heard North Watch was under new management, I *had* to come check it out for myself. And I gotta say, I like what you're doin' already! Damn, this place cleans up nicer than I woulda thought."

"I'm glad it's to your liking," I said slowly, stalling with pleasantries while I considered what to do about this. The speaker was one of four goblins. In addition to himself, he'd brought two other men, both carrying heavy cudgels, and a woman. Their proportions were . . . actually I couldn't quite put my finger on the details, besides noting that they weren't childlike and weren't exactly just shrunk-down green humans. "Obviously we have a lot of work yet to do, but it's a start. To what do I owe the unexpected pleasure, Mr. . . . ?"

"Maugro's the name," he said with outgoing good cheer, already reminding me of an aggressive salesman. "And this here's my girl, Mindzi. Don't mind the muscle; they're just along on general policy."

"Happy to meet you, Lord Seiji," the girl said, winking. "I already like you a *lot* better than the last guy." This was accompanied by a flirtatious little wiggling motion of her whole body; our relative statures made it easier for her to look coyly up at me through her thick lashes, and she leaned forward to facilitate me looking down her dress. The look Maugro gave me at the same time was just a little too acute and overtly sly.

Oho. So apparently Donon's little obsession wasn't *that* unheard of, if Maugro thought it worth the effort of bringing along goblin eye candy to dangle in front of me.

I could . . . sort of see it. The goblins were *cute*, in a way—all of them, even the sleazy salesman type I was dealing with and the two over by the tunnel trying to look intimidating. Mindzi was noticeably woman-shaped and dressed to accentuate it. Their size made their oversized pointed ears even more amusing. They had wiry black hair, which all four, including the muscle, had clearly taken pains to style carefully. Just another race of people, not monsters. I had to conclude that goblins in general weren't *unattractive*, so long as their mouths were closed so I couldn't see those frightening teeth. Big, *sharp*, triangular teeth exactly like a shark. Mentally, I upgraded Donon from "isekai sex freak" to "guy with a type," though I personally wasn't about to spring for the bait being offered. I'm not dense enough to miss a honey trap that blatant.

"Pleased to meet you both," I replied, pulling out a chair and positioning it to face the one Maugro had commandeered, alongside the table rather than across it. "And not to worry; I won't object to your muscle if you have no problem with mine." Apparently this spectacle was way better than cleaning, to judge by the way my bandits were now clustering in the doorway, spilling into the kitchen or rubbernecking over the shoulders of those in front. "I am terribly sorry about the accommodations, Maugro; I've only just inherited this fortress and barely made a start at sprucing it up. We suffer an embarrassing lack of goblin-sized amenities, which I will do my best to rectify before your next visit. In the meantime, please make yourself as comfortable as you can."

"Well." Maugro's eyebrows shot up, and Mindzi's coquettish smile faded into a much more believable expression of bemusement. "I ain't one to quibble over the niceties, Lord Seiji, so let's just say it's the thought that counts! I think you might be the first tallboy I've met who's even *had* the thought."

"Yes, this country does seem to suffer from a general lack of civilization, I've noticed. If you lot are all going to loiter around, make yourselves useful," I added over my shoulder to the scrum in the doorway while Maugro clambered back up into the chair he'd previously occupied, Mindzi sticking close by him. "Donon, break out some refreshments for our guests."

"Re . . . freshments, Lord Seiji?"

"Something to eat," I said patiently, "and a bottle of our least shitty wine."

"Uh, sure! Right away, Lord Seiji."

"We're *feeding* the goblins now?" a familiar voice muttered from within the throng. "They probably stole half the place while Goose wasn't watching 'em, anyway . . ."

"Goose," I said aloud without turning back around, "please explain the importance of hospitality to Kasser."

There came two sharp whacks, a yelp from Kasser, and a general scuffle from the vicinity of the doorway, to the intense amusement of my visitors.

"Thank you, Goose."

"My pleasure, Lord Seiji."

"Sorry about that," I said to Maugro. "They aren't all fully housebroken yet."

"Believe me when I say you've got nothing to apologize for, Lord Seiji," the goblin replied, grinning broadly. Man, that was unsettling.

Donon arrived with . . . a single uncut disc of flatbread, which he set right on the table between us with no utensils. Oh well, at least the table was clean now. He also had a bottle of something, along with three cups—also clean; I double-checked.

"Hi, Mindzi," he said bashfully, standing there twisting the bottle in his hands.

She did a little double take, then squinted up at him. "Do I know you?"

"*Thank you*, Donon," I said pointedly, taking the bottle.

"Oh, uh, sure, m'lord, I . . ."

Then Aster was there, taking him by the arm and dragging him gently but inexorably back toward the others in the doorway.

"So," I said, pouring wine, "I believe you were about to reveal the reason for your visit." Coming right to the point like that might not be good manners—at least where I'm from—but it had been a very long day already.

"Right you are!" Maugro said, accepting a cup and tilting it toward me in acknowledgment. "Y'might say I'm your neighbor, Lord Seiji. My place is just down the hall, so to speak." He waved at the broken wall with the dark tunnel beyond, currently flanked by his two pint-sized bruisers. "More relevant to your interests, I'm in the information business. Whatever you might need to know, or need someone else *not* to, Maugro's your guy. Since my established relationship with the late, unlamented Rocco was the main thing keeping this whole operation in business, clearly it's a priority for us both to check in and lay out exactly where we stand. Gotta stay solvent, Dark Lord or not!"

He gave me a particularly canny look, emphasized by the fact that his eyes were a vivid crimson. So were Mindzi's, I noticed. I also noticed that my followers had lacked the basic sense not to flap their yaps in front of miscellaneous goblins.

"I see," I said aloud. "Well, then, I'm very glad you did. Perhaps you can help lay out for me just how Rocco's operation worked." I took a sip from my cup, then had to pause and swallow laboriously. The flavor was . . . unfamiliar. Reminiscent of the jam I'd had on my bread that morning, which left me unsure if the local wine was *supposed* to be this sour. "Donon, I *did* request the *least* shitty vintage on offer, did I not?"

"That's what I got you, Lord Seiji!" he protested. "I mean, unless Rocco had something better hoarded away in his room."

"We haven't even tried to clean in there," Sakin added. "Seemed risky to poke about in your personal areas, Lord Seiji. And in Donon's defense, this isn't exactly a Lannitar teahouse we're running here."

"Hey, we've got no complaints about the hospitality," Mindzi said sweetly, giving me a long, lingering look over the rim of her cup as she took a deep sip.

"If you don't mind my asking," I said, "how does an information broker stay in business out here in the boonies? It was my impression North Watch was a stone's throw from the edge of the island."

"As the scraw flies, sure," Maugro replied. "The actual land route to the old bridge is the only passage through the mountains, and that's a winding passage a good limn long. But I take your point, Lord Seiji. See, despite what they'd like to think, the elves aren't the only people who matter on Dount, and their city-dwelling subjects aren't even the only *humans* whose business is worth considering." He winked. "Trust me, the area around North Watch is fertile ground for tunnel-grubbers like us. Ah, but I understand how you'd feel otherwise, as much as humans hate going underground."

They do? It must be cultural, I decided, remembering what Biribo had said about digging being taboo. Not unreasonable, if you lived on a broken planet. More to the point, it sounded like Maugro was the go-to intel guy for, among other things, whatever bandit gangs operated in the wilderness. He continued his account, solidifying that impression.

"So, your ol' pal Rocco carved out a real particular niche among Dount's bandit gangs, one that relied heavily on my services. Rather than try his luck with road traffic like the less *creative* gangs, he played it safe. Laid traps with no risk of combat or personal injury, and lured adventurers into 'em."

"Adventurers, specifically?" I risked a sidelong glance at Aster. Her expression had gone hard, but she didn't seem about to intervene.

"Adventurers have good shit," Maugro said, grinning. "Artifacts, quality gear, frequently a sizable amount of on-hand cash, usually some alchemicals. Most gangs give 'em a wide berth, cos most bandits ain't equipped to tangle with Blessed."

"Hence the traps."

"Exactly! So *my* role in this was to notify Rocco when adventuring parties were being hired to clear out bandits, and then arrange for a team to be given a tip directing them into one of his traps. And *that*," he added with a more serious expression, pointing at me for emphasis, "is a service Maugro does *not* provide, just so's we're clear. I'm an info man—what you hear from Maugro's own lips is the goddess's own unvarnished, stake-your-life-on-it truth. I can't be caught spreading lies or it'll ruin my business, see? *But*, for a reasonable middleman's fee, I am willing to put the likes of Rocco in contact with people in the city who *do* that kinda work, and even rent out my employees to discreetly convey messages between parties. Likewise, at the other end of the caper, in acknowledgment that artifacts are distinctive and carrying stolen ones to and from Gwyllthean is a serious risk, I also handled discreet and secure package delivery and arrangement-making between Rocco and the few fences in the area who deal in that kinda trade."

"I'm beginning to see what you mean by Rocco relying heavily on your services."

"Too right, he did!" the goblin winked.

"That's quite a bit of middle-manning. Sounds like any profit this gang made flowed right into *your* pockets, Maugro."

"Well now, you probably know the state of Rocco's personal finances better than I would," he demurred, putting on an obviously fake expression of modesty. "But yeah, I got my own overhead to consider. I'm the best info guy on Dount, Lord Seiji, and that's a straightforward fact of life. You wanna do subtle business on this island outside Gwyllthean? You're gonna need what nobody but me is selling. I'll admit, I didn't set out to diversify quite so much, y'know? Carrying messages and cargo, making introductions; it's another layer of confusion in my organization. I gotta hire on more warm bodies for those tasks, *and* make sure they're properly vetted—and believe me, that ain't a short or simple process, being that there's nothing more important than trust in my business."

"Oh, of course. That makes perfect sense. Say, Maugro, I wonder if you might enlighten me on a couple of points. How long had Rocco been running this grift, and about how often did he go out . . . trapping, so to speak?"

"Now, Lord Seiji, you're asking me for intel. I do *sell* this stuff, y'know." He put on a big grin and a teasing tone. "But, since you're easily the most well-mannered gentleman I've had to deal with, I'm willing to throw you in a freebie or two in the interests of fostering amity."

"About things I could just ask them, anyway?" I retorted, cocking a thumb at the bandits watching from the doorway.

The goblin burst out laughing, slapping his knee and almost sloshing his wine. "I knew there was a reason I liked you! But yeah, like I said, Rocco was in a *niche*. By my reckoning, he'd been at it no more'n two years, taking in a mark, say, every month or so for the most part."

It occurred to me that that might be less helpful than I'd hoped, given that I didn't even know how long years or months were on this planet. Putting that aside, I leaned forward and set my own wine on the table, barely touched. Disgusting stuff.

"That's my concern, you see. It's a fairly clever gambit, but it seems to me like the kind of thing that can only work a finite number of times before someone with real power catches on and does something about it. Not to mention that so much relying on nested layers of middlemen and outside contractors is both a security risk and a massive profit sink."

"Now, as for security," he held up one green hand, his expression going serious, "I'm not bullshitting about how important my operational security is. My people are carefully handpicked, and when I'm paid to keep a secret, it stays *kept*."

"You're quite right, though, Lord Seiji," Sakin interjected in a smooth tone. "I wouldn't exactly call Rocco's operation *profitable*. He kept us fed and equipped, more or less, and the extra bit he skimmed for himself as leader was never egregious enough to make anybody feel rebellious."

True, I hadn't found so much as a single coin in Rocco's former quarters, though admittedly I hadn't torn the place up as thoroughly as might be needed to uncover a bandit boss's secret stash.

"Artifacts are a high-value commodity, and that was most of his income," Maugro agreed, "but the legitimate sale of artifacts is rare and that was *not* the business he was in, which means there's *inherently* a lot of middlemen and overhead in the trade. Doing it long-distance the way Rocco did removed basically all the personal risk to him, but also cut deep into his profit margins."

"How many bandit gangs are operating on Dount?" I asked.

"Oh," Maugro smiled vaguely, swirling his cup, "a few."

"Ah. So when you mentioned keeping secrets for a price . . ."

"That's all part of the standard Maugro package," he said, grinning again. "Everybody who needs info—which is everybody—comes to Maugro. And Maugro is only too willing to guarantee his clients' privacy, for a nominal service fee."

The canny little bastard had discovered the ultimate protection racket; he didn't even need to use his own muscle. Just keep the location and composition of a bandit gang secret from all the *other* bandit gangs, and if one didn't pay up, they were sitting ducks for every other gang on the island.

"I was also told that Rocco paid off the local catfolk tribe to be left alone. Your doing as well?"

The goblin grimaced, which was still unsettling. Those *teeth*. "Ah, now, I'm afraid you caught me in a weak point there, Lord Seiji. I've got tenuous relations with a *few* of the beast tribes on Dount, but beastfolk in general ain't any more kindly disposed toward goblins than humans are. Couldn't tell you what arrangements Rocco had with them."

I leaned back in my chair, considering what this revealed about the racial tensions present here. I'd been told the beastfolk lived apart from humans and elves, but I was getting the impression goblins weren't well-liked anywhere. On Earth I'd assume they were just an ethnic minority getting treated the way those usually do, but could I afford to make assumptions like that on Ephemera? These were clearly a different species. Did they fundamentally *think* the same way humans did?

Maugro, apparently misinterpreting my silence, hastened to add, "I don't think you got much to worry about from the kitties, Lord Seiji. Once they don't get their regular payment of whatever, they'll probably come asking after it. And hell, lemme throw some business your way: if you *can* put me in communication with the tribe, I'm willing to pay a handsome middleman's fee, assuming I can wrangle an actual working relationship out of it."

"Oh? Are the cat people really that valuable?"

"To me, *everybody's* valuable! I deal in connections, see? Everybody I *can* dialog with is a feather in my cap and a coin in my purse, and anybody who *won't* talk to me's like an itch on my back right where I can't scratch it. But to you, I'd say they're even more valuable. The catfolk and Rocco paying 'em off are a main reason nobody's tried to contest ownership of this very convenient wilderness fortress. You're smack dab in their territory, and fighting beastfolk in the khora forest is a damn nightmare."

"Surprising that they haven't tried to seize North Watch for themselves."

"They have. Twice, in the last century. First time the local lizardfolk tribe ran 'em out—on behalf of the naga, on behalf of the dark elves. Second time

Fflyr Dlemathlys sent a battalion to do it. Bandits're one thing; the kingdom doesn't have the standing forces to throw around for piddly business like that, and as long as you're preying on humans and not their interests, the dark elves don't care. But both sides benefit from having the khora forest full of feuding beast tribes between 'em. Situation gets more complicated than either one likes it, if one of those tribes suddenly has a fortified position."

"Why, Maugro, how positively magnanimous of you," I said, smiling. "All this free information!"

He cackled, slapping his leg again. "Hey, even I ain't shameless enough to charge for basic history! I can see you're new in this part of the world; it's to my benefit to help you get caught up on how things work, if we're gonna be in business together. Speaking of which!"

"Yes, that *was* the reason for your visit, wasn't it?"

"And that brings us to the big question!" Setting his cup down on the table, he planted both hands on his knees and leaned forward, putting on an expectant expression. "What's the plan, Lord Seiji? Gonna pick up where Rocco left off?"

This had to be handled carefully. I wished it wasn't coming at the end of an exhausting day, but I was still *fairly* confident I knew what to do here.

"No, I think not. I have much grander ambitions."

"Well, naturally," Maugro said with a wink. "Can't expect the Dark Lord to just sit in his fortress, content with the easy pickings."

I smiled thinly. "To begin with, obviously I wish to continue with the arrangement ensuring your discretion."

"Yeah, I kinda assumed that one." His answering smile was just a shade too smug for an amicable negotiation, but I chose to let that pass. Mostly because he had me over a barrel on that one; word getting out about the Dark Lord at this stage would be almost as disastrous as all the other bandit gangs on Dount being informed of a dinky little eight-person outfit occupying the most desirable real estate on the island.

"As for the rest . . . no more picking on adventurers." I glanced again at Aster, whose expression was unreadable. "Instead . . . Well, there is the matter of target selection. And for that, Maugro, I'm going to have to rely on your services."

The goblin spread his hands magnanimously, Mindzi grinning over his shoulder. "That's what I'm here for! What'll it be, Lord Seiji?"

"I may soon need to significantly expand the amount of business we give you with regard to the planting of false information. I'm willing to continue relying on your middleman services, since I know you're not up for doing that in person. But that's a future stage of my plans; for now, I just need some more mundane intel."

"Music to my ears," he said, and both of said ears noticeably wiggled, twice.

"In the immediate term," I continued carefully, "I am in a . . . somewhat precarious situation. To start out on my next venture, I'm going to have to ask you to extend me a tip on credit."

Maugro leaned back, sucking in a long breath through his teeth; Mindzi openly winced. "Now, that's tricky, Lord Seiji. Don't get me wrong, I like you. Hell, you might just be my favorite human outta all my business contacts after just one conversation—and I mean that sincerely. Maugro's word is his bond, and everyone knows it. But there's liking, and then there's business, and in business, extending credit to somebody you barely know . . . Well, it ain't a winning move, see?"

Of course, I could have just paid him. But after my disastrous performance in Gwyllthean over the last two days, I was determined above all else to start being *careful*. I was lucky so far in that my impulsive actions had won Aster and Gilder to my side, both of whom had already proved valuable. But that had been pure luck, with a terrifyingly close brush with gruesome fates on the other side of that coin. I'd been stumbling from one thing to the next, acting on impulse, and by my estimate, I had exactly *no* more time in which to get away with that before the law of averages brutally caught up with me.

That meant thinking as far ahead as I could, laying my plans with care, and deliberately considering the repercussions of any action I took. I'd already spotted one pitfall just waiting to be stepped in—if an *information broker* of all people learned that Lord Seiji suddenly turned up with a lot of liquid assets after having been in Gwyllthean at the exact time a fortune in yakuza money went missing, that was going to bite me on the ass *hard* somewhere down the line. For now, I needed him to think I was cash poor.

"And that's why I'm asking for credit," I said, "not a favor. I don't think we're quite there in our relationship yet, are we? *Credit* means interest paid, which I figured you'd like. Let's be real, Maugro—this is a no-risk proposition for you. If my next plan works, you get paid—and with interest for the loan on top of your nominal fee for services rendered. If it *doesn't*, then the location of Lord Seiji's sparsely defended castle goes on the market, and you get paid anyway. There's no way for you to lose."

There was also no way for *me* to lose. If my next plan didn't go the way I hoped, when Maugro came for his money I'd just hand it over, and come up with a story explaining how I got it; by that time, it wouldn't be immediately obvious when and where that had been.

"Hmm." Maugro leaned back, folding his hands at his waist and regarding me through half-lidded eyes for a long moment. "You know how to be charming when you want to, Lord Seiji. But we're businessmen, here; much more important is whether you're *right*." After considering me during another loaded pause, he suddenly grinned. "And y'know what? You make a solid case. All right, let's talk numbers."

15

In Which the Dark Lord
is Responsible for a
Workplace Safety Violation

T*his* is a Spirit?"

"This one isn't exactly . . . typical," Aster admitted.

"These are the things that hand out spells and artifacts."

"Well . . . among other things. And, not all of them. Not this one, obviously."

Four days after my unexpected but profitable visit from the goblins, I was standing in a pleasant little meadow surrounded on three sides by the khora forest, but carpeted with nice, normal field grass and even a smattering of flowers. The last days had been spent helping clean the fortress, having Goose teach me to fight, and learning more facts about Ephemera, Fflyr Dlemathlys, and Dount from Biribo. That, and worrying about what was happening in Gwyllthean with Gilder, Clan Olumnach, and Lady Gray. All of these activities were productive except the worrying, but they had in common that there was a *lot* of progress to be made on every front, and none of my efforts felt like I was really getting anywhere yet. It was quite a relief to be here, now, in this nearly pastoral scene, even if I'd come to study more Ephemera nonsense.

In the exact center of this little meadow was a small and gently sloping hill barely taller than me, and right at the apex of that sat the Spirit.

The Spirit resembled a round, chest-high pillar of white stone, deeply engraved with geometric patterns. And it was definitely *stone*, not akorthist. It only activated when approached; this one was inert until someone drew within about two meters of it.

I studied the Spirit in silence, then set off back up the hill for my second visit to it. Biribo buzzed along at my shoulder as usual, though Aster opted to remain behind this time.

As before, once I got close enough, it lit up. The deep lines engraved in the altar began to glow with a shifting, blue-green luminescence, and a slowly rotating ring of symbols made of light appeared in a circle around its peak, like a halo. From this rose an image like a hologram, forming the shape of a somewhat stylized old woman's face.

"*Why, hello, dearie,*" the Spirit said in a creaking voice which matched the image, and additionally sounded like it had been electronically processed somehow. Electronic music isn't my forte, but I recognized the presence of deliberate audio filters that gave it an unearthly quality. "*What is your favorite color?*"

"Still gray," I replied.

"*How lovely!*" the Spirit said with apparent enthusiasm. Just like on my previous attempt, holographic butterflies and sparkling effects like tiny fireworks burst into being around the whole hill, dancing and flashing in the sunlight. It was pretty, I had to admit. Probably would've looked downright breathtaking at night. But . . .

"And that's it," I said, as the lights around the altar itself and the projection of the Spirit's face disappeared, leaving it dark and inert once more. Glowing butterflies continued to dance on the breeze around us, letting off little trails of glitter in the air.

"That's all you get from old Granny Sparkles," Aster said. "That's what she's called, locally."

"Every Spirit's different," Biribo added. "They all have their own task, and their own reward. The task can be just about anything; the reward is *usually* something related to Blessings, but there are more whimsical ones like this. Also, most of the ones with more concrete rewards will only let you complete their task once."

"Oh, but I can tell it my favorite color and get a light show as many times as I like? Useful *and* fair."

"Also, you gotta be careful if you attempt a Spirit's task. Not all of them will punish a failed attempt, but when they do, the punishments can get . . . exotic." He flicked out his tongue teasingly.

I descended back down the hill toward Aster. "Right. So when you were so insistent that I absolutely must tell the Spirit my *real* favorite color . . . ?"

"Yeah, if you lie to Granny Sparkles you get struck by lightning," Aster said, her delivery remarkably blasé for such an announcement. "That's why we've got privacy up here, Lord Seiji. This particular Spirit isn't good for anything except getting children and stupid people killed. Everybody on Dount knows to avoid it. More important ones are either tucked away in dangerous places or one of the clans has built a castle around them. So, wait, your favorite color is gray? Seriously?"

"I like simplicity," I replied. "Free lightning, huh. If only I had the faintest fucking clue how to build a battery or generator or anything electrical, I could start getting some real shit done."

"Well," Aster offered, falling into step beside me as we set off back out of the meadow, "maybe if today's plan works out, you can start buying some more scrolls! There's gotta be a lightning spell somewhere."

"Wait, you can *buy* scrolls?" I exclaimed, turning an accusing look on Biribo. "You said they were only rewards from dungeons and Spirits!"

"Not *only*," he retorted. "Of course you can buy scrolls; you got yours from a dead peddler. How do you think that happened?"

"You said Virya planted those!"

"I said she *probably* planted the Heal scroll *among* the rest of them. Remember, I made a whole big point about how it didn't fit in with the others in the selection, which I wasn't surprised to find there? You gotta start paying attention to details, boss, the nuance'll getcha killed."

Now that I thought back, he had said something like that. In my defense, it was in my first *minutes* on Ephemera, people were trying to kill me, and I was awash in a bunch of isekai exposition trying to pick out which bits would help me survive another hour. He wasn't wrong about the other part either; I really was trying to be more detail-oriented.

"Well . . . you can't exactly . . . just *buy* scrolls," Aster said more hesitantly.

This time I stopped walking and rounded on her. "You literally *just said—*"

"Sorry!" She winced, raising her hands. "I was trying to be encouraging! You can *theoretically* buy scrolls, but in practice it's more . . . complicated."

"There are very rare spells that'll let you create scrolls," Biribo explained. "Other than that, they'll be dungeon or Spirit rewards and only go to market if they're earned by somebody who doesn't need or want them for themselves. So they're either handcrafted by one of a half dozen sorcerers on the planet who can do that, or somebody with very in-demand skills risked their life to get them. You're not gonna find commodities like that just sitting on shelves in a shop. A lot of the time, there aren't even middlemen; if you wanna buy a scroll, you gotta do it directly from whoever its first owner is. That means not only having a shitload of money, but connections. There's a reason I didn't prompt you to try it when we were in town, boss."

"Yeah, joining the King's Guild would be just the *first* step toward that," Aster added. "You'd also have to build up a good reputation, get some impressive quests under your belt . . ."

"So what the hell was that peddler doing with them?"

"He's too dead to explain himself, but he probably stole them," said Biribo. We had passed into one of the arms of khora forest semi-encircling the Spirit's meadow, and I could see the rest of my bandits up ahead; Sakin waved to me from his perch in a branch of khora. "That kinda theft gets at least a clan's private army after you, if not the King's Guild itself. He was probably heading for the lake to trade the scrolls for sanctuary among the dark elves, got lost in the khora forest, stumbled onto the old road, and ended up at North Watch. Wouldn't've been the first to try that, but he wasn't gonna survive in any event. The naga would've just killed him and taken the scrolls anyway."

"That reminds me," I said, suddenly feeling a little guilty for having forgotten about this 'til now, "you lot *did* give him a respectful send-off while I was in Gwyllthean?"

"Just as you ordered, Lord Seiji," Harold said nervously, eyeing me as if expecting an attack, as usual. So far I wasn't sure if he was nervous in general or just nervous around me, which I wouldn't have blamed him for considering I'd Immolated him twice. "None of us is a priest, but we had a service. Sakin said some words."

"He did it properly, Lord Seiji," Goose added, seeing my expression. "Honestly, it was quite moving. I won't lie, I'm still a bit weirded out after hearing something that profound from *Sakin* of all people."

"And that would be exactly why he did it, Goose," I said with a sigh.

"Have I mentioned lately how much happier I am under your leadership, Lord Seiji?" Sakin asked from above us. "You *get* me."

"You're not that complicated, man." He just laughed, and I privately reminded myself to ask somebody about funerary customs here; they obviously didn't bury people if they were afraid to dig up the ground.

I made my way to the other edge of our little encampment among the khora, where Twigs was keeping watch over the distant road with the pocket-sized collapsible spyglass I'd taken from Lord Arider's corpse. Twigs tended to get stuck with watch duties, because she had the ability to focus for long periods in silence and didn't mind doing it. I had entrusted her with this task due to that, and also because my suspicions about her background suggested she would have more experience than the rest of this rabble in handling fragile and expensive objects.

"Anything?" I asked, stepping up to her perch behind a low-hanging fan of khora and leaning against it. In the raw, the stuff had an almost velvety texture over the hardness beneath.

"Looks like another caravan coming, Lord Seiji," Twigs reported quietly. "I can't tell if it's the one you want yet."

She handed me the spyglass and I settled in to examine our potential target.

According to Maugro's hot tip, the soonest we could expect a merchant caravan, which met the specifications I'd listed, was today, now, this morning. Maugro was surprisingly specific about the details; apparently shipping between Dount and the adjacent islands was monitored with more precision than I would have thought possible for the general level of technology here, and where information existed, it could be had for a price by people like me who had no business knowing it.

Raising the spyglass, I could see the caravan emerging around a bend in the road. At this angle I couldn't even count the number of wagons yet.

They were the only traffic to be seen, and only the second appearance of anyone since we'd arrived an hour before dawn; unlike the well-traveled main road, this smaller one was on the private lands of Clan Yldyllich, protected by their clansguard. Allegedly; we had yet to see any. Apparently, the private road was unpopular with merchant trains both because it added a detour to the route and because Clan Yldyllich charged a toll for using it. The way Maugro told it, merchants only brought their goods along this road if they weren't in a hurry *and* were willing to pay extra for another layer of security.

"Hmmm." I tracked their steady progress up the road as it curved slightly, bringing more of the formation into view. "Four wagons . . . I think these are our marks. Covered wagons, so it's not like I can check what they're hauling. Wait—there, I can see the logo painted on the side of the lead wagon. It looks close enough to what Maugro drew. Twigs, double-check me on this?"

"Of course, Lord Seiji," she said in her soft voice, accepting the telescope back and peering through it. Then she looked at the scrap of paper I offered, whereupon the goblin info broker had sketched the sigil of the Auldmaer Trading Company. Apparently every clan and guild and significant organization in Fflyr culture had to have its own sigil, which was constructed out of the pictographic element of their writing system. I could only read the language thanks to the Blessing of Wisdom and didn't even begin to understand cultural minutiae like this, but I suspected Twigs had the education. "The goblin's rendition is rough, but I believe it's the correct emblem."

"Then it's time for action," I said, cracking my knuckles. "Stand ready, everybody."

I reached out with my mind, a weird sensation I was only able to handle at all thanks to the practice I'd gotten in over the last few days, and felt it connect to the recipients of all the Tame Beast spells I'd cast. They were still there, all the little lumps of almost-consciousness I had meticulously created and placed under my magical control, all still following the last compulsion I had laid on them to lie still and silent in the ditch which ran alongside the road.

Now I gave them a new order, and at my mental command, hundreds of slimes boiled up out of the ditch, burbling across the road, miring the wheels, animals, and feet of the merchant caravan like a strangely cute tsunami, but gooey and as slow as molasses.

We could hear the yelling even from our distant vantage.

Controlling that many required all of my concentration, and resulted in twice as many slimes burbling around in confusion. A few managed to crawl up someone's leg or goop up a wagon wheel, and quite a few slipped my control entirely to wander off into the grass. They'd been happy enough to lie still in the ditch, since sloughing around in wet muck was their natural pattern, but they weren't interested in attacking a merchant caravan, and pushing them to do so was rapidly giving me a headache.

It did the job, though. The caravan was well and truly stopped.

Guards and teamsters were shouting, stomping, and ineffectively trying to get rid of their attackers with various weapons and tools. Slimes were weak, but practically indestructible unless you had magic. The dhawls, those shaggy goat-ox things with lizard-like faces being used to pull the wagons, had a much more stolid temperament than horses and didn't panic at unfamiliar sights, but I'd been warned that they would adamantly refuse to step on anything they didn't recognize or like, so covering the road with slimes was an effective way to stop them. The creatures didn't much care for the slimes trying to ooze up their legs either, stomping several into splatters and kicking them off, but even then their instinct was to stand in one place and do that.

No one was in danger, yet. The worst a slime could do to you was cause a chemical burn if it sat on your skin for several minutes, long enough for it to start trying to digest you. Against people actively resisting them, they were just annoying.

"C'mon," I growled against the mental strain, "this would be a good time to start chickening out . . ."

"I don't think they're going to, Lord Seiji," Aster murmured from the position she'd taken at my right. "Merchant trains deal with much more dangerous stuff than this, and possibly weirder."

"Yeah," I sighed, relaxing my mental hold. With only a distracted afterthought of influence keeping them on task, the slimes became noticeably less assertive, and the caravan crew started to make headway in driving them off the road. Silently, I held out my left hand and Twigs placed the spyglass back in it.

It took me just seconds of scanning to find my quarry. "There you are." Master Auldmaer himself, in the fashion of all managers since time immemorial, was supervising the messy work from a comfortable height. He stood on the seat of the lead wagon, well out of slime range, gesticulating and shouting at his staff without placing himself in the line of . . . slime. I could faintly hear his voice even from back here, though it was too distant to make out the words. Mostly the guards and wagon drivers seemed to be ignoring him. The man was just as Maugro described—well-dressed, with the light tan skin and medium brown hair of middle-caste blood, and young to be the owner of a trading company.

I had figured it would be the lead wagon, but now that I was certain, it was time for phase two. Focusing my mind, I shifted the spyglass to zero in on clear spots on the road around the wagon and began silently casting.

Summon Fire Slime. Tame Beast. Summon Fire Slime. Tame Beast. Summon Fire Slime. Tame Beast.

A chorus of exasperated outcries rose at this fresh nonsense. Releasing the bulk of the normal slimes to do as they would left at least half of them oozing about on the road continuing to make nuisances of themselves, even as others began slowly scattering in every direction. My focus was now on the fire slimes, even as I continued to summon more; controlling a handful was much easier than hundreds. I nudged them into a roughly circular formation, slowly closing in on the lead wagon and cutting off Auldmaer's escape.

The guards were having a much harder time dealing with this. I winced as one brought a giant mace down right on a fire slime, sending droplets of burning goo flying in every direction, followed by a shower of curses and blows from his compatriots. Slimes were just inexorable, in the way they couldn't be smashed or cut, even the pieces continuing about their business if you dismantled them. Without magic or heat, you couldn't kill a slime, just make more, smaller slimes. But set that same nuisance on fire, and what was just annoying became an actual *threat*.

There was no one Blessed with Magic among the guards, hence their failure to disperse the normal slimes, but I spied one woman with an artifact sword apparently directing them. From what I'd learned of Fflyr culture, a woman was very unlikely to be in charge of anything *unless* she had a Blessing to start with. This one kept a cool head, and seeing that their conventional methods weren't getting anywhere, tried a more effective tactic of gently prodding and nudging a fire slime away toward the edge of the road with the tip of her weapon.

I put a stop to that by directing the slime to latch onto the blade and begin crawling up it toward her hands. The sensible thing to do at that point was to drop the sword, but she wasn't willing to relinquish the artifact and stepped back, frantically flailing with it to dislodge the encroaching slime. I suspected that sword had strength-enhancing powers, to judge by how hard she was able to swing it. The slime was ripped free and went sailing away, landing beside the road and starting a small grass fire. Fortunately it was in the ditch, in which there were a few centimeters of muddy water at the bottom, an ideal environment for the slimes to hide in, and a way for me to extinguish the fiery ones when I was done here.

"That's it," I muttered. "You don't want any more of this. Come on, you bastards, time to break and run."

They weren't, though. Auldmaer was growing more frantic by the minute, nearly all the teamsters and a couple of the guards had retreated from the front wagon where the fire slimes were concentrated, and even the placid dhawls hitched to it were growing agitated. Fire has that effect on animals. Still, they were staying on task, even if for most of them that meant milling about helplessly outside of scorching range, kicking stray slimes into the ditch.

Then the adventurer discovered that with her sword's strength boost, swinging it like a golf club would wreck most of a slime and send its pieces flying. She began industriously scything them into the ditch, setting it on fire and getting rid of maybe half a slime per swing. This wasn't a winning strategy in the long run; under my direction, the pieces of slimes just crawled back up, joining back together and returning to their place in the circle, and I kept summoning more.

Until, at her apparent exhortation, some of the other guards found their nerve and started to copy her method. The guy who'd splattered the first fire slime dashed forward with his mace and chucked an entire slime clear *over* the ditch and into the grass beyond.

So now I was in a war of attrition with a less than certain outcome, and there was a grass fire creeping steadily closer to my position. Perfect.

"Uh, boss?" Biribo asked. "What're you waiting for?"

"Quiet!" I hissed. "Let me concentrate."

Finally, the first of the caravan personnel started to run—but, to my extreme annoyance, he wasn't fleeing. The adventurer in charge of the guards pointed back up the road the way they had come, shouting something indistinct from this distance, but I was definitely seeing someone dispatched to bring help.

Shit. How long would it take him to reach the Clan Yldyllich toll post from here? I'd planned to terrorize the entire staff into fleeing at once and have that much time to do what I needed to and depart before reinforcements arrived. The rest of them were swinging gamely on, though, swatting slimes as fast as I could summon them, and faster than the splattered fire slimes could re-form and rejoin the fray. Already there were enough fire slimes that it was beginning to strain my concentration to keep them in a rough circle around the wagon, and they still weren't enough to make the guards or even the teamsters give up, much less the adventurer. Also, all the grass on both sides of the road was now on fire.

Why did none of my plans ever work? It was almost as if I had no experience or aptitude for this kind of thing.

There was still phase three . . . The theoretical phase three. The last step I had told myself it probably wouldn't come to, but I could still break out in an emergency. This was quickly approaching emergency status, but now that the time was at hand, I was frozen.

My spyglass remained fixed on the adventurer, the one in charge and the only source of both backbone and direction for the caravan guards. All I had to do . . .

It wasn't even a *weapon.* It wouldn't have been as bad even if my only option had been to throw deadly fireballs. It was just . . . torture. Every previous time I'd used it had been on some murderer attempting to do violence, which I'd urgently needed to stop. This, though, was just a woman doing her job and doing it well, and being in my way.

I couldn't, not like this.

Goose's substantial muscular bulk settled in uncomfortably close on my left, between me and Twigs, resting a familiar hand on my shoulder. I'd come to like Goose over the last few days; like most of my crew, except probably Sakin, she was one of those driven to banditry by desperate circumstances whose details I didn't know, rather than any desire to prey on other people.

She had been teaching me sword fighting, knife fighting, and bare-handed fighting, and had warmed up to me considerably once I made it clear I didn't mind being smacked around when it was for a good cause.

Now she leaned in close to my ear and spoke so quietly none of the others could hear.

"It speaks well of you that you don't want to hurt anyone unnecessarily, Lord Seiji. But like it or not, you're a bandit now, and you have to make peace with the necessity. You chose to attack the caravan; letting it draw out any further is only going to make all this messier, and if we don't get what you came for, all of it was for nothing. We all have to make our choices and take responsibility for the consequences. If I'm speaking out of turn . . . well, you'll do what you need to. I understand."

What I needed to? I was not going to start punishing people for telling me uncomfortable truth when I needed to hear it; that was a strategy for quick self-destruction. I shifted my head from the spyglass to glance over my shoulder and give her a small nod; Goose withdrew, leaving only Twigs in my view looking performatively oblivious.

I looked through the lens again, once more fixing my view on the adventurer bravely smacking flaming monsters off the road, rallying her meager troops, and generally being the source of my problems right now.

God damn it. Someday, Virya was going to pay for putting me in this situation.

Immolate.

We could all hear her scream clearly across that distance.

I lowered the spyglass and closed my eyes, then immediately made myself open them and look. *No*, Seiji, you chose to do this. You will *watch* it happen.

She had fallen and dropped her sword, and was already curled into a fetal ball in the road, blazing like a bonfire and no longer able to scream. I shifted my concentration, moving the fire slimes away from her so this wouldn't get any worse than it had to be.

That had finally done the trick; the other guards had stopped playing slime golf to back up, staring in horror. Between the distance and the angle, I couldn't see the woman's entire body disintegrating into charcoal and constantly re-forming so as to keep suffering, but I remembered well what a grotesque thing that was to see. However hardened these guys might be, that was too much. The wagon drivers were already fleeing in both directions along the road, and the guards took that as permission. Nobody wanted to stay and be the next. They bolted, ignoring Mr. Auldmaer's shouted imprecations.

As Immolate faded and the healing effect started to overtake the fire, my victim's long shrieks of pain became audible again, once she had intact lungs and vocal cords. I forced myself to keep the glass fixed on her and watch the entire process. It was just a few more seconds before she was lying shivering in the road with her clothes gently smoking, but to her it probably felt like years. It felt like at least a couple of hours for me, and I was only watching.

Tremulously, she stumbled to her feet, taking stock of the mostly departed slimes, the still very much present fire slimes encircling the wagon with her employer trapped on it, and her now-complete lack of backup.

Pausing only to bend and grab her artifact sword, she turned and ran without even dignifying Auldmaer's yelling with an acknowledgment. Smart woman.

"Damn," Sakin breathed. "That is a *neat* trick."

Everyone turned to stare at him.

"What?" He shrugged. "I'm not wrong, and I didn't say it was *pleasant*. Pretty fucking impressive, though."

I finally stood from my own crouched position behind the low blade of khora that had been sheltering me and Twigs, only belatedly noting that my body was uncomfortably stiff after all that. At the moment, I was more concerned with how sick to my stomach I felt.

"All of you hold position until we beckon you over," I said. "Come on, Aster. We have an appointment with Mr. Auldmaer. It's rude to keep a businessman waiting."

16

In Which the Dark Lord
Gets Down to Business

Can I ask a favor?" Aster said quietly as we strode toward the road and the embattled wagon, where Mr. Auldmaer was now clambering back and forth seeking a gap in the encircling fire slimes. I hadn't left him one.

"Of course," I replied, hoping she wouldn't take my terse tone personally. I was still trying to push down a rising tide of self-recrimination over using my horror spell on an innocent person, and also mentally rounding up errant slimes—normal, non-fire ones—to make them ooze across the burning grass. They did *not* like that, but their gooey bodies were successfully stifling the flames wherever I could coerce them into doing it.

"It's just, uh . . ." She frowned, recollecting her thoughts, and tried again. "I understand the strategic realities we're dealing with, and I'm no stranger to having to make hard choices. No condemnation. But . . . and I'm sorry for how awful this sounds . . . please try to keep feeling terrible."

I gave her an incredulous look; she ducked her head self-consciously but continued.

"When you have to do terrible things, I mean. When I saw how much you hated it, I felt a lot better about agreeing to work for you, Lord Seiji. We all have to do things we'd rather not, and you'll no doubt have to do worse. Just . . . please try not to get used to it. Anything can start to feel normal if you do it enough. I . . . don't want you to lose the decent person you've got inside there somewhere. I know I'm asking you to make life harder on yourself, and I'm sorry. If you'll try, I promise I'll do my best to support you."

Well, I had not been expecting a heart-to-heart moment this early in our relationship, and particularly not now of all bloody times. This was not helping my tenuous control over the slimes.

"I would hope that I'd try to do that anyway," I said after considering for a moment. "I'll do my best, Aster. I don't know what's going to happen, but I have a feeling everything's going to get worse from here."

"It will," she said softly. "In some ways. In others, it'll get better. That's just how life works."

Auldmaer had given up on escaping, I think because he'd seen us. The man now sat down on the driver's bench at the front of his wagon, turned to face us with his arms folded as he waited for us to cross the half-burned field. He wasn't waving or calling for help either; I guess it made sense a man clever enough to run his own trading company would immediately realize the unprecedented slime attack had not been a natural phenomenon.

"I realize it's probably too late to matter, but are you certain about this?" Aster muttered, and I suspected she was as glad as I was for a change of topic. "Your whole plan falls apart if this guy turns out to be a man of principle."

I rolled my eyes. "He's a professional merchant, Aster."

"People are more complex than you think, Lord Seiji."

"No, they are not. People are selfish, aggressive animals who grudgingly cooperate with others when it benefits them and for no other reason. There is exactly *one* human being in existence, copied and repeated billions of times with minor cosmetic variations and always some degree of delusion that they are a unique and beautiful snowflake."

She sighed. "Why do I feel like *my* life would be a lot easier if *you* had ever been hugged as a child?"

"That's crossing a line, Aster."

"I apologize, Lord Seiji," Aster said, her tone and expression suddenly blank; she stared straight ahead, avoiding my gaze, and actually made that Fflyr folding hands gesture, the first time I'd seen it from her. "It's not my place."

Great. Something *else* to feel terrible about.

Freshly burned field grass crunched under our boots as we reached the ditch, then hopped across it to the road—me maybe not *quite* as nimbly as Aster.

"And a fine morning to you," Mr. Auldmaer called, raising a hand in greeting. In contrast to all his yelling and gesticulating when he had people to command, he now seemed quite poised. "Do forgive me for not coming to shake your hand, but . . . well." He gestured at the fire slimes now forming a burning moat around his wagon. The two dhawls hitched in front of him were pressed together now, snorting and stomping their clawed feet in displeasure.

"Yes, this does look inconvenient," I said gravely. "Allow me."

Making a hand gesture was completely unnecessary to move the slimes, as they responded to mental command, but I did it anyway because showmanship *matters*. With a broad sweep of my arm, a path opened up in the ring, fire slimes oozing over each other to form a gap.

"Well then," he said in a sardonic tone that barely managed to conceal the bitterness underneath, "it's not as if I don't *know*, but civilized people must observe the proprieties. To what do I owe this unexpected visit, Master . . . ?"

"You may call me Lord Seiji," I said, pausing at the head of his team of animals. The two dhawls shifted away from me and I considered their condition. They were famously placid beasts and these in particular would be well used to people; they must be awfully worked up if they were even this skittish.

Tame Beast. Tame Beast.

Both animals calmed noticeably, letting out heavy sighs of relief as I reached up to scratch their heads.

"And you, of course," I continued, turning back to the merchant, "are Master Cadimer Auldmaer, heir to the Auldmaer Trading Company. My condolences on your father's recent passing, sir."

"That's kind of you to say, Lord Seiji, but I have had three years to become used to his absence." He glanced at Aster, eyed her up and down, and then seemed to dismiss her as muscle. "It is probably pointless to ask, but I wonder if you'd indulge me with the knowledge of *which* of my employees has been leaking information? As a courtesy, since you do appear to appreciate them."

"And in that spirit I would, if I could," I replied, "but sadly I've no idea. The details of your work are available to anyone with coin to spend and access to certain . . . unconventional markets."

"Oh, not *so* unconventional," he sighed. "The merchant houses all keep tabs on one another's doings. Why, my company is too small to be considered competition by the most important names even on Dount, but I can obtain *their* shipping itineraries for the cost of a good meal at the Guild hall. I do say it's poor form to peddle trade information outside the fraternity of merchants," he added sourly.

"No offense intended, sir, but yours is not a profession known for its deep foundations in ethics." I glanced pointedly at Aster, who pretended she didn't notice.

Auldmaer wasn't even offended. "Oh, to be sure, but there are certain *norms*. What passes between fellow members in the trade isn't meant to involve outside players; otherwise it would lead to all but open warfare with companies hiring their own bandit gangs and bribing guards to seize shipments . . . That kind of nonsense has eviscerated entire economies, led to famines and refugee crises, and worse. *Extremely* unprofitable. I suppose if I'm being sold out to the likes of yourself—no offense, my lord—the name of Auldmaer has fallen so far that the other companies don't even see me as one of them any longer. Well! I do appreciate you taking the time to indulge me in civilized conversation, Lord Seiji. It is a rare virtue in your profession."

"Not at all; it's my pleasure. I firmly believe that life is hard enough without needless rudeness. If one must conduct unpleasant business, it behooves us to make it less so, not more."

Aster half-turned her head to give me one of those richly expressive Aster looks. This time it was my turn to ignore her.

"Well said," Auldmaer replied, reaching behind himself into the wagon. Aster tensed, her hand moving toward the handle of her sword, but what he pulled out was a bottle and two cups. "In that spirit, allow me to offer you a spot of hospitality before we conclude your business."

"Why, how very gracious of you," I said magnanimously. "I'll be pleased to accept."

"Splendid." He set the cups on the other side of the bench from us, where they were hidden from my view by his leg, and began prying loose the cork. "This is a bottle from my private stock—not the finest of vintages, I'm afraid, simply because I wouldn't bring one of those on a cargo run. But one does like to carry along a few little creature comforts even out in the wilderness. And in my view, comforts are better enjoyed in the company of someone else who appreciates the finer points of living."

While Auldmaer chattered on, he poured wine into both cups, still with his body positioned so that I couldn't see exactly what he was doing, the spiel no doubt intended to hold my attention. Aster frowned at me, and when his head was turned attending to that, nodded toward him and opened her mouth to speak. I held up a hand and winked at her. To judge by her expression, she didn't find that terribly reassuring, but stayed silent.

"To your health," the merchant said as he handed me one of the cups, lifting the other.

"Kanpai," I replied, repeating the gesture, and taking a deep sip of the wine.

And then a second. I've never been a connoisseur, but this was *good* stuff. Sweeter than I was expecting, and very rich—fortified, I suspected. Full of the kind of complex flavors that were noticeably lacking from the vinegar back at North Watch.

"Oh, that is *excellent*," I said, not having to fake a smile. "Worth the trip for this alone. Aster, care to try?"

"Thank you, Lord Seiji, but I'll pass," she said quite pointedly.

"I'm glad you approve," said Auldmaer, seeming genuinely pleased at my reaction. "The family estates aren't what they once were, but the old grounds do contain a very well-built winehouse, which I have taken pains to keep suitably stocked."

"Ah yes," I nodded, pausing to take another sip. "I'm given to understand that but for a twist of fate in your father's generation, I would be addressing Lord Cadimer of Clan Auldmaer. Alas, a random activation of recessive genes made for an unbroken sequence of siblings without so much as a lock of blonde hair between them, and thus, the loss of noble title and privileges." I paused for another sip of the really *delicious* wine, noting the way his expression had gone hard. "As you can probably tell, I'm a new arrival here in Fflyr Dlemathlys. With apologies for the disrespect to your culture, sir, that has to be the single stupidest damn thing I've ever heard of."

"I am Fflyr born and bred," he said carefully. "A loyal subject of the King and a devout follower of the Convocation. It is certainly not the place of a humble *lowborn* such as myself to challenge the dictates of the goddess, nor even her mortal representatives upon Ephemera. Still . . . I would be lying, and I suspect not convincingly so, if I did not admit to having had the same thought upon occasion, Lord Seiji."

"As well you should," I agreed. "Rules like that are always ascribed to the goddess, who I suspect would be very surprised to learn she had ever made such decisions. Ah, pardon me for a moment. **Heal**."

I wasn't feeling anything yet, but it was probably best not to wait too long anyway. Pink light flared around my body and Auldmaer jerked back in surprise, nearly spilling his wine.

"Apologies for the interruption," I said in my most pleasant tone. "As it happens, I am allergic to poison. Not to impugn your hospitality, good sir; clearly you could not have known."

Holding his gaze, I took a long, deliberate sip of the poisoned wine. Sometimes, a Dark Lord has to indulge in a blatant power move, and subtlety be damned.

Auldmaer's shoulders slumped and he set his own cup down on the bench. "Right. Well, that's that, then. I hope you won't begrudge a fellow the attempt."

"Oh, on the contrary. If you didn't have the wit and spine to try *something* of the sort, I'd be much more hesitant to go into business with you. In fact, I'm glad to see you both made preparations in advance *and* can think on your feet."

But not think *too* quickly; his desperate gambit had notably lacked a means of dealing with Aster. That was exactly how I liked my shady business partners—clever enough to be useful, not so much that I needed to be intimidated by them.

"Business?" He still looked understandably wary, but also visibly perked up. I had, after all, said the magic word.

"Of course! Or did you think I wouldn't realize all these effusive pleasantries were meant to stall me long enough for your fleeing employees to bring help? I doubt our conversation will take long enough regardless, but even if it does, I suspect by that point the clansguard would find you happily introducing me as a helpful passerby out hunting with his bodyguard who stopped to aid you when this . . . most peculiar natural phenomenon stalled your caravan."

I made another wide gesture, and all the fire slimes began oozing out of their positions, sliding down the slope of the ditch into the brackish standing water below. Steam and constant hissing plops began to emerge as they snuffed themselves out en masse.

"I . . . see," Auldmaer mused, watching this. "Forgive me, Lord Seiji, I took you for a bandit."

"That is not exactly correct, but close enough I don't consider it worth quibbling over. Suffice it to say, I am able and willing to stop a trade caravan if I find a need. You'll have observed this, of course—and also that I favor unconventional methods, keeping bloodshed to a minimum, and in general not disrupting the lives of others any more than I must."

"Well, you may consider me interested—and not just because I don't have a choice. So, you are a . . . let's say, *genteel* sort of bandit? A bandit lord?"

"Hmm, that does have a ring to it, doesn't it, Aster?"

"A most prestigious title, Lord Seiji," she said, deadpan.

"Why, then, would you choose *me*?" Auldmaer asked. "Clearly you have done your research."

"Now, correct me if I'm wrong since I'm stepping into your field here, but it seems to me the best business relationship is one of mutual advantage, right? One in which two parties have needs which can each be filled by filling each other's."

"In the best of circumstances, yes," he said with a faint smile. "Business does tend to get more . . . confrontational, sometimes. Not as much as banditry, but . . . Actually, on occasion, about as much, yes."

I nodded. "Precisely my point. You mentioned how the trading companies keep track of one another's movements, yes? I've no doubt there's a great deal of financial maneuvering based around knowing who is selling what, where, when, and to whom? There must be a thousand ways for an enterprising fellow such as yourself to profit if one has the right information."

"I suspect you don't know the half of it," he said dryly.

"And it therefore follows that if you, and you alone, know that a certain caravan is *not going* to reach its destination, you could profit considerably more, at the expense of your competitors." I paused for effect, watching his eyebrows rise. "And, for added benefit, imagine if some of the contents of such vanished caravans found their way into your warehouses, to be discreetly sold at your leisure."

"You are . . . proposing that I *hire* you?" Auldmaer drew in a deep breath, frowning. "Without addressing whether or not I might be interested, Lord Seiji, mine is a small company—one which has gambled nearly its entire assets, perhaps its very existence, on a load of trade goods, which you now see stalled on the road. Just based on the caliber of magic I have *seen* you use, and presuming I've seen barely a fraction, something tells me I can't afford you."

"Exactly. To answer your earlier question—why I chose you—it's because you and I are in similar situations—we both have a long way to climb. A smaller company with ambitions has everything to gain and comparatively little to lose, right? I'm in the same situation. You need an advantage that will let you play the game at the same level as the big syndicates, raking in the kind of profits they do without facing the same risks. *I* need an insider, someone who can direct me to the right targets—both those whose elimination will advance his interests, and those which might contain particular supplies I need. I may also need help from time to time acquiring or selling off various specific assets through discreet but non-violent channels, just as you may find it advantageous to have certain opponents removed from the board. You see my drift?"

Slowly, he nodded, frowning into the distance over my head and massaging his chin with one hand. It was an expression I related to—not only mulling the costs and benefits of this kind of business, but grappling with the stickier implications. I, for my part, suspected I was even less sanguine than the merchant about going into such dealings. Unlike him, I didn't have a choice. Either I got more comfortable with forcing my will onto others *quickly*, or I was going to end up Virya's plaything while she abducted someone more psychopathic from Japan to stick a sword in poor Yoshi.

"You would need to hit some of my shipments now and again," he mused, "and those of my business partners and allies."

"Obviously," I agreed. "Giving the Auldmaer Company special treatment would be painting a target on it. In fact, we could potentially do that to someone *else*, if there's a given company you'd like the authorities to be motivated to investigate. Don't worry—as you've seen, I can make this bloodless. At worst, your personnel will be inconvenienced."

Inconvenienced, and in some cases traumatized. For a moment I had to work to control my expression as an echo of the adventurer's scream sounded in my ears.

"Oh well," he said with a little chuckle, "if anything, you may have shaved a nice chunk off my overhead, Lord Seiji. Teamsters who abandon their cargo get a deep pay cut; guards who run from the first conflict don't get paid at all. Not to mention that the Clan Yldyllich toll comes with a guarantee of safe transit. Not only will I get refunded for this, I bet the Clan will pay me off to keep this quiet. Assuming you're *not* actually planning to rob my cargo, you've actually saved me money."

"Luxury fabrics, right?" I glanced back at the line of covered wagons, still hitched to patient dhawls standing in the road. "No offense, but I'm not even tempted. You should definitely pay your adventurer, though."

"Larinet?" Great, now I knew her name. I didn't want to know her name—which was exactly why I deserved to. "A Blessed guard who runs from battle is no different from the mundane kind, it's just a higher wage she's chosen not to receive."

"You saw what happened to her, didn't you? Never mind, I can see from your face that you did. Imagine what it must be like to *live* through. You wouldn't want someone working for you who could suffer that and not break, Mr. Auldmaer—such a person would be too insane to be trustworthy. If she were my employee I'd give her hazard pay."

I caught Aster looking at me sidelong. The merest hint of a smile quirked at the corner of her mouth, just for a second.

"Perhaps," Auldmaer allowed. "Will she . . . She had enough energy to run, but I've never seen Larinet crack like that. Is she going to be all right?"

"Physically? Better than ever. There's a touch of healing magic in that spell."

He blinked, twice, his face lengthening as he parsed the implications. "That is . . . almost impressively sadistic, Lord Seiji."

I nodded; there was no point in deflecting that accusation. "If you're dealing with people accustomed to violence? To avoid the necessity of killing sometimes requires an exercise in cruelty. No doubt some would disagree, but I consider it worth the trade-off or I wouldn't do it. A traumatized person can recover. A corpse can't do anything but feed the worms."

He leaned back from me on the bench, his expression more thoughtful than disturbed now. Picking up his abandoned cup, Auldmaer took a sip of wine, which prompted me; I had another drink of my own, then cast Heal again. Whatever he'd dosed me with didn't seem fast-acting.

"I can't believe I'm seriously considering this," Auldmaer said at last, "but goddess help me, I am . . . interested. And right after I lectured you on the perils of trade wars, too."

"There is not going to be a war, trade or otherwise." I've never been a very good liar, but it turns out it's a lot easier to say something with confidence if it's something you also desperately want to believe. "Provided we are patient, careful without being timid, and above all *smart*, there will be a . . . consolidation. A new merchant lord of Dount, and a bandit king. That, I assure you, is *going* to happen. The only question is whether you are the one to profit most from this, or simply another bystander."

"Or a loose end you need to tie up?" he said pointedly.

"I am taking the gamble that you're an intelligent enough man to seize the opportunity before you. I am absolutely confident you are intelligent enough not to cross me, whatever else happens. Not after you've seen me so vividly demonstrate my means of discouraging enmity."

He met my eyes and studied me. Openly now. I saw neither fear nor avarice in that gaze, though I knew I'd inspired both, but the cold calculation of a merchant weighing the benefits and costs, the risks against the reward.

"Most utility goods passing through Dount are just that," Auldmaer said abruptly, "passing through. Clan Aelthwyn and the King both make a handsome profit on tariffs from those, but Dount provides much of the kingdom's agriculture, and receives dungeon goods from Fflyrdylle in turn. There's little demand for imported food or basic supplies here. International trade *to* and *from* Gwyllthean is nearly all in luxury goods. The particular khora biome on this island provides a number of rare assets, which are difficult to gather and exist only in a few places, and the local nobility are both rich as a result, and hungry for fineries to flaunt at each other. This," he half-turned on the wagon seat to gesture broadly at the stalled caravan behind himself with one arm, "is a load of shimmersatin from Savindar by way of Godspire. Savindar, if you haven't heard, only recently opened to trade thanks to Godspire's expanded neutrality laws. Until this very year, the only goods from Viryan nations seen by the Dountol nobility were rare contraband from Shylverrael. Given the difficulty of passing that stuff through both Viryan and Sanorite sanctions, it all costs much more than international shipments and carries the risk of severe punishment if you're caught with it."

"So you're introducing a new commodity to market," I said. "Impressive. That sounds immensely profitable. It must've been quite a coup to position yourself to benefit from this."

"Thank you," he replied, his tone grim despite the words. "In the merchant trade, timing is everything. By being the first to market, I can set my own prices—until the competition moves in. And this time, I gambled and . . . well, I haven't lost *yet*, but only on a bare technicality. The Crown Rose Company is one of the biggest based in Fflyr Dlemathlys, and they caught wind of my gambit and are *this* close to ruining me." He held up his finger and thumb barely a centimeter apart. "Crown Rose have Blessed, and not just adventurers for caravan guards. They even have Blessed with Wisdom who can sniff out competitors' secrets. I'm almost certain that was what doomed my enterprise. And they've got sufficiently deep pockets to buy in enough bulk to get goods at a discount, which means selling at lower prices and still turning a handsome profit. A Crown Rose caravan five times the size of mine reached Godspire right before we left, and they've been gaining on us all the way back to Dount. By the last information I bought, they'll be in Gwyllthean by *tomorrow*."

"So," I said slowly, "you have one day in which to make as much money as you can, at whatever price you can get, before the contents of these wagons becomes worthless."

"Oh, not *worthless*," he said with a bitter laugh. "I'm sure Crown Rose themselves will happily buy it from me at less than cost. My entire company's assets are on the line here, Lord Seiji—if I can have the grace period I was counting on to be the sole supplier to the Gwyllthean nobility, it'll put the Auldmaer Company back on the map. The Highladies will *gladly* pay through the nose to be the only members of their singing circles dressed in shimmersatin. If I'm beaten to market . . . well, my company is dead, and it'll only be through some desperate wrangling of my own that I evade debtor's jail. Much as I'm tempted to mention that my caravan is now sitting idle on the road in the middle of nowhere thanks to *you*, the truth is, I was all but certainly beaten before you made yourself a factor. Crown Rose had plentiful ties with the nobility; they not only have buyers lined up, but rumor circulating among them that'll prevent most from buying at the prices I *need* to ask."

He drew in a shaking breath, holding my gaze.

I smiled, and sipped the poisoned wine. "Say the word."

"Nightlady take me," Auldmaer breathed. "They say a man never knows whether he'd take a devil's deal until one appears before him. Well, today I learn the weight of my soul. Get me out of this, Lord Seiji, and I'm *willing* to be greedy alongside you in the future. But first, I need to survive. You've cornered a desperate man."

I kept my smile small and polite with an effort, not revealing my triumph or relief. Sure, this meant I was going to have to take on a much bigger target with *much* better defenses, but the cold hard truth was that I could inflict far more damage if I wasn't holding back and being gentle.

More than surviving the hurdle right in front of me, this marked a turning point. By securing an income stream and necessary connections, I would make the transition from stumbling around reacting to things I didn't understand, to moving forward with plans of my own. Next step was acquiring an army, and I had an idea of where to get one that no one would notice until too late.

"Just tell me where to find them, and when," I said. "Your people should be back with Yldyllich Clansguard . . . oh, I'd say within an hour, at the most. You can still make Gwyllthean by tonight. And as for the Crown Rose's shipment . . . Well, this shimmersatin stuff is fabric, right? I assume it is *flammable*."

17

In Which the Dark Lord Plays With Fire

It took us most of a day's hike to get into position along the main trade road. The khora forest encroached onto civilized territory in the northern reaches of the island, not quite pressing against the central highway but with an arm coming close and patches of it on the eastern side. The eastern half of Dount was all agricultural land; to the west was mostly khora plantations and then the forest itself.

We reached an arm of the khora forest positioned on an overlook not too distant from the main highway, within view—with my spyglass, anyway—of the Fflyr border fortress positioned near the northern edge of the island. Well repaired, fully garrisoned, and flying colorful banners, it was a glimpse at what North Watch must have looked like in its heyday.

We were in time to observe the Crown Rose Company caravan wending its way past the border fort toward the heart of the island; it wouldn't be long before they had to stop for the night. I was all set to follow them from a distance—waiting for an opportunity when other nearby traffic was light to unleash fire slimes and wipe out their precious cargo—when Sakin just had to open his mouth. It was worse than when Donon opened his mouth, because Sakin was correct.

"So, we're going to perform a surgical strike on this caravan whose failure only benefits exactly one person? I guess if we leave no traces nobody can *prove* the Auldmaer Company is behind this, but let's face it, proof doesn't matter all that much. A big mercantile outfit like Crown Rose barely needs to bribe magistrates to retaliate against a little player like Auldmaer. I thought your plan was to make use of this guy in the longer term, Lord Seiji. For that, wouldn't he need to still be alive a month from now?"

That was not what I wanted to hear, mostly because it was accurate. In order to pull this off, I realized it couldn't look like an attack with a specific, motivated target. That meant I had to include a lot of the one thing I most wanted to avoid—collateral damage.

So we shifted position, following the caravan toward the rest area where they would stop for the night, now that they were safely in Fflyr territory, and I stewed in my ever-increasing, impotent fury the entire way.

While the Crown Rose wagon train got themselves settled in for the night at the highway waystation surrounding a crossroads, we positioned ourselves at the nearest point to it, which was sheltered by a patch of wild khora forest. Since the waystation was surrounded by an empty, well-maintained field on all sides, specifically to discourage what we'd come here to do, that put us at enough of a distance that we'd have no hope of crossing the grounds unseen on foot even in the dead of night, and no conventional weapon would reach far enough.

Fortunately, these defenses hadn't been made with me in mind. All I needed was a view of my target, and thanks to the ever-valuable spyglass, I could hit the Crown Rose wagons directly from our chosen vantage.

There was a Kingsguard post; though it was tiny, and according to my crew, the soldiers there were only interested in collecting the King's tariffs and "the King's tariffs" (bribes), not enforcing the peace. The inn had its own bouncers, and bigger caravans would always travel with dedicated guards, so that was it for defenses. Disorganized and likely to scatter to their own interests in a crisis, but still not something I wanted to take on with my pitiful handful of social rejects, so we needed to avoid being noticed. The grounds where wagons were to park were nothing but a wide area around the crossroads trampled permanently flat by use, with no discrete boundary between it and the surrounding field of grass. There was a natural spring on the grounds, with a structure built over it against the side of the inn, which provided water to outdoor ducts and the building's kitchen.

At least I had the benefit of expert advice. Sakin, as it turned out, had experience as an arsonist. None of the other bandits had known this, but absolutely no one was surprised.

"The rule of thumb for a discreet job," he lectured quietly, as we all peered across the meadow in the falling darkness, "is to make it look natural. That means the fire has to start not only at a place where fire *can*, but where it most likely *would* in an accident. You also want to only use materials already found on the site; anything you bring in to enhance the fire is a clue to its cause. Now, we're a little handicapped in that regard due to the means at your disposal of fire starting, but we'll still want to focus on a plausible target to begin with."

"Amazingly detailed," I said. "Actually, I'm really surprised to learn the Kingsguard investigates fires that diligently. From what everybody's told me, it sounds like the difference between them and the likes of us is we don't have fancy uniforms."

"Oh, not in the least. The Kingsguard won't even bother asking questions unless there's a whole *series* of fires that are incredibly obviously arson, and then only if the assets of someone important are affected. Even then, they most likely 'solve' the crime by arresting whatever random known criminal they get their hands on first. I don't think Fflyr Dlemathlys even employs any alchemists equipped for that kind of investigation."

I lowered the spyglass, staring vacantly at the sky above the distant horizon. Rationally, I knew it didn't matter and would be a waste of time, but . . . fuck it, I had to ask.

"Why, then, do you go to so much effort to make yours untraceable?"

"Lord Seiji!" Sakin turned to me, putting on a wounded expression in the dimness. "A man has to take *pride* in his work. Where's the *satisfaction* in standing over the ash and ruin of your enemy's hopes and dreams if you know, in your heart of hearts, that you half-assed it?"

Slowly, I turned to meet his eyes.

"You will either be the first to betray me, or my last loyal servant by my side as we charge into the jaws of hell."

"Right?" He grinned in sheer delight. "I don't know about you, my lord, but I'm excited to find out which! We're going places, you and I."

"First things first. Biribo, what's the situation with Blessed down there?"

"I count thirteen, boss," he reported, "among about two hundred fifty people around the buildings and encampments. I can get a more accurate head count, but I'd have to get closer."

"Shouldn't matter. Anything we should watch for from the Blessed?"

"Seven Blessed with Magic, six with Might. I can't actually see what spells a sorcerer has unless they use 'em in front of me, but none of the artifacts I've glimpsed from back here look like they have any application in fire suppression. There are combat spells using water, ice, and wind that can be applied to firefighting."

"Oh, we can only *hope* some idiot tries to fight fire with a combat wind spell," Sakin chortled. "That's likely to get everything short of the surrounding khora burned to ash. Now *that's* a show!"

Heads shifted in the dark as everyone turned to stare at him. He didn't seem to notice.

"All right, for our opening move. Lord Seiji, see that little annex sticking out from the back of the inn? Look for marks painted on it in yellow."

I trained the spyglass where he indicated, squinting. "It's dark down there, man. I don't know how—oh wait, yeah. There's something painted on the outside wall. A cross in a triangle."

"And that's why they're painted in bright yellow, so it's visible in low light. That's their asauthec storage."

"*Aha.*"

Asauthec was one of the more interesting things I'd discovered about life on Ephemera. Lacking wood to burn, Ephemerans had devised another means of controlling fire—various blends of oils made by alchemists from, of course, khora byproducts.

Which meant, of course, that every dwelling and structure on this planet contained a hearty stockpile of highly combustible fluids. If they weren't building from non-flammable khora, every city in the world would be razed to the ground every two weeks. As it was, fires tended not to spread between buildings, but would turn a house into a blast furnace once its stocks of asauthec caught flame.

"So," I said aloud, "a fire slime by the storage—"

"No, no, no!" Sakin interrupted hastily. "Remember, you want it to look accidental. Taking care around asauthec storage is one of the fundamental pillars of society, Lord Seiji; it's up there with bringing in the harvest, revering the goddess, and not digging into the earth. If a fire is set anywhere near asauthec stocks, it means it was either deliberate or multiple people were implausibly stupid. And *that* is the feature we're going to use to create our *accident.*"

He leaned forward, bracing one hand behind the outcropping of khora shell behind which we were hiding, and squinted at the dim scene before us. Here under the khora we were in the dark, but the view over the field was much better. It was a clear evening; also, it never got truly dark on Ephemera, just really dim. After some consideration, I realized sunlight must be filtering through the empty core of the planet, so the illumination didn't stop when the sun faced the other side of the world, it was just muffled by whatever was down there in the core.

"We're in luck," Sakin said, more intent and focused than I'd ever seen him, "it hasn't rained in a week. You remember how easily the grass caught during the ambush this morning. Should be the same here. So! What we are doing, Lord Seiji, is telling a story. There must be a believable narrative that ends with the Crown Rose caravan losing their cargo without anyone being personally to blame. Any number of possible things might start a fire in dry grass that tall. What we want to do is set the initial spark far enough from the waystation that it'll be seen coming and they have an opportunity to muster a response. You'll want to study the way light shimmers on the grass, see how the wind is progressing, and pick your initial spot somewhere upwind in a position the flames will naturally spread toward the asauthec storage."

"Which'll muster everybody to emergency firefighting duty to prevent that, and *away* from the caravan," I said, catching on.

"That's one purpose, an important one," he nodded. "It also creates witnesses to the fact that this started as a random grass fire. Once it's underway, you will have to maintain an active control over the scene, Lord Seiji. You must cast Spark to spread the fire in a way that is both believable as a natural spread of flames due to wind and grass, *and* lead it to the parked caravan. Their defensive actions will concentrate on preventing the asauthec from going up, which you can use to create openings. Shame there's not a caravan shipping asauthec at the moment, but ah well, can't have it all. Crown Rose personnel, and probably others, will be using water from the spring to create a firebreak protecting their interests. Ideally you'll be able to get the fire to that point before they get defenses up, but it'll depend on how things develop. Whatever happens, you'll have to get the grass fire as *close* as possible to the wagons for plausibility. I've seen sparks travel an amazing distance on the air, but we're dealing in what's believable, not what's accurate, so the closer the better."

Actually, setting fires in the Crown Rose caravan would be the easy part. From our current vantage, I had the correct angle to see into about half the wagons, which meant I could cast Spark right inside them. The wagons themselves were made of akorshil, so they wouldn't burn . . . though it occurred to me I didn't know what happened to akorshil if it got too hot. It was made from shells, so it'd probably crack and collapse . . . could I make use of that?

"Also," Sakin added, "make sure to set fire to a few other wagons. It'll still be a skeevy-looking coincidence if the Crown Rose train goes up and none of the rest are even touched."

I sighed heavily and lowered the spyglass so I could stare across the broad field and the waystation in its center without being able to pick out any details about the people whose night I was about to ruin.

"And here I was letting myself think I could maybe get through this without hurting *too* many bystanders."

"Please, they've got a sizable water source *right there*, and grass fires don't burn that hot. They're only dangerous if you get overtaken or surrounded by one, which can't happen on the packed ground of the waystation itself. If anybody gets themselves charbroiled, it's because they were so stupid they were inevitably gonna die of *something* before long, and you can't really be blamed for being the one who happened to do it."

"Sakin," I said patiently, "I get that you're trying to help, but you need to develop an instinct for when you're better off keeping your mouth shut."

"Ah, my apologies, Lord Seiji. Managing Rocco left me with some bad habits; sometimes I forget you don't need to be managed. How about this, then—ordinary folks will get themselves and their belongings out of the line of fire, which they've got plenty of room to do, the way the station is laid out. Anybody running a big enough caravan that they've got substantial assets on the line got those assets by screwing over a bunch of ordinary folks who were in no position to fight back. Why, Crown Rose alone made their initial fortune burning grain harvests so they could sell their stockpiles at a huge markup."

"It does help a little," I said, my voice as dry as the grass. "Is it even slightly true?"

He shrugged, grinning cheerfully. "I mean, probably? There's a fundamental difference in the brains between people who move money around for a living, and people who do something useful to society. A merchant is a bandit with manners. If it tells you anything, *I* considered going into the merchant trade, but it turns out I don't have a head for numbers. I am an *artist*."

"Well, I think we can call that the clincher."

I focused my spyglass back on the field, watching the way grass moved in the faint light to track the direction of the wind and decided to put off dealing with the observation that Sakin was obviously working out how to "manage" me. At some point I was going to have to seriously decide whether he was too useful to get rid of, and if not, what form that "getting rid of" would take. But, one intolerable dilemma between necessity and basic morality at a time. Better concentrate on my current crime against humanity before plotting the next one.

"**Spark.**"

In the end, it was all too easy, and that wasn't even the worst part.

After Sakin's detailed battle plan, I had expected it to be hard to manage, but the actual process of setting fires in the field was practically nothing. As it turned out, the hardest part was restraint. I had to wait, initially, for my first spark of fire to be noticed and reacted to, since the plan required attention and for the waystation's inhabitants to be rallied. I didn't even need to start as many fires as I'd expected. I had gone into this with the supposition that I would have to surreptitiously simulate the entire fire under the noses of the defenders, but in reality, fire *does* spread quite easily, especially through dry grass under a steady wind. Ultimately, I only had to cast a few additional Sparks to the sides of the rapidly expanding grass fire in order to open up new fronts and divert attention.

The whole thing went very smoothly, considering I was literally playing with fire. Two of the Blessed with Magic on site turned out to have water spells; neither were attached to the Crown Rose caravan, but one obligingly turned her focus to the wagons when I conjured fires inside them. I doubted she had any particular attachment to the Crown Rose Company or even knew who they were; it was just that wagons packed with tight rolls of cloth burned a lot higher and hotter than field grass, and once that train started going up, sparks began spreading to the point that I actually didn't have to artificially start more fires among the rest of the wagons.

By the time the grass fire was petering out for lack of anything else to burn at the edge of the hard packed earth under the wagons, most of the load of shimmersatin was ash, and every wagon in the vicinity had been soaked through the efforts of Blessed and people hauling buckets from the spring. I guess once cargo started catching fire, safeguarding it became everyone's priority. Thanks to their constant dousing, there was only minor damage to the nearby caravans, and they managed to save three of the Crown Rose wagons entirely.

I decided to let that go; it was less fabric than Auldmaer had in his shipment, which meant Crown Rose's bulk discount had gone up in smoke and they wouldn't be able to undercut him unless they were willing to give up on recouping any of their losses from this disaster. I figured I could count on the money people to choose money.

When it was all over, I stood apart from the rest of my gang under the shade of the khora, staring down at the waystation, lost inside my own head. In the near distance I could hear muted voices as the North Watch gang conversed quietly; the only sound close to me was the buzzing of Biribo's wings as he, for once saying nothing, hovered in his accustomed spot near my shoulder.

Amid the people running about, I couldn't help staring at the few sitting or standing despondently around the charred remains of the Crown

Rose caravan, staring at the sodden ashes of their paychecks. I could comfort myself, as Sakin had tried to, with the idea that the people *really* being screwed over here were the rich bosses who did shit like squeeze smaller players like Cadimer Auldmaer out of their livelihoods . . . But the reality I well knew was that in any world, the primary skill of people in power was directing profits to themselves and costs to those below them. It would be hopelessly naive to think you could stick it to the man and not have the worst of the poking felt by a hundred less important people who actually worked for a living.

I'd known that, and done it anyway. Auldmaer was right—you only found out whether you'd take the devil's deal once it was offered. If it was my ass on the line as Virya's plaything or setting fire to a waystation . . . well, I had made my choice. I was not happy about the side effects I had created. In the same dilemma, though, I'd do it again.

In fact, I was explicitly planning to. That was the whole point of forming a partnership with Auldmaer in the first place.

Boots crunched in the undergrowth as Aster came to stand beside me. She was silent, just standing there.

I probably would have let the silence hang, not feeling like talking . . . except for the way she had reached out to me that morning in our short walk across the meadow. It had subtly shifted something between us, and left me feeling a need to be understood.

"In the end, I mostly just think people are selfish. And prone to self-delusion." My voice was a bit hoarse.

"You really have a speech about how people suck for every situation, don't you. Does it make this feel better?"

"That isn't—I mean, yes, I do, but this isn't that. I don't think I want it to feel better. What I *meant* is, I'm not sure I believe in the idea of evil. If you really dig into people's motivations when they talk about evil, they're basically always referring to whatever isn't comfortable for them to think about. Something they instinctively don't like but can't be arsed to try to understand. If you look at what someone's thinking when they *do* something that is clearly wrong, they always have an explanation. A whole story, in fact; some way they've worked it around in their heads so that whatever shitty thing they've decided to do is actually right and justified. So, yeah. Selfish, deluded . . . lazy, both intellectually and morally. But *evil*, I can only comprehend that as a thing that someone fully knows is wrong, won't excuse even to themselves, and then decides to do anyway. I think . . . people will usually try to do the right thing. They rarely succeed, because people are selfish and very good at rationalizing why the right thing is to chase whatever animal impulse is flitting across their brain at a given moment. It's not common that people will just deliberately and purposely do *wrong*, without offering a pretext that it isn't."

Her head shifted in the darkness as she half-turned to look at my face.

"I only just realized *I've* never done anything I have to categorize as evil before this morning," I murmured. "I'm not a very nice person, Aster. Shut up, I don't need any of the obvious comebacks right now. I mean, I'll acknowledge being something of an asshole. But this . . . This feels different. Categorically different. I don't . . . particularly like how it feels."

She turned back to gaze out over the teeming waystation. "You must come from a very nice place, Lord Seiji. To *me* it seems like your definition of evil is a lot more common than you seem to think. It's weird how you can be so generally down on people but at the same time apparently have more faith in their basic decency than even I do."

"Don't get me wrong, I think people are more or less garbage. Just . . . self-centered, stupid garbage, not deliberately malicious. Usually."

"Can't say I agree," she mused, shaking her head, "but maybe that's for the best. What experience has taught *me* is that life is hard, and to get by you have to do a lot of things you're ashamed of. It's just . . . I think the difference is I've never really had any power over anyone. Not like you do now. Maybe you haven't either, if you were just a musician in your own country? Having to make bad choices in order to live another day must be very different when your choices only affect yourself. When you have to create consequences for a lot of people like this . . . that's got to be hard. I don't think I can judge you, except to say I'm glad it's not me."

"Hm. Maybe you have a point there."

"I'm no philosopher," she said quietly, "or priestess. I'm just someone who's survived this long and had to accept the necessity of doing some things that still cost me sleep, occasionally. I don't know the *answers*, but I've figured out the only way to make peace with it in my own mind that makes any sense to me. If . . . you're interested."

I watched one of the figures by the remains of the Crown Rose caravan get up and trudge toward the inn. Seconds later, another who'd been poking around the shell of one of the wagons just sat down in the mud.

"I think I'd like to hear it."

Aster nodded. "You do whatever you have to do, Lord Seiji, and never make excuses or justifications; never pretend you haven't *done* what you're ashamed of. And, every time you have the opportunity, be *kind*. Take any chance to put some good into the world, in payment of the bad."

"Do you think that actually balances out?"

"I'm not sure I believe balance is . . . a thing. How would you even begin calculating the weight of good and evil? Maybe the goddess . . . sorry, *goddesses* can do it, but I dunno. I just live with the fact that there's no real certainty about anything and all I can control is how much of an effort I make. So I try to do good. To be kind."

"Try to be kind," I whispered. "Huh. You know, I'm . . . not sure I'd know where to begin attempting that. I mostly just try not to deal with people or even *think* about them if I can avoid it."

"That astonishes me to hear, Lord Seiji."

"Up yours." I hesitated, then went on more quietly. "Can I rely on you to . . . help? It's not that I mean ill toward most people, Aster; I just sort of . . . don't think about ways or reasons to do nice things."

"Well, it's like any habit. Takes some practice to instill it." It was hard to read her expression in the dimness, especially with her dark complexion, but I distinctly saw the flash of teeth as she smiled. "But, sure. I can help you get started."

I nodded, then cleared my throat. That was about my tolerance of squishy feely stuff for one day. "Biribo, can you do a quick sweep of our perimeter without getting too far? As much as we've stirred up that outpost, I want to make sure we're not going to blunder into an unexpected group of bystanders when we try to leave."

"Good idea, boss," he said. "Gimme just a minute!"

I could barely see the black lizard in the dark at all, but the buzzing rapidly diminished as he shot away among the khora.

"This is never to be repeated in front of the lizard," I said very quietly, taking a step closer to Aster. "He was assigned to me by Virya and I'm *pretty* sure his only real loyalty is to her. I'm not doing this shit because I like it, Aster. I'm here because of what she threatened me with if I don't play along. *Virya* is the real enemy. I have absolutely no idea how, or even where to start, but my end goal is to stick it to *her*. I've got no quarrel with the Hero or the other goddess and no interest in world domination. We play along until I can figure out a way to turn on her without being summarily destroyed. Can I count on you?"

She nodded once, her eyes gleaming in the faint light. "I'm in, Lord Seiji. I've got your back."

I nodded back, and stepped away toward the rest of my crew without another word, Aster keeping pace alongside me. I'd just reached them and not had time to say anything when the buzzing of oversized wasp wings heralded the return of my familiar.

"Good thing you thought to check, boss. We got movement out there," he reported. "Not from the waystation, though—looks like a bandit gang. They must be based somewhere close enough to've caught wind of the fuss. About twice our numbers from what I saw, but no Blessed among 'em."

"Hm," I muttered. "This close to a Kingsguard outpost? Well, I can see it being a good spot for opportunity, if they're willing to risk it."

"The Kingsguard doesn't *patrol* in the khora forest, Lord Seiji," said Goose. "They wouldn't step foot in here unless a beast tribe tried to move in this close to the waystation. Which one wouldn't, if there's a gang camped nearby."

"All right, change of plans," I said. "I was going to send you lot back to North Watch while Aster and I make for Gwyllthean, but I don't want to risk it until we're out of range of these guys. It'll be useful to know where they are, but I'm not interested in mixing it up with another gang just yet."

"Oooh, I like the 'yet' in that sentence," Sakin chirped.

"Biribo, lead us on a course that avoids contact with anybody," I ordered. "When we're at a good distance, we'll split up. I don't want to risk you lot getting outnumbered unless you've got two Blessed here to even the odds."

"Thanks, Lord Seiji," Harold piped up.

I turned toward him, raising an eyebrow. "For what?"

"Rocco would've just left us all to fend for ourselves," Kasser answered. "In fact, he *did* that. Multiple times."

"Next time it occurs to you to compare me to Rocco, you might want to consider that his first encounter with me ended with his head rolling across the floor. Aside from the multiple things I do that aren't pants-on-head idiotic, I look after my people. Biribo, lead on. Let's move out, people. The night is young, and there's no rest for the wicked."

18

In Which the Dark Lord Meets His Match

Oh, it's all anyone's talking about down at the Trader's Guild," Cadimer Auldmaer said as he set a plate of fruit pastries between us on the desk in his office, still warm enough to be slightly steaming. "They were able to salvage a bit of their stock—but it got thoroughly soaked in the course of 'salvaging' and every bolt of fabric now has to be unwound to be dried and laboriously checked for mildew before it can be sold. To be honest, I'm rather glad you left them a bit, Lord Seiji; that was a good touch. That much shimmersatin should sell for enough to cover most of the expenses of the trip, but Crown Rose won't be pulling in a profit on it."

"And, most importantly . . . ?" I prompted.

He couldn't hide his pleased grin. "We've *already* broken even, just since I opened up the office this morning! News like what happened at the North Road waystation spreads faster than . . . well, than wildfire. Never mind setting my own prices, the news that most of the Crown Rose shipment was lost has kicked off a bidding war! And since it'll be at least two days before their stock is ready to sell, I've had customers beating down my door. It looks like I'll not have any satin left to bring to the marketplace; between the Clan Highladies and the inner ring tailors desperate to be the *first* among their peers to have real dark elf shimmersatin to show off, they've been hounding me since before dawn. This will set the Auldmaer Company up handsomely for the foreseeable future."

He took a pastry from the plate and bit into it, gesturing me to do the same.

"I'm glad this has worked out as you hoped," I said, following suit. Immediately I had to pause to collect myself before chewing. There was that flavor again . . . "Tell me something, Master Auldmaer. What local fruit is it that tastes so . . . tart? I've encountered it in jam, wine, and now pastry."

"Ah, you're becoming acquainted with a Dount specialty," he said with a pleased smile. "Did you never have the chance to try sour flavors in your home country?"

"Well, we have sour candy. It's a . . . *specific* taste, but not uncommon."

He nodded. "Then it's very likely that candy was made from Dountol sour syrup. It's one of the island's principal exports." I very much doubted that, but he was on a roll, and the last thing I wanted was to explain the lack of interplanetary trade. "It's not actually the fruit, Lord Seiji; these tarts are strawberry. It's the extra kick you're tasting, sour sap from a type of khora that grows in few places, and Dount is one of only two islands I know of that has an actual plantation to cultivate them. Alas, it doesn't travel terribly well in its raw form, so the processing is done here. What is enjoyed as a rare delicacy for the elite throughout the archipelago is a common seasoning found in practically everything on Dount. We Fflyr do enjoy our strong flavors."

"Yes, I've noticed the heavy spicing in . . . Now that I think of it, everything except the bread."

"Well, you'll only find bland bread if it's being used as a vehicle for sour jam or pepper sauce," he said, eyes glimmering with amusement. The expression faded, though, and he slowly lowered his half-eaten pastry, gazing at me seriously. "I hope you won't take offense if I abbreviate the pleasantries, Lord Seiji. I am very much cognizant that I owe my current good fortune to you, and I wouldn't want to seem ungrateful—"

"From what I've learned of Fflyr nobles, you've probably had some bad experiences with them," I said, keeping my voice mild. "Just for future reference, I won't be offended if you come right to the point, Master Auldmaer. In fact, I'm pretty hard to offend. It's my policy not to get mad at people for having reasonable concerns."

"Reasonable," he said, setting down the pastry. "Right. It's just . . . I can't help feeling *concerned* about the initial rumors I've heard about last night's events, especially as I share some responsibility for them. Burning down a whole Kingsguard waystation . . ."

"Is that what you heard?" I didn't have to fake the amused little smile this brought to my face. Ah, gossip—whether via social media or horseback messenger, some things are universal. "I'm sure that's the word going out because it makes for a better story than what happened, and that matters to the kind of people who spread stories. But no, the waystation is undamaged.

Nobody died. There were only a few injuries, and those caused by panicked animals rather than the fire directly. There was superficial damage to multiple parked caravans, but the fires were mostly put out pretty quickly, thanks to a couple of Blessed on hand and a remarkably well-organized bucket train. The Crown Rose caravan had the 'bad luck' to be right in the path of the *only* major incursion of wildfire past the firebreak the guards put up. Nor do you need to take my word for it; within a day or two you should be able to get a more accurate account of what happened from others who were there."

"Ah." Auldmaer relaxed visibly. "Well, I confess that relieves me. Somewhat."

"Nor is it my intention to sugarcoat this," I said flatly. "Last night's event was a disruption of trade, with all the repercussions that always has. People were put in danger, and property was destroyed—including that of uninvolved third parties who just had the misfortune to be nearby. You and I bear the responsibility for that, and we'll have to live with it."

"You don't favor subtlety in your methods, do you, Lord Seiji?" he asked.

"I favor it *heavily*," I countered, leaning forward. "In your line of work, is there a single tactic that always works the best in every situation, or do you need to adjust your approach to each separate event?"

"Ah." He lowered his eyes, making a rueful expression. "Yes, I see your point."

"The issue *here* was the extreme specificity of this job," I lectured. "There was *one person* exactly who benefited from the destruction of that shipment of shimmersatin. If it had been taken out on the road in any kind of targeted attack, Auldmaer, right now you'd be getting visits from thugs in the employ of the Crown Rose Company, not desperate customers. I may be new in town, but something tells me a merchant syndicate that rich wouldn't bother reporting you to the Kingsguard. As it is, I'm concerned how the outcome of the apparent natural disaster looks to them, even though I'm extremely confident no one saw solid evidence it was anything but that. Still, there was no way to do this without it looking at least *somewhat* suspicious. If I'd used a more subtle and specific approach . . . That would have been a dead giveaway."

"I see. Yes, I follow your logic, Lord Seiji." He hesitated, clearly screwing up his courage before continuing, meeting my gaze directly. "Then, with regard to the reason you approached me. You wish to make this a long-term partnership, as I understand it. Must I expect to be complicit in more attacks like this?"

"I'm not going to conclusively rule it out," I admitted, "but do understand *why* this had to happen the way it did. It was a desperate defensive action we had to take because your company's neck was on the chopping block. It would be naive to declare we'll never be in a similar situation again, but I want to be clear from the outset that I intend to avoid that if at all possible, and I'll expect you to do the same. We must be *careful*, think ahead, and avoid splashy displays of violence. With the benefit of forethought and time to plan, we can execute more targeted actions at opponents who can afford the losses, and avoid collateral damage. Partly because it's just good strategy not to create a fuss or draw attention—everything we do from here needs to look like the normal effects of Fflyr Dlemathlys not having enough standing forces to purge bandit gangs from the outskirts. But *also* because messes like the one we just made leave a bad taste in my mouth, and I just plain don't want to do that again if we can avoid it."

He let out a short breath. "Well, we're of one mind about that, Lord Seiji. Yes, I do see your point. Ah . . . I have to admit, *you* are my first ever criminal contact; I'm afraid I'm not well-positioned at the moment to take advantage of access to your talents. Not that I am putting you off!" he added hastily. "It's just going to take *time* to study the situation in Dount and its connected trade routes and identify a good next opportunity. I'll have to create a whole new strategy for my company's growth . . . Especially if, as you say, we're to take care from here on out to avoid drawing too much attention. In the short term, I . . . I'm afraid I may have little to offer you."

"That's fine," I reassured him with a smile. "In fact, I was counting on it. I need to build my own forces a bit before I'm ready to start taking on merchant trains with any regularity. Also, *you* need to lie low. You've just benefited immensely from a suspicious event; I strongly recommend you keep a squeaky-clean image for a while. In fact, the windfall you're getting from our recent success seems like a good opportunity for some nice, conservative, *boring* investments, at least until the other players in the merchant community get tired of eyeballing you."

"Again we agree," Auldmaer said in clear relief. "That being the case, what *can* I do for you? It doesn't escape me that our partnership so far has consisted of you doing all the work and me gaining all the benefit."

I had another bite of sour fruit pastry while considering my response. At this point, the challenge was keeping Auldmaer calm and optimistic enough about this not to panic, while not obscuring the seriousness of the situation. He knew how dangerous I could be, and now I needed him confident I wasn't going to turn on him, but without forgetting what would happen if *he* turned on *me*.

Damn it, I am not a people person. I'd never tried to manipulate someone before. Nobody had ever had anything important enough to me to be worth the effort.

"I sought you out because I need the economic connections you can offer, Master Auldmaer. I will need income, as everyone does, but at the moment liquid capital is less useful to me than essentials it can buy. Material supplies to keep my people safe and healthy when encamped in a khora forest, and perhaps tools and building materials to repair—that is, improve our . . . residence."

"Ah!" Auldmaer's expression brightened. "Now that I am well-positioned to aid you with, Lord Seiji. In fact, the nature of nice, conservative, *boring* investments creates opportunities to redirect supplies. The day-to-day trading and speculation between merchant companies looking to turn a quick little profit from price fluctuations involves a lot of very mundane commodities changing hands and being moved around the city in patterns that would seem arbitrary, even nonsensical to anyone not watching closely. Plentiful opportunities for the occasional shipment to appear in an unexpected place, or disappear entirely."

He stood up, turning to one of the cabinets behind him and pulled it open. Using only the hand which had not recently touched a fruit tart, the merchant began leafing through papers. I was impressed at how much paper there was in this office; if I recalled right, paper was a luxury commodity in medieval societies on Earth, but the Fflyr at least seemed to be far more literate than any comparable culture I was familiar with.

"Let's see . . . food, medicine, asauthec, clothing, tools . . . Yes, yes, plenty of that moving around. Clothing and medicine might be tricky, tools possibly, but raw staples like grains, dried meats, asauthec, beans, spices . . . easily acquired. Stockpiles like that spend as much time being traded about by the likes of me as used for their intended purpose at the end of their long journeys. Fabric and thread would be easier to obtain discreetly in quantity than finished clothes. Ah, provided you're not particular about fancy quality."

"Luxury goods would be wasted on us anyway. I won't need medicines, if that helps, and I don't believe clothing or tools are immediate concerns. Things like that I can probably just buy from shops in the Gutters—that seems least likely to attract notice. What about weapons?"

"Mmm . . . more challenging. Obtainable, though, at least in most cases." He shut the cabinet and opened another one, extracting different papers. "I can get you any number of knives, arrows, and hunting bows. Spears are military hardware and thus controlled, though there are such things as boar halberds, which I've heard of bandits using."

There were boars here? Wait, you needed *halberds* to hunt boars? "Or if it comes to that I can lash a knife to a pole."

"Well, yes," he acknowledged, grinning. "Swords are *technically* controlled tools, but the clans have been flouting that decree for so long it's practically an institution. They're obtainable even by upstanding merchants such as myself for a modest additional fee for the illegality."

"Best to hold off on that for now. We're behaving, remember?"

Auldmaer nodded, shutting the cabinet and returning to his seat behind the desk. "The one thing I unequivocally *cannot* obtain for you are crossbows. Those are restricted to military use and *that* decree is enforced. Firmly."

"Oh? What makes them such a hot commodity?"

"Why, they're a force multiplier," he said as if surprised I needed this explained. "A frighteningly user-friendly one. Using a sword, or longbow, or spear effectively requires substantial training. It's expensive to raise and then maintain an army full of men who can do it. With a crossbow, the expense is all up front in the creation of the comparatively more complex mechanism; thereafter, you just need an engineer or two to repair and maintain them, and you can put them in the hands of any idiot peasant who is then capable of killing one of your very expensively trained soldiers. Give that idiot peasant comparable training, and they can kill soldiers very *efficiently*."

I nodded slowly, digesting this. The way he described them, crossbows were sort of a precursor to firearms, the great equalizer. Was that accurate? My knowledge of military history was limited to amusing anecdotes from around the world that appealed to my sense of irony—Chamberlain's defense of Little Round Top, the campaigns of Scipio Africanus, pretty much everything Miyamoto Musashi had ever done. Isolated little stories like that with only the bare minimum of context needed to understand them. I was out of my depth in this discussion. Still, Auldmaer's description made sense. If you thought of crossbows as pre-guns . . .

Fflyr Dlemathlys was, politically speaking, a King who *barely* held a semblance of control over a patchwork of feuding noble fiefs and a peasant populace which had abundant reason to resent the lot they'd been handed, plus a generous dollop of banditry. Oh yeah, there was no way the Kingsguard could tolerate something like that getting into the hands of just anyone.

What I took away from this conversation was that *I needed crossbows*.

We settled on arrangements for my gang to be provided with some material that would be useful in the next stages of my overall plan, and regular shipments thereafter. I needed North Watch to be well stocked as much as I needed it cleaned and repaired. My "army" might be just seven people *now*, but I meant to begin gathering more immediately and I wanted to be ready. Auldmaer started to escort me politely from his office to the door, but was quickly intercepted by one of his scurrying employees, and I stepped aside to let him tend to business. I could see myself out.

I caught a glimpse of the famed shimmersatin as I was making my way around the edge of the warehouse toward the side door; a clerk was holding up a stretch of it to show a woman in a dress that already looked more expensive than anyone needed. Whatever it was made of, shimmersatin gleamed and seemed to shift in the light, its surface glimmering like water reflected from a pool. I could see why rich people would pay through the nose for this stuff.

On my way to collect Aster and go, I slowed, finding her in conversation with someone near the door. Another woman, in scuffed leather armor over a knee-length coat, with an artifact sword belted at her hip. I hadn't seen her this close previously, but I recognized her. There was no way I'd fail to.

I had heard her scream in the deepest extremity of pain. I'd been the cause of it. Her name was Larinet, and it was going to stay burned into my memory.

Fortunately, I was spared the torture of making conversation with my victim. Upon my approach, she exchanged nods with Aster, folded down hands at me, and made a discreet departure toward the back.

"Ooh, thanks!" Aster said as I handed her the spare pastry I'd taken from Auldmaer's office. She bit into it without hesitation even as we stepped out of the side door into a broad alley. "Mm, I've gotta say this job comes with nice perks. How'd you know sour strawberry was my favorite?"

"It's just what the host was serving, but I know that *now*." I fell silent, dithering over whether to ask until we had turned a corner onto a main street. Ultimately, I had to. "How is she?"

"Seems Auldmaer half-took your advice," she said after swallowing a bite. "He didn't fire her. Didn't pay her for the job, but . . . well, that's not so unreasonable. Larinet isn't complaining; I wouldn't either, in her shoes. Guards who run don't get paid. Even when running is the only sensible thing to do, the whole job is to stay and fight. A lot of employers would've sacked her, blacklisted her across the whole island, and gotten her in hot water with the King's Guild over that. Auldmaer withheld her wages for that job but is keeping her contract. Could be a hell of a lot worse."

"I guess it's a hard life all around," I murmured.

"Harder if your job involves getting set on fire," a muffled voice said from within Aster's coat.

I edged close enough to her to swat the pocket with the back of my hand. Lightly. Relatively lightly. Biribo emitted a disgruntled noise but offered no further commentary.

"Hey, hey, keep it above the waist," Aster said mildly, nibbling her tart and stepping away from me. "We're in public, here. Speaking of, what's the plan for today's trip to town, Lord Seiji?"

"I've lined up the supply shipments we need. Much as I'd like to go dither at the luthier's or stop by the King's Guild to play their keyboard, we need to start making ourselves scarce around the inner rings. Next stage of the plan will be focused on the Gutters, and I'm not going to want our activities there associated with Lord Seiji just yet. So if you have any important business here . . . ?"

"What business would *I* have?" she asked around a mouthful of strawberry tart. "Well, I guess as a Guild member I should check in from time to time, but there's no reason you particularly need to come along for that. You're a lot more recognizable in Gwyllthean than I am, Lord Seiji."

"Yeah, no kidding. To that end, the only other thing I want to get squared away before we head down to the Gutters to look for Gilder is acquiring some disguises."

"Ooh, sounds fun. Also difficult. I have to warn you, I have zero experience with, uh . . . espionage."

"Don't worry, all you'll need to do is stand back being all silent and menacing. What I have in mind is pretty simple—we should be able to put it together with bits and bobs from any clothier's shop. But *not* the guy from last time. Some place more low-class, run by somebody who'll just *sell* me shit I ask for and not turn every interaction into some kind of battle of wills."

"Funny. I had the impression from our last visit here that that's exactly how the tailor would've described you."

"No doubt, but that doesn't make him correct. I am not in the mood to be tested by idiots today."

"For you are Lord Seiji, vanquisher of tailors."

"Big talk from the vanquisher of strawberry tarts."

"That being said, wouldn't it make more sense to just buy stuff like that in the Gutters?"

"It may come to that, but we'll see. Like I said, the point is to cultivate a consistent appearance while in that district which is recognizably *not* the one I'm wearing around right now. If possible I'd prefer—"

"Omura-san?"

I slammed to a halt in the middle of the street. We were surrounded by the anonymous bustle of urban living, guaranteed a modicum of privacy even in public by the universal fact that cities are full of strangers who don't give a shit about one another's business. The voice which called out to me cut through the noise and seized my full attention, though, and not just because nobody here should know that name. I *recognized* that voice. I knew what I'd find even before I spun around to face the speaker.

"*Yoshi!*"

19

In Which the Dark Lord is Brought to Justice

There he was, in the flesh, mostly as I remembered him. It wasn't like Shinonome Yoshi's visage was burned into my brain, but there were exactly two Japanese people on this planet and only one was that chunky, and also not me.

Actually, he looked a tad less chunky than I recalled, though not so in shape that the armor he'd found fit him well. The leather armor was meant for someone smaller and was strapped awkwardly to his chest, making most of his stomach bulge out underneath it—which was unfortunately visible as the shirt and coat under the armor *had* been sized for someone larger, but large as in muscle, so it was baggy around the chest and shoulders and quite tight across the gut. And he *still* hadn't washed his hair. Poor kid couldn't have looked less heroic if he rolled in mud.

Yoshi now had an entourage, but for a few startled moments as he and I stared at each other in mutual astonishment I ignored them, even as their unsubtle conversation filled the air around us.

"So this *is* the one."

"He does have similar features . . ."

"Come on, why would the Dark Lord be in some hick-ass town in a backwater like Donut? This place is halfway to the core."

"It's Dount."

"Nobody cares, Pashi!"

"H-he recognized Yoshi, too . . . I think it has to be—"

"Oh my god, Yoshi, are you okay?" I exclaimed, overriding their chatter. I spoke half out of genuine relief and half following an instinctive drive to mischief. "After the greeting *I* got in this shithole country, I figured you'd be *dead*! Man, you've lost weight . . . I mean, you *had* it to lose, but still, it's barely been a week! Are you eating okay? Do you need money? Aster, gimme my coin pouch; we can spare Yoshi a couple gold halos. He's good people."

"I, uh . . . n-no, you don't have to do that," Yoshi stammered. He looked even more surprised than I was; clearly he hadn't come to Gwyllthean looking for me. "Please, you don't need to worry, I'm fine! It's, uh, kinda difficult *adjusting* to life here, but I've made good friends already! Oh, I'm sorry, Omura-san, these are—"

"Hold on, Yoshi," chimed a shrill little voice. "Do you really think it's *wise* to start telling . . . *this guy* in particular all about your business?"

"Holy *shit*," I exclaimed, having spotted the source of the voice after a couple seconds of searching. At issue was that it was a sunny day and she was all of ten centimeters tall, dressed in perfect sky blue to match her delicate butterfly wings, and hovering overhead where she was framed against the sky. If she hadn't fluttered lower to hang around Yoshi's shoulder, it probably would have taken me longer to spot her. "What the—you got a cute little pixie? Oh, that is just *unfair*."

"Yeah?" the tiny woman shot back. "Where's *your* familiar, Mister Dark Lord?"

Biribo was tucked in Aster's pocket as usual when we were in the city, and I hoped to god he had the sense to damn well stay there. Also, I belatedly noticed that we were drawing stares. It was a nicer area of town, and this was a loud conversation involving two obvious foreigners—one of whom lacked the basic wit to keep his familiar hidden in public—and that all-important title which had been used twice now.

I put on a confused frown. "Why do you people keep calling me that? You've got weird friends, Yoshi."

"Hey, they're good people," the Hero started to protest, but then another figure barged in front of him, planting herself square in my field of vision and pointing an artifact rapier and a scowl at me.

"Enough! If this is truly him, then the Goddess has guided our steps here. Let's be rid of this evil *before* he starts his path of conquest!"

And that was how I met my first elf.

Scowl aside, she was the most beautiful woman I had ever seen, to the point that it crested the bell curve and started to become less attractive and more unsettling. There's an uncanny valley effect that kicks in when features are a little *too* idealized. When it came to elves, in addition to the trademark long, pointed ears, this manifested in extremely refined and dainty features, which . . . Actually, she looked like a photorealistic anime character. Like she'd stepped out of one of those extremely ill-advised 3D movies the *Final Fantasy* people keep making.

Of course, all this was my perspective as someone who had seen plenty of real women, close enough to properly appreciate them. This girl undoubtedly had poor Yoshi wrapped around her little finger, whether she wanted him there or not.

"Excuse me, young woman," I said stiffly, ignoring the sword, "we are in the middle of a conversation. Were you raised in a barn?"

To judge by her expression, not only had no one ever spoken to her that way, she had never contemplated the possibility that someone *could*. Yoshi just looked (more) nervous, but his other three friends all immediately bit down on their lips to suppress outward amusement. The pixie clapped a tiny palm to her tiny forehead. And just like that, I understood most of what I needed to about this group's dynamic.

"Now hear *this*," the elf snarled, raising her sword to point at my throat.

"Come on, Highlady Flaethwyn," said the only other man in the group, a tall lowborn fellow with a ponytail carrying an artifact spear, "you can't just stab somebody in the middle of the street. This isn't your clan's territory, remember?"

"Please don't get us arrested," added another girl, sounding as nervous as Yoshi. I glanced at her, then had to do a double take; only the fact that I'd been distracted by heroes and pixies and elves had prevented this one from being the first thing to catch my notice. She seemed like a pretty average lowborn Fflyr woman, if on the short side, in her late teens at the most. Except that her hair—including eyebrows—was a vivid pink.

"Whoa," I said, blinking at her. "Hey, guys, I've spotted the main character."

At my direct attention, she immediately slid backward and ducked half-behind the guy with the spear.

"Leave her alone!" Flaethwyn barked, flicking the tip of her sword in a tight circle less than half a meter from my face. "*Your* business is with me, Champion of Virya!"

The fifth member of the group, a blonde highborn woman wearing well-fitted robes and narrow spectacles, cleared her throat pointedly. "Assuming, for the sake of argument, it's decided that having a public altercation is not the terrible idea it looks like . . . Wouldn't his business be, specifically, with *Yoshi*?"

Yoshi, I could tell by his expression, was having a moment—increasingly irritated with how he was being disregarded here, but too polite to complain and unwilling to make an issue of it. The elf herself flushed at the sudden reminder that she was upstaging the Champion of Sanora, but rallied by sticking her nose in the air and the tip of her sword perilously close to mine. I could see it was an artifact from the subtle glow around it, but not what exactly it did. For that I'd need Biribo, and right now I really preferred that he stay hidden.

"That's . . . there's no need— That is, Yoshi's still early in his training! Obviously, *this* cretin is the same. This is the chance to cut him off *before* he does any damage! You and I can handle this, Pashilyn. Be ready to support me with spells! And *you*. If you've any last words, this is the final moment to voice them!"

The silly wench actually *struck a pose*, arching her back to stick her chest out and brandishing the rapier at me in a one-handed grip, nose somehow even higher in the air than before.

I eyed her up and down as slowly and insolently as I could, just until her cheeks went scarlet with rage, then leaned to the side, talking past her entirely.

"Excuse me, miss. I don't mean to alarm you, but it appears that your hair is pink."

In hindsight, I was at fault for what followed. After only a week on Ephemera, my survival instincts hadn't fully adjusted; I failed to consider how a spoiled noblewoman in a society which probably let her do anything she wanted would react to being treated in a manner which suited her behavior.

Flaethwyn was *fast*—she moved quicker than my own eyes could follow, probably due to a combination of martial training and her sword's own power. That thing came straight at my chest at a speed that would undoubtedly have killed me, except that Aster *also* had an artifact sword, and much better social instincts than I did for dealing with Fflyr aristocracy. She must have started moving even before Flaethwyn did to intercept her, as even with the power of her greatsword, it was a much slower weapon than the rapier. But she managed it, interposing herself between us, and that one deflection was all she needed. Slow it might be, but the sheer force of its much greater weight as it connected made the elf stagger, nearly losing her grip on her rapier.

Aster planted herself between us, causing me to stumble backward and forcing all of Yoshi's group to retreat as she raised the greatsword; its considerable length was very good for enforcing personal space.

"*Back. Off.*"

I couldn't see Aster's face from behind her, but the snarl was audible.

"How *dare* you—" That was as far as Flaethwyn got before having both her arms grabbed by Yoshi and Pashilyn.

"Flaethwyn, no!"

"That's enough!"

Clearly, they weren't the only ones who thought so. Some of the onlookers had shrieked and fled when the blades came out, though others appeared to be placing bets. Much more important were the pounding boots of new arrivals in armor, brandishing weapons.

"No fighting!" bellowed the lead guard. "Weapons away, *now!*"

Aster immediately retreated two steps, fastening her greatsword onto her back again despite the continuing threat of Flaethwyn, who was now struggling against her companions' attempts to restrain her.

"Do you have any idea who I *am?*" the elf demanded as five more soldiers closed in on us from multiple directions. "Get *off* me!"

She succeeded in shrugging Yoshi loose, due to a combination of his inherent reluctance to manhandle her and the fact that he'd picked the arm in which she held the sword, which kept swinging perilously close to him as they struggled. He gave up, leaving her half-free to brandish her weapon at the military guard with all the aplomb of someone raised in such comfort that no one had thought to warn her *never* to brandish a weapon at a military guard.

"I am executing the will of the Goddess," Flaethwyn ranted, "and *you* will know your place, lowborn—"

"**Windburst!**"

I was as surprised as she to learn that the soldier was Blessed. Well, actually, probably *somewhat* less surprised, since I only got to *see* the man conjure a concentrated blast of gale-force wind. Flaethwyn was slammed across the street into an akorthist wall by it, ripped out of Pashilyn's grasp violently enough to send the other woman staggering to the pavement.

"*Wow,*" I said, peeking around Aster at the Blessed guardsman. "Hey, where'd you get the scroll for that one? Are they selling?"

His expression told me he wasn't interested in chitchat. "Quiet, foreigner. *All* of you are coming to the barracks. Weapons down, and no more nonsense, or I *will* put you down!"

Notably, Aster and the other lowborn had already placed their weapons on the ground; it was probably a well-trained instinct for them. Yoshi and I exchanged a single look, and raised our hands in unison.

Well, shit. I'd made it almost a week without getting in trouble with the law. Considering what I'd mostly been doing since I arrived here, that wasn't bad.

An hour later, I was in a much more optimistic mood.

"Once again, Lord Seiji, I apologize on behalf of Clan Aelthwyn for this embarrassment."

"On the contrary, Captain! These things happen everywhere—that's why every city needs guards. I am *quite* impressed by how professionally your men handled this unfortunate incident."

I really was, too. From what I'd been told about the Fflyr soldiers, who doubled as city guards, they normally handled civil disturbances by clubbing everyone present into compliance and then making them scrub their own blood off the street. Apparently, though, once an altercation involved multiple aristocrats and rich foreigners on both sides of the conflict, some due diligence became necessary. The Blessed lieutenant on site had actually gone so far as to interview witnesses and suspects, and quickly put together exactly what had happened.

Which put me in a good position because, somewhat to my own surprise, I wasn't even slightly in the wrong here.

"You are very gracious about this, Lord Seiji, which I appreciate," Captain Norovena replied, nodding gravely at me. "My job would be much easier if our own citizens faced such inconveniences with your equanimity." He was a lot more articulate than his subordinates, which I put down to breeding; Norovena was pale and had hair of a shade that hovered between light brown and dirty blonde. I suspected you didn't get to be a Captain in the Fflyr military without at least lower noble status, competence be damned. No wonder this country was in such shambles. "In any case, I apologize once more for the inconvenience you've suffered, and I hope it will not color your perception of our fair nation. I won't waste any more of your time, my lord; you may go at your convenience, with the goodwill of my master Archlord Caludon of Clan Aelthwyn. Rest assured, I will ensure these miscreants *repent* of their foolishness."

He finished with a glare at the miscreants in question, all five of whom were lined up against the wall in the captain's office, with their weapons piled in the corner and their hands manacled. Yoshi's pixie familiar had wisely kept her mouth shut and just fluttered aimlessly above his head, not revealing that she was sapient; the guards had been unable to do anything about her, or even figure out what she was, and so decided not to mess with what they assumed to be Spirit shenanigans. Mostly they just looked subdued, though the pink-haired girl, Amell, was visibly struggling not to burst out crying. Flaethwyn was a living portrait of the desire to throttle somebody.

"You cannot be serious!" she raged, having to lift both of her chained hands to point accusingly at Aster. "That *lowborn* raised a weapon at me!"

"Delavada Aster," Norovena said with long-suffering patience, "is a registered member in good standing of the King's Guild, whose contract as Lord Seiji's bodyguard is on record there. She defended her lord from what every witness, *including yourself*, described as an unlawful assault with murderous intent. She acted correctly for her station, as the Convocation has laid out the duties of blood, Highlady Flaethwyn. Invoking rank is not going to levy any penalty on Miss Aster; it will just entitle Lord Seiji to demand satisfaction from your clan. Is that really what you want?"

"I don't think that will be necessary," I demurred with a polite smile. Poor Flaethwyn; this was probably the worst day of her life. I was trying very hard not to enjoy it too much, because I was making an effort not to be an objectively bad person. "If I may ask, what exactly *is* going to happen to them?"

"Well, in each individual case it will depend on their station," the Captain said. He had taken a rather genial tone once it became clear I wasn't going to make his life unnecessarily difficult over this, and now seemed quite willing to hang about and chat with me, or at least in no hurry to hustle me out of his office. "Assault and attempted murder—these are not small things. In such a case, I will have to submit a report to Clan Aelthwyn. Since it involves aristocrats, Archlord Caludon will have to render judgment himself. At his convenience, of course; as the governor of all of Dount, the Archlord has countless demands upon his time and attention." He gave me a sly little half smile, which I returned because I saw an immediate benefit in maintaining rapport with this guy, which was more important than expressing my sudden disdain for his attitude. "In the meantime, they will be detained. The foreign boy will simply be held in a cell until the Archlord makes a verdict. Obviously, I can't speak for his Lordship, but it would be standard for him to be released for time served at that point. The two lowborn will receive twenty lashes by default for their complicity in this. Archlord Caludon will decide what, if any, further punishment is called for when this matter comes before him."

Amell lost her battle and broke down in quiet sobs. The other fellow, Raffan, just stared stonily at the far wall.

"High Lady Flaethwyn and Lady Pashilyn will be our . . . guests until their clans deign to retrieve them," Captain Norovena continued, ignoring Amell. "It's not for the likes of myself to impose any punishment upon highborn, of course, my lord. What happens after their time in my custody will depend on the arrangement reached between their Clans and Clan Aelthwyn. Meanwhile . . . Gwyllthean is not a *large* city, you understand, and I lack such niceties as facilities for imprisoned noblewomen specifically. The *standard* measure, of course, will be to hire a female adventurer to serve as warden of their cells."

I couldn't help noticing that Pashilyn's face had gone bone-white and even Flaethwyn was starting to look queasy. Norovena seemed increasingly smug, which only increased my growing unease.

"Do forgive me if this is a stupid question," I said aloud. "I'm not terribly familiar with Fflyr customs just yet, Captain. Why would they need an adventurer guard?"

"Oh, I don't anticipate needing an *adventurer* as such to guard them," he clarified, smirking harder. "It's just that here on Dount, the King's Guild is the only likely source of a woman capable of performing guard duty. It's a courtesy to their station, you see, Lord Seiji. I'm afraid out here in the frontier provinces we must make do with whatever louts are willing to serve in the Kingsguard, and it's not for the generous pay or cozy accommodations, I can assure you. Obviously I have *rules* concerning the treatment of prisoners, but . . . I can't be everywhere. And for some of the oafs I'm regrettably forced to rely on, this is the only chance they'll ever have to get their hands on a noblewoman. A woman adventurer monitoring their cells is to make sure nothing happens which might embarrass any of the clans involved, you see. Of course, that *is* an extraordinary expense, which would have to be approved by the Archlord. To uphold the dignity of the clans, he naturally will grant the necessary funds, of that I have no doubt."

"When he gets around to it."

"When he gets around to it," he repeated dryly.

Yoshi's expression was growing more horrified by the second as he caught on. Pashilyn was clutching her skirts in quivering fists; Flaethwyn had gone stiff as a post, glaring into space. Aster was standing behind my chair, still and silent as if extra conscious of her station in the presence of the guard captain, but I could practically feel the disgust radiating from her.

I fucking hated this country. If burning Fflyr Dlemathlys to the ground ended up providing Virya with free amusement, well . . . I decided then and there I could live with that.

I had been about to point out that only Flaethwyn had done anything wrong and the rest had been actively trying to restrain her, but at this revelation I abruptly changed tactics. The silly girl deserved a reality check, not . . . Fortunately I had anticipated the assets I would need to leverage in order to get anything done in this obviously corrupt guardhouse, and thus had already retrieved said assets from Aster.

"It sounds, Captain, as if you are forced to spend a lot of effort maintaining order *despite* a command structure disorganized by politics and a lack of resources. I am impressed that you manage it." While speaking, I idly produced a gold halo, set it on his desk, and spun it with a flick of my fingers. The coin flashed in the torchlight, making an almost melodic buzzing noise as its serrated edge danced across the polished akorshil.

"Well, I would never presume to complain, Lord Seiji." His eyes flicked to the coin, then back to my face. "It's hardly my place to criticize the decisions of my betters. Of course, sometimes it seems like my job *could* be made simpler, but isn't that true of anyone?"

"Oh, very true indeed," I agreed in my most genial tone. "I imagine it must happen from time to time that you have to make decisions outside the normal procedures just to get anything done around here."

"It does happen, now and then, that some minor detail would only be a waste of my superiors' time," Norovena agreed in a very casual tone. "It's a balancing act, you see, Lord Seiji. Ensuring the will of the highborn sometimes involves judgment calls to avoid cluttering up their agendas with trivial nonsense."

"Exactly! You took the words right out of my mouth, Captain." I stopped the spinning coin with one fingertip, then tipped it over onto the desktop. "Why, in this case . . . After all, what is this but a little kerfuffle caused by a few high-spirited youths? I already feel bad for the time your men have spent on it. I'd be *dreadfully* embarrassed to have the time of such a person as the island's governor wasted on my account."

"As courteous as you have been about this whole affair, my lord, I too would be terribly reluctant to cause you any such imposition," Norovena agreed solemnly.

I placed a second gold halo atop the first one, and then a third. "Now, if I know bureaucracies—and I do—any little deviation from procedure causes all *kinds* of extra administrative costs to pile up. If you were willing to help me avoid such awkwardness, obviously I would be only too happy to cover the necessary expenses."

With one fingertip, I pushed the stack of coins across the table. I still didn't have much economic frame of reference here, but by the best guess I'd cobbled together, a gold halo would cover the salary of a city guard for at least a week. Maybe a month? Apparently it was enough; Captain Norovena didn't hesitate, smoothly sweeping the coins off his side of the desk even as he answered.

"I can already tell you're a man of impeccable judgment, Lord Seiji. If I could trouble you for an opinion, what do *you* think would be the most reasonable way to handle these troublemakers?"

I glanced over at the Hero and his party lined up along the wall in chains, their wide eyes all fixed on me as they waited to learn what terrible fate the Dark Lord had in store for them.

"It seems to me all of this has been blown out of proportion," I said, deliberately keeping my tone light. "Yoshi's a good kid, that I can vouch for—he's just fallen in with the wrong crowd. Why, at worst, Lady Fr— Ful—ah, the young elf there seems to lack common sense and a knowledge of acceptable behavior in public. The rest of them were even trying to restrain her when your men intervened, Captain. I can only imagine how annoyed the governor would be to have his time wasted with this. I think what these kids need is a night in a cell to reinforce the fact that their *actions have consequences*. And then a . . . *reasonable* fine for the return of their weapons and belongings, yes? In fact, after that, I rather suspect they will be *model* citizens henceforth. You know how it is with the young—they just need to have boundaries set."

"A very wise assessment, Lord Seiji," the captain agreed, nodding solemnly. "Truly, I think that will be for the best—it will save effort all around! For me, and for the clans who would otherwise have to clean up after this little mishap. I will see to it the kids have to endure no more than one uncomfortable night. No doubt you're right, and that will be all the lesson they need." He finished in a hard tone, turning his glare upon the prisoners. Amell and Yoshi began babbling nearly incoherent agreement.

I interrupted by setting another gold halo on the desk with a soft *click*. "And Captain . . . I realize this will be an imposition, but I do have a request."

"Oh?" His eyes fixed on the coin for a moment before he met my gaze again. "I'm happy to accommodate you, my lord!"

I withdrew my hand slightly. "I'm sure, with a modicum of effort, it's within your power to ensure the girls are watched over such that none of the more disreputable elements within your ranks get anywhere near them. I'd hate to think of myself as having been responsible for ladies being treated in any way disrespectfully."

"That should not be a problem," he agreed, reaching for the halo. "For just one night, I can arrange that without disrupting the schedule too much, I should think—"

I slapped my hand back over it.

"Seriously." I stared at Norovena's eyes, making my tone as suddenly cold as my expression. "If I were to learn they have been mistreated *in any way*, I cannot begin to describe how *unhappy* I will be. Captain."

"We are of one mind, my lord." His appearance was so deeply serious I might even have believed it, had I not just confirmed for myself what a well-mannered sleazeball the man was. "As gentlemen and men of the world, it's incumbent upon us to protect the fairer sex from all harm."

"I knew you would understand," I said much more pleasantly, withdrawing my hand and allowing him to grab the last halo. "I had you pegged for an honorable man right from the beginning, Captain."

"That is deeply gratifying, my lord, coming from such an excellent judge of character as yourself."

There came a soft clink of chains as Pashilyn stepped forward from the wall, raised her manacled hands, and folded them down in my direction. "Thank you very much, Lord Seiji, for your graciousness. We are, all of us, *deeply* grateful."

"Seiji-san," Yoshi agreed with a solemn nod, "arigatou gozaimashita."

"*Flaethwyn*," Pashilyn added in a near growl.

The elf looked like she was about to be sick and would rather do that and then lick it up than be nice to me, but to her credit, she did step forward and offer me a jerky nod. "I . . . appreciate your forbearance. Lord Seiji."

"Least I could do," I said magnanimously, and exchanged a jovial wink with Captain Norovena.

Accidental as this whole encounter had been, and despite the money I'd just pissed away on bribes, I was counting it as a win. I now had a connection high in the Kingsguard who liked bribes; that would undoubtedly be *very* useful in the near future. And in the longer term, it meant I knew which guard captain to quietly dispose of once I was running this town.

"So, correct me if I'm wrong," Aster said later as we made our way to the city gates, "but . . . isn't that guy kind of divinely compelled to try to *kill* you? It seems odd that you'd go out of your way to help them like that. Especially from the consequences of their own actions."

"I know what I'm doing, Aster. Yoshi's a dumb kid with a good heart; the last thing I want is to play into the fantasy he thinks he's living by validating what . . . you-know-who told him. *Now* they've all got something to think about. Trust me, this will pay dividends the next time we see them. And there *will* be a next time."

"I guess I see your point," she murmured. "That was weird, though."

"How so?"

"Well, that Highlady Flaethwyn got arrested at all. This is Fflyr Dlemathlys; elves are considered the next best thing to the bloodline of the Goddess herself. Ordinarily, I'd say a city guard captain wouldn't *dare* put irons on an elf, even if she'd succeeded in murdering someone in broad daylight in the middle of the street."

"Hm. What do you make of that?"

"The only thing I can think of," Aster said slowly, "is politics. The *one* reason guards would be willing to go after an elf is if they gained favor with other, more powerful elves by doing so."

"You think she's out of favor with Clan Aelthwyn," I said, catching on.

"She's young and seems like a hothead, Lord Seiji. People like that *do* cause trouble, but at the highest levels of politics? They'd be kept well away from anything that could cause *serious* enmity. It's more likely her clan is unfriendly with Clan Aelthwyn. I wish we'd heard what clan she was in, but she never mentioned it in there. Which, now that I think about it, had to have been deliberate."

"Indeed. Well, that's definitely a lever I might be able to pull later on. Between Maugro, Auldmaer, and Gilder, I bet I can find out more. And speaking of, I hope the kid's okay and won't have much trouble finding us."

"Well, we passed into the walls late last night and it's been most of the morning. I guess how quickly he finds us will show if he's as good as he claims at spying."

"I've got a good feeling, Aster. The day started off with a distraction, but look how well it worked out! For the first time, everything's comin' up Seiji."

From inside her coat pocket came a muffled but resonant snort.

20

In Which the Dark Lord Brings Refreshments

Gilder had claimed he would find us next time we appeared in town. It was easy enough to put that to the test; I had some purchases to make anyway and capped it off with a visit to the food vendors lining the trade road, securing lunch both for us and for my spy. The kid had looked like he needed some serious feeding.

We arrived at the same secluded spot at which we'd spoken to him previously, and I took the time to look around with more care. I could tell why he'd picked this one; to judge by the weeds choking the path and the dilapidated state of the building in question, it hadn't seen much use in a while. In fact, though it was harder to tell from the main road, it looked like a lot of the Gutters was abandoned; a ring of collapsing structures encircled the inhabited part of town.

"Hey, Biribo," I said aloud, "are we alone?"

He practically exploded out of Aster's coat pocket in a furious buzz of wings. "Fuckin' *finally*! Yeah, we got privacy, there's no one within human earshot. And I got a bone to pick with you, boss man!"

"Oh, I'm sure this'll be just precious." I took a seat on the edge of the low akorthist retaining wall separating the path from the agricultural field beyond.

"I *heard* that comment back there about the Hero's familiar. *Some offense taken*, pal!"

"Cry me a river." I took a nibble of skewered meat. Not bad. Too spicy, but that was everything served in this damn country. "Did you *see* her? He gets an adorable little pixie and I'm stuck with flying vermin? Look at yourself, you little monster. I stand by what I said—*unfair*."

"What kind of Dark Lord has a pixie familiar?" Biribo demanded. "How would *that* look? You'd be a laughingstock!"

"Oh, like *you're* any more respectable."

"You know what *I'm* concerned about," Aster commented, "is a tiny woman in the custody of a teenage boy. That poor, poor pixie."

"*What* is with this outpouring of sympathy for the Hero's minions?" Biribo exclaimed. "You guys have got to be the *worst* conquerors ever to serve the name of Evil!"

"There's a badge I can wear with pride," I said. "More importantly, it's time to work. Keep an eye out and let me know if anyone approaches, especially the kid we're looking for."

"Yeah, yeah," my familiar said impatiently, "will do, but now that I'm *finally* out of the bag, there's something you need to know, boss. I *do* keep an eye out even when we're in stealth mode, and a little peek now and then was enough to show me the Hero was dressed in wall-to-wall artifacts."

"He . . . wait, what?" I narrowed my eyes, lowering my meat skewer. "Yoshi? Two of his little harem were carrying artifacts, but just one each. I didn't see any on him."

"Yeah, you probably wouldn't have. Only a familiar would be likely to notice. That's what's weird about it, boss; they were, every one of 'em, the *weakest* artifacts I have ever seen. Tiny little improvements to his stamina, or luck, or agility, stuff like that . . . the whole lot wouldn't've amounted to any measurable advantage for him. Even though it *was* a lot, because I wasn't kidding—*everything he was wearing* was an artifact."

"Okay," I said slowly, "keeping in mind that I am still new to Ephemera, put into context for me exactly *how* weird that is."

"Fuckin' very," he replied, starting to zip back and forth in the air as if this subject excited him for some reason. "Artifacts are *rare*, even the weaker ones. And yeah, they ain't all Greatswords of Mastery or Impregnable Chain Mail, but even the basic-ass beginner ones'll give their wielder *something* of clear value. Also, it's extremely uncommon for an artifact to have an even slightly plain design. The aesthetic of magic stuff is universally pretty extra, boss. That dude was wearing a bunch of cobbled-together rubbish that looked like he picked it up from low-rent adventurer supply stalls in the Gutters, except it was all artifacts, except it was without exception artifacts with the weakest, most useless powers imaginable. You seein' where this trail leads, boss?"

I exhaled sharply, having indeed realized it. "Son of a bitch. He can *make* artifacts. That's his isekai cheat power!"

"His, uh, what?" Aster asked, her eyebrows shooting up. I waved her off impatiently.

"And that's why he can't produce anything of real value yet—it's just a week in. If it's anything like my spell combination, he can't just pull whatever he imagines out of his butt. There'll be some limitation with the materials he's working with, and a *massive* learning curve when it comes to figuring out how to make the magic work. Since apparently the Blessing of Wisdom doesn't extend to magic sigils," I added pointedly.

"Hey, don't give *me* that look," Biribo protested. "Do I look like somebody who makes the rules? Not my fault the goddesses have the basic sense to keep Heroes and Dark Lords from screwing around with the source code of reality."

"Source code," I repeated. "That's an interesting way to phrase that, Biribo."

He flicked his little forked tongue out at me. It was really hard to tell, what with his triangular lizard face, but I had the strong feeling he was smirking.

"So," Aster prompted, "spell combination?"

"My . . . unique gift from Virya," I explained. "I can take the basic spells I learn and combine them into new forms, within certain limits."

"Certain limits?"

"Mostly having to do with the fact that nobody bothered to explain how it works, so I'm fumbling around blind."

"Point of order, boss: the goddess *did* try to explain—"

"Shut up, Biribo."

"Ah." Aster nodded in comprehension. "I *thought* those fire slimes were pretty exotic."

"That's one word for it. Far as I know, I'm the only person who can make 'em. Spell combination is also how I made Enjoin, which is the spell that lets you benefit from my Blessings."

"Heads up," Biribo interjected before she could render an opinion about that. "We got company heading this way. Looks like it's your boy, boss."

"Well, well, I guess the little squirt turned out to be worth the investment after all. Is he alone?"

"Come on, what kinda amateur do you think I am? If he was bringing an ambush, I'd'a *said* that in the first place."

"All right, no need to pitch a snit over it. You know the drill, Biribo—back in the pocket. I'm not ready to trust the kid with *too* many details just yet."

"Yeah, yeah, I'm goin'," he grumbled, buzzing back down to Aster's side and clambering into *his* pocket—I knew for a fact that she'd made him a comfy nest of cloth scraps and kept feeding him snacks, the little ingrate.

It was only five minutes or so before Gilder himself suddenly burst out of a large stand of weeds sprouting alongside the building, crowing "*AHA!*" at the top of his lungs.

Neither of us reacted; I finished chewing my bite of meat and some kind of tart root vegetable before bothering to answer him. "Took you longer than I'd hoped. Future reference, kiddo, I'd rather you show up punctually than waste my time setting up an ineffective jump scare."

"Aw, c'mon," the boy whined, "there's no *way* you saw me coming! I'm damn good at sneaking—I even ditched Rassin an' Kess. They been followin' me all day, but nobody out-sneaks Gilder!"

"And yet . . ."

"You got some kinda magic trick for it, right?" He shuffled forward, gazing up at me with bright, eager eyes. "Come on, spill! How'd you do it?"

"More importantly, what if it had worked? Do you think it's *really* smart to startle a man who can cast spells and is in town explicitly to kill people and cause chaos?"

His face fell slightly, but he rallied. "Aw, I knew you wouldn't slip up, Lord Seiji. You're the most powerful and in-control Blessed in all of Dount!"

"We've gotta work on your flattery, son. Points for effort, but that was *way* too ham-fisted. You'll just turn off anybody smart enough to see it coming. Here."

I proffered the remaining skewer; he darted forward with the speed of a striking cobra to snatch it and retreated just as quickly, stuffing an over-large bite in his mouth before answering.

"You sure? I ain' tol'ya anyfin' yef."

"Fuck's sake, boy, don't talk with your mouth full. Anyway, no; we'll discuss payment when you actually bring me something useful. *Feeding* you's just a perk of the job. I look after my people, that's baseline."

He gave me a look that seemed unsure whether he should be skeptical or hopeful, but it didn't stop him from cramming the rest of the meat and vegetables into his mouth at a truly alarming speed. Nor did Aster's exhortations for him to slow down. I was only partly motivated by the modern Japanese observation that bringing snacks for the staff was sound management practice. I'd been worried about the kid, a sensation exacerbated by guilt that I'd made the choice to leave him at large in his impoverished situation. There was no way he was eating enough, to judge by the size of him. Even if the harsh tactical realities prevented me from taking him in, I could at least see to it he got fed when we met up.

Aster's advice still lingered in my mind. I had to take every opportunity to dispense a little kindness in order to stay sane, given the *other* kinds of actions my role as Dark Lord would demand.

"You about ready to slow down?" I inquired once Gilder was licking the stick. His eyes zeroed in on the other package I picked up, a still-warm pastry folded up inside a broad leaf. I'd bought two of them from a stand near the meat vendor—sour strawberry tarts, Aster's favorite, just because she'd dropped the last half of hers in the street when she had to defend me from that trigger-happy elf. She had demolished hers already, and I wasn't in the mood for more sour junk, so this was the last one. I held it out toward the boy.

"Ah, ah!" Then immediately jerked it up out of his reach when he lunged for it, wagging a severe finger in his face. "*Slowly.* Never mind choking, you have to take time to appreciate the good things in life. If you get a treat, make sure you can *taste* it. Okay?"

He nodded, eyes practically bulging with avarice, and I finally handed him the tart. He did snatch it like a starving squirrel, but at least he chewed more carefully this time.

I couldn't help feeling a pang in my chest, watching the street kid enjoying the pastry. His face scrunched up like he almost couldn't bear the sheer pleasure—when he wasn't checking over his shoulder every few seconds, at least.

"Let me guess," Aster said quietly. "Usually if you get a treat, someone takes it from you."

Gilder emitted a crumb-spraying little huff, a fragment of bitter laughter only partly muffled by a mouthful of strawberry tart. "You know it, lady. Not complaining, that's just life. I never got a chance to just . . ."

He paused, and to my horror I saw tears in the corners of his eyes. Fortunately for us both, Gilder cleared his throat and half-turned away, getting himself back under control while continuing to scarf down the rest of the pastry.

Fuck. I had to think of some better way to take care of this kid. But what? Anything I gave him would just make him a target, unless it was something he could eat right in front of me while my bodyguard and I stood watch. This fucking country . . . I was starting to see the method in Virya's madness—Fflyr Dlemathlys was such an utter, appalling mess it was not only vulnerable to even an inexperienced Dark Lord, but urgently *needed* to be razed to the ground and rebuilt from scratch.

Note to self: recruit somebody who knew the slightest thing about nation-building. I sure as hell didn't.

"Better?" I asked once Gilder was licking his fingers.

"Thanks, Lord Seiji," he nodded, beaming up at me. "Best boss ever. Right, Aster?"

"He has his points," she drawled.

"Stop, I'm gonna blush. All right, now that you're slightly less starving, what have you got for me?"

"Right! I been feeling out the other kids, careful-like, just like you said. I got one name who I think you should meet, Lord Seiji—my friend Benit. She's a year younger'n me, so I look out for her. A real quiet one, but she knows how to watch and listen and *think*. People don't take her serious enough cos she keeps her mouth shut, but Benit's sharp. I've talked with her—y'know, indirectly, like you said. Not naming names or saying I got an opportunity exactly, but seeing what she might think. I bet she'd be interested. Benit's clever enough to take a chance and not fuck it up."

"Good! If you think she's ready, we'll set up a meeting. Any others?"

He winced and actually took a step back, causing me another pang at the realization that he automatically associated the delivery of bad news with punishment.

"It's . . . it's tricky, Lord Seiji. I'm sorry, but it's gonna take me longer to get more faces I can be sure of, y'know?"

"That's fine," I assured him, nodding. "That's *good*. I did tell you to move with care, remember? We're building a base here, not rushing to results. At this stage it's more important to protect yourself and not take risks."

"Okay," he said, so visibly relieved I felt my throat tighten. "Problem is, most of what I got to work with is the younger kids. And you know how it is, little kids are stupid."

"They are indeed," I said solemnly.

"I gotta be *real* selective to pick out the trustworthy ones," Gilder explained. "Most of the ones older'n me are *bigger*, and that means they ain't gonna take me seriously. Which, y'know, I can *use* that to get away with shit, but it's a drawback when I want 'em to *do* something for me. Plus, once they get like more'n a couple years older, most of the Rats start getting groomed by Lady Gray's people to join her crews, or are looking to get groomed, which means there's no way in hell they can be trusted. They'll sell you out to get any scrap of favor from her."

"Okay. Then keep going, and be as slow as you must to be careful. Results matter, but your survival is more important."

He grinned hugely, showing crumbs in his teeth. "You got it, Lord Seiji!"

"And what about the rest? Developments in the turf war between Lady Gray and Clan Olumnach?"

"Oh, that shit's on *hard*," he said with all the gleeful relish of a young boy describing violence and bloodshed. "It started pretty slow and it's still building up, but it's already at the point Olumnach and Gray's people don't meet and both of 'em walk away."

"How are the Rats faring in the middle of this?"

"Uncle Gently's playing it safe for now. He pays his protection to Lady Gray and has us do free jobs for her sometimes, but he doesn't wanna put the Rats in the middle of this. He's got us all watching everything both sides does, under strict orders not to sell either out to the other just yet."

"Mm . . . that doesn't sound like it'll hold for long."

"Well, not forever, but longer'n you might think, Lord Seiji. Uncle Gently's no fool, and he's been playing this game a long time. The fact he's got us hands-off says he doesn't know how to call it just yet, and that's bad news for Lady Gray. He'd stick with the established name if he was sure she could guarantee safety for the Rats. She's too busy keeping her own people's heads chained to their butts right now, and that right there is a shift in the whole situation."

"In broad terms," I said, affecting a casual tone, "I understand the main difference between Lady Gray's people and Clan Olumnach is that she has control over crime in the city, while the clan basically owns most of the bandit gangs operating in the countryside." That was the extent of Auldmaer's knowledge on the subject, which he insisted was just the basics anyone in Dount might have heard from rumor alone. "Any nuance you can add to that?"

"Well, that's the shape of it, Lord Seiji. I hear it gets murky where bandit crews end and the Olumnach Clansguard begins. Sorry, but the fact they *are* out of town means I don't get to overhear much about 'em. That's probably gonna change, though, with them pressing into the Gutters."

"Okay. Listen closely when you get the chance, but remember to be safe."

"You know it!" he grinned. "Anything solid you wanna know?"

"I realize you're not well-positioned for this, but I'm more interested in the outer gangs than Gray's people right now. Anything you can learn about the location or composition of other crews around Dount, I want to hear. As for Lady Gray's crews . . . by all means, pass along anything that seems particularly interesting. She's lower on my priority list, but I want to have the lay of the land before I move on her in earnest."

"Got it! Listen, if it's info on the gangs you want, I *do* know of a guy. He's a gobbo, though, and ain't based in town, so it might be hard to get an in, but I can sniff it out for you."

"I already know him," I said with a faint smile. "And believe me, I'll be following up on that. The issue is, the gangs pay him well to keep their business private."

"Oh. Damn." Gilder looked crestfallen. "But you *should* know, this city-country divide's the main reason this fight is only gonna get worse before it stops. Like, they got legit cause thanks to you—Lady Gray wants her damn money, and High Lord Caldimer's pissed as hell his kid got knifed, but they both been eyeballing each other's grift for years now. Now that it's finally on for real, neither one's gonna stop 'til the other's corebait. Whoever wins controls all crime on Dount. They *might* even be powerful enough to start making moves on Clan Aelthwyn then, and everybody knows that's what *both* dream about more than anything."

"Is that a fact," I murmured. "Well, good. I need time and room to maneuver before I'm ready to move in earnest. It sounds like I don't want to take *too* long, though."

"Longer this goes on, uglier it gets," he agreed, amazingly cheerful about it. "Course, the uglier it gets, the weaker both sides become."

"Exactly." Obviously both were still able to crush the likes of me almost without effort. I just had to build my strength without them noticing my presence while they whittled each other down. Which led me to my next order of business. "All right, Gilder, you've got your general marching orders—I want to know anything Uncle Gently knows, and ideally things he doesn't. *Especially* pertaining to the outlying gangs and the Olumnachs, but anything of value. More immediately, I'm going to call on your services as a guide to business in the Gutters."

"Gilder's your man, Lord Seiji!" he crowed. "What's it gonna be?"

I gave him my best, most mysterious smile. "Tonight, I want you to show me around the local brothels."

The boy's face lit up like I had just invented Christmas.

Aster, by contrast, very slowly turned her head to fix me with one of those oh-so-expressive looks she was so good at.

"There's no need to make that face at me, Aster," I said in a tone of indulgent geniality. "Don't worry, you get to come, too."

The Aster Look intensified.

21

In Which the Dark Lord Ministers to the Poor

In Fflyr Dlemathlys, the red-light district was actually a blue-light district. The traditional marker of a brothel, it seemed, was a lamp over the door which burned cool blue behind frosted glass; there were also paper lanterns strung on ropes across the entrances to Yrshith Street—or Cat Alley, as it was fondly called—with the same color illumination, and others here and there along its length.

Nightfall in Gwyllthean found Aster and I fully disguised and approaching the city's blue-light district from its discreet rear access. Aster was now in a coat of the same general style as the nicer one I'd bought her from the inner ring tailor, but rattier and with the addition of a deep hood—plus, of course, a scarf which doubled as a mask. I was also hooded, though I had donned a full-on cloak—for dramatic effect. I'd put together a mask from long strips of fabric, with more wrapped around my hands—again, just for effect—and under the cloak, another nondescript coat, plus a pair of scuffed leather boots because the shiny red ones I'd been wearing around were too distinctive. All of it was in nondescript shades of gray and brown.

I had been surprised to learn that the artifact greatsword was easily disguised. I'd been worried about that, but as it turned out, artifacts were very distinctive by design and we were far from the first people who'd wanted to make one harder to identify whilst engaging in subterfuge. It had been very easy to obtain the necessary bits and pieces to rewrap its grip, attach plain bits of gray akornin to its crossbar and pommel to hide their fancy design, and even smear a substance over its vivid blue blade to obscure its inlay and change the color to a murky almost-black.

So we were still a man with an accent and a woman with a greatsword, obviously disguising their identities, but . . . well, there was only so much that could be done. I just hoped the two of us hadn't made enough of an impression in the Gutters to be easily identified.

Yrshith Street was raucous and busy, with little sidewalk stands hawking a variety of portable goods, and scantily clad brothel employees lingering around the entrances of their establishments. The mostly jovial hubbub was audible all the way back where we were now, approaching from the rear. Apparently, part of the reason this had become the brothel district was because it was sandwiched between two of the canals, which gave the Gutters its name, so every building lining the street had its rear overlooking the waterfront. The grimy, stinking waterfront. There was a narrow walkway behind the brothels, reached by rickety-looking footbridges from the slum district across the canal, and even a few small boats tied up. Notably there were no women hanging out back here flashing the goods; the establishments, which had somebody covering their rear doors, had posted sinister-looking men with prominently displayed weapons.

It was one of these which we approached first. According to my intelligence from Gilder, the Alley Cat was the crown jewel of Cat Alley, such an institution that he didn't know which had been named for the other. It stood three stories, one more than any of its competitors.

A man in a sleeveless vest, which left his brawny arms exposed, was leaning against the wall next to the door, a club hanging from his belt, conspicuously cleaning his nails with a dagger way too large for that purpose. He studied the two of us pointedly at our approach, eyes narrowing as he fixed them on Aster and the wrapped greatsword handle protruding over her shoulder, but he apparently found no reason to challenge us, just nodding once as I stepped up to the door.

Opening it let a torrent of sound wash over us. The laughter and shouting I had expected, but what made me hesitate a step was the music. They were singing in there. Clearly not just a paid performer, despite the accompaniment of a guitar, and anyway not everyone participating could carry a tune, but it had to be *most* of those present joining in song. That wasn't so unusual, except for the complexity of it. This miscellaneous gaggle of hookers and johns were carrying on two distinct melodies in perfect counterpoint, one of which had people singing in dedicated harmony, as well as a baseline of baritone and alto voices keeping the rhythm along with the stomping of feet, and at least three sopranos holding prolonged high notes above the rest. This was *not* a simple or easy musical form, and the local Gutter trash were handling it with the ease of long practice. Apparently just for fun.

Well, blow me down, there just might be something of value in this godforsaken country after all. I made a mental note to begin learning about Dountol folk music at the earliest opportunity. Even though the current piece on offer was about the sexual exploits of some woman named Sabrit and apparently an entire battalion of enemy soldiers.

Putting that aside, I stepped the rest of the way in, far enough to let Aster enter behind me and pull the door shut, and paused to take stock.

The rear door opened onto a foyer area from which an upward staircase and a hallway branched off; I was just in time to see two pairs of legs vanishing up the former, to the accompaniment of feminine giggling. It opened out onto the main floor of the brothel, where a big public room contained tables around most of the floor and seating for couples along the walls, currently crowded with rowdy men and scarcely dressed young women. There was food and drink being served, though from this angle, I couldn't see where the kitchen was.

Positioned right where it had a perfect vantage over both the main public room and back door was a desk area recessed into the wall, with a beaded curtain partially concealing it from the front. It was well designed for the occupant to keep an eye on everything at once without being too accessible from the main room, which was additionally a step lower from the hall so that the desk loomed over the public area from behind its fringe of beads.

The woman sitting there regarded me and Aster with a raised eyebrow, drawing in a languid drag from the long-stemmed pipe she was smoking. I couldn't identify the substance being inhaled by its smell, though there was enough of it to form a visible haze near the ceiling. It was sweet and subtly spicy. Like the women out front, she was dressed in a distinctive kind of short robe of the style I'd seen noblewomen wearing, falling only to the knee and wide open at the neckline, with a length of ribbon wrapped around the waist. Unlike the noblewomen, the prostitutes had nothing on under theirs, showing off a lot of cleavage and leg, and the waist wrap was much wider and encircled their waists only a few times, no doubt for ease of access. This lady, too, appeared to be in her forties, with at least a decade of age on the other women I could see working the floor. Heavy cosmetics around her eyes didn't quite conceal the dark circles underneath. I couldn't see what manner of furniture she was perched upon, but it allowed her to lounge in a languorous position, which showed off that she was quite busty and constantly on the perilous edge of spilling out of her overworked neckline.

"Well, good evening, stranger," she said in a drawling purr that carried through the singing and stomping from out front, then somewhat spoiled the sultry effect by coughing. Her voice had a deep rasp to it which said she'd been at that pipe steadily for quite a few years. "The Cat welcomes all sorts. Just so you know, your lady friend there is welcome to drink, or to watch if you go to a room, but my girls don't do women. This is a Goddess-fearing establishment," she added with a deeply ironic smirk, followed by another short coughing fit. "And while we value your privacy, you *will* need to show your face before taking any girl to a room. I'll not expect them to touch gobrot or worse."

I stepped up to the desk, Aster shadowing me while the proprietess tried to eye me superciliously through another spell of coughing.

"Have you ever seen smoked meat being cured?" I asked her. My voice was slightly muffled by my mask.

The madame, or so I assumed her to be, smirked. "Stranger, I have seen more meat than you can imagine."

"Because that's the process happening to your lungs right now. You really shouldn't smoke that stuff. Or any stuff."

She took another long, slow drag, and very pointedly blew the smoke in a thin stream right into my face. Managing to make even that look seductive, I was too distracted to appreciate the effect, given I was doing my best not to give her the satisfaction of coughing.

She coughed, spoiling her own fun, but it didn't stop her from drawling at me. "You're a *bold* son, to step into a den of mortal pleasures and criticize its owner for her little pet vice."

"I am," I replied, holding up a hand. I did not speak, but just formed the word and the spell in my mind.

Heal.

Pink light flared around her. The woman straightened up and suddenly was sharp-eyed and holding a wicked-looking stiletto, which was a lot more impressive than all her seductive posturing because I legitimately couldn't conceive of where she'd been keeping it.

"Listen here, mister, you don't come into *my* place and begin flinging magic at . . ."

She trailed off, eyes going wide. I saw her fingers flex and then stop, as she wanted to touch her throat but had a pipe in one hand and a knife in the other. It was an understandable reflex; in the aftermath of the Heal, the woman spoke in a rich alto which sounded to me like that of a trained singer, with no trace at all of the smoker's rasp.

The madame's shoulders and chest moved as she inhaled slowly and deeply, then breathed out, and back in again, her expression growing more and more shocked as she breathed without difficulty for what I suspected was the first time in years. Her eyes remained fixed on me the whole time; I had deliberately arranged my hood and mask such that my face was in too much shadow for any of my features to be visible, unless someone were to shine a light straight into the hood. The woman stared, though, trying to work out who and what I was as she came to grips with what I'd done.

"I didn't ask for that," she finally said, her voice curt.

I nodded, just enough to make the motion visible even with my head covered. "Bold is the least of what I've been called."

"Magic like that . . . If this is some kind of extortion, you will leave disappointed. I *can't* pay for what that kind of healing costs. It's more than my whole establishment is worth. I know; I've checked," she added bitterly.

I shook my head once. "The price has been paid."

The madame narrowed her eyes to slits.

"What do you want here?"

"To heal," I said. "Show me any of your employees who need it."

"And what will *that* cost?"

"The price has been paid."

"By *whom*?"

I stared at her in silence until she sighed softly through her nose, realizing she wasn't going to get an actual answer.

I was proud of this gambit. I knew going in that people on the lowest rungs of the social ladder would be suspicious of a free handout no matter how desperate they were; without a doubt, everyone who came here offering anything was only looking to exploit them. My little slogan, *the price has been paid*, was my gimmick to get around this. It settled the question and raised more questions while simultaneously evading them, conjuring up mystery and intrigue around my appearance here.

I needed them curious first. And then . . . the next step. This would take time.

The brothel's owner had at least made her stiletto disappear as deftly as she had produced it, and now drummed her painted nails on the desk. She glanced at the boisterous common room, where the last refrain of Sabrit's adventure was just ending to laughter and cheers, wearing a frown of thought which looked a lot more genuine than her previously sultry expressions.

"I know when someone is up to something," she said finally, returning her stare to the darkness under my hood. "A woman doesn't prosper in the Gutters without being able to recognize that."

I didn't bother to defend myself, just regarded her in silence as she visibly decided that what I was offering was worth the risk of trusting a creepy stranger with mysterious powers.

"I don't know what other kind of magic you have, but mark me—if you harm *any* of my girls, I'll make sure you suffer for it."

"No one will be harmed unless they offer me harm first. I am only here to heal. The price—"

"Has been paid, yes, you mentioned that." She rose from her seat, the motion smooth and back to expressing over-the-top sensuality; I suspected that was a habit to which she defaulted whenever she wasn't actively shocked out of it. "Talilyn! Mind the desk."

A younger woman, no more than twenty-five, popped around the corner wearing the obligatory short robe, a flirtatious smile, and nothing else. She gave Aster and me a cursory glance that said we were an odd sight but she'd seen worse, then spoke to the madame in a pointed tone, which suggested her sweet expression was as much as mask as the fabric around my face.

"Sure thing, Miss Minifrit. Are you okay? You sound . . ."

Miss Minifrit lightly tapped Talilyn's nose with her pipe, somehow not spilling embers on her. "Later, girl. Cover 'til I come back."

"Of course."

They swapped places smoothly. Standing, Minifrit was a head shorter than me, but carried herself with a straight back and the lifted chin of a woman accustomed to being in control of her own place. I hadn't seen anyone but brown-skinned and black-haired lowborn since arriving in Yrshith Street, and she was no exception, but the madame projected more of a *presence* than some of the highborn I'd met, and most of the people I'd seen in and outside the King's Guild.

She deftly gathered myself and Aster with one gesture of her long pipe, turned, and proceeded down the hall.

We were led through another bead curtain marking off part of the hall, in front of which stood another man with a cudgel. He eyed us but did nothing else, Minifrit being all the passport we needed. Past the beads, the hall made a turn, and we continued on past a doorway into a hot, busy kitchen. Back here there were other girls in skimpy dress coming and going; they gave Aster and me curious looks, but knew better than to interfere with whatever the madame chose to do. Down we went, to the very end of the back hall.

There, Minifrit stopped before a closed door, turning a sharp look on me.

"If you want to heal," she said quietly, "this is the place to start." With that ominous pronouncement, she turned the latch, shoved the door open, and stepped inside. "Shut it after you."

We followed, Aster obeying; the soft click of the latch closed us off from the hall and left the room beyond rather cramped with the five people now in it. There were two young women present before we arrived, one of whom had stood up from her seat by the bedside with an alarmed expression; she wore one of those skimpy robes like the rest of the girls out front, but had on a kind of shawl, which concealed most of the skin it would display and suggested she wasn't working tonight.

The other woman lay in the room's sole bed, covered up to her neck with a single sheet. Her face . . . was almost unrecognizable. There were two distinct splits in her swollen lips, which looked as if they had only recently stopped bleeding. Indeed, the basin of water on the bedstand was alarmingly pink, as was the cloth sitting in it. One eye was so badly bruised it looked as if her skull around the socket had been broken. Her nose was *definitely* broken. The short, soft rasps of her labored breathing filled the room painfully.

I sucked in a short breath, frozen in place. The girl was so badly beaten I couldn't be sure, but she appeared to be no more than a teenager.

"Miss Minifrit?" the young woman who'd been tending to the injured girl asked, her tone full of wariness. "Who's this?"

Minifrit held out her hand in a limp-wristed gesture that somehow managed to be commanding, silencing the questions. The madame herself was staring at me closely with an analytical expression.

It didn't suit the Healer persona I was trying to put on, but as usual when I was shocked off my equilibrium, I instinctively took refuge in snark.

"And did the one who did *this* suffer for it?"

The other woman's face crumpled into a scowl, and she actually took a step toward me, stopping only at another gesture from Minifrit. The madame herself reacted the opposite way, her expression drawn and bitter.

"I don't suffer my girls to be mistreated," she said in a biting tone. "But if the world could ever be so sweet and simple, none of them would have fallen into this life in the first place. Most johns who dared do *half* of this would leave unconscious, head-first into the canal, and never be welcomed back, even if somebody bothered to fish them out still breathing. *But,* this is the Gutters, and there are people to whom even I cannot afford to say *no.*"

I shifted my hood to look at her, the fabric obscuring my view of the injured girl. I could still hear her labored breathing; it sounded like she could barely expand her lungs.

"People like Lady Gray."

"Oh, *that* one would make a show of sympathy to a working girl's life," Minifrit said with a mocking laugh that contained zero humor. "Out loud, and meaning not a word of it. Then again, she's no worse than some of the other matrons on this street. It's the men *under* her whom I have to deal with, the ones using her authority in the knowledge that I can't exactly walk into their mistress's lair and register a complaint. The kind of swine who gets off on doing *this* to a girl," she gestured with her pipe at the bedridden girl, "is also exactly the kind who loves nothing more than being able to impose himself where he's not welcome or wanted. Petty little creatures, permanently dissatisfied with their lot in life, and too stupid to cope with it any way other than by making someone else's lot even worse. They are . . . a *perennial* problem."

She turned to face me directly, her stare a challenge.

"But to answer your question, healer . . . it is not so simple, or so easy, to deal with such a man. That doesn't mean I can't. Just that it takes . . . time, and some doing."

I didn't bother to answer the implied warning, instead stepping forward to the bedside. Instinct wanted me to put myself anywhere but here, but I'd come here for strategic purposes, and found myself compelled to act by something deeper and more important.

"Wait, did you say healer?" the other girl asked. "Can he—"

Heal.

The flare of pink light cut her off. It was far more intense than usual—blinding in the cramped room, such that both women shied back from the bed, and I had to shut my eyes against it. Apparently, the spell had a lot more work to do than I'd ever given it before.

But work it did. With a deep gasp, the young woman sat bolt upright in bed. I immediately shifted my head away at the revelation she had nothing on under that sheet, only seeing enough to verify that every injury had been washed away from her face . . . And that she was, indeed, barely Yoshi's age. If that.

My god in heaven. I knew teenage prostitution wasn't anything new; it even happens in modern Japan, though "compensated dating" in one of the world's safest, cleanest, least violent nations isn't even in the same ballpark as what I was seeing here. Every new day brought me another reason to raze Fflyr Dlemathlys to its foundations and salt the earth. Was this how Virya convinced ordinary people from the modern world to embrace the mantle of Dark Lord and start conquering and pillaging? Just dump them in the shittiest place she could find with an overpowered set of magical skills and let nature take its course? Because if that was the plan, as much as I hated her, so help me, it was working.

"Kastrin," Minifrit said, gliding swiftly to the bedside and pulling the sheet up over the girl's chest, to my relief. "How do you feel?"

"I . . . I'm . . ." Wonderingly, she reached up to touch her own face. "Fine? I feel . . . really good, actually. Miss Minifrit, your voice! What's happening? Wait, who is this?"

Minifrit looked up at me, speculation naked on her features. "This is the Blessed who healed you, Kastrin."

"And who *paid* for that?" the recently injured girl demanded.

"The price has been paid," I intoned. Miss Minifrit pursed her lips at me, but the other two girls tilted their heads to one side in almost comedic unison.

"But . . . who *are* you?" Kastrin asked.

"A healer."

Minifrit straightened up, keeping one hand protectively upon Kastrin's shoulder, now that the girl herself was holding up the sheet.

"I still don't know what it is you're actually up to, stranger," the madame said, pointing at me with her pipe. It appeared to have gone out at some point. "But if this is what you are willing to do for my girls . . . Nightlady take me, I will risk it."

"Good." After what I'd just seen I felt sick, but I'd come here for a purpose, and it was far too late to back out. "Then who is next?"

22

In Which the Dark Lord
Pets the Dog

Over the next hour I learned that Miss Minifrit was a capable administrator, as well as someone who had the respect of her working girls and did her best to look after their interests. One by one, she singled out and brought before me women who needed medical attention of one kind or another, and also one of her bouncers who had taken a kick to the knee recently and was still limping. She did this without interrupting her business, or revealing to any of her clients that there was anything out of the ordinary going on in the back halls. Some were discreetly pulled off the main floor, some collected as they left the private rooms having finished up with clients, all brought to me with no disturbance to the Alley Cat's operations.

Early on, Minifrit asked me if I needed to see what was amiss in order to heal it. She did this in front of a woman of barely twenty who had nothing obviously wrong with her; the poor girl looked at the floor in clear mortification. I did not, and told her so. After that, at least half of the women brought to me showed no signs of anything wrong, though a few had patterns of sores along their lips, hairlines, or the backs of their hands. I'd known before coming here what prostitutes in a dump like this would mostly need healing from, and just worked my magic without comment.

There were other things, too. Nobody else had been beaten nearly as badly as Kastrin, but a handful of the women had bruises and scrapes in suggestive places. One had a bad burn on her arm from a kitchen accident; to judge by the way she burst out crying upon being Healed and had to be stopped from hugging me by both Minifrit and Aster, it must have hurt her a lot. Another just had a bad toothache, which seemed almost prosaic given the rest of what I'd seen here, but which I knew was a serious matter. In a pre-dentistry society, an untreated infection like that could eventually kill, and it would be a very painful death.

I quickly found that I preferred the suspicion to the gratitude. It was . . . sensible, even comforting, the way some of them warily watched me, waiting for the other shoe to drop, unwilling to believe anyone with this kind of power would do such a thing with no ulterior motive. Mostly, I supposed, because they were right. My ultimate intentions weren't harmful to them—or at least, I told myself, no more dangerous than the way they were living now—but I was definitely not the selfless saint I was pretending to be here.

Kastrin herself emerged from her room, dressed in one of those short robes, both so Minifrit could show her to other girls as proof of my power and apparently so she herself could stare at me as if she could figure out the mystery of the Healer by sheer force of will.

Minifrit definitely never got over her certainty that I had ulterior motives. I suspected that when she tried to offer me money, it was at least half in an attempt to square any debt so I couldn't call it in later. I had no intention of doing that anyway, but I naturally refused. In fact, in keeping with my persona and the legend I had come here to build, I declined any and all payment, no matter how mundane. Minifrit did try to bargain me down to accepting drinks or a hot meal, even hinted obliquely at sharing rumors she had acquired concerning the movements of Lady Gray and her cartel. That was the only one that even tempted me, and made me reflect that I'd made a tactical error by mentioning the criminal queen of the slums at all. I turned her down, though, as much as data to fill in the gaps of what Gilder could overhear would have helped me. I was after bigger game.

Minifrit specifically did not offer me free sex, though she didn't intervene and simply watched my reactions when half a dozen of her employees did. I enjoy getting laid as much as the next guy, but I was not even tempted. I'm sure a brothel is plenty of fun if you go there as a client and get the full treatment, but from my position behind the curtain, cleaning up the aftermath, I only found myself sickened and enraged by this whole business.

That was good, I told myself. I had to learn how to channel that, before I could teach these women to do the same.

When Minifrit decided there was no one else who immediately needed my attention, I had to disengage myself from a small adoring crowd at the back door. Not all of those who'd benefited from my magic participated; I'm sure some just took the benefit and ran back to their business, while quite a few remained wary of my motives. There were enough to make it physically hard to get out of the building, though, tearful and gazing at me as if I were the only beacon of hope in their grim world.

The guilt was crushing. I think it might've been worse than when I'd Immolated Larinet.

We made it down the boardwalk one building's distance, just out of easy earshot from the Alley Cat's backdoor bouncer, when Minifrit finally asserted her authority and ushered everyone back inside and back to their tasks. Then, I finally had to stop to breathe, and gather myself.

"Seems like that woman could've been more grateful," Aster muttered, stepping close so I could hear her voice even muffled by the scarf. "There are *kings* who'll never get that kind of treatment."

"Some people are just ingrates," I said. "Around here, though, I figure everybody's got reason to be suspicious of a free lunch."

"True enough."

"Biribo, any insight?"

He poked his triangular head out of my collar. One benefit of this cloak-and-longcoat ensemble was that, unlike the open nobleman's coat I normally wore, I could keep my familiar close enough to whisper info to me as he found a need.

"Only a couple Blessed among the patrons, boss, and they were just there to screw. No sign anybody was interested in or even aware of you. Except for one of the girls you healed—that tall number with the long nose, midtwenties, scar on her left forearm? Blessed with Might. Probably a washed-up former adventurer."

"*Adventurers* can end up working in brothels?" I demanded in muted disbelief.

"It's not an easy life," Aster said quietly. "Very dependent on luck. If you don't get the right rewards from Spirits or dungeons, you can find yourself unable to pay bills or Guild dues. Success grants equipment and breeds reputation, which means opportunities. Lack of success is a cycle going the other way."

"Shit," I muttered, then drew in a steadying breath and let it back out. "Okay, that's enough lollygagging. On to the next place."

I had not come here expecting to *enjoy* my jaunt through the sordid underbelly of the blue-light district. I'm not an idiot. And yet, once again, it seemed I had underestimated the real horror of which Ephemera was capable. I had not expected this night's work to be the most harrowing thing I'd yet experienced on this world. Eventually, surely, my expectations had to get low enough that I couldn't keep being shocked. Surely?

One after another, we went to every brothel in Cat Alley that we could reach in the course of one night.

Our reception wasn't the same everywhere, of course. A few places told me to fuck off entirely. Everyone greeted me and my gifts with suspicion, varying only by how quickly and how much it abated once I got to Healing and not accepting any payment. I just told them all, time and again, "the price has been paid." Hopefully after this night's work, it wouldn't take long for that little meme to get around. Whatever else I was doing, I *had* to be starting rumors.

I never pressed when told to leave; over future visits, I knew, I'd build a reputation which would make me more welcome here.

The quality of these brothels correlated directly with the quality of life of those working in them. Minifrit's was one of few places with workers well into their thirties; it seemed that on average, a Gwyllthean sex worker's lifespan topped out at twenty-five. It diminished all the way down to the worst establishments, in some of which I saw nothing but teenagers who looked like they'd endured at least thirty years of beating and deprivation. I didn't want to know what happened to the women after age and use wrung every last spark of profitable life out of them. Unfortunately for me, I got to learn that anyway.

The madames weren't all as protective of their girls as Minifrit. No fewer than five times I cast Heal on a woman clearly breathing her last rattling gasps, lying outside the rear door of her place of work, because at least her madame had the good taste to wait until she was dead before tipping her into the canal. I got to learn that was the designated final resting place of a dead girl, thanks to the four cases I was too late to help. The rats and crawns didn't always wait until they were dead to start scavenging.

It was ironic that after living through the aftermath of lethal fights with bandits and nobles alike, it was by providing basic medical care that I learned the limits of my supposedly world-changing Heal spell.

It didn't regrow anything—I could do nothing for missing teeth. Or fingers, toes, or eyes. Heal didn't seem to do much for sheer exhaustion, and had no effect on psychological problems at all. If there was any magic that treated PTSD, depression, or simple despair, it was clearly above my pay grade.

I saw . . . just so many cases of disease. A brothel district was practically a petri dish, and not just for STDs; anything contagious would tear through such a place like a forest fire, especially when it was a damp and narrow stretch between two fouled canals. I took to casting Heal on both myself and Aster after we exited every brothel, just on general principles. In one dim little hole literally named the Hole, I discovered they catered to a very specialized clientele, even though none of the clients were in evidence, simply because every woman working there had an advanced case of gobrot.

Almost none of the many, *many* injuries I Healed looked accidental. Not only bruises and lacerations, but multiple broken bones, obvious stab wounds, and one case of a clearly cracked skull with evidence of brain damage; the poor girl was barely responsive. I had been afraid even Heal wouldn't fix that, but she seemed fine after I cast it. A few times I was afraid my spell was starting to wear out, but no; it turned out that even with the black eyes fixed, those eyes were just too sunken and shadowed to make much of a visible difference.

For some of the men who came here, I guess it was all part of the fun. Visit Cat Alley, fuck the women, and then beat them.

One night in this place had wrung me the hell out. I felt physically nauseated that I even knew a spell like Enamor, and several times almost asked Aster to immediately kill me if she ever saw me use it on someone; though, each time I refrained from bringing it up.

Dawn found Aster and I having made our departure from Yrshith Street along the rear boardwalk on the other side from the one where we'd started. The pair of us walked in silence until we came to an intersection with one of the main trade highways running through Gwyllthean.

I stopped, and then she stopped. The city was waking up; the gates were open, traffic was already increasing, and vendors had begun hawking breakfast on the go to the passing travelers. We stood in a shady alley's mouth, watching people go by and saying nothing for a while.

"We should probably try to grab some rest. I don't think either of us has enough energy to make the whole walk back to the fortress from here."

"I don't . . . think . . . I'll be able . . . to sleep." Her delivery was halting, as if she had to grope for every word.

"Not gonna have pleasant dreams," I agreed in a dull tone. "Better an inn than collapsing on the road halfway through the khora, though."

She nodded again. That close, I could see into her hood; her eyes looked utterly shell-shocked. They looked about how I'd felt.

". . . you're going to want to do that again, aren't you."

"We are going to do that *repeatedly*," I answered.

Slowly, her hood shifted in another nod. "Well, I guess it's good that somebody does it."

"Mm." I was in no mood to dig into my real motives.

"If they can all *live* that way, we'd be pretty chickenshit to bail out after just having to *see* it."

"Yeah."

"I feel like I owe Miss Minifrit an apology. She's doing pretty good by her workers."

"Yeah."

We stood there for a few minutes longer, then silently turned and headed back into the city.

We managed a couple hours of fitful sleep, dressed in our nicer inner-ring clothes with disguises packed away in bundles, and left well before noon, which was for the best in the interests of getting back to North Watch before midnight.

For the sake of making good time, we didn't stay to eat at the inn. We just grabbed some breakfast from the stalls on the way out of town, along with some more easily carried food for the trip. Once you got used to the spicing, Fflyr street food wasn't terrible. I very determinedly did not think about the conditions in which it was cooked, and had developed a habit of casting self-Heal after meals, whenever no one was watching. No food poisoning so far.

I still didn't know these paths, but it seemed Aster had wandered all over Dount during her adventuring years and at my request took us on a different route than before; I figured it couldn't hurt to vary our paths to and from the city, even if nobody had reason to be stalking us yet. Cautious habits were good ones to get into. My earlier recklessness and how frighteningly close it had brought me to disaster still haunted me at times. Looking back, I had to wonder whether Virya had been somehow pulling strings on my behalf. Realistically, I should've gotten my ass killed at least twice in the first three days.

Today's route had us circumnavigating the outer fringes of the city for a short distance. We walked in the partial shadow of a retaining wall of akor-thist blocks, which separated the path from an agricultural field on one side, and the other consisting of vacant lots, mostly full of trash interspersed with dilapidated outbuildings. Unlike the outlying structures closer to the main road, which were used for trade, these old barns and warehouses seemed abandoned. I wondered as we walked whether Gwyllthean was suffering some kind of economic downturn to result in this, and also noted how extremely useful a variety of unoccupied structures, however rickety, would be to the likes of me, or Clan Olumnach, or Lady Gray.

While this was technically the outskirts of the city, the only "city" in sight was more or less ruins; in contrast to our time in the Gutters, this suburban footpath was as quiet as the countryside. Thus, we were both startled into freezing at a sudden growl.

Aster drew her sword, I subconsciously formed the weight of Immolate in my mind, and Biribo buzzed out of Aster's pocket and up over our heads to gain an eagle-eyed view of the battlefield.

A second later, Biribo let out a hissing little laugh and descended to rejoin us.

"Relax, guys. I think you can take 'er."

I hadn't seen the source of the growl when it first sounded, but now it moved, a shadow distinguishing itself from the overall dimness in the lee of a broken-down wagon someone had ditched here. Not approaching us, but circling to the side, and continuing to make that warning growl.

"Oh," I said, relaxing. "Wow, I hope nobody saw that."

"Don't get cocky," Aster said tersely, not putting away her sword. "Just because it's not a rampaging khorodect doesn't mean it's not dangerous. People get killed by stray dogs."

Our "foe" shifted into the sunlight, affording me a good look. Poor thing was limping and looked starved; some kind of mange-like rash had consumed what looked like half its coat. There was no foam dripping from the bared teeth, but who knew what kind of diseases it might be carrying? The Ephemera version of rabies was probably as gratuitously horrible as everything else on this asinine hell world.

If it had happened on any other morning, I probably would have just scared the dog away and gone about my business. But I was sleep-deprived and coming off a truly nightmare-inducing night of trying to aid the bedraggled and abandoned, and having to live with the reality that what I was doing was more for my own benefit than theirs.

Aster's advice rang in my ears—do what you have to, but whenever you can, be *kind*.

"Lord Seiji?" she said incredulously as I stepped forward and knelt on the path. The stray dog bared her fangs at me and let out a furious warning bark.

I held out a hand toward it. "**Tame Beast**."

"Oh yeah, *that's* a productive use of your powers," Biribo complained. I didn't dignify him with a response, busy taking in this new experience.

Immediately she relaxed, straightening up. Her ears rose, revealing one was half missing. Hesitantly at first, head lowered, she stepped toward me. Her upraised tail wagged in a jerky little motion almost as if she had forgotten how.

This was not at *all* like using that spell on a slime. Those things were basically amoebas; they didn't seem to be even conscious in any meaningful way. "Taming" them effectively put them under my intuitive mental control. My experience with Auldmaer's dhawls was another thing still; those were already tame animals that had just needed calming down, their placid dispositions regarding me as just another person once the magical shortcut had caused them to view me as such.

A dog, by contrast, was pretty smart by animal standards, with a lot of their social instincts bred over millennia specifically for interaction with humans. This one was clearly feral. I couldn't feel her mind in the same way as the slimes, but there was now a . . . familiarity. Watching her every hesitant movement as she approached me, I could interpret the nuances of her body language as if I'd raised her from a puppy. No—as if I were an expert in canine behavior who had raised and trained her from birth. It wasn't telepathy or mental control, just . . . a bond. A shortcut to achieve the same communion.

"Poor girl," I murmured. Her tail began wagging in earnest as she stepped forward and pressed her nose into my hand. "Just look what a mess you are. **Heal**."

Pink light burst; I could tell by the minute shift of her posture that she was startled, but she didn't jerk away. She knew I'd done it, and trusted me.

It made a *world* of difference. Gone was the limp; her coat was restored to a much greater plushness—no sign of that mange. The ear didn't regrow, and she was still thin, but at least the rejuvenated coat disguised her ribs. She was a sizable dog, bigger than a German Shepherd, her shaggy coat black with gray and brown markings. Unsurprisingly, centuries of evolution on Ephemera had caused some genetic drift from dogs as I knew them; she had a rather bushy tale like a fox, a triangular face that looked almost feline from some angles, and an odd combination of long, lean legs and a bulldog's burly chest. Altogether a scruffy, awkward-looking creature, even restored to good health.

"Hey, Aster, gimme one of those meat pies."

"Are you serious?"

"Don't worry, I'm not gonna feed her *your* lunch. I'll just eat when we're back at the fortress."

She handed one over without further complaint; in fact, when I glanced up, I caught her smiling.

"Don't tell me you're planning on bringing the dog with us," Biribo exclaimed while she got down to scarfing the meat pie, tail now wagging furiously.

"Dogs are very useful creatures," I said solemnly. "Aren't you, Junko?"

"*Junko?*"

"Well, I have to call her something."

"That's a name?" Aster asked uncertainly.

"A common enough girl's name, where I'm from." Still kneeling and ruffling Junko's ears while she ate, I grinned up at Aster and gestured at the lot full of old rubbish amid which the dog had been hiding. "Plus, I found her in the junk."

It took me a moment of staring at her nonplussed expression to realize what I'd said was *thwilic*, the Fflyr word for *trash*. Fluently speaking a language I had never actually *learned* caused some weird effects now and then. My brain kept assuming any language I was speaking that wasn't Japanese must be English, when neither was any use to me here.

"That's a bilingual pun," I explained.

"Ah. Impressive."

"Trust me, if you speak those two languages, that was hilarious."

"I'm sure it must be, Lord Seiji."

"You hear how she talks to me?" I complained to Junko. "She thinks I can't tell when she's being sarcastic, but *I can*."

Junko had finished my meat pie, and now barked at Aster, still wagging her tail furiously. Grinning in spite of herself, Aster leaned forward to scratch the dog's ears, causing the tail to loudly thump against her own flanks.

We had both needed this after the night we'd had. There's just something *pure* about dogs.

Aster looked up at me, her expression growing more thoughtful, and I gestured expansively as I started moving again. Junko fell into step alongside me, followed by Aster and Biribo buzzing along in the rear. "Go ahead and ask; I know you're dying to."

She sighed, then nodded. "Why prostitutes, Lord Seiji?"

"Looting caravans is all well and good for pocket change. If what you really want is to strike a blow at the foundations of society itself . . ." I turned a grin on her as we walked. "Invent feminism."

Man, that would've been such a good line on which to end the conversation, but Aster had exactly as much patience for my bullshit as usual.

"I really hope you get a lot of entertainment from dropping these arcane references to your old world, Lord Seiji, especially since it's apparently more important to you than me being able to understand what the hell we're trying to do."

I decided not to call her out for sassing me. She never did that in front of the others, and also she wasn't wrong.

"I need recruits—enough of them to form a sufficiently big force to take on the other bandit gangs."

"Right, obviously, but . . . Really, the *whores*?"

"Are you suggesting women are less valuable than men?" I asked archly.

"Junko, bite him."

Junko licked my hand.

"It's not about what they can do *now*," I said, wiping my hand on my coat. "Fighting is something you can be taught. I bet Goose and Sakin know enough about violence and skullduggery to adequately train whoever I decide to bring home. It's about finding people who've been spat on and mistreated enough that they'll be willing to not only turn bandit, but also actively work to overthrow the whole social order. And that's a *lot* of people, Fflyr Dlemathlys being the fucking mess it is. I need, specifically, to do this without drawing the attention that will inevitably come if I start removing a bunch of people from the city—and I do need to recruit a bunch at once rather than building in ones and twos over the course of years. Aside from Virya breathing down my neck, the turf war between Lady Gray and the Olumnachs is my only window of opportunity, and it won't stay open forever. Someone will *notice* if I take enough warm bodies to do what needs doing, no matter where I take them from. So I need to recruit those who won't be missed. I need to make the established powers not take me seriously. Oh, ha ha, look at this idiot Healer, trying to make an army of working girls, what a joke. This country's prejudices against women can be used to bring it down."

"Huh," Biribo commented. "Y'know what, that's actually a good angle. Sus out the situation and find an unconventional way to approach it that increases your power. A real Dark Lord move, boss."

Aster shook her head. "I think you're going to find it harder than you expect to motivate them into action, Lord Seiji. Gratitude for the healing is only going to take you so far. Not far enough, I don't think. Not *nearly* far enough."

"That's only the first step. Next I have to remind them of all the reasons they have to be *angry*."

She still didn't look convinced. "These are women who've fallen all the way down the social ladder and have been whacked by every rung they passed. All the fight was beaten out of them years ago."

"Aster," I said, staring ahead, "it's me, Seiji. One way or another, if there is one thing I can manage to inspire in people, it is *rage*."

"Hm," she mused after a long moment, "I guess that's so."

Hellish as the night had been, as we walked on, Junko pressed herself against my leg, and I felt a little bit better.

23

In Which the Dark Lord Wheels and Deals

And that squares us," Maugro said, sweeping the stacks of coins off the table into a bag, which he swiftly made disappear into his coat in an impressive feat of legerdemain. The goblin grinned up at me. "A pleasure doin' business, Lord Seiji!"

"The first of many, let's hope," I replied, lifting my cup to him in a toast and then taking a sip. Prepared now, I managed not to grimace. Fucking Fflyr, what was the matter with these people? Why would they put that sour sap in *wine*? You can just drink vinegar if you're that much of a masochist.

"Sweet music to my ears!" Maugro mimicked the gesture and had a much deeper quaff. "The more I see, the more I think you and I have a real future together."

"Oh? And here I haven't even had time to put in that goblin-sized furniture yet."

That caused a minor shift; the two goblin bruisers standing guard over the tunnel entrance turned their heads slightly to stare at me, and Mindzi's brazenly flirtatious simper faded as an analytical look peeked through her facade.

"It's a funny thing," he mused, idly swirling his wine. "Now, I know for a fact that caravan I gave you the info on made it to town fully intact, if a little behind schedule. Seems its crew were telling a really weird story about being attacked by slimes, of all the damn things. But because those idiots let themselves get chased off by *slimes*, or whatever else it actually was, the good Master Auldmaer didn't even have to pay their full wages. So he *saved* money on that debacle. What's an even *funnier* thing is the disaster that happened that very night to the much bigger Crown Rose Company caravan that was his most direct competition. Here I thought sellin' the guy out like I did was putting him over a barrel, but it seems he made out like a bandit. So to speak," he added, grinning.

"How fortuitous for him," I said in my mildest, politest, most noncommittal tone. Just because I didn't use that skill by preference didn't mean I did not have it. You don't survive in Japan without being able to put on a blank mask of courtesy at need.

"Now, I'm accustomed to dealing with people who don't have a thought in their heads beyond their next meal," said Maugro. "Not all, to be sure! You do business with enough bandits, though, you start to notice bandits are just people who've washed out of normal society, by and large."

"Do tell," I murmured, glancing aside at Aster, who was lounging against the wall by the kitchen door. She and Junko were all the guards I had with me for this meeting, and Aster was there more to enforce the rest of my bandits going about their business—they'd be rubbernecking rather than protecting me from any goblin shenanigans. The goblins seemed a lot more intimidated by the dog.

"They ain't big picture people, is what I'm saying," Maugro continued, giving me a knowing look over the rim of his cup as he took a sip of wine. "Which is how I've learned to be glad to meet those few who *are*. When a new client shows a capacity to make a long-term plan and finagle the bigger prize instead of grasping for a cheap payday . . . now, that's how I *know* we've got a profitable relationship ahead of us."

"Mm, I *love* a man with a nice, big . . . brain," Mindzi purred, lounging against the table leg in a pose that made it seem she was in danger of melting down it. I glanced again at Aster, catching her amidst an eyeroll so intense I was surprised it wasn't audible.

"Can I ask you guys a serious question?"

"Why, Lord Seiji!" Maugro spread his hands wide, nearly sloshing his wine. "Serious questions are what I *do*! As well as every other kind. What's on your mind?"

"I mean no offense, but . . ." I nodded to Mindzi. "Does this usually . . . work? I'm still acclimating to this country, but the impression I've been getting is that human/goblin . . . intermingling . . . is not socially acceptable here."

She aborted her stationary slinking so abruptly it almost looked like a stumble; her ensuing pout didn't look like the ostentatious moues of before, but an expression of genuine annoyance. I guess it's an unwritten rule of that game that you don't point out it's being played.

"If you'll forgive me for answering a question with a question," Maugro said pensively, "are human/goblin relations generally pleasant and positive where you're from?"

"Where I'm from, there are *no* goblins. You guys are the first I've ever met."

"I *see*." He took another sip of the wine, studying my face. "Well, to give you the straight answer, your impression is correct. So tallboys who have a taste for little green meat gotta be *discreet* about it, see? We've learned it's a sign of interest when a guy isn't overtly disgusted by the first attempt. But I guess a lot of the usual Fflyr rules don't apply to you, huh, Lord Seiji?"

"Indeed, it's a shame we had to meet like this," I said diplomatically, addressing Mindzi directly. "I bet it would've been quite an experience. Alas, I'm not dumb enough to get entangled with a girl introduced to me by my information broker."

Maugro brayed with laughter, but Mindzi huffed and lightly tapped his shoulder with the back of her hand. "Aw, see, and he's even a gentleman! Figures, I finally meet a tallboy who's *worth* it and the whole thing's a non-starter, thanks to *you*."

"Hah! It's only thanks to *me* you ever meet anybody at all, ungrateful wench." He swatted her rump, eliciting a squeal, and I experienced an unexpected surge of dislike.

I repressed it. This was just over-sensitivity due to spending the night seeing the worst Cat Alley had to offer. It wasn't like I'd ever been an ardent defender of women's rights, far from it; me getting pissy about little things like this would be the height of hypocrisy.

However, a side effect of my use of Tame Beast on Junko meant that she was *incredibly* sensitive to even tiny shifts of my mood. She lifted her head, pointing her nose at Maugro, and swiveled her ears partly back.

Maugro tensed, Mindzi scuttled behind his chair with wide eyes, and both of his bodyguards put hands to their clubs and took a half step forward, looking more alarmed than aggressive.

Yeah, they were *terrified* of Junko. I reached down to scratch her ears, also repressing my amusement, and she leaned into my hand, relaxing. After a moment, so did the goblins. I was really trying not to have fun at their expense, both because that would be incredibly poor manners for a host and because I was pretty sure this was exactly how *I'd* feel about meeting a dog that stood head and shoulders taller than myself on all fours.

"Since outstanding business is settled then, let's talk future business," I said aloud.

"Ah, that's just what I was hoping to hear," Maugro replied, his usual garrulous grin reasserting itself. "What'll it be, boss? We doin' long-term arrangements, or you have something in particular you wanna know?"

"Bit of both, actually. For starters, I want information on an adventuring party I encountered in Gwyllthean."

"That kinda thing's my bread and jam. How much *do* you know about 'em? As long as I can find them and they're still on Dount, I can dig up details."

"Just basic descriptions and first names, sorry. Also, they just spent a night in jail."

"Ah!" Maugro seemed genuinely pleased at that, pulling out a pocket notebook and a kind of pencil made from little akorshil slivers tied around a stick of charcoal. "More than enough! And a relief to hear, Lord Seiji. You wouldn't believe the piddly tidbits some of my clients expect me to craft a damn dossier out of. What've we got?"

I gave him a quick rundown on Yoshi and the harem; he raised his eyebrows once at the mention that Flaethwyn—whose name I had to get Aster to pronounce for me—was an elf, but aside from that was all business.

"Got it. This shouldn't even be difficult. A foreigner, an elf, and pink hair; group like that'll stick out like a broken toe. Any particular reason you're looking for their details, Lord Seiji?"

"Any particular reason you need to know that?"

He shrugged, tucking his notebook back into his coat. "Hey, it's your commission; you're the boss. You want me to dig up everything that is or can be known about this gang, I can do that. You want them stalked and get a daily report of everything they do, I can put people on it. But that shit ain't free, Lord Seiji. I find most clients want to know something *specific*, which lets me tailor my investigations. I save time, and therefore you save money, because you better believe I don't work for charity."

I hummed softly in consideration. Well, if he was going to be looking into them anyway, he'd undoubtedly hear the story.

"They accosted me on the street in Gwyllthean; that's how they ended up in jail. While I'm *fairly* sure I've dissuaded them from further nonsense like that, I remain curious and somewhat concerned. So . . . I'm not sure how much I *can* narrow down your inquiries, Maugro. I just want a more complete picture of who I'm dealing with."

"Ah, so a profile of the individuals and the group, with an emphasis on their interest in *you*, and an optional digression into anything particularly interesting that pops up?"

"That sounds about perfect, yes."

"Ain't my first trip to the races," he said, winking. "I'll get on it soon as we're done here, Lord Seiji. So, what's the rest of that 'bit o' both' you mentioned?"

"A few items I want to keep on top of as a matter of long-term interest." I set down my wine; there was a limit to how much of that stuff I could stomach at a time. Note to self: ask Auldmaer about his supplier. "First off, let me just make sure I'm all paid up on the deal whereby you ensure my privacy."

"Covered in our preceding transaction," Maugro assured me with his shark's grin. "That stipend gets tallied monthly, and don't worry, Lord Seiji; for a customer in good standing such as yourself, I offer a bit of leeway if the timing gets awkward come payday. Your continued business is more valuable to me than whatever pocket money I'd get from selling you out."

"And isn't *that* reassuring," I drawled. "To be clear—I'm not just talking about my gang's location, but *any* details about my presence. I do not want to be on anybody's radar until *I* decide to move. I am willing to pay whatever is . . . appropriate."

"Dunno what a radar is, but I got the gist. Anyway, nothing you need to worry about there, Lord Seiji. When you buy discretion from Maugro, you *get* discretion, without qualifiers. You'll see what I mean if you ask me to sell out any of the other gangs."

"Which brings us to my next standing request."

He sighed, putting on a regretful expression. "Uh-oh. Is this conversation about to get awkward?"

"No more than necessary, I hope. Relax, I'm not going to ask you to betray any confidences. I would, however, like to inquire what it would cost me to be the first notified if any of the other gangs fall behind in their payments."

Slowly, Maugro and Mindzi both raised their heads, red eyes narrowing as they studied me closely. Oh yeah, that girl was definitely a sharp operator when she wasn't putting on the floozy act.

"To be clear, I'm definitely interested in knowing where to find the other gangs, and what to expect if I should decide to pay them a visit. And since I know your professional integrity is well out of my price range, I would simply like to place myself at the top of the waiting list. If and when one of them can't pay for your discretion any longer, I want the first option to buy their details. I'm willing to negotiate a . . . reasonable retainer for this consideration."

"You know something, Lord Seiji," Maugro said, leaning back in the chair and looking pensive, "you are the first human I've done business with who asked me that."

"Oh, come on," I grinned, "no need to flatter me. I find *that* hard to believe."

"Yeah, no fuckin' kidding!" he exclaimed. "Most of the gang leaders've tried to get me to sell out the others, but not one ever thought to propose an arrangement like you just did. It's been *years* of doing this and . . . not a one! It's the *first* thing I would ask in your position. Between you and me, I've spent a fair amount of my free time just trying to wrap my head around how a person ends up in charge of a bandit gang without being able to apply such a basic amount of forethought and problem solving."

I didn't answer out loud, but now it occurred to me that he'd answered his own question—bandit leaders *ended up* in charge, they didn't aspire to it. Aside from the mysterious Lady Gray, there didn't seem to be any real criminal masterminds at work here. People just fell through the cracks of society, thanks to Fflyr Dlemathlys's society being more cracks than solid ground, and because law enforcement was a joke, culling bandit gangs usually fell to either clansguard—organized thugs serving only the desires of some spoiled aristocrat—or adventurers. Which were just *less* organized thugs, heavily armed and hungry for glory.

"I gotta say, Lord Seiji," Maugro continued after a short pause, in which all of us were apparently lost in our respective thoughts, "you think like a goblin."

"Let me guess. That is meant as a compliment—one for which most humans on Dount would draw a weapon on you."

"Right on both counts," he grinned.

I picked up my cup and toasted him. "Then I gratefully accept the sentiment in the spirit in which it's offered."

"That being said . . . y'know what, consider yourself on the list." He raised his own cup in response. "I know I said I don't do charity, but it ain't like this costs me anything. Soon as one of the gangs slips up, you'll be the first to know. And if somebody else grows an actual brain and spends money on first dibs, I'll inform you and give the chance to buy 'em out."

"Why, that's very generous of you, Maugro," I replied, deliberately keeping any irony out of my voice. Obviously, his next move would be to give someone else that idea, and thus ignite a bidding war while still earning goodwill from me. "This is all related to my next point, too. I'd like information on Clan Olumnach. Or are they also up to date on their discretion bill?"

"*Hah*," Mindzi spat, suddenly scowling. "Those stuck-up assholes wouldn't even—"

"There, there, hon," Maugro said soothingly, reaching over to pat her hip. "Bit of history there, Lord Seiji. Nah, I think you'll find the clans of Fflyr Dlemathlys think far too much of themselves to *ever* do business with goblins—at least, not without paying through the nose for an acceptably tall middleman. Olumnach's people wouldn't give me the time of day. So," he grimaced, "against my better judgment, Mindzi insisted on trying her particular method of persuasion."

"I, ah, gather the lords of Clan Olumnach don't swing that way."

"Fucker," Mindzi muttered. "Didn't need to be so *violent* about it. I barely got outta there with both my ears still on! Why do humans always have *dogs*, anyway?"

She half-hid behind Maugro again, glaring accusingly at Junko. I reached down to ruffle Junko's ears, causing her tail to thump against the floor.

"Yeah, so," Maugro drawled, "this is a bit complicated by the fact that people with whom I do business are *closely* tied to Clan Olumnach, and I'm obligated to protect their privacy by established agreements for which coin has changed hands. That hobbles me when it comes to dishing on the Olumnach's movements out here in the wilds. I get the impression you've already learned they pull the strings on the bandit gangs around Dount; Rocco's crew was the only exception I know of, and there's a reason he set up out here in Buttfuck, Nowhere. Most of what's tactically significant about what the Olumnachs do on Dount is a little too close to revealing my other clients' secrets. *However*, when it comes to the clansguard, or known movements about the noble family themselves? Oh, you better *believe* I'm glad to dish on them. Hell, if you can promise me you plan to ruin their day, I just might find it in my little green heart to give you a discount."

"That turd who got jibbed in Gwyllthean the other day?" Mindzi added with a snarl that looked way too alarming for her size, what with those shark teeth. "Lord Arider. *He's* the evil fuck who set his damn dogs on me. I hope Virya kicked his rotten soul straight to the Void."

"Oh, a Lord of Clan Olumnach died?" I asked, raising my eyebrows. "That explains some stuff. I heard a rumor around the Gutters they were in some kind of dispute with the urban gangs."

"That guy threatened to tan and emboss my tits with his signet and use 'em as coin pouches!" Mindzi exclaimed. "I mean, what the *fuck*! Who *says* that? What kind of twisted shit even *thinks* of something like that? And you know the worst part? I'm pretty sure he *actually* woulda done it!"

I had to appreciate the diligence with which Arider went out of his way to ensure I wouldn't feel bad about getting him killed.

"Okay, Zi, you're letting personal business affect our work," Maugro reproved. "Arider's dead, which means you won. Time to let it go."

"Wish I coulda at least *watched*," she muttered. "Or taken a shit on his corpse."

Junko raised her head, causing both goblins to freeze, but I patted the dog and she subsided again.

"Anyway," I said, "thank you for clarifying where you stand about that, Maugro. I'll keep it in mind. Since I'm in no position to get uppity with Clan Olumnach just yet, I'm going to choose to conserve my funds at the moment; my interest is more in the other gangs around Dount. As soon as anything changes, I'll come right to you. On to the next item . . ."

"Wow, you really are setting yourself up for the long term," Maugro said with clear approval. "That's what I like to see! What'll it be next, Lord Seiji?"

"I am in the market for scrolls and artifacts," I said. "Can you keep me appraised of the trade?"

He grimaced, sucking in air through his teeth. "Gonna have to disappoint you on that front, Lord Seiji, sorry. There just *ain't* a trade on Dount. Hell, anywhere in Fflyr Dlemathlys—you'd have to go to Lancor or Godspire to find an actual broker in commodities like that. Round here, you want a spell scroll or artifact, you either get it right from the Spirit or buy it directly off somebody who did. I got a few adventurers I do business with, but honestly, if one of them was looking to sell, it'd get snapped up before I could get word to you out here, much less set something up."

"Damn." I forgot myself so far as to take a sip of wine. Hopefully he interpreted my wince as a response to the news, not the libation I'd served him. Why had I even uncorked another bottle of this swill?

"Now, that's not to say I can't do *anything* for you," he hastened to add. "I won't sugarcoat it—your options are pretty starkly limited unless you reach out *far* beyond Dount. We don't even have an active dungeon on this island. What I *can* do is draw up a list of known Spirits on the surface, along with a description of their challenge and reward. In fact, I got a few different lists, depending on your levels of access. Y'know, cos a *lot* of those things are walled away on private grounds held by various clans."

"Mm. What about a complete list, with annotations about whoever controls access to it and known means of currying their favor—or bypassing their defenses?"

"Hah!" Again, he grinned broadly, and the animal part of my brain couldn't help interpreting the expression as a threat despite his evident good cheer. Those *teeth*. "Now that right there's a real goblin question, Lord Seiji, and yes, that is still a compliment. Yeah, I don't have such a document just lying around my office, but I *do* have all that info at my fingertips. It's just a matter of cross-referencing notes and writing shit down. I can have it to you tomorrow."

"Perfect. Then before we talk totals, there's just one other thing I want to know."

Maugro spread his arms, beaming. "So far you're the best customer I've had all month! What'll it be?"

I kept my tone as casual as the whole conversation had been thus far. "I'm hoping to call upon your services as a middleman. Can you put me into contact with a goblin alchemist? A *good* one."

Both their faces abruptly went expressionless. The two silent knee cappers by the tunnel entrance turned their heads to stare fixedly at me.

"You not satisfied with the alchemy shops in Gwyllthean?" Maugro finally asked, his voice as deliberately nonchalant as my own. "They'll set you back a lot less."

"Oh, to be sure. And if I find myself needing akorshil varnish or rat poison, I'll probably just go there and save money. But I'm afraid those aren't too helpful if I want something more interesting. Like, say . . . fireproof glue, fog dust, sleep venom . . ."

The goblin's shoulders shifted as he inhaled through his nose and let it out in a short sigh. "Aha. *You've* been asking Sakin questions. Y'know, somehow Rocco went his whole tenure without ever thinking to interrogate that guy about the stuff he knows. In hindsight, the surprising thing about Rocco's leadership here is that it lasted as long as it did."

I had indeed asked Sakin questions. I wasn't going to start up Rocco's old con, even if that wouldn't have automatically pushed Aster to mutiny, and my efforts at raiding caravans thus far had taught me that I needed a *much* more efficient way of doing that before I could make good on my arrangement with Auldmaer. Preferably one that minimized the risk to my already tiny forces, and if possible preserved my anonymity. I'd come up with no answer to this conundrum, and so I had consulted the person available to me whom I suspected knew a lot more about criminal business than he'd let on.

And indeed, Sakin had immediately proposed a source of assets, which the Fflyr of Dount, thanks to their own prejudices, either disdained to use or didn't know existed.

Of course, that fact, and now this conversation, raised another interesting line of questions.

"What kind of stuff *does* that guy know?" I asked mildly.

"Seems like you'd get a better answer to that from him."

"I am really not sure that I would."

Maugro grinned; Mindzi rolled her eyes. "Heh, probably right. Is this a formal request for information, Lord Seiji? Because if so, we need to add another item to the tally when it comes time to talk numbers."

"Mmm. What can you tell me, without putting me in debt, about *whether* it's worth paying for information on Sakin?"

The info broker shrugged, performatively casual. "Sakin's like you, Lord Seiji—a way more interesting caliber of troublemaker than this piddly little operation out here deserves. He's *unlike* you in that you seem to be trying to whip this outfit into shape, while Sakin is apparently . . . I dunno, retired? On vacation? Oddly sanguine about fuckin' around in the khora forest with miscellaneous reprobates. Personally, if I had that guy operating under my authority, I would spend coin to find out everything I could about his origins. You do you, though."

"Perhaps we'll revisit that," I hedged. I sure as hell would, but I wasn't sure how urgent it was, and it seemed like I was already racking up a bill that might make Maugro question the source of my on-hand cash. "Now, about alchemy . . ."

"Sure, I know people," he said neutrally. "That's one of the great constants of life. Maugro knows people. *This*, however, is not straightforward. Goblin business is none of human business, get me? We barely manage to eke out a living as it is, and the biggest impediment to that is humans. When they aren't pushing us out of every honest trade, they're sending adventurers into our homes to murder everybody, steal what little we've got, and generally wreck shit."

"Hm . . . I'm sorry to hear that. I thought the local humans were afraid to go underground?"

"Yeah, and that's why that isn't more of an ongoing concern than it is—why we can manage to live at *all* in human territory. Takes either fear of punishment or a shit-ton of reward money to make human adventurers do that, neither of which the big names in charge wanna provide unless they consider it important. Which basically means goblins start putting together a secure enough position to make us less easy to kick around. And that brings us to our problem, Lord Seiji. If a bandit gang started throwing around the kind of alchemy that's *known* to be a goblin specialty . . . That leads in a straight line to the King's Guild posting a reward to do to *us* what you're proposing to do to *them*."

I thought back to my own visit to the Guild, and the posted notice that they were interested in investigating goblin activity.

"I see," I said slowly. "So, not to change the subject . . . but if I were interested in getting in touch with a goblin engineer able to make crossbows, would a similar concern apply?"

Mindzi cringed outright; Maugro slapped a hand over his eyes, leaning his head back to emit a long groan.

"Lord Seiji, *please.* I was so optimistic about all this new business you're bringing me. Please don't make me regret this relationship."

"Okay, I get where you're coming from." Shit; I really did, and it was decidedly inconvenient for my own plans. "But I'm not asking *you* to sell me anything too dangerous, Maugro. Can you put me in contact with somebody who can do the kinds of things I'm asking about, and let them make their own call?"

"At the risk of having my name associated with the business if it all goes tits up, yeah," he said pointedly. "My work thrives on connections, Lord Seiji. I gotta explain how much trouble it is for me if goblin society in general blames me for an adventurer raid? I don't even need to be at fault; just having the stink on me'll be more than enough."

"Okay, how about this." Bless Sakin, he'd had the forethought to suggest a bargaining chip already in my possession. "I've recently learned some interesting things about slimes."

"Slimes," he repeated, red eyes narrowing. I could practically see him thinking back to news of the attack on Auldmaer's caravan.

"They're basically blobs of mildly corrosive goo, with interesting properties as a result of being inherently magical and only sort of technically alive. Right? I hear those are *very* useful to alchemists."

"They're a base component for a fair number of potions, yeah," he said, still aggressively noncommittal. "That's common knowledge."

"I *also* hear they're not native to Dount. Apparently they like wet environments, on hard surfaces where they're not likely to ooze through the ground if they stop moving. Which makes the only local place where they tend to live . . . the canals surrounding Gwyllthean."

"You're also describing any natural cave system," he said dryly. "Such as, y'know, where goblins live?"

"*Are* the caves on Dount natural?" I countered. "Or are they goblin-carved tunnels designed to catch thermal updrafts from the core? In other words, warm, dry, and windy, exactly the worst kind of environment for slimes to live in?"

This time Maugro managed to control his expression better, but it was Mindzi's turn to squint aggressively at me. I noticed that both of his bodyguards had shuffled forward from the tunnel, staring at me with borderline hostile faces.

Sensing the tension, Junko raised her head again, ears forward and alert. All the goblins froze. I did not pat the dog, for the moment.

"Man," Maugro said after a very loaded pause, "you *really* got Sakin flapping his yap. I wonder, did you actually have to entice or coerce him with something? Or was all that dude's nefarious expertise just waiting for somebody to ask him *nicely*? Cos, no lie, if it's the last one, I'm honestly gonna laugh."

"I think the right thing for me to do would be to respect Sakin's privacy, at least until I have a specific reason not to," I said diplomatically, causing Mindzi to snort. "But back to what I was saying, I can only imagine how difficult it is for the local goblin alchemists to catch wild slimes from the Gutters. They're already big enough to be hard for you folks to handle, and that's the *heart* of Fflyr territory where anybody who sees you scuttling around is likely to throw things or call the guard. Not to mention that the human alchemists probably feel threatened by goblin expertise to begin with; they'd have a standing motivation to—"

"Okay, with the greatest possible respect, Lord Seiji, you've made your point." He sighed, leaning back in his chair again. "You're not wrong, any alchemist I know in the tunnels would *love* a cheap, convenient source of slimes. Before I can broach the topic with any of 'em, I need a little more detail. How many can you produce, how consistently, and how fast?"

"The answer to all those questions is *yes*," I replied, smiling beatifically. "Unlimited slimes. Any slime-proof container I'm sent, I can fill, as often as they're brought to me. The only limitation is my schedule and the fact I can't always be *here* and at liberty to do it. And if the alchemist in question is willing to send along some finished products, I don't even need money for them."

The pause which ensued was even more loaded; this time, all the goblins fixed their attention on Maugro, who was staring into space, slowly working his jaw as if physically chewing on the idea.

"Not saying there ain't risks," Mindzi finally said to him, "but damn. The finder's fee alone . . ."

"All right," he agreed, his eyes focusing back on me. "You just never cease to be interesting, Lord Seiji. Tell you what, I can put you in touch with somebody. What happens after that ain't my business, though. As for the rest of it . . . Seems we've got a lot of numbers to go over."

"Of course," I said, smiling pleasantly and scratching behind Junko's ear. After my last spell of overconfidence had led directly to Cat Alley, I wasn't about to declare, even to my own inner monologue, that things were once again coming up Seiji, but still.

Progress.

24

In Which the Dark Lord Gets Cooking

I had to give Fflyr Dlemathlys credit; for as much of a borderline dystopia as it was, this culture prized reading and literature. All of the bandits here were literate, and apparently that was standard for even lowborn. The only problem was that everyone here—except me—had already read everything we had on hand, and still they fought over books. I'd resolved to improve our library as soon as I had a positive cash flow. The money taken from Arider was still . . . substantial, but I was becoming wary of the fact that I'd done nothing since getting it but spend, and my deal with Auldmaer had yet to start paying off.

"That's good to see," Goose said very quietly from behind me, after we'd finished a training session in the courtyard the next day. I glanced back, and she nodded in the direction of Twigs and Junko now running in circles, laughing and barking, respectively. "It's been a long time since I saw her like . . . Well. We've survived. You survive long enough, and you start to forget that's not the same thing as living."

I just nodded, finding nothing to say to that. Fortunately, I was rescued before the pause could grow awkward.

"Lord Seiji!" Donon came jogging out of the keep's main doors, waving a hand overhead. "Lord Seiji! You're needed in the kitchen, my lord; the goblins are back!"

"Ah! That'll be Maugro with the dossier I requested. Thanks, Donon." I picked up my coat from where it was draped over the rack where Goose was waiting patiently to replace the blunt akorshil practice swords.

"But it's not just Maugro!" Donon exclaimed, fairly dancing in excitement. "It's *new* goblins, and they want to meet you! Lord Seiji, one of 'em's a girl, and she's *gorgeous*. I wanted to—that is, Kasser insisted I be the one to come get you. He was a real dick about it."

Good man, Kasser. I had quietly made it known that I didn't want Donon unsupervised around any goblins, especially Maugro and Mindzi. None of the others had even blinked; everybody knew about his *thing* for goblin girls and his inability to keep his mouth shut. I was also concerned with the fact that Donon was one of the few who knew *exactly* where I got my money from—I suspected Sakin had pieced it together, but that one knew the value of silence—and Donon would be a sitting duck for Mindzi's vampish routine. Mindzi was only interested in flirting where she saw advantage, which around here meant only with me; the last thing I wanted was her catching on that Donon was a weak link in my organization.

"Then it sounds like I'd better not keep them waiting. Junko! Here, girl, time to work. Donon, help Goose straighten up out here."

"Aw, but Lord Seiji—"

I turned a flat stare on him, and he fell silent. I was doing my best to lead with a light touch—let the bandits go their own way where possible and not make them feel bullied the way they were under Rocco. It only worked because they all knew I was the guy who Immolated people, and a sharp look or slightly raised voice was all it took to bring that fact to mind.

"If there are new business contacts, the last thing I need is you *drooling* over one, Donon. Help Goose with her chores, and *then* you can join us. Quietly. If you manage not to embarrass me, we'll see about letting you meet more goblins."

He nodded, practically frantic. "Yes, Lord Seiji."

I felt bad—Donon was a decent guy and firmly on my side. But god damn, man, keep it in your pants.

Pausing only to give Junko a scratch behind the ears—because she was a good girl and there was never not time for skritches—I shrugged into my coat and strode back into the keep.

Kasser and Aster were on guard in the kitchen. Kasser looking sullen and hostile, and Aster just lounged by the door with a neutral expression and her sword leaning nearby. I hoped Kasser wasn't too off-putting to my guests; it took some familiarity to understand that he probably wasn't sullen and hostile at anyone in particular; the guy was just like that. Not unlike me, but without the charm.

"Hey, there he is!" Maugro called with characteristic outgoing cheer. "Glad to see you again, Lord Seiji!"

"Maugro, welcome back," I replied, nodding with all due courtesy, then turned to my subordinates. "Really, you two, am I the only one in this place who understands the meaning of hospitality? I have guests just standing around awkwardly. In the *kitchen*, where the food is."

"Hey, I'm just guarding the door," Aster said with a shrug. "That's what I do, guard stuff. I'm not your serving girl, Lord Seiji."

"All right, fair enough. I guess that makes you the serving girl."

I turned a grin on Kasser. He did not play along. The man's glower intensified by an order of magnitude and his whole body went rigid.

Belatedly, it occurred to me to add up how close he and Harold seemed, and the open question of what had driven the two of them out of normal Fflyr society, and one obvious solution to that equation suggested exactly the kind of taunts and slurs Kasser might have had thrown at him.

"Never mind," I said, crossing to the cabinet. "Thank you for delegating, Kasser. That was quick thinking. I believe you're about due for a break, yes?"

He hesitated, uncertainty overtaking anger on his features, then gave me a curt nod and strode out of the room.

"Ah, here we go," I continued, picking up the bottle and beginning to round up cups. "Same one we opened last night, Maugro; I'm not much of a drinker."

"See what I mean?" he said to the two new faces in the room. "Lord Seiji's a good sort."

Mindzi was not in evidence today. He had two hench-goblins with clubs standing guard at the tunnel entrance as usual, but I noticed that only one was familiar to me. The two other newcomers were both standing very still, staring at Junko, who was currently having her ears scratched by Aster. Panting and wagging her tail, she looked singularly unthreatening. If, I guess, you weren't a goblin.

They were a man and a woman. Both had on heavy belts, bulging with numerous closed pouches and several sheathed tools, the man also with a pair of heavy goggles perched atop his head. He had on some kind of heavy apron, while the woman wore a vest of plain leather, dyed a dark gray, and very obviously cut to fit her precisely.

I could see at a glance why Donon had called her gorgeous; that wouldn't have been my reaction, but knowing his preferences, yeah. She had eyes a shade more violet than the red of the other goblins, and her hair was styled up in a kind of curling side-tail with artful bangs hanging over half her face, dyed purple with red highlights to match her eyes. It was definitely not the hair or eyes that had caught Donon's attention, though. The girl was *stacked*. Her chest would've been fair to moderately buxom on a human; at her size, it was just short of looking awkwardly disproportionate. I could see why the taut leather vest was necessary, just for support.

Damn it. I *really* hoped Donon hadn't said something embarrassing before Kasser chased him out.

"Don't worry, Donon didn't say anything too embarrassing," Maugro said.

I coughed, pouring wine into cups. "I gather you're . . . acquainted with him."

"Heh, I been bringin' Mindzi here for a good while, Lord Seiji. He was too shy to do more than stare before you fixed up his little . . . condition. So! Your order."

"Ah, thank you! And here's your usual." I accepted a sheaf of papers in the heavy parchment folder he offered me, handing over a cup of wine in trade. It was thicker than I'd expected, probably in part due to the dimensions being smaller than the pages I was used to. Goblin sized, no doubt. I tucked it under my arm, picking up another cup. "And for . . . ?"

"You're . . . offering us wine?" the purple-haired woman asked with naked suspicion. "Seriously? Or, wait, are you *selling* it?"

"I told you, Zui," Maugro said with a chuckle, "it's simple hospitality. Man knows how to treat a guest."

"Even a goblin guest," she said, squinting up at me.

"A guest is a guest," I replied, pouring a cup. "I won't make any promises about how *good* the wine is, because I honestly can't tell. The stuff they make around here is . . . not to my taste. But isn't it traditional for business to be discussed over drinks?"

"It's a Dountol sour red," Maugro explained, sipping his own. "Probably not the kind that graces a lord's table, but Lord Seiji here just moved in; it's the best stuff Rocco had on hand."

"You say that like I should know who Rocco is."

Maugro cleared his throat, turning back to me. "Aha, well, anyway. Lord Seiji, you were looking to do business with an alchemist. This is Zui and Youda. They represent a certain business concern which has expressed an interest in reaching out to you."

"A *tentative willingness*," Zui corrected, her expression just barely short of openly unfriendly. "My boss will hear you out. We're here to decide whether she should actually be *interested*. And, ah . . . thanks, but no thanks. I never drink while I'm working."

"Ooh, I'll take a—"

Zui shoved her partner's shoulder. "You *also* don't drink while we're working!"

"Probably a wise policy," I said, setting the cup and bottle back on the counter. "Excuse me, did you say your name was . . . Youda?"

"That's me!" he said, grinning hugely. His teeth gleamed a brighter white than Maugro's, and looked more even, too. Just as murderous, though. "Personal cook to Miss Sneppit herself!"

"Her . . . cook," I said slowly. "Wait, Miss Who?"

"Miss Sneppit," Zui repeated sharply, "is our boss, the person with whom you're proposing to do business. Lord . . . Seiji, was it?"

"It was. Excuse me, I'm a little confused. I thought I'd be dealing with the alchemist herself."

"Oh, Miss Sneppit ain't the alchemist, she runs the whole show," Youda explained. "I do the brewing in Miss Sneppit's organization."

". . . you do."

"Yup!"

"The cook."

"Who better?"

"Uh . . ." I turned to Zui, noting a glint of cold amusement in her expression now. "So, if he's the alchemist, that would make you . . . ?"

"I'm just along to represent Miss Sneppit's business interests and supervise Youda on site," she said, folding her arms, which looked a trifle difficult. "His alchemical expertise will obviously be consulted here, but *I* will be making the recommendation to our boss on whether or not to pursue a business relationship between her organization and yours, Lord Seiji."

"Ah. So, you're her business manager?"

"Her hairstylist."

I had to stare at her for a few seconds, blinking.

"Right. Of course. Well, your hair *is* pretty amazing." I turned to my more longstanding goblin acquaintance, noting in passing that Aster was physically repressing laughter with only moderate success. "*Maugro?*"

"Okay, whoa, let's reel this back a bit before a misunderstanding happens," Maugro said soothingly, holding up his hands, one of which still contained a cup of wine. "Lord Seiji, I promise you're not being taken lightly here. To help you understand these staffing choices, I'd need to explain a lot about goblin culture—which, no offense, I don't intend to do, on account of one pillar of goblin culture being it's none of your business. Just know that I *get* how this probably comes across, and with all due respect, you are making the same caliber of impression right now as they are on you. Listen, everybody, it's me, Maugro. How long have we all known each other?"

"We've done business *twice* now," I exclaimed.

"I never heard of you before today," said Youda.

"You have a solid reputation," Zui said grudgingly, "or at least so Miss Sneppit says, otherwise we wouldn't be here."

"Exactly! I value my connections too much to waste everybody's time. Believe me, folks, I brought you all together because I see a golden opportunity for mutual profit here. So, instead of standing here stewing in irreconcilable cultural misunderstandings, how's about we get down to some alchemy and show everybody that everybody else means business, yeah?"

"Hey, I'm always down to brew!" Youda said with evidently unfeigned enthusiasm.

"Brew, or brew not," I replied solemnly, "there is no try."

Everybody looked at me in confusion except the self-proclaimed cook, who pointed up at me and grinned. "See? This guy gets it!"

"All right," Zui said with a lot less pep, "we were told you can furnish any amount of slimes. Before testing *that*, I trust you won't object to an analysis of a sample for quality?"

"I, uh . . . sure? I have no idea how you'd judge the quality of a slime, but knock yourself out, I guess."

Youda had already returned to the wheeled cart they'd brought; it was basically a crate of mismatched akorshil planks with a hinged lid and what looked like a harness attached to leather straps on one end. He opened the top, then had to nearly clamber inside to reach what was resting there, treating us all to a momentary show of his stubby legs kicking in the air while he balanced on the rim of the box. But then he hopped back down, holding up another, much smaller box, with a metal apparatus attached to one edge.

Metal, not akornin. It looked like polished iron. I *had* seen metal here, though the Ephemerans used their shell derivatives almost everywhere metal would ordinarily be applied. I'd wondered where it came from, if they were afraid to dig, but it now occurred to me that *goblins* obviously dug all they wanted.

"Okay!" He stepped back, looking up at me expectantly. "If you could deposit one slime in the box, please, I can get started."

"Can do," I replied, pointing at the box. Now that I looked, it was just about the perfect size to contain an average slime—which was to say, just big enough to be awkward for the goblin to pick up and maneuver.

Summon Slime.

It appeared without fanfare, right in the designated space. Youda, who had spent the preceding seconds donning a pair of heavy leather gloves and lowering his goggles over his eyes, now clapped his hands and then rubbed them together, grinning expectantly, before he got down to work.

With efficient movements, the goblin . . . alchemist? Cook? . . . scooped a clear glass beaker into the slime's body, making it wobble and try to start oozing out over the sides of the box. Youda shoved it back in with one hand, then plucked a heavy knife from his belt and used it to sever the goop surrounding his handheld container, finally pulling it away, holding a sample of detached slime. This he set in a bracket affixed to his metal apparatus, sealed the top with a lid, then—having to pause and shove the inquisitive slime back into place once more—finally closed a lid over the box itself, trapping it inside.

"You cast that silently," Zui said, catching my attention. She was regarding me with a speculative expression, which I guess was the least openly unfriendly look I'd gotten from her so far.

"But of course," I replied, putting on my most mysterious and aloof smile. Actually, other people had remarked on that. Was it supposed to be harder to cast spells without saying their names out loud? It had never made much difference to me. "Uh, apropos of nothing . . . Slimes don't feel pain, do they?"

Youda had now started a tiny contained burner directly under the sample of slime, and was apparently boiling it, causing the substance to rise into a much thinner glass tube he'd affixed to the top.

"How would they?" Zui asked dismissively. "They don't have nerves."

"No evidence of a pain response," Youda added, not looking up. "They'll move out of things that are harmful to them, but actually *slower* than they respond to food. Not much except heat, dehydration, or magic *can* harm a slime. Abrupt and escapable sources of those are rare in nature, so, stands to reason pain wouldn't be biologically useful to 'em like it is to us."

"Ahp! Back up, please," Zui ordered as I leaned in to watch what he was doing more closely. "Do not crowd an alchemist while he's working with flames and potentially unstable chemicals; that should be basic sense. Also, I realize this is a kitchen, but please keep any foodstuffs and especially *flammable liquids* like *alcohol* as far from the experiment as possible." The last was directed pointedly at Maugro, who just as pointedly took a long sip of wine and did not move.

"Nothing here's unstable, and it's not an experiment," Youda said, currently peering at the surge of boiled slime rising up through his glass tube via a magnifying lens he'd clipped to his goggles. "It's just a visual test; I could literally do it with one eye. You can relax for once, Zui."

I sauntered over to the table, which was closer to her than to him, and leaned against it. "Soooo . . . How *you* doin'?"

Slowly, Zui swiveled her head up to stare at me.

I waggled my eyebrows at her. "Come here often? What're you doing after this?"

"You're not interested in me," she said with clipped enunciation. "You are only doing that to get under my skin. You've succeeded. So you won, okay? Can you stop?"

And that was how one little goblin accomplished what no one else on Ephemera had been able to—including the very Goddess of Evil herself—shutting me up.

I knew it wasn't even her reaction that hit me, so much as lingering discomfort after my long, dark night of the soul in Cat Alley. Any time before that night, I probably would have laughed. It was the *look* on her face; the expression wasn't actually angry, barely even frustrated, just . . . tired. The weary look of someone dealing with the same exhausting shit she'd endured for who knew how long. I had recently seen that exact look on the faces of dozens of beaten-down sex workers. Worse, I had just suddenly realized I'd seen it in the expressions of women I'd approached in Tokyo.

Maugro made eye contact with me and, behind Zui's back, grimaced, then jerked his head silently toward her in universal guy sign language for "chicks, what can ya do." For some reason, that only made it feel worse.

Aster, by contrast, was now grinning like a fool, and actually straightened up from her lounging position to fold down her hands at Zui. That seemed to startle the goblin more than anything I'd done.

"Yeah, this is good stuff," said Youda, blessedly rescuing me from the social quagmire I'd created. "Damn near pure. Summoned slimes are *always* better for alchemy than the wild-caught variety, that's why that spell's so valuable. Those Gutter slimes have been crawling around in goddess knows what, and eating most of it; takes forever to process all the filth out, and by the time that's done you've lost at least a quarter of their usable mass. This stuff? I'd barely have to do more than boil it to start brewing potions." He turned to his compatriot, raising his goggles to reveal a serious expression. "If he can produce these in bulk, this is a seriously important connection,

Zui. Never mind making our in-house potions, we could start selling the raw—"

"Okay!" she interrupted loudly. "By Virya's morning breath, Youda, how many times we gotta have this talk? It is *not* necessary to explain your entire business strategy in front of random vendors!"

Maugro chuckled, earning a sour look from her, but she turned to me with a more serious attitude.

"All right, Lord Seiji, you can consider us . . . interested."

"Great! Then I'll just—"

"Now, hold on," she said, raising one hand. Despite the interruption, I couldn't help noticing her entire demeanor was suddenly a lot more polite now that I demonstrably had something of value to offer. "You understand, this was a preliminary meeting. Miss Sneppit has sole authority to finalize any deal, and she'll want us to report in before drawing one up. That will lay out the conditions of a long-term agreement—and just so you know, Miss Sneppit will undoubtedly want to do business on the condition of exclusivity."

"Sure, the value of slimes goes down if other people have the same access, I get it," I said, nodding. "As long as I get what I want out of the bargain, I've no objection to that. I will be *using* slimes for whatever purpose I may devise, but I'm willing to agree not to sell them elsewhere. So when do I get to meet the fabulous Miss Sneppit?"

Zui's lips thinned. "*If* she is impressed with our report, and *if* I am satisfied her person will not be in danger here, and *if* Maugro grants the use of his access tunnel, and *if she decides it is appropriate*, Miss Sneppit *may* visit you in person. The head of the whole organization doesn't personally chat with everybody with whom we do business, obviously."

"Aha."

Perhaps because I was clearly on the verge of taking offense, Zui moderated her delivery somewhat, becoming almost pleasant. "As for today, I am authorized to finalize the trade you were interested in. A shipment of slimes—as many as can fit in this box—in exchange for certain alchemical products. *And*," she added, going stern again, "we were assured by Maugro that you understand the value of discretion."

"Let me put it this way—I am exactly as interested as you are in having the Gwyllthean authorities visit me at home. In fact, that's precisely why I want those supplies in particular. I'd like to get my business done without having to be . . . confrontational."

"That's a start," Zui agreed, relaxing once more. "I will warn you that Miss Sneppit will likely require a contractual stipulation that you not reveal your source of these assets to any human authority. Got 'em, Youda?"

"Yup!" He had delved back into their big wheeled box, and now pulled out a bag, which he handled with care. The goblin trundled over to the kitchen table and reached up with a grunt to set his burden down there. "Sleep dust, a kinetic charge, and basalt shimmer powder."

"Do you mind if I ask where you learned the names of such reagents, Lord Seiji?" Zui asked in a deceptively mild tone.

"As I just told you," I said sweetly. "You value discretion, and so do I."

Her nostrils flared very slightly in a mute huff of annoyance, but the goblin nodded and didn't press me.

"Not sure what you're planning to *do* with it, though," Youda added.

"He wants to make a sleeping bomb that looks like a rock, obviously," said Zui.

"Well, yeah, but there's no ignition method," replied the alchemist. "Attaching a fuse would ruin the effect of disguising it, and I don't care how freakishly long your legs are, you *cannot* manually ignite this stuff and get away in time to avoid taking a nap."

"Youda," Zui barked, "you're doing it again."

"Oh, will you *relax?*" he retorted. "You don't gotta play *everything* so close to the chest, Zui! If we wanna do business with this guy, helping him screw himself over ain't exactly best practice, and I bet Miss Sneppit would back me up on that. Sorry, Lord Seiji," he added to me with a wink. "Zui's a real nice girl, actually, she's just a mother goose."

"A . . . what?" I asked, while Zui pursed her lips and looked generally displeased.

"Y'know, a little overprotective and aggressive when you go near her eggs. Doin' business with humans would put anybody on edge."

"Huh. Sorry, that expression refers to something different where I'm from."

"Really?"

"Okay, enough," Zui interjected. "This has gotten *way* off subject, and we didn't come here to socialize."

"Yes, I appreciate the warning, Youda, but I have accounted for that," I assured him. "I know what I'm doing."

Hopefully that was true.

"Righty-o then," he said, grinning cheerfully. "Hate to think my work accidentally landed you in trouble—and not just cos you're a valuable source of reagents! We goblins may be half your height, but we got just as much heart."

"Judge you by your size, I do not," I assured him gravely.

Zui loudly cleared her throat. "Right, well, anyway. I believe the proposed deal in exchange for those reagents was to fill 'any slime-proof container' we could provide?"

"Right you are," I said, stepping up to the wheeled box at which she now gestured. It was currently empty; apparently Youda would have to carry his smaller box and brewing attachment home himself. It was also fitted together from planks that didn't *look* slime-proof, but hey, if Zui was willing to let me accidentally sleep myself playing with alchemy, she could clean up her own slime trail.

Summon Slime. Summon Slime. Summon Slime. Summon Slime. Summon Slime. Summon Slime. Summon Slime . . .

That box held a lot more than it looked like it should. Even so, the task was nothing compared to the hundreds of slimes I'd summoned to ambush Auldmaer's caravan. Youda watched avidly as it quickly filled with potion-ready, marketable slimes, and even Zui looked grudgingly impressed.

They didn't stick around for small talk once it was done and the lid swung back into place. Youda requested the benefit of my height to put his smaller box on top of the closed one for the return journey, which I was glad to do because *he* was pleasant. Zui left it with a curt "We'll be in touch soon" and a respectful nod that even I could tell was an afterthought. Apparently the hairstylist/chief negotiator also served as a beast of burden; she slipped the harness over her shoulders and personally hauled the box away. Maugro designated one of his personal goons to escort them back down the tunnel, and that was that for my second group of goblin visitors.

"She's cute, though, right?" Maugro commented after they'd departed.

"Eh." I made a waffling gesture with one hand. "Cuteness is ninety percent attitude. I kept expecting her to bite me." Junko whuffed agreement, which made the remaining goblins twitch.

"Okay, fine, you caught me," Maugro admitted, covering quickly for his dog-induced lapse. "I meant, she's got amazing honkers."

How many conversations exactly like this had I had with other guys over the years? And why was it suddenly bugging me so much now? Cat Alley had really gotten under my skin. I found myself trying to deflect rather than playing along for once. "Mm. Seems like that'd be pretty inconvenient at her height."

"Well, that's just the inherent unfairness of life," he said with a genial grin. "They get the back pain, we get the benefits. Right, Aster?"

"We get some of the benefits too, y'know," she said dryly, "though I think you're the first man I've ever heard admit it, Maugro, so credit for that."

"Hey, Maugro knows how to see from everybody's perspective!" he said with an expansive gesture of both arms and an even bigger grin. "In my line of work it's a vital skill."

"Yeah, by the way," I said. "*Your* tunnel?"

"I told you when we first met, Lord Seiji, we're neighbors! Yeah, that tunnel comes out *right* in my personal residence and business headquarters. Any other goblins who wanna visit you gotta go through me."

"I did notice you seemed to pivot pretty hard from not wanting to involve me in goblin business yesterday to making *sure* this deal worked out."

"And I will continue to do so, Lord Seiji, because you're gonna need my help. That Miss Sneppit is a real monster when it comes to contracts and agreements. I mean, she's *fair*, basically, by goblin standards, but you better read that thing carefully and don't be shy about negotiating for better terms."

"Negotiating . . . which will be done through intermediaries, because this Sneppit won't come here, and they've gotta go through *you* to even send messengers. Maugro, I was looking to lock down a source of alchemy, not enter a prolonged period of arbitration."

"No, you were looking for *goblin* alchemy. You wanna do business with goblins, this is how it's gonna go; we make sure everything's laid out clearly before any goods or services change hands. Look, it ain't as bad as you're probably thinking, Lord Seiji. Sneppit will naturally give you more lenient terms than she'd offer another goblin business."

"Oh? Because she's just so *fond* of humans?"

He didn't reciprocate my grin. "Because humans break deals and get violent when they don't get their way. That's why Zui was so on edge. It wasn't personal; far as *she* knew, her and Youda's lives were in danger just by being here."

"Hm. Which brings us back to my original point—you're *awfully* eager for this deal to go down, considering how standoffish you were about it just yesterday."

"Yeah, well, business is about managing risks, know what I mean? I'm taking a gamble on you, Lord Seiji. If you decide to fuck over Sneppit's company, you'll be fucking me over, too." He grinned even more toothily than usual. "And I have you pegged as too smart a man to pull that on somebody who knows your location and approximate strength, and communicates regularly with every other bandit gang on Dount."

"Right. And this also gets you an in with Miss Sneppit and her crew, who I gather are kind of a big deal."

Again, he spread his arms wide as if to embrace the world, and his grin took on a less predatory cast—as much as it could, with those chompers. "And *that*, Lord Seiji, is how you do *business*. A successful deal is one in which everybody wins!"

"I like that philosophy," I admitted. It'd be really nice if *I* could do business that way. Thanks to Virya, though, I was locked on a path which was inevitably going to make a lot of people *very* unhappy. Starting with me.

Donon burst into the kitchen, out of breath. "Okay, I'm— Aw, is she gone?"

25

In Which the Dark Lord Unilaterally Declares Naptime

Silver, black, red, gold, blue, and white," I recited, slowly tilting my open hand so that the coins piled in it glinted in the dim light. They were *very* shiny. Ephemeran coins, aside from being made with an exquisite precision that matched and exceeded modern Earth metallurgy, never seemed to get dull or scratched. They also all had bands of vivid color just inside their outer rims. Whatever it was made of, the colored parts remained as glossy and apparently as impervious as the rest. The actual engravings depicted either abstract shapes reminiscent of sunbursts or Sanora's face from a variety of angles depending on the coin. She was immediately recognizable; whoever had designed these had clearly seen the goddess in person, as I had.

"Yep, that's the ascending order," said Aster. "Don't forget they're in pairs, too."

"That's how you calculate the values," Donon added. "There's discs, halos, and stars, see?"

There were indeed three styles of coin, each available in all six colors. Plain round coins, and then others with circular holes in the center.

"So, within a shape group, each color up in the chain is ten times the value of the previous one," Donon lectured. "So a black disc is worth ten silver discs, and a red disc is ten black discs, and so on up. But! To get the value of the next shape group, you gotta consider the positions of the pairs. The halos are the second tier up from discs, right? So you count from the second pair—but from the *first* coin *in* the second pair, cos it's from the first tier. Once you've got your starting position, you double it, so a silver halo is worth twice what a red disc is worth. Then they go up by tens; a black halo is ten silvers, and so on. Then! For the stars, it's the same deal—they're the third tier, so you calculate from the third pair, but you're counting *from* the second tier, so it's from the second coin *in* the third pair. Therefore, a silver star is worth ten white halos."

"Yeah, you'll notice a complete lack of star coins in your bag there, Lord Seiji," Sakin drawled. "People like us will probably never *see* one of those in person. There was almost no point in Donon explaining how to count them."

"Hey!" Donon protested. "It's important to know this stuff! Just cos *we* don't get to handle stars doesn't mean Lord Seiji won't."

"I'm not a hundred percent convinced white stars even exist," said Harold.

I carefully stowed my handful of coins back into their pouch, hung the pouch back on my belt, and only then clapped both hands to my forehead and dragged them down my face.

"That's the expression he makes whenever somebody mentions limns," Donon stage whispered.

"No," I said, hearing the deep spiritual exhaustion in my own voice, "no, this is *much* worse."

Eighteen different denominations of coins? No linear progression of values—or rather, three different ones, separated by weird arbitrary leaps? Not to mention the *scale* of them. I was having trouble coming up with a comparative value of Ephemera coins to any currency I knew, just because the *kinds* of things I'd bought here had almost nothing to do with anything purchasable on Earth. The only point in common I'd found was street food, so calculating roughly from that, a silver disc was worth . . . maybe one yen? One or two—small enough to be effectively not worth carrying. Then on the other end of the spectrum, there were coins apparently worth so much they couldn't be used *for* anything. Who would even accept them? What the hell could you *spend* them on if you had one? It'd be like trying to get change for a trillion-yen banknote.

"*Nonsense*," I groaned. "All of it! I can almost forgive the measuring system—*almost*—that's just the kind of thing primitive agrarian societies with no scientific tradition come up with, but this? At a certain point, someone's deliberately minimizing utility and maximizing gratuitous pains in the ass!"

"Hey, don't blame *us* for the coins," Goose protested. "Look at 'em. You don't think *we* can forge anything like that, do you? Coins come from the goddess."

"Goddesses," Biribo corrected. "Virya's coins have exactly the same values, just different artwork. A few of them trickle into circulation around here, with Shylverrael so close, but the two economies are mostly separate."

"*How*, exactly, do coins come from goddesses?"

"Dungeons," Aster said, as if this should be obvious. "Well, occasionally Spirits, I hear. But yeah, mostly dungeons. *Lots* of useful stuff comes from dungeons."

"Scrolls and artifacts and Blessings, I know."

"Nah, she means *lots* of useful stuff!" Biribo chirped. "Dungeon loot runs economies and drives civilization! Adventurer stuff like you mentioned, but also a lot of trade goods that Ephemera can't produce the old-fashioned way—or at least not easily. Metal ingots, bolts of cloth, pottery clay . . . And they increase in value as you go to the more dangerous parts of dungeons. Adventurers in the deepest depths might earn a new scroll or artifact, but they can also haul out jewels, lumber, exotic fruits that won't actually grow anywhere . . ."

"Not to mention there's a good trade in edible monster parts," Goose added. "Or medicinal. In cities that have a dungeon, there's always a whole industry of followers who go in behind the adventurers and cart out the big shipments of stuff that appears in the rooms they clear. We're talking *pallets* of metal and stone and stuff."

"I hear the Emperor of Lancor lives on an *all*-dungeon diet!" Donon chimed in enthusiastically. "Manticore steak, sazja fruit, and glittershrooms, the works!"

"Huh," I grunted, contemplating. A whole economy based on dungeon drops. My innate suspicion of otaku bullshit was jangling, but I also had the nagging feeling that this piece of information had brought me close to understanding something very important that I couldn't quite put my finger on just yet. "Well, anyway, I've got suspicions a culture at this stage of development shouldn't be able to run on fiat currency, but that's just a hunch. I'll freely admit I don't understand economics well enough to fully argue that point."

"Sorry we're so *undeveloped*, Lord Seiji," Kasser snipped.

"It's not your fault," I said kindly. "But what I *do* understand is that what you're describing can't work. If coins are just constantly generated in dungeons and flowing into the economy, even if it's just trickles of whatever fits in an adventurer's pockets, that's a recipe for infinite inflation. How are they taking money back *out* of circulation? Ceremonially dumping it into the core?"

"Not exactly, but close!" Biribo said cheerfully. "Nah, what keeps money scarce is buying miracles!"

"Wait." I held up one hand. "Hang on, I need to prepare myself emotionally for this."

I turned and trudged over to the ground-level outcropping of khora shell, which I had identified as handily bench-shaped when we picked this spot to encamp. Lowering myself onto it with a sigh, I turned sideways, stretching my legs across it, and leaned back against the bulk of the towering khora behind me. Eyes closed, I let my head come to rest against the rock-hard, slightly fuzzy outer shell, and slowly breathed in and out twice.

"Okay." Without opening my eyes, I made a beckoning gesture at Biribo. "Hit me."

Aster mumbled something as she walked off in the direction of the place where Twigs was keeping watch over the road with Arider's spyglass. I only caught "dramatic" and "big baby."

"If a given religious institution is accepted by one of the goddesses as valid," Biribo explained, "they can purchase a miracle. Of all the various Sanorite and Viryan religions across Ephemera, that's how the 'true faiths' single themselves out—they're not proven until they buy a miracle from their goddess. How *much* a miracle costs depends on a lot of factors, but let's just say you pay for something like that mostly in star coins, if not entirely."

"And that's why we put up with this monetary system," Sakin said with his usual laid-back good cheer. "Believe me, Lord Seiji, you're not the first person to notice it's unwieldy and overly complicated. Kings and popes want the official goddess-coins coming in so they can save up enough to buy miracles, therefore they conduct all their business in those coins and crack down on any alternative currencies that pop up. Fflyr Dlemathlys is one of the few countries that doesn't actually have laws on the books against bartering. They all want those coins flowing, because coin always flows upward."

"What *kinds* of miracles are we talking about?" I asked.

"Could be anything," said Biribo. "There are no rules about it. Considering the *cost* pretty much requires you to have a kingdom's worth of income at least, it's usually something on that scale. Curing a plague, ending a drought, conjuring a new island to expand your realm . . . Or *inflicting* plagues and droughts on enemy countries, if you're nasty. Some of 'em are more personal, or frivolous. Kings have gotten themselves way overtuned spells or artifacts that made them nearly as powerful as a Dark Lord or Hero, and some of the world's grandest and most beautiful cities were created in an instant by a goddess by way of miracle. And there've been some miracles that neither goddess was willing to perform at any price. But broadly? To get a miracle, you need a legitimate Viryan or Sanorite religious institution willing to intercede for you, a few literal tons of coins, and a wish that the goddess decides she's willing to grant for the price you offer. The sky's the limit."

And just like that, I understood it. The thought that had been tickling at the back of my brain crashed into full comprehension.

These "miracles" were only the most overt example. At every level, from Spirit gifts to dungeon drops, they had their fingers on the scales. A Spirit's challenge might be anything, and its reward might be anything. Dungeon rewards might scale with difficulty, but that still left a world of wiggle room. Conceptualizing Ephemera as a game world—which it was to the goddesses, even if it lacked RPG mechanics—I would say the entire magic system was a series of gimmicks that *looked* random but were opportunities for the admins to silently intercede. They controlled not only who got what Blessings and artifacts and spells, but how easily, and even more prosaic things, like how much money flowed in and out of the economy and what trade goods would be cheaply available in a given country. At a casual glance, you could mistake the magic system for fair, or at least impartial, but *everything* was under their direct control.

My god, they even made the currency so deliberately confusing it prevented everybody using it from grasping the value of what they were spending. That was *exactly* what gacha game designers did!

That was when the true, bitter reality of it sunk in fully—rather than an RPG world, I was living in a giant gacha game.

"I'm going to slaughter them both," I said aloud, my voice amazingly calm, considering.

"Heh." At Biribo's little chuckle, my eyes snapped open as I belatedly remembered I was trying not to let on in front of him that I meant to turn on Virya as soon as I could manage. *Shit.* The little lizard flicked out his tongue at me in amusement. "I think you should know, boss, that at least half of all Dark Lords and a surprising number of Heroes have set out with that exact ambition. Before you go and do anything reckless, keep in mind that not one of 'em ever made any meaningful progress toward pulling it off."

And wasn't *that* just the fucking cherry on top.

"Seemed to work out okay for the Devil King," Sakin said brightly. Immediately, everyone raised their heads and looked at him with the alarm of people who'd just heard one of their ultimate taboos broken.

Interesting.

Biribo buzzed the top of Sakin's head, making him duck. "If getting exiled to the Void is your idea of a success story, you're even more screwed up than I thought."

"And I bet that's *really* saying something," Sakin agreed.

"Lord Seiji," Twigs interrupted, "there's a wagon. I think it's . . . Yes, it has the Auldmaer Company emblem."

"Ah, thank you, Twigs." I swung my legs off my perch and picked my way over the uneven ground to join her.

We had a better vantage for this ambush than our previous one, as the khora forest came within a few meters of the road, up an incline overlooking it. I'd chosen a spot a bit more distant, where the hill was less steep, to mitigate the hassle of hauling our stolen booty up it. The wagon was indeed approaching; taking the spyglass from Twigs, I raised it to verify the Auldmaer logo on its side, then focused on the alchemical bomb Sakin had carefully planted in the road.

It consisted of a bag of the sleeping powder, surrounded by a layer of the explosive compound, which would propel the stuff in a big cloud all over the place once ignited, then a piece of fabric artfully draped over the top and coated in the basalt shimmer stuff, which made the finished product look like an innocuous, flattish rock. Sakin had assembled it with a practiced deftness that told me this wasn't his first time. Now it lurked there at the edge of the road, just waiting for our targets to come within range.

Downwind of us, of course.

"Hang on, Auldmaer?" Harold asked. "Why are we robbing them again? I thought those guys were our friends now."

"Indeed," I said, still watching through the glass as the wagon drew closer. "Master Auldmaer's struggling little trading company has just made a *killing* by cornering the market on certain rare luxury goods, thanks to us. The logical thing for him to do now is to diversify into more stable and conservative markets, like distributing mundane trade goods between villages and clan castles around Dount; this stabilizes the company's cash flow while he scouts for the next *big* investment. We're talking simple goods like food, asauthec, and other basics we'll need. Even better, if he then *loses* some of these shipments to bandit attacks, it diminishes the suspicion that naturally fell on him due to his huge stroke of luck when Crown Rose lost their competing shipment."

"So he can surreptitiously funnel materials to us and deflect unwanted attention in one move," said Sakin with clear approval. "*Nice*, Lord Seiji."

"And since Auldmaer set this up with me, it's a *relatively* safe opportunity for us to test out new methods of subduing caravans," I added. "He and I share a need to get our business done without drawing attention. Quiet now, they're almost in position."

It was too easy. As the wagon drew alongside the disguised alchemical bomb, I focused the spyglass upon the fake rock, and then focused my mind on it. This was much easier than screwing about with fire slimes.

Spark.

The thing ignited in a great *poof,* like the sound of an ox falling onto a colossal pillow, and the entire wagon was enveloped in a gout of purple smoke. There were only two people attached to the single cart, a driver and a guard; one of them got off an aborted yell before going silent. Immediately the smog began to dissipate, vanishing into the air as it drifted away from us in what gentle breeze managed to filter through the khora.

Both dhawls were slumped in the road in their harnesses; the wagon driver had fallen across his seat, while the guard was stretched out on the ground beside one wheel.

"Well, damn," said Donon. "Seems almost . . . anticlimactic. Specially after last time."

"Anticlimactic is what we *want,*" said Sakin. "Quick, quiet, and no witnesses."

"*And* as bloodless as possible," I added. "The last part is important. Won't be very realistic as we get bigger and start handling bigger threats, but it *is* part of my strategy. We need methods of dealing with enemies and not leaving a trail of bodies. Biribo, how's it look?"

"They're out cold, boss," he reported. "Not faking, and no other sapient life in the vicinity; looks like Auldmaer didn't set a trap for us."

"Wait, you were *worried* about that?" Aster demanded.

"He's a merchant." I rose and stepped out of the shadow of the khora, making my way down the slope with the rest of my gang following. "The man has a mind of numbers geared toward the singular goal of *profit.* Also, despite how squeamish he seemed to be about violence, don't forget he travels around with poison in his pocket just waiting to be slipped to whoever sits down for a civilized drink with him. As soon as associating with us becomes more inconvenient than profitable, he'll turn on us. The challenge will be to make as much use of him as possible *before* he reaches that point, and then get rid of him on our terms before he can make the first move."

"Ooh, *cold,*" Sakin crowed, full of relish.

"People are selfish and worse, Lord Seiji," Twigs spoke up unexpectedly, "but that's not all they are. People are motivated by things like gratitude and loyalty, too."

"Sure, I value gratitude and loyalty," I agreed. "That's why I got a dog; she's full of those things. And I left her guarding the fortress because this kind of discreet operation is no place for an excitable creature like that."

"So how long before *we're* not useful and you have to get rid of us?" Kasser demanded in a biting tone.

It was always something with this guy. You subject a fellow to horrible torture a time or two and he gets an attitude that just never rubs off.

"Well, let's explore that, shall we, Kasser?" I did not turn around to give him my trademark shit-eating grin, but only because I was walking downhill and needed to watch my feet. "Let's say I start casually murdering my employees to make some kind of point every time they disappoint me, classic supervillain-style. How long would you reckon I have before they start running off in the night to join up with rival factions and sell them info about me? And *then* what am I supposed to do? I know you guys have said you've got nowhere else to go, but come on. One bandit gang's pretty much like the next; shifting between gangs is pretty much a lateral move, *unless* I make sure you're getting a better deal with me. So that is the deal. Stick by me and I'll make sure you're as well-fed, sheltered, and safe as I can manage. I doubt many other gangs would offer you the same."

We arrived on the road and I bent to check on the guard and wagon driver, carefully moving their limbs into a less awkward position. It seemed like the least I could do.

"Due credit, Lord Seiji, that's a point basically no bandit leaders and very few lords ever figure out," said Goose. "All right, people, you know what we're after. Search the cargo; we want food stocks that'll keep for the long haul. Load up whatever you can carry in the sacks. Donon, you have to *hand out* the sacks, or everybody's just standing around being pretty."

"Uh, right. Sorry."

"Why did we have him carry the sacks again?"

"Hey!"

"Auldmaer said the cash box would be secured under the driver's seat," I added. "Check for that, please, Aster. Biribo, any sign of traps or . . . I dunno, tracking magic?"

"Boss, I appreciate due caution, but that's verging on paranoid. When we start going up against master sorcerers, Void witches, or major clergy, we'll need to worry about stuff like tracking charms and Flashmine spells. Right *now* we're dealing with a small business owner."

"Duly noted, now answer the question."

"No, boss, everything's on the up and up. You may loot the wagon with impunity."

"Splendid." I fished a handful of coins back out and bent over the wagon driver, searching through his coat until I found the inner pockets.

"Are you looting those poor guys, now?" Sakin asked; I wasn't looking at him but I swear I could hear him grinning. "Come on, Lord Seiji, haven't we done enough to them?"

"On the contrary, I am antilooting them." I tucked a few silver halos into the man's pocket and turned to do the same with the guard, noting that Aster had pried loose the small chest of coins allotted for their journey. "We've established that Auldmaer doesn't pay full wages for employees who lose cargo. I prefer not to screw over any more average working-class folks than I can help. It's gotta be hard enough to make an honest living in this shithole country. How we doing on time, Sakin?"

"Oh, golden, we've got at least half an hour before they wake up unless you do something daffy like cast Heal on them. Maybe longer; it's been a while since I've used this particular trick, and goblin alchemy tends to get more potent over time. They're always refining their methods."

"Good. We'll definitely reuse this strategy, but I don't want to be overly predictable, so feel free to suggest other methods we can leverage now that we've got an alchemy supplier."

"*That's* what I like to hear!" he said, straightening up from an opened barrel of dried beans to grin maniacally down at me. "I know a good handful of sneaky gimmicks, but it'll be worth getting in good enough with this crew of goblins to ask them for advice. Last time I worked with gobbos was in a different kingdom, and a few years ago. It's a safe bet this outfit will have different, and possibly better, tricks."

"Actually, that's good advice for several reasons, boss," Biribo added. "See, goblins are culturally Viryan. That's why they get such a raw deal in Sanorite kingdoms like Fflyr Dlemathlys."

"Really? I figured it was because they were small and easy to push around, and incompetent regimes like to prop themselves up by scapegoating harmless minorities for their own crimes."

"Well, yeah, but I mean the Viryan thing is the on-paper justification, usually. I would advise not trying to play the Dark Lord card until you're positioned well enough to back it up, but once you're there, goblins will very likely rally to you. And what they lack in mass, they make up for in wits. They're *great* early additions to any Dark Crusade—exactly the specialists you'll need to help you get maximum effectiveness with minimal resources."

"Dunno about the Viryan thing, but I'll back him up on their usefulness, Lord Seiji," Sakin added while shoveling beans into a sack. "It'll generally be a good use of your time to establish good relations, now that you've got an in with tunnel society."

"Yeah," Donon added enthusiastically, "goblins are the—"

He was drowned out by groans, shouted imprecations, and one thrown handful of dried beans.

"Hey!" Harold called, straightening up from a crate he'd just opened. "There's a whole box of spices here!"

"Ooh, *nice*," said Goose. "Be sure to bring that! We'll have to sacrifice a bag or two of grain, but we should have plenty."

"Or," I suggested, "we could bring the grain and just *not* eat food so full of peppers and sour sap that you can't taste the actual food."

All of them, in unison, stopped what they were doing and turned stares of blank, yet faintly accusatory, incomprehension on me. Even Aster.

"Fine, whatever," I grumbled. "You people are monsters."

"It'll be fine, Lord Seiji," Goose said with an indulgent smile. "We're not low on stocks back home yet anyway; with this we should be set up for months."

"Great, I'll make sure to get some traps and pest poison next time I'm in Gwyllthean to secure our food storage. We're gonna hit more targets in the coming weeks; I want to build a solid enough stockpile for when we've got more people."

"What more people are you expecting to get, exactly?" Kasser demanded.

"Ooh!" Aster grinned at me. "Can *I* tell them?"

26

In Which the Dark Lord Gets Hot and Steamy with Aster

Cleaning up the rest of the fortress had stalled for a day when I diverted everyone's efforts to deep-cleaning the old stable, but with all hands on deck, it had only taken an afternoon. I had done this in reaction to the dual discoveries that there was a channel of the on-site spring which could be diverted into this building, and that it emptied onto an enormous square basin against the rear wall that had served as a water trough for the animals. Now that, too, was paying off.

That evening, Aster opened the door from the mess hall to peek in and find the stable entirely transformed from the dark, stinking, crawn-infested hole in which I'd hidden from Kasser and Harold on my first day. Spotlessly clean and well-lit by reed torches soaked in asauthec, it was also noticeably damp. Fortunately the stable came with a floor which subtly sloped toward the drain channel along its center. The room was also closed off now; the iron hinges of the big stable doors had rusted to practically nothing, but the big akorshil doors themselves were intact, as apparently properly treated akorshil didn't decay, and with some help from the guys, I had gotten them propped up in place.

And then there was the centerpiece. My own masterwork.

Aster peeked in, silently took stock of the scene, and then slipped the rest of the way inside, shutting the door after herself. She approached me at the far end of the old stable, her expression even more sardonic than usual.

"I hope this is important?" I drawled.

"That's what *I* want to ask," she retorted, folding her arms.

The old water trough was, apparently quite by accident, *perfectly* designed. Deep enough to sit in with your head and shoulders over the rim, subtly rounded on the interior so there were no sharp edges, and propped up on short legs that left a space underneath so it could be drained through a plugged hole in the bottom. I had piled loose akorthist bricks, fallen from the outer walls, around the edges to enclose the space. The only tricky part had been figuring out the right number of fire slimes to put under there to get the perfect temperature.

"Yes," I said, as solemnly as I could for being so relaxed. "This is *very* important. You should try; it's extremely therapeutic."

"If that's an attempt to get me naked, I've heard better. Anyway, what's therapeutic about sitting in hot water?"

"*Everything.*" I lounged back in the bath, stretching my arms along both sides of the rim, and smiled blissfully up at her. "Also, if you can't tell from the pink glow, I've got healing slimes in here. But even so, the importance of a proper hot bath *cannot* be overstated. You know, now that I think about it, the fact that you Fflyr don't bathe must be both the cause and the effect of how generally horrible this country is. It's a vicious cycle. A vicious, stinky cycle."

"Of course we *bathe*," she said, affronted. "You've never caught *me* smelling like an abattoir! But you *bathe* in a stream, or a fountain, or with a bucket and cloth if you've got nothing else."

"Yeah, I saw those . . . stationary spigots that inn we stayed at tried to pass off as a bathhouse."

"Is that why you were so disappointed? The water has to be *flowing* in some manner to wash the dirt *off* you. That's what makes you clean! What *you* are doing is making Dark Lord soup."

Junko barked, though without disturbing the folded towel resting atop her head.

"No, Junko, I didn't forget you," Aster said patiently. "Soups are named after the main ingredient. Dark Lord, healing slime, and dog soup just doesn't roll off the tongue."

"Well, obviously, you wash yourself off before you get in the bath, otherwise yes, you'd just be stewing in your own filth. A proper shower would be helpful for that, but I don't expect miracles."

"Uh-huh. Good thing that doesn't make this completely pointless. And it's customary, where you're from, to have your dog in the bath?"

I turned a thoughtful eye on Junko, who was sitting upright with just her head and shoulders emerging from the water, serving as my very convenient towel rest. The surface behind her kept rippling due to her wagging tail, but even she seemed very relaxed.

"No . . . actually, I'm pretty sure this would get me kicked out of any onsen in Japan. But hey, she wanted to come in. I'll just have to clean the tub afterwards. Or make Donon do it. Anyway, I believe you were going to explain what was important enough to interrupt bath time?"

"Just checking on you, to be honest. You've been in here a long time, and Biribo's starting to get agitated. I think something about being a familiar makes him kinda unsettled if he's separated from you for too long."

"Meh. He'll live."

Aster tilted her head slightly to one side, her expression going pensive. This gave me about two seconds' notice that what came next was going to be way too awkward for bath time.

"Why are you so mean to Biribo?"

Yep, called it.

"Are you kidding? He's a creepy little lizard who answers to the evil goddess who abducted me to this hell world."

"And the living symbol of your frustration with this whole situation, I get it." She made a peculiar lopsided gesture combining a nod and a shrug; I'd seen a few other Fflyr do that, though not as often as their ritual hand gestures. "Is that *his* fault?"

I let out a huff through my nose. "Did you miss the part where he *answers to Virya*? The lizard *explicitly* works for the enemy, and I'm dependent on him. Just how happy do you think I am about this relationship?"

"Sure, but is *that* his fault? He's a tiny flying lizard. *You're* only working for Virya because of what she threatened to do to you if you don't, right? Well, you're a grown man with all your Dark Lord powers and the full knowledge of a futuristic utopian society. Imagine how much worse it is for a little critter like Biribo. Do you think he even *likes* Virya? Seems like you could find common ground instead of taking your stress out on him."

I could have spent the entire rest of the night refuting the notion of Japan as a utopia. Sure, compared to Fflyr Dlemathlys . . . sort of. But *still*. She had me in a corner, though; in this conversation, pursuing that tangent would be a blatant evasion of the subject, and Aster would not hesitate to gleefully call me out on it.

Instead I sighed and sunk a little deeper in the water. "Aster, bath time is for relaxation. This is a sacred thing you are defiling here."

"Oh, do excuse me, my lord," she said with deep solemnity and folded her hands down at me.

I raised one hand out of the water to make a languid gesture. "Well, since you've gone and embraced the awkwardness anyway, I've been thinking. Do you think it's weird that I don't wanna bang you?"

Aster threw up her hands in exasperation. "The *things* that come out of your mouth!"

"I'm serious! Here we are, me, dashing and altogether ravishing, and you . . . cute enough, I suppose, in the right light—"

Her hand skillfully impacted the surface at the perfect angle to slice water right into my eyes. Junko barked at her in what sounded suspiciously like encouragement.

I wiped at my face without complaining because, after all, fair enough. "But really. Not to get all mushy, but I definitely trust and *like* you more than the rest of these goons. We're kinda stuck out here with each other and this pretty fucked-up situation. Everything I understand about human psychology says this is exactly how people get together, but I dunno . . ."

"No spark?" she said wryly.

I shrugged. "It's not that you aren't pretty. It's just occurred to me . . . seems odd."

"Well, that's just how it is with men and women, Lord Seiji. Passion is unpredictable by nature. A lot of the time it rears up where it's not wanted and causes trouble. Then again, sometimes it never happens when by all accounts you'd think it should."

"Just no chemistry, huh," I murmured.

"Is that really something to be bothered by?" she prodded, smiling. "I don't know about you, but to me our situation seems complicated enough. I think I'm a lot more comfortable *not* having to add an interpersonal layer that's just guaranteed to make everything . . . sticky."

"Yeah, I suppose you're right," I agreed with a sigh. My next thought caused me to hesitate. If I revealed to her . . . But I'd been over this in my own head before. If I couldn't trust Aster, I was screwed anyway. "There's something you should know, though."

"Uh-oh," she said, raising her eyebrows. "Right on the heels of *that* conversation?"

"I told you about my spell combination. Well, Enjoin—y'know, the source of your Blessings—is based partly on Enamor."

Aster emitted a startled bark of laughter. "What, *you* know the love spell? You, of all people!"

"*Love* spell? Are you serious? I don't think you understand how that thing works."

"Hey, that's just what I've always heard it called."

"We're talking about a way to remove somebody's agency so they can be coerced into sex. *Love* isn't the word I would choose."

"So I'm under the influence of Enamor, am I?" she grinned. "Then how do you explain my complete lack of any urge to strip off and climb into this tub of soup? Aside from the dog hair."

"If you'd let me *finish*, none of the effects of Enamor are inherited by Enjoin, only the conditions. So I can only cast it on someone I'm physically attracted to—"

"Aww, I'm blushing." She wasn't.

"—even if she's a horrible wench who won't let me finish a sentence. *And* the spell's termination clause is, y'know . . . the sexual fulfillment part. And it can't be cast twice on the same target."

Her eyebrows rose again as she caught on. "Ah. So if we *did* go to bed, I'd lose all my borrowed powers and could never get them back?"

"Exactly."

And there it was. She could walk out of here right now and just keep having dual Blessings forever, regardless of anything else I did. That had been true this whole time, though; now she knew it.

Aster just grinned indulgently and splashed me again. "Well, then it seems like a *very* good thing we're not making this complicated! What the hell were you so worried about anyway?"

"Maybe I'm worried *because* it seems to work out too neatly," I said, scrubbing water out of my eyes. "I'm only realizing in hindsight how many things that've happened to me were exactly what I needed, and a lot of 'em could've spelled disaster if things had gone even *slightly* differently. It makes me worried about just how many strings Virya is pulling."

"Well . . . that's fair. But there's not much you can do about her, at least not now. I'd say just be glad you've got a goddess with a vested interest in you not being killed, even if she is the bad one."

"There aren't any good ones," I muttered. "I'm only about halfway certain she's the worst of the two."

"Always such a ray of sunshine."

"Maybe I'd be more agreeable if people didn't keep *interrupting my bath.*"

"All right, all right, I'm going. Just don't stay in there until you shrivel up."

"Just for that, I'm gonna!"

"Yeah, that'll show me."

The next day, we returned to Gwyllthean. As the sun set, a week after our "delivery" from the Auldmaer Company, Aster and I arrived in Cat Alley, ready for another round of smut and horror. Fully disguised, her black-stained greatsword at the ready, Biribo hiding inside my cloak.

Here I had my first real evidence of progress; rumor had indeed swirled in my wake after my first visit, and several of the doors that had been slammed in my face before were now opened, with varying degrees of caution. A few of the low-rent madams remained too wary of my intentions, but a handful of the others found their hearts opened to . . . well, greed. I did not delude myself that care for the well-being of their working girls was a factor in their calculations, but free healing was basically free money.

Thus, I had some new cases of disease to treat, some of them verging on the horrific, as before. Among the familiar faces I saw, though, I didn't see signs of resumed infection. Of course, I Healed them anyway. Most infectious illnesses would take longer than a week to start showing symptoms, and it was a given that some of them would have picked up *something* in the intervening days.

On the other hand, the injuries were exactly as bad as when I'd been here last. In keeping with my mysterious Healer persona, I forbore comment. It was, I remained aware, deeply hypocritical for me to take moral offense at what I was seeing here; my own goal was to use these people. I was not planning to use them anywhere near as brutally as their current exploiters, but still. Being a lesser breed of asshole doesn't mean you get to call yourself a hero. It was just . . . You couldn't see shit like this without feeling *something*, unless you were a psychopath.

Maybe I should bring Sakin down here sometime and test a theory.

Plus, and yes this was petty, I was *personally* insulted at having my own work undone. When I Healed a fresh black eye on a girl of about seventeen whose broken nose I had Healed the week before, I found I had my own beef with whatever piece of shit had done it, in addition to outrage on her behalf.

It actually verged on comforting when I stepped into the rear entrance of the Alley Cat. Even the shady-looking guy guarding the back door gave me a purely respectful nod.

"Well, well," Miss Minifrit drawled in her rejuvenated alto, pausing to inhale deeply through her pipe and blow an artful streamer of smoke toward the ceiling. "I had a feeling we hadn't seen the last of you."

I shook my head, just widely enough to make it apparent with the heavy cowl. "What did I tell you about smoking?"

"And what did I tell you about telling me about smoking?" she countered, but now there was a faint smile hovering about her lips. That was progress anyway. "But wait, let me guess. The price . . ."

". . . has been paid," I finished, inclining my head.

She exhaled smoke through her nostrils, looking like a seductive dragon. "Well, there goes one theory. It would almost be simpler if you were up to anything so mundane as getting us hooked on free healing so you could later start charging through the nose."

"That sounds like a respectable grift," I acknowledged. "Perhaps in another life I could have tried it. Alas, we are all here now, and the price—"

"Yes, I remember your slogan. *And* I gather you still won't accept remuneration for your services. *Don't* say the line again."

I hesitated, reminding myself not to break character. Minifrit had a way of drawing out some of my conversational enthusiasm; she was just fun to verbally spar with. But it was Lord Seiji who was the wiseass; the Healer was aloof and mysterious.

"To take more would make me a thief."

"Mm." She regarded me for a long moment of silence while the laughter and song from her lively common room washed over us. Then, at last, the madame found another reason to smile. "Well. Whatever it is you are actually up to, Healer . . . and however I end up feeling about you when this is all over . . . thank you, in all sincerity. Both for looking after my girls, and . . ." She lightly tapped her throat with the hand not holding her pipe.

I just nodded again. "Then, who here is in need of healing?"

"How much damage do you think we could have accrued in a week?"

"On Yrshith Street? More than anyone should."

"Too right," Minifrit agreed with a grimace. "Well then, if you are still offering your services, I'll not stop you. Just don't disrupt my clients or business. And you remain welcome to my hospitality, should you ever extract that stick from where it is stuck. I have just the girl to help you with that, if you'd like."

"Healer!" a new voice burst out as a young woman emerged from one of the back rooms and spotted me. "He's back! The Healer's here!"

Minifrit ran a tight enough ship that nobody came out of an occupied room, or stopped entertaining in the public area, but apparently that left enough of the staff at liberty for a mob of half a dozen to materialize seemingly out of every crack in the walls. My last sight of the madame before I was crowded into a corner was of her making a languorous "go ahead" gesture at me with her pipe.

There remained fairly little for me to do here, compared to some places. No one was showing any signs of disease; a few of the women requested non-specific healing anyway, and received it. There were several minor injuries, the worst of which was a combination cracked molar, dislocated jaw, and a large bruise along that entire side of her face. The woman had obviously been punched. At least nothing as bad as the savage beating which had nearly killed Kastrin had happened this week, but Cat Alley remained Cat Alley. Minifrit's bouncers would toss out a john who got rough with the personnel, but clearly some got in one good hit before that happened.

And, as the gossip which surrounded me reaffirmed, there were always Lady Gray's people, who got away with doing whatever they liked because the consequences of standing up to them were even worse.

We would soon see about that.

All told, it was by far the most pleasant—or more accurately, least unpleasant—stop of the evening; I spent at least as much time deflecting questions as administering healing. And I noticed Kastrin present and watching me. With a smile, but a muted and wary one. She had reason to be grateful for my intervention, more than most, but also had the wit and life experience to be suspicious of a free handout. I decided that made her a useful barometer for how well I was doing in my campaign to befriend the denizens of Cat Alley.

It was also Kastrin who, after disappearing for a few minutes, brought my visit to a close.

"Healer!" She squeezed past her coworkers, who were lounging in the hall chatting at me, now that it had been a few minutes since anyone actually requested healing. I turned to her expecting more conversation, which I'd have to find a way to duck out of, but her expression was far more serious. "There's trouble. Two of Lady Gray's thugs are hanging around the back entrance, asking about you."

"I'm surprised it took this long," said Minifrit, manifesting in the hallway as if summoned like a genie. At a sharp gesture from her, the girls around me crowded against the walls, clearing a path. "And of course, you picked *my* place to get cornered in."

"Point taken," I agreed. "I believe I shall make myself scarce, before something happens which proves disruptive to your clientele."

"I don't know how limber you can possibly be in that getup," Kastrin said, casting a doubtful eye over my heavy coat and cloak, "but there's a way out on the top floor. If you can jump at all, you can get to the next roof over, and from there getting down shouldn't be too hard. Might wanna hop a few more rooftops, though, just to be safe."

"Gray's people use the roofs too, Kastrin," said another woman.

"Only when they're expecting a need," she retorted. "I'm not saying it'll work *twice*, but for now . . ."

"For now," I interrupted, catching Minifrit's eye and noting her wary expression, "my mysterious disappearance from here when they think me cornered will only bring attention on this house. I'll just go out the front."

"If they have men at the back, they'll have them at the front," Minifrit warned. "I don't know who you think you're dealing with, Healer, but these men will not hesitate to accost you in full view of the public."

"No doubt," I replied. "Please don't worry about me, ladies."

"I'm sure your silent companion here knows how to use that sword," the madame said, giving Aster a sharp look, "but I *don't* recommend it. If you succeed in cutting down any of Lady Gray's men, especially if they're out on her business, that will only make her attention considerably more . . . focused."

"I appreciate the warning, Miss Minifrit. Rest assured, though, I came here to heal, not to harm. I know what I'm doing."

"I very much fear you do," she said, staring me down. "I think I'd almost rather you were a naive fool."

"I'll try not to take that personally."

"We'll see who takes what personally when it comes to pass that you've finally brought down all the trouble you're inevitably going to."

That made me crack a grin, not that she could see it. Instead, I bowed to her.

All of the women clustered in the hall reared back in surprise, several looking uneasy. Minifrit just raised one eyebrow.

"You *are* from a long way away. We don't bow in Fflyr Dlemathlys."

I actively did not give a fuck what they did in Fflyr Dlemathlys, and fully intended to do everything in my not inconsiderable power to overturn every aspect of their miserable lives. But this was not the time to say so to people's faces.

Instead, I silently and mysteriously glided down the hall, through the beaded curtain, and across the common room, where my passage gathered a lot of curious stares but did not slow down the laughter and shouting appreciably.

Minifrit, as was very much like her, was right on the money. No sooner had Aster and I emerged into the blue glow of the brothel lights than two almost exaggeratedly scruffy-looking men with clubs hanging at their belts materialized right out of the crowd in front of us.

"And this must be him!" one of them said, showing me a grin that was prominently missing a tooth. "The great and powerful Healer of Cat Alley! Sorry to interrupt your rounds, Master Healer, but my chum and I require a moment of your time."

"We represent a certain . . . business concern who has interests throughout the Gutters," his partner continued. "I gather you're new in town, but something tells me you'll have heard of her by now, even so."

"Lady Gray would like a word with you," said the first, still grinning but now adding a very pointed emphasis to his tone. "At your *earliest convenience*."

All around us, the crowd had practically stopped moving; everyone either recognized these goons or had heard the name Lady Gray and knew exactly what it portended. That suited me just fine—all of this did. I had expected something of the sort sooner or later, and not being an idiot, planned for it.

And now? It was *showtime*.

27

In Which the Dark Lord Almost Makes a Spectacle of Himself

I am only here to heal."

Even through the mask, my voice projected with a force that reached everyone on this segment of the street.

"Sure, of course," said the first thug, still grinning at me. "Nobody says you can't. But you can *also* spare some time to talk with Lady Gray, I'm sure."

"*Everybody* can spare Lady Gray whatever time she needs, trust me," added the second. These guys must have worked as a pair often; they spoke in tandem almost as if they'd rehearsed it.

"Talk . . . about what?"

"Why, that's between you and her, stranger."

"Ain't for the likes of us to ask Lady Gray her business."

"She points, we go."

"And she's pointed at you, friend. So . . . shall we go?"

Still smiling and amiable, despite their deliberately rough appearance and overtly displayed weapons. I was starting to like these guys a little bit. They shared my appreciation for theatrics.

Slowly, drawing out the moment, I tilted my head to one side, just enough to make the motion apparent even with the heavy cowl.

"This . . . Lady Gray," I finally said, enunciating carefully. "Has she paid the price?"

Tweedledee and Tweedledum looked at each other in clear uncertainty. The onlooking crowd shifted, the muttering from nearby swelling to nearly overwhelming the laughter and shouts from farther up and down the street.

"Dunno how she could've, friend, seeing as you've not met just yet."

"Lady Gray doesn't lack for means after all. Whatever coin you need . . . If you're worth it, she can pay it."

I shook my head, ponderously, watching their eyes track the darkness under my hood as it shifted back and forth.

"Money. Coins will not cover the price, only . . . impose it. I've no business with those whose business is only money."

"Well, now, here in the Gutters we're adaptable folk," the gap-toothed fellow assured me, his apparent good humor undiminished by his growing uncertainty.

"And Lady Gray *is* the Gutters, for all intents and purposes."

"Favors, commodities . . . Pick your poison, stranger."

"But you should really ask the Lady herself for your price. We're just the messengers after all."

I deliberately widened my stance, as if bracing my feet for action. My hands hung loose at my sides, fingers flexed and ready. Amid the surrounding muted hubbub, I heard the scrape of boots on akorthist as Aster adjusted her feet; I couldn't see her with the damn hood blocking my peripheral vision, but I assumed she'd reached up to grasp the handle of her sword, from the way both toughs shifted their eyes to her.

"I have come here to heal," I said, loud but calm. "Unless you wish to pay the price, you are in my way."

I could almost *feel* the indrawn breath of dozens of onlookers. Lady Gray's two thugs looked at each other again, seeming to communicate something silently with just their eyes. I flexed my hands—not because I needed them to cast magic, but just for effect.

Now the spectacle I'd planned would begin in earnest.

"Well, all right then," said the first thug, folding down his hands at me. "The request stands, Healer."

Wait. What?

"We'll just check back with you later, shall we?" the second thug added. "When you change your mind, let us know."

"Have a safe night, now. It's a rough sort of neighborhood."

"Not that you look like you'll have any trouble." He winked at Aster. And with no more ado, the two of them turned and strolled off up the street, cool and collected.

But . . . but my *showtime!*

I had spent the last *week* on this plan, going over and over in my head all the ways a crime lord's minions might attempt to subdue me, planning for every contingency I could think of. I'd freely indulged myself with ever more fanciful outcomes, just to make sure I had all possible events covered, reasoning that even if the majority of these ideas were implausible, just being prepared for numerous possible twists of fate would leave me better able to adapt if they sprung some new trick I'd somehow failed to anticipate.

Except, as it turned out, if they politely backed down. *That* one I had not seen coming, and now it left me standing there posed for my well-planned show, and no longer having any path to executing it.

This fucking world. Even when it gave me an optimal outcome, it managed to be in a way that wrecked all my planning. It was an entire planet whose every feature was meticulously crafted to *piss me off*.

I turned and glided across the street, Aster trailing silently along behind me, to the next brothel on my list.

In fact, the owner of the Jostled Jugs herself was standing just outside her doorway, watching the prematurely aborted show with her arms folded.

"Gannit," I greeted the old woman in a much less projected voice as I approached. "I hope all's been well since—"

"Yeah, yeah, get your shady ass in here, boy." She seized my arm in an amazingly solid grip and all but dragged me into the brothel. Gannit was incredibly spry for someone pushing seventy, but she was in no condition to haul me around unless I chose to go, and I wasn't interested in knocking down an old lady.

She tugged me all the way through the common room to the kitchen in the back, a short journey on which I had to endure a lot of catcalling. Yeah, yeah, a woman dragging a man through a brothel usually means one thing, and it's funny when it's a grandma and the mysterious magic Healer, I get it. Hilarious.

"Do you have any idea the shit you just did?" Gannit demanded upon releasing me, once we were safely in the kitchen away from her guests and employees—aside from the ones cooking, who watched the spectacle with open amusement but somehow didn't slow down in their work.

"Very little, it seemed."

"Oh, and you put a lot of trust in appearances, do you?" She gave my all-concealing outfit a very pointed once-over.

"How's the arthritis?"

Gannit cracked a grin at that and flexed one skinny arm like a bodybuilder. "Hah! Not a twinge. You got some serious mojo, Healer. Too bad you don't have the sense to go with it. Now sit your ass down and listen; it's time you got a rundown on how things work in Cat Alley."

"What's to know?" I asked, not moving toward the indicated stool.

"*Sit.*" The old woman folded her arms and looked imperious until I finally sat down, then nodded in satisfaction. "All right, it's story time. You've been up and down the street once, I'm sure you noticed it's only women who run brothels in this town."

"That did strike me as odd," I admitted. "This country seems even more hostile to women than it is to everyone else."

"Too right," she grinned. "Fflyr Dlemathlys has always been that way, but Cat Alley has only been *this* way the last thirty years or so. Whoring's good money—for the people who own the business, that is, not so much the ones doing the work. So naturally it was the men who owned it. At least, 'til some uppity whores managed to start a big flap among the Radiant Convocation and get themselves cast out of polite society."

"That sounds like quite a tale."

"Oh, that it is," she said with relish. "A long and complicated one, and I may tell you the whole version someday, but right now we got more pressing matters. Point is, in this country, it ain't *strictly* against the law for men to be involved in prostitution, but it's firmly against Convocation doctrine, and you don't spit right in the Convocation's eye like that. They've got *ways* of putting down people they don't approve of. And the best part is *we* did that!" She slapped her own chest just below the collarbone. "That's what we do here, boy. The game's rigged against the likes of us, so we took their own crooked rules and spun 'em to carve out our own place. Just takes some cleverness, a little work, and a willingness to bleed for what matters. You men like to think you're all big and tough, and you may be at that, but there's not a woman born who's shy about bleeding."

"I'm impressed," I said, meaning it. "Someday I *would* like to hear the full version. I don't understand what it has to do with me, though."

"It's more what *you* have to do with *it*," Gannit retorted, snatching a ladle right out of the hand of an exasperated cook to wag it at me. Droplets of soup scattered across the floor. "Cos we're right in the middle of another drug-out kerfuffle no less serious than the Liberation of the Whores, and *you* have just swished your spooky cloak right the hell into the middle of it. Lemme put it this way—the whole status quo in Cat Alley rests on our hard-won almost-law that only women in the business get to control the business. Well, last ten years or so, the Gutters have a woman who moved up through the street gangs until she got the whole lot of 'em tied together under her control. And just you guess where *she* came up from!"

". . . ah."

"*Ah*, he says," Gannit snorted. "Here's how it is, boy. There's still more madams who own their own places than not, but Lady Gray's moving in. Slowly, and starting with the cheap joints, but moving nonetheless. There's more brothels she doesn't own outright but has some kinda hold on the madame. Now, we're not helpless. The bigger places like Minifrit's and mine, we've got our own muscle . . . not to mention other means of getting things done that you don't need to concern yourself with. But that doesn't mean we've got enough muscle to *flex*. This is delicate, Healer. It's back-alley politics. Lady Gray's got enough force to move in here and force us all out in one night. She *won't*, because that would ruin all the businesses she's trying to take over, and probably scatter the trade far and wide across the Gutters rather than keep Cat Alley in one profitable concentration. We've got enough coin and bouncers to push back . . . here and there, within reason, *strategically*. Gray's bully boys still get to throw their weight around way more'n any of us likes, because anybody who stands up to her is inviting a confrontation that ends with her taking over *that* business."

To my mortification, I physically twitched as a vivid memory of the savagely beaten face of Kastrin flashed across my eyes, followed by a rapid parade of other brutalized women I'd seen and healed. Gannit was still watching me like a hawk, but if she thought anything of the abortive little movement, she didn't say so.

"And then there's *you*. You have already rustled her eggs good and proper, boy. What do you think happens when a bunch of beaten-down, pox-riddled whores are suddenly clean and hale again?"

"They're clean and hale again," I said.

"Yeah, yeah, and if that's all you care about, good on ya. But what their *owners* care about is how much they're worth—which is to say, more. A lot more. In a lot of the places you've visited, every girl is suddenly of a quality that used to mark their best girl, or better. Now, there's a few ways that can shake out. They might start bringing in more money—or less, if they raise prices accordingly and the custom goes elsewhere. I dunno how much extra coin you've made *and* cost Lady Gray in the last week, but whether the final tally's plus or minus, you've made yourself a big fat *variable* in her record books. And then, *then*, you went and stood up to her goons—the one thing we are keeping her at bay by carefully *not fucking doing*."

Gannit folded her arms, glaring at me. Seizing the opportunity, the cook snatched her ladle back and resumed stirring.

"Well, then," I said, after a pause. "Thank you for enlightening me, Gannit. I'll be careful."

"Son," she drawled, "I am very *slightly* concerned about *your* shifty ass. You need to get it into your head that this ain't a storybook. Actions have consequences, and around here? They're a lot more complicated than you might anticipate, and will affect a lot more people than just *you*. You can't just swoop in here and *save* everybody, if that's what you were trying to do."

"It wasn't."

Her eyes narrowed to slits. "Hnh. Well, guess that's as good a setup as any for the big question. Whatever you *are* trying to do—and I know you've got an agenda, boy—I ain't stupid nor blind. Whatever it is you're planning, is it going to get a lot of working girls, who've already had it bad enough, hurt or worse?"

She stared at me; the two cooks and one passing serving girl stopped what they were doing, turning to look expectantly at me as well.

I inhaled slowly, taking in the smells of food, and let the breath back out. This question, at least, I was prepared for. And not just because I anticipated having to answer it; I'd grappled with it on my own time.

"Yes," I replied finally. "But no more than the way they live now. And for most, I think, considerably less."

Gannit squinted at me, slowly working her jaw. The other three went back to their own business, the waitress vanishing through the swinging door into the common room.

"Well, shit," she said finally. "I owe Minifrit a gold disc. She *said* you were working a long-term scheme. I figured you were just a melodramatic weirdo with a Blessing and a hero complex."

"Parts of that are accurate," I admitted, "but the Hero I am not. I don't think his help would do you much good either. I came here to help, Gannit, that I promise you. You're right, though; complicated situations mean you can't just *help* without causing far-reaching consequences. Those who have paid the price are owed healing—that's the least I can do. What happens next . . . I will try to protect everyone I can. We'll see how well the world cooperates."

"You and your *price*," she snorted, shaking her head. "Well, that's more talking than I got outta you last time. I guess you're done opening up, then?"

I rose from the stool, and bowed to her. One of the cooks who was sneaking a peek gave me a wide-eyed stare, but Gannit just smirked.

"It has still been paid. *Far* in advance. I thank you for the warning, Gannit. Now, who here is in need of healing?"

At least the rest of the night went according to plan.

There was a whole new layer of tension this time, now that I knew Lady Gray's eyes were on me. Not being an utter fool, I didn't believe for a second that her goons had actually given up and gone home after one verbal rejection, especially after Gannit had laid out the political situation for me. I could practically feel the eyes on me as I finished up in the cheapest brothels—the ones Gannit had warned might be owned outright by Gray herself.

By the end of my rounds that night, I was almost irked that our constant vigilance had been for nothing. But so it was. Aster and I found ourselves back on the road, and she stopped by a vendor to get us some hot food for the trip home. There hadn't been so much as another peep out of Lady Gray or anyone purporting to work for her. Nobody had ambushed us, barred our path, or in any way made themselves an inconvenience.

And so it remained until we were a good forty-five minutes out of the city.

"Hey, boss?" Biribo piped up, buzzing out of my cloak to hover in front of me at shoulder height.

"What's up?"

"I wasn't sure until we turned onto this side trail," he said quietly, "but we're being followed."

I inhaled deeply and blew the breath back out. ". . . okay. Not unexpected. Would've been *nice* if they'd tried this back in Cat Alley so I could execute my plan."

"Yeah, what's up with enemies not walking helpfully into our traps?" Aster complained. "Foes these days. *No* respect for tradition, that's what's wrong with the world."

"Are you done?"

"I think that'll hold me for now," she said sweetly.

"What've we got, Biribo?"

"Three targets. Human, male, lowborn, no Blessed. I'm *mostly* sure they're the same three who've been behind us all the way from the city, but that was on the main highway during morning traffic, so it was less certain. But they turned onto this back road after us, so . . ."

"Mm . . . *could* still be coincidence, but I'm not gonna gamble on that. How far?"

"Close to a dhil."

"I'm gonna stab you."

"Boss, you can keep being performatively upset about the measuring system here or *learn* it. Which do you think is more useful? They're just close enough to see if you turned around, but . . . maybe don't."

"Yeah, let's not give away the game just yet," I murmured. "Thoughts?"

"If we're gonna take 'em out, the sooner the better," said Aster. "Neither of us are at our freshest and we'll only get more tired as time goes on."

"Given that you've got *me* and can keep track of them without revealing you know they're there, we've got dozens of ways of ditching 'em, especially once we get into the khora," Biribo suggested.

"Any sign they're looking to overtake us?" I asked.

"Not so far. That might change, but right now they're staying way back at the edge of visibility. That's shadowing behavior, not ambushing."

"So the goal's not to jump us, but to track us back to our lair," I murmured. "Still, I can't figure out Gray's strategy. Why'd she wait? It would have been much easier to make a move in the Gutters, where she has power. Sending people out into rural Dount is sacrificing the high ground, so to speak. This is Olumnach country and she's at war with them."

"Sounds like there's some stuff going on that we're not aware of," said Aster. "As per usual."

"Okay. Stay alert. Biribo, warn me if they try to speed up; if they wanna make this a confrontation, I mean to hit first."

"You got it, boss. But if not . . . ?"

"If not . . . I have an idea. Aster, how're you doing?"

"Tired. Physically and down to my soul. But I've been more tired than this and kept going. I repeat, if this is going to come to a fight or a run, it'd be better to do it sooner than later, but if your plan just involves walking, I can go for a while yet."

"All right. We're gonna swing north; Biribo can help navigate if you don't know the way, Aster. We'll stick to the back roads as much as possible so they don't get spooked, but our destination is toward the Kingsguard waystation."

She turned to me, raising her eyebrows. "You wanna set the Kingsguard on 'em? Ballsy."

"I don't see how much good *that* would do," I said. "I doubt we look any less shifty and disreputable than they do. Hell, the Kingsguard aren't much better, from what I hear. Just another gang. But speaking of gangs . . .

remember when we torched the Crown Rose caravan and Biribo spotted a bunch of bandits hiding in the khora nearby?"

Biribo himself began laughing quietly.

"Ah," Aster nodded. "And we've been told that the outlying gangs on Dount answer to Clan Olumnach . . ."

"There's an old saying in my mother's homeland," I said, grinning. "'Let's you and him fight.'"

28

In Which the Dark Lord Chews the Scenery

Being pursued at a sedate pace through an idyllic countryside on a sunny morning, with a miniature oracle who obviates the need to check over your shoulder, was an amazingly laid-back experience. If anything, the slight tension added just the right pinch of spice to what would've otherwise been just an aimless stroll. We even fell into casual conversation while Biribo magically kept watch on our pursuers.

"No, look. If it's a one in ten chance, it's ten percent! So it's nine times more likely to have gone the other way."

"Yeah, but a single person is one or the other, right? So it's a binary choice."

"A binary choice with one in ten odds! Listen, if you've got ten people, and only one is—"

"Yeah, but you *don't* have ten people, you only *have* the one, so it's a coin toss."

"That is *not how statistics works*! Biribo, considering I'm dependent on you for information, it is *really* disturbing that you misunderstand *math* on a basic level!"

"Assuming for the sake of argument that you're right, and that's not a concession, math has nothing to do with tactical data or general Ephemera knowledge, boss."

"*I fucking know*. I've been told about the coins."

"So," Aster interrupted, "I gather one of your reasons for recruiting your army is so you can use that Enjoin to strengthen them? Cos, let's face it, they aren't *all* lookers but enough of 'em are passably pretty . . ."

"I considered that, but there doesn't seem much point," I said, glad enough to drop the argument. "The Blessing of Wisdom does nothing without a familiar, and we have no way of getting you one, much less any-body else. The other two are dependent on scrolls and artifacts to be any use, which I already haven't found a way to get more of, and if I *do*, I'm going to need them for myself. So, no real use in Enjoining anybody else when I can't equip them to get anything out of it. To be honest, I only made that spell to test out how spell combination works; I thought at the time it was pretty useless. *You* were a supremely lucky find, Aster."

"That's the nicest thing anybody's said about me in years. Truly. And isn't *that* depressing as hell."

"If it helps, I only cast it on you to see whether it worked."

"Why would that help? Why would you even *say* that? Not every thought that drifts through your consciousness needs to come out of your mouth!"

I cleared my throat. "How're our friends back there doing, Biribo?"

"Oh sure, discussion over, I take it," Aster grumbled.

"They're keeping pace, boss. Cutting through that stretch of khora slowed them down, but they're staying with us."

"I wondered if that would throw them off . . . Visibility in there was prac-tically nil and we stopped talking for the duration. How'd they follow us?"

"The old-fashioned way; I think the third guy is a tracker. The other two are the pair who approached you outside the Alley Cat."

"Are we close to the waystation?"

"It's hard to tell, sticking to remote trails like we have been, but we should be in the vicinity by now," said Aster.

"I think so," Biribo added. "There's a big concentration of people off to our northeast. At this range I can't sense more detail than that, but that'd be the most likely source of it."

"Mm . . . Well, keep me posted. On another note, I've been meaning to ask you, what the hell is Yoshi doing here?"

"Uh, that seems like something you'd need to ask *him*, boss. I'm not a mind reader, unless you empower me the right way. Which you are nowhere near being able to do, incidentally."

"I mean, on Dount."

"Didn't you hire Maugro to find that out?" Aster asked innocently.

I drew in a deep, slow breath, as if I could absorb patience along with the musty, spicy scent of khora. "Okay, let me back up. Virya said this whole Good versus Evil bit is a game to them, right? Well, where I'm from, we have lots of games and stories like that, only not using real people's lives as playing pieces. There's a certain . . . *rhythm* to them. Usually you only start seeing a

Hero when the Dark Lord is well established, has conquered a lot of territory, and is threatening the remainder of the world. Meanwhile, here *I* am, lord of a broken-down old fortress and a handful of bandits. Why's the fucking Hero sniffing around my own backyard already?"

"Ah," said Biribo. "I dunno what to tell you, boss. You gotta understand, this cycle has been going for a *long* time, and there've been a lot of variations. For one thing, a round of the great game only ends when the Dark Lord dies; if the Hero gets murked instead, another one's called. So, lots of Dark Lords have ruled huge empires by the time they bought it. A few honestly just got tired of it all and quit. Or died of anything from natural causes to suicide. Three that I know of retired, handed the keys to power to a lieutenant, and went off by themselves to relax; two of those were still alive and enjoying their sunset well after a Hero toppled their former dominion."

"Virya didn't give me the impression *that* was going to be an option."

"If you gave *her* the same impression you give most people, boss, she was probably not dealing with you gently. Take out a few Heroes and she'll be a lot more lenient with you. But besides that, there've been a bunch of permutations over the centuries. Heroes and Dark Lords might be called decades apart, or at opposite ends of the archipelagos, or right there cheek to cheek from the beginning, like you were. Sometimes they're complete strangers, or best friends, or lovers. A few times the goddesses deliberately pushed them together to become friends before arranging circumstances to force them to fight. Some real good drama that way, you see. It's all about the spectacle for the goddesses."

"That's just *twisted*," Aster murmured.

"So yeah, there's not really some profound answer, if that's what you were wondering, boss," Biribo continued. "The reason you and Yoshi ended up starting in the same country at the same time is just . . . That's how they decided to do it this time. Heads up, we're close enough now that I'm picking up some details. Some of that big group of people I sense is a smaller group, a lot closer to us. About ten."

"*Aha*. Our bandit camp?"

"Most likely. They're deep in the khora, and this is too close to Fflyr territory to be a beastfolk encampment."

We were now on what looked like a game trail that ran through a kind of long, narrow valley, carpeted in field grass and wildflowers, with stands of khora up on ridges to either side.

"And our friends back there?"

"A little closer, but within what I'd consider normal variation of distance for tailing somebody. They don't seem to be trying to close in."

"All right, kids, that's our cue. This is gonna be delicate; we have to move quickly and navigate precisely. Biribo, we'll need you to be the eyes and ears."

"That's what I do, boss! What's the plan?"

Aster and I stepped as quietly as we could manage through the khora, though I did look behind us to take note that we were leaving a trail even I could follow. With no voices except for Biribo guiding us in a whisper barely audible above the buzz of his wings, we passed by the bandit camp as closely as we could manage without coming within range of whatever sentries they had posted. We never saw them, though we passed near enough that even Aster and I could hear voices in the distance. This would never have been possible if we'd gone in blind, but Biribo's senses made it downright easy. He even updated their numbers to a firm count of twelve as we passed by.

We came to a stop as soon as Biribo judged we were at the proper distance and turned back to face the direction from which we'd come. Aster shifted forward, placing herself a bit ahead of me, and drew her greatsword.

"All right, Biribo, you're up," I whispered. "You know the plan; don't flub the timing, and this'll go like clockwork."

"Won't letcha down, boss," he promised, and zipped away into the khora, vanishing in seconds.

Then, there was nothing to do but wait, in tense silence. I checked my hood and mask, the latter of which I'd lowered earlier for ease of breathing; everything was back in place, ready to display the Healer's mysterious persona to the fullest. To my side and ahead, Aster's shoulders shifted as she drew in a breath and let it out slowly.

"You okay?" I murmured. "Tired?"

"Tired, but not too much. I'm fine."

"Probably no need to hold that sword at the ready position. If all goes well, you won't even be using it."

"How often does all go well?"

"Hm. Now that you mention it, seems like things either blow up in our faces or go *suspiciously* smoothly, doesn't it?"

She glanced at me, and though I could see nothing but her eyes between her scarf and hood, I could swear I caught a smirk in them.

That was when the whoop came from up ahead, a loud, penetrating yell in Biribo's shrill little voice. It was immediately followed by a clamor of other voices and the crashing of people rushing about through the underbrush.

I let the yelling play out until it changed tone as a second set of voices joined in. Just after that, Biribo zipped back to us, looking hugely pleased with himself.

"Smooth as buttered satin, boss! Looks like Gray's men are goners."

"Nice work, Biribo. And now, *finally*, it is *showtime*."

"Wait, we're not gonna just let them get killed?" Aster asked. "Then what was the point?"

I just stepped forward, heading toward the sounds of confrontation. That had been my original plan, but in the interim it had occurred to me that if Lady Gray's minions vanished or turned up dead at the hands of an enemy bandit gang after trailing the Healer, I'd leap to the top of her priority list. She couldn't allow me to exist if it looked like I was working for Clan Olumnach. Thus, I'd come up with a better idea. There was no time to explain it now, though.

Biribo ducked back under my cloak just before we stepped around a huge trunk of khora into the small cleared area where he'd laid his ambush. His yell, executed just as our three pursuers had entered this space in the shelter of three huge khora formations, had brought seven of the nearby bandits out of their camp to investigate, where they found three startled Gwyllthean thugs just passing through.

"What the fuck do you think you're doing here, pissant?"

"Hey, I know that guy! He's one of Gray's crew!"

"Is that a *fucking* fact?"

"Don't even think about it!" snarled one of the toughs who'd confronted me in Cat Alley, far less amiable now. He was carrying a crossbow, and now trained it on the tall fellow who was evidently the leader of the bandits. Both of his companions had weapons out, a club and a rapier respectively, but they were badly overmatched and knew it. Apart from being outnumbered, two of the bandits had short hunting bows with arrows nocked and drawn. All of them were armed, and the whole clearing was one sudden move from exploding into violence.

The outcome of that explosion would be simple math, even I could see it at a glance. The crossbowman would kill one of the bandits, the archers would kill two of the city thugs, and then the last guy would be facing six-on-one odds.

At least, until I stepped forward, and about half the weapons were immediately turned on me.

"And what is this?" I demanded, spreading my arms in a beneficent gesture as I emerged from the shadows, my voice projecting clearly through the khora. "Wherefore this violence between countrymen? Can you not see the futility of such infighting? Are we not all brothers in the same struggle? Verily I say to you, all our foes are the same, and it is only they who prosper when we quarrel amongst ourselves."

Dead silence fell; my booming voice had momentarily scared off even the birds and bugs.

"What in Sanora's name is this idiot blathering about?" one of the local bandits finally asked aloud, sounding more confused than angry.

"Ah, ah," I chided, wagging one finger at him. "Invoke not the goddess, lest you call down her notice. For she is less benign than you have been taught."

"Are you with these fuckers?" the big fellow in the lead demanded, looking at me but pointing his ax at the Gwyllthean trio.

"I am the Healer," I intoned, folding my hands before me in a poster of prayer. "I come only to heal. I am on nobody's side, for nobody is on my side."

The bandit boss stared at me quizzically, then turned his incredulous expression on Lady Gray's men.

"I wish I could tell you, brother," the one with the crossbow said tersely. "Guy's some kinda crawnbrain. I really wouldn't fuck with him, though. He's Blessed, and powerful."

"I know a cure for that," one of the bandits growled, and even as his leader shouted a warning at him, the bowstring twanged.

There was an archery club in my high school, but I hadn't been part of it; that was the closest I've ever been to bows and arrows. If your only familiarity with archery is from movies, you're likely to underestimate just how much kinetic energy an arrow has, especially if it's fired from just a couple of meters away.

The shaft hit me right in the midsection and very nearly bowled me over. I stumbled backward, almost losing my feet, and was only saved from an embarrassing tumble by coming up against an outcropping of khora that arrested my backward momentum.

Aster had surged forward, sword upraised. Between it and the artifact armor she wore under her coat, she could very possibly wipe out the entire gang.

"Stop!" I gasped, raising a hand. It was hard to speak—hard to breathe. I straightened back up, my limbs buzzing with the lightness and energy of sheer adrenaline. Good, hopefully that would keep me going long enough to avoid shock setting in. "Be at peace! They know not what they do."

She hesitated, half-turning to keep the bandits in her field of view while checking on me.

I stepped forward, grasping the shaft now sticking out of my midsection. Hot blood was sticky on my fingers, pouring down the front of my coat. By luck or Virya's grace, it had struck me below the ribs, so there was nothing but soft tissue for the head to get stuck on. Hopefully.

You never, ever pull out a foreign object impaling your body, unless you want to bleed to death. Or unless you have ridiculous overpowered healing magic.

The buzz of adrenaline was all that kept me from collapsing or throwing up as I ripped the arrow out of my diaphragm. I felt muscle tear, felt pain spike through me abruptly; it hadn't actually hurt until that point, weirdly enough. The arrow came free cleanly, absolutely soaked crimson. I checked that I had the whole thing out and didn't have an arrowhead still in my flesh, but no, it was there at the end of the shaft. Along with a small chunk of unidentifiable meat which I looked away from and refused to think about, throwing the shaft to the side.

The blood had become a fountain. I could feel myself bleeding out.

Heal.

Gasps, curses, and a couple of shouts reacted to the burst of pink light around me.

"Yeah, I told you," the Gwyllthean thug with the crossbow said resignedly.

"Know this, my child," I intoned, holding out one bloodstained hand toward the bowman who was now gaping at me in shock. "I forgive you your transgression. For I know it was born of fear and pain, not malice."

"Oh, fuck that and fuck *you*," he growled, drawing another arrow.

"Rugin, don't you fucking dare," the bandit leader snarled. "*I* decide who gets jibbed in this outfit! Pop off without my orders again and *your* ass is next!"

"Peace!" I boomed. "Judge not, lest ye be judged."

"Okay, listen up, weirdo," the boss retorted, turning back to me. "That's some impressive mojo, but—"

"Ask yourself, what pain causes your man to lash out so?" I was actually starting to enjoy this; Heal hadn't done anything about the adrenaline still surging in me, and I felt borderline manic at this point now that I wasn't even injured. I raised both my arms skyward, really losing myself in my messianic performance. "What torment of the spirit so erodes the bond between mortal souls? What sickness of the mind assails him? Ask yourself this, but fear not! For I have come, and with me I bring healing!"

"Uh . . ." The bandit glanced at me, at the now shaken-looking archer, and at the Gwyllthean thugs, who were slowly trying to back up into the khora. "Sure, buddy. How about you settle down for a second while I deal with these townie assholes and then we can talk?"

"Behold!" I struck another pose, throwing forward my hand with such enthusiasm that droplets of blood sprayed from my fingertips in the direction of the man who'd shot me. "Your travails end, my brother, for I bring you *healing*!"

Immolate.

I'm afraid poor Rugin dropped his bow, and that was the least of his worries.

Everybody yelled and backpedaled; somebody fired an arrow, but it flew wild into the khora way over our heads. Rugin's scream of utter anguish and terror seemed to fill the clearing with a physical weight, along with the blaze of light from the inferno which consumed him from the inside out.

Two of the bandits broke and ran, as did the third guy from Gwyllthean, the tracker. Both of his companions tried to, but they both tripped over obstructions on the ground; one went sprawling while the crossbowman landed on his butt, accidentally discharging his bolt into the khora foliage above us. The rest of the bandits retreated from Rugin, as any sensible person did from a fire.

None of the rest ran, though, after the first shock, and the entire audience stared in horrified shock, seemingly frozen, as the spell ran its course. The bandit's voice gave out as the flesh which enabled it was reduced to charcoal; that period of silence in the middle there was almost the worst part before the healing magic began to take over and he recovered the ability to gasp and wail.

It ended, though, as it always did, with the victim curled up on the ground, struggling to breathe and whimpering. In better physical health than he'd likely ever been in his life, and with a new set of nightmares that wasn't going to go away anytime soon.

Also, by the smell, this one appeared to have shat himself. Poor guy. After all that, I actually was ready to forgive him for shooting me. I had definitely come out the better for the confrontation.

"Alas," I said solemnly into the terrified silence which fell, "it seems he had not paid the price. But it is done now, my child. You are cleansed by the fire, healed and born anew."

I raised my bloody hand in a gesture of grandiloquent benediction.

"Go, and sin no more."

Rugin let out another high, shrill scream, scrambling backward until he managed to get to his feet and went crashing away through the khora, leaving his fallen bow behind.

"Fuck *this*, I'm out," the bandit leader announced, following suit. The rest of his men took that as their cue and went after him.

"Hold it," I ordered as the two remaining Gwyllthean thugs started to get up to run themselves. They froze, staring at me in terror. "You two are a long way from home. Should I even bother to ask what business brings you out here?"

"L-listen, man," the crossbowman stammered, "we've got no issue with you, all right? It's just, it's Lady Gray's business. She wants to talk with you, that's all. Just talk."

And now they would live to report that I was not in league with the Olumnach-funded bandits either. And also, just as crucially, that fucking with me was not a cost-effective proposition.

"I am on no one's side but mine," I said clearly. "I serve no master but myself. I have come to this land to heal, and so long as I am not interfered with, I shall do only that. You may tell your mistress this."

"I, uh . . . Sure, Healer. I'll tell her. But . . ." He swallowed heavily, and I couldn't help noticing that he'd fitted another bolt into his crossbow and cocked the lever to prime it at some point during all the screaming. "Listen, right now Lady Gray's only curious about you. See? Somebody with your power and no attachments, that's big news. So, there's a reward out. That's it, just a reward; she'll pay whoever brings you to her. If you start doing shit like *that* around Gwyllthean, she's gonna end up issuing actual orders to deal with you."

"Then for all our sakes, I hope no one around Gwyllthean does something so unwise as attempting to stop me. Don't you?"

"Uh . . ."

"Very good, then," I said, making my voice exaggeratedly pleasant. "Since we are still friends, I'm sure you won't mind doing me the favor of spreading the word. The Healer should be left alone, by anyone who knows what is good for them."

"Sure, I can do that," he said, nodding frantically.

I started to turn away, then suddenly paused and shifted back. "Oh. And just one other thing."

"Pleased with yourself?" Aster inquired as we strolled down the road toward North Watch, enjoying the midmorning sunshine and the complete lack of anyone attempting to follow us.

"Insufferably so," I said honestly, holding up my new crossbow to admire it.

"Because I was gonna ask . . . I mean, that thing looks like it's built to take smaller ammunition than standard hunting arrows. Is there a reason you didn't think to have the guy hand over his quiver, too?"

". . . oh, goddammit."

29

In Which the Dark Lord Gets Played

There's my girl!"

Junko came barreling out of the fortress pretty much as soon as we were close enough to see it; I'd started to hear her distant barking around the same time I'd spied the watchtower through a gap in the khora foliage above. Now I knelt in the broken old road, setting down my crossbow and attempting to scratch her ears the way she liked. Only occasionally succeeding, what with the way she was jumping all over me, yipping and whining.

I'd never had a dog before; the experience of anyone or anything being *this* happy to see me was entirely new. Frankly, right now I really needed it.

"Lord Seiji," Twigs greeted me, approaching from the gates at a much more sedate pace. "We were beginning to worry. Is everything all right?" She looked pointedly at the sizable bloodstain running down the front of my clothes from the obvious hole in my shirt.

"Things did not go *quite* according to plan, but we handled it," I said, straightening up but continuing to scratch Junko's head as she pressed against my leg. "Any issues here?"

"In fact, my lord, you have visitors again. Maugro, with another goblin who's not been here before. They arrived over an hour ago; I've been up front on watch, but nobody's come to tell me they left again."

I closed my eyes, drew in a steadying breath, and let it out slowly.

I was *not* in the mood for goblin shenanigans right now. Coming up on two full days without sleep, right off an almost daylong hike, with the confrontation with the bandits before that, and before *that* another brutal traversal through the worst Cat Alley had to offer. My mental equilibrium hung in rags, and *this* was when Maugro came back with what sounded like a new goblin representative with whom I'd have to negotiate. Also, an hour ago? It was fully dark now; that would've been past dusk. These goblins were clearly trying to play head games with me.

That fact alone might have made me tell them to fuck off and come back when they were serious, if I didn't urgently need what they were selling. Goblin alchemy, and crossbows. My long-term plans *required* these assets. With my only available source of mass recruits being a bunch of prostitutes, a disturbing number of whom were teenagers, I needed combat strategies that didn't depend on upper body strength.

Pink light burst around us as I cast a quick Heal on myself, causing Twigs to squint against the glare. The soreness in my legs dissipated, but the fatigue did not. The spell didn't seem to affect "natural" conditions like weariness, hunger, thirst . . . anything you'd normally remedy yourself. And I had theorized that it didn't replace severed limbs because it couldn't create matter, but that theory was shot to hell by today's discovery that it could replenish blood; I'd been left with no signs of anemia after spewing what had to have been a couple liters from the hole in my gut. Whatever the rules of Heal were, they seemed arbitrary.

"This new goblin," I said aloud, warily. "I don't suppose it's a girl? A pretty one?"

"I haven't seen her," Twigs said solemnly. She was normally the most serious and quiet of the crew, but now her lips quivered as she clamped down on a smirk. "Don't worry, Lord Seiji, Goose and Sakin are entertaining the guests. Donon is not being left alone with them."

"Thank god for small favors," I muttered.

"What god are you talking about?" Aster asked.

"Never mind, it's just an expression." I swiftly shuffled out of my Healer getup, handing the cloak, coat, and mask to Twigs, and then retrieved my new crossbow from where I'd left it in the road. "All right, Aster, looks like there's no rest for the wicked. Let's go deal with more goblin bullshit before I pass out for the night. C'mon, Junko."

Considering who I was dealing with, obscuring the connection between the Healer and Lord Seiji might have been a futile effort, but I was making a habit of being security-conscious on general principles. Anyway, right now that wouldn't be the first thing to get anyone's attention. My nondescript shirt and trousers were made *very* descript by being soaked in a stiffened deluge of dried blood that went from the hole just below my sternum all the way down the pants.

As a distraction, it served its purpose.

"Had a little mishap with your new toy, Lord Seiji?" Maugro asked as soon as I strode into the kitchen, glancing from the huge bloodstain to the crossbow in my right hand. "I know a simple beginner's trick to help with that—try pointing it at the other guy."

"Nobody's paying you for your comedy stylings, Maugro. Not here, not anywhere."

"Aw, c'mon, you don't know that."

"I am *very* confident. Ah, I see *someone* around here has finally picked up on my rules about hospitality. *Thank* you, Donon."

"My pleasure, Lord Seiji!"

Apparently they'd been waiting long enough to get properly settled in. Maugro had his usual cup of wine; the other guest had a cup of the fragrant, spicy tea the Fflyr liked because every *fucking* thing here was spicy for some godforsaken reason, and there was even soup and sliced bread laid out on the table at which the two goblins sat. To judge by the dishes, both had partaken, and Donon was still hovering to one side like a waiter. Good; aside from being a basic virtue that all civilized people should practice, hospitality was part of my campaign to get on the goblins' collective good side.

Something told me I was gonna need every tick in the pro-Seiji column I could scrounge after tonight's work.

The new arrival was, indeed, a woman. I supposed she was pretty enough; I could probably cast Enjoin on her. Since I'd landed on Ephemera, that kind of thing was no longer one of the first data points I noticed about women, being shuffled below "how likely and able is this person to kill me?" In this case, probably more than most.

She wore a black leather trench coat and managed not to make it look like an affectation. Below it was a clearly armored leather vest over a crimson shirt. Her black trousers also had patches of leather armor sewed on over the thighs and shins; the boots looked heavy enough I wouldn't want to be kicked by them, even with her short legs. Atop all that, the woman's pixie cut hair would have looked incongruous, but something in the set of her eyes ensured I didn't even think about finding her amusing.

"Well, glad to see ya anyway, Lord Seiji," Maugro said with his usual ebullient grin. "Can't fault the way you treat guests, even when you're not here to do it in person! Sorry we caught you away on . . . uh, business." He looked speculatively at the blood again.

I glanced quickly at Goose and Sakin, the latter of whom gave me a cheerful grin. He was positioned between the two doors that opened onto the kitchen;

Aster now took up her normal post to the other side of the corridor which led to the mess hall. Goose was across the room, lounging against the wall close enough to Maugro's customary pair of bodyguards that they were watching her closely.

"Thank you for joining us, Lord Seiji," the new goblin said in a sardonic tone. "Are you in the habit of keeping your business associates waiting for hours on end?"

I swear, I felt something in the back of my head audibly *snap*.

Junko felt it, too. The dog went on point, laying her ears back and growling low in her throat. As usual, Maugro and his bodyguards twitched and shifted backward from her in alarm, but not the new girl. She just turned an icy stare on Junko and reached one hand into her coat.

Yeah, this one was trouble.

"Maugro," I said quietly, my eyes fixed on the new arrival, "do introduce me to your friend."

He cleared his throat, expression rueful. "Ahem. This is Gizmit, Lord Seiji. She's from Miss Sneppit's organization. Brought you that contract you were waiting on."

"Now that you're—"

"Shut up," I interrupted her. "Maugro, how long does it take someone like Sneppit to draw up a contract?"

"Oh, half an hour, absolute tops," he said with a knowing grin. "Sneppit's *famous* for her contract work. She's probably got templates just sitting around her office ready to have the proper nouns and exact numbers filled in, but even working from scratch she could throw together a document like that in her sleep."

"Are you being paid to divulge that information, Maugro?" Gizmit asked him coolly.

He turned his shark's grin on her, spreading his hands in a broad shrug. "Maugro doesn't tell lies at any price, hon. Maugro *does*, if so contracted, actively preserve the privacy of his clients. Lord Seiji has paid for that service. Miss Sneppit has not."

"So," I continued, still staring at her, "not only has your boss kept me waiting for a week, when you finally deign to show up, the first thing out of your mouth is a jab at *me* for not being around when you popped in with no appointment and no warning at an hour when you could reasonably expect everyone here to be asleep?"

Everyone else in the room was watching me with open wariness now. Gizmit did not seem intimidated in the slightest, either by me or by Junko's ongoing quiet growl.

"Excuse me," she said evenly, "I was not aware of any agreed upon terms dictating when you would receive Miss Sneppit's reply."

I looked her up and down, slowly; she didn't react to that either.

"So, what're you then? Sneppit's . . . gardener? Taste tester? Astrologist?"

"The maid," said the obvious assassin.

"Right. Clearly. Maugro, in your *honest* assessment, have I dealt fairly with you?"

"Absolutely," he said without hesitation. "You're straightforward, willing to work with me on unusual circumstances, and you give fair compensation for services rendered. Not to mention you're more hospitable and open to dealing with goblins than literally any other human I've dealt with on this island—and my clientele roster is *mostly* humans. I feel comfortable staking my professional reputation on recommending you as a business partner. In fact, I specifically *have* in this instance."

"There you go," I said, my eyes still on Gizmit. "I am fully willing to meet your employer halfway and establish a mutually profitable business relationship. Once we've had time to build trust, I'll even be willing to overlook the odd foible, because that is what civilized people do for each other. But right out of the gate, your Sneppit seems to have the impression that she gets to jerk me around with impunity. I need you to impress upon her that on that point she is as *wrong as she has ever been.*"

Gizmit stared up at me with the calm expression of someone who saw more threatening things on the weekly. "I will relay that message, Lord Seiji. Are you no longer interested in doing business, then?"

Christ, this one was even worse than Zui. Did Sneppit exclusively employ the most insufferable women she could find?

I held out my hand, not caring that the gesture was imperious or that I still had dried blood crusting under my nails. "Let me see the contract."

Without comment, thankfully, she withdrew a folded sheaf of paper from inside her coat and handed it over.

Anger sharpened my consciousness enough for me to focus as I read through the document, slowly and with care, not interested in the slightest with how long I was keeping my audience waiting. It wasn't too bad; I could believe Sneppit was a master of contract negotiations, given how carefully she covered all her bases, but it seemed goblins preferred to conduct their formal business in plain speech, without bogging it down in legalese.

"Most of this is agreeable to me," I said finally after reading through it twice to be sure my sleep-deprived brain hadn't missed anything important.

"As an additional stipulation, my own business takes precedence, and I may not be *here* whenever your company's representatives feel like showing up. I'd like to establish a schedule of regular appointments, with the condition that extenuating circumstances will be respected, and neither party will be held in breach of contract if either is unable to make a regular meeting for any reasonable cause."

"That's a common enough consideration," Gizmit agreed, nodding. "I doubt Miss Sneppit will object."

"Also, I would like it in writing that I have the prerogative to consult with your alchemist and receive recommendations in good faith for new wares to purchase with my slimes. I'm not interested in being locked into a single package of goods on every exchange."

She tilted her head, considering that. "Miss Sneppit will of course be the final arbiter of any such agreement, but I don't think she'll find that unreasonable. So, if there are no other stipulations you wish to add, she can draw up a revised contract. If that's agreeable?"

"Sounds good." I refolded the document and held it out to her.

Gizmit grasped the paper, but I tightened my grip.

"And one other thing. Sneppit is done wasting my time. The revised document will be here *tomorrow*, no later than sunset, or the quantity of slimes you get per exchange drops by ten percent, permanently. And then a further ten percent for every time she fails to communicate *promptly* any further revisions. If I don't hear from you for any three consecutive days prior to the finalization of our agreement, I will take my business elsewhere."

The goblin's red eyes, a shade darker than Maugro's, met mine without flinching. Neither of us let go of the folded contract. "Are you so certain you have access to another source of goblin alchemy, Lord Seiji?"

"Maugro?" I asked, still holding her stare.

"Sneppit's company is your best bet, in terms of how much they're able to offer," he said, "that's why I set you up with 'em first. But yeah, there're any number of tunnel outfits who'd *love* to have a deal with you, Lord Seiji. If you're willing to take a slight hit in quantity and quality, you've got no shortage of options. I can hook you up with another crew by tomorrow."

Gizmit broke eye contact with me to shoot him an openly annoyed look, the closest to a rise either of us had gotten out of her yet, then returned her gaze to mine. "My employer will not enjoy hearing that, Lord Seiji. You might keep in mind that if you are not going to be in business with us, the only thing of value Miss Sneppit will have gained from this interaction is knowledge of your location. Maugro may be contracted to keep that information private, but as he pointed out, we have not."

"And before you *threaten* me again," I said quietly, "you should consider that your expectation that humans won't come into your tunnels is based on general familiarity with the Fflyr. *I* am not from around here. Understand?"

We locked eyes, and the silence stretched out for long, tense seconds. Junko growled again, louder; Gizmit didn't even glance at her.

"Lord Seiji, please don't stab the messenger," Aster finally said quietly. "She's just doing her job."

"Gizmit, I do not recommend you antagonize this guy," Maugro added, "and you can repeat that to Sneppit. If she and him end up not doing business, best to leave it at that. Remember there's more at stake here than just your company, or mine."

"Very well," Gizmit said finally. "I will communicate all of this to my boss. I expect she will probably be amenable to your terms, Lord Seiji."

I released my hold on the paper, and gave her a wintry smile as she retreated with it. "Pleasure doing business."

"All right!" Maugro slapped both his thighs and hopped down from his chair as Gizmit silently withdrew to the tunnel mouth, where his bodyguards made room for her. "That leaves the other matter you hired me for. I got your dossier on that adventuring party; it took the week cos I had to reach out to my contacts on the mainland. This group's from Fflyrdylle." He pulled another folder of papers from inside his coat and offered it to me, his expression growing serious. "First things first, I need to inform you that since you didn't request this information be kept private, I've already shared it with multiple interested parties in the tunnels."

I felt my left eye begin to twitch involuntarily. That may have been why Maugro quickly backed up the second he'd released the folder into my hands. "Any particular reason for that?"

"Yeah, it's goblin business," he said seriously. "Specifically, this party is on Dount to answer the local King's Guild's call for adventurers to investigate goblin activity and possibly enter our tunnels with suppressive intent."

I narrowed my eyes, not opening the folder yet. "Odd. Why would they come all the way here for that? Why wouldn't local parties answer the call first?"

"For the second part, adventurers *don't* like taking goblin-related quests," he explained. "Like you were just mentioning, they hate going underground. It's a big fat taboo in their religion, and even the less faithful Fflyr seem to think they'll fall through the bottom of the island if they crack the surface.

So they gotta be *heavily* motivated to do so, and the King's Guild saying 'hey, maybe somebody look into this' is not enough incentive. Which is exactly what makes the first part so curious. The same is usually true of all Fflyr. We are *real* interested in learning why this group from the capital would be willing to take this on—and not just willing, but interested enough to leave the big city for a backwater like Dount."

"That didn't come up in your research?"

He spread his arms in one of those expressive shrugs of his. "What I found is all there in the dossier."

"And I will definitely be studying it in detail when I'm less dead on my feet, but would you mind running me through the high points?"

"Not at all. The foreign boy, Shinonome Yoshi, is a complete unknown. Something tells me you're more familiar with him than my people ever could be. Only thing of note is a suspicion that he may be Blessed with Wisdom, which is rare. He's followed around by a sparkly little critter nobody can identify; it *could* be a familiar. The elf is Highlady Flaethwyn of Clan Adellaird. She's a fifth daughter, not important to the succession, so she's spoiled and allowed to run around doing whatever; that's about the only reason she gets to be an adventurer. Blessed with Might, and carries a Rapier of Mastery that's a known treasure of her clan. Also, Clan Adellaird has longstanding beef with Clan Aelthwyn, so it's pretty brassy of her to show her face in their territory. Makes me even *more* curious what's so damn important to this crew about the local goblins."

"That explains some of what I saw in Gwyllthean," I murmured. "Go on."

"Right. The other noble's Lady Pashilyn of Clan Fremond. They're a subordinate clan allied with the Adellairds; she's Flaethwyn's maedhlou. Pashilyn is also an ordained priestess in the Radiant Convocation as well as a member of the King's Guild. Blessed with Magic; her spell arsenal is known to include Windburst, Soothe Wounds, Firecracker, Light Barrier, and Radiance. Seems she mostly follows Flaethwyn around, and has a reputation for being calmer and much more reasonable to deal with. That's the best news, I'm afraid; there was less information to be had about the two lowborn."

"That's not surprising."

"Yeah, they tend not to make much of a splash. The other guy, Raffan Talimonder, is basically an unknown. He's Blessed with Might and carries an artifact spear, but I wasn't able to dig up any word on what exactly it does. Run of the mill King's Guild lowborn, lucky he managed to get Blessed at his age and mostly busy with fetch quests and other grunt work. He seems to've taken Yoshi under his wing when the kid showed up in Fflyrdylle, though how that led to this party forming I wasn't able to uncover. Usually, the two noblewomen would be way out of the league of guys like that. Then there's the girl, Saviadora Amell. She's an alchemist, which is a weird choice for an adventuring party. Lots of adventurers have a preferred alchemist they go to for potions and stuff, but it's not generally smart to bring somebody like that along to fight monsters. Girl's not even Blessed. Though I did find out that the hair is the result of an experiment of hers that went wrong. Apparently it changes color every so often."

"Hm. Nothing on why they'd decide to attack me in the middle of a public street?"

"Nothing on why these kids do *anything*, and that has become a legitimate *concern*, Lord Seiji." Maugro's expression was fully serious now, quite unlike his usual amiable presentation. "Their movements in general don't make sense, and they're apparently on Dount specifically to cause trouble for goblins. So, look. I know you contracted me for info here, but you've obviously got some connection to them, or at least to the boy. It's not much of a stretch to figure he's from the same country as you. If you can offer any insight into what we can expect from this group and how to *deal* with them, I will both pay prime rates for that intel and make sure you're known as the source of it around the tunnels. That'll help you out with any further dealings you have with goblins on Dount."

Damn it, I was too tired for this . . . How to balance my interests here?

"I think . . . Yoshi is the angle you'll want to take," I said slowly. "He's a good kid. Naive, but good-hearted. Where he comes from, he'll have been raised on stories about how goblins are all monsters, and I'm sure the crowd he's fallen in with will have encouraged that, but there's no malice in the boy. What he thinks of as beginner dungeon-delving is actually breaking into people's homes to murder them and steal their stuff, right? Basically banditry. If you can get him to *see* that, you can probably nip this whole thing in the bud. The rest of his party will listen to him."

"Is he the Hero?"

I jerked my head around, only realizing—now that she'd spoken—Gizmit was still there, lurking just inside the mouth of the tunnel.

"Excuse me, the what?"

"I'm trying to imagine why else you're so confident a party like that would listen to its least experienced member," she said, watching me with a bland expression. "Here we have two mysterious young men who show up out of nowhere from a country nobody's ever heard of. One holes up in a fortress in the khora and begins gathering bandits to his side and reaching out to goblins. Another joins an adventuring party with an idiosyncratic composition, including two devout followers of Sanora who ordinarily wouldn't give him the time of day. There's a familiar story taking shape there, for those of us who've read the lore."

"Well . . . that's . . . an interesting theory," I fumbled, trying to make my tone wry. Maugro was watching this conversation with an alarming lack of expression.

"You're new at this, Lord Seiji," Gizmit said with a faint smile, which made me desire to kick her, not that I was fool enough to try. "Bold claims are easy enough to deny, if they aren't specifically true. Plus, on the subject of people being Blessed with Wisdom, it's quite fascinating that you can read Khazid."

Fuuuck. The contract. Only in hindsight did I realize that it wasn't printed in Fflyr script—a fact which any human would at least *comment* on, even if they could read it for whatever reason, considering how unlikely it seemed to be that any human would be that familiar with goblin culture. This wasn't the first time the odd experience of understanding languages I had never actually learned had tripped me up. It was the first time someone had used that to deftly set a trap for me, though.

I found myself *really* hoping I had not made a very big mistake by getting involved with the mysterious Miss Sneppit and her crew.

30

In Which the Dark Lord Takes the Kids to the Park

Yeah, I can do it," said Harold, turning the crossbow over in his hands and holding it up to peer critically at its cocking mechanism up close. "Just need the materials . . . and proper tools. It'd help if I could take it apart . . ."

"I'd rather you didn't," I said. "Not to question your skills, but just in case." It had been a surprise to learn that Harold and Kasser had been craftsmen before they'd left their village for unspecified reasons and ended up here, but definitely a stroke of luck. Harold worked with akornin, the tough and slightly flexible animal shell substance Ephemerans mostly used in place of metal, making him the equivalent of a blacksmith. Kasser was a specialist in akorshil—so basically a carpenter. "What tools and materials, specifically?"

"If you ask your merchant friend for basic sets of akornin and akorshil shaping tools, he'll be able to get what you need," Kasser answered. Unless I was imagining it, he seemed less terse with me now that the opportunity to practice his actual trade was on the table. "For materials . . . Hm, it'll depend. Harold, I think we'd better write up a list of types and grades to give Lord Seiji."

"Uh, yeah," Harold agreed, giving me a shy smile. "No offense, Lord Seiji, it's just . . . those details don't tend to stick in the mind for people who aren't trained in it."

"None taken, you're dead right. Take your time looking that over and laying plans, and get me a list before my next Gwyllthean visit tomorrow morning."

"Yes, my lord! And it shouldn't be a problem, doing it without dismantling the crossbow. Some of these components are pretty finicky-looking, but I think I can figure out the necessary shapes by examining it."

"Ah, if I may?" All of us looked up at Sakin, who was hovering off to one side of the table where we were bent over the crossbow. "What you've got there is a townie special, Lord Seiji. See the hinged bits there on the front? That's to fold up its arms so you can hang it from your belt under a long coat and hide it. All that absolutely *guts* the power of the weapon, and also adds hugely to the complexity. If you get rid of that, it's basically just a short bow fixed sideways to a stick, and the lever mechanism for cocking it should be a lot simpler for Harold to reproduce. *And* if he just makes it with a smooth arc of akornin instead of folding arms, it'll be a lot more durable and powerful."

"Hey, he's right!" Harold exclaimed. "Yeah, this folding mechanism is *really* complicated compared to the lever—and I can see how it's secured when it locks open, but still, that obviously weakens the bow part considerably. If you draw it too hard the whole thing'll break."

"I'd think about making several variations," Sakin suggested. "This is smaller than a military crossbow, for one. Perfect if you want someone not very strong to carry it around and shoot people from fairly close up—city fighting, in essence. The ones the army uses are bigger, made to punch through armor at range. I've also seen little hand-sized stinger versions; no range or stopping power to speak of, but they're meant to deliver alchemy."

"Mm," I mused, "I can see the potential in that, especially now that we've hopefully got an alchemy supplier locked down. Dunk some darts in poison for a guaranteed kill, or sleeping potion to neutralize nonlethally. That's *perfect*. Harold? Kasser?"

"Since we're planning to modify 'em from the original version anyway, it sounds like good sense to test out various models," Kasser agreed. "The biggest problem I can see is that the string looks thicker than a normal bowstring. If that's a specialty component, it'll be hard to get more without revealing to the supplier what we're making. And I've got no idea how you turn raw animal sinew into bowstrings."

"It's thicker than hunting bows like you'd normally use, sure," Sakin agreed. "Should be able to cobble it together with strings for longbows—just cut them down and rewrap the ends. I'm no fletcher, but I bet any of us can figure out how to do that much. Longbows are military hardware, but not controlled nearly as carefully as crossbows. Takes a lot of muscle and training to use one. I bet you can get the strings without too much trouble."

"I'll sound Auldmaer out," I said. "Discreetly. All right, gentlemen, sounds like we've got a plan."

And then . . . the waiting. For now I had to make slow, careful progress, and that involved a lot of downtime as days turned into weeks and the field grass began turning gold with the onset of autumn.

At least things were falling into place, bit by bit. Goblin alchemy and Auldmaer's knowledge of trade routes enabled us to begin *gently* lifting supplies from passing caravans. The tools we needed I bought from a contact to whom Auldmaer directed me; shipments of raw akornin and akorshil we lifted from rival trade companies who were cutting into his profit margins. It ended up being Maugro, not Auldmaer, who got us the right caliber of bowstrings. It seemed goblins had access to khora products from their underground root systems, which could be used to create all kinds of useful things, including bowstrings that worked just as well as the sinew variety and were also less vulnerable to temperature and moisture.

Kasser and Harold were good at their respective crafts; it took some trial and error, but they got it down pretty quickly. Soon there was a crossbow for every member of the gang. We even saw some success with smaller models, the ones Sakin called "stingers," taking out caravan guards with makeshift sleeping darts that were little more than splinters of akorshil dipped in Youda's potions. The lads kept busy making more, since I would need enough weapons to supply a much bigger force soon.

Hopefully.

Gilder kept me updated on the progress of Lady Gray's and Olumnach's feud during my visits to Gwyllthean, wearing my real face openly, as well as other interesting rumors in the Gutters, including the expanding reputation of the Healer. The gang war was steadily intensifying, and neither the corrupt lords of the island nor their inept Kingsguard were doing anything about it. Perfect.

Meanwhile, my own information network grew. Slowly and carefully, just the way I liked it. Gilder recruited two more additions to my side, which wasn't much, but I approved of his caution; first he, and then I, needed to vet them carefully before they could be entrusted with anything.

Benit was a serious and solemn girl a year younger than Gilder, with big watchful eyes that always looked somewhat haunted. I didn't inquire after her full backstory; the fact that she was a Gutter Rat pretty much covered the depressing basics. I could see why she'd tend to get overlooked in a culture like Fflyr Dlemathlys, especially its violent underbelly, but her quiet watchfulness was exactly what you wanted in a spy, and if Uncle Gently and the Rats didn't appreciate her, I was glad to take advantage.

A week after Benit, Gilder brought me Radon, a boy who didn't know how old he was, but to my eyes couldn't have been more than seven. Like Gilder and Benit, he was way too serious for his age; I didn't really want to know the kind of shit he must have seen. Where Gilder was ambitious and Benit shy, Radon was *mad*. Not angry in the lashing-out way you'd expect of a child, but carrying a deeply rooted, simmering resentment of the sheer injustice of everything. I found I related the most to this kid, even as I had to acknowledge he was probably more entitled to his anger than I was to mine.

The knowledge these kids provided of what was brewing in the Gutters was more than worth the time and money I invested in them. As they brought me more reports of clashes between Lady Gray's forces and the bandits answering to Clan Olumnach, I began to accumulate a sense of how much both could bring to bear.

I also learned from my orphans that the crossbowman whose weapon I'd confiscated had done right by the Healer's instructions in the end. Gilder related the rumors with relish, an enthusiasm I found myself sharing as they continued to pile up. Apparently, the full nature of Immolate was a bit too complex for the medium of rumor to fully convey. Instead, accounts included the spell causing people to explode, or just their heads to explode; burning people to a crisp in a single flash of light; creating a blast that threw someone half a dhil (ugh) where they landed in charred pieces . . . There was also a whole set of variants on these themes which claimed that assaulting the Healer resulted in immediate retribution from Sanora herself.

It frustrated me that I couldn't *give* the kids anything that would matter unless it was something they could eat right in front of me; anything else would just be confiscated and make them targets. So at least I made damn sure they were well-fed on the days I visited. I did end up handing over some coin to them, but all of it went right into Uncle Gently's pockets. This was necessary, as he'd just order them to ditch a contact that wasn't bringing him money, but it still rankled me. Insult upon injury.

One day, just to appease my own conscience, I took the kids inside the walls to the middle ring, where they could see the cleaner environs, get some better food in them than was available in the Gutters, and have some time to enjoy one of the parks. It was an offhanded idea, but the Rats were absolutely ecstatic, and to judge by how excited they were over everything, you'd think I'd brought them to Disneyland.

It almost hurt to watch.

Naturally, scruffy Gutter orphans were decidedly not allowed through the gates, even in the company of a well-dressed lord, but that ended up not mattering. The gate guards knew me by now; in fact, their eyes lit up when I approached with anything that wasn't supposed to pass. I think I could've marched an army of orcs into the city, so long as the orcs brought some pocket change for the guards.

It was funny how annoyed I was by the disgraceful state of law enforcement in Gwyllthean when I was constantly benefiting from it. There was a *principle* involved.

Regardless, the Gwyllthean trip was a success. On that afternoon, three weeks after finalizing my deal with the goblins, and just a few days after adding Radon to my crew, late afternoon found us in a park, watching Gilder and Radon chase each other around on the well-kept grass. Benit, already tuckered out, sat on a bench with Aster, asleep and half in her lap.

"Ah, Lord Seiji."

Standing at the edge of the park, watching the orphans enjoy what was probably the only day of fun they'd ever had, I was not expecting to be greeted by anyone I'd not brought with me. And who the hell knew my name?

I turned my scowl upon the interloper, and was immediately amazed by the fact that he'd managed to approach me unheard, wearing all that armor. It was the Goblin Slayer guy from the King's Guild, still clad head to toe in gleaming metal, and his steps were eerily quiet. The magic on that armor had to be some serious shit.

"Oh, it's . . . ah, sorry . . ."

"Rhydion," he supplied.

"Right, Rhydion. Forgive me, I am still having trouble with Fflyr names. I can't even pronounce half of them."

"Not at all. I rarely have the opportunity to meet foreigners anymore; it must be quite disorienting, to be so immersed in another culture. It seems you are managing admirably, however. How are you finding your stay in Fflyr Dlemathlys?"

"This is the worst place I have ever been," I informed him. "I am constantly in amazement that a nation's government can be this perfect storm of corrupt and incompetent at every level and still *exist*. Even knowing nothing about the surrounding international politics, I can tell that Fflyr Dlemathlys has no hostile or ambitious or merely excitable neighbors, just from the fact nobody has bothered to conquer it yet. A girls' choir armed with hand fans and insults could take the whole thing in a week and the clans would be too busy sneering at each other and molesting their citizens to notice. Honestly, what amazes me the most is how many people I hear invoking Sanora's name; if the goddess bothered to be aware of half the shit that goes on here, she would blast the whole island off the face of Ephemera just on general principle."

There was only inscrutable darkness behind the slits of Rhydion's visor; I had no clue what he was thinking for the several seconds in which he regarded me after my little therapeutic venting session. He turned his head to watch the kids playing before answering me.

"One of my favorite things about the adventuring life is how many interesting people I get to know. You are particularly fascinating, Lord Seiji. I have never met someone so constantly angry at everything, yet keeps taking opportunities to be *kind* to those he encounters."

"I'm not *constantly* angry," I said defensively. Rhydion's helmet shifted slightly to point toward the bench, where Aster was gently stroking the sleeping Benit's hair while dividing her attention between us and the boys. "Yeah, well . . . The kids were helpful to me, when I first landed here. I try to give a little back. There's not really a lot I *can* do for 'em, aside from getting them fed and the odd trip into town."

"I suppose it is true that not everyone is of the right character to be responsible for children full-time."

"It's not that," I said in annoyance. "There's this . . . Ugh. The Gutters doesn't have a proper orphanage, apparently. Just some asshole who takes in the kids and uses them for all kinds of less than savory purposes. And it seems *he* answers to the gangsters who run all the crime in this town, so. Remove orphans from the Gutters and you're cutting into the business of dangerous people who'll make their opinions of that known. You're an adventurer; I'm sure you're more aware of all this crap than I am."

The helmet shifted slightly as he shook his head. "I actively try not to be aware of business in which I would feel an ethical need to intervene."

"*Do* you, now?"

"It was a lesson hard learned. I believe a man has a responsibility to right what wrongs he can, where he is. Yet, if a man tries to right every wrong in the world, the result will be exhaustion and countless tasks left half done, in their best-case scenarios. Many will be actively exacerbated by the offhanded meddling of someone who does not understand the full depth of the situation. The effective practice of virtue, I have come to think, requires a kind of tunnel vision. Find an objective against which your abilities can do good, and dedicate yourself to it until it is done. We must have faith that the Goddess will send those of similar inclination to attend to other evils. No one can be everywhere."

I watched Gilder and Radon chase each other around a fountain, laughing shrilly, and said nothing while I digested that.

"Perhaps you disagree," Rhydion suggested after at least a full minute of silence.

"Perhaps I do," I said. "In fact, I'll go ahead and declare that's the most mealy-mouthed justification of moral laziness and intellectual cowardice I've ever heard."

Aster jerked her head around to stare at me in wide-eyed horror. Ah yes, I remembered, Rhydion was some kind of local celebrity superhero.

"I will not argue," he said, inclining his head slightly toward me. "I harbor such doubts myself. Nor are the methods I have developed any kind of ideal practice, but merely compromises experience has forced me to make with my own mortal frailty. If there is any value in my soul at all, I shall continue improving myself so long as I live."

"Well, I can respect that, at least."

"If you have a similar interest in advancing yourself, both in virtue and material standing, you might consider the offer I made you before."

"Offer? Remind me."

"To join the King's Guild. Healing magic is rare and valuable, Lord Seiji; even if your medical spells are as humble as you claimed, they would ensure you a place of great prestige within the Guild."

Oh. Right. That. "Ah . . . I think the adventuring life is not for me."

"I understand. If you are not interested in adventuring as a career, I wonder if you might deign to sell your services for a shorter duration."

I blinked at him. "Excuse me?"

"I am on Dount in response to a growing threat of necromantic events and possible Void activity. This has been a slow process, involving much careful investigation; we are not to the point of taking physical action yet, but before the time comes, I would like to retain the services of a healer."

"Ahah!" I couldn't quite restrain the incredulous bark of laughter which escaped me, not that I tried very hard. "No, I don't think so. But good luck with it, sincerely. Sounds like a worthwhile endeavor. Goddess favor you and all that."

"I hope you might reconsider before we reach the critical juncture, Lord Seiji. To face the Void without healing magic at one's side is deeply perilous."

"Come on, I can't possibly be the only healer on Dount. I'm definitely not the best." Actually, I probably was the best, but he was the last person who needed to know that.

"It is vanishingly rare to meet a healer who is not fully committed for the foreseeable future. The truth is, you may well be the best available. The options are you and a rumored madman who goes around the Gutters healing prostitutes."

"Heh. Prostitutes, hm? Well, there you go; you should ask that guy. He sounds a lot more charitable than I am."

"I am not so sure." He looked again at the playing children.

"Even so, I can't believe I'm your *best* option."

"Let me put it this way, Lord Seiji. I'm sure you have some idea how . . . pleasant you are to talk to. I am asking you anyway."

For one second, I was offended. But then, in spite of myself, I had to laugh.

31

In Which the Dark Lord
Takes Baby Steps

Over the following weeks, my continued visits to Yrshith Street progressively bore fruit. By the time a month of the Healer's presence had passed, the effects were downright transformative.

At that point, every brothel had opened its doors to the Healer, which was the benchmark I'd been shooting for and made me start to get antsy as the next development on which I'd been counting failed to materialize. Not everybody was free of suspicion, but it seemed even those who remained skeptical of my motives were glad enough to see me for the benefits I brought; and for the vast majority of the women working in Cat Alley, I was a hero.

I'll admit, it was nice being greeted like a rock star everywhere I went. Would've been nice to earn that as an actual rock star as I'd always dreamed, but if I was being honest, this work was objectively more important. Ulterior motives and all.

As everyone warmed up to me, and seemed to warm up in general now that disease had been effectively eradicated from the brothels and their injuries were remedied on a weekly basis, I had the opportunity to actually get to know some of the women. Some were still shy or suspicious around me, but in places like the better brothels clustered around the Alley Cat near the center, the madams were better about enforcing order, and I often got a chance to talk a bit with the people I was healing. More and more, as they relaxed enough around me, I got to hear their stories.

Not one of them was pleasant. People either fell into this life or were forced into it; amazingly, young girls in Fflyr Dlemathlys did not spend their childhoods dreaming of one day being worked to death before they were thirty on their backs under a succession of the sorriest goons Gwyllthean had to offer.

"Actually, I knew a girl like that," Madyn once said to me. She was a twentysomething working girl who seemed to have a hilarious and/or alarming story for any conversation. "Rich kid, brown-haired, I think she may've actually been lower nobility. No idea where her family were, but she deliberately sought out a job here in the Alley. Craziest bitch I ever met, I swear. Took the worst customers the place had; she actually got off on it. Yeah, she's dead now."

Madyn was a born storyteller and enjoyed ending her tales on a mood-altering twist like that, but . . . way too many of the stories in Cat Alley ended that way.

A lot of the women took up prostitution out of desperation after ending up alone; in Fflyr Dlemathlys, a woman without family had few other options, save the King's Guild and the Radiant Convocation, and neither of those would take just anybody off the street. That had been the fate of Adelly, who was Blessed with Might but had never managed to get her hands on an artifact before falling into debt and washing out of the King's Guild. She was actually proud of having ended up where she was rather than stealing, despite her talents being better suited to banditry.

Others, though . . . many others . . . had been forced into this life. By parents who decided they needed the money more than they needed another mouth to feed, or by relatives who ended up with custody of a new orphan and who didn't even consider that a dilemma. Sometimes, just because they caught the eye of some noble and then weren't considered good enough for anything else after he got bored.

"Chattel slavery is specifically illegal in Fflyr Dlemathlys," Miss Minifrit explained to me once when I asked about these cases, pausing as she so often did to consider her words along with a long drag from her omnipresent pipe. "It's rather a big deal. Long ago, the elves who now rule this country were slaves of the previous overlords, and after their successful uprising swore there would be no more of that evil in their land. Of course, they immediately set to committing every crime that was ever perpetrated on them, each under a new name and with a spiffy coat of fresh paint."

"Wait. Is that why you people have all these hand motions instead of bowing?"

"You catch on," she said, smirking and exhaling streamers of smoke through her nose. "Yes, Fflyr culture is full of things like that. Bowing is associated with slavery and thus forbidden—so instead there's a whole system of etiquette which sorts people *much* more unforgivingly by rank and station. Likewise, there is no slavery in Fflyr Dlemathlys. But there is indentured servitude."

I remained silent while she took another drag, shifting her gaze to stare at some infinite point through the wall behind me.

"You can't just *sell* an inconvenient daughter or niece," Minifrit continued after a moment. "What you *can* do, as her guardian, is take out a substantial loan in her name—and then, on her behalf, sign a contract with the lender defaulting upon the principal. The lender can then take this to a judge, and she can be sentenced to servitude at the lender's discretion until the principal and interest are fully repaid. And of course, these contracts can then be bought and sold."

"So . . . there is the possibility of the debt being paid off?"

Minifrit snorted, sending smoke curling toward me.

"In theory? Certainly. It would simply take a contract holder who bothers to keep track of the servant's earnings, guards interested in enforcing the proper terms, and a judge willing to hear the case. I invite you to guess how often those stars align."

"Mm," I murmured. "Slavery with extra steps, then."

"Well put. And those cases aren't even the worst. I doubt there are any judges in Fflyr Dlemathlys who would turn up their noses at an indenture case of that nature; the ones we consider actually *corrupt* are willing to sentence somebody to servitude with no money having actually changed hands—save from the alleged lender to the judge. Girls ending up in brothels or some noble's spare bedroom are only one of the more common cases of this. When men get taken, their fate is usually to labor on the farms of whatever clan snatches them. It's all very civilized; we are a nation of laws, you see. No kidnappings in the night, just court cases and paperwork. But your back gives out just the same, whether you work bent over a bed frame or in a wheat field."

I hadn't known about the farm workers; they would make much better bandits and soldiers. Well, I was committed to this course now; though, I resolved to look into that for my next big campaign.

"Have you ever taken in a girl who was falsely contracted this way?"

Minifrit stared at me for a long moment, allowing slow trickles of smoke to stream from her nostrils. "Over the years . . . several. On occasions when the opportunity arose to intervene before a girl's contract was sold to an establishment where she'd be treated worse . . . and I had the liquid capital on hand to buy it out . . . and also a spot open for another employee at the time. It's not common for those circumstances to line up so conveniently. Most of my girls I took in from the streets, where they were wandering in confusion, alone and destitute. And someday, Sanora will weigh my soul and I will finally learn whether I've done them a kindness, or if it would have been kinder to let them freeze in the gutter." She took a long drag, her eyes somewhere far distant. "We can't save everyone, Healer. No one can. Not even you."

"No," I agreed, "we can't. But . . ."

Minifrit eyed me pensively, but the conversation ended there. It wasn't time for me to reveal what I *did* intend.

I was the Dark Lord, not the Hero. I couldn't save all of the innocent; there were just too many victims. But I could sure as hell punish the guilty.

Never mind nightmares, I had started having occasional flashes of some of the horrible sicknesses and injuries I'd seen among the brothels while wide awake and otherwise occupied, causing me to freeze and break out in a sweat. If I didn't know better, I could take these episodes as a symptom of PTSD— but I *did* know better, and that was just stupid. If these dozens of women could live through this every day, I could fucking cope with only having to see it once a week.

Also, I was shadowed by obvious thugs now. Lady Gray's forces were stretched thin dealing with Clan Olumnach's incursions, but she could spare a few to keep tabs on the Healer. They tended to show up an hour or so after I arrived in Cat Alley and keep their distance. They always made sure to catch my eye, smile and fold hands politely, and display weapons. None came close or spoke to me, though.

Profits were up across the district thanks to my ministrations, which meant I was making Lady Gray money. That didn't mean she was going to leave me alone—only that for the time being she preferred to let me work under supervision than provoke me into doing something . . . expensive.

But she was a sword hanging over my head. Sooner or later, somebody would connect the dots, and I *needed* to have my mission here finished before that happened.

My unease grew as time passed. Slow and steady progress was better than none, but after six weeks had gone by since my deal with the goblins was finalized, I felt I had reached the level of esteem in Cat Alley that I needed to execute the next stage of my plan, yet the impetus I'd been counting on had not arrived. The pressure mounted until, inevitably, it suddenly broke.

I was in the back corridors of the Sizzle, healing the last injury—another kitchen burn this time. There'd been no fresh cases of disease in nearly a month, but johns continued to mistreat the women. The sick, sad truth was that the Healer was never going to run out of work in a place like this.

Just as she stepped back, a commotion from the common area occurred, and swiftly burst out of the front room into the hall in which I stood. This was unusual enough; the Sizzle was by far the quietest and most orderly joint in the Alley, as a rule. The madame kept bouncers on hand to firmly encourage her idea of proper conduct.

When three men burst through the curtain into the back area, though, I could immediately see why the hired muscle hadn't stopped them. They'd probably been afraid to try.

The two middleborn guards were all decked out in some *fancy* clothes, plus chain armor under their heavily embroidered coats. All of it had that overly embellished aesthetic of goddess-made artifacts, which the Fflyr nobility liked to emulate in their own tacky style. To my Blessed eyes, there was no giveaway glow; neither of these fellows had actual artifacts. But they were big, muscular, armed with rapiers and daggers, and both clearly rich. That was trouble in and of itself.

Their boss was even richer, by the cut of his clothes, but even more important, he was blonde and black-eyed. A nobleman of a rank which was rarely, if ever, seen in these parts.

And he was sick. With sunken cheeks, a grayish pallor, and patterns of lesions along his eyebrows, hairline, and the backs of his hands, he was clearly in the later stages of something I had repeatedly seen in Cat Alley before personally purging it from the district.

"You," the nobleman rasped, pointing a trembling finger at me. He was sweating and breathing with effort. "You're the one! The Healer. I *demand* your services."

I drew myself up to my full height, breathing in and then out slowly. It seemed rumor of the Healer's miraculous power had circulated as far as the upper city, drawing the interest of the overprivileged and entitled.

Finally.

"Have you paid the price?"

32

In Which the Dark Lord Lights Up the Town

Yes, yes, I'll pay your price," the nobleman said impatiently, dry-washing his hands. As dry as possible with how sweaty they looked, at least. "Name it, money is no object. Just heal me!"

We were still behind the curtain, separated from the Sizzle's common room. Everyone out there was surely aware of the noble and his two bodyguards, because they'd just forced their way through, and he was still carrying on in a very outside voice, but this was still less of an audience for the confrontation than I wanted. Much less. It was lucky he'd chased me down here in one of the central brothels; rather than dragging his complaining ass halfway down the street, I just needed to move the scene right outside. Should be doable.

"Money," I said in my flattest tone.

"Money, of course, however much you want," he repeated, holding out one hand and snapping his fingers impatiently. One of his fancy bully boys took a hand away from his sword handle to produce a bulging coin pouch from inside his coat.

"Do I look like I need money?" I asked.

They all froze, frowning in confusion; the nobleman's face twitched as he eyed my shabby cloak and coat, and I could see him refraining from saying that yes, of course I did. Despite his agitation, he restrained himself.

"Well . . . what *do* you want, then? I am a powerful man; I can reward you far better than this Gutter trash." He made a dismissive gesture at the cluster of sex workers huddled at the end of the hall with one pox-marked hand. None of them reacted; all of them knew better than to offend a noble.

That was what I needed to change.

"I want nothing," I stated. "And you have not paid the price."

"Wh— How dare— Wait!"

Trusting Aster to play off my lead, I made right for the thin space between the nobleman and the guard who was in the process of handing him the money. Predictably, he jerked it back to protect his master's property from the scruffy character pushing into his personal space; the noble also retreated from me, as if he might catch something even worse than what he had if he touched a poor person. In the confusion, I pushed right between them and stepped out through the curtain.

"Stop! *Stop him!*"

They tried; the guy with the money tucked it away, freeing up his hand to grab at my cloak, but by the time he managed that, his path was blocked by Aster's sword. That thing coming out in such close quarters sent the other armed man into bodyguard mode, and he interposed himself between his boss and us, inadvertently clearing the path for both of us to press through and into the common room.

It had fallen silent, girls and johns all staring wide-eyed at the confronta-tion we were now dragging past them.

"I'm telling you, I'll pay whatever you want!" the guy screeched, trail-ing along behind me while his guards awkwardly tried to keep themselves between him and everyone else while also not getting in his way. "Don't you walk away from me, lowborn! I *demand* you use your magic on me!"

I got the feeling this fellow was not used to people turning their backs and ignoring him. That, of course, was what made it satisfying.

I strode through the Sizzle's front room and pushed out the door, step-ping onto Yrshith Street. In front of me opened up the closest thing there was to a square here in the blue-light district, the slightly wider segment of street fronted by the five best brothels in the Gutters. It was maybe an hour before midnight—prime time in this neighborhood. The street was thronged, buzz-ing with voices, laughter, shouts, and music from both street performers and clusters of drunken patrons singing off-key for the sheer joy of it. Rowdy patrons and bawdy working girls catcalled each other, the latter competing to draw customers into their establishments.

Into this, the Healer strode at a speed that set his cloak flaring dramatically, shadowed by his omnipresent silent bodyguard, while behind him a man ordered of magnitude too rich to even be here trailed along, squawking helplessly.

In short, *this* was a show. We did not get immediate silence and atten-tion—that's not really how crowds work—but people began to pause their own business and turn to watch.

"Come *back* here!" the aristocrat yelled in a shrill voice. "So help me, I'll have you seized by the guard! Do you know who I *am?*"

I did stop, finally. I had made it to the center of the street. A space cleared around us, as the surrounding Gutter-dwellers wisely removed themselves from the proximity of a highborn having a tantrum. I did not turn to face him, but twisted my head to one side, such that my face would have been in profile to his eyes had my hood not obscured it. My answer was delivered in a projecting tone, powerful enough to be perfectly audible to him, and more importantly to all the onlookers despite my mask.

"A man begging for help from someone who needs nothing he can offer."

The gasps were audible; people backed up further, and the ring of quiet surrounding us expanded as more onlookers clued in to what was happening. In another time and place, I would have expected laughter at the sight of a rich and powerful man being humbled in public—and undoubtedly I would, once the drunker elements of the crowd started paying attention. This was Fflyr Dlemathlys, however, and irritating a highborn could get you killed. They didn't flee, though. Despite the danger, this was just too good not to watch, and there was a measure of safety in a crowd.

I let the nobleman sputter for another moment; poor guy was not coping well with not being catered to. What kind of upbringing must a person have to make them this unable to handle disappointment?

"You wish to pay the price, then?" I asked, finally turning to face him. Aster pivoted with me, positioning herself at my back. Quiet was progressively descending upon the street, with the show I was putting on taking precedence over the various other diversions at hand.

"What do you think I've been *saying?*" the noble screeched. "Yes! *Obviously!* I'll pay whatever it costs—I can make you a very rich man. Just work your magic, fool, before I have you flogged for disobedience to your betters!"

This time the gasps had a distinct hissing quality; everyone watching was familiar with the rumors about what happened when you pissed off the Healer, though nobody here had seen it firsthand. Now, the tipping point had been reached, and people were dropping their other various pursuits to gather closer, jostling and craning necks to see. A space had opened up in the street around myself, the aristocrat, and our respective bodyguards. All three had now drawn their weapons, Aster simply standing at the ready while the pair of guards were warily surveying the tightly-packed ring of people in which their boss had gotten us all trapped.

He didn't seem to even notice the crowd, glaring at me and absently scratching at the sores on the backs of his hands. This guy was inconveniently late; I'd been counting on an event of this type happening at least a couple of weeks ago. I decided to forgive his tardiness, however, because he played his part so perfectly. Everything would've been much more awkward if the petitioner had been pitiful, appealing, or even slightly sympathetic to my audience, but there seemed to be nothing in this man but entitlement and aggression. He couldn't have been a more ideal subject if I had designed him myself.

"Tell me." Thanks to my years of musical training, I have excellent vocal control; it was child's play to project my voice at a volume that resonated across the street while maintaining an even, calm tone. "How long do you think you could survive here on Yrshith Street?"

"What in Sanora's blinding name are you babbling about?" His rage only appeared to increase with his incredulity.

"Have you ever toiled with every ounce of your being, every last iota of your strength, drenched yourself in your own sweat and *bled* for your struggle, only to be rewarded with nothing but one more day of bare survival?"

"How dare you suggest—I am highborn! One of the goddess's chosen!"

"How much have you sacrificed, and for how little gain?" I began pacing slowly to the left, keeping my head angled so it was clear my gaze was fixed on him while I circled him like a predatory vulture. "What have you suffered?"

"*Look at me!*" he practically screamed, holding up both hands so I could see the sores along their backs, some now bleeding from just having been scratched.

"And what has that earned you, in the comfort of your mansion, protected by your guards, tended by your servants? Everyone suffers. Most suffer to an extent that would *break* you."

"I will have you—"

"Can you even imagine what it would be like to submit your body to the depredations of whoever could pay, just to earn a meal and a roof over your head?" This time I pushed on, overriding his complaints. They were getting repetitive anyway. "All with no prospects, no *hope*, and as punishment for no wrong you had done—only the accident of having been born? To rise each day and toil until you collapsed, with nothing to look forward to but another day of the same. To live under the constant sneering eye of those who presume themselves your betters while refusing to be worthy of their higher station, to suffer abuse and condemnation from petty little men who never earned a speck of their good fortune? Can you even imagine it? The humiliation. The *indignity*. Is your mind *capable* of conceiving the reality with which *most* people live?"

"You are insane," he said, eyes practically bulging with disbelieving fury now, but he seemed to have been reduced to whispering.

My prowling brought me back around to the point from which I had started, and I turned to face him full-on, standing still once more.

"The price," I thundered, ensuring my voice reached every ear on the street, "is *misery*. And you, rich boy, have not paid it."

I had apparently reduced him to silence, finally. The sick nobleman gaped at me, mouth half-open as if he'd tried to find words and come up with nothing. That was fine; he was just a prop in this drama, as far as I was concerned, not someone whose opinions mattered. With my eyes well hidden beneath my deep hood, I looked quickly around at the crowd. Unaccustomed silence reigned over Cat Alley now, everyone within earshot having come to watch, and fallen silent to listen. People were even crowding at windows, peering out.

Many of those expressions were solemnly thoughtful; more than a few were angry. Of course, there was a lot of rage buried there. My task was to dig it up, through the layers of despair and fear piled atop these people by men like the one now staring at me in stupefaction.

"So I will ask you again," I said after allowing the silence to hang for several beats. "*Will* you pay the price?"

"How many times do I have to *say* it?" he replied, sounding downright plaintive now. "I did not come here to listen to your deranged ramblings. Whatever your price, I will *pay* it. I *demand* that you *heal me*!"

"My lord," one of his bodyguards said warily. Not being highborn, he had a more well developed sense of danger. Alas, his employer cut him off with a slashing gesture rather than listen to sense.

"So be it." My voice rang out as I raised one hand to point at the lordling. All according to plan.

Immolate.

He was only the first to scream.

The sight of a man disintegrating in a column of fire right before their eyes would cause any sensible person to back up, and the crowd tried to do so, many with shrill outcries of their own. It was just a backward press, however; a few broke and pushed away through the throng to escape, but most stayed to stare in horrified fascination at the grisly spectacle, once they'd put a little more distance between it and themselves.

Lord What's-His-Name, who had probably never experienced anything more uncomfortable than the symptoms of his illness, howled in the ultimate extremity of anguish as his very flesh exploded around him, fire bursting from every fresh crack that appeared in his skin from the sheer pressure and heat. He passed through the same cycle with which I had become depressingly familiar by now, eventually falling silent as there was nothing left intact which would enable him to scream. Having stumbled to his knees under the initial onslaught, he now tumbled over onto his side, burning limbs kicking and thrashing as he tried hopelessly to put himself out by rolling on the pavement, before eventually curling up in a smoldering fetal position.

His bodyguards dithered about in a way that would've looked downright comical under less horrific circumstances, completely at a loss for what to do about this. One tried to grab his boss, then retreated, shaking his singed fingers; the other actually had the presence of mind to turn toward me and brandish his sword. That was where he stopped, however, between the sight of Aster with her huge blade out and the obvious reality that his rapier wasn't going to do much against a sorcerer who could combust people from the inside out.

And then, as always, the flames receded. The noble's voice returned, reduced to piteous, whimpering groans. His flesh restored itself as the fire faded, and soon enough, there he lay on his side. Still curled up with his arms over his head, shivering and weeping quietly.

Dead silence had fallen once again, making his soft whimpers stand out all the more. The crowd of girls, johns, and other passersby stared at the spectacle of a highborn, the living incarnation of the power that kept them where they were, sniveling at my feet. No one whispered, at least not yet; the pressure of the moment was like a physical thing keeping everyone rooted in place. But they saw, and they thought. I watched their faces as they absorbed implications.

The nobleman finally, tremulously, shifted one arm to raise his head, peeking up at me with a terrified expression. One of his guards had knelt beside him now, uncertainly touching his shoulder, while the other brandished his rapier at the onlookers as if he feared they would try to mob him.

They wouldn't, I knew. We weren't at that point, yet.

With his face exposed, all could see that the nobleman had a healthy color. It was less obvious that his breathing was less labored, given how he was still crying, but his skin conspicuously lacked any of the lesions which had been all over it seconds before.

"The price has been paid," I intoned into the terrified quiet, "and so, you are healed. Go in peace."

He stared up at me, gibbering softly; the more assertive of the two guards took one faltering step in my direction.

Then the nobleman scrambled desperately to his feet, nearly falling over again as he set off at a run. He caught himself and stumbled directly into the crowd, shrieking "Get out of my way!" They tried, but the press of bodies was too tight to create sufficient room. He had to push through, managing it only because nobody seemed to want to inconvenience a highborn, even a fleeing one. The bodyguards followed, one hesitating with a long look at me as if he felt he should do *something* in retribution, but that lasted only a second. They caught up with their master as he vanished amid the crowd, the disturbance of their flight remaining after they were lost to sight.

Muttering and whispering had sprung up now, with all eyes still on me, but no one came closer. Good; whispering was exactly what I wanted. The word would spread that the Healer held power even over the highborn. This could not have gone more flawlessly if I'd scripted it.

Making my movements steady, even casual, as if nothing of any import had just happened, I turned and continued on my rounds. In this case, that meant proceeding across the street to the next brothel on my agenda for the night, which happened to be the Jostled Jugs. At my approach, people pressed back to clear a path for me, many making obsequious Fflyr hand gestures as they retreated.

In the door of the Jugs was the first person who didn't back away from me after the show I'd put on—its owner, Gannit. She stood there, blocking the entry with her skinny body, arms folded, staring balefully at me. Behind her, patrons and prostitutes alike had been clustered near the windows, but now were in the process of retreating to the opposite side of the room. Still trying to peek past her at me as they went. I suspected she must've just banished everyone to give us space.

"I've got half a mind to bar you from my establishment for life, boy," Gannit said in a tone as grim as it was quiet. With the bubble of space around us, it was unlikely she'd be overheard at that volume.

I paused, then turned and deliberately looked in the direction the lordling had fled, then back at her. "Friend of yours?"

"Don't you get clever with me, you smug twerp. What the hell was all that jabbering? Healing whores is one thing—that was preaching *rebellion*. That's the kind of talk that riles up the clans and the Convocation alike and brings Kingsguard stomping through the whole neighborhood to put blades in anybody who's been too friendly with you. Common sense tells me I oughta kick you between the legs before you get your stink on any of my girls."

"But?"

The old woman narrowed her eyes. "But of course, you waited to bust out *that* horseshit until you've made yourself the hero of every cat in the Alley. Any madame who gives you the boot is likely to have a mutiny on her hands. Well played, you crafty little shit."

I stood in silence, aware of the eyes on us from all sides, but focused on her. This confrontation was as important in a way as the show I'd put on with the nobleman. Gannit was one of the most successful madams, and among the most liked and respected, probably second only to Minifrit. Her word was law in her establishment and commanded significant weight, even among the rest of the brothels.

If she *did* bar me, I might have trouble. But now that she could see the broad shape of what I was doing, if she threw in with me . . .

"You're still not gonna spill the beans, are you?" she said finally, scowling. "You and your precious mystery routine."

I waited.

"Tell me one thing, then," said Gannit. "Have you planned *past* what's inevitably coming down next? Do you *really* think you can survive the hive you just kicked? Much less protect any of the rest of us?"

"You have some idea how powerful my Heal spell is," I murmured, "and how rare. Do you think that is my only asset? Or even the strongest?"

Her eyes cut past me to the vacant spot in the middle of the street, where people still seemed reluctant to pass through where I had publicly unveiled Immolate at the expense of the nobility.

"How many of my girls are you planning to get killed?"

"How many are you?" I countered. "Or are you going to tell me they retire to an idyllic life in the countryside when they can't work anymore? We're all going to die, Gannit. Probably by violence; this is Ephemera. I happen to think people deserve to live with some dignity and pride before the inevitable happens. Dignity, pride, and the chance to hit back at those who would deprive them of it."

Gannit's eyes narrowed to slits. Now it was she who remained silent, all but demanding I come up with a better explanation. I was done explaining myself, though; the ball was now in her court.

"So the question is . . . Are you okay with the way things are? Just plan to live out whatever years you've got exactly like this? Or are you willing to take a risk?"

"What're you, the Hero?" she grunted, but I detected wry amusement in her face now. "Gonna save the world, is that it?"

"I can only heal, and punish. That's not going to save anything. But I still think it beats the alternative."

"Hn." She grimaced, then actually laughed softly, and shook her head. "Nightlady take my bony old ass, so do I. All right, you little freak, get your spooky butt in here. Let's ride this crazy horse 'til it tramples us both."

And just like that, after long weeks of spinning my wheels, I was two big steps closer.

33

In Which the Dark Lord Hangs Out with the Boys

After that performance, someone tried to follow us home again. Nothing came of it; Blessed with Wisdom are exceedingly difficult to track when they don't want to be, and unlike the previous time, I was not interested in playing around with whoever this was. Thanks to Biribo's senses, we ditched them amid the khora with ease, at the cost of getting our feet wet traveling up and down a few streams to wipe out our scent.

And bright and early the next day, I found myself again making use of my familiar's powers in exactly the same manner. Well, for given value of both "early" and "bright." It was the afternoon, and I was bedraggled and only somewhat less exhausted than I'd been the night before, due to having had just a few hours to sleep, and managing to spend those only getting fitful naps.

I kept having dreams. Endless parades of people injured and wounded, needing my help, and my Heal spell faltering every time. People burning alive, screaming that it was my fault.

Thanks, brain.

"But this is a narrow window of opportunity," I explained to my companions as I picked carefully through the khora forest the next day following my familiar's guidance. "According to Biribo, today's some kind of sacred festival thingy for the local beast tribes."

"Sure, the harvest celebration's coming up," Harold agreed, sounding nervous as usual. "But that's not for a few weeks . . ."

"Cos harvesting is something agricultural societies do," Biribo lectured. "The beast tribes are hunter-gatherers; theirs is right on the autumnal equinox. For *one* day, they'll be drawn back within their villages, not hunting or gathering or patrolling or doing *anything* which would make them likely to find us tiptoeing through their territory. Which isn't to say this is not a *risk*, lads. We're still on catfolk land, here, and those ears of theirs ain't for show. I don't know where the actual village *is*, but it's likely to be *fairly* near our destination, and if they find us fucking around in their territory during a sacred event, there's gonna be trouble whether or not they realize what we're up to. So quick and *quiet* are the orders of the day, got it?"

"Got it," Harold agreed.

"What *are* we up to?" Kasser demanded, albeit quietly. "I know how much you enjoy never explaining yourself until the last fucking minute, Lord Seiji, but I think we're past that point now, and I *still* don't know what the hell we're doing out here."

"Nobody appreciates my dramatic timing," I complained.

"That is correct," he agreed.

"So, remember that list I had Maugro draw up of accessible Spirits on Dount? Narrowing it down to Spirits which offer a reward that'll be useful to me, a task I can easily complete, and are in a place I can physically access, there are all of precisely *two* candidates. At least until I'm in a position to push around larger beast tribes or get access to some of the clans' fortresses. For now, there's one Spirit in the wolf tribe's territory that grants the Blessing of Might, or an artifact to people who already have it, and one here in our local cat territory that gives . . . Biribo, what was it called?"

"Reward for accumulated experience."

My left eye involuntarily twitched; fortunately both of my companions were behind me and didn't see it. They wouldn't recognize the video game terminology anyway, much less understand why it made me angry. "Right. Basically a freebie. The Spirit looks at you, considers the kind of life you've lived, and gives you something it deems appropriate."

It was so *obviously* just another mechanism for the goddesses to lean on the scales and hand out whatever they wanted to whoever they liked, just for showing up, because this game was rigged as fuck.

"The other one, in wolf lands, is both farther away and it tests you with a trial by combat. So, we're going here."

"I wouldn't mind getting Blessed with Might," Kasser muttered.

"You still could," said Biribo. "Our target Spirit might bestow pretty much anything. Also, I'm not sensing any sapient beings close enough to matter just yet, boys, but the deeper in we go, the likelier it'll be, so get your conversing over with as quick as you can."

"I, uh . . . sorry, Lord Seiji, but I don't really understand why you brought *us*," said Harold.

I was glad they couldn't see my face at that moment. "Figured you guys deserved a reward for your work on those crossbows. That's pivotal to my plans, and I know you're working hard on them. You've done a fine job. Anyway, bringing the two of you was a compromise. Biribo wanted to just bring Aster."

"No," Biribo said with open aggravation, "bringing *Aster* would've been the compromise! *I* wanted the Dark Lord to come *alone*, being that *every additional person* along on this jaunt is an extra risk of drawing the cats' attention. With me, his spells, and her artifacts, Lord Seiji could probably avoid their notice and deal with 'em if not. *This* is a case of the great and illustrious Dark Lord doing whatever the hell he wants and ignoring my advice, as per fucking usual!"

I drew in a deep breath and let it out slowly. "Don't get too busy ranting to keep watch, Biribo."

"I'm a familiar! I can multitask!"

"Well, we're . . . I mean . . . thanks." Kasser finally got the word out. Grudgingly, but he did it.

I could easily have let the conversation drop there. Probably should have, for a variety of reasons. After a pause, though, I was compelled to speak again, ignoring Biribo's exasperated tiny facepalm.

"Anyway. Crossbows aside, I feel like I owe you guys. I've only *seen* Immolate go off and it's . . . that's bad enough. It's got to have been nightmare-inducing to live through. You deserve . . . something for it. And for sticking with me afterward."

"It's not like we had a choice," Kasser muttered.

"It's fine, Lord Seiji," Harold hastened to assure me. "We *were* trying to kill you at the time. You were just defending yourself."

"Sure, I know that's what we discussed," I agreed, then turned to glance over my shoulder at them. "But I still *feel* like I owe you something. Don't you?"

They exchanged a look and then avoided eye contact with me, finding nothing to say. Which was as good as an answer.

Biribo buzzed closer to my ear as we continued on through the khora, pitching his tinny voice low. "Spirits with undefined reward systems *usually* react to Blessed with Blessing-related gifts. I've mentioned that, right?"

"Yes, I remember."

"So bringing Aster would've probably gotten her a scroll or artifact. Which could either power up your number one henchwoman or you could've taken 'em for yourself—it's not like the Spirit would've stopped you. Instead, we're gonna get party favors for these two clowns. *Great* use of time and energy, *Lord* Seiji."

I very nearly raised my arm and backhanded him. Fatigue was definitely not doing my temper any favors. Instead, I paused, breathed, and thought. Aster's pointed question about the way I treated Biribo rose to the forefront of my mind.

"Yeah, I know," I said finally. "You're right."

Whatever he was expecting, it wasn't that. He actually dropped a few centimeters in the air as if he momentarily forgot to keep flying, then zipped forward to blink owlishly at me. "You . . . do?"

I shrugged, watching my feet and keeping my voice pitched low. "It's good advice, I understand where you're coming from. It's not that simple, though. Everything on this world is horrible bullshit, *I* keep having to *do* horrible bullshit, and even the good things I find opportunities to do are full of ulterior motives that make me feel sleazy. Biribo, I have to do some things to appease my conscience once in a while, or I will go completely insane. And not the entertaining, villainous kind of insane Virya would enjoy. I'm talking hugging my knees in the corner, rocking back and forth for days on end. So, yeah, I *get* what you mean, and I don't even disagree. But I gotta give the boys something, here. I just . . . need to."

"Huh," he said. "Well, all right then, makes sense."

Now it was my turn to be surprised. "It does?"

"Sure, I understand, boss. You can't optimize your whole life for efficiency; that's just not how people work. Far as I'm concerned, what makes the difference is that you're listening to advice, thinking about stuff, and making a decision. I thought you were just stumbling around flailing in constant cranky outrage like you spent the entire first week doing."

Not the highest praise I'd ever received, but hell, I'd take it.

"Lions," I said aloud, studying the carvings. "There are *lions* here?"

The rest of our trek had taken about an hour, and we hadn't talked further. Both due to Biribo's warning about keeping quiet, and also because I suspected Kasser and Harold just didn't have much to say to me. As an unexpected benefit of the journey, we'd passed close enough to the cat tribe's village for him to sense where it was by the sheer concentration of people there. This was sure to be useful intel later, but for now, it was mostly beneficial in enabling us to swing wide and avoid it. From there, finding the Spirit had been easy; Maugro's directions were broad, but familiars were attuned to Ephemera's magic system, and Biribo made a beeline for it once we got within a general range.

He estimated the cat tribe's numbers to be around two hundred. I was curious to see a cat person for myself, but not in that quantity when I was trespassing on their land.

So now we stood before the Spirit's altar, which was inside a dead and hollowed out husk of khora shell that had been decorated with surprisingly intricate paints and hanging beads. Bracketing its entrance were two carved blocks of akorthist clearly depicting Earth creatures I knew well.

"Sure," Kasser answered quietly, coming to stand beside me. "Not *right* here, you won't find big predators this close to a beastfolk camp. But yeah, in the wilder parts of the khora forest. There aren't any khorodects on Dount, so lions and wolves are the most dangerous animals on the island. Well, aside from whatever dark elf bullshit lives in the naga lake anyway."

"Huh."

I stepped into the shade of the khora shell, Biribo buzzing along at my shoulder, leaving the lads to keep watch outside. At my approach, the subtle glow of the carvings in the altar's white stone brightened and changed, and the projected image of the Spirit itself appeared above it.

This one was different from Granny Sparkles. The face was likewise stylized, but clearly male, as was its oddly resonant voice.

"*Well, well, what have we here?*" he asked rhetorically, smiling at me. "*A young Dark Lord, no less. You're an angry lad, aren't you? But you're trying your best. Everything has been rough for you on this world, I can tell. You persevere, though—and a bit more than that. Yes, you're doing well with what you've been given.*"

I made no response to all this claptrap, pondering. The way his voice resonated . . . I knew how to create that effect myself, if I had a mixer. Could there be a technological explanation for this? I almost wanted to think so. Highly advanced alien tech was less oppressively stupid to my mind than goddesses and magic.

"*It's dangerous to go alone,*" the Spirit finally said after a pause, and then actually winked at me. "*Take this.*"

I narrowed my eyes to slits. Did that thing really just . . . ?

Light coalesced out of the air and then solidified, taking the shape of a physical object. Reaching out as it fell from head height, I barely managed to catch it.

Them, actually. There were two of them. Simple curls of yellowish parchment, bound by colored ribbons.

My gambit had paid off; Virya was watching over me after all. And now I had *two* brand new spells!

"Hey, nice," Harold said, observing them in my grasp as I stepped back outside. "Worth the trip, huh, Lord Seiji?"

"Indeed," I agreed, unable to keep the smile off my face. "Okay, you're up, lads. The thing seems harmless enough; good luck. Here's hoping you get something good."

I stepped to the side to clear the way, and the pair of them came forward with some trepidation. They went in together; I'd thought we'd do this single file, but whatever. Leaving the boys to their own Spirit adventure, I got down to unwrapping my presents.

As before, the spell scrolls reacted to thought. All I had to do was hold one up with the intent of activating it, and the gray ribbon broke and dissolved. The parchment unrolled before my eyes, the text written upon it turned to light and seemed to rise up off the surface as it melted in the air, and as the scroll itself disintegrated into motes of luminescence, I felt the pressure in my mind of the new spell forming, along with the intuitive knowledge of its working.

Orb of Light. It would conjure a ball of pure white light, which would illuminate my surroundings and float along with me so long as I maintained it. A simple utility spell, maybe a bit underwhelming, but I wasn't about to complain. The *real* fun would begin when I started combining it with the other spells in my arsenal.

Even occupied with this, I was dimly aware of lights and soft voices from inside the hollowed out khora behind me, but I figured Kasser and Harold could handle themselves. There was nothing dangerous in there. Impatiently, I held up the second scroll, this one with a gold ribbon which dissolved as soon as I focused my intent on it. The process unrolled as before, and I was left with another tool in my arsenal.

Windburst. It caused a powerful blast of air along a narrow trajectory, more than enough to knock down an average human. I felt a wild grin blossom on my face as the reality of this sank in.

Finally, an actual combat spell that wasn't horrific torture, date rape, or lighting a birthday cake! Oh, this one was a *goldmine* of potential. Just think of all the things I could do with this once I really got to working with spell combination . . . Not to mention just being able to knock some motherfuckers over.

This had been *well* worth the trip.

I was still grinning when I turned to find the lads emerging from the khora shell, looking an odd combination of pleased and shaken. Immediately I noticed that Kasser was holding a beautifully carved flute, and only secondarily that Harold didn't seem to have anything, and they were holding hands.

There was a beat of silence before Kasser noticed that I'd noticed, and his expression flattened. He tried to jerk his hand away, but Harold didn't let go.

"Hey, I didn't know you played," I said, nodding toward the flute. "That's a beautiful instrument. Maybe we can get a proper jam session going after dinner sometime, even get the rest of the crew to try singing."

"I, uh . . . sure. Maybe. Look, this isn't . . ." The guy was starting to look borderline panicked, repeatedly pulling his arm as Harold stubbornly clung to him. "Would you let—Lord Seiji, this isn't . . ."

"It's okay," Harold said. Looking more closely at him, I found myself wondering what exactly had transpired in there. "Remember what the Spirit said?"

"I—I don't—"

"Guys, relax," I said, turning to head back the way we'd come. "I don't care. Do what makes you happy. C'mon, let's haul ass outta here before the cats get done partying."

"The celebration should keep them occupied until past nightfall, but it's probably for the best to be gone as quick as possible," Biribo added. "And let's try to keep it *quiet.*"

"I uh . . ." Kasser still hadn't given up, even despite a murmured remonstration from Harold that was too soft for me to make out, given that I was facing the other way. "Look, Lord Seiji, I just don't want . . ."

"Seriously, man, don't worry about it. We're out here in the howling goddamn wilderness, living in a ruined fort, and I'm pretty sure I'm supposed to be toppling social institutions as a matter of course. If anybody gives you a hard time, punch 'em."

We proceeded in silence for over a full minute, leading me to believe the conversation was over. Then Kasser surprised me with a bitter little laugh.

"It figures. First person in the fucking world to show some compassion is the fucking Dark Lord. The guy who burns people alive."

"For the record," I clarified, "this is disinterest, not compassion. I'm a big believer in not being bothered with other people's personal business."

"It's pretty weird how you're the first person to even be *disinterested*," he said bitterly. "Everybody's always so *fucking* invested in shit that doesn't affect them at all. It kinda fits, actually. They always told us we were touched by Evil."

Okay, *this* was starting to get legitimately uncomfortable. I was just trying to look after my employees the way I figured a decent manager ought to, not take some kind of stand for justice. I'm the *last* person to do that kind of nonsense. I had spent my entire life determinedly giving no fucks about other people's problems, and that was before I started trying to actively stir up a rebellion and overthrow the regime.

"Solid ten percent, across the board," I muttered.

"What's that, Lord Seiji?" Harold asked.

"Where I'm from, science is much more advanced," I said with a sigh. "We've studied and documented a *lot* about the natural world. And about ten percent of people are gay, is all. Not just people; that's a standard average across all mammal species. One in ten, guys; it's not uncommon. We even understand the biological purpose of it. In the animal kingdom, same-sex couples are the ones that raise offspring which get orphaned. So species with the ten percent have a better overall chance of surviving than others. It's just biology."

"Huh," Kasser grunted after a short pause. "I wonder why the goddess is so dead set against it, then."

"Oh, I assure you Sanora doesn't give a shit," I said, grinning viciously at nothing in front of us. "This is just something stupid, incompetent, crooked governments do to stay in power. Pick out some harmless minority and designate them a scapegoat. Call 'em corrupt or impure, accuse them of plotting against society, whatever the fuck. That way you keep people angry at the wrong target so you can carry on oppressing everybody else. The more groups you can get riled up at each other, the better you can hold on to power without having to actually *run* things in a way that wouldn't make the whole population so angry in the first place. You know why Fflyr Dlemathlys hates *everybody* so fucking much? Women, lowborn, goblins, you guys, whoever else? It's because it's run by evil-minded *morons* who shouldn't be in charge of their own front yard, much less a country. As long as they keep everybody fighting each other instead of the people who're actually causing *all the fucking problems*, they get to stay in charge. Bunch of—"

I broke off in startlement as Biribo darted in front of my face.

"Boss," he said in a low voice, "not to throw a wheel off your rage wagon or anything, but could we maybe keep it *down?*"

Ah. Right, we were being stealthy. Belatedly, I realized my voice had begun to rise in agitation the longer I'd kept talking. *That* was embarrassing. Why did I even give a damn about Harold and Kasser's business? I didn't. It was just . . . This whole fucked-up, asinine excuse for a country. I hated to see stupid assholes in charge, that was all.

I resumed walking in silence.

It was close to dark when we got back to North Watch, and I was ragged from lack of rest, but even so, I couldn't resist playing with my new toys. And I did it in the mess hall with the full crew present, because the performer in me can never turn down an audience.

Spell combination didn't work on everything, of course. I could always tell when two spells were a complete nonmatch; the sensation of attempting to combine them was like trying to press together the same poles of two magnets. Orb of Light, which I'd experimented with first, did not seem to connect with any of my more mentally-focused spells, so I got nothing out of trying to combine it with Enamor, Spirit Bond, or Tame Beast either.

Combining it with Spark created Firelight, however, which I enjoyed. It just made a floating ball of heatless fire, which put off a warm orange glow instead of the clean white one of Orb of Light. So, pure style with no utility, but I already knew I'd be using that one instead of the vanilla spell, purely to flex on all the other poor suckers who didn't have it.

Even better, I could now Summon Light Slime. The slime resulting from this was now just chilling on one of the tables, staying put thanks to Tame Beast. It put off a pure glow of golden white light that lit the room up beautifully. Now all I needed to do was get some glass bottles to put these in and we'd save a fortune on asauthec for torches, not to mention having much better lighting in the fortress.

Everybody cheered as I fired off a blast of Sparkspray, the child of Windburst and Spark—a burst of heated wind that carried a spray of sparks. Not so much "wizard casts fireball" as "idiot drops a log on the campfire too hard." Showy, but not good for much.

"Hey, any adventuring sorcerer would love to get their hands on that one," Sakin disagreed when I commented on this. "Set that sucker off in anything's eyes and you've bought yourself an opening for whatever else you might want to do."

Windburst similarly didn't want to connect with mind spells, though I felt an odd lack of resistance when I tried to combine it with Tame Beast.

Unusually for a simple two-spell combination, I couldn't make it work, but I could *feel* the magical code shifting around and rearranging, trying to link up. I gave up on it, though; it was as hard as pulling off a three-spell combination, and I was just too tired to focus adequately.

Fittingly enough, it was my last effort of the evening that proved the most impressive. I was looking forward to being able to summon air slimes, mostly just out of curiosity at what an air slime would even look like. But though Windburst combined easily with Summon Slime, it did not grant me a new summons.

Instead . . .

"Huh," I said aloud, frowning.

"Well?" Donon asked impatiently.

"C'mon, don't keep us in suspense!" Goose added with a big grin.

I held out one hand, pointing at the far wall, and focused.

"Slimeshot!"

It just summoned a standard, useless slime—at about the velocity of a fired arrow. The slime ripped across the mess hall and hit the wall hard enough to splatter droplets in every direction.

There was a moment of stunned silence, and then wild cheering. And, from Sakin, hysterical laughter.

I slowly lowered my arm, feeling a grin of pure malicious anticipation spreading over my features. I couldn't wait to cast *that* at the next asshole who got on my nerves.

34

In Which the Dark Lord
Attempts to Civilize the Natives

I made magic my project of the week.

I was at it again the next morning, immediately following a solid night's sleep and a hearty breakfast of crawn stew. Because, oh yes, here on Ephemera we ate crawns. Lowborn did anyway; in fact, they seemed to be the chief source of protein for the lower classes in Fflyr Dlemathlys, which might explain why the peasants here were so physically robust, given how abundant they were. Skittering and crawling *everywhere*, like rats or roaches and filling more or less the same ecological niche. The umbrella term *crawn* referred to dozens of species of little arthropods ranging from mouse-sized to ferret-sized, with between four and eighteen legs, which could be found wherever there was any speck of food to be sniffed out and consumed. You didn't even have to hunt for meat, just set traps in your kitchen.

For obvious reasons I was leery of this practice; eating tiny scavengers is an excellent way to acquire diseases and parasites. Apparently, the Fflyr were aware of this, to judge by how offended Aster was when I asked if they ate rats, too. Biribo claimed the biology of crawns made them a kind of living disinfectant, turning any organic matter into safe and usable protein in which microorganisms couldn't survive. For the same reason, you had to cook them thoroughly because raw crawn meat would make a person sick.

They weren't bad. Sort of like shellfish. Once the Fflyr got finished putting all their peppers and spices in everything, it all tasted kind of the same anyhow. At least crawn stew was filling and provided a nice boost of energy to start the day.

Thus, I had a lot more strength and mental focus when I set up in the mess hall with a pot of spicy-sweet Fflyr tea to practice my spell combination.

Harold and Kasser were off to the side at another table, Harold making cross-bow parts while Kasser had switched to crafting lamp stands; already the room was lit by every scavenged wine bottle we could scrape together, each filled with a light slime and corked.

I began my morning's efforts with the last, much-anticipated simple combinations I'd been too worn out to get to last night. I had packed it in right after discovering Slimeshot and hauled myself to bed, but now I tested what I could make by combining my new base spells with Heal.

Somewhat to my surprise, they both worked.

Heal and Windburst combined to create Breath of Vitality, which was very pretty and not very useful. It created a gentle breeze, which smelled of flowers and carried lovely little curls of pink and pale green sparkles. This seemed to have the effect of boosting overall well-being and would work to heal injuries during long exposure times. It could be streamed continuously as long as I concentrated, and by focusing, I could adjust the width and range of the spray, rather like turning the nozzle on a spray bottle.

Junko really enjoyed Breath of Vitality; she liked to chase the sparkles. This was good because she *also* wanted to chase the sparkles made by Sparkspray, and at least this wouldn't set her fur on fire.

The other healing combination I produced added Heal to Orb of Light's effect to create Healing Beacon, which was just . . . an Orb of Light, but pink, and which healed you as long as you were in range of the glow. The effect was more pronounced the closer you were.

Neither was particularly impressive in effect. As Biribo had explained how healing magic worked, it mostly relied on specific spells to treat specific ailments. Vague, broad "healing" spells needed to be grossly overpowered like Heal itself to be much good, or you could find yourself taking hours to remedy a broken bone, minutes to seal a cut, or just prolong the suffering of someone dying of a terminal illness.

I got to test the potency of these new healing spells. As Sakin was passing through the mess hall on his way back to the barracks, he immediately volunteered to repeatedly injure himself. Which he then *did* with absolutely none of the hesitation a human being would normally have to break his foot under a heavy table or stab himself in the arm with a kitchen knife.

I did not ask him to do so, nor would I have, he just up and did it. Grinning cheerfully, and apparently happier to be doing *this* than cleaning the barracks. Classic Sakin.

"Well, good to know the combinations work, but those are a waste of time," I said after giving him a proper Heal. "With the original spell, piddly stuff like that is completely useless."

"I can think of a big use for 'em," said Aster, who had just come to see what was taking Sakin so long. "Remember how your cover story at the King's Guild was that you only know a few 'minor medical spells'? I thought that would be the end of it, but apparently Rhydion remembered, and we know he wants you to come heal for his zombie quest. Well, now if you're ever backed into a corner and have to bust out weak healing magic to support your claims, you *have* some. Before, you'd have been forced to reveal you've only got the single most potent healing spell in existence. Y'know, the same one the mysterious Healer uses?"

"Hm." I nodded. "Actually, you're dead right, Aster. *Okay*, so we've gained nothing in the way of healing capacity, but some useful tricks for subterfuge."

Junko barked, wagging her tail and staring expectantly at Aster with her ears up. I sighed and directed a wide stream of Breath of Vitality off to the side, and she began leaping ecstatically through it, snapping at the dissipating sparkles.

"*And* a new dog toy," Sakin said solemnly. "This is a vital addition to your resources, Lord Seiji."

"All right, fun's over," Aster ordered, giving him a light shove on the shoulder. "Back to work."

"You think that was *fun?*" Sakin protested, albeit with good humor while he headed off toward the hall alongside her. "Did you *see* what I was doing?"

"Yes, I did, and knowing you? Yes, I do."

"Well, when you're right, you're right!"

Unfortunately, that was the last experiment of the day that qualified as a success.

The next goal on which I set my sights was the combination of Spark, Summon Slime, and Windburst which Slimeshot had inspired in me, because I *wanted* my damn napalm cannon.

In short, it didn't work. No idea why; it seemed like it might be able to, as it didn't have the inherent resistance of the fundamentally incompatible spells, but I just couldn't make them click together in my mind no matter how hard I focused on the idea.

"I wish I could help you, boss," said Biribo when I complained, sounding actually sincere. "I know you're not the first champion of a goddess to have spell combination as their extra gift, but . . . uh, that makes one person every few centuries who's got it. So, nobody *does* know how it works. Even if a previous Hero or Dark Lord figured it all out and bothered to write a manual, it would be useless to basically everyone; this is not something people can *do* without the specific favor of one of the goddesses. It's not likely that knowledge would survive if it was recorded somewhere, much less find its way to one of the only people who might need it at some unknowable point in the distant future."

"You said the goddesses are playing a game, right?" Aster offered, having returned along with the rest of the crew for lunch. Which they were now setting out on one of the tables. Wait, was it already that late in the day? Yeah, now that I thought about it, I was pretty hungry. I'd completely lost track of time while wrestling with spells inside my head. "If they're just doing all this to entertain themselves . . . It makes sense to me they'd want you to fumble around first and figure out the hard way how things work."

"Yeah, if you just handed the Hero and the Dark Lord all kinds of powers up front and made 'em fight, that's a brief spectacle at best," Donon agreed, ladling soup into bowls. "You wanna make it a proper *story*, there's gotta be a, what's the word . . . progression?"

"Well, that's just tremendous," I groused, then winced as I got up from my seat at the edge of the dais. "Why the fuck is my body so stiff? I've cast Heal on myself half a dozen times this morning."

"Because you've been sitting there working yourself into a knot," said Aster with a smile. "Come have some food, Lord Seiji, you need it after all that."

"Dunno about that," I grumbled, but joined them at the table. "You guys have been doing all the work around here today."

"She ain't wrong, boss," Biribo chirped. "The brain is an organ in your body! You work too hard on any one part and you'll get tired all over."

"Yeah, what you've been doing over there is some exhausting work, Lord Seiji," Sakin agreed. "Pure concentration is difficult shit. There's a reason monks and priests and such have to train for years to meditate that deeply. And that's just meditation; the only analogs I know for what you've been trying to do is the workings of really high-level sorcerers, who have spells that let them design their own spells, or Void witches. If it was easy, everybody would be a Void witch."

"Mmf." I finished chewing a bite of soup, which was just this morning's crawn stew thinned with some more broth and extra vegetables—and extra peppers, of course. "That's another thing I've been meaning to ask. People mention this Void occasionally, but it doesn't seem to come up often. What's a Void witch? Is that extra magic I can learn?"

"*Absolutely not!*" Biribo shouted, making me rear back in surprise.

"Yeah, I was just talking hypothetically," Sakin agreed. "Anybody who messes with the Void is either desperate or suicidal. The lizard's right, Lord Seiji, that's not an avenue to anything helpful."

I opened my mouth to push further, but then noticed his expression. Sakin usually had a look on his face like he was having the time of his life, especially at moments when a normal person would be bored or upset, and I still hadn't figured out whether he was doing that deliberately or just crazy in that specific way. Now, though, he met my gaze with an intent expression, and once he was sure he had my attention, cut his eyes momentarily toward Biribo and then back to me.

Biribo himself was hovering over the table in front of me, with his back to Sakin, similarly staring as if he could impress on me the dangers of the Void by sheer force of eye contact.

Well, well, well. How about that.

"So, these limits on the Blessing of Wisdom," I said, at least as much to distract him as because I was curious. "What can you tell me about that?"

Biribo drooped in midair again; he definitely looked distracted. "Ah . . . yeah. I guess we were gonna have to have this conversation eventually."

"Well, that's good and ominous," I sighed, spearing another bite of bug meat and the stringy alien tuber that wasn't exactly a yam but seemed related. "Just when I thought I was all settled in and I'd heard all the background info that was gonna piss me off. Is this gonna piss me off, Biribo?"

"He means relative to how much everything pisses him off," Aster said gravely, causing several of the traitors surrounding me to duck their heads over their soup, as if that meant I couldn't hear the snickers.

"Yeah, may as well rip this scab off," Biribo agreed. "Okay, boss, the thing about the Blessing of Wisdom is it's not only the least defined in terms of what it can and can't do, but you, uh, sort of . . . have to learn it as you go."

I chewed, swallowed, and deliberately kept my tone even. "Go on?"

"You already know the basics. You get universal language comprehension, and a familiar who can gather intel, mostly about other people and Blessing related stuff. There's a whole *host* of other potential skills and powers that can come with the Blessing of Wisdom, *but* they're sort of situationally activated. They're different for each Blessed, and even from that baseline which ones you acquire depend on the circumstances you find yourself in and the things you accomplish. And, uh . . . fair warning, this is the part that's probably gonna piss you off."

"I am aflutter with anticipation," I said calmly, taking another bite.

"Okay, so I *do* know many, if not most, of the possible extra powers you might get, boss. Any familiar would. But we've all learned not to *tell* you in advance, because . . . if you try to go for a specific power or gift deliberately, you'll very likely find yourself blocked from attaining it. We familiars do try to guide our Blessed toward unlocking extra attributes that'll be helpful for them, but subtly. If the Blessed knows of one in advance, it almost never activates for them, even if they meet the conditions perfectly. The system sort of . . . *enforces* working blind."

I unhurriedly finished chewing and swallowed. "Sounds a lot like how my morning's been going."

"Sorry, boss," he said weakly.

"Well, it's clearly not your fault, Biribo, unless you designed the system. Just do your best."

"You bet I will, and that's a promise!" he said, zooming around my head in a complete circle. Aster was right; I got noticeably better cooperation from the little freak when I tried to be more considerate of him.

"It's like I said," Aster mused, "and like Donon said, the whole setup seems designed to make you go through a drawn-out process for the goddesses' entertainment."

Not to mention *yet another* mechanism by which they could heavily influence events without being seen brazenly doing so.

I didn't say anything further, just kept shoveling soup into my face, already scheming my next scheme.

My next scheme began with introducing my followers to Japanese culture, in a sufficiently offhanded way that it would hopefully look to everyone— even a mystically canny being like a divine familiar—like that was all I was doing.

After a frustrating afternoon, in which I wore myself out failing to either create my much-anticipated napalm cannon spell or make either of my new base spells work in *any* combination for a three-parter, I sat down to dinner with the gang, which I began with the loudest, most cheerful "Itadakimasu!" I could manage.

"Uh . . . bless you?" Goose said uncertainly while they all stared at me.

"It's a table prayer," I explained. "An expression of appreciation for the food, those who prepared it, and nature itself for providing us the resources."

"Well, hey, you're welcome," said Donon with a pleased smile. I suspected he most commonly put himself on cooking duty because he preferred it to helping clean up the fortress, but since he was the best cook, I had never bothered to call him out for it.

"It has occurred to me that among its many, and I mean *many*, shortcomings, Fflyr culture lacks the little verbal rituals to which I am accustomed that mark the many passages we make through time and the events of life. Respectful phrases which signify the beginning and ending of a meal, entering someone's home, leaving your own home or returning to it, greeting a teacher or superior, thanking coworkers for their efforts when one leaves the office for the day . . ."

"You've got ritual chants for *all* of that?" Kasser demanded, his eyebrows climbing. "And I thought we Fflyr were obsessed with everyone's social place. That sounds fucking *exhausting*."

Harold leaned over and nudged him.

"Ah, no offense, Lord Seiji," Kasser added belatedly.

"It's okay," I assured him with good humor. "I'm not going to insist any of you follow along. You're not Japanese, and trying to make you would be foolish. Hell, *I'm* such a poor example of a Japanese person in general that if my government knew I was one of our country's two representatives on an alien world, someone in the Ministry of Foreign Affairs would have a stroke. Still. Living without these things for a while has made me appreciate them, I find."

"It's funny how that can happen," Twigs murmured, eyes on her plate.

"You don't truly appreciate what you have until you lose it," I agreed. "So! I'm going to . . . *casually* institute a few practices, in which all of you are welcome to join me, but it will not be required. I think you might find they add to your quality of life. To begin with, there will be a *schedule* for the bath after dinner, since we only have the one bathing chamber. And tub, for that matter. For the sake of avoiding any embarrassment, there will be one hour assigned for men's use, and one for women's. Alternating each day for the sake of fairness. And beginning tonight, the men will go first, because I am shamelessly pulling rank."

"The . . . bath?" Harold said warily. "I, uh. I thought that was a *you* thing, Lord Seiji."

"Yeah, all due respect, we don't really have a problem getting clean the old-fashioned way," Donon added.

"Pouring and scrubbing is to clean you," I intoned. "A proper bath is to *cleanse* you. Body, mind, and spirit. Seriously, you should all try it."

A round of awkward glances passed around the table. Aster shook her head and tucked back into her food.

"This sounds like a setup for somebody to 'accidentally' walk in on the girls all naked," Goose said skeptically.

"I thought I'd made it clear that I expect there to be harmony and civility within the organization," I replied. "But to be plain, there will be *consequences* if anybody tries that. Bath time is a sacred thing. Peeking will not be tolerated. That includes familiars," I added.

"Yeah, yeah," Biribo huffed, hovering over the table as usual. "You and your bath time. D'you know how many people I've seen naked over the years?"

"That's not the point, Biribo. It's the *principle*."

"And to be extra clear," Kasser said carefully, "this is *not* mandatory?"

"No, Kasser, it is not. It's encouraged, and I'll be disappointed if you decline to share in one of the finer offerings of my culture, but it would defeat the purpose if you were forced to participate. A bath is relaxing. Just wouldn't work if you were all tense from being compelled to be there."

"Well, hey, I'll try anything once," Sakin declared lightly.

Yeah, I had a feeling he would.

"As for things which *are* mandatory," I said, noting the position of the wagging tail which emerged from behind the table, "all of you quit sneaking scraps to my dog. I feed her plenty; you're gonna make her sick."

Five pairs of hands were immediately and innocently placed on the tabletop.

"That was neatly done, Lord Seiji," Sakin said with a knowing little smirk an hour later as soon as we were both up to our shoulders in the steaming tub, with the doors to the old stable firmly shut and Biribo on the other side of them. None of the other gentlemen had decided to join us, which suited my plans perfectly. "Y'know—and I mean this quite sincerely—for an amateur, you've got good instincts for this stuff. I think we'll shape you into a properly terrifying operator yet!"

"Mmhm," I murmured, lounging back against the curved rim of the old trough. "Glad to hear it. Now that we have privacy, tell me about the Void."

35

In Which the Dark Lord Stews in His Own Juices

So the Void can refer to two things—shapeless magic, and the realm it comes from."

"*Shapeless* magic?"

Sakin nodded, and I couldn't help noticing how unusually focused he looked. Maybe because we were deliberately going behind Biribo's back; he only ever seemed to get serious when there was scheming or violence afoot.

"All the magic humans can use is in the form of Blessings, and various related paraphernalia. Spell scrolls, artifacts . . . whatever Wisdom bullshit the lizard was talking about. That's shaped magic. The power of the Void is *shapeless*, not tied to any specific forms or objects or rituals. Whatever you can imagine, the Void can do, assuming you gather up enough energy."

I straightened up in the bath, setting the water sloshing. "Now *that* sounds like exactly what I'm looking for. I'm assuming there's a big, incredibly awful caveat that prevents people from using it? A stupid one, probably."

"Okay, to explain properly I'll have to give you a quick history lesson," he said, his customary grin returning as he lounged against the side of the tub. "A long time ago, there was a particularly successful Dark Lord who was never beaten. At this point, nobody knows how long ago that was, or what his name was; every Sanorite *and* Viryan religion has worked hard to erase him, but he's . . . kind of impossible to ignore, if you deal in world affairs above a certain level. Guy beat a whole succession of Heroes, figured out how to make himself immortal, and—this is the really important part—while every other Dark Lord *eventually* fell, this one managed to escape the game."

I found myself practically vibrating with eagerness. Another Dark Lord had done *exactly* what I aspired to?

"He worked out how to corrupt a Spirit into a Void Altar, as we call them now," Sakin continued. "That enabled him to open a portal into the Void, another reality connected to Ephemera where the goddesses have no power. I don't know if they *can't* go in there, or just refuse to, or there's something in the Void they're afraid of, but the fact remains they stay out of his realm and don't even try to muster forces to march in. This Dark Lord took his *entire* organization into the Void. Using the energy there, he turned them into immortal devils who are still around today. That's why we call him the Devil King now."

"Wait, but *I'm* the—" I shut my mouth, realizing I was having another magic translation issue. In Fflyr, Dark Lord and Devil King were two different titles; my inner monologue wanted to translate them both as Maou. "Never mind. Go on."

"Well, that's it for history," Sakin said, sprawling lazily into one corner of the trough. "These days, the Void and the Devil King are just facts of life. The goddesses and all their followers *hate* him; Sanorites and Viryans will drop what they're doing and cooperate any time they have a chance to destroy Void witches or devils. Meanwhile, the Devil King has been slowly expanding his reach. Nowadays, there's at least one Void Altar on most major islands. His devils sneak into Ephemera to cut deals with people, trading the powers of the Void for the chance to corrupt more Spirits into Void Altars and collect souls."

"Wait, souls? As in, *people's* souls? What do the devils want with souls?"

"No idea," he said cheerfully. "*Maybe* some of the higher-up priests know how Void shit works, but I suspect only the goddesses and the Devil King have all the facts. The point is, the Void's power is versatile, and available to anyone able to summon a devil and willing to cut a deal."

"Is this the part where you explain the downside?"

"Well, the most obvious one is that these deals are *really* tricky. Most of them have, as a standard stipulation, that when you die, they get *your* soul. Even if you manage to negotiate out of that, they *still* get your soul if you break the contract, or just fail to fulfill your end well enough. Plus, what with the devils and their King being basically a third faction in the Sanorites versus Viryans conflict, every established power on Ephemera will come down *hard* on Void magic and those who practice it. The goddesses hate him for infringing on their power, but their propaganda happens to be objectively correct. Fucking around with the Void *always* ends badly. Those devils have their own agenda, and they tend to get what they want."

His expression sobered again and he straightened his posture subtly.

"I wasn't just spreading manure for the lizard's benefit, Lord Seiji. I *really* don't recommend trying to access the Void. Virya's likely to go completely feral on your ass if she finds another of her Dark Lords attempting to follow in the Devil King's footsteps. And as for the King himself . . . I bet he'd *love* to tie strings to a new Dark Lord, but he's not interested in sharing power. That would be a *very* one-sided relationship. This is not a resource you can use. Still . . . It's something you should definitely *know* about, and not a lot of people are willing to even talk about it. Virya and the lizard would actively try to keep you from learning about it. It's very likely you're going to have to deal with devils eventually, though, if just because they tend to meddle whenever anything important's going on. When that happens, personally I'd recommend using Immolate until they learn to stay out of your business. But hey, what do I know? I'm just a bandit."

He gave me a cheerful, self-effacing smile which I'd like to think wouldn't have fooled me even if I didn't know him better than that. For my part, I was still struggling to contain my eagerness at these revelations.

It could be done.

"You said the goddesses haven't tried to attack the Devil King directly," I said, leaning forward.

"Yeah, there's kind of an enforced stalemate, what with the inter-dimensional nature of it. I dunno exactly why they won't go into the Void, but they definitely won't, and what's more interesting is they seem reluctant to even send anybody else in there. As for the reverse, that's easier to see—magic is shaped by Blessings because the goddesses made it that way. *They* can still use magic shapelessly, and they've probably got a lot more power and control over it than the Devil King. Honestly, Lord Seiji, your revelation from their own lips that Virya and Sanora are just playing a game with this world explains a lot. When it comes to the Devil King, well, something tells me they'd stop being playful if he gave them a target to hurl islequakes and falling stars at."

"But," I said slowly, thinking out loud, "devils do come here to make deals. So . . . they're avoiding the goddesses' notice somehow, at least in small numbers."

"So it would seem." A faint smile hovered around his lips as he watched me coming to the obvious conclusion. It was possible to *hide* from the goddesses.

"So the Devil King and the goddesses each stay in their own realms where they have power. They'd probably get instantly murked if they risked crossing the barrier. That's a stalemate, like you said. He *must* have some long-term plan to retake Ephemera. Take it from another Dark Lord, revenge on both goddesses is a powerful motivator."

"Now, take this with a pinch of spice," Sakin said lazily, "cos obviously nobody *knows*, and I'm not the kinda guy who hangs out in mystical or theological circles, but of all the theories I've heard as to why devils want souls, there are two really common ones that seem the most logical to me. Either they're using the souls to fuel their Void magic, or they turn every soul they get into a new devil."

"Hm . . . That would make the difference in whether his forces are growing or shrinking, wouldn't it?"

"Exactly!" he grinned. "If they get a new devil for every soul stolen, the ranks have been swelling for however many centuries it's been now. On the other hand . . . everybody knows somebody who knows somebody whose cousin fucked around with the Void and got taken by the devils, but this stuff isn't happening at a high rate anywhere. Not with every country and religion actively suppressing it. They're getting a trickle, at best. So if their magic is powered by souls, stands to reason it's been steadily *losing* power since that old Dark Lord became the Devil King."

"That depends," I mused, frowning at the far wall. "If they're, um, *burning* souls like asauthec, then yeah. But if their magic comes from some kind of steady central power source that's somehow *augmented* by adding souls to it, they could still be growing more powerful."

"Hey, good point! I see why Virya decided you should be a sorcerer. Still, this is blind speculation. And again, Lord Seiji, I really don't wanna tell you how to run your own business, but let me reiterate that all this is for purposes of general information. Eventually, devils will undoubtedly seek you out. Best to be ready to deal with them on even footing by then. Please don't try to get favors or anything useful out of them. I've been around and seen a lot of shit in my day, but I have never heard of anybody getting the better of a devil in a deal."

"No, I see your point, don't worry." I wasn't about to risk tangling with cosmic trickster beings, no matter what they might promise me. "*But*, you said the Devil King himself started all this by figuring out how to corrupt a Spirit, right?"

"So the story goes."

"And he wasn't the Devil King then. There was no Void yet for him to use." I forced myself to lean back in the tub. "But he found a way. The system *can* be interfered with. If it could be done once, it can be done again—without putting myself in the last guy's power." My fingers began absently tapping guitar chords on the rim of the tub. "Well, this is an unfortunate evolution of the situation I've been in from day one. As usual, I don't know what the fuck is going on. But instead of general Ephemera trivia about which I can ask Biribo or Aster or whoever's nearby, now I'm dealing with the deep dark mysteries of magic which nobody has easy answers for."

"Sounds like progress to me," Sakin said cheerfully. I regarded him thoughtfully. The man was a bundle of mysteries; he kept coming through for me in surprising ways, but everything about him set off danger signals in my head.

"What's your story anyway?" I asked, keeping my tone mild and my posture relaxed. "I don't get why a versatile fellow like you is out here in some dinky-ass bandit gang in the middle of nowhere in the first place, but since you are . . . Granted, my acquaintance with Rocco was brief, but I got the distinct impression he wasn't as competent as you at . . . I'm gonna go ahead and call it 'anything.' A person might start to wonder about your circumstantial presence right in the spot where the Dark Lord landed."

"Oh, I quickly stopped worrying about that," he said in a breezy tone, grinning as usual. "At first, sure, the idea that the Nightlady might've been pulling my strings to put me here was *tense*, but I figured, hey, if I'm gonna pal around with the Dark Lord anyway, may as well get used to Virya looking over my shoulder. Figure I've got nothing she hasn't seen anyway. As for Rocco," he added, winking at me, "I don't have to tell *you* of all people what being in charge is really like, Lord Seiji. I've led a few operations in my time, and . . . never again. It's all responsibility and very little actual reward. People who want *power* are always looking to fill some emotional gap that no amount of power ever will. Guys like Rocco, who need to be able to bark orders and kick people around, well, they're always trying to prove something to *themselves*, in the end. And that's not me. One thing I've *never* lacked is satisfaction with who and what I am. I'd just as soon not have to make the decisions and keep shit organized, thanks. You have fun with that headache, m'lord."

"Thanks," I said sourly, prompting a laugh from him. Damn, he'd deflected and dodged that question very neatly, which only reinforced my concerns.

"I think you can consider me a convert, Lord Seiji. They use baths not unlike this in Lancor, but being a Fflyrdylle boy myself I never saw the point.

This is weirdly pleasant, though! I wonder how anybody does it without the fire slimes."

"Yeah, it's just too bad I've gotta conquer the world instead of going into business. I could make a killing."

"Hah! Well, what other innovations from your home country do you think we should try? After this, color me interested in your little cultural exchange program."

"Hmm. Considering winter's coming . . . I wonder if I could manage to put together a fire slime powered kotatsu? Might be too hot, though . . ."

I made myself relax in the bath, as baths are meant to be used. Later, I was going to spend some serious time alone considering the enigma of Sakin, the dangerous riddle of the Void, and how by granting me the gift of spell combination, Virya might have accidentally handed me the keys to start tearing apart her whole world.

The thought of what I'd do to her once it was *I* who had the power warmed me almost as much as the water.

"Huh."

I stared at the smoking dot on the akorthist wall of my room later that evening. Sitting on the edge of the bed, with Junko's head resting on my knee, in the relaxed state which follows a meal and a hot bath, I suddenly found that spell combination was easier to do.

I hadn't even been planning to do more of it tonight. It had just occurred to me in an embarrassing eureka moment after I retired to my room that I hadn't even thought to try combining my two new spells together yet; I'd been so excited to get new permutations of my older ones. Almost to my surprise, they worked like a charm—the fusion of Windburst and Orb of Light made Light Beam, a directional glow I could emit from my hand. It would continue as long as I held focus on it, and I found that, like Breath of Vitality, I could vary the dimensions of the beam from a diffuse glow, not unlike Orb of Light, to something with the acuity of a laser pointer.

Even better, I had finally made a new triple combo. Orb of Light, Windburst, and Spark made Heat Beam, which had all of the above properties, plus a more orange shade to the glow, and heat. The more focused the beam, the more focused the heat, until at its tightest concentration it would scorch the akorthist brick walls, and presumably ignite anything flammable. Not that I was interested in starting fires in my room.

This had all been *much* easier than anything else I'd tried to do today. It made sense, really; mood and mental state surely have an effect on any task which requires concentration. I was definitely too tired tonight, but for future reference . . . *Could* I create some of the spell combinations that had been eluding me just by eating well, having a nice bath, and cuddling with my dog?

"If that works," I said out loud, "imagine what I could accomplish if I manage to get laid."

My whole body jerked as a flash of memory overtook my consciousness for an instant. The faces of so many sick, injured, miserable people compressed into a split-second vision of human suffering that blended them all together until I couldn't have picked out a single individual.

Junko straightened up in alarm, ears perking upright, and whuffed softly at me.

"Sorry, girl," I muttered, wrapping an arm around the dog. "This place has really fucked me up. And I've barely gotten started. Sorry to say it, Junko, but your world sucks."

She licked my cheek and pressed her body against mine, her tail thumping against the covers.

With a sigh, I threw a blanket over the bottled light slime on my bedside stand, crawled into the bed, and tried to fall asleep.

Like everything else today, it took a lot more time and effort than it should have.

36

In Which the Dark Lord Gets Cornered

O h, it is sparking *off*," Gilder said with all the ghoulish relish of a young boy describing violence and chaos. "Everybody's talking about how Lady Gray's over a barrel now. This Healer shit's got her combing the Gutters to find his ass, and with the Olumnach bandits still pressing in, she's losing her grip. That's not great for all of us trying to live here," he added more soberly. "Tough people who're used to being in charge get *ugly* when they feel cornered. Her bully boys are mostly too busy to hassle people too much, but right now everybody's trying to stay out of their way even more than the usual."

"They've started making . . . *points*," Benit said quietly. "They caught one of the bandits and nailed him to a wall on the edge of town. Facing out at the countryside. To send the rest a message. I wouldn't wanna be the Healer when she catches him."

"She's gotta catch him first," I muttered. "Why's Gray reacted so violently to this guy, do you think?"

"He blew up a *highborn*," Gilder said, as if incredulous that I even needed to ask. "That's the kinda shit that brings down the clans. And if clansguard start stomping through the Gutters, let alone Kingsguard, they're gonna look for Lady Gray's businesses to smash up first. They already don't like how she calls herself Lady. That only gets tolerated cos she stays outta the inner rings and doesn't mess with their business."

"Hm. What's the reaction been from the clans?"

He shrugged. "Not a peep. So far, looks like it's just the Gutters that cares about this."

"Really? I'd have thought that noble would try to get some kind of revenge."

"He's highborn," Benit said in her quiet voice, then immediately hunched in on herself when Gilder gave her an annoyed look at the interruption.

"What do you mean, Benit?" I asked, keeping my voice calm. I'd found the girl both watchful and insightful, but she was definitely a shrinking violet. It took encouragement to get her to offer opinions. Generally I'm not great with kids; my strongest memory from childhood was overall hating how condescending adults are when they speak to children, so I'd done my best to put childhood behind me. The best thing I could think of was to not do *that*, and talk to them like I would anybody else. Except maybe a bit more polite. It seemed to be working okay.

"Highborn care about their pride the way normal people care about their lives," Benit answered, encouraged. "This guy had alleypox; he had to beg for help from a crazy street preacher, then he got burned and cried about it in front of a bunch of Gutter trash. That's all stuff he won't want to admit. He'll try to keep his clan from even finding out."

"Hey, she's got a good point, Lord Seiji," Gilder chimed in. "See, I told you Benit was smart!"

He reached over to ruffle her hair, not noticing how that immediately erased the smile his words of praise had brought to her face.

"Hm. So you think the repercussions will be limited to the Gutters?"

"Sounds like it!" Gilder said cheerfully.

"Maybe . . ."

"Go on, Benit," I encouraged.

She drew in a breath before continuing. "Way too many people saw that for it to stay secret. He probably thought they didn't matter cos they were all lowborn, but that's not how it works. Word'll get to the upper ring eventually, and *then* he'll be embarrassed and want revenge."

"Mm," Gilder mused. "Yeah . . . she's right again, Lord Seiji. Highborn do make mistakes like that. A *smart* one'll plan for it from the beginning, but they ain't all smart."

"Some highborn are smart," Benit whispered. "*Scary* smart. But only some. A lot of 'em are pretty stupid."

"They don't get left to starve if they can't figure out a way to eat, not like normal people," Gilder added with a grin.

"And how're you guys?" I prompted. "I don't see Radon today. Anything you need?"

"Don't worry, Lord Seiji; Radon's fine," Gilder assured me, showing off a grin with specks of the meat-and-pepper skewer he'd just devoured still in his teeth. "Uncle Gently's got him and some of the other little kids catching crawns today. We gotta eat."

"That reminds me," I said, frowning critically at him. "Why are you two so short and skinny? Crawns are everywhere in the Gutters, but you always act like you're starving when I buy you food."

Gilder and Benit exchanged a loaded look.

"We're not supposed to eat outside the Nest, Lord Seiji," he admitted after a pause. "We get a break when it's with you, cos you're a contact and dealing with you is bringing in money for Uncle Gently. But yeah, crawns gotta get cooked proper or you can't eat 'em, and Rats get in deep shit if we're caught cooking our own away from home. There's always tattletales looking for something to squeal to him about. Uncle Gently says we're a family and families eat together."

I didn't even try to suppress the scowl this brought to my face. Deprivation and dependence, a neat way to keep control.

"We're not stupid, Lord Seiji," Benit said in her quiet way. "We know what he's doing. Most of the Rats don't exactly *like* Nest life. But . . . enough do. Uncle Gently's got his, uh, loyalists."

"The bigger boys, mostly," Gilder added. "The ones who got a mean streak from early on. They get favored, and also more food so they grow up bigger. They get groomed to join up with Lady Gray's people. Uncle Gently tries to stay on her good side."

"All right. Both of you, be *careful*. I'm beginning to worry about how hot it's getting in the Gutters. I want you to let me know if you think it's starting to get too dangerous; if it comes to that I can pull you out. Uncle Gently has no reach at my place."

It was both heartening and heart-clenching how the kids stumbled over themselves to assure me they would keep being useful. Even after just a few weeks of this, I could tell they *liked* me more than their Uncle Gently, and boy, he must be an epic piece of shit to make that happen. I was definitely planning to have *words* with that guy, but he would have to get in line. I had more immediate problems to worry about.

I was fully ready to cut down anything Lady Gray threw at me; Aster and I heavily outclassed any of the thugs we'd seen so far. And yet, as I resumed my rounds in Cat Alley as the Healer, they failed to show. Not only was I not accosted, but the usual stalkers following me had disappeared. Despite

Gilder's warning that Lady Gray was after the Healer, it sure *looked* like she'd forgotten about me entirely.

This was not reassuring. On the contrary, it warned me that whatever was coming would probably take me by surprise no matter how carefully I watched for it.

So it was that I found myself at the Alley Cat earlier than usual, and much tenser than usual with the awareness that I was being outplayed somehow. Just waiting for the blade to fall. Still, I had an image to keep up, and made my usual conversation with the employees as I healed them, and chatted with Minifrit.

"Do cats and rats get along where *you're* from?" she asked dryly in response to my query about the Gutter Rats, who were evidently unwelcome in Cat Alley.

"Pithy," I acknowledged, "but unless you're eating the orphans, the metaphor doesn't exactly work."

Minifrit blew a long stream of smoke at the ceiling. "The Rats do two things; they steal, and they snoop. We work hard for every disc we get, and ours is a business in which discretion has high value. It's simply a matter of the madams' interests clashing with Uncle Gently's. That, and little Rats grow up to be big problems. It's a rite of passage when they graduate from their adorable little gang into one of Lady Gray's concerns that they come here and get . . ." Her lips twisted in distaste. "A *freebie*. One of those concessions we make to Gray to keep her pacified and at bay. And these . . . *inaugural* visits are frequently among the most distasteful duties the girls have to perform. After growing up being shooed away from our establishments, those ex-Rats get a little drunk on the tiny scrap of power they're granted."

I considered my response carefully; it was obvious to me, as an outsider, how this self-perpetuating cycle of hostilities kept two of the Gutters' main factions from banding together against their mutual enemy, but it was a long gap between realizing that and finding a way to point it out to Minifrit that wouldn't be arrogant and patronizing.

"Boss," Biribo suddenly hissed in my ear, "we got groups of people coming this way. Toward the front *and* back doors, from both directions. Fifteen in total."

I drew in a breath to steel myself. Showtime.

The familiar was only barely ahead of the more old-fashioned methods. Kastrin came skittering around the corner from the stairwell, rushing to her employer's side at the desk.

"*Miss Minifrit!*" she hissed. "Lady Gray's thugs are coming right toward us from both directions!"

Minifrit snapped upright out of her usual languorous pose. "The rooftops?"

"Clear, but I don't think there's time—"

From my position behind the beaded curtain, I could see into the common room and thus had a perfect view of their entrance. It was a pretty good entrance, I had to admit. The door was hurled open hard enough to bang loudly against the wall outside, and they streamed in. They had, to my eye, gone out of their way to *look* like thugs. None had any artifacts or even faux-artifact style gear like adventurers wore, but all of them had on what was unmistakably leather armor, and had weapons bared. Swords, cudgels, a couple of crossbows, and one guy carrying a big two-handed battle-axe.

Immediately, everyone already in the common room came out of their seats, moving toward the rear. That was when the back door opened and five more thugs entered, pushing Minifrit's usual bouncer ahead of them at sword point; he didn't look harmed, just furious. Perhaps warned by the sounds of heavy boots from behind the beaded curtain, the patrons and girls out front shifted aside to crowd toward the walls and corners.

"And a fine good evening to you all!" called out the fellow in front, planting the butt of his axe on the floor and grinning broadly. Yeah, this guy had a flair for the dramatic. I respected that. "Is the, heh, *lady* of the house available? We require a word."

Minifrit was already on her feet and brushing past me. She slipped through the beads and planted herself just inside the common room, adopting a stance that was both cocky and languid, omnipresent pipe dangling from her hand.

"Good evening, gentlemen," the madame greeted them. "I'm afraid we don't service groups this size. Not, at least, without an appointment."

"Well, now, that's just bad business," the lead thug chided, dragging his gaze up and down her body in a way that made *my* skin crawl, and I was pretty sure I'd looked at women that way myself. And wow, wasn't *that* an interesting combination of emotions to suddenly experience. Minifrit, of course, did not react, and the leader snapped his fingers, holding up one hand over his shoulder. "Maybe that explains why you're *in* this little predicament."

"Oh? Am I in a predicament?" she drawled. "Surely you don't think you're the first gang of jumped-up layabouts I've had to deal with. Or the most impressive."

Someone behind the leader put a heavy roll of paper in his hand, which caught my eye in its design. The Fflyr liked books; this was the first time I'd seen an actual scroll that wasn't a magical object with a spell inscribed on it. Still grinning in a distinctly alarming way, he unrolled it and held it up, facing forward, so that Minifrit and those of us behind her could see the lines of neat text. They weren't legible from this distance, but the very official-looking seals at the top and bottom were.

"Should've paid your debts, little missy. By order of Clan Aelthwyn, this establishment is now seized and remanded to your creditor in lieu of payment."

"Kastrin, *no*," Adelly hissed, seizing the younger girl before she could rush through the beads. That was probably wise, given the absolutely feral look on her face.

Minifrit actually laughed, a throaty sound heavily laced with bitterness. Her bouncer did push through the curtain, though less precipitously, coming to stand in silence behind her shoulder.

"I *gather* the fact that I owe no debts to anyone is not a real consideration here," Minifrit sneered.

"Oh, I'd save your protests, if I were you," said Gray's henchman, beaming and shuffling the scroll. There was another paper behind it, as it turned out, which he moved to the top and brandished before her. "Given the amount of your outstanding debt versus the assessed value of this business, by further order of Clan Aelthwyn, one Armondeza Minifrit is hereby remanded into custody with a contract of indentured servitude at the sole discretion of her creditor until the balance is fully repaid by time worked."

"You evil son of a *bitch*!" Kastrin screeched, wrenching herself free and tearing out through the beads.

"*Kastrin!*" Minifrit barked, bringing her up short. The girl breathed heavily through her teeth, hands clenched into claws at her sides and staring at the wall of armed thugs with an expression I could only describe as bloodlust, but at the madam's voice she stopped. Minifrit made a sharp gesture with her pipe, and Kastrin even retreated a step. "I find it quite interesting that it's *you* delivering this little practical joke, Cauth. Unless the law has changed *very* recently, orders from a magistrate are to be delivered by a duly appointed agent of the Archlord, or they are not valid."

"Why, how very embarrassing," Cauth chuckled, rolling up the scrolls again. He held them up over his shoulder, and one of his cronies reached forward to retrieve them. "I tell you what, Minnie, sweets. Next time you find yourself with a break from your new *job*, and of course permission from your *owner*, you just toddle off to the guard barracks and complain about these little irregularities. Do let me know how that works out for you."

He took two steps forward, looking her up and down again. His eyes lingered on her chest for a stretch of seconds that could only have been deliberate before he raised them to smirk at her face again. "Mm. Not bad at *all*, for an old lady. I might just buy out your contract myself."

I didn't recall deciding to move, but there I was, pushing forward through the beads.

The thugs behind me held position at the back door; those in front collectively drew in a breath at my appearance and shuffled backward slightly. Not the leader, though. Cauth turned his stare on me directly, and to my surprise, his grin did not diminish. It took on a hard cast, though, looking more like he was trying to keep it in place rather than actually enjoying this.

"Well, well! And *there* he is, the great and mysterious Healer. Patron saint of whores and losers, eh? Got something you wanna say, mister?"

I slowly swept my gaze around the room, considering. Cauth held his position, his grip white-knuckled on the haft of his axe. His followers were less skilled at controlling their expressions. They were all afraid of me; I could see it plainly. Yet they held their ground, despite knowing what I could do to them.

They wanted me to attack. No, I realized, it was worse than that. Lady Gray had planned this so that anything I did would play into her hands. If I stood by and let them do this, Minifrit would lose her establishment and her freedom, and my credibility with the denizens of Cat Alley would be destroyed. If I intervened . . . Easy as it was to bribe officials in this fucking country, those documents might well have legal weight, in which case thwarting their execution would make me an outlaw. Well, *officially* an outlaw, in my Healer persona.

"Well?" Cauth taunted me, emboldened by my silence. "Unless you got something you wanna get off your chest, Healer, you're just in the way here."

Minifrit gave me a look which said without the need for words, *This is your fault.* Which . . . yeah, it was.

Actually, I amended my assessment; anything I could do here *that Lady Gray could anticipate* would play into her hands. But she didn't know she was dealing with a Dark Lord. What could I whip out to upend this situation?

"Boss," Biribo whispered right in my ear, "I need you to trust me."

Oh, I wasn't going to like this, I already knew it.

37

In Which the Dark Lord Brings Down the House

I also knew I'd be following whatever advice he came up with, purely because I had no *other* options here.

"Get to the guitar," Biribo whispered in my ear, "and *sing*. Sing something in your own language—anything these people won't understand. And you gotta *really* sing. Put some heart in it."

The house guitar, which Minifrit's employees used to entertain the customers, was sitting propped on a chair nearby, where the last girl playing had set it down when she retreated from the drama.

"Blessing of Wisdom?" I breathed, a bare whisper that wouldn't be audible outside my mask.

"Exactly."

I still didn't know what the fuck he expected to happen, but this was at least something he had alluded to before. I just had to trust him.

Yeah, that was all . . .

Ignoring the weight of all the stares on me, I turned and stepped off to the side, picked up the guitar, and seated myself on the chair where it had been, making sure to collect the dropped pick before I sat on it. The next hurdle was my heavy gloves, which were part of the Healer disguise but weren't going to work here. I folded them carefully on my lap, behind the guitar, and began very softly checking the tuning.

"Well, okay, then," Cauth said, smugness incarnate, and turned back to Minifrit, at whose expression I did not look. I was keeping an eye on the room at large from the depths of my hood, but I'd have had to shift notably toward her to see her face from that position. Also, I frankly didn't want to face her in that moment. "Ah, ah! You wanna think *real* carefully about how much you're gettin' paid, boyo, and whether it's worth it."

Minifrit's bouncer had stepped up beside her, brandishing his club; another appeared from the stairwell as Cauth threatened his comrade. There was a third somewhere, but I was more absorbed on the guitar than the onlookers. I'd have preferred to tune it a bit more precisely; the strings had loosened a tad from being played all evening, but it was good enough for an emergency.

"You can make it as much trouble as you want if that makes you feel better, doll," Cauth was saying condescendingly to Minifrit as I strummed the opening chords. "I don't hate it when they struggle."

Biribo had better know what he was talking about.

"She can kill with a smile . . ."

The words came out of me in their original English, projected powerfully enough to be fully audible throughout the room despite my mask and without messing up the soft nature of the song, because I am a professional and such vocal control is but a parlor trick to me.

And Biribo's faith was rewarded. People had mostly shifted their attention away from the Healer to Cauth's attempted abduction of Minifrit, but suddenly I had everyone's full focus again. Cauth himself trailed off mid-threat, his stare quickly growing glassy-eyed, and more of his followers were swiftly gazing at me with such literally slack-jawed expressions it seemed they might start drooling.

Huh. Don't get me wrong, I'm *good*, but there was clearly something else going on here.

Even under these circumstances, I found myself falling into the music as I finished the first verse.

This. *This* was why I'd kept up my English; this was my stuff. I believe above all else that everyone has the right to enjoy whatever music moves their spirit, and to me, it was the American rock from the whole first decades of the genre's existence. The entire latter half of the twentieth century, from Elvis to Nirvana. It's not that there isn't fantastic music from Japan and everywhere else, but *this* was what stirred my soul to sing, and that is a thing which requires no justification. Some people argue over where the definition of "classic rock" starts and ends; me, I just play it. Billy Joel isn't even one of my favorites; some of the hipsters and purists may argue about whether he's rock at all, which is probably why he wrote a song about that. But the moment I sat down with the guitar, this was the song that sprang to mind as the right one for here and now. That's how music works—you do need to study the technique, but once you have that, you have to follow the passion.

My fingers on the strings flowed into the series of arpeggios which followed the initial verse. This was written as a piano piece; you *can* do on a guitar what's meant for piano, up to a point, but it's difficult. Which is why it's impressive, which is why I like doing it. I've never claimed *not* to be a show-off.

However, keeping a watch on the room from within my hood, I immediately noticed signs that whatever trance I'd induced was fading. Expressions sharpened, a couple of people blinked, and one guy physically shook himself. So it was the voice, not the music.

The second verse began, and they all went back under with just a few more lines. Well, mostly. Biribo's plan became clear as I watched the audience while singing and playing, which fortunately didn't strain my attention too far. I usually did that while performing; next to attempting a triple spell combination, this was nothing. But while the customers huddling against the wall and Lady Gray's impromptu army were all staring at me with raptly vacant fascination, Minifrit herself remained sharp-eyed as ever, looking around for a few seconds in clear puzzlement at this state of affairs, but she was quick to take advantage, melting backward from the main room while her foes were distracted.

I was really looking forward to having Biribo explain what the fuck was happening. Was it a gender-based hypnosis? No; both of Minifrit's bouncers remained lucid and wary, shifting to hover over her as she retreated. Also, while I could only see a few of the Alley Cat's girls from my current vantage and didn't want to shift my hood and risk drawing attention to them, I noticed that most quickly and quietly followed Minifrit up the stairs, but Adelly seemed to have been taken in by the effect. Kastrin had to clamp a hand over her mouth and give her a shake to jostle her out of it.

These women were experts at surviving in the rough part of town and knew when and how to move fast. Every one of them had disappeared up the stairs by the end of the first chorus. Both ground floor exits were still crowded with Gray's street soldiers, who probably would have been prodded out of their stupor by the women trying to push through them. I remembered that there were rooftop escapes, though. I kept playing, buying them the time I could.

It got to be downright eerie, the way all the remaining thugs gaped at me; their expressions held the strangest blend of intensity and vacuity, not at all the looks I was used to seeing on the faces of people enjoying a musical performance. An artist could almost take it personally.

But I was performing for a purpose beyond my own ego, for once, and I kept at it. I didn't know how much longer it would hold; I slowed the tempo just a hair, as much as I could without making it sound wrong, since I also didn't know what might spoil the effect. I kept on to the end of the song, though, buying Minifrit and her employees what time I could. The three to four minutes, give or take, of an average modern song would have to do.

"*. . . always a woman to me.*"

It took them a few seconds after the last chords for them to come out of it. For several seconds, that was a slow process of blinking and eyes coming gradually into focus. But then Cauth woke up enough to realize what had happened, and the ensuing bellowing brought everybody back down to Ephemera.

"What the *fuck!*" he roared, rounding on me after spinning in a futile circle to notice that his men were all dazed and his quarry all gone. "What did you *do*, you little shit?"

I slowly and deliberately lowered the guitar. "Not a music lover, I take it? You seemed to be enjoying it a minute ago."

"Listen here, corebait!" He took an aggressive step toward me, raising his axe.

Still at an even and unhurried pace, I stood upright, and stepped forward as well.

"*Yes?*"

I could literally see the moment in his eyes when Cauth remembered who he was dealing with, and I'd be lying if I said I didn't enjoy it.

"You think you're pretty fuckin' smart, don't you?" he grated. "You've only got so many tricks up your sleeve, Healer. When Lady Gray gets as tired of anybody's bullshit as she is of *yours*, they're done. It's just a matter of time."

I could've traded bluster with this guy, but really, what was the point?

"Those documents you were showing off," I said instead. "Give them to me."

He barked an incredulous laugh in my face. "Yeah? And why the fuck would I ever do that?"

"Come now, you know how this works." I turned my hood slightly to the side, addressing the whole crowd. "You take things from people all the time. Surely I don't need to explain *how*. You're going to give me what I want, because of what will *happen* to you if you don't."

All of them stiffened further, several taking steps back. Cauth flexed his grip on the handle of his axe, seeming for once to have no ready reply.

"Not only will you die," I continued in a sepulchral tone, "you will experience the furthest extremity of human anguish the *entire* time you are dying. And only if I judge that your price is *fully* paid will it stop at that. Life, death, and pain are mine to toy with. I can burn you to ash and raise you to full health . . . as many times as it takes. For the entire rest of the night, over and over, until I am satisfied that—"

"Here!" one of them practically squawked, thrusting out a double roll of paper at me. I plucked it from his hand before anybody else could intercede, tucking the documents inside my coat.

"Jakkin, you sniveling little *stain*," Cauth roared.

"Fuck you, Cauth! You can't do half the evil shit this crazy bastard can!"

"You think you can just come to this town and throw your fuckin' weight around?" Cauth snarled at me. "This is *Lady Gray's* town, fucker."

I looked at him in silence for a second, then turned to look at Aster. She had drawn her greatsword, and now casually laid it across her shoulders, ready to swing in an arc that could conceivably behead six people in this confined space. Then I looked back at Cauth, and stood there in silence for exactly four more seconds.

I turned my back on him and walked toward the door, Aster right behind me. The main bulk of Lady Gray's men were still blocking the exit.

They got out of our way.

It was a little quieter than usual out on Yrshith Street. The customary crowds were present, and had not failed to notice a bunch of armed goons entering the Alley Cat; some might have noticed its entire staff escaping via the rooftops. At any rate, folks were watching the doors, and whispers and murmurs started when I emerged with nobody but my omnipresent bodyguard.

"So," I mumbled almost silently, "you gonna explain what that was—"

"Boss!" Biribo interrupted. "Archer on the roof of the Jugs!"

I jerked my head up in time to see a man in shabby leather taking aim at me with a crossbow. I didn't know if he was just positioning his weapon to fire or simply a watcher covering me, and I didn't wait to find out.

Immolate!

He plummeted from the roof in a screaming ball of fire and impacted the pavement with an unpleasant crunch. That kind of fall would probably mess a person up, but fortunately for him he was under the influence of an extremely powerful healing spell at the moment. Not that he probably appreciated it, all things considered.

I had no more time to consider this because at that moment, an impact in my back made me stagger forward.

"Fuck," Biribo squeaked. "He was hiding in the crowd! Sorry, boss!"

Useless little . . . Why was it so hard to breathe?

"Hold still," Aster murmured right in my ear, and then there came a jerk. I enveloped myself in Heal just on instinct, only realizing exactly what happened when I turned around to find Aster holding up a crossbow quarrel drenched in my blood.

Everybody on the street was suddenly fleeing, except for the guy with the now-unloaded crossbow who had been taking shelter amid the crowd before they abandoned the scene. Apparently, he wasn't quick enough on the uptake to follow suit. Okay, I had to give it to Biribo; crowds were a known weak point of his senses. If somebody was circulating aimlessly with a bunch of other people, the familiar wouldn't be able to tell what they were up to based on movements alone.

"You shot me," I said out loud, "with a crossbow."

Eyes wide, he began scrabbling for another quarrel from inside his coat, with hands that were suddenly shaking.

"You know what I am," I stated, striding toward him. "You know what I can do. And *still*, you somehow decided that *shooting me with a crossbow* was a winning move. How *exactly* did you come to this conclusion? Please explain—be thorough, and *specific*. I *really* want to understand the thought process behind this."

Okay, I was veering out of the Healer persona now. In my defense, I was *good* and mad.

The guy let out a choked sob as he fumbled his ammunition and it fell to the ground. "W-wait! I'm sorry! Don't—"

Immolate.

Down he went in a screaming column of fire.

"Two enemies, behind and from the right!" Biribo barked.

Aster was already moving, redeeming her failure to put her artifact armored body between me and the crossbowman by sweeping her greatsword in a horizontal arc that the next guy failed to avoid, having been in the process of charging full tilt at me with a sword. He fell in two pieces, one of them with enough intact lungs to scream.

The second was a bit farther behind, enough that he saw this go down and reassessed his priorities. He managed to skid to a stop barely a meter from me, and probably would have turned to flee had I been in the mood to allow it.

Sparkspray! Windburst! Slimeshot!

He staggered backward from the sparks in his face, then was *blown* backward and hit the wall behind him. The last spell was honestly just because I felt like being an asshole. The slime, a thing with about the mass and weight of a watermelon, nailed him right in the midsection, causing him to double over and slump to the pavement. Seeing this, I reconsidered my earlier assessment that this was a nonlethal combat spell. At that range, at the speed at which it was fired . . . well, I guess it depended where it hit the target. This guy was clearly not breathing. He could've just been winded, of course.

Funny how I felt neither curious nor at all bad about this.

Everything had gone straight to shit. I was now at open hostilities with Lady Gray, which meant that every plan I'd devised for getting the workers of Cat Alley out of Gwyllthean without it being a straight-up battle, which would surely get a bunch of them killed, was now off the table. Almost two months of work, up in smoke.

Well, if there was no salvaging this anyway, may as well vent my frustration.

"Two alleys ahead, right side, two targets, one with a crossbow."

Following Biribo's indications, I beheld the pair of thugs leaning out, one taking aim at me. I took him down with a Slimeshot which smashed him skull-first into the wall behind, causing a splatter of blood. The other one turned and fled at that.

"Next alley after that, left side, four targets, about five strides deep in the alley!"

I walked past it without turning to look, simply holding out my hand and peppering them with bullet-velocity slimes as I went past.

And so it went. No one could get the drop on me thanks to Biribo and the lack of crowd cover, and it didn't take long for them to recognize futility and stop trying. I left Lady Gray's assembled street soldiers behind me—fleeing, dead, maimed, Immolated, and in one case blind because I discovered that Heat Beam's targeting was purely mental and not connected to my pointing finger, which made it very simple to nail him right in the eyeball with a focused beam.

Well before I reached the mouth of the street, the remainder had given up and run from the sight of me.

"Okay, I think we're in the clear," Biribo reported as we picked our way through the half-abandoned outskirts of the Gutters minutes later. "We're still being shadowed, off to the left in the alleys, but it's just Adelly from the brothel. There's somebody up ahead who's moving in position to intercept us, but I *think* it's Minifrit."

"That's fine," I said. "I owe them an explanation anyway. And speaking of explanations?"

"Right!" He wriggled out of my mask, the sensation making me grimace, and buzzed along beside me in the chilly night air. "I had a feeling you'd get that one, boss—people Blessed with Wisdom who're musically inclined often do. It's an extension of the language-processing application of the Blessing! If you *sing* in a foreign language, and really put your intent and emotion in it, everybody who hears will be able to understand the words."

"And that mesmerizes them, somehow?"

"It only *tends* to. The actual magic is just in the translation effect; beyond that, it's mostly just the combination of how weird it is to understand words you've never learned and the hypnotic nature of music itself. That won't work reliably, boss. It does nothing to people who're expecting it or prepared, like if they've got mental training—anybody else Blessed with Wisdom will already be used to that and won't fall for it. Keep in mind who did and didn't succumb back there—the onlookers were just waiting for a chance to leave, and the thugs were just doing their job, but Minifrit and her girls were on high alert for a way outta that situation. They kept their wits and took advantage."

"Mm. Sounds unreliable, but . . . still potentially powerful. Hell, it sure made enough of a difference in a pinch."

It was something. My first extra Wisdom power. Between that and the fact that Lady Gray's men were now universally terrified of me, I guess the night hadn't been a complete waste. It did not feel like a win, though. My plans were in ruins, and Minifrit and her girls had lost their income and home.

Well . . . I *did* have a place prepared for them after all.

"Yeah, it's definitely Minifrit up ahead, boss," Biribo reported. "She, uh, doesn't seem happy."

"No, she wouldn't, would she."

I continued in silence, Biribo ducking under my coat as we approached the spot he'd indicated. The half-ruined buildings of the outlying Gutters made for countless excellent ambush points. This one I walked into voluntarily, because it consisted of nothing more deadly than Miss Minifrit stepping out from around a corner to plant herself in my path.

Well, the look in her eyes was fairly deadly, I supposed, even in the pale illumination of Ephemeral night.

"I believe that is mine," the madame said icily.

"Ah. Right." I was still carrying the guitar from her brothel. It hadn't felt right to just abandon it. I stepped forward, holding it out, and she snatched it from my grasp in an aggressive motion. "Can you do anything with these?" I added before she could escalate, pulling the documents out of my coat and offering them as well.

She did not take them, but her eyes narrowed as she realized what I held. "It depends. If they're forgeries, they have no legal weight. If a judge was bribed to sign them, they still do, but it can be disputed. Not that I am in any position to do so. In either case, I can't go home without immediately becoming Lady Gray's personal scratching post. *Thanks to you.*"

I drew in a breath. "Right. I—"

"Miss Minifrit!"

Biribo hadn't warned me, so presumably the person who came skittering around the corner was no threat. It was just Kastrin, with Adelly a step behind her, both looking panicked. "We were followed! It's Cauth and his boys again—they've got the rest of the girls cornered in the hiding spot!"

Minifrit drew in a hissing breath, then pointed the stem of her pipe accusingly at me. "You. *You* will *fix this.*"

"Yes, ma'am," I agreed. "Kastrin, where?"

It was just a couple minutes' dash away, in a disused warehouse from which shouts and screams were audible well before we reached it. I took the lead, flanked by Aster and Kastrin, with Adelly just behind and Minifrit wisely bringing up the rear.

The double loading doors at the front were half-broken to begin with and collapsed into fragments when I impacted them with my shoulder. I burst into the chamber and conjured a Firelight, holding up the ball of flame to cast its flickering orange glow across the entire interior.

The women had been herded into one corner, but no one seemed to have been hurt yet. At my entrance, Cauth and the boys turned to brandish weapons at me.

But this time, I had them all to myself out here. Behind my mask, I felt a truly malicious grin spring unbidden to my face.

"Good evening, ladies and gentlemen," I declaimed, spreading my arms in greeting. "Do you have a moment to talk about our lord and savior, Virya?"

38

In Which the Dark Lord Repaints a Barn

D-did you just say . . ." one of the street soldiers stammered.

"Fuckin' lunatic," muttered another.

Cauth pivoted to face me fully, his battle-axe braced in both hands, ready to swing, though the look on his face told me he knew his chances against me in a fight. His voice was tense with it.

"For real, though. Who *are* you?"

"I am . . . a man of wealth and taste." They couldn't see me grin beneath my mask, but I like to think I expressed it with my insouciant saunter as I strolled closer to them. My very presence abruptly reversed the dynamic in the room, with the thugs clutching defensively together the way the cornered girls had been a moment before; Minifrit's girls now began to spread out around the walls, either deliberately or subconsciously moving to encircle the predators who had abruptly become the prey. "And what's puzzling you is the . . . *nature* of my game."

"That's for damn sure," commented Nierit, one of the Alley Cats whose sardonic humor I had come to enjoy during my visits.

"Now, I'm sure you all have many questions. I have only one."

"Yeah, yeah, the price thing," muttered one of the only two female thugs with Cauth. "We know, we've heard it."

"Oh, I think I have enough of a picture now to tell me who has paid the price," I said. "No, this is a deeper question. A challenge, and one I want you all to *really* think about." Pause for dramatic effect. Spread hands in a TV preacher gesture, then resume speaking at a lower pitch but subtly louder volume. "What would you do . . . if you *knew you could get away with it?*"

"Nobody's getting away with fuck all," Cauth stated, still all but vibrating with barely restrained tension. "You've had your fun, Healer, but you're already in deep shit. Lady Gray's dealt with more powerful enemies than *you*. Whatever you're thinking about doing next is only gonna make it worse. I suggest you back off—"

"Pardon me, my good fellow," I interrupted in my kindest, politest tone. "You seem to have misconstrued the situation. Allow me to clarify."

Immolate.

By this point I was almost . . . No, I decided—watching the leader of the street toughs scream as he dissolved in fire and his crew scattered away from the blaze—I couldn't say I was numb to it. This was still *hard* to watch, and harder to live with the reality that I had done it, on purpose, to another human being. But it was definitely not as hard as it had been . . . as it should be. Not to mention the rest of tonight's work; I was pretty sure I'd killed at least one person and definitely left quite a few more badly injured, not to mention the several I'd subjected to this grotesque torture. Thinking back to my first day, to the shock and sick terror of duking it out with Harold and Kasser, the way I had nearly lost my lunch after provoking Aster to execute Rocco . . .

Ephemera was leaving its mark on my soul. You can't survive in a violent place without becoming a violent person. And while most—not all, but *most*—of the people I'd hurt or killed had richly had it coming, I found that I very much resented it, even more than being stranded here. I'd never claimed to be a saint, but I was having to become a measurably worse human being just to get by. That was a bitter thing to live with.

While looming over Cauth's unimaginable suffering and mulling the implications, I did step forward to pick up his dropped battle-axe. I had a use for that, come the next stage of this confrontation.

"You threatening me with Lady Gray's wrath is pure comedy," I said calmly once Cauth was once again lying on the floor whole, hale, and faintly smoking. "I will deal with her soon enough, and believe me, she doesn't know what she's fucking with any more than *you* do, boy. No, your previous plan was the best one you had. I was not inclined to kick up a ruckus in Miss Minifrit's establishment. But you had to go and ruin her setup, didn't you? And now, here we are. Just you, a large group of the people whose livelihood you just ruined, and *me*. And you know what that means?"

Very slowly, I leaned forward, enjoying the way several of the bandits edged further back from me. It was now they who were pressed against the walls; when they'd fled from Cauth's pillar of fire, the girls had likewise bolted and were now clustered around Minifrit, behind me in the doorway. I spoke straight from the diaphragm as if in a concert hall, my voice deadly calm, even as it thundered through the barn and echoed off every wall.

"*I. Own. You.*"

There were two beats of silence, and then one of them started very softly crying.

"Not as funny when it happens to you, is it?" I drawled.

"You're not gonna save the world," Cauth rasped, stumbling up to his knees and glaring pure hatred at me. "That's not how the world works. Doesn't matter how much power you've got, the world *eats* idealists like you."

"That's the first correct thing I've ever heard you say," I replied. "Save the world? *Please.* Worlds are not for saving. This world is a broken wreck with nothing on it that *could* be salvaged, even if anyone had the capacity. You call me an idealist? I wasn't sent here to *fix* anything. I have the power to heal whoever is right in front of me, and to destroy . . . Well, a great deal more than that. I help wherever I can, and if that makes me an idealist, then that's a sad commentary on the state of ideals."

I moved while I spoke, ambling to one side at a languid stride that I hoped would continue to resemble an active preacher pacing behind his pulpit, though the real purpose was to shift my view so that everybody was once again in sight. They were now divided down the middle, the Alley Cat's girls on one side and Lady Gray's men on the other, with the distance between them now my invisible podium. Aster, displaying a knack for showmanship, had placed herself on the other end of the no man's land, sword at the ready.

"And when salvation is off the table, when there is nothing left but destruction, what is there for us to do, but point it where it best belongs? Nothing that's wrong with this city, or this country, or this *world*, is anything that just *happened.* You all live in misery and squalor because someone decided it served their desires for you to do so. It didn't *have* to be like this! *All* of this could have been avoided. Well, it's too late now for us to escape the fate of short lives and violent ends, so *I* mean to turn the full force of my disappointment on those who are at the root of all this misery. From your precious Lady Gray, to the clans of Fflyr Dlemathlys, to the churches and kings, and the very goddesses themselves!"

At some point, my act had faded away, leaving behind something . . . more. I felt it taking over, driving my voice to a greater speed and higher pitch, a simmering rage I hadn't even realized I was carrying, now bubbling to the surface and starting to spill over as I articulated what was actually wrong with this whole fucking planet, and what little could still be done about it.

"I'm not going to promise you anything fanciful like liberty, and certainly not justice. Realistically, not even life, because who knows what'll happen to any of us tomorrow? What I promise is some *god damned punishment.* I intend to watch everyone who *laughed* while we suffered, bleed, burn, and spend their last moments of existence in pure regret for what they've done to us all."

To my amazement, I could see from the expressions of my audience in Firelight's glow that I had swept up a lot of them—and not just the Cat's employees, but even several of the thugs I was actually threatening. Minifrit was watching me with narrow-eyed calculation, but nearly all the faces of her girls were alight with a combination of fury and hope that mirrored what I was feeling.

It was time.

"I've been hearing rumors that I'm the Hero. I assure you, nothing could be further from the truth. It wasn't Sanora who brought me here."

Reaching up to my face, I grabbed the strip of fabric covering my mouth and yanked it free, shrugging back the hood in the same motion. At the signal, Biribo buzzed out of hiding, doing a complete spin around me before coming to hover at my shoulder.

"I am the Dark Lord Seiji, and I mean to burn this entire motherfucker to the ground."

Now that the moment was here, after that speech, it was almost anticlimactic. No, I realized; this wasn't the climax. This was the final moment of tension before everything plunged one way or the other at a speed that nobody would be able to stop or control. Breaths were drawn in, eyes widened, faces creased with such a variety of expressions I couldn't even parse the whole.

And I realized, nearly too late, that it would be a mistake to simply wait and see what happened. If I was going to keep riding this crazy horse, I couldn't relinquish the reins.

"Kastrin." She was already staring at me with a kind of immobilized frenzy. I couldn't even interpret the expression on her face, but at the moment I was thinking of other looks I'd seen her throw over the course of the night, and decided to play a hunch. "The one who beat you up. Is he here?"

She twitched, physically, and jerked her head around to stare at Cauth with the same expression of vicious hatred she'd shown him earlier. Her lips drew back in an animal snarl; from deep in her throat came a rattling hiss like an angry leopard.

"Well, he has no power now," I stated. "There is nothing he can do if I decide not to let him, and no one who's capable of avenging him. Not against me. So I will ask again the question I posed to everyone. If you knew you could get away with it . . ."

I extended my arm toward her, placing the haft of Cauth's own battle-axe within her easy reach.

"*What would you do?*"

Kastrin's fingers closed over the haft, slowly, at an almost dreamlike rate that belied the intensity of her expression.

Cauth tried to draw himself back upright, bracing his fists. "Don't you even fucking think about it, bitch. A borrowed weapon doesn't make you anything more than a little whore."

Slimeshot.

He went down with another howl of agony, this time not accompanied by the roar of flames but by the brutal crack of his knee breaking right where I'd just fired a slime into it from two meters away.

"Oh, don't complain to *me*," I said, as disdainfully as I could manage. "You're a smirking little slime who needs to beat up helpless women while hiding behind Lady Gray's skirts to feel like a big man. Let's face it, you were *always* going to die on your knees."

The sound that emerged from Kastrin I can only describe as feral. It was a scream and a roar, the noise of a mountain lion promising someone's painful end. The axe was so big she visibly had trouble lifting it, but she managed on the strength of sheer rage. Surging forward with the weapon arcing overhead, she brought it down on Cauth from above.

It was a *terrible* swing; the blade wasn't even aligned properly. Half kneeling on his one good leg, he had no chance of dodging and reflexively raised one arm to block it. I heard his forearm break, then saw a spray of blood as the mis-directed blade bit into his flesh at an awkward angle. Cauth bellowed in pain, even as Kastrin howled again in pure animal fury and raised the axe once more.

The spectacle of it was brutal, ugly, the furthest possible thing from a clean beheading. She had no idea how to wield the battle-axe and was just barely strong enough to try, and he was in no shape to evade or defend. Kastrin simply brought it up and down, again and again, bludgeoning as much as slicing him. But she was, after all, bludgeoning him with a heavy axe. Messy and drawn-out as it was, it didn't take long for her to find his neck.

Once his yelling was cut off, hers faded rapidly. Kastrin was splattered liberally with blood; the pool of it spread out continuously from Cauth's mangled corpse, the coppery stink of it filling the barn. She stood there, hunched over him, with the bloodied weapon resting against the floor. All around was silence.

I stepped forward, my boots squelching in blood, and gently took the axe from her. She relinquished it without resisting.

"You swing that thing like you're beating a rug." Kastrin looked up at me, frowning, and I gave her a smile. "That's okay. Technique can be learned, after all, and I have the perfect person to teach you. What *matters* is the will to strike. I bet you can remember a time when this pile of meat seemed invincible, totally beyond your power. Well, there he lies, reduced to an object lesson. They're *all* just meat in the end. Lady Gray, the Archlord, the King, all of them. Their power depends on you not realizing how *very* easily they can die."

Chest still heaving with exertion, she finally raised her arm to scrub blood away from her lips with one sleeve. "We have to get to them first. Lord . . . Seiji."

I patted her shoulder. "Yes, that's the part that takes some doing. I'm working on it."

"I'm in."

"Uh . . . scuse me?"

I turned and raised an eyebrow at one of the thugs, who had timidly addressed me. He swallowed visibly, but continued.

"You're, uh . . . recruiting, right? Isn't that the point of this?"

He stopped, staring expectantly at me. I tilted my head slightly, staring expectantly back.

"Because," he said after another moment, "if it's between a Dark Lord and Lady Gray—"

"Jakkin, you scuttling little crawn," someone else growled.

Jakkin, why did I recognize that name? *Oh* right, he was the twitchy one who'd handed over Minifrit's papers when I threatened them.

"Well, that remains to be seen," I said aloud, then turned toward the women gathered around Minifrit, pointing at the opportunistic thug. "I promised you *punishment.* Does anyone have an outstanding grievance to settle with *this* guy in particular?"

Jakkin hunched his shoulders as a stir went through the women.

"Eh, Jakkin's a decent enough sort, as men go," said Melityn after a pause. "I never heard of him hitting anybody. Likes to do butt stuff, but that's not a crime. He's even gentle about it. Fairly."

"I'll argue against that," Iredi countered, causing Jakkin to freeze and go wide-eyed. The second woman stepped forward, leaning one elbow on Melityn's shoulder and giving him a long, cold stare. Then she smirked. "It's more like . . . I get the impression he *would* be gentle if he had the slightest fucking idea how women's bodies worked."

That prompted snorts of laughter and caused Jakkin to hunch his shoulders in mortification.

"Hell's bloody revels," one of the other bandits muttered in disgust.

I just nodded at the target of all this mockery. "Congratulations, Jakkin, and welcome to the Dark Crusade. Ladies, my question stands. Since Lady Gray has so thoughtfully sent us a veritable buffet of offerings, consider this evening's events and your own longstanding knowledge of these . . . individuals. Who else here needs to be *punished*?"

That alone caused one of them to make a break for the door. He went down with a distinctly girlish shriek when I nailed him in the leg with a Slimeshot. I was rather proud of that; my first try against a moving target, and it was a flawless hit.

"Why, *hello*, Dasker," Adelly drawled, grabbing the axe from me without asking. Hefting it with far more expertise than Kastrin, she strode across the room toward him while he tried to crab-scuttle backward with one broken leg, whimpering. "Aw, what's that look for? After all the fun we've had together? You remember the *fun*, right, Dasker? Where's that knife you like so much, Dasker?"

"Wait," he blubbered, trying to ward her off with both hands upraised, "don't! I'm sorry, I—"

It was clearly not Adelly's first time handling a weapon like that. Her swing took one of his hands entirely off and bit deep enough into his neck to reduce all his protests to gurgling.

"Well, look at that," she sneered, yanking the akornin blade out of his throat and causing his head to tumble sideways, partially detached. "He was right all along. You *can* drown in your own blood."

Another woman was already stepping forward, wearing an expression of resolute fury. Adelly held out the axe, and she grabbed the haft in passing as she strode toward the remaining thugs, who collectively retreated from her.

It occurred to me that all this was getting rather more bloodthirsty than I'd expected. I had thought I'd have to do a lot more entreating, goading, and general rabble-rousing before I moved most of these women to go on the attack, but it seemed I had underestimated the amount of suppressed anger there was just below the surface. It was more like I'd let a wrathful genie out of a bottle.

"Ridd!" barked Sicellit, the woman who currently had the axe. "Don't you try to hide, you sad little crawn, I *saw* you back there."

As she approached, the two nearest thugs to her target roughly shoved him forward, blatantly offering him as a sacrifice to her wrath. He landed on his knees, looked over at me, then up at the armed woman looming over him.

"Celly," he said, tremulously but clearly trying for bravado, "come on, it was just . . . It was your job, yeah? We all gotta—"

The man actually flinched as she moved forward, but Sicellit just knelt on one knee in front of him, holding the axe off to one side, upright with its butt on the floor.

"I just want you to know," she said, her voice quiet yet clearly audible in the suspenseful stillness, "that I forgive you. For all of it. Because I am *better* than you."

She held his gaze for three more heartbeats, then stood and stepped to the side.

Ridd let out a sigh of relief, not noticing that another woman had taken the axe from her until it came down in a swift arc that separated his head from his shoulders more successfully than Adelly had managed with Dasker. Blood sprayed across most of the remaining clear area.

Menytin straightened up, then raised the battle-axe to rest over her shoulder, heedless of the gore dripping onto her dress.

"I'm not, and I don't," she said, directing a cold smile to the rest of the bandits.

"Long overdue as this is," Minifrit commented, taking a delicate step backward from the expanding pool of blood, "I am increasingly glad it did not transpire in my place, or anywhere we might be responsible for cleaning up."

"Sorry about the mess," I agreed.

Adelly let out a scornful laugh. "Women aren't afraid of the sight of blood, Lord Seiji, lowborn women least of all."

My reply was cut off by a sudden choking gurgle; I turned just in time to see one of the only two female bandits buckling to her knees, clutching a ruined throat from which blood was pulsing. In the next second, the man next to her gasped and also pitched forward.

As he fell, the other female bandit yanked out the dagger which she'd plunged into his heart from behind. The remaining thugs retreated from her, several brandishing weapons, and Aster also raised her sword to a ready position.

"Rapist," the woman declared, pointing at the man now gasping his last, then at the twitching woman failing to do likewise. "Sadist."

"I think you misunderstand," I said. "If you are trying to curry my favor—"

She barked a harsh laugh and threw her bloodied dagger to the ground. "Fuck you, *Dark Lord*. I'm not stupid. After this night's work, either you kill me or Lady Gray does. I just had business to settle with those two first. There's others I'm sorry I won't get to finish off, but fuck it, you can't have everything. Now I'm sure your pet sluts are gonna tell you *all* about how badly *I* deserve to die, so let's get on with it." Folding her arms, she lifted her chin, staring defiantly at Minifrit. "I ain't about to beg. Hell's revels, I hope some of the rest of you fuckers can find your balls. Be a fucking joke if *I'm* the only one in this whole crew who can die like a man."

I regarded her curiously for a moment, then turned to Minifrit.

The madame had her omnipresent pipe out and had actually stuffed and lit it at some point during the proceedings; the cinnamon smell of whatever Fflyr smoked was actually a relief, what with the stink of death in the air.

"Jadrin," Minifrit said, blowing a streamer of smoke in the woman's general direction. "She never worked for me, but she was employed at three brothels over a grand total of two weeks. They all kicked her out for fighting, with patrons and other girls. Working under Lady Gray has been a much more suitable application of her . . . talents."

"I don't have a problem with Jadrin," Adelly piped up. "She doesn't pick on Alley Cats the way most of the women who work for Gray do."

Jadrin squinted at her. "Didn't I punch you once?"

"And I punched you right back," Adelly retorted. "Most of 'em use weapons."

"Jadrin's cool," added Ennid, the youngest girl in Minifrit's employ, who as usual was partly hiding behind the madame. She found enough spine to lean out and speak up, though. "She sent me to Minifrit's place when that old harpy Magdid tried to rope me into working for her. I'd probably be dead by now if she hadn't butted in."

"Well, well," I said, turning back to Jadrin, who looked utterly bemused by this turn of events. "What do you say? Want to help me bring this country to its knees?"

She met my eyes, and her gaze sharpened into something like hunger. "Will I get to kill highborn?"

"Provided you can follow orders? As many as I can arrange. I won't promise the pay is as good as—"

"Fuck that," Jadrin interrupted, her gaze growing downright avid. "I'll follow orders, do whatever you want, spread my legs for you or whoever you say. As long as I get to fuck up Gray and the clans, *I am yours.*"

Well, this was a surprising acquisition. But to judge by the nearly fanatical expression on her face, she was the living embodiment of the rage against the system I had come here to weaponize.

"That won't be necessary. Just as long as you strike when, where, and whom I tell you, there will be plenty of blood to spread around. I'm not going to have you upsetting my plans or causing a problem within the organization, however."

She grinned broadly, and I thought I discerned more than a slight glint of madness in her eyes. "I am *in*, Dark Lord. Far as I give a shit, Virya's just as good as the other one."

So, Jakkin and Jadrin. So far, Jakkin seemed borderline timid, another of those types who'd fallen into a life of crime due to bad luck and not being good for much else. And Jadrin . . . Well, it looked like I'd picked up another Donon and another Sakin.

Great.

"If I might suggest a change of approach, *Lord* Seiji?" Minifrit drawled. "I'll remind you that *all* of these cretins were just complicit in depriving all of us of our home and livelihoods. Rather than spending half the night judging each of their sins one by one, may I suggest we presume them guilty, and ask whether there are any others on whose behalf one of the girls will speak out?"

"Now, that's a fine idea," I agreed. "I appreciate your good business sense, Miss Minifrit. Well, ladies?"

In the ensuing silence, something was softly dripping.

"Listen here," one of the remaining thugs snarled, brandishing his club. "We're not just gonna line up quietly for you to butcher like sheep!"

"I respect that," I said, nodding to him. "**Immolate**. Aster, if you would assist me, please?"

I was probably going to have nightmares about this. To be honest, part of me hoped I did. I was beginning to be bothered by how little I was bothered by all the murder.

Minutes later, we retreated outside the broken-down barn to enjoy the fresh air. It *really* stank in there by the time we'd finished. Aster and I were both splattered with blood, as were several of the Alley Cat girls who'd insisted on participating. I gave everyone a quick Heal on general principles. Goddesses only knew what sort of plague was percolating in that ichor.

"So," Minifrit said, turning to fix me with that piercing look of hers. "I have to admit, Dark Lord was not one of my theories." Her eyes cut to Biribo, then back to mine. "I suppose it makes sense you don't start off at the head of an empire of monsters. Everyone must work their way up from the bottom. I see what you were doing, now; I could more or less tell the shape of it weeks ago, but there remains a question whose answer I *still* do not understand." She paused to take a long draw from her pipe and blew it out slowly, and I allowed her to do so without interruption because I sincerely admired her command of dramatic timing. Game recognizes game. "Why whores? There are more lowborn in Fflyr Dlemathlys who would turn on the regime than not, if they had the backing of someone who could actually pull it off. Just off the top of my head, the agricultural serfs alone have just as must resentment, and significantly more muscle."

And if I'd known about the agricultural serfs when I started out, I would probably have aimed for them instead for exactly that reason. Still, I did have an answer to her question, which remained true even now. I prepared to give it, waiting for her to finish her little parting shot, as she liked to do.

"If you have ideas of building yourself some manner of harem, I suggest . . ."

Groans of pain, *screams*. Eyes filled with desperate hope, or too beaten-down and weary to be filled with anything. The smell of rot and disease, sores and bruises barely visible under the dim blue lamps—

All this flashed across my vision out of nowhere, causing me to physically jerk. I don't know what Minifrit saw on my face, but she broke off speaking, her eyes wide in the first expression of unguarded surprise I'd ever seen on her.

Fuck. I didn't know why this kept happening, but I needed to get it under control somehow.

"I am, as you pointed out, just starting off," I said, covering as smoothly as I could manage. "They may or may not have more reason than others to resent the system, but no one else is treated with as much unjustified contempt. Anyone who might have the power to stop me at this early stage would *laugh* at the idea of you as a real enemy. Their arrogance will be the knife I slip into their hearts, and *you* ladies, the hand that wields it. If, that is, you will join me?"

Off to the side, Jadrin folded her arms and made a thoughtful face, nodding. Jakkin just stood there looking confused.

Minifrit regarded me thoughtfully for a moment, then turned to gaze at her assembled charges, raising one eyebrow.

"Champion of Virya, though," Sicellit said after a pause. "I mean . . . It's not like we've got anywhere else to go now. And after that little taste, if you can give us the opportunity to spread some more *punishment* around, I for one am sorely fucking tempted. It's just that . . . Virya? None of us are paragons of virtue, Lord Seiji, but I don't think any of us have ever thought of turning against the Goddess."

"The, uh, other goddess," Iredi clarified.

Adelly snorted. "Fucking Sanora, what's she ever done for any of us? The Radiant Convocation's just another thing that kicks people around and demands taxes. At least the Kingsguard don't give pompous lectures about how living in misery and squalor is our divinely ordained *place*. It wasn't the Hero who came to Cat Alley and offered us healing."

"I've met both goddesses," I informed them, "and I am here to tell you, whatever horrible things you've heard about Virya don't even *begin* to cover it. She's a fucking monstrosity, and if I could stab her in the heart, I would be doing that right now. What, were you expecting a surprising revelation about the goddesses?" I grinned bitterly at their surprised expressions. "Well, good, because I have one—Sanora isn't any better. Ephemera and everything on it is just . . . toys to them. All of it. Spirits and Blessings, artifacts and scrolls, dungeons and miracles, the *stupid fucking coins*. The goddesses are immortal, all-powerful, and *bored*. The great struggle of Good and Evil is just a game they play."

A moment of weighty silence hung over the small crowd after that pronouncement.

"Well, that makes way too much fucking sense," Nierit muttered at last.

Minifrit indulged in another long drag, then blew a stream of fragrant smoke skyward. "So. A short life and a violent end . . . Or a short life and a violent end, plus the chance at a little revenge? Well, girls, what do you say? Up for a career change?"

I studied the assembled faces as carefully as she did. Not everyone was fully enthusiastic about this, I could tell. Adelly, Kastrin, and a few others seemed to be veritably chomping at the bit. But at worst, the girls were uncertain, watching Minifrit to follow her lead. No one seemed openly apprehensive.

Dear god, I'd just cost these women their home, made them watch a literal bloodbath, and now offered to recruit them into a doomed guerrilla army, and not a one of them seemed particularly reluctant. How badly do you have to ruin your citizens' lives before they're *this* willing to turn on you? Fflyr Dlemathlys urgently needed to be scoured off the map.

And now, I was a big step closer to doing it.

"I assume," Minifrit said dryly, "you have a place for us to stay, now that we have lost ours? Your evil lair had best not be some manner of dank goblin cave, Dark Lord."

"Oh," I replied, grinning, "I can offer you a *little* better than that."

39

In Which the Dark Lord
Has Breakfast at Dusk

It was hard to say how impressed they were with North Watch. The place looked a lot better than it did when I'd arrived, but I wasn't equipped to rebuild the broken masonry. By the time we reached home, the new arrivals were too exhausted from the long hike to do much more than find the beds we'd prepared and fall into them. That had been in the early afternoon, after a trip that took significantly longer than usual, between the slow pace of all our refugees and the need to stick to the most remote paths where fifteen people stood a better chance of slipping by unnoticed.

North Watch was quiet when I awoke just a few hours after collapsing into my own bed. I definitely could've used some more rest, but I'd get that overnight; at that moment my mind was racing too fast to let me drift off again.

Donon was still at work in the kitchen, having prepared the customary pot of spicy crawn stew for dinner and then some, in case some of our new arrivals awoke and wanted to join in, along with trays of the local flatbread. When I returned to the mess hall with a bowl of stew and a piece of fresh bread, however, nobody was about except for Kasser and Harold, crafting and assembling crossbow components at their usual table.

Somewhat to my surprise, three spoonfuls in I was joined by Miss Minifrit, also carrying a meal. I noted that Donon had given her *two* pieces of bread, I suspected because she wore her customary low-cut dress. Donon's thing for goblin ladies was clearly a relative preference, not an exclusive one. He had better not get grabby with any of the new girls, or one of them would break his nose, and I'd let her.

"Konbanwa," I said as Minifrit sat down across from me.

"And to you," she replied without missing a beat. "I gather every part of this fortress which is not completely uninhabitable is to your credit?"

"Most of it. Some of the gang were here when I arrived, but they were amazingly willing to live surrounded by dust and mildew."

"Men," she sniffed, and I suppressed a smile, not raising any of the several very obvious objections that came to mind. "North Watch itself, though. For as important as it was during the Liberation, one so easily forgets this is even out here. I am surprised the beastfolk and dark elves did not try to secure it during the last century, or at least knock it down. I wonder, Lord Seiji, are you sufficiently acquainted with Fflyr history to realize the symbolic importance of launching your campaign from this base?"

"I'm afraid not. I can't even get a straight answer on how far the fortress is from the edge of the island. People say it's a limn or so, but that seems like an awfully long way from the thing it's supposed to be guarding."

"It's about a limn's *travel* from the old land bridge," said Biribo, hovering above me as usual. "But that's through a winding mountain pass. It's maybe a fifth of that if you could go straight over land. North Watch is as close to the edge as there's space to build a defensible structure. You can see the cliffs and mouth of the pass from the battlements. Well, barely, now. Back in the day they'd have kept the khora well clear of the road and the fort's walls."

"As you have installed my girls in a single barracks," Minifrit said, "I trust you've no objection to me taking over the attached officer's quarters. I am accustomed to having my own room."

"Not at all, help yourself."

"I had wondered," she said idly, eyeing me over a piece of bread, "given the circumstances and how these things *usually* go, whether I should expect to be installed in your chambers, Lord Seiji."

"Ah," I said with a wince, "no matter how long I live here, I just *keep* forgetting how things work in primitive societies. No, Miss Minifrit, I assure you nobody has any . . . untoward designs on your person, or that of any of the others. I don't think any of the lads here would cause a problem, but if they do, let me know and it will be *firmly* dealt with."

"That is . . . mostly a relief," she said mildly. "You would hardly be the first man whose bed I've warmed to secure my safety and comfort. Perhaps that can still be discussed."

I hadn't even considered such a thing. Now I suddenly couldn't help noticing the way she had subtly leaned forward over the table, hovering skillfully on the edge of spilling out of her plunging neckline. Minifrit had at least a decade on me, maybe as much as two, but she was undeniably beautiful and possessed that rare hourglass shape that one tends to see in comics more than in nature—

My fingers clawed on the smooth akorshil of the tabletop as I shut my eyes against a flash of memory. For an instant, someone's scream of pain echoed in my skull.

"And there it is again," Minifrit said softly, her gentle voice a contrast to the acute look in her eyes. "I have known men to be repulsed at the idea, but you are not the type, and this is clearly not that. Closer to what I've seen in girls after they've been cornered in an alley by a group of toughs."

Son of a bitch. The clever minx had *deliberately* prodded me to see how I'd react. I needed to stop recruiting women who were smarter than me or I was going to lose control of this whole operation.

"These things must be worked through, Lord Seiji," she said, still quietly, "not left to fester. There is no perfect process, but—"

"Minifrit," I interrupted, "I appreciate your concern, but I would appreciate it even more if you dropped the subject."

"As you wish, my lord." She was smooth and nonconfrontational, and still I had the creeping suspicion this was not the last I'd heard of the matter. "What, then, is to be my role in your burgeoning campaign of villainy? I hope you do not expect *me* to pick up a crossbow and storm the walls of Gwyllthean."

"There will be no storming of any walls," I assured her, "and no, I rather think that would be a waste of your abilities. I had in mind to leverage your management experience, actually. You know your girls better than I, and also have more experience organizing people and a business. I'd like to learn from you, in that regard, but more immediately, I'll need your help in setting up a training schedule. We've got crossbows, which everyone needs to practice with, and that'll be the backbone of our military strategy. Likewise, Sakin is going to teach everyone about guerrilla tactics. Goose will train the girls in hand-to-hand combat, both armed and unarmed. And of course, everyone needs enough time to eat and rest."

"Wise," she agreed. "Adelly and Jadrin also have fighting experience. Following an initial few tests to see who is how skilled at what, I propose that breaking the trainees into smaller groups under different coaches will enable them to learn faster."

"There, see? You're doing it already. I wouldn't have thought of that."

She smiled faintly, but pressed on. "And this . . . Sakin. Where exactly did he *learn* to carry out guerrilla warfare?"

"That's something of an open question," I said sourly.

"That guy is trouble, Lord Seiji. I can tell it at a glance, and that's the worst sign of all. Someone who's as much trouble as that and doesn't bother to hide it? Exponentially more massive trouble, unless you are *very* certain you have his loyalty. Or an unbreakable leash on him."

I wasn't about to openly admit to her that I had neither.

"Right now, I can't afford to dispense with his expertise, but . . . Listen, as we start having him coach people, I would appreciate being notified of any-thing . . . interesting that Sakin does or says. I don't expect any *specific* problem out of him, but I'm not blind to the fact that I've got a tiger by the tail."

"A tiger?" Aster inquired, sitting down next to me with a bowl of stew.

"Oh. Like a lion, but bigger and with a striped coat."

"Ah." Minifrit nodded. "I understand, my lord. What, then, is the plan? I am taking it as given that you have a *reason* for gathering the population of Cat Alley under your aegis, rather than simple kindness toward the downtrodden."

"Kindness toward the downtrodden is, in fact, a cornerstone of my strat-egy," I said. "Where I am from, there are universal standards of human rights, and great prosperity shared with the whole population. This is not because the people in charge care about anything but their own power—that's the only thing people in charge *ever* care about—but because they have the ben-efit of centuries of refining the craft of power. And the fact is that a properly cared-for populace is more productive and less likely to revolt. You *take care of your people* if you want to keep them. Otherwise, some asshole like me will come along and turn them against you."

Aster smiled; Minifrit tilted her head contemplatively to one side. Both remained silent as I continued.

"I have to get into a position to *dispense* kindness first, though. Healing is a start, but I can only Heal people right in front of me. To make broader, systemic improvements, I need a broad system."

"What about those healing slimes?" Aster asked.

"Healing *slimes?*" Minifrit echoed incredulously.

"I'm formulating a strategy to leverage those," I said, "but there's an issue of slime biology that provides a hurdle."

"Slimes are pretty easy to cultivate," Biribo explained. "Once you get one, all you gotta do is feed it and it'll eventually divide once it reaches a certain mass. So, if Lord Seiji's enemies get ahold of *any* of his special slimes, they've immediately got their own endless supply so long as they've got compost to feed 'em. Duplicating slimes starts out slow, but that's the kinda growth that increases exponentially."

"That's why I'm only trading regular slimes to the goblins," I added. "Just trying to keep some assets held back to leverage as I need them. I don't like how ruthless it is, considering how much those healing slimes could help people, but right now my position is weak, and I have to hoard every advantage I can get."

"These slimes . . ." Minifrit prompted.

"They're basically just slimes infused with my Heal spell," I said. "Living, high-quality healing potions, in essence."

Her eyebrows climbed. "Well. That *would* be a powerful thing to unleash on the world. But I do see your point about strategy."

"I have an idea for how to dispense them to the population and use that to secure my own power, but I need to be in the right position to begin with for that to work. Once I control the crime and banditry on Dount, that plus my established contacts in the merchant and goblin communities, and the leverage it'll give me over Clan Olumnach, will enable me to decide who gets robbed, and when, and how roughly. I can use that to get the general population on my side while weakening any organized opposition within the establishment. But to *get* there, I first need to bring all the outlying bandit gangs under my control. And," I added with a frown, "Lady Gray and her entire organization must be crushed. The goal for now is *surreptitious* control, of the kind that won't provoke Clan Aelthwyn or the King, but arriving at that point means we're going to have to shed a lot more blood."

"Hmm." Minifrit would never do anything so gauche as play with her food, but she leaned back in her chair, hands folded in her lap, to consider the plan I laid out. "It should go without saying that a point will inevitably come where you have to face mass armed conflict with established powers. I think, however, your strategy is the best way to aim for that position, Lord Seiji. Irrespective of the conflict between the goddesses, making yourself popular with the people is always guaranteed to invite retaliation from those in control, but also provides leverage you can use against them, because the control of nations inevitably comes down to the control of people. Then, too, when it comes to the eternal battle between the Hero and the Dark Lord, you'll be very well positioned. A Hero's real power is belief in his heroism; if he's trying to murder a ruler beloved by the people, much of his crucial support will be cut off."

"You're an educated woman, Minifrit," I acknowledged.

Her lips quirked in an ironic little smile. "For an old whore?"

"Those are two words I would never apply to you."

"Ah," said Aster, "so you *do* know when it's best to keep your mouth shut; you just sometimes refuse to?"

"On principle, yes."

"Well, at least one of them is indisputably accurate, but I will accept the compliment," said Minifrit, still smiling. "And you, Lord Seiji? I gather just from your comments last night and today that the old legend is true, about Heroes and Dark Lords being called here from another world. I would expect that to leave you very much in the dark as to how things work here, but you do seem to have some insight into current politics."

"You're not wrong," I admitted. "I'd have been dead in the first five minutes without Biribo. And the specific political structure of Fflyr Dlemathlys remains a bit over my head, aside from the basic observation that it's stupid and doesn't work and this country is perpetually one bad harvest from total collapse."

"Well, then," Minifrit said lightly, "what about our next step? You still need to extract the rest of the girls from Cat Alley, Lord Seiji."

"Yeah." I frowned down at my half-eaten food. "That's going to be harder than I originally planned. I didn't intend to be openly at war with Lady Gray until afterward, but she forced my hand. The girls are *not* ready to fight and I don't want to put them up against Gray's thugs."

"You have two weeks," Minifrit said. "In two weeks is the harvest festival; that's your big opportunity. It's a religious event, and always a dry night in the blue-light district. The only people likely to be there are Convocation preachers, come to be condescending in the guise of compassion, and perhaps some of Gray's own gangsters. I suspect she might otherwise pull them back, given the losses she's taken between the Olumnach bandits and *you*, but Lady Gray is more than canny enough to interpret your intentions from what you've done so far, and she will easily recognize that as your target date."

I drew in a breath and let it out slowly. "All right. Thanks, Minifrit, it helps a great deal to know the timetable. So what I need to *do* is put pressure on Lady Gray and keep enough of her forces distracted and pinned down elsewhere so I can personally deal with the rest."

"What's the plan?" Aster inquired.

"I have . . ." I chuckled ruefully. "Well, several half-baked, highly improbable schemes in mind. Unfortunately, our current position, the short timetable, and the lack of available resources means I'm stymied when it comes to shoring up any of these ideas."

"All right," said Minifrit. "Which of your half-baked schemes do you think the least hopeless? Perhaps we can find a way to strengthen it."

"Actually, I think I'm going to take a different approach."

"Oh no," Aster muttered. "He's pausing for effect. I always hate whatever comes next."

I winked at her. "I mean to try them all at once."

"Yep, there it is."

40

In Which the Dark Lord Baits the Hook

All right, all *right*, I hear you!" Maugro emerged from the darkness of the tunnel into my kitchen, wearing a sour expression and followed by one of his omnipresent goblin bouncers. "Future reference, Lord Seiji, I always got somebody holding down the fort. You can shout *once* and be assured I'll come see you as soon as I'm present and free."

"Holy shit, you weren't kidding," I said, impressed in spite of myself. "I literally can just yell down the tunnel to arrange a meeting! To be honest, I thought that was bravado."

The goblin information broker squinted up at me in displeasure. "Please don't tell me our first meeting *not* initiated by myself is nothin' but you checking to see if you *can* drag me outta my hole at half a bell past dinner. You got any idea what time it is? We can't even see the sun down there and *I* know what damn time it is!"

"Oh, so it's only good sport if *you* do it?"

"That was *one time*, and *for the record*, it was at Miss Sneppit's instigation! I realize you ain't schooled on tunnel politics, but believe you me, if I'll drop what I'm doing and report when summoned by *your* gangly ass, I will definitely move when Miss Sneppit snaps her fingers."

"As much as I love looking at your pretty face, Maugro, no. This is a business call. I have information to sell."

"Now *that's* more like it!" Grinning, he whipped out his pencil and notebook. "What've we got and what's it worth to you?"

"Strategic intelligence for the Olumnach-aligned bandit gangs around Dount," I said, making my expression serious. "Lady Gray just lost an entire crew at once, plus some extra casualties. She's already on the ropes, but the big opportunity is going to be in two weeks. During the harvest festival, there will be a major push against her interests in Gwyllthean. That is the moment she will be at her weakest and most distracted."

He hadn't opened his notebook; the grin faded from his green face while I talked. "Uh-huh. And lemme guess, that 'major push' will go down a lot more smoothly with the other gangs serving as a nice diversion by attacking at the same time."

"Well, I suppose that stands to reason," I said solemnly.

"So you want me to pay you for the privilege of arranging your own dirty work? Listen here, pal—"

"Hey, it's me!" I protested. "Maugro, come on. Have I ever played you false? I *guarantee* the information is good, and I'm sure you don't need me to explain how and why it would be valuable to the other gangs!"

"Oh, I believe you, all right," he shot back. "Some *big* fuckin' news outta Gwyllthean today, for those of us in the know. Lady Gray made a move to seize the most prosperous business on Yrshith Street—and more or less succeeded, but if she has any more 'successes' like that, she's gonna be *outta* business. This mysterious Healer beat the shit out of a whole force of her men, *all* the employees of said business scarpered without a trace, and then that entire crew turned up in a hideout on the outskirts, slaughtered like fuckin' sheep! And y'know what's real *interesting*, Lord Seiji? Everywhere the Healer went and left carnage behind him, there were *slimes* oozing around. Apparently the ones in the barn had absorbed so much blood they were red as juice pums and stuck to the floor!"

Well, this was embarrassing—mostly because I hadn't spared a thought for the obvious fact that using Slimeshot left behind some . . . very distinctive evidence. The slimes tended to be splattered on impact, but each droplet of a divided slime could live and move about on its own, and I'd observed that smaller ones would tend to rejoin back together. This might be a problem. Did anyone other than the goblins have reason to associate slimes with me?

"They do get everywhere," I said, still outwardly solemn. "It's honestly kind of impressive, for such slow-moving critters."

"Yeah, well, I'm not sure you realize the scope of the mess the Healer just kicked up. Going around using incredibly powerful healing magic on random prostitutes is one thing. That merely gets attention. Busting out an offensive spell arsenal that'd let him go toe to toe with the King's Guild's best? Listen, I make it my business to be the first to know, but I definitely won't be the last. Once word bubbles up to the upper ring, this guy's gonna be the subject of way more interest from the clans than he probably wants."

Nothing I hadn't anticipated and planned for, but still a smidge alarming to hear it spelled out by someone not even involved. I continued to play casual, though.

"Wow, free intel from the broker! And I haven't even busted out the wine yet!"

"Hey, I may be a disc-grubber, but I'm an honest one; it ain't good business to gouge you for rumors you won't be able to avoid hearing for free." Maugro sighed and rubbed at his eyes. "All right, look. What you've got there *is* valuable intel, but your obvious reasons for wanting it disseminated change the color of the whole affair. A broker is *neutral*, get me? I can't stay in business otherwise. Maugro buys from and sells to every player of every game; Maugro serves as nobody's personal intelligence service. What you're proposing has me effectively taking a side against Lady Gray's syndicate, and her power may be diminished, but nowhere near enough for that not to be a terrifyingly bad idea. Unless you want me sellin' this info to *her* as well as everybody else on the market? Cos, I'll tell you straight up, from my *neutral* position, my best move here is to go right to the party with the deepest pockets and greatest interest in learning this. Is that what you want?"

Shit. If Lady Gray was forewarned of my intentions, she could . . . be forced to disperse her already weakened forces to defend her whole perimeter on the festival night instead of me having to face them all before they were drawn away by bandit attacks?

Wait a second.

"Let's take a step back," I said very carefully. "Assuming you do see value in this intel and believe its veracity, how much is it worth to you?"

"You're cookin' up something," he accused, squinting up at me. "Something you weren't a second ago. I can see right through that head of yours, no matter how far off the ground it is. I got a feeling you're going for an angle that may complicate the equation, which makes me reluctant to name a figure up front."

"Not your first day on the job, I see. Ahem." I glanced over at the doorway, where I had three lackeys standing by. "Twigs, would you bring us some wine and the least cracked cups that are clean, please?"

She folded down her hands at me and glided across the room to the cupboard, which served as North Watch's wine cellar.

"All right, I don't want to put you in an intractable position, Maugro, and I can see how setting you directly against Lady Gray is just that. If you gotta sell to her, okay. I respect it and I can deal. With that said, I can't help taking note that you have a long history of offering services beyond the buying and selling of information. Allowing me and the other bandit gangs to pay a service fee to guarantee our privacy, for example. Limiting the options concerning to *whom* you'll sell, in essence, provided you get paid. Right?"

"Go on," he said in an openly wary tone while accepting a cup of wine from Twigs.

I received my cup of wine with a nod of thanks to Twigs, took a sip, and suppressed a grimace. *Every time* with this stuff. Why did I always forget?

"In addition to selling you this extremely valuable tidbit, I would like to purchase the distribution rights, so to speak. Or, I suppose, preemptively buy out anyone else's attempt to buy exclusive access. In short, the deal I want means you can sell to anyone, but nobody else can pay you not to sell to anyone. If Gray can buy, so can the other gangs. Follow me?"

"Mm." He took a lingering sip of the wine, staring pensively at the wall behind me. "A little arcane, but not wholly original; I've done deals on those terms before, almost exactly. Still. The fact remains that this is *Lady Gray*, who is not stupid and may interpret it as me taking a side if I accept that deal over her inevitable offer to buy exclusivity."

"But I'm offering you the deal now, before she's even heard about this. Not even Lady Gray can begrudge a neutral party the rule of first come, first served."

"Lady Gray can begrudge a lot," he said with a humorless grin. "Especially when she's backed into a corner."

"Then I guess what it comes down to is the fact that she *is* backed into the corner," I replied, meeting his gaze and holding it. "Don't think of it as taking a side, Maugro, but recognizing *who* you're going to be dealing with going forward. Is Lady Gray the future of crime on Dount, or am I?"

Maugro's eyes again focused elsewhere on me as he rapidly thought, covering his pause with a long sip of wine. I waited, not bothering to disguise my alert attention on him. This was a real test of my progress. If the information broker, the guy who possibly knew the overall situation better than anyone and didn't have a personal stake, ventured an opinion as to who was going to come out on top in the end . . .

"I'll call that even," he said suddenly, his red eyes zeroing back in on mine. "I will buy your intelligence, and I will sell you the guarantee of availability to anyone who's willing to pay. Same price, for a net transaction of zero. The hell I'm paying you for this, Lord Seiji."

"I accept your terms," I said, inclining my head as graciously as I could and really working to keep the satisfaction off my face. "Pleasure doing business as always, Maugro."

"Yeah, well, truth be told I was gonna come see you first thing at a *reasonable* hour tomorrow. I got something to market that you've expressed an interest in, if you wanna knock that out tonight."

"Oh?"

"You've paid for the right to be notified first if any of the other gangs fail to pay up. Well, one's come up short this month. I'm withholding a few vital details they were able to cover, but that was a fraction of my agreed upon fee for the service of discretion and it leaves quite a bit which is now up for market." He grinned knowingly. "If you're still interested?"

"Aster," I said, "please go to my room and grab my money pouch. The big one. And don't let Junko out!"

"Please," Maugro added with a pained grimace. Aster nodded at me and slipped out of the kitchen without a word.

"I remember the quoted price for this per gang," I said. "Consider it agreed to. If you prefer to wait for the coin . . . ?"

"You ain't played me false yet," he said, winking. "Also, I'm gonna shave off two red halos because, as I said, they scraped together the coin to cover what they consider the essentials, which is the identities of any of the individuals in question. No names or descriptions. However, I can give you the rundown of their operations and where to find them. Also," he added with a canny glint in his eye, "assuming you're still interested in dibs . . . I don't suppose you'd be interested in covering the rest of their privacy fee? At a discount, of course, but it'll ensure nobody *else* gets informed of this data."

I drew in a long breath, thinking rapidly. "Hm. How about we reconsider that after you tell me what you can?"

"Fair enough," he agreed. "Okay, so this is a gang of nine individuals. Their base is somewhere in a bladegrass forest near the village of Flynswith, *way* over on the eastern edge of the island. That's on the lands of Clan Thelflyn, on the southern edge of their demesne near Gwyllthean. I dunno the exact location of their camp; I meet 'em in the village, where we got a goblin tunnel entrance hidden. That's not a big area to search, but bladegrass is no joke; *I* wouldn't go pokin' around in there. But anyway, this crew is the only significant player on the island who's not beholden to Clan

Olumnach. They run an entirely different operation than most of the gangs, too. Instead of attacking travelers and raiding outlying villages and houses like most gangs, these gi—that is, this crew—specializes in poaching and cat burglary. They specifically prey on the nobility all around the island. What they poach they eat, and what they steal, they distribute among the villagers and isolated farmers. That buys 'em a *lot* of freedom to move; villagers refuse to turn 'em in no matter how insistently the clans come asking, and they've got enough contacts among servants in every keep to slip in and out without any clansguard being any the wiser."

"Huh," I mused, my mind racing. "Sounds like Robin Hood and his Merry Men."

Maugro's eyebrows rose. "Uh . . . no? I assume that's a gang from your old country?"

"Not—never mind, long story." I hesitated, considering. "Any idea why they're short on their protection money?"

"Yeah," he chuckled, "because they're trying to play renegade hero out there, and that was *always* a scheme with a limited shelf life. This crew is pissing off the people in power, specifically and personally. There've been crackdowns, and since they can't get at the l—at the bandits in question, the clans are squeezing their suspected allies. It's been a rough month. They've bled coin and resources rescuing various peasants who either stood up for 'em or were randomly targeted to discredit them. I can admire the principles involved," he added with a fatalistic shrug, "but I got mouths to feed, and let's face it, that whole idea was never gonna amount to shit. I hope they got to feel like heroes for a little while, because that was all that'll have come of it in the end."

"Hm." I frowned into my wine, forgot myself so far as to take a sip, and involuntarily puckered. Dammit.

"Excuse me?"

Maugro and I both turned in surprise to Twigs, who had interjected herself into the conversation. Very softly and diffidently, but still.

"How long has this gang been active?"

"It's been less'n a year," Maugro said, after glancing at me for approval. "Let's see . . . Eight months in business with me, maybe a month or two operating before that?" Twigs folded down her hands at him and retreated three steps, but her eyes shifted to focus on me with an intense look that was very much unlike her.

"Ah, Aster, good timing," I said as she returned and handed over my coin pouch. "All right, Maugro, I'll pay up for the tip. And . . ." I glanced again at Twigs, who was now dry-washing her hands. ". . . yeah. Let me cover the discretion fee for this gang. Just for the rest of this month."

Twigs sagged visibly in relief. I noticed that Maugro saw that; his speculative expression was a mirror of my own.

"Glad to do business as always, Lord Seiji," the goblin said moments later, tucking coins away in a pouch inside his coat and grinning up at me. "You continue to be a profitable acquaintance. I'll make the rounds over the course of tomorrow; you can expect your intel to be fully disseminated within the week at the latest. Gray'll be the first to know, of course. I really hope you're ready for the consequences of that, for both our sakes."

"Oh, don't worry," I lied with a smile, "I know exactly what I'm doing."

I waited until he and his bodyguard had vanished into the darkness of the tunnel, then waited a minute more, before turning to face Twigs. She surged toward me, opening her mouth, but I forestalled her with an upraised hand.

"Biribo?" He zipped into the room, doing a complete circuit around my head. "Are they gone?"

"Outta earshot, boss," my familiar reported. "*Although*, given what we just learned about the acoustics of that tunnel, we *may* wanna refrain from discussing *anything* of a sensitive nature in this kitchen. In fact, would it kill you to put a *door* across that thing? Preferably something that locks from this side. Now that we know we got a shilwright and ninwright on staff, it's just a matter of gettin' the raw materials."

"Good suggestions, both," I agreed. "Ladies, join me?"

I led the way through the kitchen's side door into the base of the stairwell.

Goose, Twigs, and Aster all followed, and I ignited a Firelight to chase away the darkness. Aster shut the door behind us and nodded to me.

"All right," I said to Twigs, "let's hear it."

"Lord Seiji," she burst out, "may I have your permission to leave?"

I blinked at her. I wasn't sure exactly what I'd expected, but it wasn't that. "Are you . . . unhappy with us, Twigs?" If anything, I thought she had been relaxing noticeably over the course of my tenure here.

"Oh no, I—" Twigs cut herself off, taking a deep breath. "Pray forgive me, my lord. In my eagerness I spoke with unseemly haste, at the expense of clarity."

Aster raised an eyebrow, and I nearly did the same. This distinctly formal speech was new.

"By all means, collect your thoughts," I said.

"What I meant was," Twigs continued after getting an encouraging nod from Goose, "I'd like your blessing to go on a mission on your behalf. That gang the goblin was talking about, that you bought information on—I think I know who they are."

"His name is Maugro," I said in gentle reproof. "And you figured that out based on his description alone?"

She nodded earnestly. "By the timetable, and the description of their methods and goals. Plus . . . the fact that what coin they could scrape together they spent protecting their names and descriptions. Dount has no famous bandits except for Lady Gray herself; only nobility or certain adventurers would be so recognizable as to make that a high priority, and I don't think the King's Guild is missing anyone?" She turned a questioning look on Aster, who shrugged.

"I'm a bit out of the loop, but if they've been out there for nearly a year? Yeah, that's definitely not anybody from the local Guild. They'd've been identified and prioritized on a kill quest pretty quickly."

"If I'm right," Twigs said, turning her attention back to me, "I *know* I can persuade them to come here and join you, Lord Seiji. I suspect I could, even if they were at the peak of their success, but apparently they are currently in urgent need of a protector and a new base."

"And if you're wrong?"

"Then, based just on what Maugro told us, they're still perfect recruitment targets. And almost certainly disaffected aristocrats; I know how to talk to people like that. The fact that you bought them another month of privacy will be compellingly persuasive."

I mulled for a moment, studying her. Twigs had relaxed enough to start cleaning herself properly since I'd taken over, and been less vigilant about keeping her oversized hat pulled down. Her hair was straight and medium brown; not glossy elven gold, but closer to it than the wavy black hair of Dountol lowborn. And she was definitely pale enough to fit in with the aristocracy. Nobody had poked at her about it. There seemed to be an unspoken agreement among the bandits that we didn't dig into each other's histories. Now, though . . .

"Twigs, I haven't demanded your personal story, and I'm still not interested in intruding on your privacy," I said. "But considering all this, is there something in particular you think I should know?"

She hesitated, clearly thinking, and looked again at Goose.

"No more than you can probably figure out just from looking at her," Goose answered me, stepping forward to lay one big hand on Twigs's shoulder with the surprising gentleness she always showed the girl. "I've been looking after Twigs since long before we were bandits, and she started going by that nickname. We had to leave our previous home . . . let's say quickly, and under inauspicious circumstances. All this time, we'd thought we lost somebody in the process. But she's right; it does sound a lot like they're still out there."

I sighed softly. "And *naturally*, if she goes, you'll insist on going with her."

"Yes, my lord," Goose said quietly, meeting my gaze.

"This is the worst possible timing, ladies. We've got a load of new recruits who need to get trained *quickly*. I was really counting on you to spearhead that effort, Goose."

"I appreciate your faith, Lord Seiji," she said with a slight grin. "And I'd reconsider asking if I was the only prospect. But the new girls still have plenty of prospects to get trained in fighting. You've got Sakin and Aster, and now also that Jadrin, and Adelly."

"That's—wait, *you* know Adelly?"

"She tried to hide when she saw me," Goose said with a grimace. "Probably thought I'd judge her for where she ended up working. We crossed paths a couple times when we were both in the King's Guild. And hell no, I don't look down on her or any of those women for that. To make it as an adventurer, you gotta get a Blessing, and then *also* the artifacts and scrolls to use it. Lots of people wash out, more than succeed, and if you're a woman without family to go crawling back to . . . Well, I was stupid lucky a clan took me in to guard one of its daughters. Most aren't that lucky, and everybody's gotta survive."

I nodded slowly, pondering. How much did I really know about Twigs and Goose? This was by far the most forthright they'd been with me in the whole time we'd been acquainted, and it did not escape my attention that it came up only when they were trying to persuade me to let them run off into the wild alone. They knew a *lot* about my location and operations. If . . .

"They could've just slipped away, Lord Seiji," Aster pointed out softly. "If they meant us any ill. It's not like we've got anything resembling security in this damn place. The gates don't even close."

"Right," I said with a rueful grimace. "You're right, of course. I apologize, Twigs, I didn't mean to imply any distrust."

"There's nothing to apologize for, Lord Seiji," she said, smiling. "You have to consider these things; it's part of being in charge. I understand completely."

"All right." I inhaled again and let out a sigh. "You two be *careful* out there. Take whatever you need for a journey from the supplies."

"Thank you, Lord Seiji!" Twigs exclaimed, squeezing her hands together and staring at me through eagerly shining eyes. "I promise you won't regret this!"

I wasn't willing to take *anyone's* word on that particular point. I didn't tell them so, of course. Somebody around here might as well be able to cling to some optimism.

41

In Which the Dark Lord Pokes the Bear

"**G**ood morning, ladies!"

Though it was early for breakfast, still before dawn, everyone had gathered in the mess hall and they all looked a lot more chipper than upon arrival.

For the first time, my followers occupied more than one table. Some had to twist around to look at me as I parked between Aster and Kastrin. We were all close enough together that I didn't have to project.

"How're we all settling in? I know it hasn't been the easiest couple of days. We should have plenty of supplies for now, but if you come up with any needs we haven't considered, let me know and I'll see to it."

"Gotta say, I feel better about this than last night," Jadrin commented, then paused, frowning. "Or . . . night before last, I guess. Fuck, no kidding, it's been a weird couple days. But seriously, you have a *castle*."

"Yeah, I'll admit I was expecting like a camp in the khora or something," Adelly agreed. "But holy shit, it's an actual *castle*! Guess this Dark Lord thing is serious after all."

"North Watch is really more of a fortress," said Sicellit. "An outpost, basically. And, no offense, Lord Seiji, but it's kind of a wreck."

"It's as impressive a keep as some of the clans have," Kastrin retorted defensively.

"And you should've seen it when I moved in," I added. "No offense taken, Sicellit, getting this place back in shape is an ongoing project."

"Oh, I guess I know what *we'll* be doing," muttered Iredi.

"I do expect every able pair of hands to help," I replied, "but that particular goal is over the long term, and we have more important things to focus on right now. I promised you girls the chance to strike back at our oppressors; to do that, you're going to need training. That's job one, and what we'll focus on starting today. I *really* wanted to be here to supervise and be available during these first few days," I added with a frown I didn't have to feign, "but none of this has gone *quite* according to my plans. Now I have to immediately go back to Gwyllthean to do some damage control and set the next stages in motion. I thought I'd arranged it carefully, but it turns out I underestimated Lady Gray."

"Yeah, people do that," said Jadrin. "That's a big part of why she's the top dog in the Gutters."

"My mistake," I acknowledged. "Everyone slips up, but I don't mean to make the same mistake twice. Speaking of, Jadrin and Jakkin, what do you think will be her next move?"

"Oh, she is gonna be *pissed*," Jadrin said with a blend of relish and amusement that reminded me of Gilder.

"She's gonna try to deal with you herself, uh, my lord," Jakkin said, his expression far more concerned. "That's what she does with . . . well, cases like that. Lady Gray sends her crews out to handle most things, but when it comes to Blessed making a move on her, she's gotta come out and remind everybody why she's in charge. Whenever a dangerous enough adventurer starts trying to cut into her business, she's always taken 'em down herself."

"So Lady Gray is Blessed," I said, frowning.

"With Might," said Jadrin around a mouthful of soup. "She's got this dagger that makes her invisible when it's out of the sheath."

Fuck. A perfect assassin's weapon. *That* was going to be a nightmare to fight.

"Biribo?" I turned to my familiar, who was hovering in his usual place over my shoulder.

"That's a powerful artifact," he said. "I've seen a few with similar abilities. That's actually not the biggest thing to worry about, boss. If a Blessed has the skills, wealth, or influence to possess something like that, *and* a Blessing strong enough to wield its full powers, they've probably got more than one. Lots of artifacts are small and easily concealed, and this Lady Gray strikes me as the type to keep some of her advantages hidden."

"Hm. Do you know of any other artifacts she has?"

"Not that I've seen, but lizard's right," Jadrin grunted. "Lady Gray's cagey."

"So, she could have another really powerful one, say," Biribo continued, "or three or four much less powerful artifacts to make up the difference. That's the real problem when fighting Blessed, boss. Artifacts and even some spells are so individual it can be hard to know what you're up against. It's really not smart to go in blind."

"Well, I'll do what I can. I may not know exactly what I'm dealing with, but neither does she. Does she have any other Blessed working for her?"

"A few here and there, but nobody impressive," said Jakkin.

"Yeah, I think she doesn't want potential competition in her own organization," Jadrin added. "I wouldn't either, if I was her."

"All right, thanks for the tip—I know now what gaps in my intel need filling in. But that's a problem for another day. For *today*, I am sorry to leave you ladies so soon, but it can't be helped. I'll be back as soon as I can. In the meantime, Miss Minifrit is going to help get everything organized; I know you're all accustomed to following her lead. Sakin will take point on establishing a training routine." I pointed my spoon at him, and he waved, grinning hugely. "Adelly, Jadrin, I'd like you two to step up and teach the others what you know about fighting. Sakin, work with them a bit first, then all three of you gauge everyone's current abilities and potential, figure out who needs to learn what and how close we are. Overall, until I get back, Kasser's in charge."

Kasser, the newly deputized, jumped so violently he almost spilled his soup, looking up at me in wide-eyed surprise. I gave him what I hoped was an encouraging smile.

The fact was, with Aster coming with me and Goose leaving, I had nobody else in the acceptable range on what I had mentally labeled the Donon-Sakin Axis, whose endpoints were "loyal to me" and "competent." Kasser was . . . the least terrible choice, in my judgment. At least since our visit to the Spirit, after which he'd started slowly warming up to me. And with the gang having quadrupled in size overnight, and with the new arrivals completely unfamiliar with the old, I could no longer do the same laissez-faire absentee leadership that had been working up until now. There needed to be an actual chain of command.

And I needed to keep people busy enough that they didn't have the opportunity to sit around and wonder if they'd made the wrong choice, throwing in with me. I'd already asked Sakin and Minifrit both to watch out for troublemakers, and told Harold and Kasser to start drawing up plans and get me a materials list to both repair the fortress gates and install Biribo's suggested door across the goblin tunnel. North Watch was currently about as secure as a food cart. I wanted to fix that *before* I had reason to regret it, not after.

It was Kasser himself who came to see us off at the gates. He'd been watching me with visibly gathering tension throughout breakfast and during the few minutes it took Aster, Goose, Twigs, and I to put ourselves together to set out, so I really wasn't surprised when he burst out just outside the gates, "Lord Seiji!"

"Kasser, you'll do fine," I assured him. "I know it was sudden, but I have faith in you."

"It's not that," he said, shaking his head. "I mean, I wouldn't have hated a bit of forewarning, but I'm getting used to your *dramatic timing*. But no, it's just . . ."

He trailed off, looking strangely conflicted, and half-turned to look back into the courtyard, where Sakin was marshaling the troops and having them square off with sticks of sanded akorshil. Kasser dry-washed his hands against his shirt, clearly nervous.

"They took my sister," he said suddenly, turning back to me.

"Uh . . . who did?"

"There are judges who do it practically for a living," he said, face twisting in remembered bitterness. "Some soldiers just showed up at our house one day with papers, saying she owed a debt . . . It was all bullshit, of course, but there's no point arguing with the Kingsguard. I don't even know when, but the judge must've passed through our village at some point, saw how pretty she was, figured out who she was, and . . ." He paused, swallowing painfully. "My parents never gave up. Took Dad six years just to find out where they'd taken her. She was sold to a brothel in the middle ring and . . . and by the time he tracked her that far, turned out she'd died two years ago. Nobody would ever tell him how."

"I'm sorry," I said quietly. It wasn't nearly enough for something like that, but . . . damn. What else *can* you say?

"You're doing a good thing here, Lord Seiji," Kasser said, staring intently at me now. "Thank you for this."

Awkward.

"I'm the fuckin' Dark Lord," I replied, irritated and not completely sure why. "I was sent here to conquer and bring chaos. It's not *my* fault this country is in such goddamn shambles that the most destructive thing I can unleash on it is basic human decency."

"I'll keep everything in order here, Lord Seiji," he said, nodding once. "Have a safe trip."

"Good man. I know I can count on you." I sure hoped I could; it'd be nice if it turned out to be true.

With that for a farewell, the four of us set out at as brisk a pace as we safely could on the broken and overgrown old road. We made good enough time that it was just a couple of hours until the next round of goodbyes, as we reached the first branching path where our routes diverged.

"I know I probably don't need to tell you two to be careful, but I'm saying it anyway," I stated.

"We'll look after each other, Lord Seiji," Goose promised with a smile.

"The harvest festival in two weeks is when shit's going down," I said. "I know you've gotta get all the way across the island, *find* this gang, and get a meeting with them without getting stabbed. I want you to be *cautious* above all else and prioritize your well-being, even if that means it takes longer. But if it ends up being possible, it would help a lot if you can be back here with these reinforcements by then. That's looking like the first time I'll be taking multiple combatants into what's sure to be an actual brawl, and more people with real combat experience would be a huge help."

"That won't take two weeks," said Twigs. "It's negotiations that I expect to stall things, Lord Seiji. If even half of my hunches are right, not to mention Maugro's intelligence, these people are on what they think is a righteous crusade and will be loath to give it up just because they're losing and doomed. I *can* change their minds; they wouldn't have made it this long if they were too obsessed to see reason. It may take time, though."

"And we might also get lucky," Goose added with a grin. "Maybe they'll be desperate to get outta there and pack it up to join us as soon as we arrive."

"Ganbatte," I said. "Watch your backs."

Aster and I pressed on at our harsher pace, leaving Goose and Twigs to make what was surely a more leisurely pace through the back paths. We didn't talk for a while, but by that point we were comfortable enough with each other's company that it wasn't awkward.

By pushing our pace, we made it to Gwyllthean in record time. Having set out near dawn, we arrived during the tail end of the lunch hour, where we had a stroke of luck so perfect it felt like the universe's apology for how badly that mess in Cat Alley had gone. Our quarry was in the first place we started to look, entirely sparing us the need to hunt him down.

And so, I strode up to the table in the King's Guild, at which Rhydion, the armored paladin, was sitting with two companions having lunch. Rhydion couldn't eat because, as usual, his face was fully covered by his helmet visor. I was starting to wonder if it even opened at all.

"Why do you always have that thing on indoors?" I asked, seating myself without waiting for an invitation. "And during a meal, no less. You're a famous guy; you can't possibly be ugly enough under there to make this necessary."

"*Excuse* me," the woman sitting across from me indignantly exclaimed.

"Lord Seiji," Rhydion said in a far more neutral tone. "Welcome. I hope you are well? It seems unlike you to seek me out."

"I went looking for that Healer character you mentioned," I said.

"Oh? I wonder why you might need his help, given that you yourself possess healing magic."

"Are you kidding? What *can't* you do with somebody like that in your address book?" I grinned humorlessly. "Though just for starters, I was thinking if I could throw him at you, it'd get you off *my* back."

"How *dare* you," the woman hissed, starting to rise from her seat.

"It's all right, Dhinell," Rhydion said, giving her a nod of his helmet before turning back to me. "And did you find him?"

"Almost. Apparently I just missed him, but I tracked him down to Yrshith Street in the Gutters two days ago and found where he'd been. I'm sorry to say I have to retract my recommendation of taking that guy along on your mission. To judge by the mess he left behind, Healer may not be the most appropriate moniker."

"Heard about that," grunted the other man at the table, who had not stopped chomping away at his large slab of rare meat the whole time. "Apparently he murdered half the gangs in the area and made a whole mess of whores vanish. Settin' people on fire, blasting down walls. Sounded like a better time than you can *usually* have in Cat Alley."

All of us, including Aster, who was standing behind me, gave him long looks. He was lowborn, muscular in build, with a bushy mustache and two days' worth of stubble, dressed in those overwrought clothes sold in the middle ring that were crafted to mimic the overdesigned aesthetic of artifact armor. The bow strapped to his back had the telltale glow of an *actual* artifact, though none of his clothing did.

"I see," Rhydion said after a moment. "Then I thank you for the information, Lord Seiji. Does this mean you have reconsidered my offer?"

Instead of answering that, I withdrew the two sheets of paper I'd been keeping inside my coat, unfolded them, and handed them to him silently. He accepted the documents after a moment's hesitation, and shifted his helmet to study the notices declaring Lady Gray's seizure of Minifrit's business and Minifrit herself.

"I bought those from an extremely angry woman who'd just lost her liveli-hood and home," I said. "*She* was given them by the Healer, who it seems took them by force from the local gangsters who attempted to serve them without an actual judge or Kingsguard present. Everyone I've checked with says they appear to be genuine, which means the judge whose signature that is was either the victim of forgery, or is so brazenly corrupt he's not afraid to leave a paper trail. Either way, someone should really check in on him, don't you think?"

The mustachioed man grunted again, swallowing a bite of his steak, which he appeared barely to have chewed, and with his mouth open. "Is that about the Alley Cat? Yeah, rumor 'round the Gutters is it was foreclosed by Lady Gray."

"Peculiar that the woman implicated in this would sell you these doc-uments," Rhydion said quietly, "given the power they grant the holder. It would seem quite contrary to her interests to relinquish them under any circumstances."

Dammit, why couldn't this guy be a muscle-bound brute like the com-pany he apparently liked to keep? Everything would be so much easier.

"I assume because they're illegal and unenforceable," I said, shrugging, "which makes the question how she knew that. Considering the person on whose behalf they were executed, I guess that was a foregone conclusion."

"Then it is good of you to take up this cause," Rhydion said gravely, extending the documents back toward me.

I didn't reach for them. "What, me? Believe me, I'd love to follow this through, but don't forget I'm just a guest in this country. *This* business would set me against a judge, and apparently also a local crime lord. Too rich for my blood."

"I see." He did not move his hand, just holding the documents toward me. Some undertone in his voice made the hairs on the back of my neck stand up, though. "And is there anything else you would like to tell me about this matter, Lord Seiji?"

Hm. Perhaps this guy was even more intelligent than merely "not stu-pid." Best to hedge my bets and avoid outright falsehoods as much as I could; you never knew what someone might be able to fact-check.

"Yes," I said, staring openly at his visor. "Quite a bit that I'd like to. But nothing else that I presently *can*. I have several people's privacy to consider, not least my own."

"Then I wish you well in rectifying this injustice," he said gravely, extend-ing his arm slightly more to push the papers closer to me.

Rather than taking them, I stood up. "Likewise, I'm sure."

The steak man snorted a laugh. "Wow, you weren't kidding, Dhinell. This guy's fuckin' insufferable."

I frowned at him, then at the woman, who was glaring pure outrage at me. Actually, she did look sort of familiar.

"Have we met before?" I asked her. Apparently yes, to judge by how fast the outrage on her face magnified.

"I explained to you the last time we met, Lord Seiji," Rhydion interjected calmly, "I make it a point not to intercede in every worthy cause which comes along. A person must focus their efforts, in order for them to be at their most effective. If, perhaps, you were interested in joining *my* quest, it would make sense for us to combine our goals as well as our efforts?"

"Ah, ah," I chided, wagging a finger at him. Not because I thought that would improve my case, but because it made Dhinell visibly want to lunge across the table at me, which was just good clean entertainment. "I remember the conversation better than that. What you told me is that you deliberately blind yourself to avoid *learning* about extraneous injustices, because once you're informed of them, you have the moral obligation not to let them stand. So willful blindness is the only way to avoid chasing every rabbit that crosses your path, right?"

I finally reached out for the documents he was still holding toward me, but rather than taking them, lightly flicked the papers with a fingertip.

"Well, consider yourself well and truly informed, Rhydion. There's a judge on Dount in bed with the local crime syndicate. The legitimate authorities by definition won't help, and an outsider like me can't. But a famous and powerful hero of Fflyr Dlemathlys?" I winked. "Good hunting."

"Why does this matter so much to you?" Rhydion asked. "For a man who seems to want to avoid entangling himself with me, you risk a great deal by putting yourself in my debt while also inviting me to investigate trails which have crossed your own. This seems like much more than you would do purely out of moral obligation."

Yeah, I was *really* not enjoying this guy's perceptiveness. What could I tell him that wasn't an outright lie? Well, actually, now that I thought about it, there was a truth.

"Someone I . . . like, and respect, was . . . caught up in this," I said more seriously. "Enough that I'm not willing to let it lie, even if I can't do much myself."

"Your favorite whore get sliced up?" grunted Mustache Man, carving off another bite of steak. "Hate when that happens."

Again, all of us turned stares of pure contempt on him, which he didn't seem to notice.

"Sure," I said in a tone carrying the full weight of my disdain, "let's go with that."

"You should stick to brothels on the middle ring," he suggested, pointing a forkful of meat at me. "You look like you can afford it, plus they're cleaner and safer. Prettier girls, too."

"I apologize if my companion's rough manner offends you, Lord Seiji," Rhydion said. "He is—"

"And they asked him why he ate with prostitutes, lepers, and tax collectors; he told them, 'It is not the healthy who need a doctor, but the sick.' I get it. See you around, Rhydion."

I left the paladin holding the paper trail that would set him on a collision course with Lady Gray, turned, and walked out of the King's Guild with Aster on my heels.

"I know we've been over this, and it's too late now anyway, but it bears repeating," she muttered. "You are playing with fire."

"Yeah, well, it's a relief to be only playing with metaphorical fire for once. Now step lively, my evil minion. Daylight's burning, and we've got a lot more trouble to stir up today."

42

In Which the Dark Lord Huntsfor More Bears to Poke

Captain Norovena wasn't best pleased to return to his guard post and find I'd turned it into happy hour, but that was what he got for not being there when I came calling. I didn't bother asking where he was, instead taking the opportunity to ingratiate myself a bit with the local Kingsguard. I noticed that one of them had a guitar, and that was all it took.

Obviously, I was much better with it than whichever yokel owned the thing, which of course meant I could've livened up everyone's day on pure talent, but I did not hesitate to hit them with the Blessing of Wisdom now that I had a shiny new power to exploit. I lulled the off-duty guards in the barracks effortlessly into a stupor with a rendition of "Uptown Girl;" this meant I'd performed more Billy Joel in the last week than probably the preceding five years, but I had to choose my weapons carefully. People were apparently very suggestible in a hypnotic state, and I wanted these guys relaxed and happy, not riled up the way harder rock would get them. Besides, I figured the lyrics would be relatable in a caste society like this.

I woke them up by segueing immediately into having them teach me some Fflyr folk songs before anybody could ask too many questions about what had just happened. Reel 'em in, set the hook. In no time I had the whole barracks stomping on the floor and singing along.

Looking around at the laughing, singing, cheerful lads, I wondered which of them would've gone after Flaethwyn, Pashilyn, and Amell in the jail had I not intervened. Then I kept grinning and dazzled them with a complicated series of arpeggios before launching into the chorus. I had enough enemies, and I needed the guards on my side.

For now.

Captain Norovena sent everyone scrambling about their business with an incredulous bellow upon his arrival, and rounded on the source of this disturbance as soon as his men were in motion. Recognizing me, he immediately mellowed considerably. The man was too well-bred to look openly greedy, but he was instantly *awfully* polite toward a known source of generous bribes.

Moments later, I was politely ushered into his office, where Norovena seated himself behind his desk, and I in front of it. Aster retreated to the corner and leaned against the wall unobtrusively.

"I'm terribly sorry if I distracted your men, Captain," I said innocently. "Naturally I assumed that anyone presently hanging about the barracks must not be on duty."

"You show an admirable faith in the decency of human nature," Norovena said wryly, not seeming to notice Aster's strangled cough. "In any case, no need to worry. Those louts are responsible for showing up for their own patrol shifts on time. No fault of yours, my lord. It is of course a pleasure to see you again, regardless."

"How kind," I smiled. "I've not happened across Yoshi and his little friends since I left them in your care; how did that turn out?"

"In fact, your judgment proved impeccable, Lord Seiji. We gave them a stark—but respectful—dose of reality overnight, and had not a peep of trouble out of the lot ever since. They've settled into Gwyllthean, which I'll admit I had mixed feelings about at first, but the group has been staying at the King's Guild headquarters and diligently carrying out minor quests while they investigate this goblin issue that brought them." He twisted his mouth slightly in a wry grimace. "The two lowborn were *very* well-behaved; that pair know their place, and in fact they were only in trouble thanks to Lady Flaethwyn's antics. One always feels bad for lowborn dragged into the after-effects of their betters' poor judgment, but such is life. Lady Pashilyn and the foreign boy have been positively respectful toward my men ever since. By the reports I get, Lady Flaethwyn . . . continues to be a *challenging* personality, but she has refrained from causing any further public disturbances. Thus far."

"Yes, I thought that was about how it would go down, but it's gratifying to be validated. Thank you for the update, Captain. In more recent business, I assume you're aware of the . . . kerfuffle that happened in Cat Alley the other night?"

"Ah yes, that Healer fellow," he said, frowning. "I've been hearing reports on him for a while, but he only ever seemed to be caught in the Gutters' blue-light district, or coming and going from it, and the Kingsguard tries not to be an overt presence there. The madams do a decent job of keeping order around their business, and sending in troops just riles up the local gangs. Of course, then my own superiors caught wind of the rumors there's a Blessed with exceptionally powerful healing magic running about and ordered me to investigate. But then, no sooner do I get the word than this guy goes on some kind of rampage. Nothing can ever be simple, can it?"

"I witnessed that a bit more closely than I'd like," I said, affecting a solemn expression. Best to keep my story consistent; I never knew who Rhydion might talk to. "I'd been looking for the Healer for similar reasons myself, and managed to home in on Yrshith Street right after he blasted a trail of destruction through half of it. I'm not too proud to admit I decided to leave the man alone after that."

"I strongly approve of that decision, Lord Seiji. A Blessed that powerful and unpredictable is nothing for civilians to mess about with. If he can't behave, the King's Guild will deal with him, and so much the better if the rest of us just stay out of it."

His eyes cut to Aster and then back to mine, just long enough to make certain I saw it. Norovena's expression remained unchanged and opaque, as did mine, but suddenly . . . I wondered. This could be dicier than I'd planned; I might have to spread around more coin than I'd come here intending to. Well, that was what coin was for.

"I only lingered long enough to chat with a few witnesses and put together the broad strokes of what happened," I said. "Apparently . . . Well, I don't much care about that guy and his fixation on sex workers, but . . . I assume you're aware of this Lady Gray character?"

Norovena's gaze sharpened. "Lord Seiji. I cannot recommend strongly enough that you stay as far away from that woman's business as possible."

Yeah, no kidding. For once I didn't even have to dissemble.

"Believe me, I don't want to be anywhere near somebody like that," I said fervently. "I would very much prefer that Lady Gray never become aware that I exist."

"Good," he said firmly, nodding.

"It just goes to show how unconscionably disrespected Gwyllthean's guardsmen are," I went on in a more casual tone, lounging in my chair and bringing out a couple of gold halos to idly toy with. "I realize I'm an outsider here, Captain, and it's not my place to criticize, so I hope you will not take offense. Where I'm from, we give our police the resources and support they need to take care of people like that *before* they become a problem. I am frankly appalled that your superiors are so blasé about this."

"Obviously, it is not my station to critique or even speculate about the motivations of my betters," the Captain said blandly. "The Convocation teaches us that these things are in the Goddess's hands. Her elect lead as is their right according to Her will, and even should they briefly falter, Her divine plan will see justice prevail in the end."

It didn't go so far that he could've been called out for it, but by the end of that little speech his tone had gone distinctly dry. Obviously, Captain Norovena knew better than anyone exactly how often justice prevailed in Fflyr Dlemathlys.

"I will say," he continued after a pause to clear his throat, "the most I am able to do to curtail Lady Gray's schemes is pull my recruits from the same pool of . . . ahem, *talent* . . . as her gangsters. Every man issued a uniform and a sword is one not cutting purse strings in the Gutters. And doesn't that just reveal everything about the situation in this city."

"Yes, I can well understand why you can't afford to send your lads down there in a direct confrontation. Perish the thought; bloodshed and demolishing half the city would be the only certain outcome."

"I do so appreciate your understanding nature, Lord Seiji," he said with a bland smile.

"I have to confess something to you, Captain," I said, affecting an abashed little smile. "While I like to think of myself as a civic-minded person, I only became aware enough of Lady Gray to ask questions about her because her business has cost me money."

Slowly, he raised an eyebrow. "Oh?"

This was the necessary cover—a believable motivation for Lord Seiji to take an interest in this. I required a story that Norovena would believe easily enough that he felt no need to pry into my affairs any further. With that and enough money spread around, hopefully he'd decide not to risk alienating the goose that laid the golden eggs.

"Nothing illegal, don't worry," I said with a wink. "I arrived here on Dount with some assets of my own, of course, but I like to think in the long term, and my little nest egg won't support me in the style to which I am accustomed over the span of years. Thus, I've been investing modest amounts in some ventures by the local trading companies, feeling out the local business climate and making some extra coin as the opportunity allows. It seems trade and merchant exchanges are the primary source of flowing coin on this island."

"That, and khora farming," he said with a wry smile, "and sheep. With all due respect, Lord Seiji, you don't seem the agricultural type."

"I choose to take that as a compliment, Captain! But yes, I'm afraid I received a rude awakening in some of the . . . hidden costs of doing business in Gwyllthean."

He grimaced. "I'm very sorry to hear that, my lord. Usually, such losses are inflicted by the gangs out in the countryside, which I'm glad to say is outside my purview. It's always embarrassing when the criminal element in my own city dares to importune such an upstanding member of society."

"Oh, believe me, Captain, I don't blame you at all. I can clearly see how well you're doing with the shamefully limited resources granted you. That anyone walks down the street unmugged in this city is a testament to your ingenuity." That might be laying it on a little thick; I decided to rein it in and proceed straight to my pitch. Casually, I set the two halos down on the edge of his desk, an idle motion as if just discarding the toy I was fidgeting with. "And that got me thinking. I'll be the first to admit that you've not heard from me until now because I'm not one to lean into what's none of my business. However, it seems to me that if I were to invest some capital into ensuring our hard-working city guardians were able to clean up the streets a bit more efficiently, well, that's just an investment in the future and my own prosperity, isn't it?"

"I follow your line of thinking, Lord Seiji," Norovena said noncommittally, still not glancing at the coins. "However, I am not sure I have anything to offer that would be *worth* your investment this time. There is . . . embarrassingly little I can do about Lady Gray directly, and while I'm ashamed to admit it, the truth is that it's not a question of . . . resources."

"As I said, Captain, I'm not proposing an armed march on her headquarters or anything."

He nodded once. "I'm curious, then, what you *do* have in mind, my lord."

"Now, do cut in if I'm wrong on any point; I'm only going off rumors, and I'm sure you are better-informed, Captain. From what I hear, however, Lady Gray is currently embroiled in some kind of turf war with several of the countryside bandit gangs, and now has this maniac Healer cutting her men down left and right. Would I be right in suggesting that her position right now is as weak as it has ever been?"

"Still not weak enough that I'd consider opening up a third front worth the risk," he said doubtfully.

"We are of one mind, Captain Norovena. But with all these more overt threats holding her attention, it seems to me that there are suddenly opportunities for motivated men such as ourselves to . . . *carefully* apply further pressure to her organization, in a way that won't lead right back to us. If it doesn't pan out, well, I'll be out some financial donations, and your men will have wasted a bit of time on busywork while making your own organization run a bit more smoothly. But if we're clever and a little bit lucky . . . we might just incidentally create an opportunity for one of Lady Gray's more aggressive enemies to get her out of our hair for good."

Norovena tilted his head to one side, visibly mulling for a long moment. But then a canny little smile spread across his features, and I knew I had him.

"I do appreciate the way your mind works, Lord Seiji. Let's talk more about these *careful* pressures."

As I'd said to Minifrit, these were all half-baked schemes, not worth relying on individually but hopefully aggregately amounting to something. Of the ploys I'd launched so far, I had the most hope for Maugro's angle. I thought my meeting with Norovena had gone well, but there was always the risk of him pocketing my money and then sitting on his thumbs. That would honestly be the standard move for a corrupt city guard in his position; I was gambling on him being ambitious enough to want to parlay a success against the local crime boss into career advancement and connections with the nobility. Norovena was a man dissatisfied with his genetically appointed lot in life and hungry for more.

As for Rhydion, pinning my hopes on the conscience of a man who deliberately blinkered his conscience so he didn't have to listen to it was . . . a coin toss, at best.

None of this was going to even come close to landing a deathblow on Gray's organization, but I hoped if I could keep up pressure on her from all sides, her dwindling resources and increasing desperation would lead to an opening through which I could strike.

And indeed, after spending over an hour talking over plans with Captain Norovena, I had already caught her in her first big mistake—while she had the basic intelligence to plant her fingers in the local Kingsguard, Lady Gray heavily preferred blackmail to bribery. Her men on the inside were there because they were afraid of her and the various levers she had over them, not for the chance to enrich themselves. Every guard on whom Lady Gray exerted her influence hated her guts, and with her attention fixed elsewhere, there was a *lot* the likes of Norovena could do to begin plucking her fingers out of his pie.

What it came down to was that he wasn't shy about dealing with things quietly, out of uniform, once he had a wealthy patron whose coin could help smooth things over. Some of his corrupted men, he reckoned, could be prevailed upon to turn double agent, and the rest . . . Well, Gwyllthean was a rough town; people went missing. And given Lady Gray's other problems right now, she was more likely to believe Lord Olumnach had started getting savvier and more aggressive than that the Kingsguard had suddenly grown a spine.

Our next stop took us to a dilapidated house on the outskirts of the Gutters.

As previously directed by Minifrit, we slipped around to the rear of this structure, in a cramped alley with the cracked rear wall of a warehouse behind us, and I rapped twice on the kitchen door. Hopefully we had the right place; this house didn't look like anyone had been home for a long time, but then, that was the point.

There were enough cracks between the aged akorshil planks of the door that a person on the other side could peek out and see us, though it was dark enough inside that I could not see in. Minifrit had said that my appearance would suffice to get it open. As the seconds stretched out into a minute, then two, I started to wonder if she'd called that right. She had said not to knock again . . .

The door opened a crack and a man's face appeared, one I recognized. "Are you lost . . . my lord?" he asked in an almost aggressively neutral tone.

"Are you . . . Thwyn?" I inquired pleasantly. He wasn't; he was Olyc, one of the other bouncers employed at the Alley Cat.

"Who's asking?"

I reached into my coat and pulled out a folded sheet of paper. "I'm an acquaintance of Miss Minifrit. She sent a message."

His eyes fixed on the letter for a moment, then back to my face, and after another short pause, the door opened wide enough for me to slip through as Olyc stood back in a mute invitation. I stepped inside with Aster right on my heels.

In the dingy kitchen, Thwyn was also present, idly toying with his cudgel. There was no sign of the third bouncer, Raelther, at least not at the moment.

Olyc shut the door, then accepted Minifrit's letter with a polite "Thank you, m'lord."

He read the letter quickly, then handed it to Thwyn to do the same. Of course I knew what it said, having read it myself at Minifrit's invitation.

"So, the harvest festival in almost two weeks," Olyc said while Thwyn read. The missive had identified me as someone who could be trusted and with whom they should be open, and apparently Minifrit's signature on that was enough for him. "It's a good plan, my lord; Miss Minifrit doesn't make bad plans. I don't think it's going to work this time, though. Things in Cat Alley have already gotten ugly. I don't think Lady Gray means to leave us that long to act."

No, of course she didn't. God *fucking* dammit, I was getting tired of being outmaneuvered by that woman.

"Right," I said with a sigh. "Okay. How bad is it?"

43

In Which the Dark Lord
Takes Responsibility for Once

It's pretty bad, m'lord." Olyc didn't beat around the bush. "Seems like Lady Gray's pulled almost her whole organization to focus on Cat Alley. Gotta be near every gang operating in the Gutters is hanging around there, either right in it or just outside. Me and the lads can still get in and out to check on things, being that we know all the subtle routes and have plenty of friends in there, but it's been a close thing already and it won't be long before one of us slips up."

"What are the gangs *doing*, exactly?"

"Applying pressure," he said flatly, meeting my gaze. "Every kind they can. There's been no more outright seizures like they tried with the Cat, and Gray hasn't tried to actually take over and run it as a business since all the employees scarpered, but they've trashed the place something awful. I'm just glad Miss Minifrit ain't around to see it. During night hours they hassle johns and anybody else coming into the street, all but shutting down business. The girls and bouncers who'll still talk to us said Gray's people have taken aside the lower-rent madams, probably just to give her orders that the Healer's not to be allowed on the premises. With nobody but gangsters coming through . . . They're breaking stuff, hurting people. Helping themselves to . . . freebies." Olyc tightened both hands into fists as he spoke, and Thwyn's jaw clenched so hard it looked painful. "Rough-like, even more than that needs to be."

For a second, I could barely breathe. I felt *sick*. All of this was my fault.

I wanted to charge right down there and . . . What, exactly? Aster and I could *maybe* take on Gray's organization. Well . . . part of them. I was apparently a pretty powerful sorcerer, and her artifacts were nothing to sneeze at, but we were both only human. How many enemies *could* we tackle before simple numbers won out? And that was assuming Lady Gray herself didn't take to the field with that invisibility dagger and whatever other bullshit she was hiding.

"I thought Gray kept her hands off in Cat Alley as a rule," said Aster while I struggled for self-control. "Doesn't she make money from the businesses there? This has to be hurting her own interests."

"That's always been the way," Olyc agreed, nodding at her, "but apparently she's changed her mind. Right now it looks like Lady Gray's done caring about money. What they're doing . . . She's just punishing the Alley Cats for supporting the Healer. That's the only thing that makes sense."

"And trying to draw . . . him out," Thwyn added, glancing between me and Aster.

In hindsight, my mistake was obvious. I'd assumed once Maugro spilled the beans about my plan to move on festival night, with the likelihood of the outer gangs attacking at the same time, Gray would prepare her defenses to meet the threat. But she hadn't attained her position and kept it for years by thinking defensively. She meant to have all this settled *before* that night came so she could use it to take down any gangs that tried to attack her then. Either by luring out the Healer and dealing with him—with me—or by inflicting such damage on Cat Alley that if I failed to show up, the women there who'd been the victims of my scheming would never trust me again.

"Listen, my lord," Olyc said carefully, now also looking pointedly at Aster. "I know you're—"

"We haven't met before," I interrupted sharply.

He hesitated, clenched his jaw, then nodded once. "Of course, m'lord. My mistake."

God, it really was transparent, wasn't it? There were exactly two people with Japanese accents on this island—on this *world*—and only one was followed around by a woman with a huge sword. Norovena had glanced at her exactly the same way when the subject of the Healer came up. We could obscure the details, but the disguise was paper-thin. It only worked at all because relatively few people in Gwyllthean knew Lord Seiji. Enough did; too many, in fact. Hell, I'd just personally set Rhydion on a course to figure it out (assuming he hadn't already), which was more than enough to make this good and disturbing, but—

Suddenly I felt as if I'd been dunked in ice water.

Uncle Gently knew about Lord Seiji. It was necessary for my use of his Rats to gather information. And Uncle Gently reported directly to Lady Gray.

My god, how could I have been so stupid?

The kids. Orphans in this medieval hellhole were less valued than live-stock, and someone like Lady Gray counted lives and human suffering as nothing but tallies in her ledger, to be stacked up however it best served her interests. She'd already had a couple of days to . . .

That ice water was drowning me. I felt the real world begin to slough away as an impossible, insurmountable wall of the consequences of *what I'd done* loomed up on all sides. So much pain, death, destruction . . . All unleashed because of me. I had to do something. What could I do? What could one person do, even with all the powers of a Dark Lord? I couldn't breathe. *What could I do?*

And then a strange thing happened.

It was as if my consciousness was rising up out of itself. Amid the whirl-ing chaos of my own emotions, I floated, suddenly calm. Gazing down from a bird's eye vantage at the rising torrent of panic, grief, righteous indignation, guilt, and vengeful rage, as if they were things that didn't truly concern me. More than that, I found I could see the broader situation, unencumbered by the chaos clouding my own mind.

What could I do?

From here, there was not yet a clear path to victory, or even to proper damage control, but suddenly I could plainly see the next steps to be taken.

"Do you have paper in here?" I asked Olyc. He blinked as if startled; I realized I'd been standing silent for a long stretch of seconds, and whatever was on my face must have been rather unnerving.

"Ah . . . that is, yes, m'lord. Place is kind of a dump, but it's a Dountol house after all. There's always paper."

"Good. I need you to sketch me a quick map of the districts surrounding Cat Alley. It doesn't have to be complete; I just need to know the locations nearby from which Lady Gray is staging attacks. If she's moving people in full time to pressure the blue-light district, she'll have set up field bases. Show me where they are in relation to the Alley's landmarks."

"I . . ." Olyc glanced at Thwyn, who nodded once and turned to exit the kitchen, hopefully in search of paper. "We don't know of all of 'em, obviously, and some of the likely spots are less than certain. I can think of several, though. The other lads may know of more'n I do."

"That's fine. It doesn't have to be perfect, just get me the best starting point you can."

"We can do that, my lord. Are . . . You're going to save the girls, right?"

"I'm going to do what I can," I said, hearing the inhuman iciness in my own voice and feeling too detached from myself to care. "Maybe I can't save everyone, but anyone I fail, *I will avenge tenfold*. Now. In terms of specifics, I need you to be on the lookout for three specific Gutter Rats I'll describe; they're allies. Protect them if you can, and rely on them as needed, but don't place them in further danger. Also, I need you to get a message to Gannit at the Jostled Jugs." I hesitated, rapidly considering. "Give me a moment to iron out those details. In *general*, I want you to spread the word to the Alley Cats that the Healer is coming. If the gangs hear it . . . In fact, let them. Let it spread to all of them. Lady Gray wants the Healer, and she tends to get what she wants. This time, she is going to choke on it."

After leaving the safehouse some minutes later, Aster and I made tracks for our next destination, a deserted spot amid the weed-grown foundations of some long-destroyed structure on the periphery of the Gutters with a sheep field visible half a block over. There, we set about doing the absolute last thing I wanted to be doing right then: dithering around.

The arrangement was that the Rats found *us*. There wasn't even a dedicated meeting place, and in fact, Gilder had made a point that we should pick somewhere different each time. We'd come to town and do whatever other business we had first; Gilder, Benit, and Radon insisted they were always watchful and had ways of finding us once they knew we were in town. So far, they always had, though it involved anything from five minutes to an hour of sitting around somewhere accessible but remote in the Gutters, depending on how closely they were shadowing us. The kids made a game of trying to sneak up on me, which they'd always lost thanks to Biribo.

So there was nothing to do but sit there and wait for them to show up, simmering in the very real prospect that this would be the time they didn't. Whatever that preternatural calm from before was, it had dissipated rapidly on the walk over, and now I felt like a nervous wreck.

Fortunately, Biribo had a way to distract me from my nervous pacing as soon as we'd settled in.

"So, uh, boss . . ." He buzzed out of his comfy padded pocket in Aster's coat to hover in front of me. "This is awkward."

"I'll take awkward," I said wearily. "What's on your mind?"

"Well, you just unlocked a new Wisdom perk."

I blinked, twice. "I did? When?"

"Just back there. It's, uh . . . It repurposes traumatic dissociation. Any time you experience something so emotionally painful your consciousness would shut down in self-defense, instead of actually shutting down, it puts you in a highly lucid state from which you can think coherently at the cost of being, uh . . . emotionally detached to a pathological degree."

Aster winced and avoided my eyes.

I just blinked twice more at Biribo. Then a third time. Then rubbed at the bridge of my nose with both hands, squeezing my eyes shut.

"Great. That's . . . handy. Thanks for keeping me in the loop, Biribo."

"You got it, boss!"

Biribo hovered around, on guard for anyone approaching, while Aster stood patiently with her sword drawn. I found myself pacing. Wearing out my legs right before I needed to walk halfway across the island back to North Watch wasn't exactly a solid tactical decision, but I needed to do something. I had to *move*, since I couldn't yet make any moves that were actually useful.

"I dunno how we could've handled it differently," I said suddenly, "but I keep remembering how we took out those thugs in the barn. That was . . ."

"That was pretty bad, yeah," Aster agreed softly. "It'd be weird if you *weren't* seeing that whenever you tried to sleep."

"You too, huh?"

"I know Fflyr Dlemathlys is more violent than where you come from, but I *don't* commonly execute a dozen people in a night for purely pragmatic reasons. Most people don't."

I nodded. "Yeah. Seems . . . unfair."

Aster let out a little bark of incredulous laughter. "Unfair! Yeah, that's a word."

"I know, I know. Kind of underwhelming. It's what I keep circling back to, though. Unfair, and hypocritical. I mean, hell, my first big Dark Lord speech when I arrived was about how people end up as bandits. How they slipped through the cracks of a society that failed them. It's not like that's any *less* true of the people working for Lady Gray; they just ended up positioned against me in circumstances where it's not as convenient for me to recruit them. And look at the ones we *did* get. Enough of the girls vouched for Jadrin that I'm kind of optimistic about her, but that Jakkin guy . . ."

"Is basically Donon again," she said wryly, "but not as loyal or useful?"

"Yeah, basically. Or as funny. That was objectively a *really* fucked-up thing we did." I sighed and stopped pacing. "I can't think of anything we could've done that would've worked better, is the thing. And you know what?

I'm *not* losing sleep over it, and that's the part that I find disturbing. I am bothered that I'm not more bothered."

"Boss, I don't mean to diminish what you're going through, but that's *super* common," said Biribo. "It's part of the process of getting used to violence. Everybody goes through that. It'll pass."

"I'm not sure that helps," I muttered. "If it passes, then what the hell does that make me?"

"One step closer."

In that moment I really, *really* wanted to smack him.

"While you're probably not wrong about the unfortunate circumstances that led all those people to their situations," said Aster, "that's also true of the Cat Alley girls, and our own people back at the castle. To be frank, Lord Seiji, if I thought what we did in that barn was your idea of carrying out justice, I'd be severely disturbed. What *I* thought was that we were at *war*, and that was the action that was strategically necessary in that moment. That doesn't make it any less a loss of life, but . . . Look, I'm no historian, but war is pretty much a process of slaughtering a bunch of people you don't really have any argument with, for no reason except they're between you and the person you *actually* need to kill."

"As someone who's witnessed a lot of history firsthand, that's actually a really spot-on description," said Biribo.

She nodded. "War is ugly. It'd obviously be better if it never happened. But we're *at* war because we *need* to be. It's the only way to change anything or protect anyone, and we have to see it through to the end. Otherwise everything we've done so far was for nothing."

"Perfect," I sighed. "All this wasn't nearly morally fraught enough, so let's discuss what does or doesn't make a just war."

Aster cracked a grin at that. "Well, I might just be rationalizing to make myself feel better, but the way I look at it, all the killing is the natural consequence of the mess we're in. It's the people you've managed to go out of your way to save who're the extraordinary circumstance in all this, and that's also on you."

"I didn't exactly recruit the North Watch gang out of the goodness of my heart, you know. *Or* the prostitutes."

"I know," she shrugged. "Still saved 'em, though. For a while, at least. And that's not nothing."

"It helped for a while, and that's not nothing." I looked up at the oddly purplish sky that I still wasn't used to. "Man, I really hope that doesn't end up being the best I can say about what I accomplished on this world."

"We got incoming, boss," Biribo reported. "Two juveniles. I'm *pretty* sure it's Benit and Radon."

I experienced a one-two punch of relief and terror. God, I hoped it really was those two and they were okay. But *what about Gilder?*

We had to wait only a couple more minutes for at least some of the answers. For once, instead of trying their usual stealthy approach, both kids emerged around a corner a full block distant and came toward us at a run down the narrow space that would have been an alley before half the buildings bordering it had collapsed. I could identify them both well before they reached us.

"Biribo, anybody else?" I asked quietly.

Previously he'd been hidden whenever I talked with the Rats, only muttering messages from inside Aster's pocket as needed, but this time I had directed him to stay out. A lot of cats were out of their various bags, and it was past time for dissembling.

"Nobody pursuing 'em," he reported. "Now, at least. I can't speak as to what happened before they got close, though."

Both kids were panting when they finally reached us, but it didn't stop Radon from pointing right at Biribo and demanding, "What's *that?*"

"This is Biribo," I said impatiently. "*Where's Gilder?*"

"He's okay, Lord Seiji," Benit replied. "I hope. He was a little while ago."

I drew in a steadying breath. "Okay, that's . . . Start at the beginning, please."

"We've been gone to ground since last night," she said, and indeed the poor girl looked exhausted. "Uncle Gently got one of his visits from a couple of the ex-Rats, younger guys in one of Lady Gray's crews who used to live at the Nest. Soon as they left, next thing he said to Gilder is he wants to talk to you. To Lord Seiji. So we were supposed bring you there soon as we saw you next."

"And we knew what that meant, cos we ain't *stupid,*" Radon interjected.

Benit nodded. "We know how to nod and smile and say yes, so we did, and promised we'd fetch you. All like everything was level. But Uncle Gently's not stupid either, and Gilder thought . . . Well, we decided to play it safe. We didn't sleep at the Nest last night, and we decided not to go back. We been watching for you so we could tell you what's what, Lord Seiji. Sorry for making you wait, but there was other Rats prowling after us and we had to lose 'em."

"Okay," I said with strained patience, "but *where is Gilder?*"

"He drew off the others," Radon answered, his expression far too solemn for such a young child.

"Don't worry, Gilder's better than the two squishbutts who was after us," Benit hastened to assure me. "He can lose 'em, no problem, it'll just take some minutes. But Lord Seiji . . . He told us to link up with you, said to tell you he was gonna keep on watch in the Gutters a couple days more."

"He *what*?"

"There's a lot going down," she said, small and wan and earnest. "Lady Gray is losing it, Lord Seiji. She's gone crawn mad over the Healer, and she's kicking down Cat Alley to get at him. Gilder told us to come to you. He said—he said we should ask you to hide us 'til all this blows over. But he doesn't wanna pack it in yet. He said he's gonna stay your eyes and ears in the Gutters and have fresh news for you when you're ready to make your move."

God damn that boy. If I ever saw him alive again I'd wring his scrawny neck.

"He's good, Lord Seiji," Benit said, her own fear plain on her face. "But . . . nobody's as good as . . . I mean, Gilder can manage for a couple days, probably. I don't think . . . I wouldn't leave him more than that. That is, if you . . ."

"Biribo, do you think you can find him?" I asked.

"Track *one* child who's not already within range of my senses in a city this size?" Biribo did an agitated little loop the loop. "Honestly, boss, these two would probably have a better chance of running him down."

I didn't even consider that idea. Gray was after me, and she knew these kids were a connection to me. I needed to get them *out* of Gwyllthean, immediately. Gilder . . . *Fuck*. I just had no way to *get* to him that wouldn't also endanger Radon and Benit.

"Seriously," Radon exclaimed, "what *is* that? It talks!"

"Right back atcha, kneebiter," Biribo spat.

"Biribo is my familiar," I said.

Benit's eyes widened. Yeah, she was always the one who knew more than she let on and put things together quietly.

"What's a familiar?" Radon demanded.

"It's a helper I get from having the Blessing of Wisdom."

"Wisdom?" he scoffed. "That's not a real Blessing!"

"Yes, it is," Benit whispered. "It's just really rare."

"Wait," the younger child said, frowning, "but you're Blessed with Magic."

"Yep." In spite of the dire gravity of this situation, I couldn't help enjoying this reveal as it played out. I guess showmanship is baked right into my soul.

"Are . . . are you the Hero, Lord Seiji?" Benit whispered.

I shook my head. "Nope. I'm the Dark Lord."

Both children stared up at me in pure awe. Then Radon grinned so widely it almost looked painful.

"*Awesome!*" he breathed.

Well, it was nice to be appreciated.

"Okay, look." I knelt amid the weeds, bringing my eyes closer to theirs. "Gilder was right. I mean, not about him running off to play tag with Lady Gray's gangs by himself—that's the dumbest goddamn thing I've ever heard of and I'm gonna box his ears for it when I see him again." *If I see him again.* "But about getting you two out of Gwyllthean. I know it's all you've ever known, and it's scary to leave it, but we have to go, *now*. I will come back for Gilder as soon as I can, but for now we'll have to trust that he can look after himself. Since he hasn't exactly left us with any choice."

"We can still help you, Lord Seiji!" Radon swore. "We can fight!"

Benit gave him a sidelong look which emphatically disagreed.

"Listen to me." I reached out and put a hand on each of their shoulders. "I know you're used to having to work for every scrap you get. It seems normal to you to be used by adults until you're either used up or survive to be adults yourself. But that is *not* normal. It's *fucked up*, is what it is. Anybody who puts children in danger like this for their own purposes is a complete piece of shit who deserves whatever happens to them. And yes, that includes me. I could tell you a story about how I had no other options and tried my best to look after you, but none of that really matters. What matters is I *did* it, and it was wrong as hell. And the difference between me and Uncle Gently is I'm going to take responsibility.

"As of right now, you two are retired from Rat work. Understand? When you're grown, you'll have to make yourselves useful, just like everybody does. But a child's job is to study and to *play*, and that's what I'm gonna have you get down to as soon as we're safely back at my castle."

Both of them swelled up again, Radon until I feared he might burst.

"You have a *castle*?" he squealed.

"Is it far?" Benit asked, only a trifle less breathlessly.

By contrast to their enthusiasm, the question caused me to deflate. Was it *far*? I looked the pair of them over critically; they were about nine and six, by my reckoning, and clearly both tired and hungry to begin with. For children in that condition to make a journey like that, on foot . . .

"Hey, Aster," I said, turning to look at her over my shoulder. "About how strong would you say you are?"

I'd caught her smiling fondly, no doubt at my little speech, but just like that her expression collapsed into a particularly vivid Aster Look.

44

In Which the Dark Lord
Needs a Nap

Needless to say, we did not make good time on the return trip. Having the kids along slowed us considerably, especially once their energy ran out and we had to carry them.

We actually took the risk of making camp for the night, in the middle of the khora forest. Not far off the old road, Aster found a dead khora husk that gave us an arc of something to put our backs against and only have to watch in a few directions. The kids were scared of the forest, but also exhausted, and they slept like logs while Aster and I napped in turns, one always keeping watch, familiar or no familiar.

They weren't *properly* rested when we resumed, and we were back to carrying them by the time the battlements of North Watch rose into view. I didn't even have time to point them out to the kids before the frantic barking started.

Benit hid behind my legs as Junko came barreling out of the broken gates; Radon, bless him, tried to plant himself between Benit and the dog, but I just knelt to welcome Junko with a hug, which she immediately wriggled out of in her frantic excitement.

"It's okay," Aster reassured our new charges, clearly amused. "This is Junko, she's Lord Seiji's dog. She's actually very nice as long as you're nice to her."

"Looks like one of the strays from outside the Gutters," Benit muttered, shying back again as a furiously tail-wagging Junko tried to sniff her.

"Funny story about that," I said cheerfully, still scratching the dog's ears.

"Those things have killed Rats," Radon said, calmer but still extremely wary around the excitable animal, which was about as big as he was. "I knew a girl got *eaten* by a pack."

Well, there went my nascent good mood. God *damn* it, Ephemera! Why was there *always* something horrible around every corner?

"Junko, heel." She obeyed instantly, looking up at me with those big eyes and her tail still wagging. I preferred to let her work off her energy as a rule, but the kids noticeably calmed now that the dog was calm. "We can tell stories and the like later. Right now, let's get you kids an *actual* meal and some real rest in a proper bed."

"A *bed*?" Benit asked in clear surprise. "Wait, for *us*?"

"Surely you have beds."

She shook her head. "My sleeping spot is a blanket against the wall. Usually. Sometimes it's easier to just sleep on the roof, when one of the bigger kids gets in a mood."

"I sleep on a shelf," Radon added.

I turned and started walking again toward the gates, at least in part so they wouldn't see my expression. This was what I'd left them in for weeks so I could use them to gather information for me. And what had I even gained from it, apart from some city gossip? Maybe Virya was right about me.

"We don't mind sharing, Lord Seiji," Benit said quickly, apparently misinterpreting my silence. "We're small! If there's a free bed, that's surely big enough for—"

"A bed *each*," I stated. "You've earned that, at the *very* least."

"C'mon, guys, we're almost there," Aster prompted. With Junko and the children trailing along, we crossed the last steps to the old fortress's gates, where the noise from within the walls already told me what my next headache was going to be.

We'd started out from Gwyllthean in the late morning, and thanks to the incredibly slow pace set by having to handhold the two youngsters, we were just arriving home as dawn was beginning to break. I was gratified to see, upon stepping inside the gates, that Kasser had kept the place running and the schedule intact—everyone was assembled in the courtyard for exercise and training, as I had directed. It was less gratifying to see how that was going today.

Training was suspended; my new army was clustered in two rings making various communal noises, one around Sicellit, who was on the ground bleeding from a head wound, and one around Jadrin and Adelly, who were practically nose-to-nose, screaming in borderline incoherent rage, and clearly seconds from mutually attempted homicide.

I had left them alone for *one day*.

"Lord Seiji," said Kasser in clear relief. Miss Minifrit stood next to him, idly smoking that long pipe of hers and watching the incipient fight with a wry expression.

"Kasser," I said, then ignited a burst of pink light around Sicellit which caused the women surrounding her to yelp and jump back. "**Heal**. Minifrit, were you planning to *do* anything about this?"

"Yes," she said evenly, "after it has concluded. That is the appropriate time to dispense consequences, and trying to break up a fight between two individuals who are *each* better fighters than I is a fine way to acquire a black eye and lose credibility in front of my employees. Lord Seiji, did you really just adopt two Gutter Rats?"

"Oh, you would not *believe* the stuff he drags home," Sakin said merrily, sidling up to her. Minifrit gave him a sidelong look of unvarnished dislike, earning a flirtatious wink in response.

I had successfully built myself an organization composed entirely of discipline problems. Adelly gave Jadrin a hard shove, prompting a chorus of catcalls from the onlookers. Predictably, Jadrin recovered from her stumble and surged forward with a fist and the clear intent to inflict debilitating damage.

Windburst.

I was a good ten meters from the knot of women about to dissolve into a brawl, so it merely knocked them all down.

"Ara, ara, ara," I drawled, my boots crunching on gravel in the sudden ominous quiet as I paced toward them. "What a unique method of training you've discovered. All right, who's the lucky winner; who gets to *explain* this to me?"

Jadrin was back on her feet almost immediately, followed a half second later by Adelly. It was the latter who managed to speak first.

"Lord Seiji! We'd be getting a lot more *training* done if *this* maniac wasn't using it as an excuse to beat the shit out of everyone!"

"Oh, *spare* me your *fucking* whining," Jadrin snarled back. "What kind of soft-headed corebait expects to teach people how to *fight* and not get bruised? I'm trying to keep these girls *alive*, no thanks to your sniveling—"

"*Bullshit*! What you're doing has nothing to do with necessary force. You are going out of your way to cause pain and humiliation and *you fucking know it*. Don't even pretend—"

"Sakin?" I asked loudly.

"There is an underlying difference of training methods here," he chirped, "plus a personality clash. I've seen the effectiveness of what Jadrin's been trying to do in a variety of places, and I *do* think Adelly's overstating the problem; but just for the record, I would not use such rough methods with this particular crew, Lord Seiji. You don't kick beginners around like veterans and expect them to gain more from it than a boot print on the ass and a bad attitude. They gotta internalize the fundamentals before the *real* whipping into shape can begin."

"All right, then," I said, attempting to project evenness and calm. "Much as I would like to take the time and ensure you all learn to get along, we are on a much less forgiving timetable than I'd hoped, ladies. So here's the short version. Adelly, stop taking things so personally. Jadrin, chill out. Clear? Good. Adelly, please take over here for now. Jadrin, I need—"

"You've gotta be *kidding* me!" Jadrin erupted, stomping toward me and brandishing an accusing finger at Adelly. "If she has her way, these miserable whores are *never* gonna be fit to stand—"

Slimeshot.

The slime ripped past her ear at a notable fraction of the speed of sound, barely a centimeter from grazing her head or shoulder; the passage whipped her hair instantly into complete disarray. Behind her, the slime impacted the wall of the fortress hard enough to splatter droplets of it in every direction. Jadrin froze in place, eyes bulging.

"I understand how it is, Jadrin," I said. Calmly, quietly, with a kind smile. "It's been a rough morning, you've already got your heart rate up from exercising, and that was before you had that extremely irritating shouting match. I get it; your blood's rushing, you're in the heat of the moment, and you accidentally forgot *who you are talking to.*"

I let the sudden silence hang for a beat. Jadrin remained exactly as she was, as if suddenly afraid to move. In her wide eyes, I could practically see the other night in the barn replaying. Flames, screaming, blood, and slimes.

"All's forgiven," I said after my grand pause, widening my smile. "Going forward, however, I expect you to get that temper under control. I'm only willing to repeat myself a very limited number of times, Jadrin. How limited? That's a secret. It's a guessing game with no prize, and no winners. The only question is *how badly* you lose."

She swallowed heavily, then nodded. "Yes, Lord Seiji."

Behind me, Sakin cleared his throat. "Ah, Lord Seiji. Would you mind if I tried?"

I turned to give him a speculative look, which he met with his customary expression of good-natured innocence that practically made my skin crawl.

Obviously, it was a mistake to let this guy off his leash in even a limited capacity when I didn't know *specifically* what he was planning to do. On the other hand, I had the strong sense that intimidating Jadrin was not making any constructive progress toward enforcing actual discipline around here, and Sakin knew a lot more than I did about . . . well, a lot of things.

"By all means," I said graciously, stepping aside.

"Jadrin, baby," he cooed, sauntering forward and instantly making her revert to a glare and clenched fists; I already had a bad feeling about this. "Lemme ask you a question—what did you learn just now?"

"Uh . . . what?" She squinted at him, then glanced at me. "Don't fuck with Lord Seiji? But I already—"

"You already knew that," he said, nodding. "You have seen *vividly* the consequences of fucking with Lord Seiji; that was not a useful lesson. Making him enforce discipline only helps him, it doesn't help you. And that's fine, because enforcing discipline is what he was *trying* to do. Now, if he was trying to *teach* you something constructive . . . well, that would've been a big waste of time, now wouldn't it? See what I'm getting at?"

"That's not the—" She caught herself, stiffening in visible frustration. "I don't appreciate being called a fucking bully when I'm trying to *help*. These girls are not ready for what's coming. If they don't get whipped into shape—"

"Sure, you're dead right there," he said agreeably. "It's a question of technique. *Teaching* is its own skill, Jadrin, and it's not the same as just pushing at people until learning happens. You were doing it the wrong way, not trying to do the wrong thing. I can give you pointers; so can Miss Minifrit, probably, if you ask her real nicely. For now, try watching Adelly take a turn and *think* about what she's doing instead of what you'd do differently, yeah?"

Jadrin heaved a deep sigh and let it out through her teeth, a veritable portrait of someone controlling their temper. Finally, with a jerky little shrug, she turned and stalked over to the wall of the fortress. There, she leaned against it, folding her arms and looking sullen, but at least watching in the direction of the group.

"Thank you, Sakin," I said. "Adelly, ladies, please continue. Minifrit, Kasser, would you join Aster and me in the mess hall in a few minutes? I need to discuss strategy with you; we have a problem. Aster, can you get the kids fed and settled in? Thanks. Is Donon—ah, there you are. Donon, we need a hot meal for the children, and then they've got some sleep to catch up on. Also, please brew some strong tea for this meeting, and Aster and I haven't had breakfast either, now that I think of it. Everybody, this is Benit and

Radon. They've helped me a lot in the last few weeks—more than should be asked of children. They are my guests and to be made welcome, understand? When everybody's all settled in we can discuss pitching in with chores, but for now they've got some recuperating to do."

Everyone stared at me in silence.

"*Well?*" I barked, echoed by an insistent bark from Junko, and everyone burst into a flurry of motion.

"What is this problem we have?" Minifrit murmured, drawing close enough to me that the spicy-sweet scent of her pipe was even more distracting than her deep cleavage. Sometimes I wondered how much of her presentation was just her being herself and how much was calculated to dazzle and disarm.

"Lady Gray's not waiting for me to move on the harvest festival," I said shortly. "She's taken to outright attacking all of Cat Alley in retaliation for . . . Well. The point is, we're going to have to move as quickly as possible. Every hour is being paid for in the blood of the women there, and I've already racked up more debt than is acceptable. But we need a plan."

"And you need to fully rest before enacting said plan," Aster added, managing to look severe even while holding Radon in the crook of one arm and Benit by the hand. He was outright asleep, and Benit was yawning hugely. "Me, too, for that matter. We're both gonna need to be at our best for that confrontation."

"It's not that you're wrong, Aster, but we don't have the luxury of *time*."

"Aster is right," Minifrit interjected. "I hope you don't think *I* lack sympathy for the women of Yrshith Street, Lord Seiji. For that very reason, our counterattack must *succeed*, and therefore must be carefully planned and also executed with our only two Blessed at their full strength."

"Gotta add my vote to that, boss," said Biribo.

"*Fine.*" I rubbed at my eyes with both hands. "*After* we get something to eat and work out a plan of attack, I promise to take a nap, okay? Minifrit, Kasser, I'll meet you in the mess hall in a few minutes, once Aster joins us. Kids, sorry about this, uh, rough introduction, but you'll be safe here."

"Rough?" Benit blinked sleepily up at me. "You're nicer to your crew than Uncle Gently, Lord Seiji. He *pretends* to be nicer, but that . . . looks different."

"I'll bet," I said wearily. "Go with Aster. Donon will get you set up with a proper meal. Sakin, while they're settling in, a word?"

"At your service, Lord Seiji!"

The rest of them dispersed in their various mandated directions, and I led Sakin around the corner of the fortress, with my familiar buzzing along above us, leaving behind the clack of akorshil practice sticks as Adelly started walking the girls through sword forms.

"Biribo, how're we on privacy?"

"Nobody within earshot, boss. Nobody trying either. That'd be hard to pull off with a crew this size anyway. Now, once we've got most of the population of Cat Alley in here, there'll be more opportunities for snooping."

Right, crowds were his weak point. I did not say that out loud in front of Sakin, even though I would be unsurprised to learn he already knew how to get around a familiar's senses.

"Was it like that all day yesterday?" I asked.

"It *built* up to that over the course of the day, but the seeds of it were there from the start. The problem was you weren't there, Lord Seiji. Personalities like Jadrin really need someone indisputably in charge of them. She only barely toed the line with Kasser, and that just because he had the sense not to push her."

"That's about what I figured," I sighed. "I really did not want to leave them alone so soon, but . . ."

"But the situation is what it is and you made the necessary call," Sakin said, nodding. "I think it's going to be a good long while before we're in anything resembling ideal circumstances, Lord Seiji."

"Yeah. I'll keep a closer eye on them going forward. For now, I want to ask your assessment of the new batch of recruits."

"They're hopeless," he grinned, "but in a way that's rectifiable. They've got the spirit and the anger; all that's missing is the know-how. That just takes time. Adelly's a bit stiff, but she's shaking off the moss as she goes. Oh, and that girl Kastrin is a crack shot with a crossbow."

"Wait, really? Kastrin?"

"It happens," he said, shrugging. "There are some people who're just gifted. Training will only make her more terrifying, but she could put a bolt in a bastard's eye at the weapon's maximum controllable range the moment she picked it up. Considering the small size of this recruitment pool, we *really* lucked out having that kind of savant among 'em. A nation the size of Fflyr Dlemathlys can expect maybe one of those every two to five years among its military recruits."

"Huh. How about that. Well, good, but there was one other thing I wanted your opinion about. Lady Gray keeps running circles around me, and for the most part, I'm pretty sure it's because she's just years more experienced at this kind of thing than I am."

"Good to respect your enemies, Lord Seiji," he said seriously. "Gotta give 'em credit before you can work out how to beat them."

"Right, well, more specifically, I'm wondering about the possibility that she's managed to plant an agent in our ranks, now that we've suddenly grown them so fast."

"Incredibly unlikely," Sakin said without hesitation.

"Really? Because I can't help noticing that we went and recruited two of her own people . . ."

"I wouldn't consider either of those a likely prospect, Lord Seiji. It's good that you're aware anyone *might* be a spy, but that's just the first step. The hard part is sussing out who is a probable suspect. Frankly, neither Jakkin nor Jadrin are good fits."

"Go on," I said, frowning.

"You need a spy to be unobtrusive and not draw suspicion," he explained. "That rules out Jakkin, who flipped on his boss the second you scared him enough and will without question flip on you the second someone else scares him more. He has to be the target of our suspicion from the outset. That is *not* how you position your agent. And Jadrin is just a resentful hothead, which is entirely the wrong profile for a spy."

"Unless that's an act . . ."

He chuckled, shaking his head. "Sure, that's been done. But Lord Seiji, you've gotta consider who you're dealing with, and the circumstances. For the kind of deep cover agent who can build a whole backstory and project a false front for *years*, just on the *off chance* of getting recruited by someone like you? Well, the Lancor Empire employs people like that, for example. Because an empire has a *need* for them, and the resources to support them. Somebody like Lady Gray? No chance. The trope of the multiplicitous genius who always triumphs because they have a plan for every possible situation only exists in stories. Actual, real-world pragmatists like Gray prepare *reasonable* contingencies for foreseeable problems, and build enough flexibility into their organizations to be able to react to the unexpected."

"So, no spies yet."

"*Probably* no spies," Sakin chided, grinning. "Nothing is ever certain, Lord Seiji. But yes, at this juncture I think you should reasonably focus your energies elsewhere."

"All right, good. Thanks for the update. Carry on."

"I always do, Lord Seiji."

I just nodded once, turned, and strode back into the fortress to get a head start on planning my next war crimes.

45

In Which the Dark Lord Sends a Message

After all my recent frustrations, it felt good to finally be kicking down doors. Literally.

The latch was already loose; it wrenched free of its moorings under the impact of my boot, tumbling to the ground in pieces as the door banged inward. I stepped into the room beyond, already spreading my arms in a grandiose gesture of greeting as the men inside whirled to face me.

"Good evening, gentlemen!" I called out. "Virya's blessings upon you all."

"So you can give a polite greeting, but you can't turn a door latch?" retorted the fellow I decided must be in charge on the basis of his superior poise alone. While the other three present had sprung to their feet and uncertainly raised weapons at me, he was still seated, just now setting down his hand of cards on the table before him. "Look at that, we're gonna have to have the whole door rebuilt now. Who's gonna pay for that?"

"No one," I said pleasantly. "Don't trouble yourself over it, my good man. In five minutes' time, this place will be burning down and you'll all be dead."

"Uh-huh." The leader made a wry face at me. "Caester, shank this idiot."

"Oh, fuck me," one of the other men suddenly whispered as the fellow I took to be Caester stepped forward with his sword upraised. "It's *him*."

The leader's gaze sharpened, and he finally straightened up in his chair, taking a closer look at my ragged coat and hooded cloak. "Caester, *now!*"

Slimeshot.

Caester was hurled across the room by the impact to his chest, hitting the wall with a groan and sliding down amid a puddle of destroyed slime, his sword tumbling away. The boss of the thugs scrambled to his own feet, drawing his sidearm.

"A bold move!" I congratulated him. "Let's see how it works out for you!"
Immolate.

The little sitting area in the front wasn't large; the flames and his flailing seemed to take up a lot of space, forcing the other two men to scramble back. I strode forward, ignoring the screaming thug boss.

The nearest of them rushed at me in panic and was smashed against the wall by a Windburst for his trouble; the other, near the stairs, actually dropped his sword and tried to retreat up the steps from me.

"Wait! You're a Healer, aren't you? Mercy!"

"*Ooh*, if only you'd asked me a week ago," I said apologetically. "We're fresh out of mercy. I do have a large backlog of 'no one leaves alive,' and we're running a special on 'nothing personal, but you're in my way.'"

He turned and attempted to flee up the steps. I Slimeshotted him right in the small of the back and heard a distinct cracking sound. The poor bastard flopped bonelessly down the stairs, howling bloody murder; I stepped around him to ascend the staircase, right as a man who'd been stationed above came charging down, brandishing a club.

Given our respective positions, my next Slimeshot nailed him square between the legs.

He dropped his weapon and crumpled, emitting a high-pitched wheeze and doubling over himself. I grabbed him by the collar as he started to fall toward me, hauling his dead weight up the remainder of the flight of narrow steps. That wasn't exactly easy, but I was running on adrenaline and what seemed to be a bottomless well of eternally bubbling rage.

"On the one hand, I'd feel pretty bad for doing that to another guy," I informed my whimpering victim as I deposited him on the floor at the top of the steps. "On the other, fuck you."

This was a narrow, cramped structure wedged between two others on one of Gwyllthean's backstreets, with little more than two rooms below the claustrophobic staircase, and the smaller windowless room up here on the second floor where the heart and soul of this operation sat—a large chest, locked.

"Boss, that guy you just set on fire is Blessed with Might," Biribo reported, poking his head out of my cloak. "Not a very strong Blessing, but he might have an artifact."

"Oh indeed? Thanks, Biribo, well spotted."

"That's what I'm here for, boss!"

I grabbed the chest by one of its handles and pulled. Damn thing was a *lot* heavier than the still-crying thug, who was clutching his crotch—and also bleeding from it, I noticed in passing while I dragged the chest past him. It would be a real pain in the ass to get this thing anywhere, if I was interested in doing things properly.

It was still a pain to shove it onto the staircase, but once there, gravity did the rest. After my final shove, the heavy chest clattered the rest of the way down in a cacophony of thumps, a few distinct splintering noises, and the almost musical jingle of its contents as they started to come loose.

I descended after it, finding the thing had landed upright surprisingly intact, though the lid had popped open and some of its boards were broken and bulging, emitting trickles of coin from inside.

"Jadrin, really?" I protested as she straightened up from slitting the throat of the guy whose back I'd just broken.

"Well, I mean, come on," she said with a shrug, flicking blood off her dagger. The other guy by the wall was already dead, apparently from a clean stab through the heart. "You really wanna leave 'em alive in here, considering what we're planning to do *next*? Have a heart, Lord Seiji."

"I suppose I take your point," I conceded. "Any of these acquaintances of yours?"

"Rapist, dumbass, never seen that guy before," she recited, pointing her dagger at each of the fresh corpses in turn, the last being Caester, who had taken a crossbow bolt in the throat, which Adelly was at that moment pulling out. "And that's Donon."

"Wait, really?"

"No relation," Adelly said, smirking. "It's a common enough name."

"Jadrin, you backstabbing little cunt," the new Donon wheezed. His clothes were still smoking, and in the few moments I'd been upstairs he'd been shot through both legs by a crossbow. That'd be Kastrin's work, to judge by its precision.

"Yeah, let it all out," Jadrin sneered. "Get your talking in, Donon; that's all you've got left on this world."

"Ugh, I'm *not* calling him that," I groaned. "From now on, you're Shitty Don, okay?"

"Hope you enjoy this," Shitty Don snarled, clutching one of his bleeding legs. "Lady Gray's gonna—"

"Lady Gray's gonna burn just like you did, and then some. Several times, before I decide to *finish* with her. Biribo, see anything on him?"

My familiar buzzed out into the air. "Not directly, boss, but you can hide a lot under clothes."

"You looking for his artifact?" Jadrin asked. "It's a medallion. On a chain around his neck, under the shirt."

"I shoulda porked and gutted you when I had the chance," Shitty Don growled, glaring pure hatred at her.

"Prob'ly." Jadrin gave him the sweetest grin I'd ever seen on her. "Never will now, sweetroll."

"Found it," Kastrin called, emerging from the door tucked beside the stairs, her crossbow in one hand and a hefty jug of asauthec in the other, bearing the traditional yellow warning mark.

"Ah, fine work, Kastrin," I praised her. "Would you be a dear and finish this guy off?"

"Yes, sir!" She raised the crossbow one-handed, as it had a bolt already in place, and squeezed the trigger.

This wrought a scream of outraged pain from Shitty Don as the bolt impacted his shoulder.

"I missed?" Kastrin protested, scowling in outrage. "That's not—oh, fuck you! I *never* miss!"

"That's what you get for being cocky," Adelly replied without sympathy. "Use the damn thing with *both* hands like it's designed for."

"Nah, the kid's fine," said Jadrin. "That's his artifact. It gives him luck or something, dunno exactly."

"Huh, now I wanna see how this works," I said. "**Slimeshot.**"

I was aiming for his head, which at that range would've been an instant kill. That spell was deadly precise, as it seemed to inherently direct the flying slime to whatever spot I focused on without needing to be properly aimed, but this time it just grazed the side of his head, knocking him over.

"Damn," I said, impressed. "Hey, this is fun! Who's got a throwing knife?"

"Do we really have time to fuck around all night, Lord Seiji?" Jadrin asked pointedly.

"I suppose you're right," I admitted. "Biribo?"

"This guy's Blessing is *not* strong enough for a powerful defensive arti-fact," said the familiar. "Most likely it's something affecting probability on a local scale; that's not uncommon for cheaper amulets and the like. Get close enough to take any possible randomness out of the equation and it should work normally."

"W-wait," Shitty Don rasped, trying to pull himself back upright. "Listen to me, you've got—"

He fell silent as Adelly knelt and shoved the tip of her loaded crossbow directly under his chin.

"Goodbye, Shitty Don," she simpered, and the weapon twanged. The bolt smashed cleanly up through his skull, its tip emerging from the crown of his head in a spray of blood that artfully decorated the wall behind him.

"Well, now you're down a crossbow bolt," Kastrin said, unimpressed. "*I'm* not pulling that one out."

"Relax, we've got plenty at home."

I strode over to join Adelly, bent, and reached into the neck of the dead man's shirt. My fingers closed over a chain and I pulled, carefully dragging out the diamond-shaped piece of metal and pulling the chain up over the corpse's head. And it *was* metal, not akornin; so was the chain. The thing looked rather plain—just a flat quadrangle of what looked like copper, inset with a round piece of glass in the center and with some minor decorative etching around the edges. Had I not been able to see the telltale glow of an artifact around it, I'd never have given the cheap-looking amulet a second thought.

"Meh, nothing special," Biribo said dismissively, buzzing around my head. "It's just an Amulet of Final Luck. It has a minor but relatively far-reaching deflection property; all it really does is ensure that any attack coming at you will miss a lethal blow. Does nothing to stop you from getting hurt, and if an attack is physically impossible to deflect or avoid anyway, it won't counter it, as you just saw. Also it'll tend to be less effective on spells. In short, pretty much the kind of trash-tier artifact I'd expect a goon like this to have."

"*Except*," I said slowly, "if the person wearing it has the spell of ultimate healing, *this* particular piece of crap is a game changer."

Adelly let out a low whistle. "As long as you survive the first strike, you can Heal whatever it does. Damn, Lord Seiji, that thing's almost *perfectly* designed for you."

"Must be nice, having a patron goddess," said Jadrin, "even if she is the crappy one."

"Indeed." I raised the chain and draped it around my neck, tucking the amulet inside my cloak. There was blood on it, but I'd have to clean that later. I was getting pretty accustomed to blood. "Verily, this is a boon from the goddess, whose favor we must acknowledge. Let us pray."

I spread my hands wide, raising my face to gaze solemnly at the ceiling, and all three women lowered their weapons and bowed their heads respectfully.

"Oh Virya, patroness of assholes and dickheads everywhere," I intoned, "we give thee thanks for this great bounty. In gratitude, I promise that when I rise up to destroy the gods themselves, I'll do you last. Unless it's more convenient to do you earlier; or if I'm in a real bad mood at the time, or I forget or something. I've got stuff on my mind. Amen."

"Her will be done," all three intoned, making in unison one of those Fflyr formal gestures, which I'd been told was performed in religious services.

I really liked these girls.

"All right, ladies, you remember the plan. Kastrin, slosh that stuff around, and don't forget the second floor. Oh, and be careful; I think the guy up there is still alive."

"Not for loooong," she sang, sauntering toward the staircase and somewhat awkwardly reloading her crossbow with the jug of asauthec tucked under her arm.

"Adelly, give me a hand with this." I bent to grasp one end of the ruptured chest of coins. Adelly sighed, handed her crossbow to Jadrin, who had refused one of her own, preferring her knives and cudgel, and took the other.

The thing was impressively sturdy to have survived being hurled down the stairs at all, but it was in bad shape. It creaked alarmingly as we moved it, and every motion caused glittering coins to spill out of the widening cracks, leaving a trail to mark our passage as we shuffled awkwardly out the broken door into the street. Jadrin preceded us, sweeping Adelly's crossbow this way and that, but no one was nearby.

After all, that was half the security of this little counting house of Lady Gray's, a place where much of the income from her nearby businesses was tallied and sorted. The five men standing guard were, if anything, the lesser half of the defenses; the greater was the simple fact that everyone knew what this place was, and nobody in the Gutters dared piss her off by going after her money directly. The Olumnach bandit gangs hadn't penetrated this far into the city, so there were only Gwyllthean natives who knew better. Here, her reputation was a greater deterrent than any amount of guards. Even the Kingsguard wouldn't dare antagonize her so openly.

Unfortunately for Gray, I wasn't the Kingsguard.

"Here we go." I shuffled to one side, Adelly moving opposite me as we maneuvered the chest of coins so that its length ran parallel to the street between us. "And one . . . two . . ."

We swung it back, then forward, gathering momentum as money sprayed out in every direction.

". . . and *heave!*"

On my command we let go. The thing was heavy and didn't fly far, but we managed to sling it almost to the middle of the street, where the poor beleaguered thing finally gave up the ghost. On impact it shattered, boards bursting apart and coins flying every which way, though most fell in a huge puddle amid the ruins of the chest.

"By all means, ladies, fill your pockets," I said, noting the looks Jadrin and Adelly were giving the money pile. "Remember, the courteous thing to do would be to share the bounty with the others who weren't along on this mission."

"Yeah, well, I must've left my fancy manners in my other pants, along with my wooden tea set and the pony Daddy gave me for my fifth birthday," Jadrin said cheerfully, already shoveling loose coin into her pouch.

"Bitch," Adelly snorted without any real malice.

"You say that like you're expecting me to argue."

"Done and done," Kastrin reported, emerging from the door behind us. "I used about half the jug, and left the rest where you told me—oh, come on, you're starting without me?"

She scurried forward to begin scooping up Lady Gray's money.

"Fine work, Kastrin, thank you," I said magnanimously, watching the three fill their pockets and coin pouches.

"It's a damn shame, is all," Jadrin said, straightening and regretfully tucking her bulging purse away inside her jacket. "There's no way we could carry off even *half* of this, even if we'd brought sacks."

"It's not about the money," I quoted. "It's about sending a message. All right, ladies, pack it in. You'll want to be at a safe distance for the important part."

Adelly had already retreated; Kastrin grabbed a last handful and regretfully joined the other two as they scampered a few meters up the street. I remained behind, just close enough that I had a clear line of sight through the broken door at the trashed room just inside. I fixed my attention on the shiny puddle of oil visible at the foot of the stairs, glittering with fallen coins scattered across it.

Spark.

Asauthec was serious stuff; the flames caught instantly and spread fast, rising higher and burning exceptionally bright. This particular blend was for wall torches, which meant it blazed brightly but not too hot, and would last for a long span of hours. Fire raced across the trails Kastrin had left across the walls, up the stairs to the top room.

Structures made of akorthist and akorshil weren't flammable, but a lot of the stuff *in* them was. Especially Fflyr houses, which were more often than not full of books and papers. Especially a place like this, being used for accounting purposes; there was a *lot* of paperwork jammed in there.

There was one last thing to do. **Summon Slime**, **Tame Beast**.

I sauntered away from the merrily burning building, the rapid spread of flames across the asauthec puddles causing fire to burst from the upper room's window even before I made it past the edge of the structure and the narrow alleyway separating it from the next house. All three girls fell into step with me as I reached them, and we went on our way up the street.

Behind us, a *BANG* sounded, followed by an echoing crash, as the flames reached the half-full jug of asauthec and all the oil's potential energy was released at once, blasting the broken front door out into the street along with a gout of fire and a spray of burning paperwork, the meticulous records of Lady Gray's operations disintegrating as they were flung in all directions amid the sparks.

"Ah, ah," I chided as Kastrin turned to watch. "Bad form, Kastrin. Badasses never look at explosions, especially not the ones they cause."

"Wow," she said dryly, "I have so much to learn, Lord Seiji." Jadrin snorted a derisive laugh.

My strategy meeting back at North Watch had been brief. There just wasn't much to go over. We had few resources and no time, and were up against a single stark reality—Lady Gray kept succeeding because she refused to be put on the defensive, always adjusting the situation to keep the initiative and forcing me to react to her ploys. We each had too much to protect, me with the women of Cat Alley and she her already battered organization. On the occasions I'd gotten the better of her, it had always been through the exercise of my sheer Goddess-given brute force over her admittedly superior tactics.

So I went with what worked. If I had to react to protect my territory, it would be by smashing the shit out of hers first.

"All right, back to the others," I said cheerfully. "They should be in position to launch the main event by now. If not, Lady Gray has more flammable property that she doesn't really need, and the night is young."

I did not look back at the burning carnage in my wake, because it wasn't my first night being a badass. But I knew what I had left there, held in place by my last command to it, waiting to be found when Lady Gray returned to sift through the wreckage of whatever money would still be there by the time she got around to it.

Atop the pile of coins, surrounded by burning rubble, a single slime. A little personal message from me.

No more Dark Lord Nice Guy.

46

In Which the Dark Lord Lets the Hate Flow Through Him

He just dropped to street level, spent a second with a group of four people in that alley—two alleys up from here—and is now climbing back to the rooftops," my familiar reported on the movement of the spy who'd been shadowing us from above street level since the counting house. He'd been too good to let us spot him, but not knowing who he was dealing with or what a familiar even was, his skill had ironically given him away. Biribo couldn't differentiate a person hiding among a crowd, but someone keeping pace with us along the rooftops was an easy target.

"Got it," I said, feeling that sensation rising again, the one that had been increasingly driving me ever since I left North Watch—bloodlust and euphoria. I was about to dispense some *pain*, and the anticipation fed my inner Dark Lord almost as well as actually doing it would.

The alley was dark. I couldn't even see a hint of movement as I stepped in front of the girls to draw abreast of it. Not for the first split-second anyway, before I cast Light Beam straight into it.

The four huddled shapes thus revealed reared back as they were blinded. Then a Windburst sent them hurtling away, bouncing them painfully off the walls.

"Nice night for it, eh, lads?" I called out in a jolly tone as I stepped into their erstwhile ambush spot. **Slimeshot, Slimeshot**. Two of them were down just like that, at that range severely injured if not dead; neither produced a scream. One was scrambling away down the alley, having recovered faster, while a fourth nearer at hand was trying to struggle out from under the body of his companion, which had fallen half on top of him.

It made for an awkward angle; I had to step almost past him to fire a Slimeshot right into his neck. From less than a meter away. He was just a vague shape in the renewed darkness, but I suspected the wet splattering noise which resulted wasn't entirely from the slime.

Speaking of vague shapes, the last one was getting away. I looked up to find he'd made it almost to the alley's other exit point.

Immolate.

The screaming never ceased to be annoying, but at least this gave us some light to work with.

"Jadrin, you know what to do."

"I do, Lord Seiji, but I can't very well do it if you're gonna be this thorough. These guys are all finished."

"Aw. Well, don't worry, we'll find you some new toys to play with before long."

"Ugh, do you *have* to encourage her?" Adelly groaned.

I stopped a meter away from the huddled inferno that was the last guy, patiently waiting. My three followers all drew up behind me, Adelly and Kastrin flanking me from both sides with their crossbows out, Jadrin keeping watch back down the alley the way we'd come.

As usual, it took him a minute or so to stop burning. I conjured a Firelight as the illumination from the flames of torture faded, staring down at the whimpering mess of a man now curled into the fetal position. I'd been about to deliver the coup de grace, but looking at him now it seemed . . . unsporting, somehow.

"I guess we could let this one go," I mused aloud. He peeked up from between his own arms.

"He'll just run back to Lady Gray and we'll have to kill him again later," Adelly said in a tone devoid of pity. "Maybe after he hurts one of ours."

"Either of you recognize him?"

"Meh."

"They all look alike after a while," Kastrin sneered.

"I won't," the man babbled, "I'll leave the city! Swear on the Goddess!"

"Ah, wouldn't it be nice if we could all part as friends," I sighed, and turned my back. "Sadly, I don't believe you. Kastrin, do you believe him?"

All I heard in reply was the twang of a crossbow and a hoarse gurgle.

That . . . should probably not have felt the way it did. It wasn't fun; there was no joy in this. Not like facing down the guys from the counting house, who'd had a chance to fight back, however ineffectually. But a grim satisfaction, a sense of *vindication*, yes. This fucker had misspent his life prey-ing on others in the rough streets of the Gutters, he'd been about to ambush and try to murder us, and now he was rapidly bleeding out on the ground of a filthy alley. A measure of balance was restored to the universe.

I was no longer as concerned about not being directly affected by the vio-lence, but my concern at not being concerned had faded to almost nothing, and that probably wasn't a good sign. Remorse, it seemed, was incompatible with the constantly simmering rage. Ah well, I had more immediate things to worry about.

"Off we go, ladies!" I called in a cheery singsong, and we strolled back as we'd come, past the bodies to the street beyond.

"Our buddy's still on the case," Biribo reported quietly in my ear. "Along the left side . . . he's circling around the back of that peaked roof to get an indirect view of you down the next alley!"

I flew into motion, stepping as quietly as I could while dashing across the width of the next building to place myself in full view of the alley, head tilted back to watch the rooftops. The weight of Immolate formed in the front of my brain, ready to be shoved forth into reality. Now it was the hunter who stepped into the trap.

Our persistent foe rounded the peak of the gabled roof fast, having rushed around it to get into place. Finding me already there instead of where he'd expected, and also looking right at him, he panicked, and froze.

So did I.

It was a Gutter Rat, not one of Gray's gangsters. The kid was at most a year older than Gilder. He went deathly still as we locked eyes, and in the dim but clean Ephemeral starlight, I had a clear view of the child's face as he realized he was about to die.

Immolate vanished from my mind like a popped bubble. Then, so did everything else.

I'm not sure how long I would have stood there in the street, staring witlessly at the frozen boy who gaped back, but the spell was broken by pounding feet as my posse caught up. Following the direction of my gaze, Adelly muttered a curse and raised her crossbow.

I reached out and slapped it back down, as the sudden motion finally spurred the petrified Rat into action. Scrambling so frantically he nearly slipped off the roof, he managed to pivot and vanish back around the corner.

"I'm not sure I could've made that shot anyway," Adelly said after a sec-ond, gently moving her weapon from under my hand.

"*I* could've," Kastrin muttered.

"Yeah, yeah, we know, you're a witch with crossbows," Jadrin said with the particular tone of soft derision I was starting to recognize as what passed for affection from her. "More important, Lord Sciji could've made that shot first if he wanted it made. You gotta learn to follow the boss's lead when you're out on a job, girls."

All three looked at me, waiting. I was still staring in silence at a distant section of the Gwyllthean battlements right where a moment before a child's terrified face had blocked my view.

Suddenly, I wasn't angry anymore. And that was . . . not great. It turned out all the anxiety and pain under it wasn't *gone*, just suppressed while I was riding that high. It didn't even have a chance to all come rushing back in, as I was currently standing there trying to process what I'd spent the last several minutes doing. Laughing, wisecracking, murdering. Like some cheap manga . . .

Villain.

"It's tough, with the Rats," Adelly said quietly, watching me. "They're a nuisance and a downright menace sometimes, and they usually grow up to be the worst kind of people . . . The boys anyway. A lot of the girls graduate to Cat Alley themselves. Sometimes you can't help thinking you'd be saving everybody a lot of trouble, even them, if you just put one down. But . . . it's still just a kid. Makes you wonder if they might still have a chance to become something different. Better."

Jadrin snorted loudly.

"Yeah, I know," Adelly sighed.

"He's moving off in the other direction now," Biribo reported from inside my hood, just loudly enough to be audible to them. "So, either way, we're no longer being followed."

"Then we'd better keep moving," I said, hearing the dullness in my own voice.

Catching my mood, they followed me in silence the rest of the way back to the meeting point.

Fortunately I didn't have much opportunity to be lost in my thoughts on the way back; my thoughts weren't a pleasant place at that moment. We were stalking as quickly and quietly as we could through enemy territory, and had to pay attention for the counterattacks that we had just been out deliberately provoking, which might come at any time. But since we'd scared off our Gutter Rat stalker and crushed that one would-be ambush, we met no reprisal between the counting house and our own improvised field headquarters.

I had set us up in what I figured was the last place Lady Gray would look for her enemies—one of her own strongholds. We linked up with Minifrit's bodyguards on the outskirts, and had them direct us to one of the houses close to Cat Alley—where one of her gangs was currently stationed and leaning on the women there—to clean it out.

That part was shockingly easy; after Kastrin sniped their lookout, Aster and I had barged in and demolished them. It turned out that fighting Blessed of our caliber in close quarters was a terrifying exercise in futility for the kinds of roughnecks Lady Gray mostly employed.

We filed silently past the "lookout," who was leaning against the door of the house; it was the same guy who'd been there before. Getting him posed just right had been a real pain in the ass, but with his hat pulled down you had to get close to realize he was a corpse.

In theory, nobody should be observing it that closely. Our enemies *shouldn't* know we'd taken it yet; that was the kind of thing they would inevitably discover before much time had passed, but we weren't planning to be there long. The fact that the corpse was still posed there was the signal that Aster and the others still held the house. Had it been attacked and retaken, we would have retreated to the designated spot on the outskirts.

I went right to the door and slipped in unchallenged. My actual sentries were inside, on the second floor, watching through slits in the boarded windows.

"How'd it go?" Aster asked immediately upon my entry.

I waited until my three followers had filed inside and Adelly shut the door before answering. "Message sent. How about here? I see Sakin's back. Has the scouting paid off enough for us to move, or should I go rattle Gray's cage again?"

"Oh, we have met with more success than I dared hope," Sakin declared, grinning even more maniacally than usual. "I wish I could take credit, Lord Seiji, but the next few bits of good news were served up to us on a platter before I could even get my hands properly dirty."

He paused for effect—which I clearly needed to make a rule against *other* people doing—and I was just opening my mouth to demand an explanation when the stroke of luck to which he was referring popped around the corner, wearing the usual shit-eating grin.

"*Gilder!*" For a moment, I forgot to keep my voice down.

"Hey, Lord Seiji!" the boy replied, beaming with good cheer. "I tolja I was on top of things! You can always count on Gilder to—oi! Hey, c'mon!"

He made a valorous attempt to evade me, but had realized a second too late that I wasn't charging across the room for a hug. I managed to grab the kid's collar as he tried to bolt, and a short scuffle later got him into a headlock, vigorously knuckling his hair with my free hand.

"Ow! Get off! Come on, *this* is the thanks I get?"

"You little shit! Do you know how worried I— Benit was? What's the big idea, trying to tackle Lady Gray's whole gang without support? How could *anybody* be that stupid?"

"Oi, ain't nobody *that* stupid, I wasn't tacklin' nothing! Gimme more credit than that, I was—will you let *go* of me?!"

"*Boys,*" Aster interjected firmly. "We are trying to be *discreet*, remember?"

I finally released him, giving his hair one last ruffle, which he ducked out from under, still grinning exuberantly.

"The boy's actually done some damn fine work," commented Olyc, who was leaning against the wall, watching all this unfold. "Don't get me wrong, I'm with you, Lord Seiji; kid like him trying to deal with the gangs *and* the Rats, alone in the Gutters with no support? Fuckin' crazy. Good thing he found *us* or I dunno how long he would've lasted. Still, he pulled off a real trick at the end there."

"Hey, Gilder knows what he's about!" Gilder proclaimed, puffing up his thin chest and jabbing his thumb into it. "I ain't dumb enough to try to *live* that way, but for a couple days? No sweat. I knew Lord Seiji wouldn't leave me twisting any longer'n that."

"You're goddamn lucky I was *able* to get back here with reinforcements that fast," I lectured. "It is *not* a short jaunt from my base to town. There's a reason you only saw me once a week!"

At that, Gilder's expression finally sobered. "Are Benit and Radon okay? They found you, right? Was the trip too bad on 'em?"

"They're fine," I assured him. "Yeah, it was kind of a rough journey, but they made it and were resting up at the castle when we left."

"The *castle?*" He threw up his hands. "There's a castle? You have a *castle?* Why is this the first I'm ever hearing about the castle?"

"That's where you'd be *right now* if you weren't such a cocky little dumbass!"

Aster cleared her throat loudly. "Lord Seiji, you really might want to hold off boxing his ears *until* tonight's work is done with. Not that they don't need boxing, but Olyc's right. Gilder pulled off some really good work while he was unsupervised in the Gutters the last couple days."

"Okay, fine," I said. "Let's hear it, what've you got for me?"

"I got *detailed* info on Gray's people around Cat Alley," he said proudly. "How many there are, where they're moving from, and what they been doing. Also sussed out the brothels where there's more resistance ready to get moving."

"It's solid stuff," said Sakin when I looked at him. "I haven't been able to personally verify anything beyond this little patch of streets, but the boy's apparently been living hereabouts for two days, keeping an eye on everything from cover. Aster and I already got all the details; I can give you my recommendations based on what he's brought us."

"Oh, so you can take credit for all my hard work?" Gilder huffed, folding his arms.

"Easy, kid," Sakin said with a wink. "The people who gather the intel aren't usually the ones who organize it into a plan. You did your job, lemme do mine."

"That's right," I said firmly, leveling a finger at Gilder. "You *did* your job, now I want you to hang back and stay *out* of it, clear? Soon as we're finished with this place, you're coming back with us. If anybody here needs a break, boy, it's you."

"Oh, but you haven't even seen the *best* part yet!" Gilder crowed, grinning hugely.

"Yeah, Olyc wasn't kidding," Aster agreed, giving me a wry little smile. "The boy's brought us a real coup. Or at least, he was the middleman for one."

Everybody turned to look pointedly at the room's other interior door, the one Gilder hadn't come through. That led to the room where we'd piled the bodies of the enemy street soldiers who'd been in this house before we took it over. Looking through it now, I could see the corpses against the wall where I'd left them, but also Donon, Kasser, Harold, and Thwyn, one of Minifrit's other bouncers, holding crossbows trained on the other end of the room, which was out of view from here.

At Aster's encouraging nod, I stepped over to the door and through it, then I had to stop and stare.

What was now one long room had originally been two; the wall between them was only partially knocked down, but the few planks and pillars remaining were too broken to provide much of an obstruction. The door on the other side was barricaded, making this one the only route in and out, and against the wall were nine living people. Six women and three men. Members of Gray's gang, to judge by their attire and generally scruffy appearances. They'd all been disarmed, and were warily studying me and the crossbows aimed at them.

I looked at them, then at the fourteen corpses piled like driftwood on this side of the room and the bloodstains on the floor, then at Sakin.

"This arrangement was *your* idea, wasn't it?"

"I like to think of myself as an artist at heart," he preened. "I call this piece 'The Two Fates of Those Who Fuck With My Boss.'"

"Yeah, point made," said one of the women, stepping forward. She raised her hands peaceably as all four crossbows swiveled to point at her heart. "Lord . . . Healer? I'm Khadret. These are—"

"Never mind who you are," I interrupted. "Who *are* you? I thought I left orders not to take prisoners."

One of the men cleared his throat. "Uh, the idea was that we're *recruits*, not prisoners."

"*Oh?*"

"If you listen as good as Gilder does," Gilder said, poking his head in, "you learn stuff you weren't even listening for! Like, f'rinstance, which of Lady Gray's people are sick of her shit and willing to switch teams."

"So you brought them *here?*" I grated.

"*I* brought them," Aster interjected firmly. "Gilder told us where to find the two groups. Both were close and accessible; Sakin and I agreed it was worth the risk."

"I figured, worst case, we can just kill 'em," Sakin said with a casual shrug.

"They let us take their weapons and haven't given us a peep of trouble, Lord Seiji," Donon added.

"Two groups, hm?" I said, turning back to study the new arrivals.

"*They* aren't with us," Khadret said, grimacing at the three men, who were standing a bit apart.

The fellow who'd spoken before stepped forward, also raising his hands when weapons were pointed his way. "You can call me Craed, Lord . . . Seiji, was it? I won't mince words—my boys and I here are purely self-interested fellows. We're professionals, see? We go where the work is steadiest and most profitable. You aren't the first time Lady Gray's had *competition*, but you've lasted longer and done her more damage than any of the others, and the *kind* of spells you've got . . . Well, the average run of street trash we tend to work with probably don't realize it, but I know when a new player's moved in with a caliber of firepower that Lady Gray straight up *cannot* match."

"Sicellit and the girls are upstairs keeping watch," Kasser added in a low tone, "but they said these three are . . . okay."

"I know them," Adelly added, having slipped in behind me. "They're all King's Guild rejects who fell in with Gray for lack of better options. Decent enough johns. No rough stuff, or even rudeness, really. No quibbling over prices either."

"Hey, Adelly," said one of Craed's companions, grinning. "Good to see you made it outta there okay!"

"I'm better than you've ever seen me, Smin," she replied sweetly. "And you will *never* touch me again."

"Sorry to hear that," he said, still apparently cheerful. "Still glad you're okay, though."

"All right," I said with a sigh, turning back to the women. "And what's *your* story, then?"

"We're suckers," Khadret said sourly. "Lady Gray knows how to manipulate people, Lord Healer. Me and the girls threw in with her because she promised us a chance at a better life. Played the female solidarity card. Then she did fuck all to back it up; once she had us signed up, we just got used as warm bodies and kept in line through fear like all the other trash she has working for her. It's *barely* better than whoring. Meanwhile, *you* came along and have been doing all the shit she promised us, apparently for free."

"You were all Alley Cats?" I asked.

"Yeah, I know them," Jadrin said from behind me. "Story checks out."

"Is that Jadrin?" Khadret demanded. "You miserable *cunt*, I thought you were dead!"

"You wish," Jadrin grinned, sticking her head through the door.

"Fuck yeah, I do. Hey, Adelly, glad to see you safe."

"You see how much more popular I am?" Adelly said to Jadrin. "That's a little trick I like to call 'not being an asshole to everybody.'"

"We don't all have the skills to make it as a whore, Adelly."

"Enough!" I barked. Silence descended; I had perfected the trick of projecting an edge to my tone that suddenly reminded everyone I was the guy who set people on fire with his brain. I gave them a moment to dwell on it before continuing. "I am certainly interested in acquiring new talent. *However*. I trust I don't need to explain my obvious reservations."

"Sure, you don't know if you can trust us," Craed said immediately. "That's a fair cop, Lord Seiji. Everybody's gotta prove themselves."

Khadret nodded once. "We came here expecting that. My friends and I are committed, Lord . . . Seiji. Just name what you want us to do."

Well, shit, it would've been really nice if I *had* a plan for this eventuality, but it was not something I'd expected. I studied each of them in turn, then glanced at Sakin. Under my gaze, his customary tiny smile broadened slightly, and he winked.

And I suddenly had a thought.

"All right, then," I said aloud. "For your first assignment as my followers, I want you to betray me."

47

In Which the Dark Lord Breaks and Enters and Breaks

Lady Gray had her people all up and down Cat Alley; we'd created a weak patch in their distribution by wiping out that one safehouse, and hopefully my attack on the counting house had diverted some away; but the problem remained that wherever I popped up in person, she would focus her attention. And unfortunately, Gray was smart enough to strike at my weak points rather than just throwing men at me like wheat against a scythe.

I had over a hundred weak points. Every woman in this alley who I'd come here to recruit and now had to protect. As soon as I appeared, a blood-bath would ensue, and it wouldn't be focused on me. Therefore I needed the ability to appear without it becoming known that I had. I needed confusion.

And fortunately, I now had nine people positioned to draw attention to one end of Cat Alley, and a familiar who could spot people lurking on the rooftops, whether or not they were within his line of sight.

"Oh, I thought that was a chimney," Kastrin muttered, taking aim with her crossbow.

"Yeah, that's why he picked that spot," said Biribo. "You want the chimney on the left. He's got on a big hat, so your headshot's a little below where you'd expect."

"Got it."

The crossbow twanged, and the chimney on the left slumped silently over, then tumbled off the roof.

"*Nice*," I said, patting her lightly on the back. Kastrin gave me a brilliant smile over her shoulder.

"Sakin's coming back," Biribo reported. "All three targets neutralized without a peep. That guy's *good*."

"What's his story anyway?" Jadrin asked quietly.

All of us turned to look at her in the darkness. She glanced back and forth, then shrugged.

"What? What'd I say?"

Sakin scrabbled up onto our rooftop almost silently. "How we doin', boss?"

"Biribo?" I asked.

"No scouts or lookouts within our line of sight," he said.

"Wanna keep going, Lord Seiji?" asked Sakin.

I hesitated, and looked up and down the row of dark roofs with the blue-tinged light of Cat Alley shining up from below.

"No," I said finally. "This'll have to do. We've silenced communications on half the street and at this point we're on borrowed time. Every second makes it more likely there'll be a shift change or someone'll find a body. Let's move in."

It was a risk, but there was just no way to do this without risks—worse, without the certainty of innocent casualties. Even under optimal conditions we just didn't have the manpower or time to silently pick off Lady Gray's forces one by one until they didn't have enough left to threaten the Alley Cats, and that wasn't even addressing the possibility that my nine new "recruits" would *actually* betray me rather than divert street soldiers to investigate the slaughtered and now abandoned safehouse they'd "found." I was gambling that even if they were plants, they would play along in the short term to stay on my good side long enough to get close enough to me to pull something off.

If I was wrong, Gray's people would already be beating up or killing people at that end of the street. If I was right, they'd quickly figure out from the mess we'd left in the safehouse that I was here and that would start in minutes at most. There was the possibility that the turncoats would manage to go the extra mile I'd asked of them, but it would be foolish to pin my hopes on that. Either way, we hadn't even touched Gray's forces all up and down the other half of the street, and kicking off the main event the way I was about to would immediately start the bloodshed.

I was going to get these women hurt and possibly killed no matter *what* I did. I took refuge in the pulse-pounding rage clawing its way up my throat like bile; it was easier to endure than the guilt.

Once I got my hands on Gray, her end was going to be . . . *dramatic.* Immolate was too good for that bitch.

We moved as lightly as we could, but this big a group leaping onto a roof one after another was inevitably going to create noise, so I put on a burst of speed. With me was the entire crew we'd brought—Aster, Sakin, Donon, Kasser, and Harold from North Watch; Jadrin, Kastrin, Adelly, Sicellit, and two other girls from the Alley Cat (those best qualified for violence, which most of the Cats weren't yet); and the strays we'd picked up in town, Gilder and Minifrit's three bouncers, Thwyn, Olyc, and Raelther. Fifteen people wasn't nearly enough of an army to take on Gray's massed street soldiers, but it was definitely enough that moving silently wasn't an option. We'd made it this far with the simple expediency of killing all potential witnesses, but from this point on, I was forced to rely on speed and shock.

As such, rather than waste time scouting for a discreet entrance, I picked the nearest window, yanked it open, and hopped through. As luck would have it, this landed me in an upstairs bedroom which was currently in use.

"Uh . . . Healer?" said the woman inside, staring curiously up at me from under the shocked-looking young naked man currently between her legs. "Is there something wrong with the front door?"

"Yes, it's in view of a lot of people I'd rather not meet," I explained. "Speaking of which, is this fellow *bothering* you, Tazilit?"

"Hey, *hey!*" she protested, wrapping her arms protectively around the suddenly terrified man, who couldn't have been more than twenty, and frowned at me over his shoulder.. "None of that! Kaenon's a sweet guy. My best customer!"

"Ah, my humble apologies for the interruption, then," I said politely, setting a red halo on the bedstand. "Have another hour on me, Kaenon. Terribly sorry. We'll just get out of your hair."

If all went according to plan for once, he wouldn't be getting an extra hour's worth, or even the rest of this one, but the thought counted for something, surely. I swept into the hall, the rest of us filing through the room after me. Several of my crew, I was proud to hear, also offered polite apologies. Gilder loudly said "Hah, nice!" and Sicellit stopped to demand why Kaenon hadn't visited her in two months; Aster had to collect them both by the collar, the three being last through the door. Thwyn, expressionless and used to this kind of thing, silently shut it behind us.

By that point I was already at the stairs, and accelerated my descent down them as I caught the sound of what was happening down there in the Jostled Jugs's common room.

There was no music, no exuberant shouting; there was laughter, but was all male, and it had that *edge* to it. The laughter I was hearing told me nothing was funny.

I landed at the base of the stairs, my cloak flaring behind me, and only half the room went silent at my entrance. Gannit herself paused, having picked up a fallen club and had apparently been about to launch herself at one of the miscreants; it was a damn good thing I arrived when I did. She was scrappy for a grandma, but they'd kill her. All four of her bouncers were already down, two bleeding on the floor and two backed against the wall by men with swords out, holding bleeding arms. All of them, plus the toughs looming mockingly over them, turned to face me and froze.

Not the man who'd just thrown Madyn across one of the tables and grabbed her by the neck to hold her down, nor the four holding back three of her fellow sex workers, who were trying to intervene; one already had a bloody lip for her trouble. They carried on guffawing while I began casting.

Heal, Heal, Heal, Heal, Heal.

The flashes of pink light, plus the sudden quiet, got the attention of a couple of the men currently raising hell on the opposite side of the common room. Not the guy on top of Madyn or his nearest cohorts, but one had the presence of mind to release the arms of the woman he was holding back and bolt for the door.

Slimeshot.

I nailed him right in the pelvis as he ran, sending him hurtling across the room to smash against the wall, where he slumped to the floor, whimpering in pain with a shattered femur.

"Aw, that looks uncomfortable," I said, striding toward him. Now, I had everyone's undivided attention. "Don't worry, I'll make it stop. They do call me the Healer."

I stood over him, extended my arm, and took a moment to welter in the seething fury that had risen. I felt alive, buzzing with energy, free of consequence or remorse.

Slimeshot.

At that range, the squishy slime crushed his skull. Red liquid that was only partly blood sprayed.

"Do ya *have* to make such a fuckin' mess in my common room?" Gannit demanded. "Look at that! You got any idea how hard it is to scrub blood outta the cracks in the floor? Who raised you, boy?"

"I really am terribly sorry, Gannit," I said, turning and bowing toward her. I wasn't. I was all but trembling with suspended violence; the only thing holding me in check at that moment was sheer showmanship. I was creating a *spectacle*. Timing was everything.

"Well, he finally turned up," said the fellow who had just released Madyn and turned to face me, pulling his sword free. "I hope you—"

"Aw, isn't that *precious*," I said, pointing at him. "Look at the little guy, trying so hard to pretend he's not pissing himself in terror. His knees are shaking!"

I couldn't tell if they were or not, though I did notice a glow around his boots. Blessed with Might, then. Nothing else was glowing; artifact boots likely had some kind of mobility or traction property I'd have to watch out for. Biribo would warn me as soon as he had a moment.

"Listen, you," the Blessed thug tried to bluster, pointing his weapon at me. "Lady Gray—"

"**Immolate**. Do not say that name to me. Aw, I guess he can't hear me."

Everyone scrambled away from him. By that point, my forces had fanned into the common room and raised weapons, while Gannit's people had all retreated behind them. To judge by the divide this made in the room, there were no customers here. Just the Jugs's personnel, and Lady Gray's.

That made this next part convenient.

"Here, now," said one of the thugs who was not currently thrashing around, screaming and on fire. "Look, we don't want any trouble with you, Healer."

"Oh, you *don't?*" I replied in a saccharine tone, which made them all stiffen up and back away. "Hey, Gannit. Have this lot been conducting themselves in the manner of people who don't want any trouble?"

"Son, if you're just gonna ask obvious questions, do you even need me here?" the old woman retorted.

"A fair point," I acknowledged. "A more pertinent question, then—do you mind if I make more of a mess in your place?"

Gannit took a long, sour look at the guy by the wall, and the contents of his skull all over her floor, then heaved an irritated sigh and threw her hands up. "Oh well. If you don't, some other asshole will. It's been that kinda week. Go ahead and take out the trash."

"Wait a second," squeaked one of the men, who only moments before had been menacing the women in this very room.

"I'm only glad I can be of service," I said courteously to Gannit, then turned my hood slightly toward my followers. "*Kill them all.*"

There was just . . . something . . . about giving that order. In practical terms, it was no worse than things I'd already done. But I'm not a practical person. I am a *performer*, and saying it out loud in so many words felt like crossing a line.

More oddly than the fact that I felt nothing but a muted thrill of satisfaction when crossbows sang and seven men fell.

One had been missed entirely; he let out an honest-to-god shriek and tried to run for the door. I didn't bother to do anything about it, since Aster was already moving.

"Hey, Biribo, what's with those boots?" I murmured as she cut him down, then turned and stalked toward the two others who hadn't suffered lethal wounds yet.

"Surestep boots!" Biribo said after slithering unpleasantly up to my ear so he could be heard over the diminishing noise as the Blessed thug's screams trailed off. "Nothing real fancy, but they're an adventurer's early standby. Wearing those, you'll never lose your footing or miss a step. That's not a flashy effect like some artifacts, but it can be a real game changer in a fight."

"I see. Hey there, feeling better?" I called out to the man on the ground as the flames finally died. He was the last of his gang still alive, Aster having just pulled her sword from another's chest.

"F-fuck . . . you . . ." he wheezed, laboriously rolling over and trying to push himself up with one arm.

"Glad to hear it," I said. "I respect you for having the spine not to try to schmooze me. Almost none of your comrades had even that much. **Immolate**. I'm sorry to have left you with this so long," I said, turning to Gannit and having to raise my voice above the renewed howling. "We'd have been here sooner, but Minifrit insisted we not run off in a hurry and half-ass it."

"Glad to hear she's safe an' sound," Gannit grunted, also ignoring the burning man screaming in her front room. "I see you brought a few stray Cats home with a fresh set of claws, there. All the other girls all right?"

"Everyone made it out of the city. I have a safe and defensible place for them."

"Good! Yeah, that Minifrit always was cool-headed in a crisis. It's almost as admirable as it is annoying."

"I *know*. She's got a way of being *right* that makes you just want to grab her neck and shake her."

"Heh, you should try that sometime," the old woman said, grinning with mischief. "She jiggles real nice."

I'd seen enough of Minifrit's impressive cleavage that I couldn't help immediately picturing that. And then—

Screaming, the smell of rot, agonized moans, the death rattle of a woman barely halfway through her teens—

I physically jerked and had to clench both my fists to steady myself mentally. Oh good, so *that* was still going on, and apparently it could cut right through the red fog of rage that was keeping me moving. I swear, the human brain is just . . . defective hardware. Maybe what I needed was *more* rage. If I kept myself constantly so wound up that I couldn't feel anything else, perhaps I'd be able to get through this disaster alive.

"I'm afraid all this is unfolding faster than I'd planned, thanks to Lady Gray and her bullshit," I said. My voice started out hoarse, but cleared as I spoke and recovered my equilibrium. Gannit was watching me with eyes as sharp as Minifrit's, and I had a bad feeling she had likewise singled out my problem, but for now she just listened without comment. "The problem is that Gray's people are going to go after the Alley Cats. I've done what I can to prevent that, but it's not going to be enough; there are still dozens of them around Yrshith Street at least. What I need is a way to draw their attention and *presence* to me instead of going after the women. I'm open to ideas."

"Hm, that's tricky," she grunted, stroking her chin and squinting. "Most of these goons are thick enough to buy pretty much anything you sell 'em. Gray's a clever bitch, though, and enough of her actual lieutenants are sharp enough to at least follow directions. Trick's getting 'em to react before they can consider orders and plans. Yeah, I may have a notion. Oh hey, your roast is done."

"Why, so he is." I stepped over and picked up the man's fallen sword; he scuttled back from me in a panic, having just ceased burning again. Rather than speak to him, I turned, stepped over to Madyn, and offered it to her hilt-first. "I believe you are entitled to this?"

"Oh, fuck yeah," she crowed, taking the weapon. I had to step quickly back as she made a few experimental and visibly inept swings. "Sweet! I always wanted one of these!"

"Indeed. The question now is, what do you want to *do* with it." I turned my cowled head to stare pointedly at the man who'd minutes ago been abusing her.

Madyn followed my gaze, her grin fading. She glanced over at my armed followers, specifically those who had been working girls like herself just days before, clearly putting two and two together.

"You want me to kill him?" Her tone betrayed no enthusiasm for the idea.

I shook my head. "If you *want* to kill him, his life is yours. But there is no reason you should have to. It's your choice."

"Okay." She let out a sigh of relief. "Cos, y'know, I figure that shithead is probably better off dead anyway, but I don't necessarily wanna be the one to *do* it. Know what I mean?"

"I very much do," I said feelingly. Killing got way too easy, way too fast. Turning back to the subject of our conversation, I caught him trying to creep toward the door. He froze as I strode toward him again. "Aw, now what is *that* look for? I thought we were all having *fun*? This is your idea of fun, right? Someone being helpless, tormented, and completely at the mercy of a person with incalculably greater power?" I stopped, looming over him. "Come, now. No game is properly engaging if the same person is *it* every time."

"He knows," Aster said unexpectedly. Several of the Jugs's employees turned to her in surprise; she'd never spoken when we were here. "You should save that speech for the highborn, Lord Seiji. *Every* lowborn knows what it's like. This piece of garbage chose to vent his anger at the expense of others, instead of finding people to stand with and try to make things better. But he gets it. We all do."

"Mm." I turned from her, back to the fallen man. "She has a point. Well, that's not an argument in your favor, is it? I suppose it doesn't much matter. The question now is whether I have any reason to leave you alive."

He breathed heavily, several patches of his clothing still faintly smoking, and stared up at me in silence.

"Well, if even you can't think of a reason, that pretty much settles it," I mused.

He bared his teeth viciously at me. "I'll see you in hell, you fucking freak."

"And I'll kick your ass there, too. You'll probably have to remind me who you are, though."

Slimeshot.

I sighed, regarding the mess as his brains joined his companion's all over the floor.

"Come on," Gannit protested. "And why *slimes*, for fuck's sake?"

"Take it up with Virya," I muttered, then raised my voice. "All right, somebody help me get this guy's boots off. Gannit, what was your big idea?"

Then an arm gripped me from behind, and in the next instant, a blade ripped through my throat.

I stumbled forward as I was released, spraying blood; by that point, it was pure instinct.

Heal!

Fully whole again, if blood-spattered, I spun. Everyone was staring at me in shock; several of the women screamed, and the rest raised weapons, but there was no sign of anyone near me.

"I can't sense anyone!" Biribo squawked inside my cloak. "That's powerful invisibility magic!"

"Ara, ara, ara," I said aloud. I felt it rising up, taking over. Fury so potent it made my arms tremble. *She was here.* "Lady Gray, I pr—"

That time, the knife sank straight into my chest, right between my ribs, making me stagger back and jerk violently as the weapon was ripped free.

Heal! I caught myself midstumble, grinning maniacally behind my hood as adrenaline joined the chronic fury driving me and the blood spraying from my chest ceased.

"And here I thought you were a fast learner," I chided. "What a disappointment."

"I could say the same about you, boy," a woman's voice answered me out of thin air.

I turned in a slow circle, keeping my head up but watching the floor. There was enough blood everywhere . . . I could see footprints in it. All I needed was for her to make a fresh one while I was looking.

"And next, because you're a sad, predictable little creature, you'll go for one of the others," I said. "And then I'll save them as easily as I can think about it. We can do this literally all night, and it won't be me who gets tired first. It wouldn't be even if you weren't an old woman."

Her answering chuckle was low, throaty . . . and holy shit, *projected*. It bounced off the walls, such that even my trained ear couldn't pinpoint her location. She'd had vocal training.

And apparently a knack for showmanship; Lady Gray waited until my slow rotation had brought me back around to face the proper way such that when she suddenly appeared, it was right in front of me, framed by the door of the brothel. Surrounded by the bloody carnage that minutes ago had been one of her gangs, with my fully intact forces at my back.

The way she projected confidence in a situation that *should* have placed her at a massive disadvantage was downright inspiring. This woman was almost . . . Hell, she *was* in my league. I wondered if she'd had some kind of stage experience before turning to crime.

Her hand was still on the heavy dagger sheathed at her belt, the glow around it telling me that was a *powerful* artifact indeed.

Lady Gray was a woman in her fifties, at a guess, with a brown lowborn face, slightly lined, and black hair dusted with silver. Her knee-length coat was charcoal gray and there were plates of bloodred akornin stitched onto her heavy leather boots and gloves.

The criminal leader of the Gutters, and architect of so many of my problems, eyed me insolently up and down, in exactly the way I'd done to others recently, and was visibly unimpressed.

"I'll give you this much credit, boy," she said, thumb subtly caressing the pommel of her artifact dagger, "you have caused me more pain in the ass than I think any *three* other idiots who've tried to make a play for what's mine. And that's *really* unfortunate, you see. Because after the mess you've made, now I have to waste even more time and resources creating such a monument of your suffering that nobody even *dreams* about pissing me off to this degree again. I am going to disassemble your entire life like a clockwork mechanism and replace each individual piece with a new flavor of anguish, handcrafted to the specifications that will hurt you most. As if I don't have anything *better* to do! Perhaps that'll bring you some comfort when you're kneeling alone in the ruins of what used to be your existence, cursed by the memory of everyone you ever cared about. You, out of all the other jumped-up little shits, warranted that much of my attention. Good job, Healer."

I raised my hands and slapped them together. Then again, and again, slowly, filling the room with the echoes of sarcastic applause.

"Wow," I drawled, "what a beautiful speech. I had one prepared, too, but now that I've met you? I think I'm gonna save it to use on somebody actually impressive. **Immolate**."

Lady Gray held my gaze, and a smug grin languorously stretched across her features. She adjusted the position of her feet and flexed her fingers on the handle of her dagger, visibly in control and very much not on fire.

"I'm sorry, *boy*, did you just say something? You'll have to speak up. I'm just an old lady, you know."

Ah, shit.

48

In Which the Dark Lord Takes a Leap of Faith

For once, I didn't waste time shooting off my mouth, not when I had better things to shoot.

Slimeshot!

I was focused right on Lady Gray's grinning face with my hand still extended from trying to cast Immolate, but the slime did not emerge. In fact, the spell did nothing; there was no sensation of the magic activating at all. Its familiar weight remained there in my mind, but it wouldn't fire. As if I were trying to use it on an invalid target, like casting Heal on a brick.

I zeroed my focus onto her left eye and switched spells, activating Heat Beam at its narrowest intensity, which should have fried her cornea. It also failed to activate. Complete no sell.

The whole process took no more than a couple of seconds, but they were seconds passing in silence, during which I stood pointing at the woman and clearly accomplishing nothing, all in front of an audience. Lady Gray's smug little grin widened another fraction.

"All right, that's a neat trick," I finally admitted. "You should just stick to that instead of trying to make speeches."

She had the temerity to wink at me. "Wait'll you see my next one."

With her hand already on the handle of the dagger, she only had to flex her arm to yank it from the sheath, activating its invisibility effect.

"Boss! Sparkspray!" Biribo hissed in my ear, and then I was somewhat distracted by a blow to the chest toppling me backward. Even as I was falling, the knife sank into my gut and ripped out sideways, a sadistic and truly lethal wound to anyone who couldn't cast Heal, which I did before I hit the ground.

I tried to roll the way Goose had taught me, and somehow my recovery put me directly into the path of a vicious kick. Almost as if she had anticipated that move before I even made it and positioned herself accordingly. Invisibility aside, it turned out that my few weeks of practice at hand-to-hand fighting were not going to make me a match for somebody who'd been doing it for longer than I'd been alive.

However, even as the air was driven from my chest, the direction from which the kick came told me where my opponent was, and I didn't need to breathe to cast.

Sparkspray!

I had the satisfaction of hearing Lady Gray yelp in annoyed surprise as the burst of sparks momentarily revealed her invisible shape in their midst, raising one arm to protect her eyes. As an even more useful side effect of showering someone in sparks, a few landed on her clothes and continued to smolder, giving away her position for seconds longer.

And fortunately, I wasn't in this alone.

A crossbow bolt impacted her midsection. It didn't penetrate far—yeah, that coat was definitely armored underneath—and she didn't act injured, just grabbing the thing and ripping it loose with no evidence of blood, but even that just served to reveal where she was. Crossbows twanged and four more bolts ripped at her—two clean misses, another glancing hit off an armor panel in her coat, and the fourth sinking into her arm. She stayed invisible, but weirdly enough, the blood welling along the bolt itself came into view.

"It's a targeting blocker!" Biribo hissed. "Area-of-effect spells should still work!"

I rose back to my knees as Lady Gray ripped the bolt out of her arm and retreated. She threw it to the side, and undoubtedly was going to run in a different direction to throw off detection, but luckily *my* next trick didn't need to be precisely aimed.

Windburst!

A table was knocked over, chairs tossed to the side, and something invisible sprayed droplets of blood as it was flung across the room, and straight through the front windows with a crash of shattering glass and thin akorshil blinds.

"Oh, for fuck's sake!" Gannit shouted. "When I said you could make a mess, I didn't mean bust up the entire place!"

"Thousand pardons," I wheezed, straightening up painfully, "I'll try to get murdered more discreetly next time. **Heal**. Now if you'll excuse me, that woman is still alive and in not nearly enough pain; two errors I intend to correct."

"Why didn't you just set her on fire?" Adelly demanded.

"Because it seems she is immune to magic," I growled, "at least up to a point. Wide-range spells connected with her, but nothing aimed *at* her would even activate. Biribo, is it another property of that dagger?"

"No, all the dagger has is invisibility," he reported. "She must have another artifact hidden under all those clothes; I can't analyze what I can't see. But I *can* tell you that based on the strength of her Blessing of Might and how powerful that dagger is and her spell-blocker *has* to be, she hasn't got the energy left to wear another artifact. Just the two."

Oh, was that all.

"You wanna tell me why you got a second squeaky voice inside your hood, there?" Gannit inquired.

"Lady Gray's probably got several other artifacts lying around," said Sakin. "She chose this loadout to deal with a powerful sorcerer."

"It was a good choice," I had to admit. I was carefully watching the door and windows for any signs of movement, not that anything would stop her from circling invisibly around and coming in through another entrance. "I'm not sure how to fight that, exactly, but I can't afford to get pinned down or go on the defensive. She's probably already tearing into the girls elsewhere on the street. Everybody with me; if you get stabbed, try to make a noise. As long as I can see you, I can heal you."

"Hang on!" Aster caught my arm as I started toward the door. "Remember to grab that guy's boots. You'll need every possible advantage out there."

"Oh. Good point. Okay, everybody circle up while I loot this corpse and change my shoes, and *then* we'll go kill the invisible assassin. And on that note, fuck me running, why is this my life?"

It was quick enough to get the boots off the dead guy and onto me, ignoring Gannit's cackling. Every second I wasn't repeatedly slamming Lady Gray into a wall with Windburst until her skull squelched like a watermelon was a second in which I could feel the rage rising higher up the back of my throat as if it wanted to choke me.

It was already fairly obvious just from the sounds we could hear, but stepping out the front door of the Jostled Jugs immediately confirmed that all hell was breaking loose out on the street.

There were sounds of fighting, shouts and screams and impacts, and little sign of the people who would normally be about Yrshith Street at night.

No doubt many of them had been driven off by the last few days of thugs terrorizing the whole area, but the few customers and pedestrians who might have ventured here were probably down to the three people I saw fleeing into nearby alleys. I couldn't exactly see who was fighting whom, thanks to the sizable knot of men and a few women with swords and clubs coming up the street at me; they filled the available space, denying me a view of what was going on behind them.

Not that there was much question.

I stepped off the Jugs's front walkway and into the street. Smooth and unhurried, despite the seething cocktail of adrenaline and anger buzzing in all my limbs. I could ride that sensation, channel it into my performance as I'd learned to on countless stages. Aster stepped down after me, bringing her huge sword up in a broad gesture to rest its blunt edge across her shoulders. Behind us, the people I'd brought with me fanned out to cover the front of the Jugs, bouncers with clubs taking the front, ex-Alley Cats aiming crossbows through the gaps between them, as Sakin had coached us.

More goons were coming from the other side—the side toward which I'd sent my "traitors." There were fewer than from the other side, and now that I looked . . . yes, I picked out familiar faces among the ranks closing in. Positioned to cut down their former fellows as I'd ordered, or having brought them to kill me? The next moments would tell.

No sign of Lady Gray. She was here, though. That one wouldn't just be watching for an opening; she would be working to *make* one.

Both ranks of thugs slowed as they approached, weapons upraised, but none coming within a few paces of us, not close enough for Aster's sword to swing into them. Despite the sounds of violence from all around, a momentary stillness fell.

I looked straight across from the Jugs, where the Alley Cat, Minifrit's proud center of the blue-light district, stood open and empty. All its windows shattered and its door torn off, the blue lantern reduced to shards of glass in the street. All the work she'd put in, not only surviving but finding a way to *thrive* in this filthy, squalid hole, smashed just to make a point.

The rage in me *sang*.

Several of the front ranks of thugs jumped when I burst out laughing. I spread my arms, turning in a full circle to embrace all of Cat Alley and those within.

"Figured it out, haven't you? That's right—*somebody* has to be first. Well? Let's see the brave volunteers step forward! Who's in a hurry to die tonight?"

They hesitated. Shuffling their feet and glancing at once another with wide eyes. A few actually tried to back up into their comrades.

I sighed heavily, shaking my head in a broad pantomime of disappointment. "Really? Must I start the festivities myself?"

Then, to my right, one woman smoothly reversed the grip on the dagger she held in her left hand and plunged it backward into the throat of the man next to her. On that signal, more followed suit, swiftly cutting down their unprepared cohorts. That was the side of the street with significantly fewer people to begin with; in seconds, there were only nine of them, standing with bloodied weapons.

"Oh, Craed, you *cocksucker*," spat one of the men to my left.

"Nothin' personal, Cwyndon," Craed said with a shrug. "Business is business."

"Don't speak for us," Khadret sneered. "This is personal as *hell*. Ask Gray why, if any of you survive the night."

Whether on purpose or in a panicked twitch, one of them fired a crossbow at me. The bolt went clean through my forearm; I felt my hand go slack as a tendon was severed. Rage spiked in me so brilliantly I felt sure I would combust.

I grabbed the bolt by its pointed head and ripped it the rest of the way through, then tossed it to the street.

Heal.

"You," I said, pointing my freshly restored hand at a weaselly-looking man now holding an unloaded crossbow. "I want you to know I *respect* you for that. When you get to hell, tell Virya I said so. **Immolate**."

Up he went, in fire and agony, and the brawl began. It *had* to; their options were to attack or wait to be slaughtered. With a unified roar they charged, and made it maybe four steps closer before even the sheer weight of the bodies behind them couldn't stand up against the onslaught of magic they plowed into.

Windburst, Slimeshot, Slimeshot, Windburst, Slimeshot, Windburst, Immolate, Sparkspray, Sparkspray, Slimeshot, Immolate, Slimeshot, Immolate, Slimeshot, Slimeshot, Immolate, Immolate.

The thugs' charge broke five seconds after it began; they had actually *lost* ground, hurled backward by multiple Windbursts. More than half of them were down—dead, maimed, or burning.

I was not dealing with hardened troops here. Those who could still stand up now bravely charged in the opposite direction.

"Is that all?" I roared, stalking toward them with my arms stretched wide. Fallen men, those not screaming as they burned alive, tried to scrabble backward from my approach. "You boys do so enjoy picking on the weak.

This is your own game, played better than you've ever seen it! Are we not *enjoying* ourselves? Can't you at least appreciate the superior technique?"

Somebody summoned up the courage or sheer panic to charge at me with an animal scream, sword upraised to swing. He died of a slime to the face at bullet speed.

Then Aster jabbed me in the back with the pommel of her greatsword.

"Stop having fun," she growled.

I half-turned from the scene of carnage to stare incredulously at her.

Aster met my gaze, shifting her eyes only momentarily to nod at the display of destruction I'd just spread across Yrshith Street. "Those are human beings," she said in a voice low enough not to be audible beyond the two of us. "They've made some shitty choices, but they chose from the same hand of shitty options as the people we came here to save. Kill who you have to, but they aren't *toys*. You know who thinks all this is a game, and what she's trying to turn *you* into. Are you going to make it that easy for her?"

Well, that was a bucket of ice water down the pants.

For a second there I'd felt on the verge of lashing out at her, but staring into Aster's golden eyes, I felt the anger starting to melt from me. Part of me didn't want to let it go, even as I recognized this was for the best. Far from raining on my parade, I recognized that Aster had thrown me a lifeline. I might well be unable to stave off the effects that life on Ephemera and the things I had to do were having on me, but I could always remember that my becoming a cackling villain was exactly what Virya wanted. For that reason alone, I would fall no further than I had to.

I'm Omura Seiji, damn it, and what I can't do through strength or cleverness alone, I can accomplish out of *sheer fucking spite*.

I breathed in and out a couple of times, then nodded once at Aster, turning back to regard the mess I'd made with fresh eyes. The street was awash in blood and slimes; no one else was offering to attack me. The men I'd Immolated were flickering out; a couple lay on the pavement in sobbing fetal balls, but the rest of the injured and traumatized were trying to retreat, some crawling on their bellies.

Looking at this now, I couldn't find it in me to be pleased with myself. I hadn't *won* this, hadn't earned the victory. All I'd done was unleash unearned power they had no chance of matching. I might as well have mowed down these medieval peasants with an AK-47 for how honorable it was.

Funny how honor can seem like a silly, antiquated concept until you catch yourself being a despicable little shit.

"Thanks, Aster," I said quietly. "I don't like to think what I'd do without you."

Coming to stand beside me, she nodded once.

"And yet," I mused, "still don't wanna bang you."

I'm Omura Seiji, damn it. When I feel awkward or off-balance, I talk shit.

Her nostrils flared in a silent snort of annoyance. "I really appreciate how you keep bringing that up."

"It's *weird* if you think about it! You are objectively the whole package. You're gonna make some poor henpecked bastard very happy someday. Or at least . . . resigned."

"Remind me to ask Sakin if he wants any help when he inevitably betrays you."

"My current theory is he never will, just for the fun of watching me welter in the anticipation."

Above us, on the roof of the Alley Cat, a figure in a dark coat rose up.

"There she is!" someone shouted, and multiple crossbows were discharged. On the rooftops it was darker than down here among the lamps, and the figure itself was dark gray, but even in the dimness, I recognized that coat. The dimness successfully disguised its unnatural motion until it was too late. Crossbow bolts tore around, past, and into it, and then the coat fell . . .

Lady Gray stood up on the lip of the roof, catching her coat as it descended from the upward trajectory on which she'd thrown it. A few crossbow bolts stuck through it at odd angles, which didn't seem to bother her as she deftly swirled it around her shoulders, slipping her arms into the sleeves and letting it settle over her from that one dramatic swish, which was too impressive *not* to have been practiced. It looked like something out of an anime. Even the bolts still dangling from it looked more like trophies from fallen enemies than evidence she'd been shot at, and the difference was purely in the assertive confidence with which she held herself.

Damn, this woman understood the power of *presentation*. I was forced to respect that about her, which annoyed me to no end.

Presentation and tactics, I mentally amended. Now my trigger-happy followers all had unloaded crossbows, which would take an all-important few seconds to rectify. Turning the cranks on those things was easier than drawing a bowstring, but not nearly as quick.

Lady Gray raised her fingers to her lips and let out a piercing whistle which echoed over the street, then planted one boot on the lip of the roof and leaned over to smirk down at us.

"So it's personal, is it, Khadret? I will remember that."

At her signal, her men were regrouping. Nobody from behind Craed and Khadret's gangs, I saw; they had clearly done their work well. But on the other side, boots pounded as men streamed forward in groups of anywhere from two to ten. Clearly *most* of Gray's organization was out to play tonight, and now they came pouring in from whatever cruel mischief they'd been up to among the brothels down that way. Looking at the imbalance, I surmised my new recruits had engaged in some clever misdirection to divert everybody from their end of the street. There was no way they could've killed this many people alone, not without being caught and overwhelmed.

And now we were being swamped with fresh enemies.

Wait . . . not *that* fresh.

Lots of them were limping, bleeding, bruised, holding dangling arms. A couple of guys had singed clothing.

And behind them came women. Armed with weapons as makeshift as they were utterly vicious—chair legs covered in broken glass, mop handles with kitchen knives affixed to their ends to make improvised polearms, large pot lids bristling with nails. *Lots* of them dripping with blood. These women hadn't just impetuously grabbed objects and started hitting back; they had prepared and *planned* for this.

Somehow it was made all the more dramatic by the fact that they were armored only in the traditional uniform of sex workers everywhere, short and strategically slitted dresses that showed off a lot of chest and leg. Many of them were also limping, bloodied, and beaten, but they came anyway, making another line behind Gray's thugs, or so I could briefly see before the men closer at hand blocked off my view down the street with their own bodies again.

"Well, blow me down," I muttered.

Behind me, Gannit leaned out of the broken front window of her brothel and cackled. "Oh, did you think you were the only game in town, Mister Big Scary Healer? You didn't *teach* these girls to stick up for themselves; you just reminded 'em it was on the table. Don't nobody need your permission to knife a bastard!"

"Unbelievable," Gray said from the roof, her tone dripping with sheer disgust. "By Sanora's *tits*, why do I even pay you clods? Men, *slaughter those whores!*"

I inhaled deeply, raised my head, and projected from the diaphragm as powerfully as I physically could, which was a lot.

"WHORES, SLAUGHTER THOSE MEN!"

Lady Gray's men obeyed, charging both backward at the prostitutes and forward at Aster and myself, but they did so in grim silence. From behind them came a furious roar of female voices before the clashing of weapons resumed.

I felt that roar ignite the fury in me again, but differently this time. Just as angry, but now there was something else in it. Something strangely optimistic.

Aster stepped past me, swinging her greatsword in a broad horizontal arc that felled three men who were trying to rush us. Behind her, I knelt and picked up a curved sword of striated green akornin from beside a corpse I'd recently made. Straightening, looted blade in hand, I looked up at Lady Gray, who was still looming over the roof like a gargoyle.

Meeting my gaze, she grinned. Secure in her vantage point.

I stretched out my hand toward the pavement at my feet.

Windburst!

Immediately I realized why nobody had mentioned this possibility to me; local sorcerers doubtless had better sense than to do it.

Yes, you *can* fling yourself three stories straight up by directing a gale-force blast of air at the ground right under yourself, but it won't be with anything resembling a controlled trajectory. I went tumbling ass-over-hairdo into the sky, utterly disoriented and suddenly violently dizzy. My aim had been good enough; I did appear to be arcing in the right direction, and indeed I came plummeting back down right onto the roof of the Alley Cat, getting a good look at Lady Gray's startled expression as I descended.

This would ordinarily be the part where I smashed through the shingles in a mess of broken roofing and my own blood, but now there came the catch—all those sorcerers who had better sense than to try this would be Blessed with Magic—and therefore, by definition, not wearing Surestep Boots.

Despite the graceless tumble that had brought me there, I landed with my feet under me like a cat. My boots hit the slope of the roof, my legs flexed with perfect balance, and I turned the remaining momentum of my fall into a controlled slide. Straight down the slant of the roof until I shifted my footing at the last moment, regaining traction and coming to a stop at the very edge, right in front of Lady Gray.

I had the distinct pleasure of seeing her look shocked.

Below us, the roar of battle echoed from Yrshith Street as her forces and mine tore Cat Alley apart. I didn't spare it a glance, raising my sword to point at her.

"*Have you paid the price?*"

49

In Which the Dark Lord Shows a Lady a Good Time

Lady Gray did not have the courtesy to acknowledge or react to my catch-phrase. Her face was half in shadow due to the night's darkness, but in the blue and orange lights of Cat Alley below us, I saw her eyebrows draw together in confusion as her eyes flicked down to examine my feet.

Then her expression flashed in a handful of instants through realization, shock, dread, and then the blank neutrality of self-control followed by a sly little smile, which I now knew she was using as a facade.

Ah, right. She was Blessed with Might, able to see the glow around the artifact boots—and also frustratingly intelligent. I probably should've expected she would put it together.

"So that's how it is," she murmured, and grabbed the hilt of her dagger.

This time I was abuzz with adrenaline and on high alert; even as she vanished, I was pointing and casting.

Light Beam, **Sparkspray**!

And then a more prosaic incantation I decided to call Cut a Bitch.

Blinded by the flash of light and taking a burst of sparks right to the face, she lost control of her charge at me, having to cover her eyes with both arms and veering off target. Even with the sparks lingering on her clothes, she was still functionally invisible, and I wasn't nearly good enough in hand-to-hand combat to strike such a vague target with any precision. Thus, I went for a wide slash rather than the efficient stab Goose had taught me, which would have done much more damage. The cut wouldn't mess her up as much, but at least it was more likely to *hit* something.

Specifically, it raked across her upraised forearms, slicing the fabric of her coat to reveal the akornin-backed bracers underneath.

Lady Gray hopped backward out of my range, and then, to my surprise, resheathed her dagger.

She stood there fully visible, hand on the hilt, semicrouched and ready to strike again, staring at me through narrowed eyes as if watching for an opportunity. I stared back, sword at the ready, hoping my own stance didn't reveal my ineptitude too badly. Goose and Sakin both said I was shaping up well for an amateur, but there was no question I was nowhere near Gray's league.

Why didn't she stay invisible? Why sacrifice her major advantage? Well, it gave me a moment to consider my options. I was limited to nontargeted spells . . . A wide-focus Light Beam would blind her, and Sparkspray did little damage but had utility in both disrupting her actions and revealing her position. Windburst would launch her clear off the roof and *over* the next brothel at this range, and I formed the spell in my mind before thinking better of it.

Then somebody shot me in the side with a crossbow.

I ripped the bolt out, cast Heal, shifted my head to see who had done it, and then saw Gray vanish again.

I hit her with another Sparkspray, and this time she kept circling around me, ignoring the sparks lingering on her coat, even as I kept casting it at her. Despite the heat and the burst of air pushing at her, she darted up the roof behind us, regaining the high ground, and only then did I understand her strategy as I was shot in the back, twice.

Members of both our factions were shooting at the pair of us now; she'd stayed visible to goad them, then angled her position to be both farther out of range and to use *me* as a shield. And then she'd be invisible again.

And now I was also shot. One had been a glancing hit, but I now had a bolt lodged right in what felt like my kidney, which was a debilitating level of pain I'd never imagined. I couldn't even cast Heal without removing the bolt; sealing it in there would put me out of this fight and require actual surgery to fix.

This was exhausting. It was *insufferable*. I had enough power at my fingertips to massacre an entire street full of enemies, and I was *losing* here, because I was dealing with someone who was just . . . better. Smarter, faster, more prepared, more experienced, *better*.

Fuck it, **Windburst**.

I knew that was going to cause me bigger problems in the near future, but Gray had won this round; I desperately needed to gain some distance, and so I sent her spark-spangled shape tumbling the entire rest of the way up the roof and over its peak. Then I threw myself forward and flat against the shingles to minimize my target profile.

If not for the constant buzz of rage and adrenaline, I'm not sure I would have been able to yank that bolt out of my back. It came free with a *tearing* sensation that made all my primitive self-preservation instincts scream in alarm, but once it was out a quick Heal fixed everything. At least it was in my lower back and *reachable*. If it had been behind my shoulder, I might've been screwed.

"Biribo! No more time for subtlety. *Find her.*"

He clawed his way free and buzzed out into the air, darting back and forth in front of me for a moment as if trying to catch a scent. Behind and below me, all was noise, screams, crashes, and the chaos of battle. People were bleeding and dying down there—*my* people, those I'd brought and those I'd come to help. If Gray had given me the slip, I was going to drop right off the roof and start Healing—

"She landed on the other side of the roof, boss!" Biribo reported. "Just went visible again; she needed her hands off the knife to get something from her pocket, I think. Boss, we got other problems—five people Blessed with Might coming at us over the roofs to the right!"

Fucking hell, of *course* she had an ambush prepared. If she was planning to corner the Healer and it didn't go perfectly on the first strike, bring in a squad of her heavy-hitters to finish him off. And getting something from her pockets? In the last few weeks I'd learned enough about the capabilities of goblin alchemy that I did *not* like the sound of that.

I made a snap decision, rolled to my feet, and charged up the roof. It was steep enough to make this difficult and unwise, but my Surestep Boots won out over mere physics and I crested the peak in seconds with no trouble, throwing myself down the other side in a slide that sent me sliding down the slope right at Lady Gray.

Too late. She was just discarding a tiny bottle over the edge, and now jumped back from me again, grabbing at her dagger.

"She's chugging healing potions," Biribo said. In the dimness, Gray directed a piercing look at him before focusing back on me; she did not look surprised by the flying, talking lizard. Yeah, she'd already figured me out, clearly.

"Potions," I sneered. "How quaint." Actually, this highlighted a blind spot in my knowledge; I had no idea how available and/or effective those were, since my own magic made them redundant. It did explain why she had been so spry after being shot in the arm and then flung right through a glass window.

"No!" Gray suddenly shouted, pointing at me—no, past me. "Back off! He's mine!"

I risked repositioning myself so I could see both her and what was behind me peripherally. There were the five people Biribo had predicted, coming to a stop at the edge of the next rooftop over at Lady Gray's command. I could see the visible glow of artifacts around three of them. Why would she—

Of course. Blessed with Might to counter a Blessed with Wisdom. But she'd planned that before realizing she was dealing with somebody who could not only kill her heavy-hitters, but then *take* their artifacts—and unlike most people whose Blessings were of limited strength, *use them all at once.*

Lady Gray had practically ordered me a buffet.

I gave her a cheeky grin, then turned and dashed right at the confused Blessed on the other rooftop.

"No you don't!" she snarled, lunging after me and pulling out her dagger.

Thanks to the Surestep Boots, it was child's play to spin completely around while running; thanks to Gray's own agility and speed, when I fired off the Sparkspray behind me, it hit her right in the face at point-blank range. She went down, invisible but smoldering and coughing.

Immolate, Slimeshot, Immolate, Slimeshot!

Casting mentally as I ran, I managed to take down four of the Blessed hit squad before I reached the edge of the roof. The last one remaining was holding an artifact sword and seemed to be of pretty stern stuff; he didn't react to the burning and screaming of two of his friends, retaining the presence of mind to step forward with his weapon upraised and deliver a lethal blow even as I lunged across the alley at him.

With me in midair, there was really no way to avoid it. Thanks to my own artifact, the tip of his sword wavered and he missed my heart. The blade punched right into my chest just below it, my own momentum carrying me all the way down it until the cross hilt was pressed against my ribs.

He grinned at me in malicious triumph from centimeters away, at least until I dropped my own sword and reached out to grab his face with my right hand. My fingers closed across his mouth, leaving his eyes to bulge in incredulous outrage at this.

"Thanks for the sword," I wheezed around the blood filling my lung. **"Slimeshot."**

I'd never fired one at that range before. It took his head entirely *off.* Blood fountained from torn arteries, splattering me, and his twitching corpse fell, losing its grip on the hilt of the rapier now embedded in me. Thanks to my boots, I stepped adroitly aside and let it tumble off the edge of the roof without tripping me up.

Incredibly, I had an urge to giggle which I barely managed to repress. Cool, so we were past bloodlust and into straight up hysteria now. A person could almost infer that constant stress and brutal violence was bad for one's mental health or something.

I grabbed the rapier's hilt and pulled it out of my body, which was a little challenging as it was almost the whole way in, and the long, straight blade exceeded the reach of my arm; I had to yank the last few centimeters sideways, cutting more deeply into my own flesh. Oh well, not that it mattered.

Heal.

"Ooh, *nice* find!" Biribo crowed. "Rapier of Mastery! That's the same kind Lady Flaethwyn had."

Two of the others were still burning, and one was dead with the artifact glow around his shirt, which would've taken way too long to drag off him right now. The last had fallen off the roof, so I didn't know if the Slimeshot had killed her—or if the fall had—but she'd dropped her artifact staff and it had rolled to rest in the rain gutter.

Nah, no matter what the staff did, there was no way I could wield one of those *and* a sword. And I *liked* this sword.

I turned to find Lady Gray having recovered during the scant few seconds all this had taken, but she'd come to a stop on the other roof, staring at the sight of me—a dangerous spellcaster, now armed with an artifact weapon that closed the gap between our levels of martial skill, not to mention boots that gave me even better footing on the treacherous rooftops than *she* had.

Sensibly, she turned and dashed in the opposite direction.

"No, you *don't!*"

I turned, took the two steps to the steep slope of the roof I was on—steeper than that of Minifrit's place, nearly vertical—and pressed my left hand against it.

Windburst.

The blast sent me rocketing backward across the alley gap; there wasn't even a chance for me to get my fancy magic boots under me before my back impacted the Alley Cat's shingles and my momentum was translated into a brutal sideways slide along the slope.

With no credit to my own agility, the trajectory on which I found myself helplessly careening nailed Lady Gray dead-on as she tried to escape. My body swept her legs out from under her in passing, the impact slowing me enough to plant my boots and drag myself to a stop. I couldn't see what it had done to her for another few precious seconds until I could drag myself upright, Heal the damage of that landing, and turn to look. At least I managed to keep a grip on my shiny new rapier, and not impale myself on it.

In those few seconds, Gray had managed to right herself, turn, and run back the way I had come. I didn't realize what had just happened until she was vaulting across the alley to the other roof, where two of her compatriots were just now beginning to fizzle out. I didn't put together *why* until she reached down and grabbed the artifact staff, which had apparently been sheltered enough by the depth of the gutter that Windburst hadn't sent it flying.

Ugh, of fucking course. No wonder she hadn't gone invisible; she'd wanted me to see what she was doing, *so she could bait me.* Hell, she might've even anticipated I'd repeat my Windburst launch trick, which I'd thought was so clever.

I really needed less competent enemies.

Lady Gray vaulted back to the Cat's roof, and I moved to intercept her. She angled herself sideways, forcing me to follow, and bringing us both over the edge of the slope back to the side facing Cat Alley.

It sounded like a real mess down there, but I didn't have time to focus on it, because Lady Gray suddenly stopped, whirled, and one end of the staff flashed right at my face.

Artifact-given instinct took over; I flowed into stance, whipping up the rapier to parry it. The sword was light and the staff capable of delivering heavy blows, so I caught and deflected it near the base of the blade where I had the most leverage. Even if I hadn't learned fencing the proper way, I understood that much.

I was less prepared for the fountain of sparks and miniature arcs of lightning, which flashed between our weapons when they connected. So *that* was what the staff's enchantment did. A jolt of electricity like that would stun anybody it struck—or if they were small or had a heart condition, possibly kill them. Luckily my new artifact sword was an Ephemeral classic, crafted of akornin. Had it been a metal blade, that would've fried me.

Having lunged forward for that deflection, I was within range to go for a killing stab, which I did before I could even think about it. Gray had a two-handed grip on the staff, though, and could reverse it much faster, so she managed to deflect my strike with another flash and fountain of sparks.

She forced me back; I fired a Sparkspray at her and lunged in again. She deflected, I parried, stabbed, dodged, took advantage of a feint to lunge at her midsection. She parried that . . .

We danced along the roof's edge, blade and staff flicking and crashing against each other, surrounded by the flash and sparkle of the lightning enchantment and my own spells. Apparently matched. I was running on the power of three artifacts and augmented by spells and she was *holding me off*. No wonder this woman had been giving me such a hard time. She was way out of my league.

Biribo dived in to grab the edge of my hood so he could speak right into my ear, low enough that Gray couldn't overhear him.

"Boss, her Blessing isn't strong enough to run all three of those artifacts at the same time! She's stuck visible unless she gives up the staff; if she draws that dagger, all three will lose most of their power."

Good to know, though I couldn't spare the focus at that moment to reply to him. I had barely enough spare room in my head to wonder why she was engaging me in a duel; in her position, I'd have relied on the invisibility dagger to try to put a quick end to this. She probably knew something I didn't, as usual.

At least nobody was shooting at us now. Most likely they were all occupied shooting each other. I didn't dare take my eyes off Lady Gray to check.

No sooner had I thought that than she bounded back, holding the staff forward to enforce distance between us, and suddenly an object soared through the spot where she'd been standing. It shattered against the shingles, splattering foul-smelling sludge.

Someone had just thrown a *chamber pot* at Lady Gray.

Being mutually out of the range of each other's weapons, we both turned to look incredulously across the street.

In an upstairs window of the Jostled Jugs, Gannit let out a braying cackle, turned, bent over, and waggled her bony old ass at Gray.

"You have to realize there's no way you can *actually* win here," Gray called at me, shifting sideways up the slope of the Cat's roof. I kept pace with her, rapier extended to point at her heart while she held the quarterstaff in a defensive position. What was her angle? She *appeared* to be moving us onto terrain which would favor me in my artifact boots, which meant something else was going on here. "Your best-case scenario is . . . what? Liberate all the whores? Trust me, boy, the next thing you'll learn is exactly how far gratitude will get you. There's no loyalty to be had from people like that."

"Ah yes, that must be right," I said sagely. "You've never managed to inspire loyalty in anyone; therefore it can't be done."

Lady Gray laughed, loudly and bitterly. "I have seen and done more than you know, you arrogant brat. Loyalty? Oh, I know loyalty. It lasts until someone has an empty belly, or a splinter. There's *nothing* to be gained by gathering Gutter trash under your banner. I don't know if you've got some grand dream of raising up the downtrodden classes to overthrow the unjust rule of the clans or what, but did you ever stop to think they might be downtrodden for a reason? Those cretins will shatter the second they have to face off with real soldiers. They're all just people, and in the end . . . people are selfish, craven, greedy, and *stupid*. I could almost wish you victory here, just so you'll be doomed to deal with herding these witless fucking *livestock* until you've learned how badly Sanora fucked you over by bringing you here."

She had stopped moving, keeping the distance of two rapier lengths between us. Now, as her little speech paused, I let my outstretched blade fall to my side. Lady Gray narrowed her eyes suspiciously, bracing her feet but not yet trying to take advantage of the opening. She smelled a trap.

"You're doing it wrong."

"I beg your pardon?" she replied dryly. "Do correct me, I'm sure this will be fascinating."

"I can't put my finger on how, exactly, but . . . that's all wrong. It's all *true*, but for some reason when you say it, it just sounds . . . pathetic, and gross."

"Awww." Gray's mouth twisted in a grin that was more than half a sneer. "Poor little Hero. Have your sterling ideals been challenged by the sight of life in the Gutters? Get used to it, boy. It's all downhill from here. If you think *I'm* bad, wait till the Viryans start—"

She had to break off, to her visible annoyance, when I burst out laughing.

"Ahh, *so* close!" I congratulated her. "Really, I'm impressed you put it together—nobody else has had the wits to do it so fast. But it's funny, my dear Lady Gray, how even the cleverest person can be so very wrong. Shall I enlighten you as to your one teensy little mistake?"

With the rapier still pointed harmlessly down at my side, I stepped toward her. Gray backed up, staff at the ready, clearly unsure what I was up to. While I passively pushed her back with my mere presence, I reached up with my free hand and lowered my hood, just so she could see me grin, and wink.

"*I am not the Hero.*"

I stopped, smiling a wolf's smile, and watched the composure drain from her face as the final realization set in.

"I'll tell you what," I said, after giving that a moment to settle. "Despite the enormous pain in my ass you've been, *Lady Gray*, mine is a game of organization building, not monster-slaying. As skilled a character as you are, you're a lot more valuable serving me than bleeding to death in some alley—as satisfying as that would be to watch. What do you say? It'll be *difficult*, given how much hatred you've earned from . . . well, basically everyone. I'll have to do quite a bit of damage control and persuasion to keep everybody happy with having you on the team. But I think I have enough credibility to pull it off, and you just might be worth the effort."

I spread my arms wide, rapier pointed harmlessly at empty space, smiling magnanimously.

"All you'll have to do is *kneel before the Dark Lord.*"

We stared each other down, the night wind tugging at us and the noise of battle still drifting up from the street, though even that was starting to peter out. When she answered, it was quietly enough I almost had trouble hearing.

"Really, now, Seiji. After all the games we've played, you *can't* think I'm that stupid. My feelings are hurt."

"You've had a long and interesting life, I'll bet," I replied, just as softly. "It must be a great story. But you haven't begun to know what *hurt* is. Even if you die before I can teach you, you've placed yourself in Virya's way. By the time I see you in hell, you'll be ready to spend eternity licking my boots."

She bared her teeth at me, and suddenly threw the artifact staff. I instinctively caught it with my free hand; fortunately it seemed the enchantment only activated when someone holding it struck someone else, so my reflexes didn't get me electrocuted.

The momentary distraction was all she needed to reach into her pocket with one hand and grab her dagger with the other. I lunged forward with the rapier, even as Gray hopped nimbly backward and threw something to the ground between us. Whatever it was impacted the shingles with a sharp *pop* and a huge gout of acrid white smoke swelled up directly around me, thanks to my own forward momentum.

Coughing, I frantically backpedaled out of the worst of it. That stuff lingered heavily despite the breeze; I had to cast Windburst to get rid of it.

There was no telltale *thump* of a body being caught in the blast of wind, even as it effectively cleared the smoke away. She'd gone invisible, dodged to the side, and done who knows what to get out of there. Not a trace of her to be seen.

After all that, Lady Gray had managed to escape me. And that meant that this wasn't done with. Worse, she now knew exactly how cornered she was. As if she wasn't a dangerous enough animal to begin with.

I didn't even spare the time to curse, turning and dropping off the roof into what remained of the melee below. At least there was *something* to which I could put an end tonight.

50

In Which the Dark Lord Rises

It was easily my best landing so far, which wasn't much to brag about considering how many shingles I'd crashed through in the last few minutes. Thanks to the Surestep Boots, I hit the ground in a perfect roll and came up on my feet, neat as a professional stunt actor.

I landed in what was clearly the bedraggled end of a battle. The good news was that I could see at a glance we'd won. The bad news was . . . Looking around, I found myself questioning whether anybody ever "won" a battle. Bodies lay everywhere; blood splattered the street and the walls, the stench of it hung in the air, along with the fouler smell of excrement—evidence of human intestines having been slashed open.

For a span of three seconds, I stood there, paralyzed by the horror of the spectacle, and my own sudden feeling of helpless uncertainty about what I could *do*. The last of the armed men I could see were in the process of slipping away into various alleys. A vengeful corner of my mind wanted to shoot them in the back, war crimes be damned, but I didn't conjure a single Slimeshot.

Then Aster appeared from the crowd of bloodied women surrounding the space in front of the Alley Cat, her oversized sword held at her side dripping with blood.

Her appearance, and the small but visible sigh of relief she let out at the sight of me, made my brain snap back into focus. People were hurt, all around me. I *knew* what to do about that, it was my whole shtick.

Heal!

Pink light burst around a woman leaning weakly against a wall, clutching a bloody patch on her side. There were more all around; I held the spell in the forefront of my brain, casting as rapidly as I could focus my eyes on anybody.

Heal, Heal, Heal, Heal Heal Heal Heal HealHealHealHealHealHeal Heal . . .

My god, they were everywhere. I started walking forward to reach more, my pace rapidly increasing until I was at a near run, pausing only to check down alleys with a quick Light Beam and occasionally finding people in need.

Increasingly frantic, I didn't discriminate, trying to get everyone. Some of Lady Gray's fallen forces got a free Healing, and I didn't have time to begrudge them. Sometimes I would miss a beat when I tried to cast Heal on an unmoving woman, but the spell didn't react. You can't Heal the dead. Each time I pressed on. I *couldn't* stop to deal with that, not when my help was needed. Once I let myself really feel that guilt, there was no telling how long it'd be before I was any use to anyone again.

"If you're healed up and able to move, we need help!" Aster called aloud as she paced along at my side. "Check inside buildings and down alleys, look behind the brothels and don't forget the canals! Find the wounded who aren't out on the street! If they can be moved, bring them out here; if not, yell until we get to you. The Healer is working as fast as he can!"

It wasn't as bad as it could have been. As it *should* have been. These women had gone up against roughly their number in hardened thugs, unarmored and wielding nothing but improvised weapons and curses. I didn't see a single one uninjured; though they'd done surprisingly well, to judge by how many only had relatively minor wounds.

As I rushed from one end of the street to the other, the women organized around me, mostly centering on Gannit and some of the less successful madams and veteran sex workers who had some experience in herding their comrades into line. By the time Aster and I had made one breakneck triage circuit, more victims had been brought forward from the systematic search of the brothels. Only some of the fighting had spilled indoors, but there it had been bloodiest, usually amounting to one side cornering one or a few members of the other. The second pass was slower, though I kept my feet moving as rapidly as they could. We had to divert into the brothels, at which the search parties flagged me down, dashing to the rescue of women too badly mangled to make it outside. Several times Aster slipped on blood, trying to keep up with me, but my artifact boots kept me going.

I saw some truly horrible things in there. The really sick part, though, was that I didn't see anything worse than I'd encountered as a result of Cat Alley's business as usual. Just . . . a lot more of it, all at once.

Maybe that was why these women were able to stay active and quickly organize themselves; as far as I could tell, nobody was as close as I felt to breaking from the sheer stress of it. Seeing that, I pushed myself to keep going. If they could tough it out, so could I.

Our final route was the slowest, due to involving a lot of improvised surgery. A number of the women I had hastily Healed now had crossbow bolts, knives, and bits of glass sealed in their skin; those had to be cut out and Healed again. I was amazed at how little complaining resulted from this. Some had to bite down on strips of leather or wads of cloth, as they were carefully cut into, but nobody even blamed me. They were accustomed to pain around here.

During this last, ugliest phase, Madyn joined my side as designated surgeon. For as squeamish as she'd been back at the Jugs about killing that guy, she sure didn't shy away from blood or taking a blade to flesh. Well, good on her. At this point I could only envy someone who could still hold on to principles like that. A rotating circle of girls brought her water and pungent alcohol to repeatedly clean the kitchen knife she was using to cut debris out of victims' skin.

When I finished, it was sudden. I hadn't been looking ahead or trying to guess how close we were to the end. I just Healed the fresh wound Madyn had cut in a woman's arm to extract a crossbow bolt, looked for the next victim, and . . . there wasn't one.

Standing there, looking around to verify this, I found my view of the street wavering. What was . . . oh, I was actually swaying on my feet. That was odd. Oh well, the boots would . . .

"Okay, now it's your turn," Gannit ordered, taking my other arm. Aster had grabbed the left one, I blearily realized. She was probably the reason I hadn't fallen down. "Back to the Jugs; we gotta get some sustenance into you."

"I'm—"

"Boy, you know what's nice about you being able to heal literally anything?" the old madame said lightly as she led me away. "If you try to stand there and tell me you're fine, I get to smack you as hard as you deserve for once. It's damn well refreshing; most men are such delicate creatures. Now come on, you've done your job and several other people's tonight. Ahp! Shut it, I'm in no mood for backtalk. Left foot, right foot, there we go."

Turned out I didn't care for what they called blood tea. Whatever it was made from, it was deep crimson in color, with little shifting swirls of black particulate matter on top; fortunately, it was actually tea, the liquid not nearly as thick as blood, otherwise I wouldn't have been able to get it down after as much of the real thing as I'd seen tonight. Also, it had a deep bitter taste, which was compensated for by more of whatever the Fflyr put in their tea to make it spicy and sweet.

But whatever else it was, blood tea seemed to have at least as much caffeine as coffee. After two cups, a mug of water, and some crawn stew, I was improved from being as exhausted as I had ever been in my life to feeling . . . well, functional.

Gannit set me up in her common room, which seemed to be the new de facto administrative center of the whores' revolution. I was tucked away in a corner table being hovered over protectively by Aster, Sakin, Donon, Kastrin and Adelly. Gilder was holding court in another, brashly flirting with several women who had clearly chosen to find him amusing rather than offensive.

I made a mental note to have a talk with him about how to treat women, and then a second one to first have a talk with Minifrit about that because what the fuck did I know? Far from being proud that I wasn't as sexist as a bunch of the literal rapists I'd been dealing with recently, I was left with a lot of uncomfortable realizations about how I'd acted toward my girlfriends and other women I'd known back in Japan.

But that was an issue for another day.

Gannit was pooling together resources from the nearby brothels to make sure everybody got fed and hydrated, while the remaining sex workers and madams got people organized. For what purpose I didn't yet know; I was busy surviving my brush with exhaustion and an adrenaline crash, and was doing well to have gotten a meal and some tea into me without passing out or sobbing. Adrenaline, it turns out, is a hell of a drug, and the withdrawal's a bitch.

I did note from conversations I'd overheard that apparently there were few madams left on Cat Alley—just Gannit and a handful from the poorer brothels near the ends of the street. As it turned out, most of those who profited from the status quo had resisted any change to it, and their own workers turned on them when rebel furor swept Yrshith Street. A few of the madams who'd tried to throw in with Lady Gray had actually been lynched and dumped in the canals, after which the others from the richer brothels here in the center had fled or been chased out.

Just as I pushed away my empty bowl, Gannit stopped by my table, giving me a critical once-over. Nodding to herself in satisfaction that I was apparently replenished enough to be given shit, she prodded me aggressively with a ladle.

"You lied to me, boy."

"Did not." I was still tired and somewhat out of it, but that much I was sure of. I had been very careful to dissemble and deflect every time I was here, never saying anything to anyone that could be found untrue.

Gannit snorted and folded her arms. "Listen here, Spooky, I know the only reason you'd have wanted a pair of artifact boots, and I *saw* you pick up that swishy little sword you've got, and suddenly you didn't suck at fighting anymore. Not to mention *that* fuckin' thing," she added, jabbing the ladle at Biribo, who swooped out of range. He hadn't bothered hiding again after my rooftop duel with Lady Gray. "Just cos I've never seen a familiar in person doesn't mean I dunno what one is, and I ain't enough of a hick not to know what it *means* when someone obviously has all three Blessings."

"Mm." I took another sip of my third cup of blood tea, grimacing at the taste. "And?"

"And, you *told* me right to my face that you're not the Hero. Remember?"

I shrugged and sipped again, too weary to give this moment the gravitas it probably warranted. "I'm not."

Gannit stared at me, narrowing her eyes. After a moment she let out a little huff, nodded, and then chuckled ruefully. "Well. Well, well. No wonder Gray cut and ran from you. I was just thinkin', up there, it was pretty in character for her to think she could kill an actual Hero. This is another matter, ain't it?"

"Is this going to be a problem, Gannit?" I asked quietly.

The old woman cackled, slapping her thigh. "Is it gonna be a problem, he asks me! You bet your creepy ass, boy. It's gonna be the kind of problem that gets books written about it! This is closer to history than I ever wanted to be. But now we're all here? Fuck it, you've been straighter and kinder to me and mine than any pompous fuckheads from the Convocation. Yeah, you're good with me, Healer. I've only got so many years left anyway, an' after tonight? Turns out I've got a mind to see more shit burned down before I join Hell's revels. It's not like there isn't plenty in Fflyr Dlemathlys that needs burning."

With a final wink, she turned and strode off to resume browbeating her employees into order.

"Okay," I said to those around me, setting down the cup. "Thanks for standing by, everyone. What's our situation like now?"

"Lady Gray got away, as you saw in person," said Aster. "At a rough guess, I think a bit more than half her men did, too. The damage we and the Alley Cats did to them tonight has probably ended them as an organization. It'd be a massive loss at the best of times, but the Olumnach bandits are going to be pushing aggressively into town as soon as they learn of this. Which'll be soon, given how fast Maugro works."

"And our losses?"

"Not bad," she said, placing a hand on my forearm. "You did the best—"

"Fourteen dead," Sakin interrupted bluntly. "Aster, my love, I appreciate your good intentions but don't coddle him. A commander needs accurate intel or everyone following him is fucked. That said, bossman, she's right. It is *miraculous* how few losses the whores took, and that's entirely on you and that Heal spell. Infection, trauma, blood loss, disease, and a host of after-the-fact problems like that are the lion's share of fatalities from a pitched battle, and you completely eliminated that as a factor here. Lady Gray's people not only took about the same in direct losses, but we've got at least twenty-five being held prisoner by the girls, and most of the rest are nursing wounds. Some will die in the coming days, and a *lot* are gonna be functionally out of commission."

"Right. Prisoners." I rubbed my forehead. "We need to do something about—"

"Done and done," Gannit called, passing by. "They weren't *your* prisoners, boy. While I wasn't lookin', apparently some of the girls decided to unheal the lot. More fodder for the crawns."

"Good," Kastrin muttered, fondling the butt of her beloved crossbow. "Sorry I missed that."

I hesitated, then decided to let it go. I couldn't exactly complain about these women being bloodthirsty when a cornerstone of my whole strategy here was to provoke them to it. Not like I had any right to throw stones anyway.

"In your opinion," I asked Sakin, "what's Lady Gray's next move?"

"If Gannit knows you're the Dark Lord, so does she," he said. "The good news is she'll keep that to herself. The rumor will spread; enough people saw tonight's events to put two and two together, but *none* of them are going to be considered credible witnesses, and that rumor spreads whenever there's an especially successful bandit leader, warlord, or royal usurper anywhere. Lady Gray's motivation will be to quash it. She rules by fear, and after the licking she and hers took tonight, she'll be barely holding them together as it is. If they get a credible tip that they're facing off with an actual, honest-to-goddess Dark Lord, most of 'em will flee the city rather than fuck with that."

"I'm honestly curious how she's gonna motivate her people to try attacking something they all saw her run away from," Adelly added.

"She'll gather up any Blessed with Magic she's got and throw them at you," Sakin continued seriously, holding my gaze. "Standard strategy for fighting Blessed on an organizational level is to do so asymmetrically. Sorcerers against physical fighters and vice versa; matching them with their own kind usually turns into a war of attrition whose only certainty is collateral damage. *Now*, though, she knows you can slaughter the caliber of Blessed she's got, and that sending Blessed with Might at you is just hand-feeding you artifacts."

I nodded, glancing at the Lightning Staff and what Biribo had identified as a Featherweight Tunic which had been retrieved by my people and laid next to me on the table. The other two, whose owners had been merely Immolated and thus survived, had vanished.

"She'll most likely lose the Blessed with Magic she sends at you," said Sakin, "but after tonight she'll consider any loss acceptable if it means putting you down. Best move will be to use them to put pressure on you and try to create an opening to get a swift kill herself. Without knowing what *other* artifacts she's got, it's impossible to say what specifically she'll try, but that's the most viable strategy in her position. And another reason she won't want it getting out that you're the Dark Lord; her remaining Blessed are not going to toss themselves on a sacrificial altar if they know that's what it is."

"Hm. So . . . I could counter her by publicly declaring myself . . ."

"Whoa!" Biribo objected. "Trust me, boss, you're *not* there yet!"

"Lizard's right," Sakin agreed, nodding. "As soon as there's a verified Dark Lord, *everyone* will come at you. You're good, Lord Seiji, and you've gained a lot of in-person power with the artifacts from tonight, but you're not ready to personally fend off the *entire* King's Guild, and that would just be the first wave. The last Dark Lord stomped through what's now Fflyr Dlemathlys, and the clans won't have forgotten that she's what made the previous regime collapse. Nothing motivates powerful people like a threat to their power, and the clans are just Lady Gray with better table manners. They'll unite to put you down, and the King might actually be able to solidify his own rule if he's got a compelling threat like a Dark Lord to rally everyone against."

I drew in a deep breath and let it out slowly. "So . . . That being the case, Lady Gray could really fuck me over by letting them know."

"That's pretty much the one thing she *can't* do," Sakin disagreed. "She's got negative credibility with any legit authority to begin with. If she tried to start that rumor about her obvious rival for power being the Dark Lord . . . Well, that's way too convenient to be believable. The fact that it's the literal truth is just hilarious." He grinned broadly in apparently genuine mirth.

"Dark Lord or no, after tonight we're going to be a very much more identifiable group," Aster murmured, frowning out at the common room. "There's just no way to move this many people at once without leaving a huge trail. Anybody who wants to know where the Healer is based will be able to find North Watch pretty easily after that."

"Yeah, we need to get to work properly fortifying it," Sakin agreed. "Fortunately, the necessary work should be doable, Lord Seiji. I'll give you my recommendations; with Harold and Kasser's skills and all these extra hands, we can get it done, probably with the materials we have on hand."

Given the state of North Watch, with its broken gates and crumbling walls, I was skeptical of that, but decided to take him at his word for the time being.

"All right. I think that's enough dallying." I pushed back from the table, standing up. "What exactly has been the purpose of all this running back and forth I'm seeing?"

"Whaddaya think?" Gannit asked, coming over again. Now, I saw, she had a leather satchel slung over her bony shoulder. "Everybody's gettin' packed and organized. Your boy here let slip that you've got a defensible base, and after tonight's work, it ain't like we can all stay in Gwyllthean. Gray ain't dead, and she's as pissed as anyone has ever been. She'll go right to work picking off whoever she can get her little claws on. Not everybody's coming, Healer, but I'll eat my own ass if you got less than fifty women out there ready to march."

I took a deep breath and blew it out slowly. "All right. Then I'd better not keep them waiting any longer."

She wasn't kidding. They were not only ready, but waiting. The last occupants of the Jostled Jug's common room trickled out while I gathered myself; and when I stepped onto the street with Aster and the others behind me, it was to find a crowd already formed. They'd made a semicircle around the front of the Jugs, most carrying bundles and many still holding their cobbled-together weapons. No one was still actively hurt anymore, but the night's brutal work still showed in torn and bloodstained clothing.

Gilder stood grinning hugely in the front row, both arms raised to wrap around the waists of the two amused-looking women bracketing him, one of whom I noted had a grip on his collar. I was gonna have to do something with that boy.

I'd kept my hood down, and now turned my head slowly, taking in as many faces as I could. I didn't know everybody's names after just two months of weekly visits, but I recognized all the women I could see.

I had recognized those who had died, too.

"Khadret," I said, stepping off the Jugs's stoop and nodding to her. "You and your friends joined me out of principle and did good work under pressure. I will *remember* that. In fact, going forward, I may find myself relying on you—because I know, now, that you ladies have a limited tolerance for bullshit. That is immensely valuable to me. I am just beginning to learn how easily violence and power can lead to a self-destructive spiral, and I need people around me who'll say so when things go too far. I want you to always feel free to speak up if you see a need. If you have concerns, over anything, I'll hear them out."

Khadret was smiling by the end of that little speech, as were four of her five cohorts, none of whose names I'd learned yet. The fifth had folded her arms and was regarding me with a pensive expression, but at last she didn't look openly skeptical.

"Glad to hear that, Lord Seiji," said Khadret, nodding. "We won't let you down."

"I believe you won't. Now, Craed." I turned to him; he immediately stepped forward out of the crowd, followed by his two friends. I really needed to start learning names, especially of this group. "*You* lads joined up in the middle of a fight out of simple opportunism. I'm going to have to remember that, too. You've done right by me and mine, and helped turn the tide, and I honor good work."

Craed nodded, the ghost of a smile flitting across his lips. "But?"

"But things aren't always going to go my way," I said, holding his gaze. "Eventually, a time will come when I'm in the position Lady Gray was— against the ropes, beset by an enemy I can't easily defeat. I don't know when that time will come—it likely won't be for years—but it's one of the inevitabilities of life. There's always a bigger fish. However long it takes, *that's* how long you boys have got to make yourselves absolutely indispensable."

Belatedly, I remembered they didn't know what fish were. Nobody commented, though; apparently my meaning was clear.

"We can do that, Lord Seiji," Craed said with utter self-confidence, nodding again. "Especially with the kind of opportunities a boss like you creates. You'll be impressed, I guarantee it."

"I hope so." I drew in a slow breath and let it out before continuing in a carrying tone, now constantly moving my eyes to keep watch over the whole group.

"If there's one thing I know about life, on this world or any other, it's that there's *always* another bastard. You deal with a crook, and then there's a corrupt guard. And behind him a merchant, a priest . . . a lord. A king, an emperor, even a goddess. It just never *stops*. From the alleys and brothels to the halls of heaven itself, it's *bastards* all the way down. Well, look who I'm telling."

That got me a stir of grim chuckles from the crowd. Folding my hands behind me, I found myself beginning to pace up and down in front of the Jugs.

"This is where I'd like to promise you all something better. And, don't mistake me, I intend to do the best I can to help *whoever* I can. All of you know what I can do. I will heal whoever I can reach, and protect whoever my power can extend to cover." I hesitated, drew in another breath and let it out. "But you've all seen tonight that there are limits to my power, as there are to anyone else's. I can't be everywhere, or do everything. Sometimes, the bastards win. That . . . will never change. I am not here to save the world. I don't really think that's how worlds *work*. As long as there are people on it, no matter what we do, eventually things will crumble and go to shit. As long as there are goddesses looming over us all . . . well, there's no telling what we might suffer just because one of them has a whim."

I paused, both in speaking and pacing, feeling my hands clench involuntarily into fists at my sides.

"I'm fucking sick of it."

This got me a lot of nods and some angry mutters of agreement.

"That's not an excuse not to try! Because . . . hell, what *else* are we gonna do? Just lie down and take it?" I spread my arms in a wide shrug. "I won't promise you safety, or justice, or certainty of anything. In the end, we all come up against something we can't defeat. Everybody's blood spills just the same. The *bastards* stay in power because they keep us all too afraid and desperate to take a risk of reaching for something better—but you see, that's their mistake. They take *too much*. They can't help themselves—it's a sick compulsion, for people who have power over others. The bastards always want more, and more, until finally they've driven us to a point where we have *nothing left to lose*. Not even our own lives, not when the only certainty is a cruel death at the end of all this.

"I'm not going to save the world, no. I'm going to do what I can, to heal and to help and to protect whoever I can along the way. But that is not the *point*. I will assure you of my best efforts and intentions, but you all know what those amount to in the end. I will *promise* you only one thing, *vengeance*. Not equity, not justice, not the victory of good in the end—because what is good without evil, and what is evil but a word the powerful use to describe whatever threatens them?"

I pointed up and behind me, where the outward-arching walls of Gwyllthean loomed over us all in the darkness, the eternal and implacable fact of life for everyone scraping out an existence in the Gutters.

"If you want to run away and hide, know that I have *nothing* bad to say about that decision. Hell, I'll respect your common sense. But if you're as *sick and fucking tired* as I am of all this bullshit, if you just don't have the strength for more common sense and patience while you're getting pissed on by smirking morons who dedicate their whole lives to *pretending* they're better than us, then you come with me. We're not going to save the world, oh no. We're going to go find the bastards who *broke* it, and *fuck 'em up*."

The roar of approval that erupted was a physical thing, very nearly pushing me back. It didn't, though, and I held my arms wide, letting their rage wash over me, nourishing and stoking my own back to life. I was only the catalyst; the rage was *there*, the result of everything wrong with this horrible, stupid world, just waiting for someone to come along and forge it into a weapon.

I'd done that, and now I had to wield it, because tonight's events had proven that what I'd unleashed couldn't be contained. If I didn't take the lead, the rage animating these people would find another outlet—and I had much better plans for them than to let their lives be squandered on the spears of a few crooked soldiers in this miserable backwater town.

This scream of primal rage was the sound of change—the promise of a reckoning that would roar across this island and every other. It was the sound of the Dark Lord rising.

"I know you're watching, Virya," I whispered to the sky, inaudible beneath the still-swelling cheer of victory and fury that rose throughout Cat Alley. "Enjoying the show, right? Laugh while you can. You're on my list."

About the Author

D. D. Webb is a highly suspicious character widely believed to be up to no good. Any information on his misdeeds should be reported to the requisite authorities.